Fu-Manchu

FOUR CLASSIC NOVELS BY

SAX ROHMER

Citadel Press   Secaucus, N.J.

First paperbound printing
Copyright © 1983 by Castle, a division of Book Sales Inc.
All rights reserved
Published by Citadel Press
A division of Lyle Stuart Inc.
120 Enterprise Ave., Secaucus, N.J. 07094
In Canada: Musson Book Company.
A division of General Publishing Co. Limited
Don Mills, Ontario
Manufactured in the United States of America
ISBN 0-8065-0899-X

Originally published by Castle as *Sax Rohmer's Collected Novels*

TABLE OF
CONTENTS

The Hand of Fu Manchu 1941
1

The Return of Dr. Fu-Manchu 1916
91

The Yellow Claw 1915
189

Dope 1919
313

The
Hand of
Fu-Manchu

The Chinaman lifted the lamp and directed its light fully
upon me

Chapter I

THE TRAVELER FROM TIBET

"Who's there?" I called sharply.

I turned and looked across the room. The window had been widely opened when I entered, and a faint fog haze hung in the apartment, seeming to veil the light of the shaded lamp. I watched the closed door intently, expecting every moment to see the knob turn. But nothing happened.

"Who's there?" I cried again, and, crossing the room, I threw open the door.

The long corridor without, lighted only by one inhospitable lamp at a remote end, showed choked and yellowed with this same fog so characteristic of London in November. But nothing moved to right nor left of me. The New Louvre Hotel was in some respects yet incomplete, and the long passage in which I stood, despite its marble facings, had no air of comfort or good cheer; palatial it was, but inhospitable.

I returned to the room, reclosing the door behind me, then for some five minutes or more I stood listening for a repetition of that mysterious sound, as of something that both dragged and tapped, which already had arrested my attention. My vigilance went unrewarded. I had closed the window to exclude the yellow mist, but subconsciously I was aware of its encircling presence, walling me in, and now I found myself in such a silence as I had known in deserts but could scarce have deemed possible in fog-bound London, in the heart of the world's metropolis, with the traffic of the Strand below me upon one side and the restless life of the river upon the other.

It was easy to conclude that I had been mistaken, that my nervous system was somewhat overwrought as a result of my hurried return from Cairo—from Cairo where I had left behind me many a fondly cherished hope. I addressed myself again to the task of unpacking my steamer-trunk and was so engaged when again a sound in the corridor outside brought me upright with a jerk.

A quick footstep approached the door, and there came a muffled rapping upon the panel.

This time I asked no question, but leapt across the room and threw the door open. Nayland Smith stood before me, muffled up in a heavy traveling coat, and with his hat pulled down over his brows.

"At last!" I cried, as my friend stepped in

and quickly reclosed the door.

Smith threw his hat upon the settee, stripped off the great-coat, and pulling out his pipe began to load it in feverish haste.

"Well," I said, standing amid the litter cast out from the trunk, and watching him eagerly, "what's afoot?"

Nayland Smith lighted his pipe, carelessly dropping the match-end upon the floor at his feet.

"God knows what *is* afoot this time, Petrie!" he replied. "You and I have lived no commonplace lives; Dr. Fu-Manchu has seen to that; but if I am to believe what the Chief has told me to-day, even stranger things are ahead of us!"

I stared at him wonder-stricken.

"That is almost incredible," I said; "terror can have no darker meaning than that which Dr. Fu-Manchu gave to it. Fu-Manchu is dead, so what have we to fear?"

"We have to fear," replied Smith throwing himself into a corner of the settee, "the Si-Fan!"

I continued to stare, uncomprehendingly.

"The Si-Fan——"

"I always knew and you always knew," interrupted Smith in his short, decisive manner, "that Fu-Manchu, genius though he was, remained nevertheless the servant of another or others. He was not the head of that organization which dealt in wholesale murder, which aimed at upsetting the balance of the world. I even knew the name of one, a certain mandarin, and member of the Sublime Order of the White Peacock, who was his immediate superior. I had never dared to guess at the identity of what I may term the Head Center."

He ceased speaking, and sat gripping his pipe grimly between his teeth, whilst I stood staring at him almost fatuously. Then—

"Evidently you have much to tell me," I said, with forced calm.

I drew up a chair beside the settee and was about to sit down.

"Suppose you bolt the door," jerked my friend.

I nodded, entirely comprehending, crossed the room and shot the little nickle bolt into its socket.

"Now," said Smith as I took my seat, "the story is a fragmentary one in which there are many gaps. Let us see what we know. It seems that the despatch which led to my sudden recall (and incidentally yours) from Egypt to London and which only reached me as I was on the point of embarking at Suez for Rangoon, was prompted by the arrival here of Sir Gregory Hale, whilom attaché at the British Embassy, Peking. So much, you will remember, was conveyed in my instructions."

"Quite so."

"Furthermore, I was instructed, you'll remember, to put up at the New Louvre Hotel; therefore you came here and engaged this suite whilst I reported to the chief. A stranger business is before us, Petrie, I verily believe, than any we have known hitherto. In the first place, Sir Gregory Hale is here——"

"Here?"

"In the New Louvre Hotel. I ascertained on the way up, but not by direct inquiry, that he occupies a suite similar to this, and incidentally on the same floor."

"His report to the India Office, whatever its nature, must have been a sensational one."

"He has made no report to the India Office."

"What! made no report?"

"He has not entered any office whatever, nor will he receive any representative. He's been playing at Robinson Crusoe in a private suite here for close upon a fortnight—*id est* since the time of his arrival in London!"

I suppose my growing perplexity was plainly visible, for Smith suddenly burst out with his short, boyish laugh.

"Oh! I told you it was a strange business," he cried.

"Is he mad?"

Nayland Smith's gaiety left him; he became suddenly stern and grim.

"Either mad, Petrie, stark raving mad, or the savior of the Indian Empire—perhaps of all Western civilization. Listen. Sir Gregory Hale, whom I know slightly and who honors me, apparently, with a belief that I am the only man in Europe worthy of his confidence, resigned his appointment at Peking some time ago, and set out upon a private expedition to the Mongolian frontier with the avowed intention of visiting some place in the Gobi Desert. From the time that he actually crossed the frontier he disappeared for nearly six months, to reappear again suddenly and dramatically in London. He buried himself in this hotel, refusing all visitors and only advising the authorities of his return by telephone. He demanded that I should be sent to see him; and—despite his eccentric methods—so great is the Chief's faith in Sir Gregory's knowledge of matters Far Eastern,

that behold, here I am."

He broke off abruptly and sat in an attitude of tense listening. Then—

"Do you hear anything, Petrie?" he rapped.

"A sort of tapping?" I inquired, listening intently myself the while.

Smith nodded his head rapidly.

We both listened for some time, Smith with his head bent slightly forward and his pipe held in his hands; I with my gaze upon the bolted door. A faint mist still hung in the room, and once I thought I detected a slight sound from the bedroom beyond, which was in darkness. Smith noted me turn my head, and for a moment the pair of us stared into the gap of the doorway. But the silence was complete.

"You have told me neither much nor little, Smith," I said, resuming for some reason, in a hushed voice. "Who or what is this Si-Fan at whose existence you hint?"

Nayland Smith smiled grimly.

"Possibly the real and hitherto unsolved riddle of Tibet, Petrie," he replied—"a mystery concealed from the world behind the veil of Lamaism." He stood up abruptly, glancing at a scrap of paper which he took from his pocket—"Suite Number 14a," he said. "Come along! We have not a moment to waste. Let us make our presence known to Sir Gregory—the man who has dared to raise that veil."

Chapter II

THE MAN WITH THE LIMP

"Lock the door!" said Smith significantly, as we stepped into the corridor.

I did so and had turned to join my friend when, to the accompaniment of a sort of hysterical muttering, a door further along, and on the opposite side of the corridor, was suddenly thrown open, and a man whose face showed ghastly white in the light of the solitary lamp beyond, literally hurled himself out. He perceived Smith and myself immediately. Throwing one glance back over his shoulder he came tottering forward to meet us.

"My God! I can't stand it any longer!" he babbled, and threw himself upon Smith, who was foremost, clutching pitifully at him for support. "Come in and see him, sir—for

Heaven's sake come in! I think he's dying; and he's going mad. I never disobeyed an order in my life before, but I can't help myself—I can't help myself!"

"Brace up!" I cried, seizing him by the shoulders as, still clutching at Nayland Smith, he turned his ghastly face to me. "Who are you, and what's your trouble?"

"I'm Beeton, Sir Gregory Hale's man."

Smith started visibly, and his gaunt, tanned face seemed to me to have grown perceptibly paler.

"Come on, Petrie!" he snapped. "There's some devilry here."

Thrusting Beeton aside he rushed in at the open door—upon which, as I followed him, I had time to note the number, 14a. It communicated with a suite of rooms almost identical with our own. The sitting-room was empty and in the utmost disorder, but from the direction of the principal bedroom came a most horrible mumbling and gurgling sound—a sound utterly indescribable. For one instant we hesitated at the threshold—hesitated to face the horror beyond; then almost side by side we came into the bedroom. . . .

Only one of the two lamps was alight—that above the bed; and on the bed a man lay writhing. He was incredibly gaunt, so that the suit of tropical twill which he wore hung upon him in folds, showing, if such evidence were necessary, how terribly he was fallen away from his constitutional habit. He wore a beard of at least ten days' growth, which served to accentuate the cavitous hollowness of his face. His eyes seemed starting from their sockets as he lay upon his back uttering inarticulate sounds and plucking with skinny fingers at his lips.

Smith bent forward peering into the wasted face; and then started back with a suppressed cry.

"Merciful God! can it be Hale?" he muttered. "What does it mean? what does it mean?"

I ran to the opposite side of the bed, and placing my arms under the writhing man, raised him and propped a pillow at his back. He continued to babble, rolling his eyes from side to side hideously; then by degrees they seemed to become less glazed, and a light of returning sanity entered them. They became fixed; and they were fixed upon Nayland Smith, who, bending over the bed, was watching Sir Gregory (for Sir Gregory I concluded this pitiable wreck to be) with an expression upon his face compound of many emotions.

"A glass of water," I said, catching the glance of the man Beeton, who stood trembling at the open doorway.

Spilling a liberal quantity upon the carpet, Beeton ultimately succeeded in conveying the glass to me. Hale, never taking his gaze from Smith, gulped a little of the water and then thrust my hand away. As I turned to place the tumbler upon a small table he resumed the wordless babbling, and now, with his index finger, pointed to his mouth.

"He has lost the power of speech!" whispered Smith.

"He was stricken dumb, gentlemen, ten minutes ago," said Beeton in a trembling voice. "He dropped off to sleep out there on the floor, and I brought him in here and laid him on the bed. When he woke up he was like that!"

The man on the bed ceased his inchoate babbling and now, gulping noisily, began to make quick nervous movements with his hands.

"He wants to write something," said Smith in a low voice. "Quick! hold him up!"

He thrust his notebook, open at a blank page, before the man whose moments were numbered, and placed a pencil in the shaking right hand.

Faintly and unevenly Sir Gregory commenced to write—whilst I supported him. Across the bent shoulders Smith silently questioned me, and my reply was a negative shake of the head.

The lamp above the bed was swaying as if in a heavy draught; I remembered that it had been swaying as we entered. There was no fog in the room, but already from the bleak corridor outside it was entering; murky, yellow clouds steaming in at the open door. Save for the gulping of the dying man, and the sobbing breaths of Beeton, there was no sound. Six irregular lines Sir Gregory Hale scrawled upon the page; then suddenly his body became a dead weight in my arms. Gently I laid him back upon the pillows, gently disengaged his fingers from the notebook, and, my head almost touching Smith's as we both craned forward over the page, read, with great difficulty, the following:—

"Guard my diary. . . .Tibetan frontier . . . Key of India. Beware man . . . with the limp. Yellow . . . rising. Watch Tibet . . . the *Si-Fan.* . . ."

From somewhere outside the room, whether above or below I could not be sure, came a faint dragging sound, accompanied by a *tap—tap—tap*. . . .

Chapter III

"SÂKYA MÛNI"

The faint disturbance faded into silence again. Across the dead man's body I met Smith's gaze. Faint wreaths of fog floated in from the outer room. Beeton clutched the foot of the bed, and the structure shook in sympathy with his wild trembling. That was the only sound now; there was absolutely nothing physical so far as my memory serves to signalize the coming of the brown man.

Yet, stealthy as his approach had been, something must have warned us. For suddenly, with one accord, we three turned our eyes away from the bed, and stared out into the room from which the fog wreaths floated in.

Beeton stood nearest to the door, but, although he turned, he did not go out, but with a smothered cry crouched back against the bed. Smith it was who moved first, then I followed, and close upon his heels burst into the disordered sitting-room. The outer door had been closed but not bolted, and what with the tinted light, diffused through the silken Japanese shade, and the presence of fog in the room, I was almost tempted to believe myself the victim of a delusion. What I saw or thought I saw was this:—

A tall screen stood immediately inside the door, and around its end, like some materialization of the choking mist, glided a lithe, yellow figure, a slim, crouching figure, wearing a sort of loose robe. An impression I had of jet-black hair, protruding from beneath a little cap, of finely chiseled features and great, luminous eyes, then, with no sound to tell of a door opened or shut, the apparition was gone.

"You saw him, Petrie!—you saw him!" cried Smith.

In three bounds he was across the room, had tossed the screen aside and thrown open the door. Out he sprang into the yellow haze of the corridor, tripped, and, uttering a cry of pain, fell sprawling upon the marble floor. Hot with apprehension I joined him, but he looked up with a wry smile and began furiously rubbing his left shin.

"A queer trick, Petrie," he said, rising to

his feet; "but nevertheless effective."

He pointed to the object which had occasioned his fall. It was a small metal chest, evidently of very considerable weight, and it stood immediately outside the door of Number 14a.

"That was what he came for, sir! That was what he came for! You were too quick for him!"

Beeton stood behind us, his horror-bright eyes fixed upon the box.

"Eh?" rapped Smith, turning upon him.

"That's what Sir Gregory brought to England," the man ran on almost hysterically; "that's what he's been guarding this past two weeks, night and day, crouching over it with a loaded pistol. That's what cost him his life, sir. He's had no peace, day or night, since he got it. . . ."

We were inside the room again now, Smith bearing the coffer in his arms, and still the man ran on:

"He's never slept for more than an hour at a time, that I know of, for weeks past. Since the day we came here he hasn't spoken to another living soul, and he's lain there on the floor at night with his head on that brass box, and sat watching over it all day.

" 'Beeton!' he'd cry out, perhaps in the middle of the night—'Beeton—do you hear that damned woman!' But although I'd begun to think I could hear something, I believe it was the constant strain working on my nerves and nothing else at all.

"Then he was always listening out for some one he called 'the man with the limp.' Five and six times a night he'd have me up to listen with him. 'There he goes, Beeton!' he'd whisper, crouching with his ear pressed flat to the door. 'Do you hear him dragging himself along?'

"God knows how I've stood it as I have; for I've known no peace since we left China. Once we got here I thought it would be better, but it's been worse.

"Gentlemen have come (from the India Office, I believe), but he would not see them. Said he would see no one but Mr. Nayland Smith. He had never lain in his bed until tonight, but what with taking no proper food nor sleep, and some secret trouble that was killing him by inches, he collapsed altogether a while ago, and I carried him in and laid him on the bed as I told you. Now he's dead—now he's dead."

Beeton leant up against the mantelpiece

and buried his face in his hands, whilst his shoulders shook convulsively. He had evidently been greatly attached to his master, and I found something very pathetic in this breakdown of a physically strong man. Smith laid his hand upon his shoulders.

"You have passed through a very trying ordeal," he said, "and no man could have done his duty better; but forces beyond your control have proved too strong for you. I am Nayland Smith."

The man spun around with a surprising expression of relief upon his pale face.

"So that whatever can be done," continued my friend, "to carry out your master's wishes, will be done now. Rely upon it. Go into your room and lie down until we call you."

"Thank you, sir, and thank God you are here," said Beeton dazedly, and with one hand raised to his head he went, obediently, to the smaller bedroom and disappeared within.

"Now, Petrie," rapped Smith, glancing around the littered floor, "since I am empowered to deal with this matter as I see fit, and since you are a medical man, we can devote the next half-hour, at any rate, to a strictly confidential inquiry into this most perplexing case. I propose that you examine the body for any evidences that may assist you in determining the cause of death, whilst I make a few inquiries here."

I nodded, without speaking, and went into the bedroom. It contained not one solitary item of the dead man's belongings, and in every way bore out Beeton's statement that Sir Gregory had never inhabited it. I bent over Hale, as he lay fully dressed upon the bed.

Saving the singularity of the symptom which had immediately preceded death—viz., the paralysis of the muscles of articulation—I should have felt disposed to ascribe his end to sheer inanition; and a cursory examination brought to light nothing contradictory to that view. Not being prepared to proceed further in the matter at the moment I was about to rejoin Smith, whom I could hear rummaging about amongst the litter of the outer room, when I made a curious discovery.

Lying in a fold of the disordered bed linen were a few petals of some kind of blossom, three of them still attached to a fragment of slender stalk.

I collected the tiny petals, mechanically,

and held them in the palm of my hand studying them for some moments before the mystery of their presence there became fully appreciable to me. Then I began to wonder. The petals (which I was disposed to class as belonging to some species of *Curcas* or Physic Nut), though bruised, were fresh, and therefore could not have been in the room for many hours. How had they been introduced, and by whom? Above all, what could their presence there at that time portend?

"Smith," I called, and walked towards the door carrying the mysterious fragments in my palm. "Look what I have found upon the bed."

Nayland Smith, who was bending over an open despatch case which he had placed upon a chair, turned—and his glance fell upon the petals and tiny piece of stem.

I think I have never seen so sudden a change of expression take place in the face of any man. Even in that imperfect light I saw him blanch. I saw a hard glitter come into his eyes. He spoke, evenly, but hoarsely:

"Put those things down—there, on the table; anywhere."

I obeyed him without demur; for something in his manner had chilled me with foreboding.

"You did not break that stalk?"

"No. I found it as you see it."

"Have you smelt the petals?"

I shook my head. Thereupon, having his eyes fixed upon me with the strangest expression in their gray depths, Nayland Smith said a singular thing.

"Pronounce, slowly, the words 'Sâkya Mûni,' " he directed.

I stared at him, scarce crediting my senses; but—

"I mean it!" he rapped. "Do as I tell you."

"Sâkya Mûni," I said, in ever increasing wonder. Smith laughed unmirthfully.

"Go into the bathroom and thoroughly wash your hands," was his next order. "Renew the water at least three times." As I turned to fulfil his instructions, for I doubted no longer his deadly earnestness: "Beeton!" he called.

Beeton, very white-faced and shaky, came out from the bedroom as I entered the bathroom, and whilst I proceeded carefully to cleanse my hands I heard Smith interrogating him.

"Have any flowers been brought into the room to-day, Beeton?"

"Flowers, sir? Certainly not. Nothing has ever been brought in here but what I have brought myself."

"You are certain of that?"

"Positive."

"Who brought up the meals, then?"

"If you'll look into my room here, sir, you'll see that I have enough tinned and bottled stuff to last us for weeks. Sir Gregory sent me out to buy it on the day we arrived. No one else had left or entered these rooms until you came to-night."

I returned to find Nayland Smith standing tugging at the lobe of his left ear in evident perplexity. He turned to me.

"I find my hands over full," he said. "Will you oblige me by telephoning for Inspector Weymouth? Also, I should be glad if you would ask M. Samarkan, the manager, to see me here immediately."

As I was about to quit the room—

"Not a word of our suspicions to M. Samarkan," he added; "nor a word about the brass box."

I was far along the corridor ere I remembered that which, remembered earlier, had saved me the journey. There was a telephone in every suite. However, I was not indisposed to avail myself of an opportunity for a few moments' undisturbed reflection, and, avoiding the lift, I descended by the broad, marble staircase.

To what strange adventure were we committed? What did the brass coffer contain which Sir Gregory had guarded night and day? Something associated in some way with Tibet, something which he believed to be "the key of India" and which had brought in its train, presumably, the sinister "man with a limp."

Who was the "man with the limp"? What was the Si-Fan? Lastly, by what conceivable means could the flower, which my friend evidently regarded with extreme horror, have been introduced into Hale's room, and why had I been required to pronounce the words "Sâkya Mûni"?

So ran my reflections—at random and to no clear end; and, as is often the case in such circumstances, my steps bore them company; so that all at once I became aware that instead of having gained the lobby of the hotel, I had taken some wrong turning and was in a part of the building entirely unfamiliar to me.

A long corridor of the inevitable white marble extended far behind me. I had evidently traversed it. Before me was a heavily curtained archway. Irritably, I pulled the curtain aside, learnt that it masked a glass-paneled door, opened this door—and found myself in a small court, dimly lighted and redolent of some pungent, incense-like perfume.

One step forward I took, then pulled up abruptly. A sound had come to my ears. From a second curtained doorway, close to my right hand, it came—a sound of muffled *tapping*, together with that of something which dragged upon the floor.

Within my brain the words seemed audibly to form: "The man with the limp!"

I sprang to the door; I had my hand upon the drapery . . . when a woman stepped out, barring the way!

No impression, not even a vague one, did I form of her costume, save that she wore a green silk shawl, embroidered with raised white figures of birds, thrown over her head and shoulders and draped in such fashion that part of her face was concealed. I was transfixed by the vindictive glare of her eyes, of her huge dark eyes.

They were ablaze with anger—but it was not this expression within them which struck me so forcibly as the fact that they were in some way familiar.

Motionless, we faced one another. Then—

"You go away," said the woman—at the same time extending her arms across the doorway as barriers to my progress.

Her voice had a husky intonation; her hands and arms, which were bare and of old ivory hue, were laden with barbaric jewelry, much of it tawdry silverware of the bazaars. Clearly she was a half caste of some kind; probably a Eurasian.

I hesitated. The sounds of dragging and tapping had ceased. But the presence of this grotesque Oriental figure only increased my anxiety to pass the doorway. I looked steadily into the black eyes; they looked into mine unflinchingly.

"You go away, please," repeated the woman, raising her right hand and pointing to the door whereby I had entered. "These private rooms. What you doing here?"

Her words, despite her broken English, served to recall to me the fact that I was, beyond doubt, a trespasser! By what right did I presume to force my way into other people's apartments?

"There is some one in there whom I must see," I said, realizing, however, that my chance of doing so was poor.

"You see nobody," she snapped back uncompromisingly. "You go away!"

She took a step towards me, continuing to point to the door. Where had I previously encountered the glance of those splendid, savage eyes?

So engaged was I with this taunting, partial memory, and so sure, if the woman would but uncover her face, of instantly recognizing her, that still I hesitated. Whereupon, glancing rapidly over her shoulder into whatever place lay beyond the curtained doorway, she suddenly stepped back and vanished, drawing the curtains to with an angry jerk.

I heard her retiring footsteps; then came a loud bang. If her object in intercepting me had been to cover the slow retreat of some one she had succeeded.

Recognizing that I had cut a truly sorry figure in the encounter, I retraced my steps.

By what route I ultimately regained the main staircase I have no idea; for my mind was busy with that taunting memory of the two dark eyes looking out from the folds of the green embroidered shawl. Where, and when, had I met their glance before? To that problem I sought an answer in vain.

The message despatched to New Scotland Yard, I found M. Samarkan, long famous as a *maître d'hôtel* in Cairo, and now host of London's newest and most palatial *khan*. Portly, and wearing a gray imperial, M. Samarkan had the manners of a courtier, and the smile of a true Greek.

I told him what was necessary, and no more, desiring him to go to suite 14a without delay and also without arousing unnecessary attention. I dropped no hint of foul play, but M. Samarkan expressed profound (and professional) regret that so distinguished, though unprofitable, a patron should have selected the New Louvre, thus early in its history, as the terminus of his career.

"By the way," I said, "have you Oriental guests with you, at the moment?"

M. Samarkan raised his heavy eyebrows.

"No, monsieur," he assured me.

"Not a certain Oriental lady?" I persisted.

M. Samarkan slowly shook his head.

"Possibly monsieur has seen one of the *ayahs*? There are several Anglo-Indian families resident in the New Louvre at present."

An *ayah*? It was just possible, of course. Yet . . .

Chapter IV

THE FLOWER OF SILENCE

"We are dealing now," said Nayland Smith, pacing restlessly up and down our sitting-room, "not, as of old, with Dr. Fu-Manchu, but with an entirely unknown quantity—the Si-Fan."

"For Heaven's sake!" I cried, "what is the Si-Fan?"

"The greatest mystery of the mysterious East, Petrie. Think. You know, as I know, that a malignant being, Dr. Fu-Manchu, was for some time in England, engaged in 'paving the way' (I believe those words were my own) for nothing less than a giant Yellow Empire. That dream is what millions of Europeans and Americans term 'the Yellow Peril'! Very good. Such an empire needs must have—"

"An emperor!"

Nayland Smith stopped his restless pacing immediately in front of me.

"Why not an *empress*, Petrie!" he rapped.

His words were something of a verbal thunderbolt; I found myself at loss for any suitable reply.

"You will perhaps remind me," he continued rapidly, "of the lowly place held by women in the East. I can cite notable exceptions, ancient and modern. In fact, a moment's consideration will reveal many advantages in the creation by a hypothetical body of Eastern dynast-makers not of an emperor but of an empress. Finally, there is a persistent tradition throughout the Far East that such a woman will one day rule over the known peoples. I was assured some years ago, by a very learned pundit, that a princess of incalculably ancient lineage, residing in some secret monastery in Tartary or Tibet, was to be the future empress of the world. I believe this tradition, or the extensive group who seek to keep it alive and potent, to be what is called the Si-Fan!"

I was past greater amazement; but—

"This lady can be no longer young, then?" I asked.

"On the contrary, Petrie, she remains always young and beautiful by means of a continuous series of reincarnations; also she thus conserves the collated wisdom of many ages. In short, she is the archetype of Lamaism. The real secret of Lama celibacy is the existence of this immaculate ruler, of whom the Grand Lama is merely a high priest. She has, as attendants, maidens of good family, selected for their personal charms, and rendered dumb in order that they may never report what they see and hear."

"Smith!" I cried, "this is utterly incredible!"

"Her body slaves are not only mute, but blind; for it is death to look upon her beauty unveiled."

I stood up impatiently.

"You are amusing yourself," I said.

Nayland Smith clapped his hands upon my shoulders, in his own impulsive fashion, and looked earnestly into my eyes.

"Forgive me, old man," he said, "if I have related all these fantastic particulars as though I gave them credence. Much of this is legendary, I know, some of it mere superstition, but—I am serious now, Petrie—*part of it is true.*"

I stared at the square-cut, sun-tanned face; and no trace of a smile lurked about that grim mouth.

"Such a woman may actually exist, Petrie, only in legend; but, nevertheless, she forms the head center of that giant conspiracy in which the activities of Dr. Fu-Manchu were merely a part. Hale blundered on to this stupendous business; and from what I have gathered from Beeton and what I have seen for myself, it is evident that in yonder coffer"—he pointed to the brass chest standing hard by—"Hale got hold of something indispensable to the success of this vast Yellow conspiracy. That he was followed here, to the very hotel, by agents of this mystic Unknown is evident. But," he added grimly, "they have failed in their object!"

A thousand outrageous possibilities fought for precedence in my mind.

"Smith!" I cried, "the half-caste woman whom I saw in the hotel . . ."

Nayland Smith shrugged his shoulders.

"Probably, as M. Samarkan suggests, an *ayah!*" he said; but there was an odd note in his voice and an odd look in his eyes.

"Then again, I am almost certain that Hale's warning concerning 'the man with the limp' was no empty one. Shall you open the brass chest?"

"At present, decidedly *no.* Hale's fate renders his warning one that I dare not neglect. For I was with him when he died; and they cannot know how much *I* know. How did he die? How did he die? How was the Flower of Silence introduced into his closely guarded room?"

"The Flower of Silence?"

Smith laughed shortly and unmirthfully.

"I was once sent for," he said, "during the time that I was stationed in Upper Burma, to see a stranger—a sort of itinerant Buddhist priest, so I understood, who had desired to communicate some message to me personally. He was dying—in a dirty hut on the outskirts of Manipur, up in the hills. When I arrived I saw at a glance that the man was a Tibetan monk. He must have crossed the river and come down through Assam; but the nature of his message I never knew. He had lost the power of speech! He was gurgling, inarticulate, just like poor Hale. A few moments after my arrival he breathed his last. The fellow who had guided me to the place bent over him—I shall always remember the scene—then fell back as though he had stepped upon an adder.

" 'He holds the Flower of Silence in his hand!' he cried—'the Si-Fan! the Si-Fan!'—and bolted from the hut.

"When I went to examine the dead man, sure enough he held in one hand a little crumpled spray of flowers. I did not touch it with my fingers naturally, but I managed to loop a piece of twine around the stem, and by that means I gingerly removed the flowers and carried them to an orchid-hunter of my acquaintance who chanced to be visiting Manipur.

"Grahame—that was my orchid man's name—pronounced the specimen to be an unclassified species of *jatropha;* belonging to the *Curcas* family. He discovered a sort of hollow thorn, almost like a fang, amongst the blooms, but was unable to surmise the nature of its functions. He extracted enough of a certain fixed oil from the flowers, however, to have poisoned the pair of us!"

"Probably the breaking of a bloom . . ."

"Ejects some of this acrid oil through the thorn? Practically the uncanny thing stings when it is hurt? That is my own idea, Petrie. And I can understand how these Eastern fanatics accept their sentence—silence and death—when they have deserved it, at the hands of their mysterious organization, and commit this novel form of *hara-kiri.* But I shall not sleep soundly with that brass coffer in my possession until I know by what means Sir Gregory was induced to touch a Flower of Silence, and by what means it was placed in his room!"

"But, Smith, why did you direct me tonight to repeat the words, 'Sâkya Mûni'?"

Smith smiled in a very grim fashion.

"It was after the episode I have just related that I made the acquaintance of that pundit, some of whose statements I have already quoted for your enlightenment. He admitted that the Flower of Silence was an instrument frequently employed by a certain group, adding that, according to some authorities, one who had touched the flower might escape death by immediately pronouncing the sacred name of Buddha. He was no fanatic himself, however, and, marking my incredulity, he explained that the truth was this:—

"No one whose powers of speech were imperfect could possibly pronounce correctly the words 'Sâkya Mûni.' Therefore, since the first effects of this damnable thing is instantly to tie the tongue, the uttering of the sacred name of Buddha becomes practically a test whereby the victim may learn whether the venom has entered his system or not!"

I repressed a shudder. An atmosphere of horror seemed to be enveloping us, foglike.

"Smith," I said slowly, "we must be on our guard," for at last I had run to earth that elusive memory. "Unless I am strangely mistaken, the 'man' who so mysteriously entered Hale's room and the supposed *ayah* whom I met downstairs are one and the same. Two, at least, of the Yellow group are actually here in the New Louvre!"

The light of the shaded lamp shone down upon the brass coffer on the table beside me. The fog seemed to have cleared from the room somewhat, but since in the midnight stillness I could detect the muffled sounds of sirens from the river and the reports of fog signals from the railways, I concluded that the night was not yet wholly clear of the choking mist. In accordance with a prearranged scheme we had decided to guard "the key of India" (whatever it might be) turn and turn about throughout the night. In a word—we feared to sleep unguarded. Now my watch informed me that four o'clock approached, at which hour I was to arouse Smith and retire to sleep to my own bedroom.

Nothing had disturbed my vigil—that is, nothing definite. True once, about half an hour earlier, I had thought I heard the dragging and tapping sound from somewhere up above me; but since the corridor overhead was unfinished and none of the rooms opening upon it yet habitable, I concluded that I had been mistaken. The stairway at the end of our corridor, which communicated with that above, was still blocked with bags of cement and slabs of marble, in fact.

Faintly to my ears came the booming of London's clocks, beating out the hour of four. But still I sat beside the mysterious coffer, indisposed to awaken my friend any sooner than was necessary, particularly since I felt in no way sleepy myself.

I was to learn a lesson that night: the lesson of strict adherence to a compact. I had arranged to awaken Nayland Smith at four; and because I dallied, determined to finish my pipe ere entering his bedroom, almost it happened that Fate placed it beyond my power ever to awaken him again.

At ten minutes past four, amid a stillness so intense that the creaking of my slippers seemed a loud disturbance, I crossed the room and pushed open the door of Smith's bedroom. It was in darkness, but as I entered I depressed the switch immediately inside the door, lighting the lamp which swung from the center of the ceiling.

Glancing towards the bed, I immediately perceived that there was something different in its aspect, but at first I found this difference difficult to define. I stood for a moment in doubt. Then I realized the nature of the change which had taken place.

A lamp hung above the bed, attached to a moveable fitting, which enabled it to be raised or lowered at the pleasure of the occupant. When Smith had retired he was in no reading mood, and he had not even lighted the reading-lamp, but had left it pushed high up against the ceiling.

It was the position of this lamp which had changed. For now it swung so low over the pillow that the silken fringe of the shade almost touched my friend's face as he lay soundly asleep with one lean brown hand outstretched upon the coverlet.

I stood in the doorway staring, mystified, at this phenomenon; I might have stood there without intervening, until intervention had been too late, were it not that, glancing upward toward the wooden block from which ordinarily the pendant hung, I perceived that no block was visible, but only a round, black cavity from which the white flex supporting the lamp swung out.

Then, uttering a hoarse cry which rose unbidden to my lips, I sprang wildly across the room . . . for now I had seen something else!

Attached to one of the four silken tassels

which ornamented the lamp-shade, so as almost to rest upon the cheek of the sleeping man, was a little corymb of bloom . . . the *Flower of Silence!*

Grasping the shade with my left hand I seized the flex with my right, and as Smith sprang upright in bed, eyes wildly glaring, I wrenched with all my might. Upward my gaze was set; and I glimpsed a yellow hand, with long, pointed finger nails. There came a loud resounding snap; an electric spark spat venomously from the circular opening above the bed; and, with the cord and lamp still fast in my grip, I went rolling across the carpet—as the other lamp became instantly extinguished.

Dimly I perceived Smith, arrayed in pajamas, jumping out upon the opposite side of the bed.

"Petrie, Petrie!" he cried, "where are you? what has happened?"

A laugh, little short of hysterical, escaped me. I gathered myself up and made for the lighted sitting-room.

"Quick, Smith!" I said—but I did not recognize my own voice. "Quick—come out of that room."

I crossed to the settee, and shaking in every limb, sank down upon it. Nayland Smith, still wild-eyed, and his face a mask of bewilderment, came out of the bedroom and stood watching me.

"For God's sake what has happened, Petrie?" he demanded, and began clutching at the lobe of his left ear and looking all about the room dazedly.

"The Flower of Silence!" I said; "some one has been at work in the top corridor. . . . Heaven knows when, for since we engaged these rooms we have not been much away from them . . . the same device as in the case of poor Hale. . . . You would have tried to brush the thing away . . ."

A light of understanding began to dawn in my friend's eyes. He drew himself stiffly upright, and in a loud, harsh voice uttered the words: "Sâkya Mûni"—and again: "Sâkya Mûni."

"Thank God!" I said shakily. "I was not too late."

Nayland Smith, with much rattling of glass, poured out two stiff pegs from the decanter. Then—

"*Ssh!* what's that?" he whispered.

He stood, tense, listening, his head cast slightly to one side.

A very faint sound of shuffling and tapping was perceptible, coming, as I thought, from the incomplete stairway communicating with the upper corridor.

"The man with the limp!" whispered Smith.

He bounded to the door and actually had one hand upon the bolt, when he turned, and fixed his gaze upon the brass box.

"No!" he snapped; "there are occasions when prudence should rule. Neither of us must leave these rooms to-night!"

Chapter V

JOHN KI'S

"What is the meaning of Si-Fan?" asked Detective-sergeant Fletcher.

He stood looking from the window at the prospect below; at the trees bordering the winding embankment; at the ancient monolith which for unnumbered ages had looked across desert sands to the Nile, and now looked down upon another river of many mysteries. The view seemed to absorb his attention. He spoke without turning his head.

Nayland Smith laughed shortly.

"The Si-Fan are the natives of Eastern Tibet," he replied.

"But the term has some other significance, sir?" said the detective; his words were more of an assertion than a query.

"It has," replied my friend grimly. "I believe it to be the name, or perhaps the sigil, of an extensive secret society with branches stretching out into every corner of the Orient."

We were silent for awhile. Inspector Weymouth, who sat in a chair near the window, glanced appreciatively at the back of his subordinate, who still stood looking out. Detective-sergeant Fletcher was one of Scotland Yard's coming men. He had information of the first importance to communicate, and Nayland Smith had delayed his departure upon an urgent errand in order to meet him.

"Your case to date, Mr. Smith," continued Fletcher, remaining with hands locked behind him, staring from the window, "reads something like this, I believe: A brass box, locked, contents unknown, has come into your possession. It stands now upon the table there. It was brought from Tibet by a man who evidently thought that it had something to do with the Si-Fan. He is dead, possibly by the agency of members of this group. No arrests have been made. You know that there are people here in London who are anxious to regain the box. You have theories respecting the identity of some of them, but there are practically no facts."

Nayland Smith nodded his head.

"Exactly!" he snapped.

"Inspector Weymouth, here," continued Fletcher, "has put me in possession of such facts as are known to him, and I believe that I have had the good fortune to chance upon a valuable one."

"You interest me, Sergeant Fletcher," said Smith. "What is the nature of this clue?"

"I will tell you," replied the other, and turned briskly upon his heel to face us.

He had a dark, clean-shaven face, rather sallow complexion, and deep-set, searching eyes. There was decision in the square, cleft chin and strong character in the cleanly chiseled features. His manner was alert.

"I have specialized in Chinese crime," he said; "much of my time is spent amongst our Asiatic visitors. I am fairly familiar with the Easterns who use the port of London, and I have a number of useful acquaintances among them."

Nayland Smith nodded. Beyond doubt Detective-sergeant Fletcher knew his business.

"To my lasting regret," Fletcher continued, "I never met the late Dr. Fu-Manchu. I understand, sir, that you believe him to have been a high official of this dangerous society? However, I think we may get in touch with some other notabilities; for instance, I'm told that one of the people you're looking for has been described as 'the man with the limp'?"

Smith, who had been about to relight his pipe, dropped the match on the carpet and set his foot upon it. His eyes shone like steel.

" 'The man with the limp,' " he said, and slowly rose to his feet—"what do you know of the man with the limp?"

Fletcher's face flushed slightly; his words had proved more dramatic than he had anticipated.

"There's a place down Shadwell way," he replied, "of which, no doubt, you will have heard; it has no official title, but it is known to habitués as the Joy-Shop. . . ."

Inspector Weymouth stood up, his burly figure towering over that of his slighter confrère.

"I don't think you know John Ki's, Mr. Smith," he said. "We keep all those places pretty well patrolled, and until this present business cropped up, John's establishment

had never given us any trouble."

"What is this Joy-Shop?" I asked.

"A resort of shady characters, mostly Asiatics," replied Weymouth. "It's a gambling-house, an unlicensed drinking-shop, and even worse—but it's more use to us open than it would be shut."

"It is one of my regular jobs to keep an eye on the visitors to the Joy-Shop," continued Fletcher. "I have many acquaintances who use the place. Needless to add, they don't know my real business! Well, lately several of them have asked me if I know who the man is that hobbles about the place with two sticks. Everybody seems to have heard him, but no one has seen him."

Nayland Smith began to pace the floor restlessly.

"I have heard him myself," added Fletcher, "but never managed to get so much as a glimpse of him. When I learnt about this Si-Fan mystery, I realized that he might very possibly be the man for whom you're looking—and a golden opportunity has cropped up for you to visit the Joy-Shop, and, if our luck remains in, to get a peep behind the scenes."

"I am all attention," snapped Smith.

"A woman called Zarmi has recently put in an appearance at the Joy-Shop. Roughly speaking, she turned up at about the same time as the unseen man with the limp. . . ."

Nayland Smith's eyes were blazing with suppressed excitement; he was pacing quickly up and down the floor, tugging at the lobe of his left ear.

"She is—different in some way from any other woman I have ever seen in the place. She's a Eurasian and good-looking, after a tigerish fashion. I have done my best"—he smiled slightly—"to get in her good books, and up to a point I've succeeded. I was there last night, and Zarmi asked me if I knew what she called a 'strong feller.'

" 'These,' she informed me, contemptuously referring to the rest of the company, 'are poor weak Johnnies!'

"I had nothing definite in view at the time, for I had not then heard about your return to London, but I thought it might lead to something anyway, so I promised to bring a friend along to-night. I don't know what we're wanted to do, but . . ."

"Count upon me!" snapped Smith. "I will leave all details to you and to Weymouth, and I will be at New Scotland Yard this evening in time to adopt a suitable disguise.

Petrie"—he turned impetuously to me—"I fear I shall have to go without you; but I shall be in safe company, as you see, and doubtless Weymouth can find you a part in his portion of the evening's program."

He glanced at his watch.

"Ah! I must be off. If you will oblige me, Petrie, by putting the brass box into my smaller portmanteau, whilst I slip my coat on, perhaps Weymouth, on his way out, will be good enough to order a taxi. I shall venture to breathe again once our unpleasant charge is safely deposited in the bank vaults!"

Chapter VI

THE SI-FAN MOVE

A slight drizzling rain was falling as Smith entered the cab which the hall-porter had summoned. The brown bag in his hand contained the brass box which actually was responsible for our presence in London. The last glimpse I had of him through the glass of the closed window showed him striking a match to light his pipe—which he rarely allowed to grow cool.

Oppressed with an unaccountable weariness of spirit, I stood within the lobby looking out upon the grayness of London in November. A slight mental effort was sufficient to blot out that drab prospect and to conjure up before my mind's eye a balcony overlooking the Nile—a glimpse of dusty palms, a white wall overgrown with purple blossoms, and above all the dazzling vault of Egypt. Upon the balcony my imagination painted a figure, limning it with loving details, the figure of Kâramanèh; and I thought that her glorious eyes would be sorrowful and her lips perhaps a little tremulous, as, her arms resting upon the rail of the balcony, she looked out across the smiling river to the domes and minarets of Cairo—and beyond, into the hazy distance; seeing me in dreary, rain-swept London, as I saw her, at Gezîra, beneath the cloudless sky of Egypt.

From these tender but mournful reflections I aroused myself, almost angrily, and set off through the muddy streets towards Charing Cross; for I was availing myself of the opportunity to call upon Dr. Murray, who had purchased my small suburban practise when (finally, as I thought at the time) I had left London.

This matter occupied me for the greater part of the afternoon, and I returned to the New Louvre Hotel shortly after five, and seeing no one in the lobby whom I knew, proceeded immediately to our apartment. Nayland Smith was not there, and having made some changes in my attire I descended again and inquired if he had left any message for me.

The booking-clerk informed me that Smith had not returned; therefore I resigned myself to wait. I purchased an evening paper and settled down in the lounge where I had an uninterrupted view of the entrance doors. The dinner hour approached, but still my friend failed to put in an appearance. Becoming impatient, I entered a call-box and rang up Inspector Weymouth.

Smith had not been to Scotland Yard, nor had they received any message from him.

Perhaps it would appear that there was little cause for alarm in this, but I, familiar with my friend's punctual and exact habits, became strangely uneasy. I did not wish to make myself ridiculous, but growing restlessness impelled me to institute inquiries regarding the cabman who had driven my friend. The result of these was to increase rather than to allay my fears.

The man was a stranger to the hall-porter, and he was not one of the taximen who habitually stood upon the neighboring rank; no one seemed to have noticed the number of the cab.

And now my mind began to play with strange doubts and fears. The driver, I recollected, had been a small, dark man, possessing remarkably well-cut olive-hued features. Had he not worn spectacles he would indeed have been handsome, in an effeminate fashion.

I was almost certain, by this time, that he had not been an Englishman; I was almost certain that some catastrophe had befallen Smith. Our ceaseless vigilance had been momentarily relaxed—and this was the result!

At some large bank branches there is a resident messenger. Even granting that such was the case in the present instance, I doubted if the man could help me, unless, as was possible, he chanced to be familiar with my friend's appearance, and had actually seen him there that day. I determined, at any rate, to make the attempt; reentering the call-box, I asked for the bank's number.

There proved to be a resident messenger, who, after a time, replied to my call. He knew

Nayland Smith very well by sight, and as he had been on duty in the public office of the bank at the time that Smith should have arrived, he assured me that my friend had not been there that day!

"Besides, sir," he said, "you say he came to deposit valuables of some kind here?"

"Yes, yes!" I cried eagerly.

"I take all such things down on the lift to the vaults at night, sir, under the supervision of the assistant manager—and I can assure you that nothing of the kind has been left with us to-day."

I stepped out of the call-box unsteadily. Indeed, I clutched at the door for support.

"What is the meaning of Si-Fan?" Detective-sergeant Fletcher had asked that morning. None of us could answer him; none of us knew. With a haze seeming to dance between my eyes and the active life in the lobby before me, I realized that the Si-Fan—that unseen, sinister power—had reached out and plucked my friend from the very midst of this noisy life about me, into its own mysterious, deathly silence.

Chapter VII

CHINATOWN

"It's no easy matter," said Inspector Weymouth, "to patrol the vicinity of John Ki's Joy-Shop without their getting wind of it. The entrance, as you'll see, is a long, narrow rat-hole of a street running at right angles to the Thames. There's no point, so far as I know, from which the yard can be overlooked; and the back is on a narrow cutting belonging to a disused mill."

I paid little attention to his words. Disguised beyond all chance of recognition even by one intimate with my appearance, I was all impatience to set out. I had taken Smith's place in the night's program; for, every possible source of information having been tapped in vain, I now hope against hope that some clue to the fate of my poor friend might be obtained at the Chinese den which he had designed to visit with Fletcher.

The latter, who presented a strange picture in his make-up as a sort of half-caste sailor, stared doubtfully at the Inspector; then—

"The River Police cutter," he said, "can drop down on the tide and lie off under the

Surrey bank. There's a vacant wharf facing the end of the street, and we can slip through and show a light there, to let you know we've arrived. You reply in the same way. If there's any trouble, I shall blaze away with this"— he showed the butt of a Service revolver protruding from his hip-pocket—"and you can be ashore in no time."

The plan had one thing to commend it, viz., that no one could devise another. Therefore it was adopted, and five minutes later a taxi-cab swung out of the Yard containing Inspector Weymouth and two ruffianly looking companions—myself and Fletcher.

Any zest with which, at another time, I might have entered upon such an expedition, was absent now. I bore with me a gnawing anxiety and sorrow that precluded all conversation on my part, save monosyllabic replies, to questions that I comprehended but vaguely.

At the River Police Depot we found Inspector Ryman, an old acquaintance, awaiting us. Weymouth had telephoned from Scotland Yard.

"I've got a motor-boat at the breakwater," said Ryman, nodding to Fletcher, and staring hard at me.

Weymouth laughed shortly.

"Evidently you don't recognize Dr. Petrie!" he said.

"Eh!" cried Ryman—"Dr. Petrie! why, good heavens, Doctor, I should never have known you in a month of Bank holidays! What's afoot, then?"—and he turned to Weymouth, eyebrows raised interrogatively.

"It's the Fu-Manchu business again, Ryman."

"Fu-Manchu! But I thought the Fu-Manchu case was off the books long ago? It was always a mystery to me; never a word in the papers; and we as much in the dark as everybody else—but didn't I hear that the Chinaman, Fu-Manchu, was dead?"

Weymouth nodded.

"Some of his friends seem to be very much alive, though!" he said. "It appears that Fu-Manchu, for all his genius—and there's no denying he was a genius, Ryman—was only the agent of somebody altogether bigger."

Ryman whistled softly.

"Has the real head of affairs arrived, then?"

"We find we are up against what is known as the Si-Fan."

At that it came to the inevitable, unanswerable question.

"What is the Si-Fan?" asked Ryman blankly.

I laughed, but my laughter was not mirthful. Inspector Weymouth shook his head.

"Perhaps Mr. Nayland Smith could tell you that," he replied; "for the Si-Fan got him to-day!"

"Got him!" cried Ryman.

"Absolutely! He's vanished! And Fletcher here has found out that John Ki's place is in some way connected with this business."

I interrupted—impatiently, I fear.

"Then let us set out, Inspector," I said, "for it seems to me that we are wasting precious time—and you know what that may mean." I turned to Fletcher. "Where is this place situated, exactly? How do we proceed?"

"The cab can take us part of the way," he replied, "and we shall have to walk the rest. Patrons of John's don't turn up in taxis, as a rule!"

"Then let us be off," I said, and made for the door.

"Don't forget the signal!" Weymouth cried after me, "and don't venture into the place until you've received our reply. . . ."

But I was already outside, Fletcher following; and a moment later we were both in the cab and off into a maze of tortuous streets toward John Ki's Joy-Shop.

With the coming of nightfall the rain had ceased, but the sky remained heavily overcast and the air was filled with clammy mist. It was a night to arouse longings for Southern skies; and when, discharging the cabman, we set out afoot along a muddy and ill-lighted thoroughfare bordered on either side by high brick walls, their monotony occasionally broken by gateways, I felt that the load of depression which had settled upon my shoulders must ere long bear me down.

Sounds of shunting upon some railway siding came to my ears; train whistles and fog signals hooted and boomed. River sounds there were, too, for we were close beside the Thames, that gray old stream which has borne upon its bier many a poor victim of underground London. The sky glowed sullenly red above.

"There's the Joy-Shop, along on the left," said Fletcher, breaking in upon my reflections. "You'll notice a faint light; it's shining out through the open door. Then, here is the wharf."

He began fumbling with the fastenings of a dilapidated gateway beside which we were standing; and a moment later—

"All right—slip through," he said.

I followed him through the narrow gap which the ruinous state of the gates had enabled him to force, and found myself looking under a low arch, with the Thames beyond, and a few hazy lights coming and going on the opposite bank.

"Go steady!" warned Fletcher. "It's only a few paces to the edge of the wharf."

I heard him taking a box of matches from his pocket.

"Here is my electric lamp," I said. "It will serve the purpose better."

"Good," muttered my companion. "Show a light down here, so that we can find our way."

With the aid of the lamp we found our way out on to the rotting timbers of the crazy structure. The mist hung denser over the river, but through it, as through a dirty gauze curtain, it was possible to discern some of the greater lights on the opposite shore. These, without exception, however, showed high up upon the fog curtain; along the water level lay a belt of darkness.

"Let me give them the signal," said Fletcher, shivering slightly and taking the lamp from my hand.

He flashed the light two or three times. Then we both stood watching the belt of darkness that followed the Surrey shore. The tide lapped upon the timbers supporting the wharf and little whispers and gurgling sounds stole up from beneath our feet. Once there was a faint splash from somewhere below and behind us.

"There goes a rat," said Fletcher vaguely, and without taking his gaze from the darkness under the distant shore. "It's gone into the cutting at the back of John Ki's."

He ceased speaking and flashed the lamp again several times. Then, all at once out of the murky darkness into which we were peering, looked a little eye of light—once, twice, thrice it winked at us from low down upon the oily waters; then was gone.

"It's Weymouth with the cutter," said Fletcher; "they are ready . . . now for John Ki's."

We stumbled back up the slight acclivity beneath the archway to the street, leaving the ruinous gates as we had found them. Into the uninviting little alley immediately opposite we plunged, and where the faint yellow luminance showed upon the muddy path before us, Fletcher paused a moment, whispering to me warningly.

"Don't speak if you can help it," he said; "if you do, mumble any old jargon in any language you like, and throw in plenty of cursing!"

He grasped me by the arm, and I found myself crossing the threshold of the Joy-Shop—I found myself in a meanly furnished room no more than twelve feet square and very low ceiled, smelling strongly of paraffin oil. The few items of furniture which it contained were but dimly discernible in the light of a common tin lamp which stood upon a packing-case at the head of what looked like cellar steps.

Abruptly, I pulled up; for this stuffy little den did not correspond with pre-conceived ideas of the place for which we were bound. I was about to speak when Fletcher nipped my arm—and out from the shadows behind the packing-case a little bent figure arose!

I started violently, for I had had no idea that another was in the room. The apparition proved to be a Chinaman, and judging from what I could see of him, a very old Chinaman, his bent figure attired in a blue smock. His eyes were almost invisible amidst an intricate map of wrinkles which covered his yellow face.

"Evening, John," said Fletcher—and, pulling me with him, he made for the head of the steps.

As I came abreast of the packing-case, the Chinaman lifted the lamp and directed its light fully upon my face.

Great as was the faith which I reposed in my make-up, a doubt and a tremor disturbed me now, as I found myself thus scrutinized by those cunning old eyes looking out from the mask-like, apish face. For the first time the Chinaman spoke.

"You blinger fliend, Charlie?" he squeaked in a thin, piping voice.

"Him play piecee card," replied Fletcher briefly. "Good fellow, plenty much money."

He descended the steps, still holding my arm, and I perforce followed him. Apparently John's scrutiny and Fletcher's explanation respecting me, together had proved satisfactory; for the lamp was replaced upon the lid of the packing-case, and the little bent figure dropped down again into the shadows from which it had emerged.

"Allee lightee," I heard faintly as I stumbled downward in the wake of Fletcher.

I had expected to find myself in a cellar, but instead discovered that we were in a small square court with the mist of the night about us again. On a doorstep facing us stood a duplicate of the lamp upon the box upstairs. Evidently this was designed to indicate the portals of the Joy-Shop, for Fletcher pushed open the door, whose threshold accommodated the lamp, and the light of the place beyond shone out into our faces. We entered and my companion closed the door behind us.

Before me I perceived a long low room lighted by flaming gas-burners, the jets hissing and spluttering in the draught from the door, for they were entirely innocent of shades or mantles. Wooden tables, their surfaces stained with the marks of countless wet glasses, were ranged about the place, café fashion; and many of these tables accommodated groups, of nondescript nationality for the most part. One or two there were in a distant corner who were unmistakably Chinamen; but my slight acquaintance with the races of the East did not enable me to classify the greater number of those whom I now saw about me. There were several unattractive-looking women present.

Fletcher walked up the center of the place, exchanging nods of recognition with two hang-dog poker-players, and I was pleased to note that our advent had apparently failed to attract the slightest attention. Through an opening on the right-hand side of the room, near the top, I looked into a smaller apartment, occupied exclusively by Chinese. They were playing some kind of roulette and another game which seemed wholly to absorb their interest. I ventured no more than a glance, then passed on with my companion.

"Fan-tan!" he whispered in my ear.

Other forms of gambling were in progress at some of the tables; and now Fletcher silently drew my attention to yet a third dimly lighted apartment—this opening out from the left-hand corner of the principal room. The atmosphere of the latter was sufficiently abominable; indeed, the stench was appalling; but a wave of choking vapor met me as I paused for a moment at the threshold of this inner sanctuary. I formed but the vaguest impression of its interior; the smell was sufficient. This annex was evidently reserved for opium-smokers.

Fletcher sat down at a small table near by,

and I took a common wooden chair which he thrust forward with his foot. What should be our next move I could not conjecture. I was looking around at the sordid scene, filled with a bitter sense of my own impotency to aid my missing friend, when that occurred which set my heart beating wildly at once with hope and excitement. Fletcher must have seen something of this in my attitude, for—

"Don't forget what I told you," he whispered. "Be cautious!—be very cautious! . . ."

Chapter VIII

ZARMI OF THE JOY-SHOP

Down the center of the room came a girl carrying the only ornamental object which thus far I had seen in the Joy-Shop: a large Oriental brass tray. She was a figure which must have formed a center of interest in any place, trebly so, then, in such a place as this. Her costume consisted in a series of incongruities, whilst the entire effect was barbaric and by no means unpicturesque. She wore high-heeled red slippers, and, as her short gauzy skirt rendered amply evident, black silk stockings. A brilliantly colored Oriental scarf was wound around her waist and knotted in front, its tasseled ends swinging girdle fashion. A sort of chemise—like the 'anteree of Egyptian women—completed her costume, if I except a number of barbaric ornaments, some of them of silver, with which her hands and arms were bedecked.

But strange as was the girl's attire, it was to her face that my gaze was drawn irresistibly. Evidently, like most of those around us, she was some kind of half-caste; but, unlike them, she was wickedly handsome. I use the adverb *wickedly* with deliberation; for the pallidly dusky, oval face, with the full red lips, between which rested a large yellow cigarette, and the half-closed almond-shaped eyes, possessed a beauty which might have appealed to an artist of one of the modern perverted schools, but which filled me less with admiration than with horror. For I *knew* her—I recognized her, from a past, brief meeting; I knew her, beyond all possibility of doubt, to be one of the Si-Fan group!

This strange creature, tossing back her jet-black, frizzy hair, which was entirely innocent of any binding or ornament, advanced along the room towards us, making unhes-

itatingly for our table, and carrying her lithe body with the grace of a *Ghâzeeyeh.*

I glanced at Fletcher across the table.

"Zarmi!" he whispered.

Again I raised my eyes to the face which now was close to mine, and became aware that I was trembling with excitement. . . .

Heavens! why did enlightenment come too late! Either I was the victim of an odd delusion, or Zarmi had been the driver of the cab in which Nayland Smith had left the New Louvre Hotel!

Zarmi placed the brass tray upon the table and bent down, resting her elbows upon it, her hands upturned and her chin nestling in her palms. The smoke from the cigarette, now held in her fingers, mingled with her dishevelled hair. She looked fully into my face, a long, searching look; then her lips parted in the slow, voluptuous smile of the Orient. Without moving her head she turned the wonderful eyes (rendered doubly luminous by the *kohl* with which her lashes and lids were darkened) upon Fletcher.

"What you and your strong friend drinking?" she said softly.

Her voice possessed a faint husky note which betrayed her Eastern parentage, yet it had in it the siren lure which is the ancient heritage of the Eastern woman—a heritage more ancient than the tribe of the *Ghâzeeyeh,* to one of whom I had mentally likened Zarmi.

"Same thing," replied Fletcher promptly; and, raising his hand, he idly toyed with a huge gold ear-ring which she wore.

Still resting her elbows upon the table and bending down between us, Zarmi turned her slumbering, half-closed black eyes again upon me, then slowly, languishingly, upon Fletcher. She replaced the yellow cigarette between her lips. He continued to toy with the ear-ring.

Suddenly the girl sprang upright, and from its hiding-place within the silken scarf, plucked out a Malay *krîs* with a richly jeweled hilt. Her eyes now widely opened and blazing, she struck at my companion!

I half rose from my chair, stifling a cry of horror; but Fletcher, regarding her fixedly, never moved . . . and Zarmi stayed her hand just as the point of the dagger had reached his throat!

"You see," she whispered softly but intensely, "how soon I can kill you."

Ere I had overcome the amazement and horror with which her action had filled me, she had suddenly clutched me by the shoulder, and, turning from Fletcher, had the point of the *krîs* at *my* throat!

"You, too!" she whispered, "you too!"

Lower and lower she bent, the needle point of the weapon pricking my skin, until her beautiful, evil face almost touched mine. Then, miraculously, the fire died out of her eyes; they half closed again and became languishing, luresome *Ghâzeeyeh* eyes. She laughed softly, wickedly, and puffed cigarette smoke into my face.

Thrusting her dagger into her waist-belt, and snatching up the brass tray, she swayed down the room, chanting some barbaric song in her husky Eastern voice.

I inhaled deeply and glanced across at my companion. Beneath the make-up with which I had stained my skin, I knew that I had grown more than a little pale.

"Fletcher!" I whispered, "we are on the eve of a great discovery—that girl . . ."

I broke off, and clutching the table with both hands, sat listening intently.

From the room behind me, the opium-room, whose entrance was less than two paces from where we sat, came a sound of dragging and tapping! Slowly, cautiously, I began to turn my head; when a sudden outburst of simian chattering from the *fan-tan* players drowned that other sinister sound.

"You heard it, Doctor!" hissed Fletcher.

"The man with the limp!" I said hoarsely; "he is in there! Fletcher! I am utterly confused. I believe this place to hold the key to the whole mystery, I believe . . ."

Fletcher gave me a warning glance—and, turning anew, I saw Zarmi approaching with her sinuous gait, carrying two glasses and a jug upon the ornate tray. These she set down upon the table; then stood spinning the salver cleverly upon the point of her index finger and watching us through half-closed eyes.

My companion took out some loose coins, but the girl thrust the proffered payment aside with her disengaged hand, the salver still whirling upon the upraised finger of the other.

"Presently you pay for drink," she said. "You do something for me—eh?"

"Yep," replied Fletcher nonchalantly, watering the rum in the tumblers. "What time?"

"Presently I tell you. You stay here. This one a strong feller?"—indicating myself.

"Sure," drawled Fletcher; "strong as a mule he is."

"All right. I give him one little kiss if he good boy!"

Tossing the tray in the air she caught it, rested its edge upon her hip, turned, and walked away down the room, puffing her cigarette.

"Listen," I said, bending across the table, "it was Zarmi who drove the cab that came for Nayland Smith to-day!"

"My God!" whispered Fletcher, "then it was nothing less than the hand of Providence that brought us here to-night. Yes! I know how you feel, Doctor!—but we must play our cards as they're dealt to us. We must wait—wait."

Out from the den of the opium-smokers came Zarmi, one hand resting upon her hip and the other uplifted, a smoldering yellow cigarette held between the first and second fingers. With a movement of her eyes she summoned us to join her, then turned and disappeared again through the low doorway.

The time for action was arrived—we were to see behind the scenes of the Joy-Shop! Our chance would come—I never doubted it—our chance to revenge poor Smith even if we could not save him. I became conscious of an inward and suppressed excitement; surreptitiously I felt the hilt of the Browning pistol in my pocket. The shadow of the dead Fu-Manchu seemed to be upon me. God! how I loathed and feared that memory!

"We can make no plans," I whispered to Fletcher, as together we rose from the table; "we must be guided by circumstance."

In order to enter the little room laden with those sickly opium fumes we had to lower our heads. Two steps led down into the place, which was so dark that I hesitated, momentarily, peering about me.

Apparently some four or five persons squatted and lay in the darkness about me. Some were couched upon rough wooden shelves ranged around the walls, others sprawled upon the floor, in the center whereof, upon a small tea-chest, stood a smoky brass lamp. The room and its occupants alike were indeterminate, sketchy; its deadly atmosphere seemed to be suffocating me. A sort of choking sound came from one of the bunks; a vague, obscene murmuring filled the whole place revoltingly.

Zarmi stood at the further end, her lithe figure silhouetted against the vague light coming through an open doorway. I saw her raise her hand, beckoning to us.

Circling around the chest supporting the lamp we crossed the foul den and found ourselves in a narrow, dim passage-way, but in cleaner air.

"Come," said Zarmi, extending her long, slim hand to me.

I took it, solely for guidance in the gloom, and she immediately drew my arm about her waist, leant back against my shoulder and, raising her pouted red lips, blew a cloud of tobacco smoke fully into my eyes!

Momentarily blinded, I drew back with a muttered exclamation. Suspecting what I did of this tigerish half-caste, I could almost have found it in my heart to return her savage pleasantries with interest.

As I raised my hands to my burning eyes, Fletcher uttered a sharp cry of pain. I turned in time to see the girl touch him lightly on the neck with the burning tip of her cigarette.

"You jealous, eh, Charlie?" she said. "But I love you, too—see! Come along, you strong fellers. . . ."

And away she went along the passage, swaying her hips lithely and glancing back over her shoulders in smiling coquetry.

Tears were still streaming from my eyes when I found myself standing in a sort of rough shed, stone-paved, and containing a variety of nondescript rubbish. A lantern stood upon the floor; and beside it . . .

The place seemed to be swimming around me, the stone floor to be heaving beneath my feet. . . .

Beside the lantern stood a wooden chest, some six feet long, and having strong rope handles at either end. Evidently the chest had but recently been nailed up. As Zarmi touched it lightly with the pointed toe of her little red slipper I clutched at Fletcher for support.

Fletcher grasped my arm in a vice-like grip. To him, too, had come the ghastly conviction—the gruesome thought that neither of us dared to name.

It was Nayland Smith's coffin that we were to carry!

"Through here," came dimly to my ears, "and then I tell you what to do. . . ."

Coolness returned to me, suddenly, unaccountably. I doubted not for an instant that the best friend I had in the world lay dead there at the feet of the hellish girl who called herself Zarmi, and I knew since it was she, disguised, who had driven him to his doom, that she must have been actively concerned in his murder.

But, I argued, although the damp night air was pouring in through the door which Zarmi now held open, although sound of Thames-side activity came stealing to my ears, we were yet within the walls of the Joy-Shop, with a score or more Asiatic ruffians at the woman's beck and call. . . .

With perfect truth I can state that I retain not even a shadowy recollection of aiding Fletcher to move the chest out on to the brink of the cutting—for it was upon this that the door directly opened. The mist had grown denser, and except a glimpse of slowly moving water beneath me, I could discern little of our surroundings.

So much I saw by the light of a lantern which stood in the stern of a boat. In the bows of this boat I was vaguely aware of the presence of a crouched figure enveloped in rugs—vaguely aware that two filmy eyes regarded me out of the darkness. A man who looked like a lascar stood upright in the stern.

I must have been acting like a man in a stupor; for I was aroused to the realities by the contact of a burning cigarette with the lobe of my right ear!

"Hurry, quick, strong feller!" said Zarmi softly.

At that it seemed as though some fine nerve of my brain, already strained to utmost tension, snapped. I turned, with a wild, inarticulate cry, my fists raised frenziedly above my head.

"You fiend!" I shrieked at the mocking Eurasian, "you yellow fiend of hell!"

I was beside myself, insane. Zarmi fell back a step, flashing a glance from my own contorted face to that, now pale even beneath its artificial tan, of Fletcher.

I snatched the pistol from my pocket, and for one fateful moment the lust of slaying claimed my mind. . . . Then I turned towards the river, and, raising the Browning, fired shot after shot in the air.

"Weymouth!" I cried. "Weymouth!"

A sharp hissing sound came from behind me; a short, muffled cry . . . and something descended, crushingly, upon my skull. Like a wild cat Zarmi hurled herself past me and leapt into the boat. One glimpse I had of her pallidly dusky face, of her blazing black eyes, and the boat was thrust off into the waterway . . . was swallowed up in the mist.

I turned, dizzily, to see Fletcher sinking to his knees, one hand clutching his breast.

"She got me . . . with the knife," he whispered. "But . . . don't worry . . . look to yourself, and . . . *him*. . . ."

He pointed, weakly—then collapsed at my feet. I threw myself upon the wooden chest with a fierce, sobbing cry.

"Smith, Smith!" I babbled, and knew myself no better, in my sorrow, than an hysterical woman. "Smith, dear old man! speak to me! speak to me! . . ."

Outraged emotion overcame me utterly, and with my arms thrown across the box, I slipped into unconsciousness.

Chapter IX

FU-MANCHU

Many poignant recollections are mine, more of them bitter than sweet; but no one of them all can compare with the memory of that moment of my awakening.

Weymouth was supporting me, and my throat still tingled from the effects of the brandy which he had forced between my teeth from his flask. My heart was beating irregularly; my mind yet partly inert. With something compound of horror and hope I lay staring at one who was anxiously bending over the Inspector's shoulder, watching me.

It was Nayland Smith.

A whole hour of silence seemed to pass, ere speech became possible; then—

"Smith!" I whispered, "are you . . ."

Smith grasped my outstretched, questing hand, grasped it firmly, warmly; and I saw his gray eyes to be dim in the light of the several lanterns around us.

"Am I alive?" he said. "Dear old Petrie! Thanks to you, I am not only alive, but free!"

My head was buzzing like a hive of bees, but I managed, aided by Weymouth, to struggle to my feet. Muffled sounds of shouting and scuffling reached me. Two men in the uniform of the Thames Police were carrying a limp body in at the low doorway communicating with the infernal Joy-Shop.

"It's Fletcher," said Weymouth, noting the anxiety expressed in my face. "His missing lady friend has given him a nasty wound, but he'll pull round all right."

"Thank God for that," I replied, clutching my aching head. "I don't know what weapon she employed in my case, but it narrowly missed achieving her purpose."

My eyes, throughout, were turned upon Smith, for his presence there, alive, still seemed to me miraculous.

"Smith," I said, "for Heaven's sake enlighten me! I never doubted that you were . . ."

"In the wooden chest!" concluded Smith grimly. "Look!"

He pointed to something that lay behind me. I turned, and saw the box which had occasioned me such anguish. The top had been wrenched off and the contents exposed to view. It was filled with a variety of gold ornaments, cups, vases, silks, and barbaric brocaded raiment; it might well have contained the loot of a cathedral. Inspector Weymouth laughed gruffly at my surprise.

"What is it?" I asked, in a voice of amazement.

"It's the treasure of the Si-Fan, I presume," rapped Smith. "Where it has come from and where it was going to, it must be my immediate business to ascertain."

"Then you . . ."

"I was lying, bound and gagged, upon one of the upper shelves in the opium-den! I heard you and Fletcher arrive. I saw you pass through later with that she-devil who drove the cab to-day . . ."

"Then the cab . . ."

"The windows were fastened, unopenable, and some anæsthetic was injected into the interior through a tube—the speaking-tube. I know nothing further, except that our plans must have leaked out in some mysterious fashion. Petrie, my suspicions point to high quarters. The Si-Fan score thus far, for unless the search now in progress brings it to light, we must conclude that they have the brass coffer."

He was interrupted by a sudden loud crying of his name.

"Mr. Nayland Smith!" came from somewhere within the Joy-Shop. "This way, sir!"

Off he went, in his quick, impetuous manner, whilst I stood there, none too steadily, wondering what discovery this outcry portended. I had not long to wait. Out by the low doorway came Smith, a grimly triumphant smile upon his face, carrying the missing brass coffer!

He set it down upon the planking before me.

"John Ki," he said, "who was also on the missing list, had dragged the thing out of the cellar where it was hidden, and in another minute must have slipped away with it. Detective Deacon saw the light shining through a crack in the floor. I shall never forget the look John gave us when we came upon him, as, lamp in hand, he bent over the precious chest."

"Shall you open it now?"

"No." He glanced at me oddly. "I shall have it valued in the morning by Messrs. Meyerstein."

He was keeping something back; I was sure of it.

"Smith," I said suddenly, "the man with the limp! I heard him in the place where you were confined! Did you . . ."

Nayland Smith clicked his teeth together sharply, looking straightly and grimly into my eyes.

"I *saw* him!" he replied slowly; "and unless the effects of the anæsthetic had not wholly worn off . . ."

"Well!" I cried.

"The man with the limp is *Dr. Fu-Manchu!*"

Chapter X

THE TÛLUN-NÛR CHEST

"This box," said Mr. Meyerstein, bending attentively over the carven brass coffer upon the table, "is certainly of considerable value, and possibly almost unique."

Nayland Smith glanced across at me with a slight smile. Mr. Meyerstein ran one fat finger tenderly across the heavily embossed figures, which, like barnacles, encrusted the sides and lid of the weird curio which we had summoned him to appraise.

"What do you think, Lewison?" he added, glancing over his shoulder at the clerk who accompanied him.

Lewison, whose flaxen hair and light blue eyes almost served to mask his Semitic origin, shrugged his shoulders in a fashion incongruous in one of his complexion, though characteristic in one of his name.

"It is as you say, Mr. Meyerstein, an example of early Tûlun-Nûr work," he said. "It may be sixteenth century or even earlier. The Kûren treasure-chest in the Hague Collection has points of similarity, but the workmanship of this specimen is infinitely finer."

"In a word, gentlemen," snapped Nayland Smith, rising from the arm-chair in which he had been sitting, and beginning restlessly to pace the room, "in a word, you would be prepared to make me a substantial offer for this box?"

Mr. Meyerstein, his shrewd eyes twinkling behind the pebbles of his pince-nez, straightened himself slowly, turned in the ponderous manner of a fat man, and re-adjusted the pince-nez upon his nose. He cleared his throat.

"I have not yet seen the interior of the box, Mr. Smith," he said.

Smith paused in his perambulation of the carpet and stared hard at the celebrated art dealer.

"Unfortunately," he replied, "the key is missing."

"Ah!" cried the assistant, Lewison, excitedly, "you are mistaken, sir! Coffers of this description and workmanship are nearly always complicated conjuring tricks; they rarely open by any such rational means as lock and key. For instance, the Kûren treasure-chest to which I referred, opens by an intricate process involving the pressing of certain knobs in the design, and the turning of others."

"It was ultimately opened," said Mr. Meyerstein, with a faint note of professional envy in his voice, "by one of Christie's experts."

"Does my memory mislead me," I interrupted, "or was it not regarding the possession of the chest to which you refer, that the celebrated case of 'Hague versus Jacobs' arose?"

"You are quite right, Dr. Petrie," said Meyerstein, turning to me. "The original owner, a member of the Younghusband Expedition, had been unable to open the chest. When opened at Christie's it proved to contain jewels and other valuables. It was a curious case, wasn't it, Lewison?" turning to his clerk.

"Very," agreed the other absently; then— "Have you endeavored to open this box, Mr. Smith?"

Nayland Smith shook his head grimly.

"From its weight," said Meyerstein, "I am inclined to think that the contents might prove of interest. With your permission I will endeavor to open it."

Nayland Smith, tugging reflectively at the lobe of his left ear, stood looking at the expert. Then—

"I do not care to attempt it at present," he said.

Meyerstein and his clerk stared at the speaker in surprise.

"But you would be mad," cried the former, "if you accepted an offer for the box, whilst ignorant of the nature of its contents."

"But I have invited no offer," said Smith. "I do not propose to sell."

Meyerstein adjusted his pince-nez again.

"I am a business man," he said, "and I will make a business proposal: A hundred guineas for the box, cash down, and our commission to be ten per cent on the proceeds of the contents. You must remember," raising a fat forefinger to check Smith, who was about to interrupt him, "that it may be necessary to force the box in order to open it, thereby decreasing its market value and making it a bad bargain at a hundred guineas."

Nayland Smith met my gaze across the room; again a slight smile crossed the lean, tanned face.

"I can only reply, Mr. Meyerstein," he said, "in this way: if I desire to place the box on the market, you shall have first refusal, and the same applies to the contents, if any. For the moment if you will send me a note of your fee, I shall be obliged." He raised his hand with a conclusive gesture. "I am not prepared to discuss the question of sale any further at present, Mr. Meyerstein."

At that the dealer bowed, took up his hat from the table, and prepared to depart. Lewison opened the door and stood aside.

"Good morning, gentlemen," said Meyerstein.

As Lewison was about to follow him—

"Since you do not intend to open the box," he said, turning, his hand upon the door knob, "have you any idea of its contents?"

"None," replied Smith; "but with my present inadequate knowledge of its history, I do not care to open it."

Lewison smiled skeptically.

"Probably you know best," he said, bowed to us both, and retired.

When the door was closed—

"You see, Petrie," said Smith, beginning to stuff tobacco into his briar, "if we are ever short of funds, here's something"—pointing to the Tûlun-Nûr box upon the table—"which would retrieve our fallen fortunes."

He uttered one of his rare, boyish laughs, and began to pace the carpet again, his gaze always set upon our strange treasure. What did it contain?

The manner in which it had come into our possession suggested that it might contain something of the utmost value to the Yellow group. For we knew the house of John Ki to be, if not the head-quarters, certainly a meeting-place of the mysterious organiza- tion the Si-Fan; we knew that Dr. Fu-Manchu used the place—Dr. Fu-Manchu, the uncanny being whose existence seemingly proved him immune from natural laws, a deathless incarnation of evil.

My gaze set upon the box, I wondered anew what strange, dark secrets it held; I wondered how many murders and crimes greater than murder blackened its history.

"Smith," I said suddenly, "now that the mystery of the absence of a key-hole is explained, I am sorely tempted to essay the task of opening the coffer. I think it might help us to a solution of the whole mystery."

"And I think otherwise!" interrupted my friend grimly. "In a word, Petrie, I look upon this box as a sort of hostage by means of which—who knows—we might one day buy our lives from the enemy. I have a sort of fancy, call it superstition if you will, that nothing—not even our miraculous good luck—could save us if once we ravished its secret."

I stared at him amazedly; this was a new phase in his character.

"I am conscious of something almost like a spiritual unrest," he continued. "Formerly you were endowed with a capacity for divining the presence of Fu-Manchu or his agents. Some such second-sight would appear to have visited me now, and it directs me forcibly to avoid opening the box."

His steps as he paced the floor grew more and more rapid. He relighted his pipe, which had gone out as usual, and tossed the match-end into the hearth.

"To-morrow," he said, "I shall lodge the coffer in a place of greater security. Come along, Petrie, Weymouth is expecting us at Scotland Yard."

Chapter XI

IN THE FOG

"But, Smith," I began, as my friend hurried me along the corridor, "you are not going to leave the box unguarded?"

Nayland Smith tugged at my arm, and, glancing at him, I saw him frowningly shake his head. Utterly mystified, I nevertheless understood that for some reason he desired me to preserve silence for the present. Accordingly I said no more until the lift brought us down into the lobby and we had passed out from the New Louvre Hotel, crossed the busy thoroughfare and entered the buffet of an establishment not far distant. My friend having ordered cocktails—

"And now perhaps you will explain to me the reason for your mysterious behavior?" said I.

Smith, placing my glass before me, glanced about him to right and left, and having satisfied himself that his words could not be overheard—

"Petrie," he whispered, "I believe we are spied upon at the New Louvre."

"What!"

"There are spies of the Si-Fan—of Fu-Manchu—amongst the hotel servants! We have good reason to believe that Dr. Fu-Manchu at one time was actually in the building, and we have been compelled to draw attention to the state of the electric fittings in our apartments, which enables any one in the corridor above to spy upon us."

"Then why do you stay?"

"For a very good reason, Petrie, and the same that prompts me to retain the Tûlun-Nûr box in my own possession rather than to deposit it in the strong-room of my bank."

"I begin to understand."

"I trust you do, Petrie; it is fairly obvious. Probably the plan is a perilous one, but I hope, by laying myself open to attack, to apprehend the enemy—perhaps to make an important capture."

Setting down my glass, I stared in silence at Smith.

"I will anticipate your remark," he said, smiling dryly. "I am aware that I am not entitled to expose *you* to these dangers. It is *my* duty and I must perform it as best I can; you, as a volunteer, are perfectly entitled to withdraw."

As I continued silently to stare at him, his expression changed; the gray eyes grew less steely, and presently, clapping his hand upon my shoulder in his impulsive way—

"Petrie!" he cried, "you know I had no intention of hurting your feelings, but in the circumstances it was impossible for me to say less."

"You have said enough, Smith," I replied shortly. "I beg of you to say no more."

He gripped my shoulder hard, then plunged his hand into his pocket and pulled out the blackened pipe.

"We see it through together, then, though God knows whither it will lead us."

"In the first place," I interrupted, "since

you have left the chest unguarded——"

"I locked the door."

"What is a mere lock where Fu-Manchu is concerned?"

Nayland Smith laughed almost gaily.

"Really, Petrie," he cried, "sometimes I cannot believe that you mean me to take you seriously. Inspector Weymouth has engaged the room immediately facing our door, and no one can enter or leave the suite unseen by him."

"Inspector Weymouth?"

"Oh! for once he has stooped to a disguise: spectacles, and a muffler which covers his face right up to the tip of his nose. Add to this a prodigious overcoat and an asthmatic cough, and you have a picture of Mr. Jonathan Martin, the occupant of room No. 239."

I could not repress a smile upon hearing this description.

"No. 239," continued Smith, "contains two beds, and Mr. Martin's friend will be joining him there this evening."

Meeting my friend's questioning glance, I nodded comprehendingly.

"Then what part do *I* play?"

"Ostensibly we both leave town this evening," he explained; "but I have a scheme whereby you will be enabled to remain behind. We shall thus have one watcher inside and two out."

"It seems almost absurd," I said incredulously, "to expect any member of the Yellow group to attempt anything in a huge hotel like the New Louvre, here in the heart of London!"

Nayland Smith, having lighted his pipe, stretched his arms and stared me straight in the face.

"Has Fu-Manchu never attempted outrage, murder, in the heart of London before?" he snapped.

The words were sufficient. Remembering black episodes of the past (one at least of them had occurred not a thousand yards from the very spot upon which we now stood), I knew that I had spoken folly.

Certain arrangements were made then, including a visit to Scotland Yard; and a plan—though it sounds anomalous—at once elaborate and simple, was put into execution in the dusk of the evening.

London remained in the grip of fog, and when we passed along the corridor communicating with our apartments, faint streaks of yellow vapor showed in the light of the lamp suspended at the further end. I knew that Nayland Smith suspected the presence of some spying contrivance in our rooms, although I was unable to conjecture how this could have been managed without the connivance of the management. In pursuance of his idea, however, he extinguished the lights a moment before we actually quitted the suite. Just within the door he helped me to remove the somewhat conspicuous check traveling-coat which I wore. With this upon his arm he opened the door and stepped out into the corridor.

As the door slammed upon his exit, I heard him cry: "Come along, Petrie! we have barely five minutes to catch our train."

Detective Carter of New Scotland Yard had joined him at the threshold, and muffled up in the gray traveling-coat was now hurrying with Smith along the corridor and out of the hotel. Carter, in build and features, was not unlike me, and I did not doubt that any one who might be spying upon our movements would be deceived by this device.

In the darkness of the apartment I stood listening to the retreating footsteps in the corridor. A sense of loneliness and danger assailed me. I knew that Inspector Weymouth was watching and listening from the room immediately opposite; that he held Smith's key; that I could summon him to my assistance, if necessary, in a matter of seconds.

Yet, contemplating the vigil that lay before me in silence and darkness, I cannot pretend that my frame of mind was buoyant. I could not smoke; I must make no sound.

As pre-arranged, I cautiously removed my boots, and as cautiously tiptoed across the carpet and seated myself in an arm-chair. I determined there to await the arrival of Mr. Jonathan Martin's friend, which I knew could not now be long delayed.

The clocks were striking eleven when he arrived, and in the perfect stillness of that upper corridor, I heard the bustle which heralded his approach, heard the rap upon the door opposite, followed by a muffled "Come in" from Weymouth. Then, as the door was opened, I heard the sound of a wheezy cough.

A strange cracked voice (which, nevertheless, I recognized for Smith's) cried, "Hullo, Martin!—cough no better?"

Upon that the door was closed again, and as the retreating footsteps of the servant died away, complete silence—that peculiar silence which comes with fog—descended once more upon the upper part of the New Louvre Hotel.

Chapter XII

THE VISITANT

That first hour of watching, waiting, and listening in the lonely quietude passed drearily; and with the passage of every quarter—signalized by London's muffled clocks—my mood became increasingly morbid. I peopled the silent rooms opening out of that wherein I sat, with stealthy, murderous figures; my imagination painted hideous yellow faces upon the draperies, twitching yellow hands protruding from this crevice and that. A score of times I started nervously, thinking I heard the pad of bare feet upon the floor behind me, the suppressed breathing of some deathly approach.

Since nothing occurred to justify these tremors, this apprehensive mood passed; I realized that I was growing cramped and stiff, that unconsciously I had been sitting with my muscles nervously tensed. The window was open a foot or so at the top and the blind was drawn; but so accustomed were my eyes now to peering through the darkness, that I could plainly discern the yellow oblong of the window, and, though very vaguely, some of the appointments of the room—the Chesterfield against one wall, the lamp-shade above my head, the table with the Tûlun-Nûr box upon it.

There was fog in the room, and it was growing damply chill, for we had extinguished the electric heater some hours before. Very few sounds penetrated from outside. Twice or perhaps thrice people passed along the corridor, going to their rooms; but, as I knew, the greater number of the rooms along that corridor were unoccupied.

From the Embankment far below me, and from the river, faint noises came at long intervals it is true; the muffled hooting of motors, and yet fainter ringing of bells. Fog signals boomed distantly, and train whistles shrieked, remote and unreal. I determined to enter my bedroom and, risking any sound which I might make, to lie down upon the bed.

I rose carefully and carried this plan into

execution. I would have given much for a smoke, although my throat was parched; and almost any drink would have been nectar. But although my hopes (or my fears) of an intruder had left me, I determined to stick to the rules of the game as laid down. Therefore I neither smoked nor drank, but carefully extended my weary limbs upon the coverlet, and telling myself that I could guard our strange treasure as well from there as from elsewhere . . . slipped off into a profound sleep.

Nothing approaching in acute and sustained horror to the moment when next I opened my eyes exists in all my memories of those days.

In the first place I was aroused by the shaking of the bed. It was quivering beneath me as though an earthquake disturbed the very foundations of the building. I sprang upright and into full consciousness of my lapse. . . . My hands clutching the coverlet on either side of me, I sat staring, staring, staring . . . at *that* which peered at me over the foot of the bed.

I knew that I had slept at my post; I was convinced that I was now widely awake; yet I *dared* not admit to myself that what I saw was other than a product of my imagination. I dared not admit the physical quivering of the bed, for I could not, with sanity, believe its cause to be anything human. But what I saw, yet could not credit seeing, was this:

A ghostly white face, which seemed to glisten in some faint reflected light from the sitting-room beyond, peered over the bedrail; gibbered at me demoniacally. With quivering hands this night-mare horror, which had intruded where I believed human intrusion to be all but impossible, clutched the bedposts so that the frame of the structure shook and faintly rattled. . . .

My heart leapt wildly in my breast, then seemed to suspend its pulsations and to grow icily cold. My whole body became chilled horrifically. My scalp tingled: I felt that I must either cry out or become stark, raving mad!

For this clammily white face, those staring eyes, that wordless gibbering, and the shaking, shaking, shaking of the bed in the clutch of the nameless visitant—prevailed, refused to disperse like the evil dream I had hoped it all to be; manifested itself, indubitably, as something tangible—objective. . . .

Outraged reason deprived me of coherent speech. Past the clammy white face I could see the sitting-room illuminated by a faint light; I could even see the Tûlun-Nûr box upon the table immediately opposite the door.

The thing which shook the bed was actual, existent—to be counted with!

Further and further I drew myself away from it, until I crouched close up against the head of the bed. Then, as the thing reeled aside, and—merciful Heaven!—made as if to come around and approach me yet closer, I uttered a hoarse cry and hurled myself out upon the floor and on the side remote from that pallid horror which I thought was pursuing me.

I heard a dull thud . . . and the thing disappeared from my view. Yet—and remembering the supreme terror of that visitation I am not ashamed to confess it—I dared not move from the spot upon which I stood, I dared not make to pass that which lay between me and the door.

"Smith!" I cried, but my voice was little more than a hoarse whisper—"Smith! Weymouth!"

The words became clearer and louder as I proceeded, so that the last—"Weymouth!"—was uttered in a sort of falsetto scream.

A door burst open upon the other side of the corridor. A key was inserted in the lock of the door. Into the dimly lighted arch which divided the bedroom from the sitting-room, sprang the figure of Nayland Smith!

"Petrie! Petrie!" he called—and I saw him standing there looking from left to right.

Then, ere I could reply, he turned, and his gaze fell upon whatever lay upon the floor at the foot of the bed.

"My God!" he whispered—and sprang into the room.

"Smith! Smith!" I cried, "what is it? what is it?"

He turned in a flash, as Weymouth entered at his heels, saw me, and fell back a step; then looked again down at the floor.

"God's mercy!" he whispered, "I thought it was you—I thought it was you!"

Trembling violently, my mind a feverish chaos, I moved to the foot of the bed and looked down at what lay there.

"Turn up the light!" snapped Smith.

Weymouth reached for the switch, and the room became illuminated suddenly.

Prone upon the carpet, hands outstretched and nails dug deeply into the pile of the fabric, lay a dark-haired man having his head twisted sideways so that the face showed a ghastly pallid profile against the rich colorings upon which it rested. He wore no coat, but a sort of dark gray shirt and black trousers. To add to the incongruity of his attire, his feet were clad in drab-colored shoes, rubber-soled.

I stood, one hand raised to my head, looking down upon him, and gradually regaining control of myself. Weymouth, perceiving something of my condition, silently passed his flask to me; and I gladly availed myself of this.

"How in Heaven's name did he get in?" I whispered.

"How, indeed!" said Weymouth, staring about him with wondering eyes.

Both he and Smith had discarded their disguises; and, a bewildered trio, we stood looking down upon the man at our feet. Suddenly Smith dropped to his knees and turned him flat upon his back. Composure was nearly restored to me, and I knelt upon the other side of the white-faced creature whose presence there seemed so utterly outside the realm of possibility, and examined him with a consuming and fearful interest; for it was palpable that, if not already dead, he was dying rapidly.

He was a slightly built man, and the first discovery that I made was a curious one. What I had mistaken for dark hair was a wig! The short black mustache which he wore was also factitious.

"Look at this!" I cried.

"I am looking," snapped Smith.

He suddenly stood up, and, entering the room beyond, turned on the light there. I saw him staring at the Tûlun-Nûr box, and I knew what had been in his mind. But the box, undisturbed, stood upon the table as we had left it. I saw Smith tugging irritably at the lobe of his ear, and staring from the box towards the man beside whom I knelt.

"For God's sake, what does it mean?" said Inspector Weymouth in a voice hushed with wonder. "How did he get in? What did he come for?—and what has happened to him?"

"As to what has happened to him," I replied, "unfortunately I cannot tell you. I only know that unless something can be done his end is not far off."

"Shall we lay him on the bed?"

I nodded, and together we raised the slight figure and placed it upon the bed where so recently I had lain.

As we did so, the man suddenly opened his eyes, which were glazed with delirium.

He tore himself from our grip, sat bolt upright, and holding his hands, fingers outstretched, before his face, stared at them frenziedly.

"The golden pomegranates!" he shrieked, and a slight froth appeared on his blanched lips. "The golden pomegranates!"

He laughed madly, and fell back inert.

"He's dead!" whispered Weymouth; "he's dead!"

Hard upon his words came a cry from Smith:

"Quick! Petrie!—Weymouth!"

Chapter XIII

THE ROOM BELOW

I ran into the sitting-room, to discover Nayland Smith craning out of the now widely opened window. The blind had been drawn up, I did not know by whom; and, leaning out beside my friend, I was in time to perceive some bright object moving down the gray stone wall. Almost instantly it disappeared from sight in the yellow banks below.

Smith leapt around in a whirl of excitement.

"Come on, Petrie!" he cried, seizing my arm. "You remain here, Weymouth; don't leave these rooms whatever happens!"

We ran out into the corridor. For my own part I had not the vaguest idea what we were about. My mind was not yet fully recovered from the frightful shock which it had sustained; and the strange words of the dying man—"the golden pomegranates"—had increased my mental confusion. Smith apparently had not heard them, for he remained grimly silent, as side by side we raced down the marble stairs to the corridor immediately below our own.

Although, amid the hideous turmoil to which I had awakened, I had noted nothing of the hour, evidently the night was far advanced. Not a soul was to be seen from end to end of the vast corridor in which we stood . . . until on the right-hand side and about half-way along, a door opened and a woman came out hurriedly, carrying a small handbag.

She wore a veil, so that her features were but vaguely distinguished, but her every movement was agitated; and this agitation perceptibly increased when, turning, she perceived the two of us bearing down upon her.

Nayland Smith, who had been audibly counting the doors along the corridor as we passed them, seized the woman's arm without ceremony, and pulled her into the apartment she had been on the point of quitting, closing the door behind us as we entered.

"Smith!" I began, "for Heaven's sake what are you about?"

"You shall see, Petrie!" he snapped.

He released the woman's arm, and pointing to an arm-chair near by—

"Be seated," he said sternly.

Speechless with amazement, I stood, with my back to the door, watching this singular scene. Our captive, who wore a smart walking costume and whose appearance was indicative of elegance and culture, so far had uttered no word of protest, no cry.

Now, whilst Smith stood rigidly pointing to the chair, she seated herself with something very like composure and placed the leather bag upon the floor beside her. The room in which I found myself was one of a suite almost identical with our own, but from what I had gathered in a hasty glance around, it bore no signs of recent tenancy. The window was widely opened, and upon the floor lay a strange-looking contrivance apparently made of aluminum. A large grip, open, stood beside it, and from this some portions of a black coat and other garments protruded.

"Now, madame," said Nayland Smith, "will you be good enough to raise your veil?"

Silently, unprotestingly, the woman obeyed him, raising her gloved hands and lifting the veil from her face.

The features revealed were handsome in a hard fashion, but heavily made-up. Our captive was younger than I had hitherto supposed; a blonde, her hair artificially reduced to the so-called Titian tint. But, despite her youth, her eyes, with the blackened lashes, were full of a world weariness. Now she smiled cynically.

"Are you satisfied," she said, speaking unemotionally, "or," holding up her wrists, "would you like to handcuff me?"

Nayland Smith, glancing from the open grip and the appliance beside it to the face of the speaker, began clicking his teeth together, whereby I knew him to be perplexed. Then he stared across at me.

"You appear bemused, Petrie," he said, with a certain irritation. "Is this what mystifies you?"

Stooping, he picked up the metal contrivance, and almost savagely jerked open the top section. It was a telescopic ladder, and more ingeniously designed than anything of the kind I had seen before. There was a sort of clamp attached to the base, and two sharply pointed hooks at the top.

"For reaching windows on an upper floor," snapped my friend, dropping the thing with a clatter upon the carpet. "An American device which forms part of the equipment of the modern hotel thief!"

He seemed to be disappointed—fiercely disappointed; and I found his attitude inexplicable. He turned to the woman—who sat regarding him with that fixed cynical smile.

"Who are you?" he demanded; "and what business have you with the Si-Fan?"

The woman's eyes opened more widely, and the smile disappeared from her face.

"The Si-Fan!" she repeated slowly. "I don't know what you mean, Inspector."

"I am not an Inspector," snapped Smith, "and you know it well enough. You have one chance—your last. To whom were you to deliver the box? when and where?"

But the blue eyes remained upraised to the grim tanned face with a look of wonder in them, which, if assumed, marked the woman a consummate actress.

"Who are you?" she asked in a low voice, "and what are you talking about?"

Inactive, I stood by the door watching my friend, and his face was a fruitful study in perplexity. He seemed upon the point of an angry outburst, then, staring intently into the questioning eyes upraised to his, he checked the words he would have uttered and began to click his teeth together again.

"You are some servant of Dr. Fu-Manchu!" he said.

The girl frowned with a bewilderment which I could have sworn was not assumed. Then—

"You said I had one chance a moment ago," she replied. "But if you referred to my answering any of your questions, it is no chance at all. We have gone under, and I know it. I am not complaining; it's all in the game. There's a clear enough case against us, and I am sorry"—suddenly, unexpectedly, her eyes became filled with tears, which coursed down her cheeks, leaving little wakes of blackness from the make-up upon her lashes. Her lips trembled, and her voice shook. "I am sorry I let him do it. He'd never done anything—not anything big like this—before, and he never would have done if he had not met me. . . ."

The look of perplexity upon Smith's face was increasing with every word that the girl uttered.

"You don't seem to know me," she continued, her emotion momentarily growing greater, "and I don't know you; but they will know me at Bow Street. I urged him to do it, when he told me about the box to-day at lunch. He said that if it contained half as much as the Kûren treasure-chest, we could sail for America and be on the straight all the rest of our lives. . . ."

And now something which had hitherto been puzzling me became suddenly evident. I had not removed the wig worn by the dead man, but I knew that he had fair hair, and when in his last moments he had opened his eyes, there had been in the contorted face something faintly familiar.

"Smith!" I cried excitedly, "it is Lewison, Meyerstein's clerk! Don't you understand? don't you understand?"

Smith brought his teeth together with a snap and stared me hard in the face.

"I do, Petrie. I have been following a false scent. I do!"

The girl in the chair was now sobbing convulsively.

"He was tempted by the possibility of the box containing treasure," I ran on, "and his acquaintance with this—lady—who is evidently no stranger to felonious operations, led him to make the attempt with her assistance. But"—I found myself confronted by a new problem—"what caused his death?"

"His . . . *death!*"

As a wild, hysterical shriek the words smote upon my ears. I turned, to see the girl rise, tottering, from her seat. She began groping in front of her, blindly, as though a darkness had descended.

"You did not say he was dead?" she whispered, "not dead!—not . . ."

The words were lost in a wild peal of laughter. Clutching at her throat she swayed and would have fallen had I not caught her in my arms. As I laid her insensible upon the settee I met Smith's glance.

"I think I know that, too, Petrie," he said gravely.

Chapter XIV

THE GOLDEN POMEGRANATES

"What was it that he cried out?" demanded Nayland Smith abruptly. "I was in the sitting-room and it sounded to me like 'pomegranates'!"

We were bending over Lewison; for now, the wig removed, Lewison it proved unmistakably to be, despite the puffy and pallid face.

"He said 'the golden pomegranates,' " I replied, and laughed harshly. "They were words of delirium and cannot possibly have any bearing upon the manner of his death."

"I disagree."

He strode out into the sitting-room.

Weymouth was below, supervising the removal of the unhappy prisoner, and together Smith and I stood looking down at the brass box. Suddenly—

"I propose to attempt to open it," said my friend.

His words came as a complete surprise.

"For what reason?—and why have you so suddenly changed your mind?"

"For a reason which I hope will presently become evident," he said; "and as to my change of mind, unless I am greatly mistaken, the wily old Chinaman from whom I wrested this treasure was infinitely more clever than I gave him credit for being!"

Through the open window came faintly to my ears the chiming of Big Ben. The hour was a quarter to two. London's pulse was dimmed now, and around about us the great city slept as soundly as it ever sleeps. Other sounds came vaguely through the fog, and beside Nayland Smith I sat and watched him at work upon the Tûlun-Nûr box.

Every knob of the intricate design he pushed, pulled and twisted; but without result. The night wore on, and just before three o'clock Inspector Weymouth knocked upon the door. I admitted him, and side by side the two of us stood watching Smith patiently pursuing his task.

All conversation had ceased, when, just as the muted booming of London's clocks reached my ears again and Weymouth pulled out his watch, there came a faint click . . . and I saw that Smith had raised the lid of the coffer!

Weymouth and I sprang forward with one accord, and over Smith's shoulders peered into the interior. There was a second lid of some dull, black wood, apparently of great age, and fastened to it so as to form knobs or handles was an exquisitely carved pair of *golden pomegranates!*

"They are to raise the wooden lid, Mr. Smith!" cried Weymouth eagerly. "Look! there is a hollow in each to accommodate the fingers!"

"Aren't you going to open it?" I demanded excitedly—"aren't you going to open it?"

"Might I invite you to accompany me into the bedroom yonder for a moment?" he replied in a tone of studied reserve. "You also, Weymouth?"

Smith leading, we entered the room where the dead man lay stretched upon the bed.

"Note the appearance of his fingers," directed Nayland Smith.

I examined the peculiarity to which Smith had drawn my attention. The dead man's fingers were swollen extraordinarily, the index finger of either hand especially being oddly discolored, as though bruised from the nail upward. I looked again at the ghastly face, then, repressing a shudder, for the sight was one not good to look upon, I turned to Smith, who was watching me expectantly with his keen, steely eyes.

From his pocket he took out a knife containing a number of implements, amongst them a hook-like contrivance.

"Have you a button-hook, Petrie," he asked, "or anything of that nature?"

"How will this do?" said the Inspector, and he produced a pair of handcuffs. "They were not wanted," he added significantly.

"Better still," declared Smith.

Reclosing his knife, he took the handcuffs from Weymouth, and, returning to the sitting-room, opened them widely and inserted two steel points in the hollows of the golden pomegranates. He pulled. There was a faint sound of moving mechanism and the wooden lid lifted, revealing the interior of the coffer. It contained three long bars of lead—and nothing else!

Supporting the lid with the handcuffs— "Just pull the light over here, Petrie," said Smith.

I did as he directed.

"Look into these two cavities where one is expected to thrust one's fingers!"

Weymouth and I craned forward so that our heads came into contact.

"My God!" whispered the Inspector, "we know now what killed him!"

Visible, in either little cavity against the edge of the steel handcuff, was the point of a needle, which evidently worked in an exquisitely made socket through which the action of raising the lid caused it to protrude. Underneath the lid, midway between the two pomegranates, as I saw by slowly moving the lamp, was a little receptacle of metal communicating with the base of the hollow needles.

The action of lifting the lid not only protruded the points but also operated the hypodermic syringe!

"Note," snapped Smith—but his voice was slightly hoarse.

He removed the points of the bracelets. The box immediately reclosed with no other sound than a faint click.

"God forgive him," said Smith, glancing toward the other room, "for he died in my stead!—and Dr. Fu-Manchu scores an undeserved failure!"

Chapter XV

ZARMI REAPPEARS

"Come in!" I cried. The door opened and a page-boy entered.

"A cable for Dr. Petrie."

I started up from my chair. A thousand possibilities—some of a sort to bring dread to my heart—instantly occurred to me. I tore open the envelope and, as one does, glanced first at the name of the sender.

It was signed "Kâramanèh!"

"Smith!" I said hoarsely, glancing over the message, "Kâramanèh is on her way to England. She arrives by the *Nicobar* to-morrow!"

"Eh?" cried Nayland Smith, in turn leaping to his feet. "She had no right to come alone, unless——"

The boy, open-mouthed, was listening to our conversation, and I hastily thrust a coin into his hand and dismissed him. As the door closed—

"Unless what, Smith?" I said, looking my friend squarely in the eyes.

"Unless," he rapped, "she has learnt something, or—is flying from some one!"

My mind set in a whirl of hopes and fears, longings and dreads.

"What do you mean, Smith?" I asked. "This is the place of danger, as we know to our cost; she was safe in Egypt."

Nayland Smith commenced one of his restless perambulations, glancing at me from time to time and frequently tugging at the lobe of his ear.

"*Was* she safe in Egypt?" he rapped. "We are dealing, remember, with the Si-Fan, which, if I am not mistaken, is a sort of Eleusinian Mystery holding some kind of dominion over the Eastern mind, and boasting initiates throughout the Orient. It is almost certain that there is an Egyptian branch, or group—call it what you will—of the damnable organization."

"But Dr. Fu-Manchu——"

"Dr. Fu-Manchu—for he lives, Petrie! my own eyes bear witness to the fact—Dr. Fu-Manchu is a sort of delegate from the headquarters. His prodigious genius will readily enable him to keep in touch with every branch of the movement, East and West."

He paused to knock out his pipe into an ashtray and to watch me for some moments in silence.

"He may have instructed his Cairo agents," he added significantly.

"God grant she get to England in safety," I whispered. "Smith! can we make no move to round up the devils who defy us, here in the very heart of civilized England? Listen. You will not have forgotten the wild-cat Eurasian Zarmi?"

Smith nodded. "I recall the lady perfectly!" he snapped.

"Unless my imagination has been playing me tricks, I have seen her twice within the last few days—once in the neighborhood of this hotel and once in a cab in Piccadilly."

"You mentioned the matter at the time," said Smith shortly; "but although I made inquiries, as you remember, nothing came of them."

"Nevertheless, I don't think I was mistaken. I feel in my very bones that the Yellow hand of Fu-Manchu is about to stretch out again. If only we could apprehend Zarmi."

Nayland Smith lighted his pipe with care. "If only we could, Petrie!" he said; "but, damn it!"—he dashed his left fist into the palm of his right hand—"we are doomed to remain inactive. We can only await the arrival of Kâramanèh and see if she has anything to tell us. I must admit that there are certain theories of my own which I haven't yet had an opportunity of testing. Perhaps in the near future such an opportunity may arise."

How soon that opportunity was to arise neither of us suspected then; but Fate is a merry trickster, and even as we spoke of these matters events were brewing which were to lead us along strange paths.

With such glad anticipations as my pen cannot describe, their gladness not unmixed with fear, I retired to rest that night, scarcely expecting to sleep, so eager was I for the morrow. The musical voice of Kâramanèh seemed to ring in my ears; I seemed to feel the touch of her soft hands and to detect, as I drifted into the borderland betwixt reality and slumber, that faint, exquisite perfume which from the first moment of my meeting with the beautiful Eastern girl, had become to me inseparable from her personality.

It seemed that sleep had but just claimed me when I was awakened by some one roughly shaking my shoulder. I sprang upright, my mind alert to sudden danger. The room looked yellow and dismal, illuminated as it was by a cold light of dawn which crept through the window and which competed the luminance of the electric lamps.

Nayland Smith stood at my bedside, partially dressed!

"Wake up, Petrie!" he cried; "your instincts serve you better than my reasoning. Hell's afoot, old man! Even as you predicted it, perhaps in that same hour, the yellow fiends were at work!"

"What, Smith, what!" I said, leaping out of bed; "you don't mean——"

"Not that, old man," he replied, clapping his hand upon my shoulder; "there is no further news of *her*, but Weymouth is waiting outside. Sir Baldwin Frazer has disappeared!"

I rubbed my eyes hard and sought to clear my mind of the vapors of sleep.

"Sir Baldwin Frazer!" I said, "of Half-Moon Street? But what——"

"God knows *what*," snapped Smith; "but our old friend Zarmi, or so it would appear, bore him off last night, and he has completely vanished, leaving practically no trace behind."

Only a few sleeping servants were about as we descended the marble stairs to the lobby of the hotel where Weymouth was awaiting us.

"I have a cab outside from the Yard," he said. "I came straight here to fetch you before going on to Half-Moon Street."

"Quite right!" snapped Smith; "but you

are sure the cab is from the Yard? I have had painful experience of strange cabs recently!"

"You can trust this one," said Weymouth, smiling slightly. "It has carried me to the scene of many a crime."

"Hem!" said Smith—"a dubious recommendation."

We entered the waiting vehicle and soon were passing through the nearly deserted streets of London. Only those workers whose toils began with the dawn were afoot at that early hour, and in the misty gray light the streets had an unfamiliar look and wore an aspect of sadness in ill accord with the sentiments which now were stirring within me. For whatever might be the fate of the famous mental specialist, whatever the mystery before us—even though Dr. Fu-Manchu himself, malignantly active, threatened our safety—Kâramanèh would be with me again that day—Kâramanèh, my beautiful wife to be!

So selfishly occupied was I with these reflections that I paid little heed to the words of Weymouth, who was acquainting Nayland Smith with the facts bearing upon the mysterious disappearance of Sir Baldwin Frazer. Indeed, I was almost entirely ignorant upon the subject when the cab pulled up before the surgeon's house in Half-Moon Street.

Here, where all else spoke of a city yet sleeping or but newly awakened, was wild unrest and excitement. Several servants were hovering about the hall eager to glean any scrap of information that might be obtainable; wide-eyed and curious, if not a little fearful. In the somber dining-room with its heavy oak furniture and gleaming silver, Sir Baldwin's secretary awaited us. He was a young man, fair-haired, clean-shaven and alert; but a real and ever-present anxiety could be read in his eyes.

"I am sorry," he began, "to have been the cause of disturbing you at so early an hour, particularly since this mysterious affair may prove to have no connection with the matters which I understand are at present engaging your attention."

Nayland Smith raised his hand deprecatingly.

"We are prepared, Mr. Logan," he replied, "to travel to the uttermost ends of the earth at all times, if by doing so we can obtain even a meager clue to the enigma which baffles us."

"I should not have disturbed Mr. Smith," said Weymouth, "if I had not been pretty sure that there was Chinese devilry at work here: nor should I have told you as much as I have, Mr. Logan," he added, a humorous twinkle creeping into his blue eyes, "if I had thought you could not be of use to us in unraveling our case!"

"I quite understand that," said Logan, "and now, since you have voted for the story first and refreshments afterward, let me tell you what little I know of the matter."

"Be as brief as you can," snapped Nayland Smith, starting up from the chair in which he had been seated and beginning restlessly to pace the floor before the open fireplace—"as brief as is consistent with clarity. We have learnt in the past that an hour or less sometimes means the difference between——"

He paused, glancing at Sir Baldwin's secretary.

"Between life and death," he added.

Mr. Logan started perceptibly.

"You alarm me, Mr. Smith," he declared; "for I can conceive of no earthly manner in which this mysterious Eastern organization of which Inspector Weymouth speaks, could profit by the death of Sir Baldwin."

Nayland Smith suddenly turned and stared grimly at the speaker.

"I call it death," he said harshly, "to be carried off to the interior of China, to be made a mere slave, having no will but the will of the great and evil man who already—already, mark you!—has actually accomplished such things."

"But Sir Baldwin——"

"Sir Baldwin Frazer," snapped Smith, "is the undisputed head of his particular branch of surgery. Dr. Fu-Manchu may have what he deems useful employment for such skill as his. But," glancing at the clock, "we are wasting time. Your story, Mr. Logan."

"It was about half-past twelve last night," began the secretary, closing his eyes as if he were concentrating his mind upon certain past events, "when a woman came here and inquired for Sir Baldwin. The butler informed her that Sir Baldwin was entertaining friends and that he could receive no professional visitors until the morning. She was so insistent, however, absolutely declining to go away, that I was sent for—I have rooms in the house—and I came down to interview her in the library."

"Be very accurate, Mr. Logan," interrupted Smith, "in your description of this visitor."

"I shall do my best," pursued Logan, closing his eyes again in concentrated thought. "She wore evening dress, of a fantastic kind, markedly Oriental in character, and had large gold rings in her ears. A green embroidered shawl, with raised figures of white birds as a design, took the place of a cloak. It was certainly of Eastern workmanship, possibly Arab; and she wore it about her shoulders with one corner thrown over her head—again, something like a *burnous*. She was extremely dark, had jet-black, frizzy hair and very remarkable eyes, the finest of their type I have ever seen. She possessed beauty of a sort, of course, but without being exactly vulgar, it was what I may term *ostentatious*; and as I entered the library I found myself at a loss to define her exact place in society—you understand what I mean?"

We all nodded comprehendingly and awaited with intense interest the resumption of the story. Mr. Logan had vividly described the Eurasian Zarmi, the creature of Dr. Fu-Manchu.

"When the woman addressed me," he continued, "my surmise that she was some kind of half-caste, probably a Eurasian, was confirmed by her broken English. I shall not be misunderstood"—a slight embarrassment became perceptible in his manner—"if I say that the visitor quite openly tried to bewitch me; and since we are all human, you will perhaps condone my conduct when I add that she succeeded, in a measure, inasmuch as I consented to speak to Sir Baldwin, although he was actually playing bridge at the time.

"Either my eloquence, or, to put it bluntly, the extraordinary fee which the woman offered, resulted in Sir Baldwin's agreeing to abandon his friends and accompany the visitor in a cab which was waiting to see the patient."

"And who was the patient?" rapped Smith.

"According to the woman's account, the patient was her mother, who had met with a street accident a week before. She gave the name of the consultant who had been called in, and who, she stated, had advised the opinion of Sir Baldwin. She represented that the matter was urgent, and that it might be necessary to perform an operation immediately in order to save the patient's life."

"But surely," I interrupted, in surprise,

"Sir Baldwin did not take his instruments?"

"He took his case with him—yes," replied Logan; "for he in turn yielded to the appeals of the visitor. The very last words that I heard him speak as he left the house were to assure her that no such operation could be undertaken at such short notice in that way."

Logan paused, looking around at us a little wearily.

"And what aroused your suspicions?" said Smith.

"My suspicions were aroused at the very moment of Sir Baldwin's departure, for as I came out onto the steps with him I noticed a singular thing."

"And that was?" snapped Smith.

"Directly Sir Baldwin had entered the cab the woman got out," replied Logan with some excitement in his manner, "and reclosing the door took her seat beside the driver of the vehicle—which immediately moved off."

Nayland Smith glanced significantly at me.

"The cab trick again, Petrie!" he said; "scarcely a doubt of it." Then, to Logan: "Anything else?"

"This," replied the secretary: "I thought, although I could not be sure, that the face of Sir Baldwin peered out of the window for a moment as the cab moved away from the house, and that there was a strange expression upon it, almost a look of horror. But of course as there was no light in the cab and the only illumination was that from the open door, I could not be sure."

"And now tell Mr. Smith," said Weymouth, "how you got confirmation of your fears."

"I felt very uneasy in my mind," continued Logan, "for the whole thing was so irregular, and I could not rid my memory of the idea of Sir Baldwin's face looking out from the cab window. Therefore I rang up the consultant whose name our visitor had mentioned."

"Yes?" cried Smith eagerly.

"He knew nothing whatever of the matter," said Logan, "and had no such case upon his books! That of course put me in a dreadful state of mind, but I was naturally anxious to avoid making a fool of myself and therefore I waited for some hours before mentioning my suspicions to any one. But when the morning came and no message was received I determined to communicate with Scotland Yard. The rest of the mystery it is for you, gentlemen, to unravel."

Chapter XVI

I TRACK ZARMI

"What does it mean?" said Nayland Smith wearily, looking at me through the haze of tobacco smoke which lay between us. "A well-known man like Sir Baldwin Frazer is decoyed away—undoubtedly by the woman Zarmi; and up to the present moment not so much as a trace of him can be found. It is mortifying to think that with all the facilities of New Scotland Yard at our disposal we cannot trace that damnable cab! We cannot find the headquarters of the group—we cannot *move!* To sit here inactive whilst Sir Baldwin Frazer—God knows for what purpose!— is perhaps being smuggled out of the country, is maddening—maddening!" Then, glancing quickly across to me: "To think . . ."

I rose from my chair, head averted. A tragedy had befallen me which completely overshadowed all other affairs, great and small. Indeed, its poignancy was not yet come to its most acute stage; the news was too recent for that. It had numbed my mind; dulled the pulsing life within me.

The s.s. *Nicobar*, of the Oriental Navigation Line, had arrived at Tilbury at the scheduled time. My heart leaping joyously in my bosom, I had hurried on board to meet Kâramanèh. . . .

I have sustained some cruel blows in my life; but I can state with candor that this which now befell me was by far the greatest and the most crushing I had ever been called upon to bear; a calamity dwarfing all others which I could imagine.

She had left the ship at Southampton— and had vanished completely.

"Poor old Petrie," said Smith, and clapped his hands upon my shoulders in his impulsive, sympathetic way. "Don't give up hope! We are not going to be beaten!"

"Smith," I interrupted bitterly, "what chance have we? what chance have we? We know no more than a child unborn where these people have their hiding-place, and we haven't a shadow of a clue to guide us to it."

His hands resting upon my shoulders and his gray eyes looking straightly into mine.

"I can only repeat, old man," said my friend, "don't abandon hope. I must leave you for an hour or so, and, when I return, possibly I may have some news."

For long enough after Smith's departure I sat there, companioned only by wretched reflections; then, further inaction seemed impossible; to move, to be up and doing, to be seeking, questing, became an imperative necessity. Muffled in a heavy traveling coat I went out into the wet and dismal night, having no other plan in mind than that of walking on through the rain-swept streets, on and always on, in an attempt, vain enough, to escape from the deadly thoughts that pursued me.

Without having the slightest idea that I had done so, I must have walked along the Strand, crossed Trafalgar Square, proceeded up the Haymarket to Piccadilly Circus, and commenced to trudge along Regent Street; for I found myself staring vaguely at the Oriental rugs displayed in Messrs. Liberty's window, when an incident aroused me from the apathy of sorrow in which I was sunken.

"Tell the cab feller to drive to the north side of Wandsworth Common," said a woman's voice—a voice speaking in broken English, a voice which electrified me, had me alert and watchful in a moment.

I turned, as the speaker, entering a taxicab that was drawn up by the pavement, gave these directions to the door-porter, who with open umbrella was in attendance. Just one glimpse I had of her as she stepped into the cab, but it was sufficient. Indeed, the voice had been sufficient; but that sinuous shape and that lithe swaying movement of the hips removed all doubt.

It was Zarmi!

As the cab moved off I ran out into the middle of the road, where there was a rank, and sprang into the first taxi waiting there.

"Follow the cab ahead!" I cried to the man, my voice quivering with excitement. "Look! you can see the number! There can be no mistake. But don't lose it for your life! It's worth a sovereign to you!"

The man, warming to my mood, cranked his engine rapidly and sprang to the wheel. I was wild with excitement now, and fearful lest the cab ahead should have disappeared; but fortune seemingly was with me for once, and I was not twenty yards behind when Zarmi's cab turned the first corner ahead. Through the gloomy street, which appeared to be populated solely by streaming umbrellas, we went. I could scarcely keep my seat; every nerve in my body seemed to be dancing—twitching. Eternally I was peering ahead; and when, leaving the well-lighted West End thoroughfares, we came to the comparatively gloomy streets of the suburbs, a hundred times I thought we had lost the track. But always in the pool of light cast by some friendly lamp, I would see the quarry again speeding on before us.

At a lonely spot bordering the common the vehicle which contained Zarmi stopped. I snatched up the speaking-tube.

"Drive on," I cried, "and pull up somewhere beyond! Not too far!"

The man obeyed, and presently I found myself standing in what was now become a steady downpour, looking back at the headlights of the other cab. I gave the driver his promised reward.

"Wait for ten minutes," I directed; "then if I have not returned, you need wait no longer."

I strode along the muddy, unpaved path, to the spot where the cab, now discharged, was being slowly backed away into the road. The figure of Zarmi, unmistakable by reason of the lithe carriage, was crossing in the direction of a path which seemingly led across the common. I followed at a discreet distance. Realizing the tremendous potentialities of this rencontre I seemed to rise to the occasion; my brain became alert and clear; every faculty was at its brightest. And I felt serenely confident of my ability to make the most of the situation.

Zarmi went on and on along the lonely path. Not another pedestrian was in sight, and the rain walled in the pair of us. Where comfort-loving humanity sought shelter from the inclement weather, we two moved out there in the storm, linked by a common enmity.

I have said that my every faculty was keen, and have spoken of my confidence in my own alertness. My condition, as a matter of fact, must have been otherwise, and this belief in my powers merely symptomatic of the fever which consumed me; for, as I was to learn, I had failed to take the first elementary precaution necessary in such case. I, who tracked another, had not counted upon being tracked myself! . . .

A bag or sack, reeking of some sickly perfume, was dropped silently, accurately, over my head from behind; it was drawn closely about my throat. One muffled shriek, strangely compound of fear and execration, I uttered. I was stifling, choking . . . I staggered—and fell. . . .

Chapter XVII

I MEET DR. FU-MANCHU

My next impression was of a splitting headache, which, as memory remounted its throne, brought up a train of recollections. I found myself to be seated upon a heavy wooden bench set flat against a wall, which was covered with a kind of straw matting. My hands were firmly tied behind me. In the first agony of that reawakening I became aware of two things.

I was in an operating-room, for the most conspicuous item of its furniture was an operating-table! Shaded lamps were suspended above it; and instruments, antiseptics, dressings, etc., were arranged upon a glass-topped table beside it. Secondly, I had a companion.

Seated upon a similar bench on the other side of the room, was a heavily built man, his dark hair splashed with gray, as were his short, neatly trimmed beard and mustache. He, too, was pinioned; and he stared across the table with a glare in which a sort of stupefied wonderment predominated, but which was not free from terror.

It was Sir Baldwin Frazer!

"Sir Baldwin!" I muttered, moistening my parched lips with my tongue—"Sir Baldwin! —how——"

"It is Dr. Petrie, is it not?" he said, his voice husky with emotion. "Dr. Petrie!—my dear sir, in mercy tell me—what does this mean? I have been kidnaped—drugged; made the victim of an inconceivable outrage at the very door of my own house. . . ."

I stood up unsteadily.

"Sir Baldwin," I interrupted, "you ask me what it means. It means that we are in the hands of Dr. Fu-Manchu!"

Sir Baldwin stared at me wildly; his face was white and drawn with anxiety.

"Dr. Fu-Manchu!" he said; "but, my dear sir, this name conveys nothing to me—nothing!" His manner momentarily was growing more distrait. "Since my captivity began I have been given the use of a singular suite of rooms in this place, and received, I must confess, every possible attention. I have been waited upon by the she-devil who lured me here, but not one word other than a species of coarse badinage has she spoken to me. At times I have been tempted to believe that the fate which frequently befalls the specialist had befallen me. You understand?"

"I quite understand," I replied dully.

"There have been times in the past when I, too, have doubted my sanity in my dealings with the group who now hold us in their power."

"But," reiterated the other, his voice rising higher and higher, "what does it mean, my dear sir? It is incredible—fantastic! Even now I find it difficult to disabuse my mind of that old, haunting idea."

"Disabuse it at once, Sir Baldwin," I said bitterly. "The facts are as you see them; the explanation, at any rate in your own case, is quite beyond me. I was tracked . . ."

"Hush! some one is coming!"

We both turned and stared at an opening before which hung a sort of gaudily embroidered mat, as the sound of dragging footsteps, accompanied by a heavy tapping, announced the approach of *some one.*

The mat was pulled aside by Zarmi. She turned her head, flashing around the apartment a glance of her black eyes, then held the drapery aside to admit the entrance of another. . . .

Supporting himself by the aid of two heavy walking sticks and painfully dragging his gaunt frame along, *Dr. Fu-Manchu entered!*

I think I have never experienced in my life a sensation identical to that which now possessed me. Although Nayland Smith had declared that Fu-Manchu was alive, yet I would have sworn upon oath before any jury summonable that he was dead; for with my own eyes I had seen the bullet enter his skull. Now, whilst I crouched against the matting-covered wall, teeth tightly clenched and my very hair quivering upon my scalp, he dragged himself laboriously across the room, the sticks going *tap—tap—tap* upon the floor, and the tall body, enveloped in a yellow robe, bent grotesquely, gruesomely, with every effort which he made. He wore a surgical bandage about his skull and its presence seemed to accentuate the height of the great domelike brow, to throw into more evil prominence the wonderful, Satanic countenance of the man. His filmed eyes turning to right and left, he dragged himself to a wooden chair that stood beside the operating-table and sank down upon it, breathing sibilantly, exhaustedly.

Zarmi dropped the curtain and stood before it. She had discarded the dripping overall which she had been wearing when I had followed her across the common, and now stood before me with her black, frizzy hair unconfined and her beautiful, wicked face uplifted in a sort of cynical triumph. The big gold rings in her ears glittered strangely in the light of the electric lamps. She wore a garment which looked like a silken shawl wrapped about her in a wildly picturesque fashion, and, her hands upon her hips, leant back against the curtain glancing defiantly from Sir Baldwin to myself.

Those moments of silence which followed the entrance of the Chinese Doctor live in my memory and must live there for ever. Only the labored breathing of Fu-Manchu disturbed the stillness of the place. Not a sound penetrated to the room, no one uttered a word; then—

"Sir Baldwin Frazer," began Fu-Manchu in that indescribable voice, alternating between the sibilant and the guttural, "you were promised a certain fee for your services by my servant who summoned you. It shall be paid and the gift of my personal gratitude be added to it."

He turned himself with difficulty to address Sir Baldwin; and it became apparent to me that he was almost completely paralyzed down one side of his body. Some little use he could make of his hand and arm, for he still clutched the heavy carven stick, but the right side of his face was completely immobile; and rarely had I seen anything more ghastly than the effect produced upon that wonderful, Satanic countenance. The mouth, from the center of the thin lips, opened only to the left, as he spoke; in a word, seen in profile from where I sat, or rather crouched, it was the face of a dead man. Sir Baldwin Frazer uttered no word, but, crouching upon the bench even as I crouched, stared—horror written upon every lineament—at Dr. Fu-Manchu. The latter continued:—

"Your experience, Sir Baldwin, will enable you readily to diagnose my symptoms. Owing to the passage of a bullet along a portion of the third left frontal into the postero-parietal convolution—upon which, from its lodgment in the skull, it continues to press—hemiplegia of the right side has supervened. Aphasia is present also. . . ."

The effort of speech was ghastly. Beads of perspiration dewed Fu-Manchu's brow, and I marveled at the iron will of the man, whereby alone he forced his half-numbed brain to perform its functions. He seemed to select his words elaborately and by this monstrous effort of will to compel his partially paralyzed tongue to utter them. Some of the syllables were slurred; but nevertheless distinguishable. It was a demonstration of sheer *Force* unlike any I had witnessed, and it impressed me unforgettably.

"The removal of this injurious particle," he continued, "would be an operation which I myself could undertake to perform successfully upon another. It is a matter of some delicacy as you, Sir Baldwin, and"—slowly, horribly, turning the half-dead and half-living head towards me—"you, Dr. Petrie, will appreciate. In the event of clumsy surgery, death may supervene; failing this, permanent hemiplegia—or"—the film lifted from the green eyes, and for a moment they flickered with transient horror—"idiocy! Any one of three of my pupils whom I might name could perform this operation with ease, but their services are not available. Only one English surgeon occurred to me in this connection, and you, Sir Baldwin"—again he slowly turned his head—"were he. Dr. Petrie will act as anæsthetist, and, your duties completed, you shall return to your home richer by the amount stipulated. I have suitably prepared myself for the operation, and I can assure you of the soundness of my heart. I may advise you, Dr. Petrie"—again turning to me—"that my constitution is inured to the use of opium. You will make due allowance for this. Mr. Li-King-Su, a graduate of Canton, will act as dresser."

He turned laboriously to Zarmi. She clapped her hands and held the curtain aside. A perfectly immobile Chinaman, whose age I was unable to guess, and who wore a white overall, entered, bowed composedly to Frazer and myself and began in a matter-of-fact way to prepare the dressings.

Chapter XVIII

QUEEN OF HEARTS

"Sir Baldwin Frazer," said Fu-Manchu, interrupting a wild outburst from the former, "your refusal is dictated by insufficient knowledge of your surroundings. You find yourself in a place strange to you, a place to which no clue can lead your friends; in the absolute power of a man—myself—who knows no law other than his own and that of those associated with him. Virtually, Sir Baldwin, you stand in China; and in China we know how to *exact* obedience. You will not refuse, for Dr. Petrie will tell you some-

thing of my *wire-jackets* and my *files*. . . ."

I saw Sir Baldwin Frazer blanch. He could not know what I knew of the significance of those words—"my wire-jackets, my files"—but perhaps something of my own horror communicated itself to him.

"You will not *refuse*," continued Fu-Manchu softly; "my only fear for you is that the operation may prove unsuccessful! In that event not even my own great clemency could save you, for by virtue of your failure I should be powerless to intervene." He paused for some moments, staring directly at the surgeon. "There are those within sound of my voice," he added sibilantly, "who would flay you alive in the lamentable event of your failure, who would cast your flayed body"—he paused, waving one quivering fist above his head, and his voice rose in a sudden frenzied shriek—"to the rats—to the rats!"

Sir Baldwin's forehead was bathed in perspiration now. It was an incredible and a gruesome situation, a nightmare become reality. But, whatever my own case, I could see that Sir Baldwin Frazer was convinced, I could see that his consent would no longer be withheld.

"You, my dear friend," said Fu-Manchu, turning to me and resuming his studied and painful composure of manner, "will also consent. . . ."

Within my heart of hearts I could not doubt him; I knew that my courage was not of a quality high enough to sustain the frightful ordeals summoned up before my imagination by those words—"my files, my wire-jackets!"

"In the event, however, of any little obstinacy," he added, "another will plead with you."

A chill like that of death descended upon me—as, for the second time, Zarmi clapped her hands, pulled the curtain aside . . . and Kâramanèh was thrust into the room!

* * * * * *

There comes a blank in my recollections. Long after Kâramanèh had been plucked out again by the two muscular brown hands which clutched her shoulders from the darkness beyond the doorway, I seemed to see her standing there, in her close-fitting traveling dress. Her hair was unbound, dishevelled, her lovely face pale to the lips—and her eyes, her glorious, terror-bright eyes, looked fully into mine. . . .

Not a word did she utter, and I was stricken dumb as one who has plucked the Flower of

Silence. Only those wondrous eyes seemed to look into my soul, searing, consuming me.

Fu-Manchu had been speaking for some time ere my brain began again to record his words.

"——and this magnanimity," came dully to my ears, "extends to you, Dr. Petrie, because of my esteem. I have little cause to love Kâramanèh"—his voice quivered furiously—"but she can yet be of use to me, and I would not harm a hair of her beautiful head—except in the event of your obstinacy. Shall we then determine your immediate future upon the turn of a card, as the gamester within me, within every one of my race, suggests?"

"Yes, yes!" came hoarsely.

I fought mentally to restore myself to a full knowledge of what was happening, and I realized that the last words had come from the lips of Sir Baldwin Frazer.

"Dr. Petrie," Frazer said, still in the same hoarse and unnaturaal voice, "what else can we do? At least take the chance of recovering your freedom, for how otherwise can you hope to serve—your friend. . . ."

"God knows!" I said dully; "do as you wish"—and cared not to what I had agreed.

Plunging his hand beneath his white overall, the Chinaman who had been referred to as Li-King-Su calmly produced a pack of cards, unemotionally shuffled them and extended the pack to me.

I shook my head grimly, for my hands were tied. Picking up a lancet from the table, the Chinaman cut the cords which bound me, and again extended the pack. I took a card and laid it on my knee without even glancing at it. Fu-Manchu, with his left hand, in turn selected a card, looked at it and then turned its face towards me.

"It would seem, Dr. Petrie," he said calmly, "that you are fated to remain here as my guest. You will have the felicity of residing beneath the same roof with Kâramanèh."

The card was the Knave of Diamonds.

Conscious of a sudden excitement, I snatched up the card from my knee. It was the Queen of Hearts! For a moment I tasted exultation, then I tossed it upon the floor. I was not fool enough to suppose that the Chinese Doctor would pay his debt of honor and release me.

"Your star above mine," said Fu-Manchu, his calm unruffled. "I place myself in your hands, Sir Baldwin."

Assisted by his unemotional compatriot,

Fu-Manchu discarded the yellow robe, revealing himself in a white singlet in all his gaunt ugliness, and extended his frame upon the operating-table.

Li-King-Su ignited the large lamp over the head of the table, and from his case took out a trephine.

*   *   *   *   *   *   *

"Other points for your guidance from my own considerable store of experience"—Fu-Manchu was speaking—"are written out clearly in the notebook which lies upon the table. . . ."

His voice, now, was toneless, emotionless, as though his part in the critical operation about to be performed were that of a spectator. No trace of nervousness, of fear, could I discern; his pulse was practically normal.

How I shuddered as I touched his yellow skin! how my very soul rose in revolt! . . .

*   *   *   *   *   *   *

"There is the bullet!—quick! . . . Steady, Petrie!"

Sir Baldwin Frazer, keen, cool, deft, was metamorphosed, was the enthusiastic, brilliant surgeon whom I knew and revered, and another than the nerveless captive who, but a few minutes ago, had stared, panic-stricken, at Dr. Fu-Manchu.

Although I had met him once or twice professionally, I had never hitherto seen him operate; and his method was little short of miraculous. It was stimulating, inspiring. With unerring touch he whittled madness, death, from the very throne of reason, of life.

Now was the crucial moment of his task . . . and, with its coming, every light in the room suddenly failed—went out!

"My God!" whispered Frazer, in the darkness, "quick! quick! lights! a match!—a candle!—something, anything!"

There came a faint click, and a beam of white light was directed, steadily, upon the patient's skull. Li-King-Su—unmoved—held an electric torch in his hand!

Frazer and I set to work, in a fierce battle to fend off Death, who already outstretched his pinions over the insensible man—to fend off Death from the arch-murderer, the enemy of the white races, who lay there at our mercy! . . .

*   *   *   *   *   *   *

"It seems you want a pick-me-up!" said Zarmi.

Sir Baldwin Frazer collapsed into the cane arm-chair. Only a matting curtain separated us from the room wherein he had success-fully performed perhaps the most wonderful operation of his career.

"I could not have lasted out another thirty seconds, Petrie!" he whispered. "The events which led up to it had exhausted my nerves and I had no reserve to call upon. If that last . . ."

He broke off, the sentence uncompleted, and eagerly seized the tumbler containing brandy and soda, which the beautiful, wicked-eyed Eurasian passed to him. She turned, and prepared a drink for me, with the insolent *insouciance* which had never deserted her.

I emptied the tumbler at a draught.

Even as I set the glass down I realized, too late, that it was the first drink I had ever permitted to pass my lips within an abode of Dr. Fu-Manchu. . . .

I started to my feet.

"Frazer!" I muttered—"we've been drugged! we . . ."

"You sit down," came Zarmi's husky voice, and I felt her hands upon my breast, pushing me back into my seat. "You very tired, indeed . . . you go to sleep. . . ."

* * * * * * *

"Petrie! Dr. Petrie!"

The words broke in through the curtain of unconsciousness. I strove to arouse my-self. I felt cold and wet. I opened my eyes—and the world seemed to be swimming diz-zily about me. Then a hand grasped my arm, roughly.

"Brace up! Brace up, Petrie—and thank God you are alive! . . ."

I was sitting beside Sir Baldwin Frazer on a wooden bench, under a leafless tree, from the ghostly limbs whereof rain trickled down upon me! In the gray light, which, I thought, must be the light of dawn, I discerned other trees about us and an open expanse, tree-dotted, stretching into the misty grayness.

"Where are we?" I muttered—"where . . ."

"Unless I am greatly mistaken," replied my bedraggled companion, "and I don't think I am, for I attended a consultation in this neighborhood less than a week ago, we are somewhere on the west side of Wandsworth Common!"

He ceased speaking; then uttered a sup-pressed cry. There came a jangling of coins, and dimly I saw him to be staring at a canvas bag of money which he held.

"Merciful heavens!" he said, "am I mad—or did I *really* perform that operation? And can this be my fee? . . ."

I laughed loudly, wildly, plunging my wet, cold hands into the pockets of my rain-soaked overcoat. In one of them, my fingers came in contact with a piece of cardboard. It had an unfamiliar feel, and I pulled it out, peer-ing at it in the dim light.

"Well, I'm damned!" muttered Frazer—"then I'm not mad, after all!"

It was the Queen of Hearts!

Chapter XIX

"ZAGAZIG"

Fully two weeks elapsed ere Nayland Smith's arduous labors at last met with a slight re-ward. For a moment, the curtain of mystery surrounding the Si-Fan was lifted, and we had a glimpse of that organization's elabo-rate mechanism. I cannot better commence my relation of the episodes associated with the Zagazig cryptogram than from the mo-ment when I found myself bending over a prostrate form extended upon the table in the Inspector's room at the River Police De-pôt. It was that of a man who looked like a Lascar, who wore an ill-fitting slop-shop suit of blue, soaked and stained and clinging hid-eously to his body. His dank black hair was streaked upon his low brow; and his face, although it was notable for a sort of evil leer, had assumed in death another and more dreadful expression.

Asphyxiation had accounted for his end beyond doubt, but there were marks about his throat of clutching fingers, his tongue protruded, and the look in the dead eyes was appalling.

"He was amongst the piles upholding the old wharf at the back of the Joy-Shop?" said Smith tersely, turning to the police officer in charge.

"Exactly!" was the reply. "The in-coming tide had jammed him right up under a cross-beam."

"What time was that?"

"Well, at high tide last night. Hewson, returning with the ten o'clock boat, noticed the moonlight glittering upon the knife."

The knife to which the Inspector referred possessed a long curved blade of a kind with which I had become terribly familiar in the past. The dead man still clutched the hilt of the weapon in his right hand, and it now lay with the blade resting crosswise upon his breast. I stared in a fascinated way at this mysterious and tragic flotsam of old Thames.

Glancing up, I found Nayland Smith's gray eyes watching me.

"You see the mark, Petrie?" he snapped.

I nodded. The dead man upon the table was a Burmese dacoit!

"What do you make of it?" I said slowly.

"At the moment," replied Smith, "I scarcely know what to make of it. You are agreed with the divisional surgeon that the man—unquestionably a dacoit—died, not from drowning, but from strangulation. From evidence we have heard, it would appear that the encounter which resulted in the body being hurled in the river, actually took place upon the wharf-end beneath which he was found. And we know that a place formerly used by the Si-Fan group—in other words, by Dr. Fu-Manchu—adjoins the wharf. I am tempted to believe that this"—he nodded towards the ghastly and sinister object upon the table—"was a servant of the Chinese Doctor. In other words, we see before us one whom Fu-Manchu has rebuked for some shortcoming."

I shuddered coldly. Familiar as I should have been with the methods of the dread Chinaman, with his callous disregard of human suffering, of human life, of human law, I could not reconcile my ideas—the ideas of a modern, ordinary middle-class practitioner—with these Far Eastern devilries which were taking place in London.

Even now I sometimes found myself doubting the reality of the whole thing; found myself reviewing the history of the Eastern doctor and of the horrible group of murderers surrounding him, with an incredulity almost unbelievable in one who had been actually in contact not only with the servants of the Chinaman, but with the sinister Fu-Manchu himself. Then, to restore me to grips with reality, would come the thought of Kâramanèh, of the beautiful girl whose love had brought me seemingly endless sorrow and whose love for me had brought her once again into the power of that mysterious, implacable being.

This thought was enough. With its coming, fantasy vanished; and I knew that the dead dacoit, his great curved knife yet clutched in his hand, the Yellow menace hanging over London, over England, over the civilized world, the absence, the heart-breaking absence, of Kâramanèh—all were real, all were true, all were part of my life.

Nayland Smith was standing staring vaguely before him and tugging at the lobe of his left ear.

"Come along!" he snapped suddenly. "We have no more to learn here: the clue to the mystery must be sought elsewhere."

There was that in his manner whereby I knew that his thoughts were far away, as we filed out from the River Police Depôt to the cab which awaited us. Pulling from his overcoat pocket a copy of a daily paper—

"Have you seen this, Weymouth?" he demanded.

With a long, nervous index finger he indicated a paragraph on the front page which appeared under the heading of "Personal." Weymouth bent frowningly over the paper, holding it close to his eyes, for this was a gloomy morning and the light in the cab was poor.

"Such things don't enter into my sphere, Mr. Smith," he replied, "but no doubt the proper department at the Yard have seen it."

"I *know* they have seen it!" snapped Smith; "but they have also been unable to read it!"

Weymouth looked up in surprise.

"Indeed," he said. "You are interested in this, then?"

"Very! Have you any suggestion to offer respecting it?"

Moving from my seat I, also, bent over the paper and read, in growing astonishment, the following:—

ZAGAZIG—Z,–a–·g·–a;–z:–I–g,z,–a,–g·–a,z;–I;–g:–z·a·g·A–z;i–:g;–Z,–a;–g·a·z·i;–G;–z–,a·g–:a–z·I;–g:–z·–a·g;–a–: Z–i·g:z,a·g,–a:z,i–:g·

"This is utterly incomprehensible! It can be nothing but some foolish practical joke! It consists merely of the word 'Zagazig' repeated six or seven times—which can have no possible significance!"

"Can't it!" snapped Smith.

"Well," I said, "what has Zagazig to do with Fu-Manchu, or to do with us?"

"Zagazig, my dear Petrie, is a very unsavory Arab town in Lower Egypt, as you know!"

He returned the paper to the pocket of his overcoat, and, noting my bewildered glance, burst into one of his sudden laughs.

"You think I am talking nonsense," he said; "but, as a matter of fact, that message in the paper has been puzzling me since it appeared—yesterday morning—and at last I think I see light."

He pulled out his pipe and began rapidly to load it.

"I have been growing careless of late, Petrie," he continued; and no hint of merriment remained in his voice. His gaunt face was drawn grimly, and his eyes glittered like steel. "In future I must avoid going out alone at night as much as possible."

Inspector Weymouth was staring at Smith in a puzzled way; and certainly I was every whit as mystified as he.

"I am disposed to believe," said my friend, in his rapid, incisive way, "that the dacoit met his end at the hands of a tall man, possibly dark and almost certainly clean-shaven. If this missing peronage wears, on chilly nights, a long, tweed traveling coat and affects soft gray hats of the Stetson pattern, I shall not be surprised."

Weymouth stared at me in frank bewilderment.

"By the way, Inspector," added Smith, a sudden gleam of inspiration entering his keen eyes—"did I not see that the s.s. *Andaman* arrived recently?"

"The Oriental Navigation Company's boat?" inquired Weymouth in a hopeless tone. "Yes. She docked yesterday evening."

"If Jack Forsyth is still chief officer, I shall look him up," declared Smith. "You recall his brother, Petrie?"

"Naturally; since he was done to death in my presence," I replied; for the words awoke memories of one of Dr. Fu-Manchu's most ghastly crimes, always associated in my mind with the cry of a night-hawk.

"The divine afflatus should never be neglected," announced Nayland Smith didactically, "wild though its promptings may seem."

Chapter XX

THE NOTE ON THE DOOR

I saw little of Nayland Smith for the remainder of that day. Presumably he was following those "promptings" to which he had referred, though I was unable to conjecture whither they were leading him. Then, towards dusk he arrived in a perfect whirl, figuratively sweeping me off my feet.

"Get your coat on, Petrie!" he cried; "you forget that we have a most urgent appointment!"

Beyond doubt I had forgotten that we had any appointment whatever that evening, and some surprise must have shown upon my face, for—

"Really you are becoming very forgetful!" my friend continued. "You know we can no longer trust the 'phone. I have to leave certain instructions for Weymouth at the rendezvous!"

There was a hidden significance in his manner, and, my memory harking back to an adventure which we had shared in the past, I suddenly glimpsed the depths of my own stupidity.

He suspected the presence of an eavesdropper! Yes! incredible though it might appear, we were spied upon in the New Louvre; agents of the Si-Fan, of Dr. Fu-Manchu, were actually within the walls of the great hotel!

We hurried out into the corridor, and descended by the lift to the lobby. M. Samarkan, long famous as *maître d'hôtel* of one of Cairo's fashionable *khans*, and now principal of the New Louvre, greeted us with true Greek courtesy. He trusted that we should be present at some charitable function or other to be held at the hotel on the following evening.

"If possible, M. Samarkan—if possible," said Smith. "We have many demands upon our time." Then, abruptly, to me: "Come, Petrie, we will walk as far as Charing Cross and take a cab from the rank there."

"The hall-porter can call you a cab," said M. Samarkan, solicitous for the comfort of his guests.

"Thanks," snapped Smith; "we prefer to walk a little way."

Passing along the Strand, he took my arm, and speaking close to my ear—

"That place is alive with spies, Petrie," he said; "or if there are only a few of them they are remarkably efficient!"

Not another word could I get from him, although I was eager enough to talk; since one dearer to me than all else in the world was in the hands of the damnable organization we knew as the Si-Fan; until, arrived at Charing Cross, he walked out to the cab rank, and—

"Jump in!" he snapped.

He opened the door of the first cab on the rank.

"Drive to J—— Street, Kennington," he directed the man.

In something of a mental stupor I entered and found myself seated beside Smith. The cab made off towards Trafalgar Square, then swung around into Whitehall.

"Look behind!" cried Smith, intense excitement expressed in his voice—"look behind!"

I turned and peered through the little square window.

The cab which had stood second upon the rank was closely following us!

"We are tracked!" snapped my companion. "If further evidence were necessary of the fact that our every movement is watched, here it is!"

I turned to him, momentarily at a loss for words; then—

"Was this the object of our journey?" I said. "Your reference to a 'rendezvous' was presumably addressed to a hypothetical spy?"

"Partly," he replied. "I have a plan, as you will see in a moment."

I looked again from the window in the rear of the cab. We were now passing between the House of Lords and the back of Westminster Abbey . . . and fifty yards behind us the pursuing cab was crossing from Whitehall! A great excitement grew up within me, and a great curiosity respecting the identity of our pursuer.

"What is the place for which we are bound, Smith?" I said rapidly.

"It is a house which I chanced to notice a few days ago, and I marked it as useful for such a purpose as our present one. You will see what I mean when we arrive."

On we went, following the course of the river, then turned over Vauxhall Bridge and on down Vauxhall Bridge Road into a very dreary neighborhood where gasometers formed the notable feature of the landscape.

"That's the Oval just beyond," said Smith suddenly, "and—here we are."

In a narrow *cul de sac* which apparently communicated with the boundary of the famous cricket ground, the cabman pulled up. Smith jumped out and paid the fare.

"Pull back to that court with the iron posts," he directed the man, "and wait there for me." Then: "Come on, Petrie!" he snapped.

Side by side we entered the wooden gate of a small detached house, or more properly cottage, and passed up the tiled path towards a sort of side entrance which apparently gave access to the tiny garden. At this moment I became aware of two things; the

first, that the house was an empty one, and the second, that some one—some one who had quitted the second cab (which I had heard pull up at no great distance behind us) was approaching stealthily along the dark and uninviting street, walking upon the opposite pavement and taking advantage of the shadow of a high wooden fence which skirted it for some distance.

Smith pushed the gate open, and I found myself in a narrow passageway in almost complete darkness. But my friend walked confidently forward, turned the angle of the building and entered the miniature wilderness which once had been a garden.

"In here, Petrie!" he whispered.

He seized me by the arm, pushed open a door and thrust me forward down two stone steps into absolute darkness.

"Walk straight ahead!" he directed, still in the same intense whisper, "and you will find a locked door having a broken panel. Watch through the opening for any one who may enter the room beyond, but see that your presence is not detected. Whatever I say or do, don't stir until I actually rejoin you."

He stepped back across the floor and was gone. One glimpse I had of him, silhouetted against the faint light of the open door, then the door was gently closed, and I was left alone in the empty house.

Smith's methods frequently surprised me, but always in the past I had found that they were dictated by sound reasons. I had no doubt that an emergency unknown to me dictated his present course, but it was with my mind in a wildly confused condition, that I groped for and found the door with the broken panel and that I stood there in the complete darkness of the deserted house listening.

I can well appreciate how the blind develop an unusually keen sense of hearing; for there, in the blackness, which (at first) was entirely unrelieved by any speck of light, I became aware of the fact, by dint of tense listening, that Smith was retiring by means of some gateway at the upper end of the little garden, and I became aware of the fact that a lane or court, with which this gateway communicated, gave access to the main road.

Faintly, I heard our discharged cab backing out from the *cul de sac*; then, from some nearer place, came Smith's voice speaking loudly.

"Come along, Petrie!" he cried; "there is

no occasion for us to wait. Weymouth will see the note pinned on the door."

I started—and was about to stumble back across the room, when, as my mind began to work more clearly, I realized that the words had been spoken as a ruse—a favorite device of Nayland Smith's.

Rigidly I stood there, and continued to listen.

"All right, cabman!" came more distantly now; "back to the New Louvre—jump in, Petrie!"

The cab went rattling away . . . as a faint light became perceptible in the room beyond the broken panel.

Hitherto I had been able to detect the presence of this panel only by my sense of touch and by means of a faint draught which blew through it; now it suddenly became clearly perceptible. I found myself looking into what was evidently the principal room of the house—a dreary apartment with tatters of paper hanging from the walls and litter of all sorts lying about upon the floor and in the rusty fireplace.

Some one had partly raised the front window and opened the shutters. A patch of moonlight shone down upon the floor immediately below my hiding-place and furthermore enabled me vaguely to discern the disorder of the room.

A bulky figure showed silhouetted against the dirty panes. It was that of a man who, leaning upon the window sill, was peering intently in. Silently he had approached, and silently had raised the sash and opened the shutters.

For thirty seconds or more he stood so, moving his head from right to left . . . and I watched him through the broken panel, almost holding my breath with suspense. Then, fully raising the window, the man stepped into the room, and, first reclosing the shutters, suddenly flashed the light of an electric lamp all about the place. I was enabled to discern him more clearly, this mysterious spy who had tracked us from the moment that we had left the hotel.

He was a man of portly build, wearing a heavy fur-lined overcoat and having a soft felt hat, the brim turned down so as to shade the upper part of his face. Moreover, he wore his fur collar turned up, which served further to disguise him, since it concealed the greater part of his chin. But the eyes which now were searching every corner of the room, the alert, dark eyes, were strangely familiar. The black

mustache, the clear-cut, aquiline nose, confirmed the impression.

Our follower was M. Samarkan, manager of the New Louvre.

I suppressed a gasp of astonishment. Small wonder that our plans had leaked out. This was a momentous discovery indeed.

And as I watched the portly Greek who was not only one of the most celebrated *maîtres d'hôtel* in Europe, but also a creature of Dr. Fu-Manchu, he cast the light of his electric lamp upon a note attached by means of a drawing-pin to the inside of the room door. I immediately divined that my friend must have pinned the note in its place earlier in the day; even at that distance I recognized Smith's neat, illegible writing.

Samarkan quickly scanned the message scribbled upon the white page; then, exhibiting an agility uncommon in a man of his bulk, he threw open the shutters again, having first replaced his lamp in his pocket, climbed out into the little front garden, reclosed the window, and disappeared!

A moment I stood, lost to my surroundings, plunged in a sea of wonderment concerning the damnable organization which, its tentacles extending I knew not whither, since new and unexpected limbs were ever coming to light, sought no less a goal than Yellow dominion of the world! I reflected how one man—Nayland Smith—alone stood between this powerful group and the realization of their projects . . . when I was aroused by a hand grasping my arm in the darkness!

I uttered a short cry, of which I was instantly ashamed, for Nayland Smith's voice came:—

"I startled you, eh, Petrie?"

"Smith," I said, "how long have you been standing there?"

"I only returned in time to see our Fenimore Cooper friend retreating through the window," he replied; "but no doubt you had a good look at him?"

"I had!" I answered eagerly. "It was Samarkan!"

"I thought so! I have suspected as much for a long time."

"Was this the object of our visit here?"

"It was one of the objects," admitted Nayland Smith evasively.

From some place not far distant came the sound of a restarted engine.

"The other," he added, "was this: to enable M. Samarkan to read the note which I had pinned upon the door!"

Chapter XXI

THE SECOND MESSAGE

"Here you are, Petrie," said Nayland Smith—
and he tossed across the table the folded copy
of a morning paper. "This may assist you in
your study of the first Zagazig message."

I set down my cup and turned my attention to the "Personal" column on the front
page of the journal. A paragraph appeared
therein conceived as follows:—

ZAGAZIG–Z,–a-·g·– a;–z:–I:–g;z·–a,g;–
    A–,z;i–:G,–z:–a;g–A,z–i;–g·z·
    A;g,a·Z–·i;g,z:a,g–:a z i g·

I stared across at my friend in extreme
bewilderment.

"But, Smith!" I cried, "these messages are
utterly meaningless!"

"Not at all," he rapped back. "Scotland
Yard thought they were meaningless at first,
and I must admit that they suggested nothing to me for a long time; but the dead dacoit
was the clue to the first, Petrie, and the note
pinned upon the door of the house near the
Oval is the clue to the second."

Stupidly I continued to stare at him until
he broke into a grim smile.

"Surely you understand?" he said. "You
remember where the dead Burman was
found?"

"Perfectly."

"You know the street along which, ordinarily, one would approach the wharf?"

"Three Colt Street?"

"Three Colt Street; exactly. Well, on the
night that the Burman met his end I had an
appointment in Three Colt Street with Weymouth. The appointment was made by
'phone, from the New Louvre! My cab broke
down and I never arrived. I discovered later
that Weymouth had received a telegram pur-
porting to come from me, putting off the
engagement."

"I am aware of all this!"

Nayland Smith burst into a loud laugh.

"But *still* you are fogged!" he cried. "Then
I'm hanged if I'll pilot you any farther! You
have all the facts before you. There lies the
first Zagazig message; here is the second;
and you know the context of the note pinned

upon the door? It read, if you remember,
'Remove patrol from Joy-Shop neighborhood. Have a theory. Wish to visit place alone
on Monday night after one o'clock.' "

"Smith," I said dully, "I have a heavy
stake upon this murderous game."

His manner changed instantly; the tanned
face grew grim and hard, but the steely eyes
softened strangely. He bent over me, clapping his hands upon my shoulders.

"I know it, old man," he replied; "and
because it may serve to keep your mind busy
during hours when otherwise it would be
engaged with profitless sorrows, I invite you
to puzzle out this business for yourself. You
have nothing else to do until late tonight,
and you can work undisturbed, here, at any
rate!"

His words referred to the fact that, without surrendering our suite at the New Louvre Hotel, we had gone upon a visit, of
indefinite duration, to a mythical friend; and
now were quartered in furnished chambers
adjoining Fleet Street.

We had remained at the New Louvre long
enough to secure confirmation of our belief
that a creature of Fu-Manchu spied upon us
there; and now we only awaited the termination of the night's affair to take such steps
as Smith might consider politic in regard to
the sardonic Greek who presided over London's newest and most palatial hotel.

Smith setting out for New Scotland Yard
in order to make certain final arrangements
in connection with the business of the night,
I began closely to study the mysterious Zagazig messages, determined not to be beaten,
and remembering the words of Edgar Allan
Poe—the strange genius to whom we are indebted for the first workable system of de-
ciphering cryptograms: "It may well be
doubted whether human ingenuity can con-
struct an enigma of the kind which human
ingenuity may not, by proper application,
resolve."

The first conclusion to which I was borne
was this: that the letters comprising the word
"Zagazig" were designed merely to confuse
the reader, and might be neglected; since,
occurring as they did in regular sequence,
they could possess no significance. I became
quite excited upon making the discovery that
the *punctuation marks* varied in almost every
case!

I immediately assumed that these constituted the cipher; and, seeking for my key-
letter, *e* (that which most frequently occurs

in the English language), I found the sign of a full-stop to appear more frequently than any other in the first message, namely, ten times, although it only occurred thrice in the second. Nevertheless, I was hopeful . . . until I discovered that in two cases it appeared three times *in succession!*

There is no word in English, nor, so far as I am aware, in any language, where this occurs, either in regard to *e* or any other letter!

That unfortunate discovery seemed so wholly to destroy the very theory upon which I relied, that I almost abandoned my investigation there and then. Indeed, I doubt if I ever should have proceeded were it not that by a piece of pure guesswork I blundered on to a clue.

I observed that certain letters, at irregularly occurring intervals, were set in capitals, and I divided up the message into corresponding sections, in the hope that the capitals might indicate the commencements of words. This accomplished, I set out upon a series of guesses, basing these upon Smith's assurance that the death of the dacoit afforded a clue to the first message and the note which he (Smith) had pinned upon the door a clue to the second.

Such being my system—if I can honor my random attempts with the title—I take little credit to myself for the fortunate result. In short, I determined (although *e* twice occurred where *r* should have been!) that the first message from the thirteenth letter, onwards to the twenty-seventh (*id est*: I;–g;–z·a·g·A·z;i–:g;–Z,–a;–g·a·z·i;–) read:—

"Three Colt Street."

Endeavoring, now, to eliminate the *e* where *r* should appear, I made another discovery. The presence of a letter in *italics* altered the value of the sign which followed it!

From that point onward the task became child's-play, and I should merely render this account tedious if I entered into further details. Both messages commenced with the name "Smith" as I early perceived, and half an hour of close study gave me the complete sentences, thus:—

1. *Smith passing Three Colt Street twelve-thirty Wednesday.*
2. *Smith going Joy-Shop after one Monday.*

The word "Zagazig" was completed, al-

ways, and did not necessarily terminate with the last letter occurring in the cryptographic message. A subsequent inspection of this curious code has enabled Nayland Smith, by a process of simple deduction, to compile the entire alphabet employed by Dr. Fu-Manchu's agent, Samarkan, in communicating with his awful superior. With a little patience, any one of my readers may achieve the same result (and I should be pleased to hear from those who succeed!).

This, then, was the outcome of my labors; and although it enlightened me to some extent, I realized that I still had much to learn.

The dacoit, apparently, had met his death at the very hour when Nayland Smith should have been passing along Three Colt Street—a thoroughfare with an unsavory reputation. Who had killed him?

To-night, Samarkan advised the Chinese doctor, Smith would again be in the same dangerous neighborhood. A strange thrill of excitement swept through me. I glanced at my watch. Yes! It was time for me to repair, secretly, to my post. For I, too, had business on the borders of Chinatown tonight.

Chapter XXII

THE SECRET OF THE WHARF

I sat in the evil-smelling little room with its low, blackened ceiling, and strove to avoid making the slightest noise; but the crazy boards creaked beneath me with every movement. The moon hung low in an almost cloudless sky; for, following the spell of damp and foggy weather, a fall in temperature had taken place, and there was a frosty snap in the air tonight.

Through the open window the moonlight poured in and spilled its pure luminance upon the filthy floor; but I kept religiously within the shadows, so posted, however, that I could command an uninterrupted view of the street from the point where it crossed the creek to that where it terminated at the gates of the deserted wharf.

Above and below me the crazy building formerly known as the Joy-Shop and once the nightly resort of the Asiatic riff-raff from the docks—was silent, save for the squealing and scuffling of the rats. The melancholy lapping of the water frequently reached my ears, and a more or less continuous din from the wharves and workshops upon the further bank of the Thames; but in the narrow, dingy streets immediately surrounding the house, quietude reigned and no solitary footstep disturbed it.

Once, looking down in the direction of the bridge, I gave a great start, for a black patch of shadow moved swiftly across the path and merged into the other shadows bordering a high wall. My heart leapt momentarily, then, in another instant, the explanation of the mystery became apparent—in the presence of a gaunt and prowling cat. Bestowing a suspicious glance upward in my direction, the animal slunk away toward the path bordering the cutting.

By a devious route amid ghostly gasometers I had crept to my post in the early dusk, before the moon was risen, and already I was heartily weary of my passive part in the affair of the night. I had never before appreciated the multitudinous sounds, all of them weird and many of them horrible, which are within the compass of those great black rats who find their way to England with cargoes from Russia and elsewhere. From the rafters above my head, from the wall recesses about me, from the floor beneath my feet, proceeded a continuous and nerve-shattering concert, an unholy symphony which seemingly accompanied the eternal dance of the rats.

Sometimes a faint splash from below would tell of one of the revelers taking the water, but save for the more distant throbbing of riverside industry, and rarer note of shipping, the mad discords of this rat saturnalia alone claimed the ear.

The hour was nigh now, when matters should begin to develop. I followed the chimes from the clock of some church nearby—I have never learnt its name; and was conscious of a thrill of excitement when they warned me that the hour was actually arrived. . . .

A strange figure appeared noiselessly, from I knew not where, and stood fully within view upon the bridge crossing the cutting, peering to right and left, in an attitude of listening. It was the figure of a bedraggled old woman, gray-haired, and carrying a large bundle tied up in what appeared to be a red shawl. Of her face I could see little, since it was shaded by the brim of her black bonnet, but she rested her bundle upon the low wall of the bridge, and, to my intense surprise, sat down beside it!

She evidently intended to remain there.

I drew back further into the darkness; for the presence of this singular old woman at such a place, and at that hour, could not well be accidental. I was convinced that the first actor in the drama had already taken the stage. Whether I was mistaken or not must shortly appear.

Crisp footsteps sounded upon the roadway; distantly, and from my left. Nearer they approached and nearer. I saw the old woman, in the shadow of the wall, glance once rapidly in the direction of the approaching pedestrian. For some occult reason, the chorus of the rats was stilled. Only that firm and regular tread broke the intimate silence of the dreary spot.

Now the pedestrian came within my range of sight. It was Nayland Smith!

He wore a long tweed overcoat with which I was familiar, and a soft felt hat, the brim pulled down all around in a fashion characteristic of him, and probably acquired during the years spent beneath the merciless sun of Burma. He carried a heavy walking-cane which I knew to be a formidable weapon that he could wield to good effect. But, despite the stillness about me, a stillness which had reigned uninterruptedly (save for the *danse macabre* of the rats) since the coming of dusk, some voice within, ignoring these physical evidences of solitude, spoke urgently of lurking assassins; of murderous Easterns armed with those curved knives which sometimes flashed before my eyes in dreams; of a deathly menace which hid in the shadows about me, in the many shadows cloaking the holes and corners of the ramshackle buildings, draping arches, crannies and portals to which the moonlight could not penetrate.

He was abreast of the Joy-Shop now, and in sight of the ominous old witch huddled upon the bridge. He pulled up suddenly and stood looking at her. Coincident with his doing so, she began to moan and sway her body to right and left as if in pain; then—

"Kind gentleman," she whined in a sing-song voice, "thank God you came this way to help a poor old woman."

"What is the matter?" said Smith tersely, approaching her.

I clenched my fists. I could have cried out; I was indeed hard put to it to refrain from crying out—from warning him. But his injunctions had been explicit, and I restrained myself by a great effort, preserving silence and crouching there at the window, but with every muscle tensed and a desire for action strong upon me.

"I tripped up on a rough stone, sir," whined the old creature, "and here I've been sitting waiting for a policeman or some one to help me, for more than an hour, I have."

Smith stood looking down at her, his arms behind him, and in one gloved hand swinging the cane.

"Where do you live, then?" he asked.

"Not a hundred steps from here, kind gentleman," she replied in the monotonous voice; "but I can't move my left foot. It's only just through the gates yonder."

"What!" snapped Smith, "on the wharf?"

"They let me have a room in the old building until it's let," she explained. "Be helping a poor old woman, and God bless you."

"Come along, then!"

Stooping, Smith placed his arm around her shoulders, and assisted her to her feet. She groaned as if in great pain, but gripped her red bundle, and, leaning heavily upon the supporting arm, hobbled off across the bridge in the direction of the wharf gates at the end of the lane.

Now at last a little action became possible, and having seen my friend push open one of the gates and assist the old woman to enter, I crept rapidly across the crazy floor, found the doorway, and, with little noise, for I wore rubber-soled shoes, stole down the stairs into what had formerly been the reception-room of the Joy-Shop, the malodorous sanctum of the old Chinaman, John Ki.

Utter darkness prevailed there, but momentarily flicking the light of a pocket-lamp upon the floor before me, I discovered the further steps that were to be negotiated, and descended into the square yard which gave access to the path skirting the creek.

The moonlight drew a sharp line of shadow along the wall of the house above me, but the yard itself was a well of darkness. I stumbled under the rotting brick archway, and stepped gingerly upon the muddy path that I must follow. One hand pressed to the damp wall, I worked my way cautiously along, for a false step had precipitated me into the foul water of the creek. In this fashion and still enveloped by dense shadows, I reached the angle of the building. Then—at risk of being perceived, for the wharf and the river both were bathed in moonlight—I peered along

to the left. . . .

Out onto the paved pathway communicating with the wharf came Smith, shepherding his tottering charge. I was too far away to hear any conversation that might take place between the two, but, unless Smith gave the pre-arranged signal, I must approach no closer. Thus, as one sees a drama upon the screen, I saw what now occurred—occurred with dramatic, lightning swiftness.

Releasing Smith's arm, the old woman suddenly stepped back . . . at the instant that another figure, a repellent figure which approached, stooping, apish, with a sort of loping gait, crossed from some spot invisible to me, and sprang like a wild animal upon Smith's back!

It was a Chinaman, wearing a short loose garment of the smock pattern, and having his head bare, so that I could see his pigtail coiled upon his yellow crown. That he carried a cord, I perceived in the instant of his spring, and that he had whipped it about Smith's throat with unerring dexterity was evidenced by the one, short, strangled cry that came from my friend's lips.

Then Smith was down, prone upon the crazy planking, with the ape-like figure of the Chinaman perched between his shoulders—bending forward—the wicked yellow fingers at work, tightening—tightening—tightening the strangling-cord!

Uttering a loud cry of horror, I went racing along the gangway which projected actually over the moving Thames waters, and gained the wharf. But, swift as I had been, another had been swifter!

A tall figure (despite the brilliant moon, I doubted the evidence of my sight), wearing a tweed overcoat and a soft felt hat with the brim turned down, sprang up, from nowhere as it seemed, swooped upon the horrible figure squatting, simianesque, between Smith's shoulder-blades, and grasped him by the neck.

I pulled up shortly, one foot set upon the wharf. The new-comer was the double of Nayland Smith!

Seemingly exerting no effort whatever, he lifted the strangler in that remorseless grasp, so that the Chinaman's hands, after one quick convulsive upward movement, hung limply beside him like the paws of a rat in the grip of a terrier.

"You damned murderous swine!" I heard in a repressed, savage undertone. "The knife failed, so now the cord has an innings! Go after your pal!"

Releasing one hand from the neck of the limp figure, the speaker grasped the Chinaman by his loose, smock-like garment, swung him back, once—a mighty swing—and hurled him far out into the river as one might hurl a sack of rubbish!

Chapter XXIII

ARREST OF SAMARKAN

"As the high gods willed it," explained Nayland Smith, tenderly massaging his throat, "Mr. Forsyth, having just left the docks, chanced to pass along Three Colt Street on Wednesday night at exactly the hour that *I* was expected! The resemblance between us is rather marked and the coincidence of dress completed the illusion. That devilish Eurasian woman, Zarmi, who has escaped us again—of course you recognized her?—made a very natural mistake. Mr. Forsyth, however, made no mistake!"

I glanced at the chief officer of the *Andaman*, who sat in an armchair in our new chambers, contentedly smoking a black cheroot.

"Heaven has blessed me with a pair of useful hands!" said the seaman, grimly, extending his horny palms. "I've an old score against those yellow swine; poor George and I were twins."

He referred to his brother who had been foully done to death by one of the creatures of Dr. Fu-Manchu.

"It beats me how Mr. Smith got on the track!" he added.

"Pure inspiration!" murmured Nayland Smith, glancing aside from the siphon wherewith he now was busy. "The divine afflatus—and the same whereby Petrie solved the Zagazig cryptogram!"

"But," concluded Forsyth, "I am indebted to you for an opportunity of meeting the Chinese strangler, and sending him to join the Burmese knife expert!"

Such, then, were the episodes that led to the arrest of M. Samarkan, and my duty as narrator of these strange matters now bears me on to the morning when Nayland Smith was hastily summoned to the prison into which the villainous Greek had been cast.

We were shown immediately into the Governor's room and were invited by that much disturbed official to be seated. The news which he had to impart was sufficiently startling.

Samarkan was dead.

"I have Warder Morrison's statement here," said Colonel Warrington, "if you will be good enough to read it——"

Nayland Smith rose abruptly, and began to pace up and down the little office. Through the open window I had a glimpse of a stooping figure in convict garb, engaged in liming the flower-beds of the prison Governor's garden.

"I should like to see this Warder Morrison personally," snapped my friend.

"Very good," replied the Governor, pressing a bell-push placed close beside his table.

A man entered, to stand rigidly at attention just within the doorway.

"Send Morrison here," ordered Colonel Warrington.

The man saluted and withdrew. As the door was reclosed, the Colonel sat drumming his fingers upon the table, Nayland Smith walked restlessly about tugging at the lobe of his ear, and I absently watched the convict gardener pursuing his toils. Shortly, sounded a rap at the door, and—

"Come in," cried Colonel Warrington.

A man wearing warder's uniform appeared, saluted the Governor, and stood glancing uneasily from the Colonel to Smith. The latter had now ceased his perambulations, and, one elbow resting upon the mantelpiece, was staring at Morrison—his penetrating gray eyes as hard as steel. Colonel Warrington twisted his chair around, fixing his monocle more closely in its place. He had the wiry white mustache and fiery red face of the old-style Anglo-Indian officer.

"Morrison," he said, "Mr. Commissioner Nayland Smith has some questions to put to you."

The man's uneasiness palpably was growing by leaps and bounds. He was a tall and intelligent-looking fellow of military build, though spare for his height and of an unhealthy complexion. His eyes were curiously dull, and their pupils interested me, professionally, from the very moment of his entrance.

"You were in charge of the prisoner Samarkan?" began Smith harshly.

"Yes, sir," Morrison replied.

"Were you the first to learn of his death?"

"I was, sir. I looked through the grille in the door and saw him lying on the floor of the cell."

"What time was that?"

"Half-past four A.M."

"What did you do?"

"I went into the cell and then sent for the head warder."

"You realized at once that Samarkan was dead?"

"At once, yes."

"Were you surprised?"

Nayland Smith subtly changed the tone of his voice in asking the last question, and it was evident that the veiled significance of the words was not lost upon Morrison.

"Well, sir," he began, and cleared his throat nervously.

"Yes, or no!" snapped Smith.

Morrison still hesitated, and I saw his underlip twitch. Nayland Smith, taking two long strides, stood immediately in front of him, glaring grimly into his face.

"This is your chance," he said emphatically; "I shall not give you another. You had met Samarkan before?"

Morrison hung his head for a moment, clenching and unclenching his fists; then he looked up swiftly, and the light of a new resolution was in his eyes.

"I'll take the chance, sir," he said, speaking with some emotion, "and I hope, sir"—turning momentarily to Colonel Warrington—"that you'll be as lenient as you can; for I didn't know there was any harm in what I did."

"Don't expect any leniency from me!" cried the Colonel. "If there has been a breach of discipline there will be punishment, rely upon it!"

"I admit the breach of discipline," pursued the man doggedly; "but I want to say, here and now, that I've no more idea than anybody else how the——"

Smith snapped his fingers irritably.

"The facts—the facts!" he demanded. "What you don't know cannot help us!"

"Well, sir," said Morrison, clearing his throat again, "when the prisoner, Samarkan, was admitted, and I put him safely into his cell, he told me that he suffered from heart trouble, that he'd had an attack when he was arrested and that he thought he was threatened with another, which might kill him——"

"One moment," interrupted Smith, "is this confirmed by the police officer who made the arrest?"

"It is, sir," replied Colonel Warrington, swinging his chair around and consulting some papers upon his table. "The prisoner was overcome by faintness when the officer showed him the warrant and asked to be given some cognac from the decanter which stood in his room. This was administered, and he then entered the cab which the officer had waiting. He was taken to Bow Street, remanded, and brought here in accordance with some one's instructions."

"My instructions," said Smith. "Go on, Morrison."

"He told me," continued Morrison more steadily, "that he suffered from something that sounded to me like apoplexy."

"Catalepsy!" I suggested, for I was beginning to see light.

"That's it, sir! He said he was afraid of being buried alive! He asked me, as a favor, if he should die in prison to go to a friend of his and get a syringe with which to inject some stuff that would do away with all chance of his coming to life again after burial."

"You had no right to talk to the prisoner!" roared Colonel Warrington.

"I know that, sir, but you'll admit that the circumstances were peculiar. Anyway, he died in the night, sure enough, and from heart failure, according to the doctor. I managed to get a couple of hours' leave in the evening, and I went and fetched the syringe and a little tube of yellow stuff."

"Do you understand, Petrie?" cried Nayland Smith, his eyes blazing with excitement. "Do you understand?"

"Perfectly."

"It's more than I do, sir," continued Morrison, "but as I was explaining, I brought the little syringe back with me and I filled it from the tube. The body was lying in the mortuary, which you've seen, and the door not being locked, it was easy for me to slip in there for a moment. I didn't fancy the job, but it was soon done. I threw the syringe and the tube over the wall into the lane outside, as I'd been told to do."

"What part of the wall?" asked Smith.

"Behind the mortuary."

"That's where they were waiting!" I cried excitedly. "The building used as a mortuary is quite isolated, and it would not be a difficult matter for some one hiding in the lane outside to throw one of those ladders of silk and bamboo across the top of the wall."

"But, my good sir," interrupted the Governor irascibly, "whilst I admit the possibility to which you allude, I do not admit that a dead man, and a heavy one at that, can be carried up a ladder of silk and bamboo! Yet, on the evidence of my own eyes, the body of the prisoner, Samarkan, was removed from the mortuary last night!"

Smith signaled to me to pursue the subject no further; and indeed I realized that it would have been no easy matter to render the amazing truth evident to a man of the Colonel's type of mind. But to me the facts of the case were now clear enough.

That Fu-Manchu possessed a preparation for producing artificial catalepsy, of a sort indistinguishable from death, I was well aware. A dose of this unknown drug had doubtless been contained in the cognac (if, indeed, the decanter had held cognac) that the prisoner had drunk at the time of his arrest. The "yellow stuff" spoken of by Morrison I recognized as the antidote (another secret of the brilliant Chinese doctor), a portion of which I had once, some years before, actually had in my possession. The "dead man" had not been carried up the ladder; he had climbed up!

"Now, Morrison," snapped Nayland Smith, "you have acted wisely thus far. Make a clean breast of it. How much were you paid for the job?"

"Twenty pounds, sir!" answered the man promptly, "and I'd have done it for less, because I could see no harm in it, the prisoner being dead, and this his last request."

"And who paid you?"

Now we were come to the nub of the matter, as the change in the man's face revealed. He hesitated momentarily, and Colonel Warrington brought his fist down on the table with a bang. Morrison made a sort of gesture of resignation at that, and—

"When I was in the Army, sir, stationed at Cairo," he said slowly, "I regret to confess that I formed a drug habit."

"Opium?" snapped Smith.

"No, sir, hashish."

"Good God! Go on."

"There's a place in Soho, just off Frith Street, where hashish is supplied, and I go there sometimes. Mr. Samarkan used to come, and bring people with him—from the New Louvre Hotel, I believe. That's where I met him."

"The exact address?" demanded Smith.

"Café de l'Egypte. But the hashish is only sold upstairs, and no one is allowed up that isn't known personally to Ismail."

"Who is this Ismail?"

"The proprietor of the café. He's a Greek Jew of Salonica. An old woman used to attend to the customers upstairs, but during the last few months a young one has sometimes taken her place."

"What is she like?" I asked eagerly.

"She has very fine eyes, and that's about all I can tell you, sir, because she wears a yashmak. Last night there were two women there, both veiled, though."

"Two women!"

Hope and fear entered my heart. That Kâramanèh was again in the power of the Chinese Doctor I knew to my sorrow. Could it be that the Café de l'Egypte was the place of her captivity?

Chapter XXIV

CAFÉ DE L'EGYPTE

I could see that Nayland Smith counted the escape of the prisoner but a trivial matter by comparison with the discovery to which it had led us. That the Soho café should prove to be, if not the head-quarters at least a regular resort of Dr. Fu-Manchu, was not too much to hope. The usefulness of such a haunt was evident enough, since it might conveniently be employed as a place of rendezvous for Orientals—and furthermore enable the cunning Chinaman to establish relations with persons likely to prove of service to him.

Formerly, he had used an East End opium den for this purpose, and, later, the resort known as the Joy-Shop. Soho, hitherto, had remained outside the radius of his activity, but that he should have embraced it at last was not surprising; for Soho is the Montmartre of London and a land of many secrets.

"Why," demanded Nayland Smith, "have I never been told of the existence of this place?"

"That's simple enough," answered Inspector Weymouth. "Although we knew of this Café de l'Egypte, we have never had the slightest trouble there. It's a Bohemian resort, where members of the French Colony, some of the Chelsea art people, professional models, and others of that sort, foregather at night. I've been there myself as a matter of fact, and I've seen people well known in the artistic world come in. It has much the same clientele as, say, the Café Royal, with a rather heavier sprinkling of Hindu students, Japanese, and so forth. It's celebrated for Turkish coffee."

"What do you know of this Ismail?"

"Nothing much. He's a Levantine Jew."

"And something more!" added Smith, surveying himself in the mirror, and turning to nod his satisfaction to the well-known perruquier whose services are sometimes requisitioned by the police authorities.

We were ready for our visit to the Café de l'Egypte, and Smith having deemed it inadvisable that we should appear there openly, we had been transformed, under the adroit manipulation of Foster, into a pair of Futurists oddly unlike our actual selves. No wigs, no false mustaches had been employed; a change of costume and a few deft touches of some water-color paint had rendered us unrecognizable by our most intimate friends.

It was all very fantastic, very reminiscent of Christmas charades, but the farce had a grim, murderous undercurrent; the life of one dearer to me than life itself hung upon our success; the swamping of the White world by Yellow hordes might well be the price of our failure.

Weymouth left us at the corner of Frith Street. This was no more than a reconnaissance, but—

"I shall be within hail if I'm wanted," said the burly detective; and although we stood not in Chinatown but in the heart of Bohemian London, with popular restaurants about us, I was glad to know that we had so stanch an ally in reserve.

The shadow of the great Chinaman was upon me. That strange, subconscious voice, with which I had become familiar in the past, awoke within me tonight. Not by logic, but by prescience, I knew that the Yellow doctor was near.

Two minutes' walk brought us to the door of the café. The upper half was of glass, neatly curtained, as were the windows on either side of it; and above the establishment appeared the words: "Café de l'Egypte." Between the second and third word was inserted a gilded device representing the crescent of Islâm.

We entered. On our right was a room furnished with marble-topped tables, cane-seated chairs and plush-covered lounges set against the walls. The air was heavy with tobacco smoke; evidently the café was full, although the night was young.

Smith immediately made for the upper end of the room. It was not large, and at first glance I thought that there was no vacant place. Presently, however, I espied two unoccupied chairs; and these we took, finding ourselves facing a pale, bespectacled young man, with long, fair hair and faded eyes, whose companion, a bold brunette, was smoking one of the largest cigarettes I had ever seen, in a gold and amber cigar-holder.

A very commonplace Swiss waiter took our orders for coffee, and we began discreetly to survey our surroundings. The only touch of Oriental color thus far perceptible in the Café de l'Egypte was provided by a red-capped Egyptian behind a narrow counter, who presided over the coffee pots. The patrons of the establishment were in every way typical of Soho, and in the bulk differed not at all from those of the better known café restaurants.

There were several Easterns present; but Smith, having given each of them a searching glance, turned to me with a slight shrug of disappointment. Coffee being placed before us, we sat sipping the thick, sugary beverage, smoking cigarettes and vainly seeking for some clue to guide us to the inner sanctuary consecrated to hashish. It was maddening to think that Kâramanèh might be somewhere concealed in the building, whilst I sat there, inert, amongst this gathering whose conversation was of abnormalities in art, music, and literature.

Then, suddenly, the pale young man seated opposite paid his bill, and with a word of farewell to his companion, went out of the café. He did not make his exit by the door through which we had entered, but passed up the crowded room to the counter whereat the Egyptian presided. From some place hidden in the rear, emerged a black-haired, swarthy man, with whom the other exchanged a few words. The pale young artist raised his wide-brimmed hat, and was gone—through a curtained doorway on the left of the counter.

As he opened it, I had a glimpse of a narrow court beyond; then the door was closed again . . . and I found myself thinking of the peculiar eyes of the departed visitor. Even through the thick pebbles of his spectacles, although for some reason I had thought little of the matter at the time, his oddly contracted pupils were noticeable. As the girl, in turn, rose and left the café—but by the ordinary door—I turned to Smith.

"That man . . ." I began, and paused.

Smith was watching covertly, a Hindu seated at a neighboring table, who was about to settle his bill. Standing up, the Hindu made for the coffee counter, the swarthy man appeared out of the background—and the Asiatic visitor went out by the door opening into the court.

One quick glance Smith gave me, and raised his hand for the waiter. A few minutes later we were out in the street again.

"We must find our way to that court!" snapped my friend. "Let us try back. I noted a sort of alley-way which we passed just before reaching the café."

"You think the hashish den is in some adjoining building?"

"I don't know where it is, Petrie, but I know the way to it!"

Into a narrow, gloomy court we plunged, hemmed in by high walls, and followed it for ten yards or more. An even narrower and less inviting turning revealed itself on the left. We pursued our way, and presently found ourselves at the back of the Café de l'Egypte.

"There's the door," I said.

It opened into a tiny cul de sac, flanked by dilapidated hoardings, and no other door of any kind was visible in the vicinity. Nayland Smith stood tugging at the lobe of his ear almost savagely.

"Where the devil do they go?" he whispered.

Even as he spoke the words, came a gleam of light through the upper curtained part of the door, and I distinctly saw the figure of a man in silhouette.

"Stand back!" snapped Smith.

We crouched back against the dirty wall of the court, and watched a strange thing happen. The back door of the Café de l'Egypte opened outward, simultaneously a door, hitherto invisible, set at right angles in the hoarding adjoining, opened *inward!*

A man emerged from the café and entered the secret doorway. As he did so, the café door swung back . . . and closed the door in the hoarding!

"Very good!" muttered Nayland Smith. "Our friend Ismail, behind the counter, moves some lever which causes the opening of one door automatically to open the other. Failing his kindly offices, the second exit from the Café de l'Egypte is innocent enough. Now— what is the next move?"

"I have an idea, Smith!" I cried. "According to Morrison, the place in which the hashish may be obtained has no windows but is lighted from above. No doubt it was built for a studio and has a glass roof. Therefore——"

"Come along!" snapped Smith, grasping my arm; "you have solved the difficulty, Petrie."

Chapter XXV

THE HOUSE OF HASHISH

Along the leads from Frith Street we worked our perilous way. From the top landing of a French restaurant we had gained access, by means of a trap, to the roof of the building. Now, the busy streets of Soho were below me, and I clung dizzily to telephone standards and smoke stacks, rarely venturing to glance downward upon the cosmopolitan throng, surging, dwarfish, in the lighted depths.

Sometimes the bulky figure of Inspector Weymouth would loom up grotesquely against the star-sprinkled blue, as he paused to take breath; the next moment Nayland Smith would be leading the way again, and I would find myself contemplating some sheer well of blackness, with nausea threatening me because it had to be negotiated.

None of these gaps were more than a long stride from side to side; but the sense of depth conveyed in the muffled voices and dimmed footsteps from the pavements far below was almost overpowering. Indeed, I am convinced that for my part I should never have essayed that nightmare journey were it not that the musical voice of Kâramanèh seemed to be calling to me, her little white hands to be seeking mine, blindly, in the darkness.

That we were close to a haunt of the dreadful Chinamen I was persuaded; therefore my hatred and my love cooperated to lend me a coolness and address which otherwise I must have lacked.

"Hullo!" cried Smith, who was leading— "what now?"

We had crept along the crown of a sloping roof and were confronted by the blank wall of a building which rose a story higher than that adjoining it. It was crowned by an iron railing, showing blackly against the sky. I paused, breathing heavily, and seated astride that dizzy perch. Weymouth was immediately behind me, and—

"It's the Café de l'Egypte, Mr. Smith!" he said, "If you'll look up, you will see the reflection of the lights shining through the glass roof."

Vaguely I discerned Nayland Smith rising to his feet.

"Be careful!" I said. "For God's sake don't slip!"

"Take my hand," he snapped energetically.

I stretched forward and grasped his hand. As I did so, he slid down the slope on the right, away from the street, and hung perilously for a moment over the very cul de sac upon which the secret door opened.

"Good!" he muttered. "There is, as I had hoped, a window lighting the top of the staircase. Ssh!—ssh!"

His grip upon my hand tightened; and there aloft, above the teemful streets of Soho, I sat listening . . . whilst very faint and muffled footsteps sounded upon an uncarpeted stair, a door banged, and all was silent again, save for the ceaseless turmoil far below.

"Sit tight, and catch!" rapped Smith.

Into my extended hands he swung his boots, fastened together by the laces! Then, ere I could frame any protest, he disengaged his hand from mine, and, pressing his body close against the angle of the building, worked his way around to the staircase window, which was invisible from where I crouched.

"Heavens!" muttered Weymouth, close to my ear, "I can never travel that road!"

"Nor I!" was my scarcely audible answer.

In an anguish of fearful anticipation I listened for the cry and the dull thud which should proclaim the fate of my intrepid friend; but no such sounds came to me. Some thirty seconds passed in this fashion, when a subdued call from above caused me to start and look aloft.

Nayland Smith was peering down from the railing on the roof.

"Mind your head!" he warned—and over the rail swung the end of a light wooden ladder, lowering it until it rested upon the crest astride of which I sat.

"Up you come!—then Weymouth!"

Whilst Smith held the top firmly, I climbed up rung by rung, not daring to think of what lay below. My relief when at last I grasped the railing, climbed over, and found myself upon a wooden platform, was truly inexpressible.

"Come on, Weymouth!" rapped Nayland Smith. "This ladder has to be lowered back down the trap before another visitor arrives!"

Taking short, staccato breaths at every step, Inspector Weymouth ascended, ungainly, that frail and moving stair. Arrived beside me, he wiped the perspiration from his face and forehead.

"I wouldn't do it again for a hundred pounds!" he said hoarsely.

"You don't have to!" snapped Smith.

Back he hauled the ladder, shouldered it, and stepping to a square opening in one corner of the rickety platform, lowered it cautiously down.

"Have you a knife with a corkscrew in it?" he demanded.

Weymouth had one, which he produced. Nayland Smith screwed it into the weatherworn frame, and by that means reclosed the trapdoor softly, then—

"Look," he said, "there is the house of hashish!"

Chapter XXVI

"THE DEMON'S SELF"

Through the glass panes of the skylight I looked down upon a scene so bizarre that my actual environment became blotted out, and I was mentally translated to Cairo—to that quarter of Cairo immediately surrounding the famous Square of the Fountain—to those indescribable streets, wherefrom arises the perfume of deathless evil, wherein, to the wailing, luresome music of the reed pipe, painted dancing-girls sway in the wild abandon of dances that were ancient when Thebes was the City of a Hundred Gates; I seemed to stand again in el Wasr.

The room below was rectangular, and around three of the walls were divans strewn with garish cushions, whilst highly colored Eastern rugs were spread about the floor. Four lamps swung on chains, two from either of the beams which traversed the apartment. They were fine examples of native perforated brasswork.

Upon the divans some eight or nine men were seated, fully half of whom were Orientals or half-castes. Before each stood a little inlaid table bearing a brass tray; and upon the trays were various boxes, some apparently containing sweetmeats, others cigarettes. One or two of the visitors smoked curious, long-stemmed pipes and sipped coffee.

Even as I leaned from the platform, surveying that incredible scene (incredible in a street of Soho), another devotee of hashish entered—a tall, distinguished-looking man, wearing a light coat over his evening dress.

"Gad!" whispered Smith, beside me—"Sir Byngham Pyne of the India Office! You see, Petrie! You see! This place is a lure. My God! . . ."

He broke off, as I clutched wildly at his arm.

The last arrival having taken his seat in a corner of the divan, two heavy curtains draped before an opening at one end of the room parted, and a girl came out, carrying a tray such as already reposed before each of the other men in the room.

She wore a dress of dark lilac-colored gauze, banded about with gold tissue and embroidered with gold thread and pearls; and around her shoulders floated, so ethereally that she seemed to move in a violet cloud, a scarf of Delhi muslin. A white yashmak trimmed with gold tissue concealed the lower part of her face.

My heart throbbed wildly; I seemed to be choking. By the wonderful hair alone I must have known her, by the great, brilliant eyes, by the shape of those slim white ankles, by every movement of that exquisite form. It was Kâramanèh!

I sprang madly back from the rail . . . and Smith had my arm in an iron grip.

"Where are you going?" he snapped.

"Where am I going?" I cried. "Do you think——"

"What do you propose to do?" he interrupted harshly. "Do you know so little of the resources of Dr. Fu-Manchu that you would throw yourself blindly into that den? Damn it all, man! I know what you suffer!—but wait—wait. We must not act rashly; our plans must be well considered."

He drew me back to my former post and clapped his hand on my shoulder sympathetically. Clutching the rail like a man frenzied, as indeed I was, I looked down into that infamous den again, striving hard for composure.

Kâramanèh listlessly placed the tray upon the little table before Sir Byngham Pyne and withdrew without vouchsafing him a single glance in acknowledgment of his unconcealed admiration.

A moment later, above the dim clamor of London far below, there crept to my ears a sound which completed the magical quality of the scene, rendering that sky platform on a roof of Soho a magical carpet bearing me to the golden Orient. This sound was the wailing of a reed pipe.

"The company is complete," murmured Smith. "I had expected this."

Again the curtains parted, and a *ghazeeyeh* glided out into the room. She wore a white dress, clinging closely to her figure from shoulders to hips, where it was clasped by an ornate girdle, and a skirt of sky-blue gauze which clothed her as Io was clothed of old. Her arms were covered with gold bangles, and gold bands were clasped about her ankles. Her jet-black, frizzy hair was unconfined and without ornament, and she wore a sort of highly colored scarf so arranged that it effectually concealed the greater part of her face, but served to accentuate the brightness of the great flashing eyes. She had unmistakable beauty of a sort, but how different from the sweet witchery of Kâramanèh!

With a bold, swinging grace she walked down the center of the room, swaying her arms from side to side and snapping her fingers.

"Zarmi!" exclaimed Smith.

But his exclamation was unnecessary, for already I had recognized the evil Eurasian who was so efficient a servant of the Chinese doctor.

The wailing of the pipes continued, and now faintly I could detect the throbbing of a *darabûkeh*. This was el Wasr indeed. The dance commenced, its every phase followed eagerly by the motley clientele of the hashish house. Zarmi danced with an insolent nonchalance that nevertheless displayed her barbaric beauty to greatest advantage. She was lithe as a serpent, graceful as a young panther, another Lamia come to damn the souls of men with those arts denounced in a long dead age by Apollonius of Tyana.

"She seemed, at once, some penanced lady elf,
Some demon's mistress, or the demon's self . . . ."

Entranced against my will, I watched the Eurasian until, the barbaric dance completed, she ran from the room, and the curtains concealed her from view. How my mind was torn between hope and fear that I should see Kâramanèh again! How I longed for one more glimpse of her, yet loathed the thought of her presence in that infamous house.

She was a captive; of that there could be no doubt, a captive in the hands of the giant criminal whose wiles were endless, whose resources were boundless, whose intense cunning had enabled him, for years, to weave his nefarious plots in the very heart of civilization, and remain immune. Suddenly—

"That woman is a sorceress!" muttered Nayland Smith. "There is about her something serpentine, at once repelling and fascinating. It would be of interest, Petrie, to learn what State secrets have been filched from the brains of habitués of this den, and interesting to know from what unsuspected spy-hole Fu-Manchu views his nightly catch. If . . ."

His voice died away, in a most curious fashion. I have since thought that here was a case of true telepathy. For, as Smith spoke of Fu-Manchu's spy-hole, the idea leapt instantly to my mind that this was it—this strange platform upon which we stood!

I drew back from the rail, turned, and stared at Smith. I read in his face that our suspicions were identical. Then—

"Look! Look!" whispered Weymouth.

He was gazing at the trapdoor—which was slowly rising; inch by inch . . . inch by inch . . . Fascinatedly, raptly, we all gazed. A head appeared in the opening—and some vague, reflected light revealed two long, narrow, slightly oblique eyes watching us. They were brilliantly green.

"By God!" came in a mighty roar from Weymouth. "It's Dr. Fu-Manchu!"

As one man we leapt for the trap. It dropped, with a resounding bang—and I distinctly heard a bolt shot home.

A guttural voice—the unmistakable, unforgettable voice of Fu-Manchu—sounded dimly from below. I turned and sprang back to the rail of the platform, peering down into the hashish house. The occupants of the divans were making for the curtained doorway. Some, who seemed to be in a state of stupor, were being assisted by the others and by the man, Ismail, who had now appeared upon the scene.

Of Kâramanèh, Zarmi, or Fu-Manchu there was no sign.

Suddenly, the lights were extinguished.

"This is maddening!" cried Nayland Smith—"maddening! No doubt they have

some other exit, some hiding-place—and they are slipping through our hands!"

Inspector Weymouth blew a shrill blast upon his whistle, and Smith, running to the rail of the platform, began to shatter the panes of the skylight with his foot.

"That's hopeless, sir!" cried Weymouth. "You'd be torn to pieces on the jagged glass."

Smith desisted, with a savage exclamation, and stood beating his right fist into the palm of his left hand, and glaring madly at the Scotland Yard man.

"I know I'm to blame," admitted Weymouth; "but the words were out before I knew I'd spoken. Ah!"—as an answering whistle came from somewhere in the street below. "But will they ever find us?"

He blew again shrilly. Several whistles replied . . . and a wisp of smoke floated up from the shattered pane of the skylight.

"I can smell *petrol!*" muttered Weymouth.

An ever-increasing roar, not unlike that of an approaching storm at sea, came from the streets beneath. Whistles skirled, remotely and intimately, and sometimes one voice, sometimes another, would detach itself from this stormy background with weird effect. Somewhere deep in the bowels of the hashish house there went on ceaselessly a splintering and crashing as though a determined assault were being made upon a door. A light shone up through the skylight.

Back once more to the rail I sprang, looked down into the room below—and saw a sight never to be forgotten.

Passing from divan to curtained door, from piles of cushions to stacked-up tables, and bearing a flaming torch hastily improvised out of a roll of newspaper, was Dr. Fu-Manchu. Everything inflammable in the place had been soaked with petrol, and, his gaunt, yellow face lighted by the evergrowing conflagration, so that truly it seemed not the face of a man, but that of a demon of the hells, the Chinese doctor ignited point after point. . . .

"Smith!" I screamed, "we are trapped! that fiend means to burn us alive!"

"And the place will flare like matchwood! It's touch and go this time, Petrie! To drop to the sloping roof underneath would mean almost certain death on the pavement. . . ."

I dragged my pistol from my pocket and began wildly to fire shot after shot into the holocaust below. But the awful Chinaman had escaped—probably by some secret exit reserved for his own use; for certainly he must have known that escape into the court was now cut off.

Flames were beginning to hiss through the skylight. A tremendous crackling and crashing told of the glass destroyed. Smoke spurted up through the cracks of the boarding upon which we stood—and a great shout came from the crowd in the streets. . . .

In the distance—a long, long way off, it seemed—was born a new note in the stormy human symphony. It grew in volume, it seemed to be sweeping down upon us—nearer—nearer—nearer. Now it was in the streets immediately adjoining the Café de l'Egypte . . . and now, blessed sound! it culminated in a mighty surging cheer.

"The fire-engines," said Weymouth coolly—and raised himself on to the lower rail, for the platform was growing uncomfortably hot.

Tongues of fire licked out, venomously, from beneath my feet. I leapt for the railing in turn, and sat astride it . . . as one end of the flooring burst into flame.

The heat from the blazing room above which we hung suspended was now all but insupportable, and the fumes threatened to stifle us. My head seemed to be bursting; my throat and lungs were consumed by internal fires.

"Merciful heavens!" whispered Smith. "Will they reach us in time?"

"Not if they don't get here within the next thirty seconds!" answered Weymouth grimly—and changed his position, in order to avoid a tongue of flame that hungrily sought to reach him.

Nayland Smith turned and looked me squarely in the eyes. Words trembled on his tongue; but those words were never spoken . . . for a brass helmet appeared suddenly out of the smoke banks, followed almost immediately by a second. . . .

"Quick, sir! this way! Jump! I'll catch you!"

Exactly what followed I never knew; but there was a mighty burst of cheering, a sense of tension released, and it became a task less agonizing to breathe.

Feeling very dazed, I found myself in the heart of a huge, excited crowd, with Weymouth beside me, and Nayland Smith holding my arm. Vaguely, I heard:—

"They have the man Ismail, but . . ."

A hollow crash drowned the end of the sentence. A shower of sparks shot up into the night's darkness high above our heads.

"That's the platform gone!"

Chapter XXVII

ROOM WITH THE GOLDEN DOOR

One night early in the following week I sat at work upon my notes dealing with our almost miraculous escape from the blazing hashish house when the clock of St. Paul's began to strike midnight.

I paused in my work, leaning back wearily and wondering what detained Nayland Smith so late. Some friends from Burma had carried him off to a theater, and in their good company I had thought him safe enough; yet, with the omnipresent menace of Fu-Manchu hanging over our heads, always I doubted, always I feared, if my friend should chance to be delayed abroad at night.

What a world of unreality was mine, in those days! Jostling, as I did, commonplace folk in commonplace surroundings, I yet knew myself removed from them, knew myself all but alone in my knowledge of the great and evil man, whose presence in England had diverted my life into these strange channels.

But, despite of all my knowledge, and despite the infinitely greater knowledge and wider experience of Nayland Smith, what did I know, what did he know, of the strange organization called the Si-Fan, and of its most formidable member, Dr. Fu-Manchu? Where did the dreadful Chinaman hide, with his murderers, his poisons, and his nameless death agents? What roof in broad England sheltered Kâramanèh, the companion of my dreams, the desire of every waking hour?

I uttered a sigh of despair, when, to my unbounded astonishment, there came a loud rap upon the window pane!

Leaping up, I crossed to the window, threw it widely open and leant out, looking down into the court below. It was deserted. In no other window visible to me was any light to be seen, and no living thing moved in the shadows beneath. The clamor of Fleet Street's diminishing traffic came dimly to my ears; the last stroke from St. Paul's quivered through the night.

What was the meaning of the sound which had disturbed me? Surely I could not have imagined it? Yet, right, left, above and below, from the cloisteresque shadows on the east of the court to the blank wall of the building on the west, no living thing stirred.

Quietly, I reclosed the window, and stood by it for a moment listening. Nothing occurred, and I returned to the writing-table, puzzled, but in no sense alarmed. I resumed the seemingly interminable record of the Si-Fan mysteries, and I had just taken up my pen, when . . . two loud raps sounded upon the pane behind me.

In a trice I was at the window, had thrown it open, and was craning out. Practical joking was not characteristic of Nayland Smith, and I knew of none other likely to take such a liberty. As before, the court below proved to be empty. . . .

Some one was softly rapping at the door of the chambers!

I turned swiftly from the open window; and now, came *fear*. Momentarily, the icy finger of panic touched me, for I thought myself invested upon all sides. Who could this late caller be, this midnight visitor who rapped, ghostly, in preference to ringing the bell?

From the table drawer I took out a Browning pistol, slipped it into my pocket and crossed to the narrow hallway. It was in darkness, but I depressed the switch, lighting the lamp. Toward the closed door I looked—as the soft rapping was repeated.

I advanced; then hesitated; and, strung up to a keen pitch of fearful anticipation, stood there in doubt. The silence remained unbroken for the space, perhaps, of half a minute. Then again came the ghostly rapping.

"Who's there?" I cried loudly.

Nothing stirred outside the door, and still I hesitated. To some who read, my hesitancy may brand me childishly timid; but I, who had met many of the dreadful creatures of Dr. Fu-Manchu, had good reason to fear whomsoever or whatsoever rapped at midnight upon my door. Was I likely to forget the great half-human ape, with the strength of four lusty men, which once he had loosed upon us?—had I not cause to remember his Burmese dacoits and Chinese stranglers?

No, I had just cause for dread, as I fully recognized when, snatching the pistol from my pocket, I strode forward, flung wide the door, and stood peering out into the black gulf of the stairhead.

Nothing, no one, appeared!

Conscious of a longing to cry out—if only that the sound of my own voice might reassure me—I stood listening. The silence was complete.

"Who's there?" I cried again, and loudly enough to arrest the attention of the occupant of the chambers opposite if he chanced to be at home.

None replied; and, finding this phantom silence more nerve-racking than any clamor, I stepped outside the door—and my heart gave a great leap, then seemed to remain suspended inert, in my breast. . . .

Right and left of me, upon either side of the doorway, stood a dim figure: I had walked deliberately into a trap!

The shock of the discovery paralyzed my mind for one instant. In the next, and with the sinister pair closing swiftly upon me, I stepped back—I stepped into the arms of some third assailant, who must have entered the chambers by way of the open window and silently crept up behind me!

So much I realized, and no more. A bag, reeking of some hashish-like perfume, was clapped over my head and pressed firmly against mouth and nostrils. I felt myself to be stifling—dying—and dropping into a bottomless pit.

When I opened my eyes I failed for some time to realize that I was conscious in the true sense of the word, that I was really awake.

I sat upon a bench covered with a red carpet, in a fair-sized room, very simply furnished, in the Chinese manner, but having a two-leaved, gilded door, which was shut. At the further end of this apartment was a dais some three feet high, also carpeted with red, and upon it was placed a very large cushion covered with a tiger skin.

Seated cross-legged upon the cushion was a Chinaman of most majestic appearance. His countenance was truly noble and gracious and he was dressed in a yellow robe lined with marten-fur. His hair, which was thickly splashed with gray, was confined upon the top of his head by three golden combs, and a large diamond was suspended from his left ear. A pearl-embroidered black cap, surmounted by the red coral ball denoting the mandarin's rank, lay upon a second smaller cushion beside him.

Leaning back against the wall, I stared at his personage with a dreadful fixity, for I counted him the figment of a disarranged mind. But palpably he remained before me, fanning himself complacently, and watching me with every mark of kindly interest. Evidently perceiving that I was fully alive to my surroundings, the Chinaman addressed a remark to me in a tongue quite unfamiliar.

I shook my head dazedly.

"Ah," he commented in French, "you do not speak my language."

"I do not," I answered, also in French; "but since it seems we have one common tongue, what is the meaning of the outrage to which I have been subjected, and who are you?"

As I spoke the words I rose to my feet, but was immediately attacked by vertigo, which compelled me to resume my seat upon the bench.

"Compose yourself," said the Chinaman, taking a pinch of snuff from a silver vase which stood convenient to his hand. "I have been compelled to adopt certain measures in order to bring about this interview. In China, such measures are not unusual, but I recognize that they are out of accordance with your English ideas."

"Emphatically they are!" I replied.

The placid manner of this singularly imposing old man rendered proper resentment difficult. A sense of futility, and of unreality, claimed me; I felt that this was a dream-world, governed by dream-laws.

"You have good reason," he continued, calmly raising the pinch of snuff to his nostrils, "good reason to distrust all that is Chinese. Therefore, when I despatched my servants to your abode (knowing you to be alone) I instructed them to observe every law of courtesy, compatible with the Sure Invitation. Hence, I pray you, absolve me, for I intended no offense."

Words failed me altogether; wonder succeeded wonder! What was coming? What did it all mean?

"I have selected you, rather than Mr. Commissioner Nayland Smith," continued the mandarin, "as the recipient of those secrets which I am about to impart, for the reason that your friend might possibly be acquainted with my appearance. I will confess that there was a time when I must have regarded you with animosity, as one who sought the destruction of the most ancient and potent organization in the world—the Si-Fan."

As he uttered the words he raised his right hand and touched his forehead, his mouth, and finally his breast—a gesture reminiscent of that employed by Moslems.

"But my first task is to assure you," he resumed, "that the activities of that Order are in no way inimical to yourself, your country or your King. The extensive ramifications of the Order have recently been employed by a certain Dr. Fu-Manchu for his own ends, and, since he was (I admit it) a high official, a schism has been created in our ranks. Exactly a month ago, sentence of death was passed upon him by the Sublime Prince, and, since I myself must return immediately to China, I look to Mr. Nayland Smith to carry out that sentence."

I said nothing; I remained bereft of the power of speech.

"The Si-Fan," he added, repeating the gesture with his hand, "disown Dr. Fu-Manchu and his servants; do with them what you will. In this envelope"—he held up a sealed package—"is information which should prove helpful to Mr. Smith. I have now a request to make. You were conveyed here in the garments which you wore at the time that my servants called upon you." (I was hatless and wore red leathern slippers.) "An overcoat and a hat can doutless be found to suit you, temporarily, and my request is that you close your eyes until permission is given to open them."

Is there any one of my readers in doubt respecting my reception of this proposal? Remember my situation, remember the bizarre happenings that had led up to it; remember, too, ere judging me, that whilst I could not doubt the unseen presence of Chinamen unnumbered surrounding that strange apartment with the golden door, I had not the remotest clue to guide me in determining where it was situated. Since the duration of my unconsciousness was immeasurable, the place in which I found myself might have been anywhere, within say, thirty miles of Fleet Street!

"I agree," I said.

The mandarin bowed composedly.

"Kindly close your eyes, Dr. Petrie," he requested, "and fear nothing. No danger threatens you."

I obeyed. Instantly sounded the note of a gong, and I became aware that the golden door was open. A soft voice, evidently that of a cultured Chinaman, spoke quite close to my ear—

"Keep your eyes tightly closed, please, and I will help you on with this coat. The envelope you will find in the pocket and here is a tweed cap. Now take my hand."

Wearing the borrowed garments, I was led from the room, along a passage, down a flight of thickly carpeted stairs, and so out of the house into the street. Faint evidences of remote traffic reached my ears as I was assisted into a car and placed in a cushioned corner. The car moved off, proceeding for some distance; then—

"Allow me to help you to descend," said the soft voice. "You may open your eyes in thirty seconds."

I was assisted from the step on to the pavement—and I heard the car being driven back. Having slowly counted thirty I opened my eyes, and looked about me. This, and not the fevered moment when first I had looked upon the room with the golden door, seemed to be my true awakening, for about me was a comprehensible world, the homely streets of London, with deserted Portland Place stretching away on the one hand and a glimpse of midnight Regent Street obtainable on the other! The clock of the neighboring church struck one.

My mind yet dull with wonder of it all, I walked on to Oxford Circus and there obtained a taxicab, in which I drove to Fleet Street. Discharging the man, I passed quickly under the time worn archway into the court and approached our stair. Indeed, I was about to ascend when some one came racing down and almost knocked me over.

"Petrie! Petrie! Thank God you're safe!"

It was Nayland Smith, his eyes blazing with excitement, as I could see by the dim light of the lamp near the archway, and his hands, as he clapped them upon my shoulders, quivering tensely.

"Petrie!" he ran on impulsively, and speaking with extraordinary rapidity, "I was detained by a most ingenious trick and arrived only five minutes ago, to find you missing, the window wide open, and signs of hooks, evidently to support a rope ladder, having been attached to the ledge."

"But where were you going?"

"Weymouth has just rung up. We have indisputable proof that the mandarin Ki-Ming, whom I had believed to be dead, and whom I know for a high official of the Si-Fan, is actually in London! It's neck or nothing this time, Petrie! I'm going straight to Portland Place!"

"To the Chinese Legation?"

"Exactly!"

"Perhaps I can save you a journey," I said slowly. "I have just come from there!"

Chapter XXVIII

THE MANDARIN KI-MING

Nayland Smith strode up and down the little sitting-room, tugging almost savagely at the lobe of his left ear. To-night his increasing grayness was very perceptible, and with his feverishly bright eyes staring straightly before him, he looked haggard and ill, despite the deceptive tan of his skin.

"Petrie," he began in his abrupt fashion, "I am losing confidence in myself."

"Why?" I asked in surprise.

"I hardly know; but for some occult reason I feel afraid."

"Afraid?"

"Exactly; afraid. There is some deep mystery here that I cannot fathom. In the first place, if they had really meant you to remain ignorant of the place at which the episodes described by you occurred, they would scarcely have dropped you at the end of Portland Place."

"You mean . . . ?"

"I mean that I don't believe you were taken to the Chinese Legation at all. Undoubtedly you saw the mandarin Ki-Ming; I recognize him from your description."

"You have met him, then?"

"No; but I know those who have. He is undoubtedly a very dangerous man, and it is just possible——"

He hesitated, glancing at me strangely.

"It is just possible," he continued musingly, "that his presence marks the beginning of the end. Fu-Manchu's health may be permanently impaired, and Ki-Ming may have superseded him."

"But, if what you suspect, Smith, be only partly true, with what object was I seized and carried to that singular interview? What was the meaning of the whole solemn farce?"

"Its meaning remains to be discovered," he answered; "but that the mandarin is amicably disposed I refuse to believe. You may dismiss the idea. In dealing with Ki-Ming we are to all intents and purposes dealing with Fu-Manchu. To me, this man's presence means one thing: we are about to be subjected to attempts along slightly different lines."

I was completely puzzled by Smith's tone.

"You evidently know more of this man, Ki-Ming, than you have yet explained to me," I said.

Nayland Smith pulled out the blackened briar and began rapidly to load it.

"He is a graduate," he replied, "of the Lama College, or monastery, of Rachë-Churân."

"This does not enlighten me."

Having got his pipe going well—

"What do you know of animal magnetism?" snapped Smith.

The question seemed so wildly irrelevant that I stared at him in silence for some moments. Then—

"Certain powers sometimes grouped under that head are recognized in every hospital to-day," I answered shortly.

"Quite so. And the monastery of Rachë-Churân is entirely devoted to the study of the subject."

"Do you mean that that gentle old man——"

"Petrie, a certain M. Sokoloff, a Russian gentleman whose acquaintance I made in Mandalay, related to me an episode that took place at the house of the mandarin Ki-Ming in Canton. It actually occurred in the presence of M. Sokoloff, and therefore is worthy of your close attention.

"He had had certain transactions with Ki-Ming, and at their conclusion received an invitation to dine with the mandarin. The entertainment took place in a sort of loggia or open pavilion, immediately in front of which was an ornamental lake, with numerous waterlilies growing upon its surface. One of the servants, I think his name was Li, dropped a silver bowl containing orange-flower water for pouring upon the hands, and some of the contents lightly sprinkled M. Sokoloff's garments.

"Ki-Ming spoke no word of rebuke, Petrie; he merely *looked* at Li, with those deceptive, gazelle-like eyes. Li, according to my acquaintance's account, began to make palpable and increasingly anxious attempts to look anywhere rather than into the mild eyes of his implacable master. M. Sokoloff, who, up to that moment, had entertained similar views to your own respecting his host, regarded this unmoving stare of Ki-Ming's as a sort of kindly, because silent, reprimand. The behavior of the unhappy Li very speedily served to disabuse his mind of that delusion.

"Petrie—the man grew livid, his whole body began to twitch and shake as though an ague had attacked him; and his eyes protruded hideously from their sockets! M. Sokoloff assured me that he *felt* himself turning pale—when Ki-Ming, very slowly, raised his right hand and pointed to the pond.

"Li began to pant as though engaged in a life and death struggle with a physically superior antagonist. He clutched at the posts of the loggia with frenzied hands and a bloody froth came to his lips. He began to move backward, step by step, step by step, all the time striving, with might and main, to *prevent* himself from doing so! His eyes were set rigidly upon Ki-Ming, like the eyes of a rabbit fascinated by a python. Ki-Ming continued to point.

"Right to the brink of the lake the man retreated, and there, for one dreadful moment, he paused and uttered a sort of groaning sob. Then, clenching his fists frenziedly, he stepped back into the water and immediately sank among the lilies. Ki-Ming continued to gaze fixedly—at the spot where bubbles were rising; and presently up came the livid face of the drowning man, still having those glazed eyes turned, immovably, upon the mandarin. For nearly five seconds that hideous, distorted face gazed from amid the mass of blooms, then it sank again . . . and rose no more."

"What!" I cried, "do you mean to tell me——"

"Ki-Ming struck a gong. Another servant appeared with a fresh bowl of water; and the mandarin calmly resumed his dinner!"

I drew a deep breath and raised my hand to my head.

"It is almost unbelievable," I said. "But what completely passes my comprehension is his allowing me to depart unscathed, having once held me in his power. Why the long harangue and the pose of friendship?"

"That point is not so difficult."

"What!"

"That does not surprise me in the least. You may recollect that Dr. Fu-Manchu entertains for you an undoubted affection, distinctly Chinese in its character, but nevertheless an affection! There is no intention of assassinating *you*, Petrie; *I* am the selected victim."

I started up.

"Smith! what do you mean? What danger, other than that which has threatened us for over two years, threatens us to-night?"

"Now you come to the point which *does*

puzzle me. I believe I stated awhile ago that I was afraid. You have placed your finger upon the cause of my fear. *What* threatens us to-night?"

He spoke the words in such a fashion that they seemed physically to chill me. The shadows of the room grew menacing; the very silence became horrible. I longed with a terrible longing for company, for the strength that is in numbers; I would have had the place full to overflowing—for it seemed that we two, condemned by the mysterious organization called the Si-Fan, were at that moment surrounded by the entire arsenal of horrors at the command of Dr. Fu-Manchu. I broke that morbid silence. My voice had assumed an unnatural tone.

"Why do you dread this man, Ki-Ming, so much?"

"Because he must be aware that I know he is in London."

"Well?"

"Dr. Fu-Manchu has no official status. Long ago, his Legation denied all knowledge of his existence. But the mandarin Ki-Ming is known to every diplomat in Europe, Asia and America almost. Only *I*, and now yourself, know that he is a high official of the Si-Fan; Ki-Ming is aware that I know. Why, therefore, does he risk his neck in London?"

"He relies upon his national cunning."

"Petrie, he is aware that I hold evidence to hang him, either here or in China! He relies upon one thing; upon striking first and striking surely. Why is he so confident? I do not know. Therefore I am afraid."

Again a cold shudder ran icily through me. A piece of coal dropped lower into the dying fire—and my heart leapt wildly. Then, in a flash, I remembered something.

"Smith!" I cried, "the letter! We have not looked at the letter."

Nayland Smith laid his pipe upon the mantelpiece and smiled grimly. From his pocket he took out a square piece of paper, and thrust it close under my eyes.

"I remembered it as I passed your borrowed garments—which bear no maker's name—on my way to the bedroom for matches," he said.

The paper was covered with Chinese characters!

"What does it mean?" I demanded breathlessly.

Smith uttered a short, mirthless laugh.

"It states that an attempt of a particularly dangerous nature is to be made upon my life to-night, and it recommends me to guard the door, and advises that you watch the window overlooking the court, and keep your pistol ready for instant employment." He stared at me oddly. "How should you act in the circumstances, Petrie?"

"I should strongly distrust such advice. Yet—what else can we *do*?"

"There are several alternatives, but I prefer to follow the advice of Ki-Ming."

The clock of St. Paul's chimed the half-hour: half-past two.

Chapter XXIX

LAMA SORCERY

From my post in the chair by the window I could see two sides of the court below; that immediately opposite, with the entrance to some chambers situated there, and that on the right, with the cloisteresque arches beyond which lay a maze of old-world passages and stairs whereby one who knew the tortuous navigation might come ultimately to the Embankment.

It was this side of the court which lay in deepest shadow. By altering my position quite slightly I could command a view of the arched entrance on the left with its pale lamp in an iron bracket above, and of the high blank wall whose otherwise unbroken expanse it interrupted. All was very still; only on occasions the passing of a vehicle along Fleet Street would break the silence.

The nature of the danger that threatened I was wholly unable to surmise. Since, my pistol on the table beside me, I sat on guard at the window, and Smith, also armed, watched the outer door, it was not apparent by what agency the shadowy enemy could hope to come at us.

Something strange I had detected in Nayland Smith's manner, however, which had induced me to believe that he suspected, if he did not know, what form of menace hung over us in the darkness. One thing in particular was puzzling me extremely: if Smith doubted the good faith of the sender of the message, why had he acted upon it?

Thus my mind worked—in endless and profitless cycles—whilst my eyes were ever searching the shadows below me.

And, as I watched, wondering vaguely why Smith at his post was so silent, presently I became aware of the presence of a slim figure over by the arches on the right. This discovery did not come suddenly, nor did it surprise me; I merely observed without being conscious of any great interest in the matter, that some one was standing in the court below, looking up at me where I sat.

I cannot hope to explain my state of mind at that moment, to render understandable by contrast with the cold fear which had visited me so recently, the utter apathy of my mental attitude. To this day I cannot recapture the mood—and for a very good reason, though one that was not apparent to me at the time.

It was the Eurasian girl Zarmi, who was standing there, looking up at the window! Silently I watched her. Why was I silent?— why did I not warn Smith of the presence of one of Dr. Fu-Manchu's servants? I cannot explain, although, later, the strangeness of my behavior may become in some measure understandable.

Zarmi raised her hand, beckoning to me, then stepped back, revealing the presence of a companion, hitherto masked by the dense shadows that lay under the arches. This second watcher moved slowly forward, and I perceived him to be none other than the mandarin Ki-Ming.

This I noted with interest, but with a sort of *impersonal* interest, as I might have watched the entrance of a character upon the stage of a theater. Despite the feeble light, I could see his benign countenance very clearly; but, far from being excited, a dreamy contentment possessed me; I actually found myself hoping that Smith would not intrude upon my reverie!

What a fascinating pageant it had been— the Fu-Manchu drama—from the moment that I had first set eyes upon the Yellow doctor. Again I seemed to be enacting my part in that scene, two years ago and more, when I had burst into the bare room above Shen-Yan's opium den and had stood face to face with Dr. Fu-Manchu. He wore a plain yellow robe, its hue almost identical with that of his gaunt, hairless face; his elbows rested upon the dirty table and his pointed chin upon his long, bony hands.

Into those uncanny eyes I stared, those eyes, long, narrow, and slightly oblique, their brilliant, catlike greenness sometimes horribly filmed, like the eyes of some grotesque bird. . . .

Thus it began; and from this point I was carried on, step by step, through every episode, great and small. It was such a retrospect as passes through the mind of one drowning.

With a vividness that was terrible yet exquisite, I saw Kâramanèh, my lost love; I saw her first wrapped in a hooded opera-cloak, with her flower-like face and glorious dark eyes raised to me; I saw her in the gauzy Eastern raiment of a slave-girl, and I saw her in the dress of a gipsy.

Through moments sweet and bitter I lived again, through hours of suspense and days of ceaseless watching; through the long months of that first summer when my unhappy love came to me, and on, on, interminably on. For years I lived again beneath that ghastly Yellow cloud. I searched throughout the land of Egypt for Kâramanèh and knew once more the sorrow of losing her. Time ceased to exist for me.

Then, at the end of these strenuous years, I came at last to my meeting with Ki-Ming in the room with the golden door. At this point my visionary adventures took a new turn. I sat again upon the red-covered couch and listened, half stupefied, to the placid speech of the mandarin. Again I came under the spell of his singular personality, and again, closing my eyes, I consented to be led from the room.

But, having crossed the threshold, a sudden awful doubt passed through my mind, arrow-like. The hand that held my arm was bony and clawish; I could detect the presence of incredibly long finger nails—nails long as those of some buried vampire of the black ages!

Choking down a cry of horror, I opened my eyes—heedless of the promise given but a few moments earlier—and looked into the face of my guide.

It was Dr. Fu-Manchu! . . .

Never, dreaming or waking, have I known a sensation identical with that which now clutched my heart; I thought that it must be death. For ages, untold ages—æons longer than the world has known—I looked into that still, awful face, into those unnatural green eyes. I jerked my hand free from the Chinaman's clutch and sprang back.

As I did so, I became miraculously translated from the threshold of the room with the golden door to our chambers in the court adjoining Fleet Street; I came into full possession of my faculties (or believed so at the time); I realized that I had nodded at my post, that I had dreamed a strange dream . . . but I realized something else. A ghoulish presence was in the room.

Snatching up my pistol from the table I turned. Like some evil jinn of Arabian lore, Dr. Fu-Manchu, surrounded by a slight mist, stood looking at me!

Instantly I raised the pistol, leveled it steadily at the high, dome-like brow—and fired! There could be no possibility of missing at such short range, no possibility whatever . . . and in the very instant of pulling the trigger the mist cleared, the lineaments of Dr. Fu-Manchu melted magically. This was not the Chinese doctor who stood before me, at whose skull I still was pointing the deadly little weapon, into whose brain I had fired a bullet; *it was Nayland Smith!*

Ki-Ming, by means of the unholy arts of the Lamas of Rachë-Churân, had caused me to murder my best friend!

"Smith!" I whispered huskily—"God forgive me, what have I done? What have I done?"

I stepped forward to support him ere he fell; but utter oblivion closed down upon me, and I knew no more.

* * * * * * *

"He will do quite well now," said a voice that seemed to come from a vast distance. "The effects of the drug will have entirely worn off when he wakes, except that there may be nausea, and possibly muscular pains for a time. . . ."

I opened my eyes; they were throbbing agonizingly. I lay in bed, and beside me stood Murdoch McCabe, the famous toxicological expert from Charing Cross Hospital—and Nayland Smith!

"Ah, that's better!" cried McCabe cheerily. "Here—drink this."

I drank from the glass which he raised to my lips. I was too weak for speech, too weak for wonder. Nayland Smith, his face gray and drawn in the cold light of early morning, watched me anxiously. McCabe, in a matter of fact way that acted upon me like a welcome tonic, put several purely medical questions, which at first by dint of a great effort, but, with ever-increasing ease, I answered.

"Yes," he said musingly at last. "Of course it is all but impossible to speak with certainty, but I am disposed to think that you have been drugged with some preparation of hashish. The most likely is that known in Eastern countries as *maagûn* or *barsh*, composed of equal parts of *cannabis indica* and opium, with hellebore and two other constituents, which vary according to the purpose which the *maagûn* is intended to serve. This renders the subject particularly open to subjective hallucinations, and a pliable instrument in the hands of a hypnotic operator, for instance."

"You see, old man?" cried Smith eagerly. "You see?"

But I shook my head weakly.

"I shot you," I said. "It is impossible that I could have missed."

"Mr. Smith has placed me in possession of the facts," interrupted McCabe, "and I can outline with reasonable certainty what took place. Of course, it's all very amazing, utterly fantastic in fact, but I have met with almost parallel cases in Egypt, in India, and elsewhere in the East: never in London, I'll confess. You see, Dr. Petrie, you were taken into the presence of a very accomplished hypnotist, having been previously prepared by a stiff administration of *maagûn*. You are doubtless familiar with the remarkable experiments in psycho-therapeutics conducted at the Salpêtrière in Paris, and you will readily understand me when I say that, prior to your recovering consciousness in the presence of the mandarin Ki-Ming, you had received your hypnotic instructions.

"These were to be put into execution either at a certain time (duly impressed upon your drugged mind) or at a given signal. . . ."

"It was a signal," snapped Smith. "Ki-Ming stood in the court below and looked up at the window."

"But *I* might not have been stationed at the window," I objected.

"In that event," snapped Smith, "he would have spoken, softly, through the raised letter-box of the door!"

"You immediately resumed your interrupted trance," continued McCabe, "and by hypnotic suggestion impressed upon you earlier in the evening, you were ingeniously led up to a point at which, under what delusion I know not, you fired at Mr. Smith. I had the privilege of studying an almost parallel case in Simla, where an officer was fatally stabbed by his *khitmatgar* (a most faithful servant) acting under the hypnotic promptings of a certain *fakîr* whom the officer had been unwise enough to chastise. The *fakîr* paid for the crime with his life, I may add. The *khitmatgar* shot him, ten minutes later."

"I had no chance at Ki-Ming," snapped Smith. "He vanished like a shadow. But he has played his big card and lost! Henceforth he is a hunted man; and he knows it! Oh!" he cried, seeing me watching him in bewilderment, "I suspected some Lama trickery, old man, and I stuck closely to the arrangements proposed by the mandarin, but kept you under careful observation!"

"But, Smith — I shot you! It was humanly impossible to miss!"

"I agree. But do you recall the *report?*"

"The report? I was too dazed, too horrified, by the discovery of what I had done ."

"There was no report, Petrie. I am not entirely a stranger to Indo-Chinese jugglery, and you had a very strange look in your eyes. Therefore I took the precaution of unloading your Browning!"

Chapter XXX

MEDUSA

Legal business, connected with the estate of a distant relative, deceased, necessitated my sudden departure from London, within twenty-four hours of the events just narrated; and at a time when London was for me the center of the universe. The business being terminated—and in a manner financially satisfactory to myself—I discovered that with luck I could just catch the fast train back. Amid a perfect whirl of hotel porters and taxi-drivers worthy of Nayland Smith I departed for the station . . . to arrive at the entrance to the platform at the exact moment that the guard raised his green flag!

"Too late, sir! Stand back, if you please!"

The ticket-collector at the barrier thrust out his arm to stay me. The London express was moving from the platform. But my determination to travel by that train and by no other over-rode all obstacles; if I missed it, I should be forced to wait until the following morning.

I leapt past the barrier, completely taking the man by surprise, and went racing up the platform. Many arms were outstretched to detain me, and the gray-bearded guard stood fully in my path; but I dodged them all, collided with and upset a gigantic negro who wore a chauffeur's uniform—and found myself level with a first-class compartment; the window was open.

Amid a chorus of excited voices, I tossed my bag in at the window, leapt upon the footboard and turned the handle. Although the entrance to the tunnel was perilously near now, I managed to wrench the door open and to swing myself into the carriage. Then, by means of the strap, I reclosed the door in the nick of time, and sank, panting, upon the seat. I had a vague impression that the black chauffeur, having recovered himself, had raced after me to the uttermost point of the platform, but, my end achieved, I was callously indifferent to the outrageous means thereto which I had seen fit to employ. The express dashed into the tunnel. I uttered a great sigh of relief.

With Kâramanèh in the hands of the Si-Fan, this journey to the north had indeed been undertaken with the utmost reluctance. Nayland Smith had written to me once during my brief absence, and his letter had inspired a yet keener desire to be back and at grips with the Yellow group; for he had hinted broadly that a tangible clue to the whereabouts of the Si-Fan head-quarters had at last been secured.

Now I learnt that I had a traveling companion—a woman. She was seated in the further, opposite corner, wore a long, loose motor-coat, which could not altogether conceal the fine lines of her lithe figure, and a thick veil hid her face. A motive for the excited behavior of the negro chauffeur suggested itself to my mind; a label, "Engaged," was pasted to the window!

I glanced across the compartment. Through the closely woven veil the woman was watching me. An apology clearly was called for.

"Madame," I said, "I hope you will forgive this unfortunate intrusion; but it was vitally important that I should not miss the London train."

She bowed, very slightly, very coldly—and turned her head aside.

The rebuff was as unmistakable as my offense was irremediable. Nor did I feel justified in resenting it. Therefore, endeavoring to dismiss the matter from my mind, I placed my bag upon the rack, and unfolding the newspaper with which I was provided, tried to interest myself in the doings of the world at large.

My attempt proved not altogether successful; strive how I would, my thoughts persistently reverted to the Si-Fan, the evil, secret society who held in their power one dearer to me than all the rest of the world; to Dr. Fu-Manchu, the genius who darkly controlled my destiny; and to Nayland Smith, the barrier between the White races and the devouring tide of the Yellow.

Sighing again, involuntarily, I glanced up . . . to meet the gaze of a pair of wonderful eyes.

Never, in my experience, had I seen their like. The dark eyes of Kâramanèh were wonderful and beautiful, the eyes of Dr. Fu-Manchu sinister and wholly unforgettable; but the eyes of this woman who was to be my traveling companion to London were incredible. Their glance was all but insupportable; they were the eyes of a Medusa!

Since I had met, in the not distant past, the soft gaze of Ki-Ming, the mandarin whose phenomenal hypnotic powers rendered him capable of transcending the achievements of the celebrated Cagliostro, I knew much of the power of the human eye. But these were unlike any human eyes I had ever known.

Long, almond-shaped, bordered by heavy jet-black lashes, arched over by finely penciled brows, their strange brilliancy, as of a fire within, was utterly uncanny. They were the eyes of some beautiful wild creature rather than those of a woman.

Their possessor had now thrown back her motorveil, revealing a face Orientally dark and perfectly oval, with a clustering mass of dull gold hair, small, aquiline nose, and full, red lips. Her weird eyes met mine for an instant, and then the long lashes drooped quickly, as she leant back against the cushions, with a graceful languor suggestive of the East rather than of the West.

Her long coat had fallen partly open, and I saw, with surprise, that it was lined with leopard-skin. One hand was ungloved, and lay on the arm-rest—a slim hand of the hue of old ivory, with a strange, ancient ring upon the index finger.

This woman obviously was not a European, and I experienced great difficulty in determining with what Asiatic nation she could claim kinship. In point of fact I had never seen another who remotely resembled her; she was a fit employer for the gigantic negro with whom I had collided on the platform.

I tried to laugh at myself, staring from the window at the moon-bathed landscape; but the strange personality of my solitary companion would not be denied, and I looked quickly in her direction—in time to detect her glancing away; in time to experience the uncanny fascination of her gaze.

The long slim hand attracted my attention again, the green stone in the ring affording a startling contrast against the dull cream of the skin.

Whether the woman's personality, or a vague perfume of which I became aware, were responsible, I found myself thinking of a flower-bedecked shrine, wherefrom arose the smoke of incense to some pagan god.

In vain I tld myself that my frame of mind was contemptible, that I should be ashamed of such weakness. Station after station was left behind, as the express sped through moonlit England towards the smoky metropolis. Assured that I was being furtively watched, I grew more and more uneasy.

It was with a distinct sense of effort that I withheld my gaze, forcing myself to look out of the window. When, having reasoned against the mad ideas that sought to obsess me, I glanced again across the compartment, I perceived, with inexpressible relief, that my companion had lowered her veil.

She kept it lowered throughout the remainder of the journey; yet during the hour that ensued I continued to experience sensations of which I have never since been able to think without a thrill of fear. It seemed that I had thrust myself, not into a commonplace railway compartment, but into a Cumæan cavern.

If only I could have addressed this utterly mysterious stranger, have uttered some word of commonplace, I felt that the spell might have been broken. But, for some occult reason, in no way associated with my first rebuff, I found myself tongue-tied; I sustained, for an hour (the longest I had ever known), a silent watch and ward over my reason; I seemed to be repelling, fighting against, some subtle power that sought to flood my brain, swamp my individuality, and enslave me to another's will.

In what degree this was actual, and in what due to a mind overwrought from endless conflict with the Yellow group, I know not to this day, but you who read these records of our giant struggle with Fu-Manchu and his satellites shall presently judge for yourselves.

When, at last, the brakes were applied, and the pillars and platforms of the great terminus glided into view, how welcome was the smoky glare, how welcome the muffled roar of busy London!

A huge negro—the double of the man I

had overthrown—opened the door of the compartment, bestowing upon me a glance in which enmity and amazement were oddly blended, and the woman, drawing the cloak about her graceful figure, stood up composedly.

She reached for a small leather case on the rack, and her loose sleeve fell back, to reveal a bare arm—soft, perfectly molded, of the even hue of old ivory. Just below the elbow a strange-looking snake bangle clasped the warm-flesh; the eyes, dull green, seemed to hold a slumbering fire—a spark of living light.

Then—she was gone!

"Thank Heaven!" I muttered, and felt like another Dante emerging from the Hades.

As I passed out of the station, I had a fleeting glimpse of a gray figure stepping into a big car, driven by a black chauffeur.

Chapter XXXI

THE MARMOSET

Half-past twelve was striking as I came out of the terminus, buttoning up my overcoat, and pulling my soft hat firmly down upon my head, started to walk to Hyde Park Corner.

I had declined the services of the several taxi-drivers who had accosted me and had determined to walk a part of the distance homeward, in order to check the fever of excitement which consumed me.

Already I was ashamed of the strange fears which had been mine during the journey, but I wanted to reflect, to conquer my mood, and the midnight solitude of the land of Squares which lay between me and Hyde Park appealed quite irresistibly.

There is a distinct pleasure to be derived from a solitary walk through London, in the small hours of an April morning, provided one is so situated as to be capable of enjoying it. To appreciate the solitude and mystery of the sleeping city, a certain sense of prosperity—a knowledge that one is immune from the necessity of being abroad at that hour—is requisite. The tramp, the night policeman and the coffee-stall keeper know more of London by night than most people—but of the romance of the dark hours they know little. Romance succumbs before necessity.

I had good reason to be keenly alive to the aroma of mystery which pervades the most commonplace thoroughfare after the hum of the traffic has subsided—when the rare pedestrian and the rarer cab alone traverse the deserted highway. With more intimate cares seeking to claim my mind, it was good to tramp along the echoing, empty streets and to indulge in imaginative speculations regarding the strange things that night must shroud in every big city. I have known the solitude of deserts, but the solitude of London is equally fascinating.

He whose business or pleasure has led him to traverse the route which was mine on this memorable night must have observed how each of the squares composing that residential chain which links the outer with the inner Society has a popular and an exclusive side. The angle used by vehicular traffic in crossing the square from corner to corner invariably is rich in a crop of black boards bearing house-agents' announcements.

In the shadow of such a board I paused, taking out my case and leisurely selecting a cigar. So many of the houses in the southwest angle were unoccupied, that I found myself taking quite an interest in one a little way ahead; from the hall door and from the long conservatory over the porch light streamed out.

Excepting these illuminations, there was no light elsewhere in the square to show which houses were inhabited and which vacant. I might have stood in a street of Pompeii or Thebes—a street of the dead past. I permitted my imagination to dwell upon this idea as I fumbled for matches and gazed about me. I wondered if a day would come when some savant of a future land, in a future age, should stand where I stood and endeavor to reconstruct, from the crumbling ruins, this typical London square. A slight breeze set the hatchet-board creaking above my head, as I held my gloved hands about the pine-vesta.

At that moment some one or something whistled close beside me!

I turned, in a flash, dropping the match upon the pavement. There was no lamp near the spot whereat I stood, and the gateway and porch of the deserted residence seemed to be empty. I stood there peering in the direction from which the mysterious whistle had come.

The drone of a taxicab, approaching from the north, increased in volume, as the vehicle came spinning around the angle of the square, passed me, and went droning on its way. I watched it swing around the distant corner . . . and, in the new stillness, the whistle was repeated!

This time the sound chilled me. The whistle was pitched in a curious, unhuman key, and it possessed a mocking note that was strangely uncanny.

Listening intently and peering towards the porch of the empty house, I struck a second match, pushed the iron gate open and made for the steps, sheltering the feeble flame with upraised hand. As I did so, the whistle was again repeated, but from some spot further away, to the left of the porch, and from low down upon the ground.

Just as I glimpsed something moving under the lee of the porch, the match was blown out, for I was hampered by the handbag which I carried. Thus reminded of its presence, however, I recollected that my pocket-lamp was in it. Quickly opening the bag, I took out the lamp, and, passing around the corner of the steps, directed a ray of light into the narrow passage which communicated with the rear of the building.

Half-way along the passage, looking back at me over its shoulder, and whistling angrily, was a little marmoset!

I pulled up as sharply as though the point of a sword had been held at my throat. One marmoset is sufficiently like another to deceive the ordinary observer, but unless I was permitting a not unnatural prejudice to influence my opinion, this particular specimen was the pet of Dr. Fu-Manchu!

Excitement, not untinged with fear, began to grow up within me. Hyde Park was no far cry, this was near to the heart of social London; yet, somewhere close at hand, it might be, watching me as I stood—lurked, perhaps, the great and evil being who dreamed of overthrowing the entire white race!

With a grotesque grimace and a final, chattering whistle, the little creature leapt away out of the beam of light cast by my lamp. Its sudden disappearance brought me to my senses and reminded me of my plain duty. I set off along the passage briskly, arrived at a small, square yard . . . and was just in time to see the ape leap into a well-like opening before a basement window. I stepped to the brink, directing the light down into the well.

I saw a collection of rotten leaves, waste paper, and miscellaneous rubbish—but the marmoset was not visible. Then I perceived that practically all the glass in the window had been broken. A sound of shrill chatter-ing reached me from the blackness of the undergound apartment.

Again I hesitated. What did the darkness mask?

The note of a distant motor-horn rose clearly above the vague throbbing which is the only silence known to the town-dweller.

Gripping the unlighted cigar between my teeth, I placed my bag upon the ground and dropped into the well before the broken window. To raise the sash was a simple matter, and, having accomplished it, I inspected the room within.

The light showed a large kitchen, with torn wallpaper and decorators' litter strewn about the floor, a whitewash pail in one corner, and nothing else.

I climbed in, and, taking from my pocket the Browning pistol without which I had never traveled since the return of the dreadful Chinaman to England, I crossed to the door, which was ajar, and looked out into the passage beyond.

Stifling an exclamation, I fell back a step. Two gleaming eyes stared straightly into mine!

The next moment I had forced a laugh to my lips . . . as the marmoset turned and went gambolling up the stairs. The house was profoundly silent. I crossed the passage and followed the creature, which now was proceeding, I thought, with more of a set purpose.

Out into a spacious and deserted hallway it led me, where my cautious footsteps echoed eerily, and ghostly faces seemed to peer down upon me from the galleries above. I should have liked to have unbarred the street door, in order to have opened a safe line of retreat in the event of its being required, but the marmoset suddenly sprang up the main stairway at a great speed, and went racing around the gallery overhead toward the front of the house.

Determined, if possible, to keep the creature in view, I started in pursuit. Up the uncarpeted stairs I went, and, from the rail of the landing, looked down into the blackness of the hallway apprehensively. Nothing stirred below. The marmoset had disappeared between the half-opened leaves of a large folding door. Casting the beam of light ahead of me I followed. I found myself in a long, lofty apartment, evidently a drawing-room.

Of the quarry I could detect no sign; but the only other door of the room was closed; therefore, since the creature had entered, it must, I argued, undoubtedly be concealed somewhere in the apartment. Flashing the light about to right and left, I presently perceived that a conservatory (no doubt facing on the square) ran parallel with one side of the room. French windows gave access to either end of it; and it was through one of these, which was slightly open, that the questioning ray had intruded.

I stepped into the conservatory. Linen blinds covered the windows, but a faint light from outside found access to the bare, tiled apartment. Ten paces on my right, from an aperture once closed by a square wooden panel that now lay upon the floor, the marmoset was grimacing at me.

Realizing that the ray of my lamp must be visible through the blinds from outside, I extinguished it . . . and, a moving silhouette against a faintly luminous square, I could clearly distinguish the marmoset watching me.

There was a light in the room beyond!

The marmoset disappeared—and I became aware of a faint, incense-like perfume. Where had I met with it before? Nothing disturbed the silence of the empty house wherein I stood; yet I hesitated for several seconds to pursue the chase further. The realization came to me that the hole in the wall communicated with the conservatory of the corner house in the square, the house with the lighted windows.

Determined to see the thing through, I discarded my overcoat—and crawled through the gap. The smell of burning perfume became almost overpowering, as I stood upright, to find myself almost touching curtains of some semi-transparent golden fabric draped in the door between the conservatory and the drawing-room.

Cautiously, inch by inch, I approached my eyes to the slight gap in the draperies, as, from somewhere in the house below, sounded the clangor of a brazen gong. Seven times its ominous note boomed out. I shrank back into my sanctuary; the incense seemed to be stifling me.

Chapter XXXII

SHRINE OF SEVEN LAMPS

Never can I forget that nightmare apartment, that efreet's hall. It was identical in shape with the room of the adjoining house through which I had come, but its walls were draped in somber black and a dead black carpet covered the entire floor. A golden curtain—similar to that which concealed me—broke the somber expanse of the end wall to my right, and the door directly opposite my hiding-place was closed.

Across the gold curtain, wrought in glittering black, were seven characters, apparently Chinese; before it, supported upon seven ebony pedestals, burned seven golden lamps; whilst, dotted about the black carpet, were seven gold-lacquered stools, each having a black cushion set before it. There was no sign of the marmoset; the incredible room of black and gold was quite empty, with a sort of stark emptiness that seemed to oppress my soul.

Close upon the booming of the gong followed a sound of many footsteps and a buzz of subdued conversation. Keeping well back in the welcome shadows I watched, with bated breath, the opening of the door immediately opposite.

The outer sides of its leaves proved to be of gold, and one glimpse of the room beyond awoke a latent memory and gave it positive form. I had been in this house before; it was in that room with the golden door that I had had my memorable interview with the mandarin Ki-Ming! My excitement grew more and more intense.

Singly, and in small groups, a number of Orientals came in. All wore European, or semi-European garments, but I was enabled to identify two for Chinamen, two for Hindus and three for Burmans. Other Asiatics there were, also, whose exact place among the Eastern races I could not determine; there was at least one Egyptian and there were several Eurasians; no women were present.

Standing grouped just within the open door, the gathering of Orientals kept up a ceaseless buzz of subdued conversation; then, abruptly, stark silence fell, and through a lane of bowed heads, Ki-Ming, the famous Chinese diplomat, entered, smiling blandly, and took his seat upon one of the seven golden stools. He wore the picturesque yellow robe, trimmed with marten fur, which I had seen once before, and he placed his pearl-encircled cap, surmounted by the coral ball denoting his rank, upon the black cushion beside him.

Almost immediately afterwards entered a second and even more striking figure. It was that of a Lama monk! He was received with the same marks of deference which had been accorded the mandarin; and he seated himself upon another of the golden stools.

Silence, a moment of hushed expectancy, and . . . yellow-robed, immobile, his wonderful, evil face emaciated by illness, but his long, magnetic eyes blazing greenly, as though not a soul but an elemental spirit dwelt within that gaunt, high-shouldered body, Dr. Fu-Manchu entered, slowly, leaning upon a heavy stick!

The realities seemed to be slipping from me; I could not believe that I looked upon a material world. This had been a night of wonders, having no place in the life of a sane, modern man, but belonging to the days of the jinn and the Arabian necromancers.

Fu-Manchu was greeted by a universal raising of hands, but in complete silence. He also wore a cap surmounted by a coral ball, and this he placed upon one of the black cushions set before a golden stool. Then, resting heavily upon his stick, he began to speak—in French!

As one listens to a dream-voice, I listened to that, alternately guttural and sibilant, of the terrible Chinese doctor. He was defending himself! With what he was charged by his sinister brethren I knew not nor could I gather from his words, but that he was rendering account of his stewardship became unmistakable. Scarce crediting my senses, I heard him unfold to his listeners details of crimes successfully perpetrated, and with the results of some of these I was but too familiar; others there were in the ghastly catalogue which had been accomplished secretly. Then my blood froze with horror. My own name was mentioned—and that of Nayland Smith! We two stood in the way of the coming of one whom he called the Lady of the Si-Fan, in the way of Asiatic supremacy.

A fantastic legend once mentioned to me by Smith, of some woman cherished in a secret fastness of Hindustan who was destined one day to rule the world, now appeared to my benumbed senses, to be the unquestioned creed of the murderous, cosmopolitan group known as the Si-Fan! At every mention of her name all heads were bowed in reverence.

Dr. Fu-Manchu spoke without the slightest trace of excitement; he assured his auditors of his fidelity to their cause and proposed to prove to them that he enjoyed the complete confidence of the Lady of the Si-Fan.

And with every moment that passed the giant intellect of the speaker became more and more apparent. Years ago Nayland Smith had assured me that Dr. Fu-Manchu was a linguist who spoke with almost equal facility in any of the civilized languages and in most of the barbaric; now the truth of this was demonstrated. For, following some passage which might be susceptible of misconstruction, Fu-Manchu would turn slightly, and elucidate his remarks, addressing a Chinaman in Chinese, a Hindu in Hindustanee, or an Egyptian in Arabic.

His auditors were swayed by the magnetic personality of the speaker, as reeds by a breeze; and now I became aware of a curious circumstance. Either because they and I viewed the character of this great and evil man from a widely dissimilar aspect, or because, my presence being unknown to him, I remained outside the radius of his power, it seemed to me that these members of the evidently vast organization known as the Si-Fan were dupes, to a man, of the Chinese orator! It seemed to me that he used them as an instrument, playing upon their obvious fanaticism, string by string, as a player upon an Eastern harp, and all the time weaving harmonies to suit some giant, incredible scheme of his own—a scheme over and beyond any of which they had dreamed, in the fruition whereof they had no part—of the true nature and composition of which they had no comprehension.

"Not since the day of the first Yüan Emperor," said Fu-Manchu sibilantly, "has Our Lady of the Si-Fan—to look upon whom, unveiled, is death—crossed the sacred borders. To-day I am a man supremely happy and honored above my deserts. You shall all partake with me of that happiness, that honor . . . ."

Again the gong sounded seven times, and a sort of magnetic thrill seemed to pass throughout the room. There followed a faint, musical sound, like the tinkle of a silver bell.

All heads were lowered, but all eyes upturned to the golden curtain. Literally holding my breath, in those moments of intense expectancy, I watched the draperies parted from the center and pulled aside by unseen agency.

A black covered dais was revealed, bearing an ebony chair. And seated in the chair, enveloped from head to feet in a shimmering white veil, was a woman. A sound like a great sigh arose from the gathering. The woman rose slowly to her feet, and raised her arms, which were exquisitely formed, and of the uniform hue of old ivory, so that the veil fell back to her shoulders, revealing the green snake bangle which she wore. She extended her long, slim hands as if in benediction; the silver bell sounded . . . and the curtain dropped again, entirely obscuring the dais!

Frankly, I thought myself mad; for this "lady of the Si-Fan" was none other than my mysterious traveling companion! This was some solemn farce with which Fu-Manchu sought to impress his fanatical dupes. And he had succeeded; they were inspired, their eyes blazed. Here were men capable of any crime in the name of the Si-Fan!

Every face within my ken I had studied individually, and now slowly and cautiously I changed my position, so that a group of three members standing immediately to the right of the door came into view. One of them—a tall, spare, and closely bearded man whom I took for some kind of Hindu—had removed his gaze from the dais and was glancing furtively all about him. Once he looked in my direction, and my heart leapt high, then seemed to stop its pulsing.

An overpowering consciousness of my danger came to me; a dim envisioning of what appalling fate would be mine in the event of discovery. As those piercing eyes were turned away again, I drew back, step by step.

Dropping upon my knees, I began to feel for the gap in the conservatory wall. The desire to depart from the house of the Si-Fan was become urgent. Once safely away, I could take the necessary steps to ensure the apprehension of the entire group. What a triumph would be mine!

I found the opening without much difficulty and crept through into the empty house. The vague light which penetrated the linen blinds served to show me the length of the empty, tiled apartments. I had actually reached the French window giving access to the drawing-room, when—the skirl of a police whistle split the stillness . . . and the sound came from the house which I had just quitted!

To write that I was amazed were to achieve the banal. Rigid with wonderment I stood, and clutched at the open window. So I was standing, a man of stone, when the voice, the high-pitched, imperious, unmistakable voice of *Nayland Smith*, followed sharply upon the skirl of the whistle:—

"Watch those French windows, Weymouth! I can hold the door!"

Like a lightning flash it came to me that the tall Hindu had been none other than Smith disguised. From the square outside came a sudden turmoil, a sound of racing feet, of smashing glass, of doors burst forcibly open. Palpably, the place was surrounded; this was an organized raid.

Irresolute, I stood there in the semi-gloom—inactive from amaze of it all—whilst sounds of a tremendous struggle proceeded from the square gap in the partition.

"Lights!" rose a cry, in Smith's voice again—"they have cut the wires!"

At that I came to my senses. Plunging my hand into my pocket, I snatched out the electric lamp . . . and stepped back quickly into the utter gloom of the room behind me.

Some one was crawling through the aperture into the conservatory!

As I watched I saw him, in the dim light, stoop to replace the movable panel. Then, tapping upon the tiled floor as he walked, the fugitive approached me. He was but three paces from the French window when I pressed the button of my lamp and directed its ray fully upon his face.

"Hands up!" I said breathlessly. "I have you covered, Dr. Fu-Manchu!"

Chapter XXXIII

AN ANTI-CLIMAX

One hour later I stood in the entrance hall of our chambers in the court adjoining Fleet stairs. Some one who had come racing up the stairs, now had inserted a key in the lock. Open swung the door—and Nayland Smith entered, in a perfect whirl of excitement.

"Petrie! Petrie!" he cried, and seized both my hands—"you have missed a night of nights! Man alive! we have the whole gang—the great Ki-Ming included!" His eyes were blazing. "Weymouth has made no fewer than twenty-five arrests, some of the prisoners being well-known Orientals. It will be the devil's own work to keep it all quiet, but Scotland Yard has already advised the Press."

"Congratulations, old man," I said, and looked him squarely in the eyes.

Something there must have been in my glance at variance with the spoken words.

His expression changed; he grasped my shoulder.

"She was not there," he said, "but, please God, we'll find her now. It's only a question of time."

But, even as he spoke, the old, haunted look was creeping back into the lean face. He gave me a rapid glance; then:—

"I might as well make a clean breast of it," he rapped. "Fu-Manchu escaped! Furthermore, when we got lights, the woman had vanished, too."

"The woman!"

"There was a woman at this strange gathering, Petrie. Heaven only knows who she really is. According to Fu-Manchu she is that woman of mystery concerning whose existence strange stories are current in the East; the future Empress of a universal empire! But of course I decline to accept the story. Petrie! if ever the Yellow races overran Europe, I am in no doubt respecting the identity of the person who would ascend the throne of the world!"

"Nor I, Smith!" I cried excitedly. "Good God! he holds them all in the palm of his hand! He has welded together the fanatics of every creed of the East into a giant weapon for his personal use! Small wonder that he is so formidable. But, Smith—*who* is that woman?"

Nayland Smith was staring at me in blank amazement.

"Petrie!" he said slowly, and I knew that I had betrayed my secret, "Petrie—where did you learn all this?"

I returned his steady gaze.

"I was present at the meeting of the Si-Fan," I replied steadily.

"What? What? *You* were present?"

"I was present! Listen, and I will explain."

Standing there in the hallway I related, as briefly as possible, the astounding events of the night. As I told of the woman in the train—

"That confirms my impression that Fu-Manchu was imposing upon the others!" he snapped. "I cannot conceive of a woman recluse from some Lamaserie, surrounded by silent attendants and trained for her exalted destiny in the way that the legendary veiled woman of Tibet is said to be trained, traveling alone in an English railway carriage! Did you observe, Petrie, if her eyes were *oblique* at all?"

"They did not strike me as being oblique. Why do you ask?"

"Because I strongly suspect that we have to do with none other than Fu-Manchu's daughter! But go on."

"By heavens, Smith! You may be right! I possess such features."

"She may not have had a Chinese mother; furthermore, there are pretty women in China as well as in other countries; also, there are hair dyes and cosmetics. But for Heaven's sake go on!"

I continued my all but incredible narrative; came to the point where I discovered the straying marmoset and entered the empty house, without provoking any comment from my listener. He stared at me with something very like surprised admiration when I related how I had become an unseen spectator of that singular meeting.

"And I thought I had achieved the triumph of my life in gaining admission and smuggling Weymouth and Carter into the roof, armed with hooks land rope-ladders!" he murmured.

Now I came to the moment when, having withdrawn into the empty house, I had heard the police whistle and had heard Smith's voice; I came to the moment when I had found myself face to face with Dr. Fu-Manchu.

Nayland Smith's eyes were on fire now; he literally quivered with excitement, when—

"Ssh! what's that?" he whispered, and grasped my arm. "I heard something move in the sitting-room, Petrie!"

"It was a coal dropping from the grate, perhaps," I said—and rapidly continued my story, telling how, with my pistol to his head, I had forced the Chinese doctor to descend into the hallway of the empty house.

"Yes, yes," snapped Smith. "For God's sake go on, man! What have you done with him? Where is he?"

I clearly detected a movement myself immediately behind the half-open door of the sitting-room. Smith started and stared intently across my shoulder at the doorway; then his gaze shifted and became fixed upon my face.

"He bought his life from me, Smith."

Never can I forget the change that came over my friend's tanned features at those words; never can I forget the pang that I suffered to see it. The fire died out of his eyes and he seemed to grow old and weary in a moment. None too steadily I went on:—

"He offered a price that I could not resist, Smith. Try to forgive me, if you can. I know that I have done a dastardly thing, but—

perhaps a day may come in your own life when you will understand. He descended with me to a cellar under the empty house, in which some one was locked. Had I arrested Fu-Manchu this poor captive must have died there of starvation; for no one would ever have suspected that the place had an occupant. . . ."

The door of the sitting-room was thrown open, and, wearing my great-coat over the bizarre costume in which I had found her, with her bare ankles and little red slippers peeping grotesquely from below, and her wonderful cloud of hair rippling over the turned-up collar, Kâramanèh came out!

Her great dark eyes were raised to Nayland Smith's face with such an appeal in them—an appeal for *me*—that emotion took me by the throat and had me speechless. I could not look at either of them; I turned aside and stared into the lighted sitting-room.

How long I stood so God knows, and I never shall; but suddenly I found my hand seized in a vice-like grip, I looked around . . . and Smith, holding my fingers fast in that iron grasp, had his left arm about Kâramanèh's shoulders, and his gray eyes were strangely soft, whilst hers were hidden behind her upraised hands.

"Good old Petrie!" said Smith hoarsely. "Wake up, man; we have to get her to a hotel before they all close, remember. I understand, old man. That day came in my life long years ago!"

Chapter XXXIV

GRAYWATER PARK

"This is a singular situation in which we find ourselves," I said, "and one that I'm bound to admit I don't appreciate."

Nayland Smith stretched his long legs, and lay back in his chair.

"The sudden illness of Sir Lionel is certainly very disturbing," he replied, "and had there been any possibility of returning to London to-night, I should certainly have availed myself of it, Petrie. I share your misgivings. We are intruders at a time like this."

He stared at me keenly, blowing a wreath of smoke from his lips, and then directing his attention to the cone of ash which crowned his cigar. I glanced, and not for the first time,

toward the quaint old doorway which gave access to a certain corridor. Then—

"Apart from the feeling that we intrude," I continued slowly, "there is a certain sense of unrest."

"Yes," snapped Smith, sitting suddenly upright—"yes! You experience this? Good! You are happily sensitive to this type of impression, Petrie, and therefore quite as useful to me as a cat is useful to a physical investigator."

He laughed in his quick, breezy fashion.

"You will appreciate my meaning," he added; "therefore I offer no excuse for the analogy. Of course, the circumstances, as we know them, may be responsible for this consciousness of unrest. We are neither of us likely to forget the attempt upon the life of Sir Lionel Barton two years ago or more. Our attitude toward sudden illnesses is scarcely that of impartial observers."

"I suppose not," I admitted, glancing yet again at the still vacant doorway by the foot of the stairs, which now the twilight was draping in mysterious shadows.

Indeed, our position was a curious one. A welcome invitation from our old friend, Sir Lionel Barton, the world-famous explorer, had come at a time when a spell of repose, a glimpse of sea and awakening countryside, and a breath of fair, untainted air were very desirable. The position of Kâramanèh, who accompanied us, was sufficiently unconventional already, but the presence of Mrs. Oram, the dignified housekeeper, had rendered possible her visit to this bachelor establishment. In fact it was largely in the interests of the girl's health that we had accepted.

On our arrival at Graywater Park we had learnt that our host had been stricken down an hour earlier by sudden illness. The exact nature of his seizure I had thus far been unable to learn; but a local doctor, who had left the Park barely ten minutes before our advent, had strictly forbidden visitors to the sick-room. Sir Lionel's man, Kennedy, who had served him in many strange spots of the world, was in attendance.

So much we gathered from Homopoulo, the Greek butler (Sir Lionel's household had ever been eccentric). Furthermore, we learned that there was no London train that night and no accommodation in the neighboring village.

"Sir Lionel urgently requests you to remain," the butler had assured us, in his flawless, monotonous English. "He trusts that you will not be dull, and hopes to be able to see you to-morrow and to make plans for your entertainment."

A ghostly, gray shape glided across the darkened hall—and was gone. I started involuntarily. Then remote, fearsome, came muted howling to echo through the ancient apartments of Graywater Park. Nayland Smith laughed.

"That was the civet cat, Petrie!" he said. "I was startled, for a moment, until the lamentations of the leopard family reminded me of the fact that Sir Lionel had transferred his menagerie to Graywater!"

Truly, this was a singular household. In turn, Graywater Park had been a fortress, a monastery, and a manor-house. Now, in the extensive crypt below the former chapel, in an atmosphere artificially raised to a suitably stuffy temperature, were housed the strange pets brought by our eccentric host from distant lands. In one cage was an African lioness, a beautiful and powerful beast, docile as a cat. Housed under other arches were two surly hyenas, goats from the White Nile, and an antelope of Kordofan. In a stable opening upon the garden were a pair of beautiful desert gazelles, and, near to them, two cranes and a marabout. The leopards, whose howling now disturbed the night, were in a large, cell-like cage immediately below the spot where of old the chapel altar had stood.

And here were we an odd party in odd environment. I sought to make out the time by my watch, but the growing dusk rendered it impossible. Then, unheralded by any sound, Kâramanèh entered by the door which during the past twenty minutes had been the focus of my gaze. The gathering darkness precluded the possibility of my observing with certainty, but I think a soft blush stole to her cheeks as those glorious dark eyes rested upon me.

The beauty of Kâramanèh was not of the type which is enhanced by artificial lighting; it was the beauty of the palm and the pomegranate blossom, the beauty which flowers beneath merciless suns, which expands, like the lotus, under the skies of the East. But there, in the dusk, as she came towards me, she looked exquisitely lovely, and graceful with the grace of the desert gazelles which I had seen earlier in the evening. I cannot describe her dress; I only know that she seemed very wonderful—so wonderful that a pang, almost of terror, smote my heart, because such sweetness should belong to *me*.

And then, from the shadows masking the other side of the old hall, emerged the black figure of Homopoulo, and our odd trio obediently paced into the somber dining-room.

A large lamp burned in the center of the table; a shaded candle was placed before each diner; and the subdued light made play upon the snowy napery and fine old silver without dispersing the gloom about us. Indeed, if anything, it seemed to render it the more remarkable, and the table became a lighted oasis in the desert of the huge apartment. One could barely discern the suits of armor and trophies which ornamented the paneled walls; and I never failed to start nervously when the butler appeared, somber and silent, at my elbow.

Sir Lionel Barton's *penchant* for strange visitors, of which we had had experience in the past, was exemplified in the person of Homopoulo. I gathered that the butler (who, I must admit, seemed thoroughly to comprehend his duties) had entered the service of Sir Lionel during the time that the latter was pursuing his celebrated excavations upon the traditional site of the Dædalian Labyrinth in Crete. It was during this expedition that the death of a distant relative had made him master of Graywater Park; and the event seemingly had inspired the eccentric baronet immediately to engage a suitable factotum.

His usual retinue of Malay footmen, Hindu grooms and Chinese cooks, was missing apparently, and the rest of the household, including the charming old housekeeper, had been at the Park for periods varying from five to five-and-twenty years. I must admit that I welcomed the fact; my tastes are essentially insular.

But the untimely illness of our host had cast a shadow upon the party. I found myself speaking in a church-whisper, whilst Kâramanèh was quite silent. That curious dinner party in the shadow desert of the huge apartment frequently recurs in my memories of those days because of the uncanny happening which terminated it.

Nayland Smith, who palpably had been as ill at ease as myself, and who had not escaped the contagious habit of speaking in a hushed whisper, suddenly began, in a loud and cheery manner, to tell us something of the history of Graywater Park, which in his methodical way he had looked up. It was a desperate revolt, on the part of his strenuous spirit, against the phantom of gloom which threatened to obsess us all.

Parts of the house, it appeared, were of very great age, although successive owners had added portions. There were fascinating traditions connected with the place; secret rooms walled up since the Middle Ages, a private stair whose entrance, though undiscoverable, was said to be somewhere in the orchard to the west of the ancient chapel. It had been built by an ancestor of Sir Lionel who had flourished in the reign of the eighth Henry. At this point in his reminiscences (Smith had an astonishing memory where recondite facts were concerned) there came an interruption.

The smooth voice of the butler almost made me leap from my chair, as he spoke out of the shadows immediately behind me.

"The '45 port, sir," he said—and proceeded to place a crusted bottle upon the table. "Sir Lionel desires me to say that he is with you in spirit and that he proposes the health of Dr. Petrie and his fiancée, whom he hopes to have the pleasure of meeting in the morning."

Truly it was a singular situation, and I am unlikely ever to forget the scene as the three of us solemnly rose to our feet and drank our host's toast, thus proposed by proxy, under the eye of Homopoulo, who stood a shadowy figure in the background.

The ceremony solemnly performed and the gloomy butler having departed with a suitable message to Sir Lionel—

"I was about to tell you," resumed Nayland Smith, with a gaiety palpably forced, "of the traditional ghost of Graywater Park. He is a black clad priest, said to be the Spanish chaplain of the owner of the Park in the early days of the Reformation. Owing to some little misunderstanding with His Majesty's commissioners, this unfortunate churchman met with an untimely death, and his shade is said to haunt the secret room—the site of which is unknown—and to clamor upon the door, and upon the walls of the private stair."

I thought the subject rather ill chosen, but recognized that my friend was talking more or less at random and in desperation; indeed, failing his reminiscences of Graywater Park, I think the demon of silence must have conquered us completely.

"Presumably," I said, unconsciously speaking as though I feared the sound of my own voice, "this Spanish priest was confined at some time in the famous hidden chamber?"

"He was supposed to know the secret of a hoard of church property, and tradition has it, that he was put to the question in some gloomy dungeon . . ."

He ceased abruptly; in fact the effect was that which must have resulted had the speaker been suddenly stricken down. But the deadly silence which ensued was instantly interrupted. My heart seemed to be clutched as though by fingers of ice; a stark and supernatural horror held me riveted in my chair.

For as though Nayland Smith's words had been heard by the ghostly inhabitant of Graywater Park, as though the tortured priest sought once more release from his age-long sufferings—there came echoing, hollowly and remotely, as if from a subterranean cavern, the sound of *knocking*.

From whence it actually proceeded I was wholly unable to determine. At one time it seemed to surround us, as though not one but a hundred prisoners were beating upon the paneled walls of the huge, ancient apartment.

Faintly, so faintly, that I could not be sure if I heard aright, there came, too, a stifled cry. Louder grew the frantic beating and louder . . . then it ceased abruptly.

"Merciful God!" I whispered—"what was it? What was it?"

Chapter XXXV

THE EAST TOWER

With a cigarette between my lips I sat at the open window, looking out upon the skeleton trees of the orchard; for the buds of early spring were only just beginning to proclaim themselves.

The idea of sleep was far from my mind. The attractive modern furniture of the room could not deprive the paneled walls of the musty antiquity which was their birthright. This solitary window deeply set and overlooking the orchard upon which the secret stair was said to open, struck a note of more remote antiquity, casting back beyond the carousing days of the Stuart monarchs to the troublous times of the Middle Ages.

An air of ghostly evil had seemed to arise

like a miasma within the house from the moment that we had been disturbed by the unaccountable rapping. It was at a late hour that we had separated, and none of us, I think, welcomed the breaking up of our little party. Mrs. Oram, the housekeeper, had been closely questioned by Smith—for Homopoulo, as a new-comer, could not be expected to know anything of the history of Graywater Park. The old lady admitted the existence of the tradition which Nayland Smith had in some way unearthed, but assured us that never, in her time, had the uneasy spirit declared himself. She was ignorant (or like the excellent retainer that she was, professed to be ignorant) of the location of the historic chamber and staircase.

As for Homopoulo, hitherto so irreproachably imperturbable, I had rarely seen a man in such a state of passive panic. His dark face was blanched to the hue of dirty parchment and his forehead dewed with cold perspiration. I mentally predicted an early resignation in the household of Sir Lionel Barton. Homopoulo might be an excellent butler, but his superstitious Greek nature was clearly incapable of sustaining existence beneath the same roof with a family ghost, hoary though the specter's antiquity might be.

Where the skeleton shadows of the fruit trees lay beneath me on the fresh green turf my fancy persistently fashioned a black-clad figure flitting from tree to tree. Sleep indeed was impossible. Once I thought I detected the howling of the distant leopards.

Somewhere on the floor above me, Nayland Smith, I knew, at that moment would be restlessly pacing his room, the exact situation of which I could not identify, because of the quaint, rambling passages whereby one approached it. It was in regard to Kâramanèh, however, that my misgivings were the keenest. Already her position had been strange enough, in those unfamiliar surroundings, but what tremors must have been hers now in the still watches of the night, following the ghostly manifestations which had so dramatically interrupted Nayland Smith's story, I dared not imagine. She had been alloted an apartment somewhere upon the ground floor, and Mrs. Oram, whose motherly interest in the girl had touched me deeply, had gone with her to her room, where no doubt her presence had done much to restore the girl's courage.

Graywater Park stood upon a well-wooded slope, and, to the southwest, starting above the trees almost like a giant Spanish priest, showed a solitary tower. With a vague and indefinite interest I watched it. It was Monkswell, an uninhabited place belonging to Sir Lionel's estate and dating, in part, to the days of King John. Flicking the ash from my cigarette, I studied the ancient tower, wondering idly what deeds had had their setting within its shadows, since the Angevin monarch, in whose reign it saw the light, had signed Magna Charta.

This was a perfect night, and very still. Nothing stirred, within or without Graywater Park. Yet I was conscious of a definite disquietude which I could only suppose to be ascribable to the weird events of the evening, but which seemed rather to increase than to diminish.

I tossed the end of my cigarette out into the darkness, determined to turn in, although I had never felt more wide awake in my life. One parting glance cast into the skeleton orchard and was on the point of standing up, when—although no breeze stirred—a shower of ivy leaves rained down upon my head!

Brushing them away irritably, I looked up—and a second shower dropped fully upon my face and filled my eyes with dust. I drew back, checking an exclamation. What with the depth of the embrasure, due to the great thickness of the wall, and the leafy tangle above the window, I could see for no great distance up the face of the building; but a faint sound of rustling and stumbling which proceeded from somewhere above me proclaimed that some one, or something, was climbing either up or down the wall of the corner tower in which I was housed!

Partially removing the dust from my smarting eyes, I returned to the embrasure, and stepping from the chair on to the deep ledge, I grasped the corner of the quaint, diamond-paned window, which I had opened to its fullest extent, and craned forth.

Now I could see the ivy-grown battlements surmounting the tower (the east wing, in which my room was situated, was the oldest part of Graywater Park). Sharply outlined against the cloudless sky they showed . . . and the black silhouette of a man's head and shoulders leant over directly above me!

I drew back sharply. The climber, I thought, had not seen me, although he was evidently peering down at my window. What did it mean?

As I crouched in the embrasure, a sudden

giddiness assailed me, which at first I ascribed to a sympathetic nervous action due to having seen the man poised there at that dizzy height. But it increased. I swayed forward, and clutched at the wall to save myself. A deadly nausea overcame me . . . and a deadly doubt leapt to my mind.

In the past, Sir Lionel Barton had had spies in his household; what if the dark-faced Greek, Homopoulo, were another of these? I thought of the '45 port, of the ghostly rapping; and I thought of the man who crouched upon the roof of the tower above my open window.

My symptoms now were unmistakable; my head throbbed and my vision grew imperfect; there had been an opiate in the wine!

I almost fell back into the room. Supporting myself by means of the chair, the chest of drawers, and finally, the bed-rail, I got to my grip, and with weakening fingers, extracted the little medicine-chest which was invariably my traveling companion. . . .

*   *   *   *   *   *   *

Grimly pitting my will against the drug, but still trembling weakly from the result of the treatment, internal and subcutaneous, which I had adopted, I staggered to the door, out into the corridor and up the narrow, winding stairs to Smith's room. I carried an electric pocket-lamp, and by its light I found my way to the triangular, paneled landing.

I tried the handle. As I had expected, the door was locked. I beat upon it with my fist. "Smith!" I cried—"Smith!"

There was no reply.

Again I clamored; awaking ancient echoes within the rooms and all about me. But nothing moved and no answering voice rewarded my efforts; the other rooms were seemingly unoccupied, and Smith—was drugged!

My senses in disorder, and a mist dancing before my eyes, I went stumbling down into the lower corridor. At the door of my own room I paused; a new fact had suddenly been revealed to me, a fact which the mazy windings of the corridors had hitherto led me to overlook. Smith's room was also in the east tower, and must be directly above mine!

"My God!" I whispered, thinking of the climber—"he has been murdered!"

I staggered into my room and clutched at the bedrail to support myself, for my legs threatened to collapse beneath me. How should I act? That we were the victims of a cunning plot, that the deathful Si-Fan had at last wreaked its vengeance upon Nayland Smith I could not doubt.

My brain reeled, and a weakness, mental and physical, threatened to conquer me completely. Indeed, I think I must have succumbed, sapped as my strength had been by the drug administered to me, if the sound of a creaking stair had not arrested my attention and by the menace which it conveyed afforded a new stimulus.

Some one was creeping down from the landing above—coming to my room! The creatures of the Yellow doctor, having despatched Nayland Smith, were approaching stealthily, stair by stair, to deal with *me!*

From my grip I took out the Browning pistol. The Chinese doctor's servants should have a warm reception. I burned to avenge my friend, who I was persuaded, lay murdered in the room above. I partially closed the door and took up a post immediately behind it. Nearer came the stealthy footsteps—nearer. . . . Now the one who approached had turned the angle of the passage. . . .

Within sight of my door he seemed to stop; a shaft of white light crept through the opening, across the floor and on to the wall beyond. A moment it remained so—then was gone. The room became plunged in darkness.

Gripping the Browning with nervous fingers I waited, listening intently; but the silence remained unbroken. My gaze set upon the spot where the head of this midnight visitant might be expected to appear, I almost held my breath during the ensuing moments of frightful suspense.

The door was opening: slowly—slowly—by almost imperceptible degrees. I held the pistol pointed rigidly before me and my gaze remained fixed intently on the dimly seen opening. I suppose I acted as ninety-nine men out of a hundred would have done in like case. Nothing appeared.

Then a voice—a voice that seemed to come from somewhere under the floor snapped:—

"Good God! it's Petrie!"

I dropped my gaze instantly . . . and there, looking up at me from the floor at my feet, I vaguely discerned the outline of a human head!

"Smith!" I whispered.

Nayland Smith—for indeed it was none other—stood up and entered the room.

"Thank God you are safe, old man," he said. "But in waiting for one who is stealthily entering a room, don't, as you love me, take it for granted that he will enter *upright*. I could have shot you from the floor with ease! But, mercifully, even in the darkness, I recognized your Arab slippers!"

"Smith," I said, my heart beating wildly, "I thought you were drugged—murdered. The port contained an opiate."

"I guessed as much!" snapped Smith. "But despite the excellent tuition of Dr. Fu-Manchu, I am still childishly trustful; and the fact that I did not partake of the crusted '45 was not due to any suspicions which I entertained at that time."

"But, Smith, I saw you drink some port."

"I regret to contradict you, Petrie, but you must be aware that the state of my liver—due to a long residence in Burma—does not permit me to indulge in the luxury of port. My share of the '45 now reposes amid the moss in the tulip-bowl, which you may remember decorated the dining table! Not desiring to appear churlish, by means of a simple feat of legerdemain I drank your health and future happiness in claret!"

"For God's sake what is going on, Smith? Some one climbed from your window."

"I climbed from my window!"

"What!" I said dazedly—"it was you! But what does it all mean? Kâramanèh——"

"It is for her I fear, Petrie, now. We have not a moment to waste!"

He made for the door.

"Sir Lionel must be warned at all cost!" I cried.

"Impossible!" snapped Smith.

"What do you mean?"

"Sir Lionel has disappeared!"

Chapter XXXVI

THE DUNGEON

We were out in the corridor now, Smith showing the way with the light of his electric pocket-lamp. My mind was clear enough, but I felt as weak as a child.

"You look positively ghastly, old man," rapped Smith, "which is no matter for wonder. I have yet to learn how it happened that you are not lying insensible, or dead, as a result of the drugged wine. When I heard some one moving in your room, it never occurred to me that it was you."

"Smith," I said—"the house seems as still as death."

"You, Kâramanèh, and myself are the only occupants of the east wing. Homopoulo saw to that."

"Then he——"

"He is a member of the Si-Fan, a creature of Dr. Fu-Manchu—yes, beyond all doubt! Sir Lionel is unfortunate—as ever—in his choice of servants. I blame my own stupidity entirely, Petrie ; and I pray that my enlightenment has not come too late."

"What does it all mean?—what have you learnt?"

"Mind these three steps," warned Smith, glancing back. "I found my mind persistently dwelling upon the matter of that weird rapping, Petrie, and I recollected the situation of Sir Lionel's room, on the southeast front. A brief inspection revealed the fact that, by means of a kindly branch of ivy, I could reach the roof of the east tower from my window."

"Well?"

"One may walk from there along the roof of the southeast front, and by lying face downwards at the point where it projects above the main entrance look into Sir Lionel's room!"

"I saw you go!"

"I feared that some one was watching me, but that it was you I had never supposed. Neither Barton nor his man are in that room, Petrie! They have been spirited away! This is Kâramanèh's door."

He grasped me by the arm, at the same time directing the light upon a closed door before which we stood. I raised my fist and beat upon the panels; then, every muscle tensed and my heart throbbing wildly, I listened for the girl's voice.

Not a sound broke that deathly stillness except the beating of my own heart, which, I thought, must surely be audible to my companion. Frantically I hurled myself against the stubborn oak, but Smith thrust me back.

"Useless, Petrie!" he said—"useless. This room is in the base of the east tower, yours is above it and mine at the top. The corridors approaching the three floors deceive one, but the fact remains. I have no positive evidence, but I would wager all I possess that there is a stair in the thickness of the wall, and hidden doors in the paneling of the three apartments. The Yellow group has somehow obtained possession of a plan of the historic secret passages and chambers of Graywater Park. Homopoulo is the spy in the household; and Sir Lionel, with his man Kennedy, was removed directly the invitation to us had been posted. The group will know by now that we have escaped them, but Kâramanèh . . ."

"Smith!" I groaned, "Smith! What can we do? What has befallen her? . . ."

"This way!" he snapped. "We are not beaten yet!"

"We must arouse the servants!"

"Why? It would be sheer waste of priceless time. There are only three men who actually sleep in the house (excepting Homopoulo) and these are in the northwest wing. No, Petrie; we must rely upon ourselves."

He was racing recklessly along the tortuous corridors and up the oddly placed stairways of that old-world building. My anguish had reenforced the atrophine which I had employed as an antidote to the opiate in the wine, and now my blood, that had coursed sluggishly, leapt through my veins like fire and I burned with a passionate anger.

Into a large and untidy bedroom we burst. Books and papers littered the floor; curios, ranging from mummied cats and ibises to Turkish yataghans and Zulu assegais, surrounded the place in riotous disorder. Beyond doubt this was the apartment of Sir Lionel Barton. A lamp burned upon a table near to the disordered bed, and a discolored Greek statuette of Orpheus lay overturned on the carpet close beside it.

"Homopoulo was on the point of leaving this room at the moment that I peered in at the window," said Smith, breathing heavily. "From here there is another entrance to the secret passages. Have your pistol ready."

He stepped across the disordered room to a little alcove near the foot of the bed, directing the ray of the pocket-lamp upon the small, square paneling.

"Ah!" he cried, a note of triumph in his voice—"he has left the door ajar! A visit of inspection was not anticipated to-night, Petrie! Thank God for an Indian liver and a suspicious mind."

He disappeared into a yawning cavity which now I perceived to exist in the wall. I hurried after him, and found myself upon roughly fashioned stone steps in a very low and narrow descending passage. Over his shoulder—

"Note the direction," said Smith breathlessly. "We shall presently find ourselves at the base of the east tower."

Down we went and down, the ray of the electric lamp always showing more steps ahead, until at last these terminated in a level, arched passage, curving sharply to the right. Two paces more brought us to a doorway, less than four feet high, approached by two wide steps. A blackened door, having a most cumbersome and complicated lock, showed in the recess.

Nayland Smith bent and examined the mechanism intently.

"Freshly oiled!" he commented. "You know into whose room it opens?"

Well enough I knew, and, detecting that faint, haunting perfume which spoke of the dainty personality of Kâramanèh, my anger blazed up anew. Came a faint sound of metal grating upon metal, and Smith pulled open the door, which turned outward upon the steps, and bent further forward, sweeping the ray of light about the room beyond.

"Empty, of course!" he muttered. "Now for the base of these damned nocturnal operations."

He descended the steps and began to flash the light all about the arched passageway wherein we stood.

"The present dining-room of Graywater Park lies almost due south of this spot," he mused. "Suppose we try back."

We retraced our steps to the foot of the stair. In the wall on their left was an opening, low down against the floor and little more than three feet high; it reminded me of some of the entrances to those seemingly interminable passages whereby one approaches the sepulchral chambers of the Egyptian Pyramids.

"Now for it!" snapped Smith. "Follow me closely.

Down he dropped, and, having the lamp thrust out before him, began to crawl into the tunnel. As his heels disappeared, and only a faint light outlined the opening, I dropped upon all fours in turn, and began laboriously to drag myself along behind him. The atmosphere was damp, chilly, and evil-smelling; therefore, at the end of some ten or twelve yards of this serpentine crawling, when I saw Smith, ahead of me, to be standing erect, I uttered a stifled exclamation of relief. The thought of Kâramanèh having been dragged through this noisome hole was one I dared not dwell upon.

A long, narrow passage now opened up, its end invisible from where we stood. Smith hurried forward. For the first thirty or forty paces the roof was formed of massive stone slabs; then its character changed; the passage became lower, and one was compelled frequently to lower the head in order to avoid the oaken beams which crossed it.

"We are passing under the dining-room," said Smith. "It was from here the sound of beating first came!"

"What do you mean?"

"I have built up a theory, which remains to be proved, Petrie. In my opinion a captive of the Yellow group escaped to-night and sought to summon assistance, but was discovered and overpowered."

"Sir Lionel?"

"Sir Lionel, or Kennedy—yes, I believe so."

Enlightenment came to me, and I understood the pitiable condition into which the Greek butler had been thrown by the phenomenon of the ghostly knocking. But Smith hurried on, and suddenly I saw that the passage had entered upon a sharp declivity; and now both roof and walls were composed of crumbling brickwork. Smith pulled up, and thrust back a hand to detain me.

"Ssh!" he hissed, and grasped my arm.

Silent, intently still, we stood and listened. The sound of a guttural voice was clearly distinguishable from somewhere close at hand!

Smith extinguished the lamp. A faint luminance proclaimed itself directly ahead. Still grasping my arm, Smith began slowly to advance toward the light. One—two—three—four—five paces we crept onward . . . and I found myself looking through an archway into a medieval torture-chamber!

Only a part of the place was visible to me, but its character was unmistakable. Leg-irons, boots and thumb-screws hung in racks upon the fungi-covered wall. A massive, iron-studded door was open at the further end of the chamber, and on the threshold stood Homopoulo, holding a lantern in his hand.

Even as I saw him, he stepped through, followed by one of those short, thick-set Burmans of whom Dr. Fu-Manchu had a number among his entourage ; they were members of the villainous robber bands notorious in India as the dacoits. Over one broad shoulder, slung sackwise, the dacoit carried a girl clad in scanty white drapery. . . .

Madness seized me, the madness of sorrow and impotent wrath. For, with Kâramanèh being borne off before my eyes, I dared

not fire at her abductors lest I should strike her!

Nayland Smith uttered a loud cry, and together we hurled ourselves into the chamber. Heedless of what, of whom, else it might shelter, we sprang for the group in the distant doorway. A memory is mine of the dark, white face of Homopoulo, peering, wild-eyed, over the lantern, of the slim, white-clad form of the lovely captive seeming to fade into the obscurity of the passage beyond.

Then, with bleeding knuckles, with wild imprecations bubbling from my lips, I was battering upon the mighty door—which had been slammed in my face at the very instant that I had gained it.

"Brace up, man!—Brace up!" cried Smith, and in his strenuous, grimly purposeful fashion, he shouldered me away from the door. "A batteringram could not force that timber; we must seek another way!"

I staggered, weakly, back into the room. Hand raised to my head, I looked about me. A lantern stood in a niche in one wall, weirdly illuminating that place of ghastly memories; there were braziers, branding-irons, with other instruments dear to the Black Ages, about me—and gagged, chained side by side against the opposite wall, lay Sir Lionel Barton and another man unknown to me!

Already Nayland Smith was bending over the intrepid explorer, whose fierce blue eyes glared out from the sun-tanned face madly, whose gray hair and mustache literally bristled with rage long repressed. I choked down the emotions that boiled and seethed within me, and sought to release the second captive, a stockily-built, clean-shaven man. First I removed the length of toweling which was tied firmly over his mouth; and—

"Thank you, sir," he said composedly. "The keys of these irons are on the ledge there beside the lantern. I broke the first ring I was chained to, but the Yellow devils overhauled me, all manacled as I was, half-way along the passage before I could attract your attention, and fixed me up to another and stronger ring!"

Ere he had finished speaking, the keys were in my hands, and I had unlocked the gyves from both the captives. Sir Lionel Barton, his gag removed, unloosed a torrent of pent-up wrath.

"The hell-fiends drugged me!" he shouted. "That black villain Homopoulo doctored my tea! I woke in this damnable cell, the secret of which has been lost for generations!" He turned blazing blue eyes upon Kennedy. "How did *you* come to be trapped?" he demanded unreasonably. "I credited you with a modicum of brains!"

"Homopoulo came running from your room, sir, and told me you were taken suddenly ill and that a doctor must be summoned without delay."

"Well, well, you fool!"

"Dr. Hamilton was away, sir."

"A false call beyond doubt!" snapped Smith.

"Therefore I went for the new doctor, Dr. Magnus, in the village. He came at once and I showed him up to your room. He sent Mrs. Oram out, leaving only Homopoulo and myself there, except yourself."

"Well?"

"Sandbagged!" explained the man nonchalantly. "Dr. Magnus who is some kind of dago, is evidently one of the gang."

"Sir Lionel!" cried Smith—"where does the passage lead to beyond that doorway?"

"God knows!" was the answer, which dashed my last hope to the ground. "I have no more idea than yourself. Perhaps . . ."

He ceased speaking. A sound had interrupted him, which, in those grim surroundings, lighted by the solitary lantern, translated my thoughts magically to Ancient Rome, to the Rome of Tigellinus, to the dungeons of Nero's Circus. Echoing eerily along the secret passages it came—the roaring and snarling of the lioness and the leopards.

Nayland Smith clapped his hand to his brow and stared at me almost frenziedly, then—

"God guard her!" he whispered. "Either their plans, wherever they got them, are inaccurate, or in their panic they have mistaken the way." . . . Wild cries now were mingling with the snarling of the beasts. . . . "They have blundered into the old crypt!"

How we got out of the secret labyrinth of Graywater Park into the grounds and around the angle of the west wing to the ivy-grown, pointed door, where once the chapel had been, I do not know. Lights seemed to spring up about me, and half-clad servants to appear out of the void. Temporarily I was insane.

Sir Lionel Barton was behaving like a madman too, and like a madman he tore at the ancient bolts and precipitated himself into the stone-paved cloister barred with the mooncast shadows of the Norman pillars. From behind the iron bars of the home of the leopards came now a fearsome growling and scuffling.

Smith held the light with steady hand, whilst Kennedy forced the heavy bolts of the crypt door.

In leapt the fearless baronet among his savage pets, and in the ray of light from the electric lamp I saw that which turned me sick with horror. Prone beside a yawning gap in the floor lay Homopoulo, his throat torn indescribably and his white shirtfront smothered in blood. A black leopard, having its fore-paws upon the dead man's breast, turned blazing eyes upon us; a second crouched beside him.

Heaped up in a corner of the place, amongst the straw and litter of the lair, lay the Burmese dacoit, his sinewy fingers embedded in the throat of the third and largest leopard—which was dead—whilst the creature's gleaming fangs were buried in the tattered flesh of the man's shoulder.

Upon the straw beside the two, her slim, bare arms outstretched and her head pillowed upon them, so that her rippling hair completely concealed her face, lay Kâramanèh. . . .

In a trice Barton leapt upon the great beast standing over Homopoulo, had him by the back of the neck and held him in his powerful hands whining with fear and helpless as a rat in the grip of a terrier. The second leopard fled into the inner lair.

So much I visualized in a flash; then all faded, and I knelt alone beside her whose life was my life, in a world grown suddenly empty and still.

Through long hours of agony I lived, hours contained within the span of seconds, the beloved head resting against my shoulder, whilst I searched for signs of life and dreaded to find ghastly wounds. . . . At first I could not credit the miracle; I could not receive the wondrous truth.

Kâramanèh was quite uninjured and deep in drugged slumber!

"The leopards thought her dead," whispered Smith brokenly, "and never touched her!"

Chapter XXXVII

THREE NIGHTS LATER

"Listen!" cried Sir Lionel Barton.

He stood upon the black rug before the massive, carven mantelpiece, a huge man in an appropriately huge setting.

I checked the words on my lips, and listened intently. Within Graywater Park all was still, for the hour was late. Outside, the rain was descending in a deluge, its continuous roar drowning any other sound that might have been discernible. Then, above it, I detected a noise that at first I found difficult to define.

"The howling of the leopards!" I suggested.

Sir Lionel shook his tawny head with impatience. Then, the sound growing louder and louder, suddenly I knew it for what it was.

"Some one shouting!" I exclaimed—"some one who rides a galloping horse!"

"Coming here!" added Sir Lionel. "Hark! he is at the door!"

A bell rang furiously, again and again sending its brazen clangor echoing through the great apartments and passages of Graywater.

"There goes Kennedy."

Above the sibilant roaring of the rain I could hear some one releasing heavy bolts and bars. The servants had long since retired, as also had Kâramanèh; but Sir Lionel's man remained wakeful and alert.

Sir Lionel made for the door, and I, standing up, was about to follow him, when Kennedy appeared, in his wake a bedraggled groom, hatless, and pale to the lips. His frightened eyes looked from face to face.

"Dr. Petrie?" he gasped interrogatively.

"Yes!" I said, a sudden dread assailing me. "What is it?"

"Gad! it's Hamilton's man!" cried Barton.

"Mr. Nayland Smith, sir," continued the groom brokenly—and all my fears were realized. "He's been attacked, sir, on the road from the station, and Dr. Hamilton, to whose house he was carried——"

"Kennedy!" shouted Sir Lionel, "get the Rolls-Royce out! Put your horse up here, my man, and come with us!"

He turned abruptly . . . as the groom, grasping at the wall, fell heavily to the floor.

"Good God!" I cried—"What's the matter with him?"

I bent over the prostrate man, making a rapid examination.

"His head! A nasty blow. Give me a hand, Sir Lionel; we must get him on to a couch."

The unconscious man was laid upon a Chesterfield, and, ably assisted by the explorer, who was used to coping with such hurts as this, I attended to him as best I could. One of the men-servants had been aroused, and, just as he appeared in the doorway, I had the satisfaction of seeing Dr. Hamilton's groom open his eyes, and look about him, dazedly.

"Quick," I said. "Tell me—what hurt you?"

The man raised his hand to his head and groaned feebly.

"Something came *whizzing*," he answered. "There was no report, and I saw nothing. I don't know what it can have been——"

"Where did this attack take place?"

"Between here and the village, sir; just by the coppice at the cross-roads on top of Raddon Hill."

"You had better remain here for the present," I said, and gave a few words of instruction to the man whom we had aroused.

"This way," cried Barton, who had rushed out of the room, his huge frame reappearing in the doorway; "the car is ready."

My mind filled with dreadful apprehensions, I passed out on to the carriage sweep. Sir Lionel was already at the wheel.

"Jump in, Kennedy," he said, when I had taken a seat beside him; and the man sprang into the car.

Away we shot, up the narrow lane, lurched hard on the bend—and were off at ever growing speed toward the hills, where a long climb awaited the car.

The head-light picked out the straight road before us, and Barton increased the pace, regardless of regulations, until the growing slope made itself felt and the speed grew gradually less; above the throbbing of the motor, I could hear, now, the rain in the overhanging trees.

I peered through the darkness, up the road, wondering if we were near to the spot where the mysterious attack had been made upon Dr. Hamilton's groom. I decided that we were just passing the place, and to confirm my opinion, at that moment Sir Lionel swung the car round suddenly, and plunged headlong into the black mouth of a narrow lane.

Hitherto, the roads had been fair, but now

the jolting and swaying became very pronounced.

"Beastly road!" shouted Barton—"and stiff gradient!"

I nodded.

That part of the way which was visible in front had the appearance of a muddy cataract, through which we must force a path.

Then, as abruptly as it had commenced, the rain ceased; and at almost the same moment came an angry cry from behind.

The canvas hood made it impossible to see clearly in the car, but, turning quickly, I perceived Kennedy, with his cap off, rubbing his close-cropped skull. He was cursing volubly.

"What is it, Kennedy?"

"Somebody sniping!" cried the man. "Lucky for me I had my cap on!"

"Eh, sniping?" said Barton, glancing over his shoulder. "What d'you mean? A stone, was it?"

"No, sir," answered Kennedy. "I don't know what it was—but it wasn't a stone."

"Hurt much?" I asked.

"No, sir! nothing at all." But there was a note of fear in the man's voice—fear of the unknown.

Something struck the hood with a dull drumlike thud.

"There's another, sir!" cried Kennedy. "There's some one following us!"

"Can you see any one?" called Barton sharply.

"Don't know, sir!" came the reply. "I thought I saw something then, about twenty yards behind. It's so dark."

"Try a shot!" I said, passing my Browning to Kennedy.

The next moment, the crack of the little weapon sounded sharply, and I thought I detected a vague, answering cry.

"See anything?" came from Barton.

Neither Kennedy nor I made reply; for we were both looking back down the hill. Momentarily, the moon had peeped from the cloud-banks, and where, three hundred yards behind, the bordering trees were few, a patch of dim light spread across the muddy road—and melted away as a new blackness gathered.

But, in the brief space, three figures had shown, only for an instant—but long enough for us both to see that they were those of three gaunt men, seemingly clad in scanty garments. What weapons they employed I could not conjecture; but we were pursued by three of Dr. Fu-Manchu's dacoits!

Barton growled something savagely, and ran the car to the left of the road, as the gates of Dr. Hamilton's house came in sight.

A servant was there, ready to throw them open; and Sir Lionel swung around on to the drive, and drove ahead, up the elm avenue to where the light streamed through the open door on to the wet gravel. The house was a blaze of lights, every window visible being illuminated; and Mrs. Hamilton stood in the porch to greet us.

"Doctor Petrie?" she asked, nervously, as we descended.

"I am he," I said. "How is Mr. Smith?"

"Still insensible," was the reply.

Passing a knot of servants who stood at the foot of the stairs like a little flock of frightened sheep—we made our way into the room where my poor friend lay.

Dr. Hamilton, a gray-haired man of military bearing, greeted Sir Lionel, and the latter made me known to my fellow practitioner, who grasped my hand, and then went straight to the bedside, tilting the lampshade to throw the light directly upon the patient.

Nayland Smith lay with his arms outside the coverlet and his fists tightly clenched. His thin, tanned face wore a grayish hue, and a white bandage was about his head. He breathed stentoriously.

"We can only wait," said Dr. Hamilton, "and trust that there will be no complications."

I clenched my fists involuntarily, but, speaking no word, turned and passed from the room.

Downstairs in Dr. Hamilton's study was the man who had found Nayland Smith.

"We don't know when it was done, sir," he said, answering my first question. "Staples and me stumbled on him in the dusk, just by the big beech—a good quarter-mile from the village. I don't know how long he'd laid there, but it must have been for some time, as the last train arrived an hour earlier. No, sir, he hadn't been robbed; his money and watch were on him but his pocketbook lay open beside him;—though, funny as it seems, there were three five-pound notes in it!"

"Do you understand, Petrie?" cried Sir Lionel. "Smith evidently obtained a copy of the old plan of the secret passages of Graywater and Monkswell, sooner than he expected, and determined to return to-night. They left him for dead, having robbed him of the plans!"

"But the attack on Dr. Hamilton's man?"

"Fu-Manchu clearly tried to prevent communication with us to-night! He is playing for time. Depend upon it, Petrie, the hour of his departure draws near and he is afraid of being trapped at the last moment."

He began taking huge strides up and down the room, forcibly reminding me of a caged lion.

"To think," I said bitterly, "that all our efforts have failed to discover the secret——"

"The secret of my own property!" roared Barton—"and one known to that damned, cunning Chinese devil!"

"And in all probability now known also to Smith——"

"And he cannot speak! . . ."

"Who cannot speak?" demanded a hoarse voice.

I turned in a flash, unable to credit my senses—and there, holding weakly to the doorpost, stood Nayland Smith!

"Smith!" I cried reproachfully—"you should not have left your room!"

He sank into an arm-chair, assisted by Dr. Hamilton.

"My skull is fortunately thick!" he replied, a ghostly smile playing around the corners of his mouth—"and it was a physical impossibility for me to remain inert considering that Dr. Fu-Manchu proposes to leave England to-night!"

Chapter XXXVIII

THE MONK'S PLAN

"My inquiries in the Manuscript Room of the British Museum," said Nayland Smith, his voice momentarily growing stronger and some of the old fire creeping back into his eyes, "have proved entirely successful."

Sir Lionel Barton, Dr. Hamilton, and myself hung upon every word; and often I found myself glancing at the old-fashioned clock on the doctor's mantelpiece.

"We had very definite proof," continued Smith, "of the fact that Fu-Manchu and company were conversant with that elaborate system of secret rooms and passages which forms a veritable labyrinth in, about, and beneath Graywater Park. Some of the passages we explored. That Sir Lionel should be ignorant of the system was not strange, considering that he had but recently inherited the property, and that the former owner, his kinsman, regarded the secret as lost. A start-

ing-point was discovered, however, in the old work on haunted manors unearthed in the library, as you remember. There was a reference, in the chapter dealing with Graywater, to a certain monkish manuscript said to repose in the national collection and to contain a plan of these passages and stairways.

"The Keeper of the Manuscripts at the Museum very courteously assisted me in my inquiries, and the ancient parchment was placed in my hands. Sure enough, it contained a carefully executed drawing of the hidden ways of Graywater, the work of a monk in the distant days when Graywater was a priory. This monk, I may add—a certain Brother Anselm—afterwards became Abbot of Graywater."

"Very interesting!" cried Sir Lionel loudly; "very interesting indeed."

"I copied the plan," resumed Smith, "with elaborate care. That labor, unfortunately, was wasted, in part, at least. Then, in order to confirm my suspicions on the point, I endeavored to ascertain if the monk's MS. had been asked for at the Museum recently. The Keeper of the Manuscripts could not recall that any student had handled the work, prior to my own visit, during the past ten years.

"This was disappointing, and I was tempted to conclude that Fu-Manchu had blundered on to the secret in some other way, when the Assistant Keeper of Manuscripts put in an appearance. From him I obtained confirmation of my theory. Three months ago a Greek gentleman—possibly, Sir Lionel, your late butler, Homopoulo—obtained permission to consult the MS., claiming to be engaged upon a paper for some review or another.

"At any rate, the fact was sufficient. Quite evidently, a servant of Fu-Manchu had obtained a copy of the plan—and this within a day or so of the death of Mr. Brangholme Burton—whose heir, Sir Lionel, you were! I became daily impressed anew with the omniscience, the incredible genius, of Dr. Fu-Manchu.

"The scheme which we know of to compass the death, or captivity, of our three selves and Kâramanèh was put into operation, and failed. But, with its failure, the utility of the secret chambers was by no means terminated. The local legend, according to which a passage exists, linking Graywater and Monkswell, is confirmed by the monk's plan."

"What?" cried Sir Lionel, springing to his feet—"a passage between the Park and the old tower! My dear sir, it's impossible! Such a passage would have to pass under the River Starn! It's only a narrow stream, I know, but——"

"It *does*, or *did*, pass under the River Starn!" said Nayland Smith coolly. "That it is still practicable I do not assert; what interests me is the spot at which it terminates."

He plunged his hand into the pocket of the light overcoat which he wore over the borrowed suit of pyjamas in which the kindly Dr. Hamilton had clothed him. He was seeking his pipe!

"Have a cigar, Smith!" cried Sir Lionel, proffering his case—"if you *must* smoke; although I think I see our medical friends frowning!"

Nayland Smith took a cigar, bit off the end, and lighted up. He began to surround himself with odorous clouds, to his evident satisfaction.

"To resume," he said; "the Spanish priest who was persecuted at Graywater in early Reformation days and whose tortured spirit is said to haunt the Park, held the secret of this passage, and of the subterranean chamber in Monkswell, to which it led. His confession—which resulted in his death at the stake!—enabled the commissioners to recover from his chamber a quantity of church ornaments. For these facts I am indebted to the author of the work on haunted manors.

"Our inquiry at this point touches upon things sinister and incomprehensible. In a word, although the passage and a part of the underground room are of unknown antiquity, it appears certain that they were improved and enlarged by one of the abbots of Monkswell—at a date much later than Brother Anselm's abbotship—and the place was converted into a secret chapel——"

"A *secret* chapel!" said Dr. Hamilton.

"Exactly. This was at a time in English history when the horrible cult of Asmodeus spread from the Rhine monasteries and gained proselytes in many religious houses of England. In this secret chapel, wretched Churchmen, seduced to the abominable views of the abbot, celebrated the Black Mass!"

"My God!" I whispered—"small wonder that the place is reputed to be haunted!"

"Small wonder," cried Nayland Smith, with all his old, nervous vigor, "that Dr. Fu-Manchu selected it as an ideal retreat in times of danger!"

"What! the chapel?" roared Sir Lionel.

"Beyond doubt! Well knowing the penalty of discovery, those old devil-worshipers

had chosen a temple from which they could escape in emergency. There is a short stair from the chamber into the cave which, as you may know, exists in the cliff adjoining Monkswell."

Smith's eyes were blazing now, and he was on his feet, pacing the floor, an odd figure, with his bandaged skull and inadequate garments, biting on the already extinguished cigar as though it had been a pipe.

"Returning to our rooms, Petrie," he went on rapidly, "who should I run into but Summers! You remember Summers, the Suez Canal pilot whom you met at Ismailia two years ago? He brought the yacht through the Canal, from Suez, on which I suspect Ki-Ming came to England. She is a big boat—used to be on the Port Said and Jaffa route before a wealthy Chinaman acquired her—through an Egyptian agent—for his personal use.

"All the crews, Summers told me, were Asiatics, and little groups of natives lined the Canal and performed obeisances as the vessel passed. Undoubtedly they hid that woman on board, Petrie, the Lady of the Si-Fan, who escaped, together with Fu-Manchu, when we raided the meeting in London! Like a fool I came racing back here without advising you; and, all alone, my mind occupied with the tremendous import of these discoveries, started, long after dusk, to walk to Graywater Park."

He shrugged his shoulders whimsically, and raised one hand to his bandaged head.

"Fu-Manchu employs weapons both of the future and of the past," he said. "My movements had been watched, of course; I was mad. Some one, probably a dacoit, laid me low with a ball of clay propelled from a sling of the Ancient Persian pattern! I actually saw him . . . then saw, and knew, no more!"

"Smith!" I cried—whilst Sir Lionel Barton and Dr. Hamilton stared at one another, dumbfounded—"you think *he* is on the point of flying from England——"

"The Chinese yacht, *Chanak-Kampo*, is lying two miles off the coast and in the sight of the tower of Monkswell!"

Chapter XXXIX

THE SHADOW ARMY

The scene of our return to Graywater Park is destined to live in my memory for ever.

The storm, of which the violent rainfall had been a prelude, gathered blackly over the hills. Ebon clouds lowered upon us as we came racing to the gates. Then the big car was spinning around the carriage sweep, amid a deathly stillness of Nature indescribably gloomy and ominous. I have said, a stillness of nature; but, as Kennedy leapt out and ran up the steps to the door, from the distant cages wherein Sir Lionel kept his collection of rare beasts proceeded the angry howling of the leopards and such a wild succession of roars from the African lioness that I stared at our eccentric host questioningly.

"It's the gathering storm," he explained. "These creatures are peculiarly susceptible to atmospheric disturbances."

Now the door was thrown open, and, standing in the lighted hall, a picture fair to look upon in her dainty kimono and little red, high-heeled slippers, stood Kâramanèh!

I was beside her in a moment; for the lovely face was pale and there was a wildness in her eyes which alarmed me.

"*He* is somewhere near!" she whispered, clinging to me. "Some great danger threatens. Where have you been?—what has happened?"

How I loved her quaint, musical accent! How I longed to take her in my arms!

"Smith was attacked on his way back from London," I replied. "But, as you see, he is quite recovered. We are in no danger; and I insist that you go back to bed. We shall tell you all about it in the morning."

Rebellion blazed up in her wonderful eyes instantly—and as quickly was gone, leaving them exquisitely bright. Two tears, like twin pearls, hung upon the curved black lashes. It made my blood course faster to watch this lovely Eastern girl conquering the barbaric impulses that sometimes flamed up within her, because *I* willed it; indeed this was a miracle that I never tired of witnessing.

Mrs. Oram, the white-haired housekeeper, placed her arm in motherly fashion about the girl's slim waist.

"She wants to stay in my room until the trouble is all over," she said in her refined, sweet voice.

"You are very good, Mrs. Oram," I replied. "Take care of her."

One long, reassuring glance I gave Kâramanèh, then turned and followed Smith and Sir Lionel up the winding oak stair. Kennedy came close behind me, carrying one of the acetylene head-lamps of the car. And—

"Just listen to the lioness, sir!" he whispered. "It's not the gathering storm that's making her so restless. Jungle beasts grow quiet, as a rule, when there's thunder about."

The snarling of the great creature was plainly audible, distant though we were from her cage.

"Through your room, Barton!" snapped Nayland Smith, when we gained the top corridor.

He was his old, masterful self once more, and his voice was vibrant with that suppressed excitement which I knew so well. Into the disorderly sleeping apartment of the baronet we hurried, and Smith made for the recess near the bed which concealed a door in the paneling.

"Cautiously here!" cried Smith. "Follow immediately behind me, Kennedy, and throw the beam ahead. Hold the lamp well to the left."

In we filed, into that ancient passage which had figured in many a black deed but had never served the ends of a more evil plotter than the awful Chinaman who so recently had rediscovered it.

Down we marched, and down, but not to the base of the tower, as I had anticipated. At a point which I judged to be about level with the first floor of the house, Smith—who had been audibly counting the steps—paused, and begin to examine the seemingly unbroken masonry of the wall.

"We have to remember," he muttered, "that this passage may be blocked up or otherwise impassable, and that Fu-Manchu may know of another entrance. Furthermore, since the plan is lost, I have to rely upon my memory for the exact position of the door."

He was feeling about in the crevices between the stone blocks of which the wall was constructed.

"Twenty-one steps," he muttered; "I feel certain."

Suddenly it seemed that his quest had proved successful.

"Ah!" he cried—"the ring!"

I saw that he had drawn out a large iron ring from some crevice in which it had been concealed.

"Stand back, Kennedy!" he warned.

Kennedy moved on to a lower step—as Smith, bringing all his weight to bear upon the ring, turned the huge stone slab upon its hidden pivot, so that it fell back upon the stair with a reverberating boom.

We all pressed forward to peer into the black cavity. Kennedy moving the light, a square well was revealed, not more than three feet across. Foot-holes were cut at intervals down the further side.

"H'm!" said Smith—"I was hardly prepared for this. The method of descent that occurs to me is to lean back against one side and trust one's weight entirely to the foot-holes on the other. A shaft appeared in the plan, I remember, but I had formed no theory respecting the means provided for descending it. Tilt the lamp forward, Kennedy. Good! I can see the floor of the passage below; only about fifteen feet or so down."

He stretched his foot across, placed it in the niche and began to descend.

"Kennedy next!" came his muffled voice, "with the lamp. Its light will enable you others to see the way."

Down went Kennedy without hesitation, the lamp swung from his right arm.

"I will bring up the rear," said Sir Lionel Barton.

Whereupon I descended. I had climbed down about half-way when, from below, came a loud cry, a sound of scuffling, and a savage exclamation from Smith. Then——

"We're right, Petrie! This passage was recently used by Fu-Manchu!"

I gained the bottom of the well, and found myself standing in the entrance to an arched passage. Kennedy was directing the light of the lamp down upon the floor.

"You see, the door was guarded!" said Nayland Smith.

"What!"

"Puff adder!" he snapped, and indicated a small snake whose head was crushed beneath his heel.

Sir Lionel now joined us; and, a silent quartette, we stood staring from the dead reptile into the damp and evil-smelling tunnel. A distant muttering and rumbling rolled, echoing awesomely along it.

"For Heaven's sake what was that, sir?" whispered Kennedy.

"It was the thunder," answered Nayland Smith. "The storm is breaking over the hills. Steady with the lamp, my man."

We had proceeded for some three hundred yards, and, according to my calculations, were clear of the orchard of Graywater Park and close to the fringe of trees beyond; I was taking note of the curious old brickwork of the passage, when—

"Look out, sir!" cried Kennedy—and the light began dancing madly. "Just under your feet! Now it's up the wall!—mind your hand, Dr. Petrie! . . ."

The lamp was turned, and, since it shone fully into my face, temporarily blinded me.

"On the roof over your head, Barton!"—this from Nayland Smith. "What can we kill it with?"

Now my sight was restored to me, and looking back along the passage, I saw, clinging to an irregularity in the moldy wall, the most gigantic scorpion I had ever set eyes upon! It was fully as large as my opened hand.

Kennedy and Nayland Smith were stealthily retracing their steps, the former keeping the light directed upon the hideous insect, which now began running about with that horrible, febrile activity characteristic of the species. Suddenly came a sharp, staccato report. . . . Sir Lionel had scored a hit with his Browning pistol.

In waves of sound, the report went booming along the passage. The lamp, as I have said, was turned in order to shine back upon us, rendering the tunnel ahead a mere black mouth—a veritable inferno, held by inhuman guards. Into that black cavern I stared, gloomily fascinated by the onward rolling sound storm; into that blackness I looked . . . to feel my scalp tingle horrifically, to know the crowning horror of the horrible journey.

The blackness was spangled with watching, diamond eyes!—with tiny insect eyes that moved; upon the floor, upon the walls, upon the ceiling! A choking cry rose to my lips.

"Smith! Barton! for God's sake, look! The place is *alive* with scorpions!"

Around we all came, panic plucking at our hearts, around swept the beam of the big lamp; and there, retreating before the light, went a veritable army of venomous creatures! I counted no fewer than three of the giant red centipedes whose poisonous touch, called "the zayat kiss," is certain death; several species of scorpion were represented; and some kind of bloated, unwieldy spider, so gross of body that its short, hairy legs could scarce support it, crawled, hideous, almost at my feet.

What other monstrosities of the insect kingdom were included in that obscene host I know not; my skin tingled from head to feet; I experienced a sensation as if a million venomous things already clung to me—unclean things bred in the malarial jungles of Burma, in the corpse-tainted mud of China's rivers, in the fever spots of that darkest East from which Fu-Manchu recruited his shadow army.

I was perilously near to losing my nerve

when the crisp, incisive tones of Nayland Smith's voice came to stimulate me like a cold douche.

"This wanton sacrifice of horrors speaks eloquently of a forlorn hope! Sweep the walls with light, Kennedy; all those filthy things are nocturnal and they will retreat before us as we advance."

His words proved true. Occasioning a sort of *rustling* sound—a faint sibilance indescribably loathsome—the creatures gray and black and red darted off along the passage. One by one, as we proceeded, they crept into holes and crevices of the ancient walls, sometimes singly, sometimes in pairs—the pairs locked together in deadly embrace."

"They cannot live long in this cold atmosphere," cried Smith. "Many of them will kill one another—and we can safely leave the rest to the British climate. But see that none of them drops upon you in passing."

Thus we pursued our nightmare march, on through that valley of horror. Colder grew the atmosphere and colder. Again the thunder boomed out above us, seeming to shake the roof of the tunnel fiercely, as with Titan hands. A sound of falling water, audible for some time, now grew so loud that conversation became difficult. All the insects had disappeared.

"We are approaching the River Starn!" roared Sir Lionel. "Note the dip of the passage and the wet walls!"

"Note the type of brickwork!" shouted Smith.

Largely as a sedative to the feverish excitement which consumed me, I forced myself to study the construction of the tunnel; and I became aware of an astonishing circumstance. Partly the walls were natural, a narrow cavern traversing the bed of rock which upcropped on this portion of the estate, but partly, if my scanty knowledge of archæology did not betray me, they were *Phœnician!*

"This stretch of passage," came another roar from Sir Lionel, "dates back to Roman days or even earlier! By God! it's almost incredible!"

And now Smith and Kennedy, who led, were up to their knees in a running tide. An icy showerbath drenched us from above; ahead was a solid wall of falling water. Again, and louder, nearer, boomed and rattled the thunder; its mighty voice was almost lost in the roar of that subterranean cataract. Nayland Smith, using his hands as a megaphone, cried:—

"Failing the evidence that others have passed this way, I should not dare to risk it! But the river is less than forty feet wide at the point below Monkswell; a dozen paces should see us through the worst!"

I attempted no reply. I will frankly admit that the prospect appalled me. But, bracing himself up as one does preparatory to a high dive, Smith, nodding to Kennedy to proceed, plunged into the cataract ahead. . . .

Chapter XL

THE BLACK CHAPEL

Of how we achieved that twelve or fifteen yards below the rocky bed of the stream the Powers that lent us strength and fortitude alone hold record. Gasping for breath, drenched, almost reconciled to the end which I thought was come—I found myself standing at the foot of a steep flight of stairs roughly hewn in the living rock.

Beside me, the extinguished lamp still grasped in his hand, leant Kennedy, panting wildly and clutching at the uneven wall. Sir Lionel Barton had sunk exhausted upon the bottom step, and Nayland Smith was standing near him, looking up the stairs. From an arched doorway at their head light streamed forth!

Immediately behind me, in the dark place where the waters roared, opened a fissure in the rock, and into it poured the miniature cataract; I understood now the phenomenon of minor whirlpools for which the little river above was famous. Such were my impressions of that brief breathing-space; then—

"Have your pistols ready!" cried Smith. "Leave the lamp, Kennedy. It can serve us no further."

Mustering all the reserve that remained to us, we went, pell-mell, a wild, bedraggled company, up that ancient stair and poured into the room above. . . .

One glance showed us that this was indeed the chapel of Asmodeus, the shrine of Satan where the Black Mass had been sung in the Middle Ages. The stone altar remained, together with certain Latin inscriptions cut in the wall. Fu-Manchu's last home in England had been within a temple of his only Master.

Save for nondescript litter, evidencing a hasty departure of the occupants, and a ship's lantern burning upon the altar, the chapel was unfurnished. Nothing menaced us, but the thunder hollowly crashed far above. To cover his retreat, Fu-Manchu had relied upon the noxious host in the passage and upon the wall of water. Silent, motionless, we four stood looking down at that which lay upon the floor of the unholy place.

In a pool of blood was stretched the Eurasian girl, Zarmi. Her picturesque finery was reft into tatters and her bare throat and arms were covered with weals and bruises occasioned by ruthless, clutching fingers. Of her face, which had been notable for a sort of devilish beauty, I cannot write; it was the awful face of one who had died from strangulation.

Beside her, with a Malay *krîs* in his heart— a little, jeweled weapon that I had often seen in Zarmi's hand—sprawled the obese Greek, Samarkan, a member of the Si-Fan group and sometime manager of a great London hotel!

It was ghastly, it was infinitely horrible, that tragedy of which the story can never be known, never be written; that fiendish fight to the death in the black chapel of Asmodeus.

"We are too late!" said Nayland Smith. "The stair behind the altar!"

He snatched up the lantern. Directly behind the stone altar was a narrow, pointed doorway. From the depths with which it communicated proceeded vague, awesome sounds, as of waves breaking in some vast cavern. . . .

We were more than half-way down the stair when, above the muffled roaring of the thunder, I distinctly heard the voice of *Dr. Fu-Manchu!*

"By God!" shouted Smith, "perhaps they are trapped! The cave is only navigable at low tide and in calm weather!"

We literally fell down the remaining steps . . . and were almost precipitated into the water!

The light of the lantern showed a lofty cavern tapering away to a point at its remote end, pear-fashion. The throbbing of an engine and churning of a screw became audible. There was a faint smell of petrol.

"Shoot! shoot!"—the frenzied voice was that of Sir Lionel—"Look! they can just get through! . . ."

Crack! Crack! Crack!

Nayland Smith's Browning spat death across the cave. Then followed the report of Barton's pistol; then those of mine and Kennedy's.

A small motor-boat was creeping cautiously out under a low, natural archway which evidently gave access to the sea! Since the tide was incoming, a few minutes more of delay had rendered the passage of the cavern impossible. . . .

The boat disappeared.

"We are not beaten!" snapped Nayland Smith. "The *Chanak-Kampo* will be seized in the Channel!"

*   *   *   *   *   *   *

"There were formerly steps, in the side of the well from which this place takes its name," declared Nayland Smith dully. "This was the means of access to the secret chapel employed by the devil-worshipers."

"The top of the well (alleged to be the deepest in England)," said Sir Lionel, "is among a tangle of weeds close by the ruined tower."

Smith, ascending three stone steps, swung the lantern out over the yawning pit below; then he stared long and fixedly upwards.

Both thunder and rain had ceased; but even in those gloomy depths we could hear the coming of the tempest which followed upon that memorable storm.

"The steps are here," reported Smith; "but without the aid of a rope from above, I doubt if they are climbable."

"It's that or the way we came, sir!" said Kennedy. "I was five years at sea in windjammers. Let me swarm up and go for a rope to the Park."

"Can you do it?" demanded Smith. "Come and look!"

Kennedy craned from the opening, staring upward and downward ; then—

"I can do it, sir," he said quietly.

Removing his boots and socks, he swung himself out from the opening into the well and was gone.

*   *   *   *   *   *   *

The story of Fu-Manchu, and of the organization called the Si-Fan which he employed as a means to further his own vast projects, is almost told.

Kennedy accomplished the perilous climb to the lip of the well, and sped barefooted to Graywater Park for ropes. By means of these we all escaped from the strange chapel of the devil-worshipers. Of how we arranged for the removal of the bodies which lay in the place I need not write. My record advances twenty-four hours.

The great storm which burst over England in the never-to-be-forgotten spring when Fu-

Manchu fled our shores has become historical. There were no fewer than twenty shipwrecks during the day and night that it raged.

Imprisoned by the elements in Graywater Park, we listened to the wind howling with the voice of a million demons around the ancient manor, to the creatures of Sir Lionel's collection swelling the unholy discord. Then came the news that there was a big steamer on the Pinion Rocks—that the lifeboat could not reach her.

As though it were but yesterday I can see us, Sir Lionel Barton, Nayland Smith and I, hurrying down into the little cove which sheltered the fishing-village; fighting our way against the power of the tempest. . . .

Thrice we saw the rockets split the inky curtain of the storm; thrice saw the gallant lifeboat crew essay to put their frail craft to sea . . . thrice the mighty rollers hurled them contemptuously back. . . .

Dawn—a gray, eerie dawn—was creeping ghostly over the iron-bound shore, when the fragments of wreckage began to drift in. Such are the currents upon those coasts that bodies are rarely recovered from wrecks on the cruel Pinion Rocks.

In the dim light I bent over a battered and torn mass of timber—that once had been the bow of a boat; and in letters of black and gold I read: "S.Y. *Chanak-Kampo*."

The Return of
Dr. Fu-Manchu

"Fu Manchu, for once in an otherwise blameless career, has left a clue!"

Chapter I

A MIDNIGHT SUMMONS

"When did you last hear from Nayland Smith?" asked my visitor.

I paused, my hand on the syphon, reflecting for a moment.

"Two months ago," I said; "he's a poor correspondent and rather soured, I fancy."

"What—a woman or something?"

"Some affair of that sort. He's such a reticent beggar, I really know very little about it."

I placed a whisky and soda before the Rev. J. D. Eltham, also sliding the tobacco jar nearer to his hand. The refined and sensitive face of the clergyman offered no indication of the truculent character of the man. His scanty fair hair, already gray over the temples, was silken and soft-looking; in appearance he was indeed a typical English churchman; but in China he had been known as "the fighting missionary," and had fully deserved the title. In fact, this peaceful-looking gentleman had directly brought about the Boxer Risings!

"You know," he said, in his clerical voice, but meanwhile stuffing tobacco into an old pipe with fierce energy, "I have often wondered, Petrie—I have never left off wondering—"

"What?"

"That accursed Chinaman! Since the cellar place beneath the site of the burnt-out cottage in Dulwich Village—I have wondered more than ever."

He lighted his pipe and walked to the hearth to throw the match in the grate.

"You see," he continued, peering across at me in his oddly nervous way, "one never knows, does one? If I thought that Dr. Fu-Manchu lived; if I seriously suspected that that stupendous intellect, that wonderful genius, Petrie, er—" he hesitated characteristically—"survived, I should feel it my duty—"

"Well?" I said, leaning my elbows on the table and smiling slightly.

"If that Satanic genius were not indeed destroyed, then the peace of the world may be threatened anew at any moment!"

He was becoming excited, shooting out his jaw in the truculent manner I knew, and snapping his fingers to emphasize his words; a man composed of the oddest complexities that ever dwelt beneath a clerical frock.

"He may have got back to China, Doctor!" he cried, and his eyes had the fighting glint in them. "Could you rest in peace if you thought that he lived? Should you not fear for your life every time that a night-call took you out alone? Why, man alive, it is only two years since he was here among us, since we were searching every shadow for those awful green eyes! What became of his band of assassins—his stranglers, his dacoits, his damnable poisons and insects and what-not—the army of creatures—"

He paused, taking a drink.

"You—" he hesitated diffidently—"searched in Egypt with Nayland Smith, did you not?"

I nodded.

"Contradict me if I am wrong," he continued; "but my impression is that you were searching for the girl—the girl—Kâramanèh, I think she was called?"

"Yes," I replied shortly; "but we could find no trace—no trace."

"You—er—were interested?"

"More than I knew," I replied, "until I realized that I had—lost her."

"I never met Kâramanèh, but from your account, and from others, she was quite unusually—"

"She was very beautiful," I said, and stood up, for I was anxious to terminate that phase of the conversation.

Eltham regarded me sympathetically; he knew something of my search with Nayland Smith for the dark-eyed, Eastern girl who had brought romance into my drab life; he knew that I treasured my memories of her as I loathed and abhorred those of the fiendish, brilliant Chinese doctor who had been her master.

Eltham began to pace up and down the rug, his pipe bubbling furiously; and something in the way he carried his head reminded me momentarily of Nayland Smith. Certainly, between this pink-faced clergyman, with his deceptively mild appearance, and the gaunt, bronzed, and steely-eyed Burmese commissioner, there was externally little in common; but it was some little nervous trick in his carriage that conjured up through the smoky haze one distant summer evening when Smith had paced that very room as Eltham paced it now, when before my startled eyes he had rung up the curtain upon the savage drama in which, though I little suspected it then, Fate had cast me for a leading rôle.

I wondered if Eltham's thoughts ran parallel with mine. My own were centered upon the unforgettable figure of the murderous Chinaman. These words, exactly as Smith had used them, seemed once again to sound in my ears: "Imagine a person tall, lean, and feline, high shouldered, with a brow like Shakespeare and a face like Satan, a close-shaven skull, and long magnetic eyes of the true cat green. Invest him with all the cruel cunning of an entire Eastern race accumulated in one giant intellect, with all the resources of science, past and present, and you have a mental picture of Dr. Fu-Manchu, the 'Yellow Peril' incarnate in one man."

This visit of Eltham's no doubt was responsible for my mood; for this singular clergyman had played his part in the drama of two years ago.

"I should like to see Smith again," he said suddenly; "it seems a pity that a man like that should be buried in Burma. Burma makes a mess of the best of men, Doctor. You said he was not married?"

"No," I replied shortly, "and is never likely to be, now."

"Ah, you hinted at something of the kind."

"I know very little of it. Nayland Smith is not the kind of man to talk much."

"Quite so—quite so! And, you know, Doctor, neither am I; but"—he was growing painfully embarrassed—"it may be your due—I—er—I have a correspondent, in the interior of China—"

"Well?" I said, watching him in sudden eagerness.

"Well, I would not desire to raise—vain hopes—nor to occasion, shall I say, empty fears; but—er . . . no, Doctor!" He flushed like a girl—"It was wrong of me to open this conversation. Perhaps, when I know more—will you forget my words, for the time?"

The telephone bell rang.

"Hullo!" cried Eltham—"hard luck, Doctor!"—but I could see that he welcomed the interruption. "Why!" he added, "it is one o'clock!"

I went to the telephone.

"Is that Dr. Petrie?" inquired a woman's voice.

"Yes; who is speaking?"

"Mrs. Hewett has been taken more seriously ill. Could you come at once?"

"Certainly," I replied, for Mrs. Hewett was not only a profitable patient but an estimable lady—"I shall be with you in a quarter of an hour."

I hung up the receiver.

"Something urgent?" asked Eltham, emptying his pipe.

"Sounds like it. You had better turn in."

"I should much prefer to walk over with you, if it would not be intruding. Our conversation has ill prepared me for sleep."

"Right!" I said; for I welcomed his company; and three minutes later we were striding across the deserted common.

A sort of mist floated amongst the trees, seeming in the moonlight like a veil draped from trunk to trunk, as in silence we passed the Mound pond, and struck out for the north side of the common.

I suppose the presence of Eltham and the irritating recollection of his half-confidence were the responsible factors, but my mind persistently dwelt upon the subject of Fu-Manchu and the atrocities which he had committed during his sojourn in England. So actively was my imagination at work that I felt again the menace which so long had hung over me; I felt as though that murderous yellow cloud still cast its shadow upon England. And I found myself longing for the company of Nayland Smith. I cannot state what was the nature of Eltham's reflections, but I can guess; for he was as silent as I.

It was with a conscious effort that I shook myself out of this morbidly reflective mood, on finding that we had crossed the common and were come to the abode of my patient.

"I shall take a little walk," announced Eltham; "for I gather that you don't expect to be detained long? I shall never be out of sight of the door, of course."

"Very well," I replied, and ran up the steps.

There were no lights to be seen in any of the windows, which circumstance rather surprised me, as my patient occupied, or had occupied when last I had visited her, a first-floor bedroom in the front of the house. My knocking and ringing produced no response for three or four minutes; then, as I persisted, a scantily clothed and half awake maid servant unbarred the door and stared at me stupidly in the moonlight.

"Mrs. Hewett requires me?" I asked abruptly.

The girl stared more stupidly than ever.

"No, sir," she said, "she don't, sir; she's fast asleep!"

"But some one 'phoned me!" I insisted, rather irritably, I fear.

"Not from here, sir," declared the now

wide-eyed girl. "We haven't got a telephone, sir."

For a few moments I stood there, staring as foolishly as she; then abruptly I turned and descended the steps. At the gate I stood looking up and down the road. The houses were all in darkness. What could be the meaning of the mysterious summons? I had made no mistake respecting the name of my patient; it had been twice repeated over the telephone; yet that the call had not emanated from Mrs. Hewett's house was now palpably evident. Days had been when I should have regarded the episode as preluding some outrage, but to-night I felt more disposed to ascribe it to a silly practical joke.

Eltham walked up briskly.

"You're in demand to-night, Doctor," he said. "A young person called for you almost directly you had left your house, and, learning where you were gone, followed you."

"Indeed!" I said, a trifle incredulously. "There are plenty of other doctors if the case is an urgent one."

"She may have thought it would save time as you were actually up and dressed," explained Eltham; "and the house is quite near to here, I understand."

I looked at him a little blankly. Was this another effort of the unknown jester?

"I have been fooled once," I said. "That 'phone call was a hoax—"

"But I feel certain," declared Eltham, earnestly, "that this is genuine! The poor girl was dreadfully agitated; her master has broken his leg and is lying helpless: number 280, Rectory Grove."

"Where is the girl?" I asked, sharply.

"She ran back directly she had given me her message."

"Was she a servant?"

"I should imagine so: French, I think. But she was so wrapped up I had little more than a glimpse of her. I am sorry to hear that some one has played a silly joke on you, but believe me—" he was very earnest—"this is no jest. The poor girl could scarcely speak for sobs. She mistook me for you, of course."

"Oh!" said I grimly; "well, I suppose I must go. Broken leg, you said?—and my surgical bag, splints and so forth, are at home!"

"My dear Petrie!" cried Eltham, in his enthusiastic way—"you no doubt can do something to alleviate the poor man's suffering immediately. I will run back to your rooms for the bag and rejoin you at 280, Rectory Grove."

"It's awfully good of you, Eltham—"

He held up his hand.

"The call of suffering humanity, Petrie, is one which I may no more refuse to hear than you."

I made no further protest after that, for his point of view was evident and his determination adamant, but told him where he would find the bag and once more set out across the moonbright common, he pursuing a westerly direction and I going east.

Some three hundred yards I had gone, I suppose, and my brain had been very active the while, when something occurred to me which placed a new complexion upon this second summons. I thought of the falsity of the first, of the improbability of even the most hardened practical joker practising his wiles at one o'clock in the morning. I thought of our recent conversation; above all I thought of the girl who had delivered the message to Eltham, the girl whom he had described as a French maid—whose personal charm had so completely enlisted his sympathies. Now, to this train of thought came a new one, and, adding it, my suspicion became almost a certainty.

I remembered (as, knowing the district, I should have remembered before) that there was no number 280 in Rectory Grove.

Pulling up sharply I stood looking about me. Not a living soul was in sight; not even a policeman. Where the lamps marked the main paths across the common nothing moved; in the shadows about me nothing stirred. But something stirred within me—a warning voice which for long had lain dormant.

What was afoot?

A breeze caressed the leaves overhead, breaking the silence with mysterious whisperings. Some portentous truth was seeking for admittance to my brain. I strove to reassure myself, but the sense of impending evil and of mystery became heavier. At last I could combat my strange fears no longer. I turned and began to run toward the south side of the common—toward my rooms—and after Eltham.

I had hoped to head him off, but came upon no sign of him. An all-night tramcar passed at the moment that I reached the high road, and as I ran around behind it I saw that my windows were lighted and that there was a light in the hall.

My key was yet in the lock when my housekeeper opened the door.

"There's a gentleman just come, Doctor," she began—

I thrust past her and raced up the stairs into my study.

Standing by the writing-table was a tall, thin man, his gaunt face brown as a coffee-berry and his steely gray eyes fixed upon me. My heart gave a great leap—and seemed to stand still.

It was Nayland Smith!

"Smith," I cried. "Smith, old man, by God, I'm glad to see you!"

He wrung my hand hard, looking at me with his searching eyes; but there was little enough of gladness in his face. He was altogether grayer than when last I had seen him—grayer and sterner.

"Where is Eltham?" I asked.

Smith started back as though I had struck him.

"Eltham!" he whispered—"Eltham! is Eltham here?"

"I left him ten minutes ago on the common—"

Smith dashed his right fist into the palm of his left hand and his eyes gleamed almost wildly.

"My God, Petrie!" he said, "am I fated *always* to come too late?"

My dreadful fears in that instant were confirmed. I seemed to feel my legs totter beneath me.

"Smith, you don't mean—"

"I do, Petrie!" His voice sounded very far away. "Fu-Manchu is here; and Eltham, God help him . . . is his first victim!"

Chapter II

ELTHAM VANISHES

Smith went racing down the stairs like a man possessed. Heavy with such a foreboding of calamity as I had not known for two years, I followed him—along the hall and out into the road. The very peace and beauty of the night in some way increased my mental agitation. The sky was lighted almost tropically with such a blaze of stars as I could not recall to have seen since, my futile search concluded, I had left Egypt. The glory of the moonlight yellowed the lamps speckled across the expanse of the common. The night was as still as night can ever be in London. The

dimming pulse of a cab or car alone disturbed the stillness.

With a quick glance to right and left, Smith ran across on to the common, and, leaving the door wide open behind me, I followed. The path which Eltham had pursued terminated almost opposite to my house. One's gaze might follow it, white and empty, for several hundred yards past the pond, and further, until it became overshadowed and was lost amid a clump of trees.

I came up with Smith, and side by side we ran on, whilst pantingly, I told my tale.

"It was a trick to get you away from him!" cried Smith. "They meant no doubt to make some attempt at your house, but as he came out with you, an alternative plan—"

Abreast of the pond, my companion slowed down, and finally stopped.

"Where did you last see Eltham?" he asked rapidly.

I took his arm, turning him slightly to the right, and pointed across the moonbathed common.

"You see that clump of bushes on the other side of the road?" I said. "There's a path to the left of it. I took that path and he took this. We parted at the point where they meet—"

Smith walked right down to the edge of the water and peered about over the surface.

What he hoped to find there I could not imagine. Whatever it had been he was disappointed, and he turned to me again, frowning perplexedly, and tugging at the lobe of his left ear, an old trick which reminded me of gruesome things we had lived through in the past.

"Come on," he jerked. "It may be amongst the trees."

From the tone of his voice I knew that he was tensed up nervously, and his mood but added to the apprehension of my own.

"*What* may be amongst the trees, Smith?" I asked.

He walked on.

"God knows, Petrie; but I fear—"

Behind us, along the highroad, a tramcar went rocking by, doubtless bearing a few belated workers homeward. The stark incongruity of the thing was appalling. How little those weary toilers, hemmed about with the commonplace, suspected that almost within sight from the car windows, in a place of prosy benches, iron railings, and unromantic, flickering lamps, two fellow men moved upon the border of a horror-land!

Beneath the trees a shadow carpet lay, its edges tropically sharp; and fully ten yards from the first of the group, we two, hatless both, and sharing a common dread, paused for a moment and listened.

The car had stopped at the further extremity of the common, and now with a moan that grew to a shriek was rolling on its way again. We stood and listened until silence reclaimed the night. Not a footstep could be heard. Then slowly we walked on. At the edge of the little coppice we stopped again abruptly.

Smith turned and thrust his pistol into my hand. A white ray of light pierced the shadows; my companion carried an electric torch. But no trace of Eltham was discoverable.

There had been a heavy shower of rain during the evening just before sunset, and although the open paths were dry again, under the trees the ground was still moist. Ten yards within the coppice we came upon tracks—the tracks of one running, as the deep imprints of the toes indicated.

Abruptly the tracks terminated; others, softer, joined them, two sets converging from left and right. There was a confused patch, trailing off to the west; then this became indistinct, and was finally lost, upon the hard ground outside the group.

For perhaps a minute, or more, we ran about from tree to tree, and from bush to bush, searching like hounds for a scent, and fearful of what we might find. We found nothing; and fully in the moonlight we stood facing one another. The night was profoundly still.

Nayland Smith stepped back into the shadows, and began slowly to turn his head from left to right, taking in the entire visible expanse of the common. Toward a point where the road bisected it he stared intently. Then, with a bound, he set off.

"Come on, Petrie!" he cried. "There they are!"

Vaulting a railing he went away over a field like a madman. Recovering from the shock of surprise, I followed him, but he was well ahead of me, and making for some vaguely seen object moving against the lights of the roadway.

Another railing was vaulted, and the corner of a second, triangular grass patch crossed at a hot sprint. We were twenty yards from the road when the sound of a starting motor broke the silence. We gained the graveled footpath only to see the taillight of the car dwindling to the north!

Smith leaned dizzily against a tree.

"Eltham is in that car!" he gasped. "Just God! are we to stand here and see him taken away to—"

He beat his fist upon the tree, in a sort of tragic despair. The nearest cab-rank was no great distance away, but, excluding the possibility of no cab being there, it might, for all practical purposes, as well have been a mile off.

The beat of the retreating motor was scarcely audible; the lights might but just be distinguished. Then, coming in an opposite direction, appeared the headlamp of another car, of a car that raced nearer and nearer to us, so that, within a few seconds of its first appearance, we found ourselves bathed in the beam of its headlights.

Smith bounded out into the road, and stood, a weird silhouette, with upraised arms, fully in its course!

The brakes were applied hurriedly. It was a big limousine, and its driver swerved perilously in avoiding Smith and nearly ran into me. But, the breathless moment past, the car was pulled up, head on to the railings; and a man in evening clothes was demanding excitedly what had happened. Smith, a hatless, disheveled figure, stepped up to the door.

"My name is Nayland Smith," he said rapidly—"Burmese Commissioner." He snatched a letter from his pocket and thrust it into the hands of the bewildered man. "Read that. It is signed by another Commissioner—the Commissioner of Police."

With amazement written all over him, the other obeyed.

"You see," continued my friend, tersely—"it is *carte blanche*. I wish to commandeer your car, sir, on a matter of life and death!"

The other returned the letter.

"Allow me to offer it!" he said, descending. "My man will take your orders. I can finish my journey by cab. I am—"

But Smith did not wait to learn whom he might be.

"Quick!" he cried to the stupefied chauffeur—"You passed a car a minute ago—yonder. Can you overtake it?"

"I can try, sir, if I don't lose her track."

Smith leaped in, pulling me after him.

"Do it!" he snapped. "There are no speed

limits for me. Thanks! Good night, sir!"

We were off! The car swung around and the chase commenced.

One last glimpse I had of the man we had dispossessed, standing alone by the roadside, and at ever increasing speed, we leaped away in the track of Eltham's captors.

Smith was too highly excited for ordinary conversation, but he threw out short, staccato remarks.

"I have followed Fu-Manchu from Hong-kong," he jerked. "Lost him at Suez. He got here a boat ahead of me. Eltham has been corresponding with some mandarin up-country. Knew that. Came straight to you. Only got in this evening. He—Fu-Manchu—has been sent here to get Eltham. My God! and he has him! He will question him! The interior of China—a seething pot, Petrie! They had to stop the leakage of information. *He* is here for that."

The car pulled up with a jerk that pitched me out of my seat, and the chauffeur leaped to the road and ran ahead. Smith was out in a trice, as the man, who had run up to a constable, came racing back.

"Jump in, sir—jump in!" he cried, his eyes bright with the lust of the chase; "they are making for Battersea!"

And we were off again.

Through the empty streets we roared on. A place of gasometers and desolate waste lots slipped behind and we were in a narrow way where gates of yards and a few lowly houses faced upon a prospect of high blank wall.

"Thames on our right," said Smith, peering ahead. "His rathole is by the river as usual. *Hi!*"—he grabbed up the speaking-tube—"Stop! Stop!"

The limousine swung in to the narrow sidewalk, and pulled up close by a yard gate. I, too, had seen our quarry—a long, low bodied car, showing no inside lights. It had turned the next corner, where a street lamp shone greenly, not a hundred yards ahead.

Smith leaped out, and I followed him.

"That must be a *cul de sac*," he said, and turned to the eager-eyed chauffeur. "Run back to that last turning," he ordered, "and wait there, out of sight. Bring the car up when you hear a police-whistle."

The man looked disappointed, but did not question the order. As he began to back away, Smith grasped me by the arm and drew me forward.

"We must get to that corner," he said,

"and see where the car stands, without showing ourselves."

Chapter III

THE WIRE JACKET

I suppose we were not more than a dozen paces from the lamp when we heard the thudding of the motor. The car was backing out!

It was a desperate moment, for it seemed that we could not fail to be discovered. Nayland Smith began to look about him, feverishly, for a hiding-place, a quest in which I seconded with equal anxiety. And Fate was kind to us—doubly kind as after events revealed. A wooden gate broke the expanse of wall hard by upon the right, and, as the result of some recent accident, a ragged gap had been torn in the panels close to the top.

The chain of the padlock hung loosely; and in a second Smith was up, with his foot in this as in a stirrup. He threw his arm over the top and drew himself upright. A second later he was astride the broken gate.

"Up you come, Petrie!" he said, and reached down his hand to aid me.

I got my foot into the loop of chain, grasped at a projection in the gatepost and found myself up.

"There is a crossbar on this side to stand on," said Smith.

He climbed over and vanished in the darkness. I was still astride the broken gate when the car turned the corner, slowly, for there was scanty room; but I was standing upon the bar on the inside and had my head below the gap ere the driver could possibly have seen me.

"Stay where you are until he passes," hissed my companion, below. "There is a row of kegs under you."

The sound of the motor passing outside grew loud—louder—then began to die away. I felt about with my left foot; discerned the top of a keg, and dropped, panting, beside Smith.

"Phew!" I said—"that was a close thing! Smith—how do we know—"

"That we have followed the right car?" he interrupted. "Ask yourself the question: what would any ordinary man be doing motoring in a place like this at two o'clock in the morning?"

"You are right, Smith," I agreed. "Shall we get out again?"

"Not yet. I have an idea. Look yonder."

He grasped my arm, turning me in the desired direction.

Beyond a great expanse of unbroken darkness a ray of moonlight slanted into the place wherein we stood, spilling its cold radiance upon rows of kegs.

"That's another door," continued my friend—I now began dimly to perceive him beside me. "If my calculations are not entirely wrong, it opens on a wharf gate—"

A steam siren hooted dismally, apparently from quite close at hand.

"I'm right!" snapped Smith. "That turning leads down to the gate. Come on, Petrie!"

He directed the light of the electric torch upon a narrow path through the ranks of casks, and led the way to the further door. A good two feet of moonlight showed along the top. I heard Smith straining; then—

"These kegs are all loaded with grease!" he said—"and I want to reconnoiter over that door."

"I am leaning on a crate which seems easy to move," I reported. "Yes, it's empty. Lend a hand."

We grasped the empty crate, and between us, set it up on a solid pedestal of casks. Then Smith mounted to this observation platform and I scrambled up beside him, and looked down upon the lane outside.

It terminated as Smith had foreseen at a wharf gate some six feet to the right of our post. Piled up in the lane beneath us, against the warehouse door, was a stack of empty casks. Beyond, over the way, was a kind of ramshackle building that had possibly been a dwelling-house at some time. Bills were stuck in the ground-floor window indicating that the three floors were to let as offices; so much was discernible in that reflected moonlight.

I could hear the tide lapping upon the wharf, could feel the chill from the river and hear the vague noises which, night nor day, never cease upon the great commercial waterway.

"Down!" whispered Smith. "Make no noise! I suspected it. They heard the car following!"

I obeyed, clutching at him for support; for I was suddenly dizzy, and my heart was leaping wildly—furiously.

"You saw her?" he whispered.

Saw her! yes, I had seen her! And my poor dream-world was toppling about me, its cities, ashes and its fairness, dust.

Peering from the window, her great eyes wondrous in the moonlight and her red lips parted, hair gleaming like burnished foam and her anxious gaze set upon the corner of the lane—was Kâramanèh . . . Kàramanèh whom once we had rescued from the house of this fiendish Chinese doctor; Kâramanèh who had been our ally; in fruitless quest of whom,—when, too late, I realized how empty my life was become—I had wasted what little of the world's goods I possessed;—Kâramanèh!

"Poor old Petrie," murmured Smith—"I knew, but I hadn't the heart—*He* has her again—God knows by what chains he holds her. But she's only a woman, old boy, and women are very much alike—very much alike from Charing Cross to Pagoda Road."

He rested his hand on my shoulder for a moment; I am ashamed to confess that I was trembling; then, clenching my teeth with that mechanical physical effort which often accompanies a mental one, I swallowed the bitter draught of Nayland Smith's philosophy. He was raising himself, to peer, cautiously, over the top of the door. I did likewise.

The window from which the girl had looked was nearly on a level with our eyes, and as I raised my head above the woodwork, I quite distinctly saw her go out of the room. The door, as she opened it, admitted a dull light, against which her figure showed silhouetted for a moment. Then the door was reclosed.

"We must risk the other windows," rapped Smith.

Before I had grasped the nature of his plan he was over and had dropped almost noiselessly upon the casks outside. Again I followed his lead.

"You are not going to attempt anything, single-handed—against *him*?" I asked.

"Petrie—Eltham is in that house. He has been brought here to be put to the question, in the medieval, and Chinese, sense! Is there time to summon assistance?"

I shuddered. This had been in my mind, certainly, but so expressed it was definitely horrible—revolting, yet stimulating.

"You have the pistol," added Smith—"follow closely, and quietly."

He walked across the tops of the casks and leaped down, pointing to that nearest to the closed door of the house. I helped him place it under the open window. A second we set beside it, and not without some noise, got a third on top.

Smith mounted.

His jaw muscles were very prominent and his eyes shone like steel; but he was as cool as though he were about to enter a theater and not the den of the most stupendous genius who ever worked for evil. I would forgive any man who, knowing Dr. Fu-Manchu, feared him; I feared him myself—feared him as one fears a scorpion; but when Nayland Smith hauled himself up on the wooden ledge above the door and swung thence into the darkened room, I followed and was in close upon his heels. But I admired him, for he had every ampère of his self-possession in hand; my own case was different.

He spoke close to my ear.

"Is your hand steady? We may have to shoot."

I thought of Kâramanèh, of lovely dark-eyed Kâramanèh, whom this wonderful, evil product of secret China had stolen from me—for so I now adjudged it.

"Rely upon me!" I said grimly. "I . . ."

The words ceased—frozen on my tongue.

There are things that one seeks to forget, but it is my lot often to remember the sound which at that moment literally struck me rigid with horror. Yet it was only a groan; but, merciful God! I pray that it may never be my lot to listen to such a groan again.

Smith drew a sibilant breath.

"It's Eltham!" he whispered hoarsely—"they're torturing—"

"No, no!" screamed a woman's voice—a voice that thrilled me anew, but with another emotion—"Not that, not—"

I distinctly heard the sound of a blow. Followed a sort of vague scuffling. A door somewhere at the back of the house opened—and shut again. Some one was coming along the passage toward us!

"Stand back!" Smith's voice was low, but perfectly steady. "Leave it to me!"

Nearer came the footsteps and nearer. I could hear suppressed sobs. The door opened, admitting again the faint light—and Kâramanèh came in. The place was quite unfurnished, offering no possibility of hiding; but to hide was unnecessary.

Her slim figure had not crossed the threshold ere Smith had his arm about the girl's waist and one hand clapped to her mouth. A stifled gasp she uttered, and he lifted her into the room.

I stepped forward and closed the door. A faint perfume stole to my nostrils—a vague, elusive breath of the East, reminiscent of strange days that, now, seemed to belong to a remote past. Kâramanèh! that faint, indefinable perfume was part of her dainty personality; it may appear absurd—impossible—but many and many a time I had dreamt of it.

"In my breast pocket," rapped Smith; "the light."

I bent over the girl as he held her. She was quite still, but I could have wished that I had had more certain mastery of myself. I took the torch from Smith's pocket, and, mechanically, directed it upon the captive.

She was dressed very plainly, wearing a simple blue skirt, and white blouse. It was easy to divine that it was she whom Eltham had mistaken for a French maid. A brooch set with a ruby was pinned at the point where the blouse opened—gleaming fierily and harshly against the soft skin. Her face was pale and her eyes wide with fear.

"There is some cord in my right-hand pocket," said Smith; "I came provided. Tie her wrists."

I obeyed him, silently. The girl offered no resistance, but I think I never essayed a less congenial task than that of binding her white wrists. The jeweled fingers lay quite listlessly in my own.

"Make a good job it it!" rapped Smith, significantly.

A flush rose to my cheeks, for I knew well enough what he meant.

"She is fastened," I said, and I turned the ray of the torch upon her again.

Smith removed his hand from her mouth but did not relax his grip of her. She looked up at me with eyes in which I could have sworn there was no recognition. But a flush momentarily swept over her face, and left it pale again.

"We shall have to—gag her—"

"Smith, I can't do it!"

The girl's eyes filled with tears and she looked up at my companion pitifully.

"Please don't be cruel to me," she whispered, with that soft accent which always played havoc with my composure. "Every one—every one—is cruel to me. I will promise—indeed I will swear, to be quiet. Oh, believe me, if you can save him I will do nothing to hinder you." Her beautiful head drooped. "Have some pity for me as well."

"Kâramanèh," I said. "We would have

believed you once. We cannot, now."

She started violently.

"You know my name!" Her voice was barely audible. "Yet I have never seen you in my life—"

"See if the door locks," interrupted Smith harshly.

Dazed by the apparent sincerity in the voice of our lovely captive—vacant from wonder of it all—I opened the door, felt for, and found, a key.

We left Kâramanèh crouching against the wall; her great eyes were turned towards me fascinatedly. Smith locked the door with much care. We began a tip-toed progress along the dimly lighted passage.

From beneath a door on the left, and near the end, a brighter light shone. Beyond that again was another door. A voice was speaking in the lighted room; yet I could have sworn that Kâramanèh had come, not from there but from the room beyond—from the far end of the passage.

But the voice!—who, having once heard it, could ever mistake that singular voice, alternately guttural and sibilant!

Dr. Fu-Manchu was speaking!

"I have asked you," came with ever-increasing clearness (Smith had begun to turn the knob), "to reveal to me the name of your correspondent in Nan-Yang. I have suggested that he may be the Mandarin Yen-Sun-Yat, but you have declined to confirm me. Yet I know" (Smith had the door open a good three inches and was peering in) "that some official, some high official, is a traitor. Am I to resort again to *the question* to learn his name?"

Ice seemed to enter my veins at the unseen inquisitor's intonation of the words *"the question."* This was the Twentieth Century, yet there, in that damnable room . . .

Smith threw the door open.

Through a sort of haze, born mostly of horror, but not entirely, I saw Eltham, stripped to the waist and tied, with his arms upstretched, to a rafter in the ancient ceiling. A Chinaman who wore a slop-shop blue suit and who held an open knife in his hand, stood beside him. Eltham was ghastly white. The appearance of his chest puzzled me momentarily, then I realized that a sort of *tourniquet* of wire-netting was screwed so tightly about him that the flesh swelled out in knobs through the mesh. There was blood—

"God in heaven!" screamed Smith frenziedly—*'they have the wire jacket on him! Shoot*

down that damned Chinaman, Petrie! Shoot! Shoot!"

Lithely as a cat the man with the knife leaped around—but I raised the Browning, and deliberately—with a cool deliberation that came to me suddenly—shot him through the head. I saw his oblique eyes turn up to the whites; I saw the mark squarely between his brows; and with no word nor cry he sank to his knees and toppled forward with one yellow hand beneath him and one outstretched, clutching—clutching—convulsively. His pigtail came unfastened and began to uncoil, slowly, like a snake.

I handed the pistol to Smith; I was perfectly cool, now; and I leaped forward and, took up the bloody knife from the floor and cut Eltham's lashings. He sank into my arms.

"Praise God," he murmured, weakly. "He is more merciful to me than perhaps I deserve. Unscrew . . . the jacket, Petrie . . . I think . . . I was very near to . . . weakening. Praise the good God, Who . . . gave me . . . fortitude . . ."

I got the screw of the accursed thing loosened, but the act of removing the jacket was too agonizing for Eltham—man of iron though he was. I laid him swooning on the floor.

"Where is Fu-Manchu?"

Nayland Smith, from just within the door, threw out the query in a tone of stark amaze. I stood up—I could do nothing more for the poor victim at the moment—and looked about me.

The room was innocent of furniture, save for heaps of rubbish on the floor, and a tin oil-lamp hung on the wall. The dead Chinaman lay close beside Smith. There was no second door, the one window was barred, and from this room we had heard the voice, the unmistakable, unforgettable voice, of Dr. Fu-Manchu.

But Dr. Fu-Manchu was not there!

Neither of us could accept the fact for a moment; we stood there, looking from the dead man to the tortured man who only swooned, in a state of helpless incredulity.

Then the explanation flashed upon us both, simultaneously, and with a cry of baffled rage Smith leaped along the passage to the second door. It was wide open. I stood at his elbow when he swept its emptiness with the ray of his pocket-lamp.

There was a speaking-tube fixed between the two rooms!

Smith literally ground his teeth.

"Yet, Petrie," he said, "we have learnt

something. Fu-Manchu had evidently promised Eltham his life if he would divulge the name of his correspondent. He meant to keep his word; it is a sidelight on his character."

"How so?"

"Eltham has never seen Dr. Fu-Manchu, but Eltham knows certain parts of China better than you know the Strand. Probably, if he saw Fu-Manchu, he would recognize him for whom he really is, and this, it seems, the Doctor is anxious to avoid."

We ran back to where we had left Kâramanèh.

The room was empty!

"Defeated, Petrie!" said Smith, bitterly. "The Yellow Devil is loosed on London again!"

He leaned from the window and the skirl of a police whistle split the stillness of the night.

Chapter IV

THE CRY OF A NIGHTHAWK

Such were the episodes that marked the coming of Dr. Fu-Manchu to London, that awakened fears long dormant and reopened old wounds—nay, poured poison into them. I strove desperately, by close attention to my professional duties, to banish the very memory of Kâramanèh from my mind; desperately, but how vainly! Peace was for me no more, joy was gone from the world, and only mockery remained as my portion.

Poor Eltham we had placed in a nursing establishment, where his indescribable hurts could be properly tended: and his uncomplaining fortitude not infrequently made me thoroughly ashamed of myself. Needless to say, Smith had made such other arrangements as were necessary to safeguard the injured man, and these proved so successful that the malignant being whose plans they thwarted abandoned his designs upon the heroic clergyman and directed his attention elsewhere, as I must now proceed to relate.

Dusk always brought with it a cloud of apprehensions, for darkness must ever be the ally of crime; and it was one night, long after the clocks had struck the mystic hour "when churchyards yawn," that the hand of Dr. Fu-Manchu again stretched out to grasp a victim. I was dismissing a chance patient.

"Good night, Dr. Petrie," he said.

"Good night, Mr. Forsyth," I replied; and,

having conducted my late visitor to the door, I closed and bolted it, switched off the light and went upstairs.

My patient was chief officer of one of the P. and O. boats. He had cut his hand rather badly on the homeward run, and signs of poisoning having developed, had called to have the wound treated, apologizing for troubling me at so late an hour, but explaining that he had only just come from the docks. The hall clock announced the hour of one as I ascended the stairs. I found myself wondering what there was in Mr. Forsyth's appearance which excited some vague and elusive memory. Coming to the top floor, I opened the door of a front bedroom and was surprised to find the interior in darkness.

"Smith!" I called.

"Come here and watch!" was the terse response.

Nayland Smith was sitting in the dark at the open window and peering out across the common. Even as I saw him, a dim silhouette, I could detect that tensity in his attitude which told of high-strung nerves.

I joined him.

"What is it?" I said, curiously.

"I don't know. Watch that clump of elms."

His masterful voice had the dry tone in it betokening excitement. I leaned on the ledge beside him and looked out. The blaze of stars almost compensated for the absence of the moon and the night had a quality of stillness that made for awe. This was a tropical summer, and the common, with its dancing lights dotted irregularly about it, had an unfamiliar look to-night. The clump of nine elms showed as a dense and irregular mass, lacking detail.

Such moods as that which now claimed my friend are magnetic. I had no thought of the night's beauty, for it only served to remind me that somewhere amid London's millions was lurking an uncanny being, whose life was a mystery, whose very existence was a scientific miracle.

"Where's your patient?" rapped Smith.

His abrupt query diverted my thoughts into a new channel. No footstep disturbed the silence of the highroad; where *was* my patient?

I craned from the window. Smith grabbed my arm.

"Don't lean out," he said. I drew back, glancing at him surprisedly.

"For Heaven's sake, why not?"

"I'll tell you presently, Petrie. Did you see him?"

"I did, and I can't make out what he is doing. He seems to have remained standing at the gate for some reason."

"He has seen it!" snapped Smith. "Watch those elms."

His hand remained upon my arm, gripping it nervously. Shall I say that I was surprised? I can say it with truth. But I shall add that I was thrilled, eerily; for this subdued excitement and alert watching of Smith could only mean one thing:

Fu-Manchu!

And that was enough to set me watching as keenly as he; to set me listening; not only for sounds outside the house but for sounds within. Doubts, suspicions, dreads, heaped themselves up in my mind. Why was Forsyth standing there at the gate? I had never seen him before, to my knowledge, yet there was something oddly reminiscent about the man. Could it be that his visit formed part of a plot? Yet his wound had been genuine enough. Thus my mind worked, feverishly; such was the effect of an unspoken thought—Fu-Manchu.

Nayland Smith's grip tightened on my arm. "There it is again, Petrie!" he whispered. "Look, look!"

His words were wholly unnecessary. I, too, had seen it; a wonderful and uncanny sight. Out of the darkness under the elms, low down upon the ground, grew a vaporous blue light. It flared up, elfinish, then began to ascend. Like an igneous phantom, a witch flame, it rose, high—higher—higher, to what I adjudged to be some twelve feet or more from the ground. Then, high in the air, it died away again as it had come!

"For God's sake, Smith, what was it?"

"Don't ask me, Petrie. I have seen it twice. We—"

He paused. Rapid footsteps sounded below. Over Smith's shoulder I saw Forsyth cross the road, climb the low rail, and set out across the common.

Smith sprang impetuously to his feet. "We must stop him!" he said hoarsely; then, clapping a hand to my mouth as I was about to call out—"Not a sound, Petrie!"

He ran out of the room and went blundering downstairs in the dark, crying:

"Out through the garden—the side entrance!"

I overtook him as he threw wide the door of my dispensing room. Through it he ran and opened the door at the other end. I followed him out, closing it behind me. The smell from some tobacco plants in a neighboring flower-bed was faintly perceptible; no breeze stirred; and in the great silence I could hear Smith, in front of me, tugging at the bolt of the gate.

Then he had it open, and I stepped out, close on his heels, and left the door ajar.

"We must not appear to have come from your house," explained Smith rapidly. "I will go along the highroad and cross to the common a hundred yards up, where there is a pathway, as though homeward bound to the north side. Give me half a minute's start, then you proceed in an opposite direction and cross from the corner of the next road. Directly you are out of the light of the street lamps, get over the rails and run for the elms!"

He thrust a pistol into my hand and was off.

While he had been with me, speaking in that incisive, impetuous way of his, with his dark face close to mine, and his eyes gleaming like steel, I had been at one with him in his feverish mood, but now, when I stood alone, in that staid and respectable byway, holding a loaded pistol in my hand, the whole thing became utterly unreal.

It was in an odd frame of mind that I walked to the next corner, as directed; for I was thinking, not of Dr. Fu-Manchu, the great and evil man who dreamed of Europe and America under Chinese rule, not of Nayland Smith, who alone stood between the Chinaman and the realization of his monstrous schemes, not even of Kâramanèh, the slave girl, whose glorious beauty was a weapon of might in Fu-Manchu's hand, but of what impression I must have made upon a patient had I encountered one then.

Such were my ideas up to the moment that I crossed to the common and vaulted into the field on my right. As I began to run toward the elms I found myself wondering what it was all about, and for what we were come. Fifty yards west of the trees it occurred to me that if Smith had counted on cutting Forsyth off we were too late, for it appeared to me that he must already be in the coppice.

I was right. Twenty paces more I ran, and ahead of me, from the elms, came a sound. Clearly it came through the still air—the eerie hoot of a nighthawk. I could not recall ever to have heard the cry of that bird on the common before, but oddly enough I attached little significance to it until, in the ensuing instant, a most dreadful scream—a scream in which fear, and loathing, and anger were hideously blended—thrilled me with horror.

After that I have no recollection of anything until I found myself standing by the southernmost elm.

"Smith!" I cried breathlessly. "Smith! my God! where are you?"

As if in answer to my cry came an indescribable sound, a mingled sobbing and choking. Out from the shadows staggered a ghastly figure—that of a man whose face appeared to be *streaked*. His eyes glared at me madly and he mowed the air with his hands like one blind and insane with fear.

I started back; words died upon my tongue. The figure reeled and the man fell babbling and sobbing at my very feet.

Inert I stood, looking down at him. He writhed a moment—and was still. The silence again became perfect. Then, from somewhere beyond the elms, Nayland Smith appeared. I did not move. Even when he stood beside me, I merely stared at him fatuously.

"I let him walk to his death, Petrie," I heard dimly. "God forgive me—God forgive me!"

The words aroused me.

"Smith"—my voice came as a whisper—"for one awful moment I thought—"

"So did some one else," he rapped. "Our poor sailor has met the end designed for *me*, Petrie!"

At that I realized two things: I knew why Forsyth's face had struck me as being familiar in some puzzling way, and I knew why Forsyth now lay dead upon the grass. Save that he was a fair man and wore a slight mustache, he was, in features and build, the double of Nayland Smith!

Chapter V

THE NET

We raised the poor victim and turned him over on his back. I dropped upon my knees, and with unsteady fingers began to strike a match. A slight breeze was arising and sighing gently through the elms, but, screened by my hands, the flame of the match took life. It illuminated wanly the sun-baked face of Nayland Smith, his eyes gleaming with unnatural brightness. I bent forward, and the dying light of the match touched that other face.

"Oh, God!" whispered Smith.

A faint puff of wind extinguished the match.

In all my surgical experience I had never met with anything quite so horrible. Forsyth's livid face was streaked with tiny streams of blood, which proceeded from a series of irregular wounds. One group of these clustered upon his left temple, another beneath his right eye, and others extended from the chin down to the throat. They were black, almost like tattoo marks, and the entire injured surface was bloated indescribably. His fists were clenched; he was quite rigid.

Smith's piercing eyes were set upon me eloquently as I knelt on the path and made my examination—an examination which that first glimpse when Forsyth came staggering out from the trees had rendered useless—a mere matter of form.

"He's quite dead, Smith," I said huskily. "It's—unnatural—it—"

Smith began beating his fist into his left palm and taking little, short, nervous strides up and down beside the dead man. I could hear a car humming along the highroad, but I remained there on my knees staring dully at the disfigured bloody face which but a matter of minutes since had been that of a clean-looking British seaman. I found myself contrasting his neat, squarely trimmed mustache with the bloated face above it, and counting the little drops of blood which trembled upon its edge. There were footsteps approaching. I stood up. The footsteps quickened; and I turned as a constable ran up.

"What's this?" he demanded gruffly, and stood with his fists clenched, looking from Smith to me and down at that which lay between us. Then his hand flew to his breast; there was a silvern gleam and—

"Drop that whistle!" snapped Smith—and struck it from the man's hand. "Where's your lantern? Don't ask questions!"

The constable started back and was evidently debating upon his chances with the two of us, when my friend pulled a letter from his pocket and thrust it under the man's nose.

"Read that!" he directed harshly, "and then listen to my orders."

There was something in his voice which changed the officer's opinion of the situation. He directed the light of his lantern upon the open letter and seemed to be stricken with wonder.

"If you have any doubts," continued Smith—"you may not be familiar with the Commissioner's signature—you have only to ring up Scotland Yard from Dr. Petrie's house, to which we shall now return, to disperse them." He pointed to Forsyth. "Help us to carry him there. We must not be seen; this must be hushed up. You understand? It must not get into the press—"

The man saluted respectfully; and the three of us addressed ourselves to the mournful task. By slow stages we bore the dead man to the edge of the common, carried him across the road and into my house, without exciting attention even on the part of those vagrants who nightly slept out in the neighborhood.

We laid our burden upon the surgery table.

"You will want to make an examination, Petrie," said Smith in his decisive way, "and the officer here might 'phone for the ambulance. I have some investigations to make also. I must have the pocket lamp."

He raced upstairs to his room, and an instant later came running down again. The front door banged.

"The telephone is in the hall," I said to the constable.

"Thank you, sir."

He went out of the surgery as I switched on the lamp over the table and began to examine the marks upon Forsyth's skin. These, as I have said, were in groups and nearly all in the form of elongated punctures; a fairly deep incision with a pear-shaped and superficial scratch beneath it. One of the tiny wounds had penetrated the right eye.

The symptoms, or those which I had been enabled to observe as Forsyth had first staggered into view from among the elms, were most puzzling. Clearly enough, the muscles of articulation and the respiratory muscles had been affected; and now the livid face, dotted over with tiny wounds (they were also on the throat), set me mentally groping for a clue to the manner of his death.

No clue presented itself; and my detailed examination of the body availed me nothing. The gray herald of dawn was come when the police arrived with the ambulance and took Forsyth away.

I was just taking my cap from the rack when Nayland Smith returned.

"Smith!" I cried—"have you found anything?"

He stood there in the gray light of the hallway, tugging at the lobe of his left ear— an old trick of his.

The bronzed face looked very gaunt, I thought, and his eyes were bright with that febrile glitter which once I had disliked, but which I had learned from experience were due to tremendous nervous excitement. At such times he could act with icy coolness and his mental faculties seemed temporarily to acquire an abnormal keenness. He made no direct reply; but—

"Have you any milk?" he jerked abruptly.

So wholly unexpected was the question, that for a moment I failed to grasp it. Then—

"Milk!" I began.

"Exactly, Petrie! If you can find me some milk, I shall be obliged."

I turned to descend to the kitchen, when—

"The remains of the turbot from dinner, Petrie, would also be welcome, and I think I should like a trowel."

I stopped at the stairhead and faced him.

"I cannot suppose that you are joking, Smith," I said, "but—"

He laughed dryly.

"Forgive me, old man," he replied. "I was so preoccupied with my own train of thought that it never occurred to me how absurd my request must have sounded. I will explain my singular tastes later; at the moment, hustle is the watchword."

Evidently he was in earnest, and I ran downstairs accordingly, returning with a garden trowel, a plate of cold fish and a glass of milk.

"Thanks, Petrie," said Smith—"If you would put the milk in a jug—"

I was past wondering, so I simply went and fetched a jug, into which he poured the milk. Then, with the trowel in his pocket, the plate of cold turbot in one hand and the milk jug in the other, he made for the door. He had it open when another idea evidently occurred to him.

"I'll trouble you for the pistol, Petrie."

I handed him the pistol without a word.

"Don't assume that I want to mystify you," he added, "but the presence of any one else might jeopardize my plan. I don't expect to be long."

The cold light of dawn flooded the hallway momentarily; then the door closed again and I went upstairs to my study, watching Nayland Smith as he strode across the common in the early morning mist. He was making for the Nine Elms, but I lost sight of him before he reached them.

I sat there for some time, watching for the first glow of sunrise. A policeman tramped past the house, and, a while later, a belated reveler in evening clothes. That sense of unreality assailed me again. Out there in the gray mists a man who was vested with powers which rendered him a law unto himself, who had the British Government behind him in all that he might choose to do, who had been summoned from Rangoon to London on singular and dangerous business, was employing himself with a plate of cold turbot, a jug of milk, and a trowel!

Away to the right, and just barely visible, a tramcar stopped by the common; then proceeded on its way, coming in a westerly direction. Its lights twinkled yellowly through the grayness, but I was less concerned with the approaching car than with the solitary traveler who had descended from it.

As the car went rocking by below me, I strained my eyes in an endeavor more clearly to discern the figure, which, leaving the highroad, had struck out across the common. It was that of a woman, who seemingly carried a bulky bag or parcel.

One must be a gross materialist to doubt that there are latent powers in man which man, in modern times, neglects, or knows not how to develop. I became suddenly conscious of a burning curiosity respecting this lonely traveler who traveled at an hour so strange. With no definite plan in mind, I went downstairs, took a cap from the rack, and walked briskly out of the house and across the common in a direction which I thought would enable me to head off the woman.

I had slightly miscalculated the distance, as Fate would have it, and with a patch of gorse effectually screening my approach, I came upon her, kneeling on the damp grass and unfastening the bundle which had attracted my attention. I stopped and watched her.

She was dressed in bedraggled fashion in rusty black, wore a common black straw hat and a thick veil; but it seemed to me that the dexterous hands at work untying the bundle were slim and white; and I perceived a pair of hideous cotton gloves lying on the turf beside her. As she threw open the wrappings and lifted out something that looked like a small shrimping net, I stepped around the bush, crossed silently the intervening patch of grass, and stood beside her.

A faint breath of perfume reached me—of a perfume which, like the secret incense of Ancient Egypt, seemed to assail my soul. The glamour of the Orient was in that subtle essence; and I only knew one woman who used it. I bent over the kneeling figure.

"Good morning," I said; "can I assist you in any way?"

She came to her feet like a startled deer, and flung away from me with the lithe movement of some Eastern dancing girl.

Now came the sun, and its heralding rays struck sparks from the jewels upon the white fingers of this woman who wore the garments of a mendicant. My heart gave a great leap. It was with difficulty that I controlled my voice.

"There is no cause for alarm," I added.

She stood watching me; even through the coarse veil I could see how her eyes glittered. I stooped and picked up the net.

"Oh!" The whispered word was scarcely audible, but it was enough; I doubted no longer.

"This is a net for bird snaring," I said. "What strange bird are you seeking—*Kâramanèh?*"

With a passionate gesture Kâramanèh snatched off the veil, and with it the ugly black hat. The cloud of wonderful, intractable hair came rumpling about her face, and her glorious eyes blazed out upon me. How beautiful they were, with the dark beauty of an Egyptian night; how often had they looked into mine in dreams!

To labor against a ceaseless yearning for a woman whom one knows, upon evidence that none but a fool might reject, to be worthless—evil; is there any torture to which the soul of man is subject, more pitiless? Yet this was my lot, for what past sins assigned to me I was unable to conjecture; and this was the woman, this lovely slave of a monster, this creature of Dr. Fu-Manchu.

"I suppose you will declare that you do not know me!" I said harshly.

Her lips trembled, but she made no reply.

"It is very convenient to forget, sometimes," I ran on bitterly, then checked myself; for I knew that my words were prompted by a feckless desire to hear her defense, by a fool's hope that it might be an acceptable one.

I looked again at the net contrivance in my hand; it had a strong spring fitted to it and a line attached. Quite obviously it was intended for snaring.

"What were you about to do?" I demanded sharply—but in my heart, poor fool that I was, I found admiration for the exquisite arch of Kâramanèh's lips, and reproach because they were so tremulous.

She spoke then.

"Dr. Petrie—"

"Well?"

"You seem to be—angry with me, not so much because of what I do, as because I do not remember you. Yet—"

"Kindly do not revert to the matter," I interrupted. "You have chosen, very conveniently, to forget that once we were friends. Please yourself. But answer my question."

She clasped her hands with a sort of wild abandon.

"Why do you treat me so!" she cried; she had the most fascinating accent imaginable. "Throw me into prison, kill me if you like, for what I have done!" She stamped her foot. "For what I have done! But do not torture me, try to drive me mad with your reproaches—that I forget you! I tell you—again I tell you—that until you came one night, last week, to rescue some one from—" There was the old trick of hesitating before the name of Fu-Manchu—"from *him*, I had never, never seen you!"

The dark eyes looked into mine, afire with a positive hunger for belief—or so I was sorely tempted to suppose. But the facts were against her.

"Such a declaration is worthless," I said, as coldly as I could. "You are a traitress; you betray those who are mad enough to trust you—"

"I am no traitress!" she blazed at me; her eyes were magnificent.

"This is mere nonsense. You think that it will pay you better to serve Fu-Manchu than to remain true to your friends. Your 'slavery'—for I take it you are posing as a slave again—is evidently not very harsh. You serve Fu-Manchu, lure men to their destruction, and in return he loads you with jewels, lavishes gifts—"

"Ah! so!"

She sprang forward, raising flaming eyes to mine; her lips were slightly parted. With that wild abandon which betrayed the desert blood in her veins, she wrenched open the neck of her bodice and slipped a soft shoulder free of the garment. She twisted around, so that the white skin was but inches removed from me.

"These are some of the gifts that he lavishes upon me!"

I clenched my teeth. Insane thoughts flooded my mind. For that creamy skin was red with the marks of the lash!

She turned, quickly rearranging her dress, and watching me the while. I could not trust myself to speak for a moment, then:

"If I am a stranger to you, as you claim, why do you give me your confidence?" I asked.

"I have known you long enough to trust you!" she said simply, and turned her head aside.

"Then why do you serve this inhuman monster?"

She snapped her fingers oddly, and looked up at me from under her lashes. "Why do you question me if you think that everything I say is a lie?"

It was a lesson in logic—from a woman! I changed the subject.

"Tell me what you came here to do," I demanded.

She pointed to the net in my hands.

"To catch birds; you have said so yourself."

"What bird?"

She shrugged her shoulders.

And now a memory was born within my brain; it was that of the cry of the nighthawk which had harbingered the death of Forsyth! The net was a large and strong one; could it be that some horrible fowl of the air—some creature unknown to Western naturalists—had been released upon the common last night? I thought of the marks upon Forsyth's face and throat; I thought of the profound knowledge of obscure and dreadful things possessed by the Chinaman.

The wrapping, in which the net had been, lay at my feet. I stooped and took out from it a wicker basket. Kâramanèh stood watching me and biting her lip, but she made no move to check me. I opened the basket. It contained a large phial, the contents of which possessed a pungent and peculiar smell.

I was utterly mystified.

"You will have to accompany me to my house," I said sternly.

Kâramanèh upturned her great eyes to mine. They were wide with fear. She was on the point of speaking when I extended my hand to grasp her. At that, the look of fear was gone and one of rebellion held its place. Ere I had time to realize her purpose, she flung back from me with that wild grace which I had met with in no other woman, turned—and ran!

Fatuously, net and basket in hand, I stood

looking after her. The idea of pursuit came
to me certainly; but I doubted if I could have
outrun her. For Kâramanèh ran, not like a
girl used to town or even country life, but
with the lightness and swiftness of a gazelle;
ran like the daughter of the desert that she
was.

Some two hundred yards she went,
stopped, and looked back. It would seem
that the sheer joy of physical effort had
aroused the devil in her, the devil that must
lie latent in every woman with eyes like the
eyes of Kâramanèh.

In the ever brightening sunlight I could
see the lithe figure swaying; no rags imaginable could mask its beauty. I could see the
red lips and gleaming teeth. Then—and it
was music good to hear, despite its taunt—
she laughed defiantly, turned, and ran again!

I resigned myself to defeat; I blush to add,
gladly! Some evidences of a world awakening were perceptible about me now. Feath-
ered choirs hailed the new day joyously.
Carrying the mysterious contrivance which
I had captured from the enemy, I set out in
the direction of my house, my mind very
busy with conjectures respecting the link between this bird snare and the cry like that of
a nighthawk which we had heard at the moment of Forsyth's death.

The path that I had chosen led me around
the border of the Mound Pond—a small pool
having an islet in the center. Lying at the
margin of the pond I was amazed to see the
plate and jug which Nayland Smith had borrowed recently!

Dropping my burden, I walked down to
the edge of the water. I was filled with a
sudden apprehension. Then, as I bent to pick
up the now empty jug, came a hail:

"All right, Petrie! Shall join you in a moment!"

I started up, looked to right and left; but,
although the voice had been that of Nayland
Smith, no sign could I discern of his presence!

"Smith!" I cried—"Smith!"

"Coming!"

Seriously doubting my senses, I looked in
the direction from which the voice had seemed
to proceed—and there was Nayland Smith.

He stood on the islet in the center of the
pond, and, as I perceived him, he walked
down into the shallow water and waded
across to me!

"Good heavens!" I began—

One of his rare laughs interrupted me.

"You must think me mad this morning,
Petrie!" he said. "But I have made several
discoveries. Do you know what that islet in
the pond really is?"

"Merely an islet, I suppose—"

"Nothing of the kind; it is a burial mound,
Petrie! It marks the site of one of the Plague
Pits where victims were buried during the
Great Plague of London. You will observe
that, although you have seen it every morning for some years, it remains for a British
Commissioner resident in Burma to acquaint
you with its history! Hullo!"—the laughter
was gone from his eyes, and they were steely
hard again—"what the blazes have we here!"

He picked up the net. "What! a bird trap!"

"Exactly!" I said.

Smith turned his searching gaze upon me.
"Where did you find it, Petrie?"

"I did not exactly find it," I replied; and
I related to him the circumstances of my
meeting with Kâramanèh.

He directed that cold stare upon me
throughout the narrative, and when, with
some embarrassment, I had told him of the
girl's escape—

"Petrie," he said succinctly, "you are an
imbecile!"

I flushed with anger, for not even from
Nayland Smith, whom I esteemed above all
other men, could I accept such words uttered
as he had uttered them. We glared at one
another.

"Kâramanèh," he continued coldly, "is a
beautiful toy, I grant you; but so is a cobra.
Neither is suitable for playful purposes."

"Smith!" I cried hotly—"drop that! Adopt
another tone or I cannot listen to you!"

"You *must* listen," he said, squaring his
lean jaw truculently. "You are playing, not
only with a pretty girl who is the favorite of
a Chinese Nero, but with *my* life! And I object, Petrie, on purely personal grounds!"

I felt my anger oozing from me; for this
was strictly just. I had nothing to say, and
Smith continued:

"You *know* that she is utterly false, yet a
glance or two from those dark eyes of hers
can make a fool of you! A woman made a
fool of me, once; but I learned my lesson;
you have failed to learn yours. If you are
determined to go to pieces on the rock that
broke up Adam, do so! But don't involve me
in the wreck, Petrie—for that might mean a
yellow emperor of the world, and you know
it!"

"Your words are unnecessarily brutal,

Smith," I said, feeling very crestfallen, "but there—perhaps I fully deserve them all."

"You *do!*" he assured me, but he relaxed immediately. "A murderous attempt is made upon my life, resulting in the death of a perfectly innocent man in no way concerned. Along you come and let an accomplice, perhaps a participant, escape, merely because she has a red mouth, or black lashes, or whatever it is that fascinates you so hopelessly!"

He opened the wicker basket, sniffing at the contents.

"Ah!" he snapped, "do you recognize this odor?"

"Certainly."

"Then you have some idea respecting Kâramanèh's quarry?"

"Nothing of the kind!"

Smith shrugged his shoulders.

"Come along, Petrie," he said, linking his arm in mine.

We proceeded. Many questions there were that I wanted to put to him, but one above all.

"Smith," I said, "what, in Heaven's name, were you doing on the mound? Digging something up?"

"No," he replied, smiling dryly; "burying something!"

Chapter VI

UNDER THE ELMS

Dusk found Nayland Smith and me at the top bedroom window. We knew, now that poor Forsyth's body had been properly examined, that he had died from poisoning. Smith, declaring that I did not deserve his confidence, had refused to confide in me his theory of the origin of the peculiar marks upon the body.

"On the soft ground under the trees," he said, "I found his tracks right up to the point where—something happened. There were no other fresh tracks for several yards around. He was attacked as he stood close to the trunk of one of the elms. Six or seven feet away I found some other tracks, very much like this."

He marked a series of dots upon the blotting pad at his elbow.

"Claws!" I cried. "That eerie call! like the call of a nighthawk—is it some unknown species of—flying thing?"

"We shall see, shortly; possibly to-night," was his reply. "Since, probably owing to the absence of any moon, a mistake was made," his jaw hardened at the thoughts of poor Forsyth—"another attempt along the same lines will almost certainly follow—you know Fu-Manchu's system?"

So in the darkness, expectant, we sat watching the group of nine elms. To-night the moon was come, raising her Aladdin's lamp up to the star world and summoning magic shadows into being. By midnight the highroad showed deserted, the common was a place of mystery; and save for the periodical passage of an electric car, in blazing modernity, this was a fit enough stage for an eerie drama.

No notice of the tragedy had appeared in print; Nayland Smith was vested with powers to silence the press. No detectives, no special constables, were posted. My friend was of opinion that the publicity which had been given to the deeds of Dr. Fu-Manchu in the past, together with the sometimes clumsy co-operation of the police, had contributed not a little to the Chinaman's success.

"There is only one thing to fear," he jerked suddenly; "he may not be ready for another attempt to-night."

"Why?"

"Since he has only been in England for a short time, his menagerie of venomous things may be a limited one at present."

Earlier in the evening there had been a brief but violent thunderstorm, with a tropical downpour of rain, and now clouds were scudding across the blue of the sky. Through a temporary rift in the veiling the crescent of the moon looked down upon us. It had a greenish tint, and it set me thinking of the filmed, green eyes of Fu-Manchu.

The cloud passed and a lake of silver spread out to the edge of the coppice, where it terminated at a shadow bank.

"There it is, Petrie!" hissed Nayland Smith.

A lambent light was born in the darkness; it rose slowly, unsteadily, to a great height, and died.

"It's under the trees, Smith!"

But he was already making for the door. Over his shoulder:

"Bring the pistol, Petrie!" he cried; "I have another. Give me at least twenty yards' start or no attempt may be made. But the instant I'm under the trees, join me."

Out of the house we ran, and over onto the common, which latterly had been a pageant ground for phantom warring. The light did not appear again; and as Smith plunged off toward the trees, I wondered if he knew what uncanny thing was hidden there. I more than suspected that he had solved the mystery.

His instructions to keep well in the rear I understood. Fu-Manchu, or the creature of Fu-Manchu, would attempt nothing in the presence of a witness. But we knew full well that the instrument of death which was hidden in the elm coppice could do its ghastly work and leave no clue, could slay and vanish. For had not Forsyth come to a dreadful end while Smith and I were within twenty yards of him?

Not a breeze stirred, as Smith, ahead of me—for I had slowed my pace—came up level with the first tree. The moon sailed clear of the straggling cloud wisps which alone told of the recent storm; and I noted that an irregular patch of light lay silvern on the moist ground under the elms where otherwise lay shadow.

He passed on, slowly. I began to run again. Black against the silvern patch, I saw him emerge—and look up.

"Be careful, Smith!" I cried—and I was racing under the trees to join him.

Uttering a loud cry, he leaped—away from the pool of light.

"Stand back, Petrie!" he screamed—"Back! further!"

He charged into me, shoulder lowered, and sent me reeling!

Mixed up with his excited cry I had heard a loud splintering and sweeping of branches overhead; and now as we staggered into the shadows it seemed that one of the elms was reaching down to touch us! So, at least, the phenomenon presented itself to my mind in that fleeting moment while Smith, uttering his warning cry, was hurling me back.

Then the truth became apparent.

With an appalling crash, a huge bough fell from above. One piercing, awful shriek there was, a crackling of broken branches, and a choking groan . . .

The crack of Smith's pistol close beside me completed my confusion of mind.

"Missed!" he yelled. "Shoot it, Petrie! On your left! For God's sake don't miss it!"

I turned. A lithe black shape was streaking past me. I fired—once—twice. Another frightful cry made yet more hideous the nocturne.

Nayland Smith was directing the ray of a pocket torch upon the fallen bough.

"Have you killed it, Petrie?" he cried.

"Yes, yes!"

I stood beside him, looking down. From the tangle of leaves and twigs an evil yellow face looked up at us. The features were contorted with agony, but the malignant eyes, wherein light was dying, regarded us with inflexible hatred. The man was pinned beneath the heavy bough; his back was broken; and as we watched, he expired, frothing slightly at the mouth, and quitted his tenement of clay, leaving those glassy eyes set hideously upon us.

"The pagan gods fight upon our side," said Smith strangely. "Elms have a dangerous habit of shedding boughs in still weather—particularly after a storm. Pan, god of the woods, with this one has performed justice's work of retribution."

"I don't understand. Where was this man—"

"Up the tree, lying along the bough which fell, Petrie! That is why he left no footmarks. Last night no doubt he made his escape by swinging from bough to bough, ape fashion, and descending to the ground somewhere at the other side of the coppice."

He glanced at me.

"You are wondering, perhaps," he suggested, "what caused the mysterious light? I could have told you this morning, but I fear I was in a bad temper, Petrie. It's very simple: a length of tape soaked in spirit or something of the kind, and sheltered from the view of any one watching from your windows, behind the trunk of the tree; then, the end ignited, lowered, still behind the tree, to the ground. The operator swinging it around, the flame ascended, of course. I found the unburned fragment of the tape last night, a few yards from here."

I was peering down at Fu-Manchu's servant, the hideous yellow man who lay dead in a bower of elm leaves.

"He has some kind of leather bag beside him," I began—

"Exactly!" rapped Smith. "In that he carried his dangerous instrument of death; from that he released it!"

"Released what?"

"What your fascinating friend came to recapture this morning."

"Don't taunt me, Smith!" I said bitterly. "Is it some species of bird?"

"You saw the marks on Forsyth's body, and I told you of those which I had traced upon the ground here. They were caused by *claws*, Petrie!"

"Claws! I thought so! But *what* claws?"

"The claws of a poisonous thing. I recaptured the one used last night, killed it—against my will—and buried it on the mound. I was afraid to throw it in the pond, lest some juvenile fisherman should pull it out and sustain a scratch. I don't know how long the claws would remain venomous."

"You are treating me like a child, Smith," I said slowly. "No doubt I am hopelessly obtuse, but perhaps you will tell me what this Chinaman carried in a leather bag and released upon Forsyth. It was something which you recaptured, apparently with the aid of a plate of cold turbot and a jug of milk! It was something, also, which Kâramanèh had been sent to recapture with the aid—"

I stopped.

"Go on," said Nayland Smith, turning the ray to the left, "what did she have in the basket?"

"Valerian," I replied mechanically.

The ray rested upon the lithe creature that I had shot down.

It was a black cat!

"A cat will go through fire and water for valerian," said Smith; "but I got first innings this morning with fish and milk! I had recognized the imprints under the trees for those of a cat, and I knew that if a cat had been released here it would still be hiding in the neighborhood, probably in the bushes. I finally located a cat, sure enough, and came for bait! I laid my trap, for the animal was too frightened to be approachable, and then shot it; I had to. That yellow fiend used the light as a decoy. The branch which killed him jutted out over the path at a spot where an opening in the foliage above allowed some moon rays to penetrate. Directly the victim stood beneath, the Chinaman uttered his bird cry; the one below looked up, and the cat, previously held silent and helpless in the leather sack, was dropped accurately upon his head!"

"But"—I was growing confused.

Smith stooped lower.

"The cat's claws are sheathed now," he said; "but if you could examine them you would find that they are coated with a shining black substance. Only Fu-Manchu knows what that substance is, Petrie; but you and I know what it can do!"

Chapter VII

ENTER MR. ABEL SLATTIN

"I don't blame you!" rapped Nayland Smith. "Suppose we say, then, a thousand pounds if you show us the present hiding-place of Fu-Manchu, the payment to be in no way subject to whether we profit by your information or not?"

Abel Slattin shrugged his shoulders, racially, and returned to the armchair which he had just quitted. He reseated himself, placing his hat and cane upon my writing-table.

"A little agreement in black and white?" he suggested smoothly.

Smith raised himself up out of the white cane chair, and, bending forward over a corner of the table, scribbled busily upon a sheet of notepaper with my fountain-pen.

The while he did so, I covertly studied our visitor. He lay back in the armchair, his heavy eyelids lowered deceptively. He was a thought overdressed—a big man, dark-haired and well groomed, who toyed with a monocle most unsuitable to his type. During the preceding conversation, I had been vaguely surprised to note Mr. Abel Slattin's marked American accent.

Sometimes, when Slattin moved, a big diamond which he wore upon the third finger of his right hand glittered magnificently. There was a sort of bluish tint underlying the dusky skin, noticeable even in his hands but proclaiming itself significantly in his puffy face and especially under the eyes. I diagnosed a laboring valve somewhere in the heart system.

Nayland Smith's pen scratched on. My glance strayed from our Semitic caller to his cane, lying upon the red leather before me. It was of most unusual workmanship, apparently Indian, being made of some kind of dark brown, mottled wood, bearing a marked resemblance to a snake's skin; and the top of the cane was carved in conformity, to represent the head of what I took to be a puff-adder, fragments of stone, or beads, being inserted to represent the eyes, and the whole thing being finished with an artistic realism almost startling.

When Smith had tossed the written page to Slattin, and he, having read it with an appearance of carelessness, had folded it neatly and placed it in his pocket, I said:

"You have a curio here?"

Our visitor, whose dark eyes revealed all the satisfaction which, by his manner, he sought to conceal, nodded and took up the cane in his hand.

"It comes from Australia, Doctor," he replied; "it's aboriginal work, and was given to me by a client. You thought it was Indian? Everybody does. It's my mascot."

"Really?"

"It is indeed. Its former owner ascribed magical powers to it! In fact, I believe he thought that it was one of those staffs mentioned in biblical history—"

"Aaron's rod?" suggested Smith, glancing at the cane.

"Something of the sort," said Slattin, standing up and again preparing to depart.

"You will 'phone us, then?" asked my friend.

"You will hear from me to-morrow," was the reply.

Smith returned to the cane armchair, and Slattin, bowing to both of us, made his way to the door as I rang for the girl to show him out.

"Considering the importance of his proposal," I began, as the door closed, "you hardly received our visitor with cordiality."

"I hate to have any relations with him," answered my friend; "but we must not be squeamish respecting our instruments in dealing with Dr. Fu-Manchu. Slattin has a rotten reputation—even for a private inquiry agent. He is little better than a blackmailer—"

"How do you know?"

"Because I called on our friend Weymouth at the Yard yesterday and looked up the man's record."

"Whatever for?"

"I knew that he was concerning himself, for some reason, in the case. Beyond doubt he has established some sort of communication with the Chinese group; I am only wondering—"

"You don't mean—"

"Yes—I do, Petrie! I tell you he is unscrupulous enough to stoop even to that."

No doubt, Slattin knew that this gaunt, eager-eyed Burmese commissioner was vested with ultimate authority in his quest of the mighty Chinaman who represented things unutterable, whose potentialities for evil were boundless as his genius, who personified a secret danger, the extent and nature of which none of us truly understood. And, learning of these things, with unerring Semitic in-

stinct he had sought an opening in this glittering Rialto. But there were *two* bidders!

"You think he may have sunk so low as to become a creature of Fu-Manchu?" I asked, aghast.

"Exactly! If it paid him well I do not doubt that he would serve that master as readily as any other. His record is about as black as it well could be. Slattin is of course an assumed name; he was known as Lieutenant Pepley when he belonged to the New York Police, and he was kicked out of the service for complicity in an unsavory Chinatown case."

"Chinatown!"

"Yes, Petrie, it made me wonder, too; and we must not forget that he is undeniably a clever scoundrel."

"Shall you keep any appointment which he may suggest?"

"Undoubtedly. But I shall not wait until tomorrow."

"What!"

"I propose to pay a little informal visit to Mr. Abel Slattin, to-night."

"At his office?"

"No; at his private residence. If, as I more than suspect, his object is to draw us into some trap, he will probably report his favorable progress to his employer to-night!"

"Then we should have followed him!"

Nayland Smith stood up and divested himself of the old shooting-jacket.

"He *has* been followed, Petrie," he replied, with one of his rare smiles. "Two C. I. D. men have been watching the house all night!"

This was entirely characteristic of my friend's far-seeing methods.

"By the way," I said, "you saw Eltham this morning. He will soon be convalescent. Where, in heaven's name, can he—"

"Don't be alarmed on his behalf, Petrie," interrupted Smith. "His life is no longer in danger."

I stared, stupidly.

"No longer in danger!"

"He received, some time yesterday, a letter, written in Chinese, upon Chinese paper, and enclosed in an ordinary business envelope, having a typewritten address and bearing a London postmark."

"Well?"

"As nearly as I can render the message in English, it reads: 'Although, because you are a brave man, you would not betray your correspondent in China, he has been discovered. He was a mandarin, and as I cannot write the name of a traitor, I may not name him. He was executed four days ago. I salute you and pray for your speedy recovery. Fu-Manchu.' "

"Fu-Manchu! But it is almost certainly a trap."

"On the contrary, Petrie—Fu-Manchu would not have written in Chinese unless he were sincere; and, to clear all doubt, I received a cable this morning reporting that the Mandarin Yen-Sun-Yat was assassinated in his own garden, in Nan-Yang, one day last week."

Chapter VIII

DR. FU-MANCHU STRIKES

Together we marched down the slope of the quiet, suburban avenue; to take pause before a small, detached house displaying the hatchet boards of the Estate Agent. Here we found unkempt laurel bushes and acacias run riot, from which arboreal tangle protruded the notice—"To be Let or Sold."

Smith, with an alert glance to right and left, pushed open the wooden gate and drew me in upon the gravel path. Darkness mantled all; for the nearest street lamp was fully twenty yards beyond.

From the miniature jungle bordering the path, a soft whistle sounded.

"Is that Carter?" called Smith, sharply.

A shadowy figure uprose, and vaguely I made it out for that of a man in the unobtrusive blue serge which is the undress uniform of the Force.

"Well?" rapped my companion.

"Mr. Slattin returned ten minutes ago, sir," reported the constable. "He came in a cab which he dismissed—"

"He has not left again?"

"A few minutes after his return," the man continued, "another cab came up, and a lady alighted."

"A lady!"

"The same, sir, that has called upon him before."

"Smith!" I whispered, plucking at his arm—"is it—"

He half turned, nodding his head; and my heart began to throb foolishly. For now the manner of Slattin's campaign suddenly was revealed to me. In our operations against the Chinese murder-group two years before, we

had had an ally in the enemy's camp—Kâramanèh, the beautiful slave, whose presence in those happenings of the past had colored the sometimes sordid drama with the opulence of old Arabia; who had seemed a fitting figure for the romances of Bagdad during the Caliphate—Kâramanèh, whom I had thought sincere, whose inscrutable Eastern soul I had presumed, fatuously, to have laid bare and analyzed.

Now, once again she was plying her old trade of go-between; professing to reveal the secrets of Dr. Fu-Manchu, and all the time—I could not doubt it—inveigling men into the net of this awful fisher.

Yesterday, I had been her dupe; yesterday, I had rejoiced in my captivity. To-day, I was not the favored one; to-day I had not been selected recipient of her confidences—confidences sweet, seductive, deadly: but Abel Slattin, a plausible rogue, who, in justice, should be immured in Sing Sing, was chosen out, was enslaved by those lovely mysterious eyes, was taking to his soul the lies which fell from those perfect lips, triumphant in a conquest that must end in his undoing; deeming, poor fool, that for love of him this pearl of the Orient was about to betray her master, to resign herself a prize to the victor!

Companioned by these bitter reflections, I had lost the remainder of the conversation between Nayland Smith and the police officer; now, casting off the succubus memory which threatened to obsess me, I put forth a giant mental effort to purge my mind of this uncleanness, and became again an active participant in the campaign against the Master—the director of all things noxious.

Our plans being evidently complete, Smith seized my arm, and I found myself again out upon the avenue. He led me across the road and into the gate of a house almost opposite. From the fact that two upper windows were illuminated, I adduced that the servants were retiring; the other windows were in darkness, except for one on the ground floor to the extreme left of the building, through the lowered venetian blinds whereof streaks of light shone out.

"Slattin's study!" whispered Smith. "He does not anticipate surveillance, and you will note that the window is wide open!"

With that my friend crossed the strip of lawn, and careless of the fact that his silhouette must have been visible to any one passing the gate, climbed carefully up the artificial rockery intervening, and crouched upon the window-ledge peering into the room.

A moment I hesitated, fearful that if I followed, I should stumble or dislodge some of the larva blocks of which the rockery was composed.

Then I heard that which summoned me to the attempt, whatever the cost.

Through the open window came the sound of a musical voice—a voice possessing a haunting accent, possessing a quality which struck upon my heart and set it quivering as though it were a gong hung in my bosom. Kâramanèh was speaking.

Upon hands and knees, heedless of damage to my garments, I crawled up beside Smith. One of the laths was slightly displaced and over this my friend was peering in. Crouching close beside him, I peered in also.

I saw the study of a business man, with its files, neatly arranged works of reference, roll-top desk, and Milner safe. Before the desk, in a revolving chair, sat Slattin. He sat half turned toward the window, leaning back and smiling; so that I could note the gold crown which preserved the lower left molar. In an armchair by the window, close, very close, and sitting with her back to me, was Kâramanèh!

She, who, in my dreams, I always saw, was ever seeing, in an Eastern dress, with gold bands about her white ankles, with jewel-laden fingers, with jewels in her hair, wore now a fashionable costume and a hat that could only have been produced in Paris. Kâramanèh was the one Oriental woman I had ever known who could wear European clothes; and as I watched that exquisite profile, I thought that Delilah must have been just such another as this, that, excepting the Empress Poppæa, history has record of no woman, who, looking so innocent, was yet so utterly vile.

"Yes, my dear," Slattin was saying, and through his monocle ogling his beautiful visitor, "I shall be ready for you tomorrow night."

I felt Smith start at the words.

"There will be a sufficient number of men?" Kâramanèh put the question in a strangely listless way.

"My dear little girl," replied Slattin, rising and standing looking down at her, with his gold tooth twinkling in the lamplight, "there will be a whole division, if a whole division is necessary."

He sought to take her white gloved hand, which rested upon the chair arm; but she evaded the attempt with seeming artlessness, and stood up. Slattin fixed his bold gaze upon her.

"So now, give me my orders," he said.

"I am not prepared to do so, yet," replied the girl, composedly; "but now that I know you are ready, I can make my plans."

She glided past him to the door, avoiding his outstretched arm with an artless art which made me writhe; for once I had been the willing victim of all these wiles.

"But—" began Slattin.

"I will ring you up in less than half an hour," said Kâramanèh; and without further ceremony, she opened the door.

I still had my eyes glued to the aperture in the blind, when Smith began tugging at my arm.

"Down! you fool!" he hissed harshly—"if she sees us, all is lost!"

Realizing this, and none too soon, I turned, and rather clumsily followed my friend. I dislodged a piece of granite in my descent; but, fortunately, Slattin had gone out into the hall and could not well have heard it.

We were crouching around an angle of the house, when a flood of light poured down the steps, and Kâramanèh rapidly descended. I had a glimpse of a dark-faced man who evidently had opened the door for her, then all my thoughts were centered upon that graceful figure receding from me in the direction of the avenue. She wore a loose cloak, and I saw this fluttering for a moment against the white gate posts; then she was gone.

Yet Smith did not move. Detaining me with his hand he crouched there against a quick-set hedge; until, from a spot lower down the hill, we heard the start of the cab which had been waiting. Twenty seconds elapsed, and from some other distant spot a second cab started.

"That's Weymouth!" snapped Smith. "With decent luck, we should know Fu-Manchu's hiding-place before Slattin tells us!"

"But—"

"Oh! as it happens, he's apparently playing the game."—In the half-light, Smith stared at me significantly—"Which makes it all the more important," he concluded, "that we should not rely upon his aid!"

Those grim words were prophetic.

My companion made no attempt to communicate with the detective (or detectives) who shared our vigil; we took up a position close under the lighted study window and waited—waited.

Once, a taxi-cab labored hideously up the steep gradient of the avenue . . . It was gone. The lights at the upper windows above us became extinguished. A policeman tramped past the gateway, casually flashing his lamp in at the opening. One by one the illuminated windows in other houses visible to us became dull; then lived again as mirrors for the pallid moon. In the silence, words spoken within the study were clearly audible; and we heard some one—presumably the man who had opened the door—inquire if his services would be wanted again that night.

Smith inclined his head and hung over me in a tense attitude, in order to catch Slattin's reply.

"Yes, Burke," it came—"I want you to sit up until I return; I shall be going out shortly."

Evidently the man withdrew at that; for a complete silence followed which prevailed for fully half an hour. I sought cautiously to move my cramped limbs, unlike Smith, who seeming to have sinews of piano-wire, crouched beside me immovable, untiringly. Then loud upon the stillness, broke the strident note of the telephone bell.

I started, nervously, clutching at Smith's arm. It felt hard as iron to my grip.

"Hullo!" I heard Slattin call—"who is speaking? . . . Yes, yes! This is Mr. A. S. . . . I am to come at once? . . . I know where—yes . . . you will meet me there? . . . Good!—I shall be with you in half an hour. . . . Good-by!"

Distinctly I heard the creak of the revolving office-chair as Slattin rose; then Smith had me by the arm, and we were flying swiftly away from the door to take up our former post around the angle of the building. This gained:

"He's going to his death!" rapped Smith beside me; "but Carter has a cab from the Yard waiting in the nearest rank. We shall follow to see where he goes—for it is possible that Weymouth may have been thrown off the scent; then, when we are sure of his destination, we can take a hand in the game! We . . ."

The end of the sentence was lost to me—drowned in such a frightful wave of sound as I despair to describe. It began with a high, thin scream, which was choked off staccato fashion; upon it followed a loud and dreadful cry uttered with all the strength of Slattin's lungs—

"Oh, God!" he cried, and again—"Oh, God!"

This in turn merged into a sort of hysterical sobbing.

I was on my feet now, and automatically making for the door. I had a vague impression of Nayland Smith's face beside me, the eyes glassy with a fearful apprehension. Then the door was flung open, and, in the bright light of the hall-way, I saw Slattin standing—swaying and seemingly fighting with the empty air.

"What is it? For God's sake, what has happened!" reached my ears dimly—and the man Burke showed behind his master. White-faced I saw him to be; for now Smith and I were racing up the steps.

Ere we could reach him, Slattin, uttering another choking cry, pitched forward and lay half across the threshold.

We burst into the hall, where Burke stood with both his hands raised dazedly to his head. I could hear the sound of running feet upon the gravel, and knew that Carter was coming to join us.

Burke, a heavy man with a lowering, bull-dog type of face, collapsed onto his knees beside Slattin, and began softly to laugh in little rising peals.

"Drop that!" snapped Smith, and grasping him by the shoulders, he sent him spinning along the hallway, where he sank upon the bottom step of the stairs, to sit with his outstretched fingers extended before his face, and peering at us grotesquely through the crevices.

There were rustlings and subdued cries from the upper part of the house. Carter came in out of the darkness, carefully stepping over the recumbent figure; and the three of us stood there in the lighted hall looking down at Slattin.

"Help us to move him back," directed Smith, tensely; "far enough to close the door."

Between us we accomplished this, and Carter fastened the door. We were alone with the shadow of Fu-Manchu's vengeance; for as I knelt beside the body on the floor, a look and a touch sufficed to tell me that this was but clay from which the spirit had fled!

Smith met my glance as I raised my head, and his teeth came together with a loud snap; the jaw muscles stood out prominently beneath the dark skin; and his face was grimly set in that odd, half-despairful expression which I knew so well but which boded so ill for whomsoever occasioned it.

"Dead, Petrie!—already?"

"Lightning could have done the work no better. Can I turn him over?"

Smith nodded.

Together we stooped and rolled the heavy body on its back. A flood of whispers came sibilantly from the stairway. Smith spun around rapidly, and glared upon the group of half-dressed servants.

"Return to your rooms!" he rapped, imperiously; "let no one come into the hall without my orders."

The masterful voice had its usual result; there was a hurried retreat to the upper landing. Burke, shaking like a man with an ague, sat on the lower step, pathetically drumming his palms upon his uplifted knees.

"I warned him, I warned him!" he mumbled monotonously, "I warned him, oh, I warned him!"

"Stand up!" shouted Smith—"stand up and come here!"

The man, with his frightened eyes turning to right and left, and seeming to search for something in the shadows about him, advanced obediently.

"Have you a flask?" demanded Smith of Carter.

The detective silently administered to Burke a stiff restorative.

"Now," continued Smith, "you, Petrie, will want to examine him, I suppose?" He pointed to the body. "And in the meantime I have some questions to put to you, my man."

He clapped his hand upon Burke's shoulder.

"My God!" Burke broke out, "I was ten yards from him when it happened!"

"No one is accusing you," said Smith, less harshly; "but since you were the only witness, it is by your aid that we hope to clear the matter up."

Exerting a gigantic effort to regain control of himself, Burke nodded, watching my friend with a childlike eagerness. During the ensuing conversation, I examined Slattin for marks of violence; and of what I found, more anon.

"In the first place," said Smith, "you say that you warned him. When did you warn him, and of what?"

"I warned him, sir, that it would come to this—"

"That *what* would come to this?"

"His dealings with the Chinaman!"

"He had dealings with Chinamen?"

"He accidentally met a Chinaman at an East End gaming-house, a man he had known in Frisco—a man called Singapore Charlie—"

"What! Singapore Charlie!"

"Yes, sir, the same man that had a dope-shop, two years ago, down Ratcliffe way—"

"There was a fire—"

"But Singapore Charlie escaped, sir."

"And he is one of the gang?"

"He is one of what we used to call in New York, the Seven Group."

Smith began to tug at the lobe of his left ear, reflectively, as I saw out of the corner of my eye.

"The Seven Group!" he mused. "That is significant. I always suspected that Dr. Fu-Manchu and the notorious Seven Group were one and the same. Go on, Burke."

"Well, sir," the man continued, more calmly, "the lieutenant—"

"The lieutenant!" began Smith; then: "Oh! of course; Slattin used to be a police lieutenant!"

"Well, sir, he—Mr. Slattin—had a sort of hold on this Singapore Charlie, and two years ago, when he first met him, he thought that with his aid he was going to pull off the biggest thing of his life—"

"Forestall *me*, in fact?"

"Yes, sir; but you got in first with the big raid—and spoiled it."

Smith nodded grimly, glancing at the Scotland Yard man, who returned his nod with equal grimness.

"A couple of months ago," resumed Burke, "he met Charlie again down East, and the Chinaman introduced him to a girl—some sort of an Egyptian girl."

"Go on!" snapped Smith—"I know her."

"He saw her a good many times—and she came here once or twice. She made out that she and Singapore Charlie were prepared to give away the boss of the Yellow gang—"

"For a price, of course?"

"I suppose so," said Burke; "but I don't know. I only know that I warned him."

"H'm!" muttered Smith. "And now, what took place to-night?"

"He had an appointment here with the girl," began Burke—

"I know all that," interrupted Smith. "I merely want to know, what took place after the telephone call?"

"Well, he told me to wait up, and I was dozing in the next room to the study—the dining-room—when the 'phone bell aroused me. I heard the lieutenant—Mr. Slattin, coming out, and I ran out too, but only in time to see him taking his hat from the rack—"

"But he wears no hat!"

"He never got it off the peg! Just as he reached up to take it, he gave a most frightful scream, and turned around like lightning as though some one had attacked him from behind!"

"There was no one else in the hall?"

"No one at all. I was standing down there outside the dining-room just by the stairs, but he didn't turn in my direction, he turned and looked right behind him—where there was no one—nothing. His cries were frightful." Burke's voice broke, and he shuddered feverishly. "Then he made a rush for the front door. It seemed as though he had not seen me. He stood there screaming; but, before I could reach him, he fell. . . ."

Nayland Smith fixed a piercing gaze upon Burke.

"Is that all you know?" he demanded slowly.

"As God is my judge, sir, that's all I know, and all I saw. There was no living thing near him when he met his death."

"We shall see," muttered Smith. He turned to me—"What killed him?" he asked, shortly.

"Apparently, a minute wound on the left wrist," I replied, and, stooping, I raised the already cold hand in mine.

A tiny, inflamed wound showed on the wrist; and a certain puffiness was becoming observable in the injured hand and arm. Smith bent down and drew a quick, sibilant breath.

"You know what this is, Petrie?" he cried.

"Certainly. It was too late to employ a ligature and useless to inject ammonia. Death was practically instantaneous. His heart . . ."

There came a loud knocking and ringing.

"Carter!" cried Smith, turning to the detective, "open that door to no one—no one. Explain who I am—"

"But if it is the inspector?—"

"I said, open the door to *no one!*" snapped Smith. "Burke, stand exactly where you are! Carter, you can speak to whoever knocks, through the letter-box. Petrie, don't move for your life! It may be here, in the hallway!—"

Chapter IX

THE CLIMBER

Our search of the house of Abel Slattin ceased only with the coming of the dawn, and yielded nothing but disappointment. Failure followed upon failure; for, in the gray light of the morning, our own quest concluded, Inspector Weymouth returned to report that the girl, Kâramanèh, had thrown him off the scent.

Again he stood before me, the big, burly friend of old and dreadful days, a little grayer above the temples, which I set down for a record of former horrors, but deliberate, stoical, thorough, as ever. His blue eyes melted in the old generous way as he saw me, and he gripped my hand in greeting.

"Once again," he said, "your dark-eyed friend has been too clever for me, Doctor. But the track as far as I could follow, leads to the old spot. In fact,"—he turned to Smith, who, grim-faced and haggard, looked thoroughly ill in that gray light—"I believe Fu-Manchu's lair is somewhere near the former opium-den of Shen-Yan—'Singapore Charlie.' "

Smith nodded.

"We will turn our attention in that direction," he replied, "at a very early date."

Inspector Weymouth looked down at the body of Abel Slattin.

"How was it done?" he asked softly.

"Clumsily for Fu-Manchu," I replied. "A snake was introduced into the house by some means—"

"By Kâramanèh!" rapped Smith.

"Very possibly by Kâramanèh," I continued firmly. "The thing has escaped us."

"My own idea," said Smith, "is that it was concealed about his clothing. When he fell by the open door it glided out of the house. We must have the garden searched thoroughly by daylight."

"*He*"—Weymouth glanced at that which lay upon the floor—"must be moved; but otherwise we can leave the place untouched, clear out the servants, and lock the house up."

"I have already given orders to that effect," answered Smith. He spoke wearily and with a note of conscious defeat in his voice. "Nothing has been disturbed;"—he swept his arm around comprehensively—"papers and so forth you can examine at leisure."

Presently we quitted that house upon which the fateful Chinaman had set his seal, as the suburb was awakening to a new day. The clank of milk-cans was my final impression of the avenue to which a dreadful minister of death had come at the bidding of the death lord. We left Inspector Weymouth in charge and returned to my rooms, scarcely exchanging a word upon the way.

Nayland Smith, ignoring my entreaties, composed himself for slumber in the white cane chair in my study. About noon he retired to the bathroom, and returning, made a pretense of breakfast; then resumed his seat in the cane armchair. Carter reported in the afternoon, but his report was merely formal. Returning from my round of professional visits at half past five, I found Nayland Smith in the same position; and so the day waned into evening, and dusk fell uneventfully.

In the corner of the big room by the empty fireplace, Nayland Smith lay, with his long, lean frame extended in the white cane chair. A tumbler, from which two straws protruded, stood by his right elbow, and a perfect continent of tobacco smoke lay between us, wafted toward the door by the draught from an open window. He had littered the hearth with matches and tobacco ash, being the most untidy smoker I have ever met; and save for his frequent rapping-out of his pipe bowl and perpetual striking of matches, he had shown no sign of activity for the past hour. Collarless and wearing an old tweed jacket, he had spent the evening, as he had spent the day, in the cane chair, only quitting it for some ten minutes, or less, to toy with dinner.

My several attempts at conversation had elicited nothing but growls; therefore, as dusk descended, having dismissed my few patients, I busied myself collating my notes upon the renewed activity of the Yellow Doctor, and was thus engaged when the 'phone bell disturbed me. It was Smith who was wanted, however; and he went out eagerly, leaving me to my task.

At the end of a lengthy conversation, he returned from the 'phone and began, restlessly, to pace the room. I made a pretense of continuing my labors, but covertly I was watching him. He was twitching at the lobe of his left ear, and his face was a study in perplexity. Abruptly he burst out:

"I shall throw the thing up, Petrie! Either I am growing too old to cope with such an adversary as Fu-Manchu, or else my intellect has become dull. I cannot seem to think clearly or consistently. For the Doctor, this crime, this removal of Slattin, is clumsy—unfinished. There are two explanations. Either he, too, is losing his old cunning or he has been interrupted!"

"Interrupted!"

"Take the facts, Petrie,"—Smith clapped his hands upon my table and bent down, peering into my eyes—"is it characteristic of Fu-Manchu to kill a man by the direct agency of a snake and to implicate one of his own damnable servants in this way?"

"But we have found no snake!"

"Kâramanèh introduced one in some way. Do you doubt it?"

"Certainly Kâramanèh visited him on the evening of his death, but you must be perfectly well aware that even if she had been arrested, no jury could convict her."

Smith resumed his restless pacings up and down.

"You are very useful to me, Petrie," he replied; "as a counsel for the defense you constantly rectify my errors of prejudice. Yet I am convinced that our presence at Slattin's house last night prevented Fu-Manchu from finishing off this little matter as he had designed to do."

"What has given you this idea?"

"Weymouth is responsible. He has rung me up from the Yard. The constable on duty at the house where the murder was committed, reports that some one, less than an hour ago, attempted to break in."

"Break in!"

"Ah! you are interested? *I* thought the circumstance illuminating, also!"

"Did the officer see this person?"

"No; he only heard him. It was some one who endeavored to enter by the bathroom window, which, I am told, may be reached fairly easily by an agile climber."

"The attempt did not succeed?"

"No; the constable interrupted, but failed to make a capture or even to secure a glimpse of the man."

We were both silent for some moments; then:

"What do you propose to do?" I asked.

"We must not let Fu-Manchu's servants know," replied Smith, "but to-night I shall conceal myself in Slattin's house and remain there for a week or a day—it matters not how long—until that attempt is repeated. Quite obviously, Petrie, we have overlooked something which implicates the murderer with the murder! In short, either by accident, by reason of our superior vigilance, or by the clumsiness of his plans, Fu-Manchu for once in an otherwise blameless career, has left a *clue!*"

Chapter X

THE CLIMBER RETURNS

In utter darkness we groped our way through into the hallway of Slattin's house, having entered, stealthily, from the rear; for Smith had selected the study as a suitable base of operations. We reached it without mishap, and presently I found myself seated in the very chair which Kâramanèh had occupied; my companion took up a post just within the widely opened door.

So we commenced our ghostly business in the house of the murdered man—a house from which, but a few hours since, his body had been removed. This was such a vigil as I had endured once before, when, with Nayland Smith and another, I had waited for the coming of one of Fu-Manchu's death agents.

Of all the sounds which, one by one, now began to detach themselves from the silence, there was a particular sound, homely enough at another time, which spoke to me more dreadfully than the rest. It was the ticking of the clock upon the mantelpiece; and I thought how this sound must have been familiar to Abel Slattin, how it must have formed part and parcel of his life, as it were, and how it went on now—*tick-tick-tick-tick*—whilst he, for whom it had ticked, lay unheeding—would never heed it more.

As I grew more accustomed to the gloom, I found myself staring at his office chair; once I found myself expecting Abel Slattin to enter the room and occupy it. There was a little China Buddha upon the bureau in one corner, with a gilded cap upon its head, and as some reflection of the moonlight sought out this little cap, my thoughts grotesquely turned upon the murdered man's gold tooth.

Vague creakings from within the house, sounds as though of stealthy footsteps upon the stair, set my nerves tingling; but Nayland Smith gave no sign, and I knew that my imagination was magnifying these ordinary night sounds out of all proportion to their actual significance. Leaves rustled faintly outside the window at my back: I construed their sibilant whispers into the dreaded name—*Fu-Manchu—Fu-Manchu—Fu-Manchu!*

So wore on the night; and, when the ticking clock hollowly boomed the hour of one, I almost leaped out of my chair, so highly strung were my nerves, and so appallingly did the sudden clangor beat upon them.

Smith, like a man of stone, showed no sign. He was capable of so subduing his constitutionally high-strung temperament, at times, that temporarily he became immune from human dreads. On such occasions he would be icily cool amid universal panic; but, his object accomplished, I have seen him in such a state of collapse, that utter nervous exhaustion is the only term by which I can describe it.

Tick-tick-tick-tick went the clock, and, with my heart still thumping noisily in my breast, I began to count the tickings; one, two, three, four, five, and so on to a hundred, and from one hundred to many hundreds.

Then, out from the confusion of minor noises, a new, arresting sound detached itself. I ceased my counting; no longer I noted the *tick-tick* of the clock; nor the vague creakings, rustlings and whispers. I saw Smith, shadowly, raise his hand in warning—in needless warning, for I was almost holding my breath in an effort of acute listening.

From high up in the house this new sound came—from above the topmost room, it seemed, up under the roof; a regular squeaking, oddly familiar, yet elusive. Upon it followed a very soft and muffled thud; then a metallic sound as of a rusty hinge in motion; then a new silence, pregnant with a thousand possibilities more eerie than any clamor.

My mind was rapidly at work. Lighting the topmost landing of the house was a sort of glazed trap, evidently set in the floor of a loft-like place extending over the entire building. Somewhere in the red-tiled roof above, there presumably existed a corresponding skylight or lantern.

So I argued; and, ere I had come to any proper decision, another sound, more intimate, came to interrupt me.

This time I could be in no doubt; some one was lifting the trap above the stairhead—slowly, cautiously, and all but silently. Yet to my ears, attuned to trifling disturbances, the trap creaked and groaned noisily.

Nayland Smith waved to me to take a stand on the other side of the opened door—behind it, in fact, where I should be concealed from the view of any one descending the stair.

I stood up and crossed the floor to my new post.

A dull thud told of the trap fully raised and resting upon some supporting joist. A faint rustling (of discarded garments, I told myself) spoke to my newly awakened, acute perceptions, of the visitor preparing to lower himself to the landing. Followed a groan of woodwork submitted to sudden strain—and the unmistakable pad of bare feet upon the linoleum of the top corridor.

I knew now that one of Dr. Fu-Manchu's uncanny servants had gained the roof of the house by some means, had broken through the skylight and had descended by means of the trap beneath on to the landing.

In such a tensed-up state as I cannot describe, nor, at this hour mentally reconstruct, I waited for the creaking of the stairs which should tell of the creature's descent.

I was disappointed. Removed scarce a yard from me as he was, I could hear Nayland Smith's soft, staccato breathing; but my eyes were all for the darkened hallway, for the smudgy outline of the stair-rail with the faint patterning in the background which, alone, indicated the wall.

It was amid an utter silence, unheralded by even so slight a sound as those which I had acquired the power of detecting—that I saw the continuity of the smudgy line of stair-rail to be interrupted.

A dark patch showed upon it, just within my line of sight, invisible to Smith on the other side of the doorway, and some ten or twelve stairs up.

No sound reached me, but the dark patch vanished—and reappeared three feet lower down.

Still I knew that this phantom approach must be unknown to my companion—and I knew that it was impossible for me to advise him of it unseen by the dreaded visitor.

A third time the dark patch—the hand of one who, ghostly, silent, was creeping down into the hallway—vanished and reappeared on a level with my eyes. Then a vague shape became visible; no more than a blurr upon the dim design of the wall-paper . . . and Nayland Smith got his first sight of the stranger.

The clock on the mantelpiece boomed out the half-hour.

At that, such was my state (I blush to relate it) I uttered a faint cry!

It ended all secrecy—that hysterical weakness of mine. It might have frustrated our hopes; that it did not do so was in no measure due to me. But in a sort of passionate whirl, the ensuing events moved swiftly.

Smith hesitated not one instant. With a pantherlike leap he hurled himself into the hall.

"The lights, Petrie!" he cried—"the lights! The switch is near the street-door!"

I clenched my fists in a swift effort to regain control of my treacherous nerves, and, bounding past Smith, and past the foot of the stair, I reached out my hand to the switch, the situation of which, fortunately, I knew.

Around I came, in response to a shrill cry from behind me—an inhuman cry, less a cry than the shriek of some enraged animal. . . .

With his left foot upon the first stair, Nayland Smith stood, his lean body bent periously backward, his arms rigidly thrust out, and his sinewy fingers gripping the throat of an almost naked man—a man whose brown body glistened unctuously, whose shaven head was apish low, whose bloodshot eyes were the eyes of a mad dog! His teeth, upper and lower, were bared; they glistened, they gnashed, and a froth was on his lips. With both his hands, he clutched a heavy stick, and once—twice, he brought it down upon Nayland Smith's head!

I leaped forward to my friend's aid; but as though the blows had been those of a feather, he stood like some figure of archaic statuary, nor for an instant relaxed the death grip which he had upon his adversary's throat.

Thrusting my way up the stairs, I wrenched the stick from the hand of the dacoit—for in this glistening brown man, I recognized one of that deadly brotherhood who hailed Dr. Fu-Manchu their Lord and Master.

. . . .

I cannot dwell upon the end of that encounter; I cannot hope to make acceptable to my readers an account of how Nayland Smith, glassy-eyed, and with consciousness ebbing from him instant by instant, stood there, a realization of Leighton's "Athlete," his arms rigid as iron bars even after Fu-Manchu's servant hung limply in that frightful grip.

In his last moments of consciousness, with the blood from his wounded head trickling down into his eyes, he pointed to the stick which I had torn from the grip of the dacoit, and which I still held in my hand.

"Not Aaron's rod, Petrie!" he gasped hoarsely—"the rod of Moses!—Slattin's stick!"

Even in upon my anxiety for my friend, amazement intruded.

"But," I began—and turned to the rack in which Slattin's favorite cane at that moment reposed—had reposed at the time of his death.

Yes!—there stood Slattin's cane; we had

not moved it; we had disturbed nothing in that stricken house; there it stood, in company with an umbrella and a malacca.

I glanced at the cane in my hand. Surely there could not be two such in the world?

Smith collapsed on the floor at my feet. "Examine the one in the rack, Petrie," he whispered, almost inaudibly, "but do not touch it. It may not be yet. . . ."

I propped him up against the foot of the stairs, and as the constable began knocking violently at the street door, crossed to the rack and lifted out the replica of the cane which I held in my hand.

A faint cry from Smith—and as if it had been a leprous thing, I dropped the cane instantly.

"Merciful God!" I groaned.

Although, in every other particular, it corresponded with that which I held—which I had taken from the dacoit—which he had come to substitute for the cane now lying upon the floor—in one dreadful particular it differed.

Up to the snake's head it was an accurate copy; *but the head lived!*

Either from pain, fear or starvation, the thing confined in the hollow tube of this awful duplicate was become torpid. Otherwise, no power on earth could have saved me from the fate of Abel Slattin; for the creature was an Australian death-adder.

Chapter XI

THE WHITE PEACOCK

Nayland Smith wasted no time in pursuing the plan of campaign which he had mentioned to Inspector Weymouth. Less than forty-eight hours after quitting the house of the murdered Slattin, I found myself bound along Whitechapel Road upon strange enough business.

A very fine rain was falling, which rendered it difficult to see clearly from the windows; but the weather apparently had little effect upon the commercial activities of the district. The cab was threading a hazardous way through the cosmopolitan throng crowding the street. On either side of me extended a row of stalls, seemingly established in opposition to the more legitimate shops upon the inner side of the pavement.

Jewish hawkers, many of them in their shirtsleeves, acclaimed the rarity of the bargains which they had to offer; and, allowing for the difference of costume, these tireless Israelites, heedless of climatic conditions, sweating at their mongery, might well have stood, not in a squalid London thoroughfare, but in an equally squalid market-street of the Orient.

They offered linen and fine raiment; from footgear to hair-oil their wares ranged. They enlivened their auctioneering with conjuring tricks and witty stories, selling watches by the aid of legerdemain, and fancy vests by grace of a seasonable anecdote.

Poles, Russians, Serbs, Roumanians, Jews of Hungary, and Italians of Whitechapel mingled in the throng. Near East and Far East rubbed shoulders. Pidgin English contested with Yiddish for the ownership of some tawdry article offered by an auctioneer whose nationality defied conjecture, save that always some branch of his ancestry had drawn nourishment from the soil of Eternal Judea.

Some wearing mens' caps, some with shawls thrown over their oily locks, and some, more true to primitive instincts, defying, bareheaded, the unkindly elements, bedraggled women—more often than not burdened with muffled infants—crowded the pavements and the roadway, thronged about the stalls like white ants about some choicer carrion.

And the fine drizzling rain fell upon all alike, pattering upon the hood of the taxicab, trickling down the front windows; glistening upon the unctuous hair of those in the street who were hatless; dewing the bare arms of the auctioneers, and dripping, melancholy, from the tarpaulin coverings of the stalls. Heedless of the rain above and of the mud beneath, North, South, East, and West mingled their cries, their bids, their blandishments, their raillery, mingled their persons in that joyless throng.

Sometimes a yellow face showed close to one of the streaming windows; sometimes a black-eyed, pallid face, but never a face wholly sane and healthy. This was an underworld where squalor and vice went hand in hand through the beautiless streets, a melting-pot of the world's outcasts; this was the shadowland, which last night had swallowed up Nayland Smith.

Ceaselessly I peered to right and left, searching amid that rain-soaked company for any face known to me. Whom I expected to find there, I know not, but I should have counted it no matter for surprise had I detected amid that ungracious ugliness the beautiful face of Kâramanèh, the Eastern slave-girl, the leering yellow face of a Burmese dacoit, the gaunt, bronzed features of Nayland Smith; a hundred times I almost believed that I had seen the ruddy countenance of Inspector Weymouth, and once (at which instant my heart seemed to stand still) I suffered from the singular delusion that the oblique green eyes of Dr. Fu-Manchu peered out from the shadows between two stalls.

It was mere phantasy, of course, the sick imaginings of a mind overwrought. I had not slept and had scarcely tasted food for more than thirty hours; for, following up a faint clue supplied by Burke, Slattin's man, and, like his master, an ex-officer of New York Police, my friend, Nayland Smith, on the previous evening had set out in quest of some obscene den where the man called Shen-Yan—former keeper of an opium-shop—was now said to be in hiding. Shen-Yan we knew to be a creature of the Chinese doctor, and only a most urgent call had prevented me from joining Smith upon this promising, though hazardous expedition.

At any rate, Fate willing it so, he had gone without me; and now—although Inspector Weymouth, assisted by a number of C. I. D. men, was sweeping the district about me—to the time of my departure nothing whatever had been heard of Smith. The ordeal of waiting finally had proved too great to be borne. With no definite idea of what I proposed to do, I had thrown myself into the search, filled with such dreadful apprehensions as I hope never again to experience.

I did not know the exact situation of the place to which Smith was gone, for owing to the urgent case which I have mentioned, I had been absent at the time of his departure; nor could Scotland Yard enlighten me upon this point. Weymouth was in charge of the case—under Smith's direction—and since the inspector had left the Yard, early that morning, he had disappeared as completely as Smith, no report having been received from him.

As my driver turned into the black mouth of a narrow, ill-lighted street, and the glare and clamor of the greater thoroughfare died behind me, I sank into the corner of the cab burdened with such a sense of desolation as mercifully comes but rarely.

We were heading now for that strange settlement off the West India Dock Road, which, bounded by Limehouse Causeway and Pennyfields, and narrowly confined within four streets, composes an unique Chinatown, a miniature of that at Liverpool, and of the greater one in San Francisco. Inspired with an idea which promised hopefully, I raised the speaking-tube.

"Take me first to the River Police Station," I directed; "along Ratcliffe Highway."

The man turned and nodded comprehendingly, as I could see through the wet pane.

Presently we swerved to the right and into an even narrower street. This inclined in an easterly direction, and proved to communicate with a wide thoroughfare along which passed brilliantly lighted electric trams. I had lost all sense of direction, and when, swinging to the left and to the right again, I looked through the window and perceived that we were before the door of the Police Station, I was dully surprised.

In quite mechanical fashion I entered the depôt. Inspector Ryman, our associate in one of the darkest episodes of the campaign with the Yellow Doctor two years before, received me in his office.

By a negative shake of the head, he answered my unspoken question.

"The ten o'clock boat is lying off the Stone Stairs, Doctor," he said, "and co-operating with some of the Scotland Yard men who are dragging that district—"

I shuddered at the word "dragging"; Ryman had not used it literally, but nevertheless it had conjured up a dread possibility— a possibility in accordance with the methods of Dr. Fu-Manchu. All within space of an instant I saw the tide of Limehouse Reach, the Thames lapping about the green-coated timbers of a dock pier; and rising—falling—sometimes disclosing to the pallid light a rigid hand, sometimes a horribly bloated face—I saw the body of Nayland Smith at the mercy of those oily waters. Ryman continued:

"There is a launch out, too, patrolling the riverside from here to Tilbury. Another lies at the breakwater"—he jerked his thumb over his shoulder. "Should you care to take a run down and see for yourself?"

"No, thanks," I replied, shaking my head. "You are doing all that can be done. Can you give me the address of the place to which Mr. Smith went last night?"

"Certainly," said Ryman; "I thought you knew it. You remember Shen-Yan's place—by Limehouse Basin? Well, further east—east of the Causeway, between Gill Street and

Three Colt Street—is a block of wooden buildings. You recall them?"

"Yes," I replied. "Is the man established there again, then?"

"It appears so, but, although you have evidently not been informed of the fact, Weymouth raided the establishment in the early hours of this morning!"

"Well?" I cried.

"Unfortunately with no result," continued the inspector. "The notorious Shen-Yan was missing, and although there is no real doubt that the place is used as a gaming-house, not a particle of evidence to that effect could be obtained. Also—there was no sign of Mr. Nayland Smith, and no sign of the American, Burke, who had led him to the place."

"Is it certain that they went there?"

"Two C. I. D. men who were shadowing, actually saw the pair of them enter. A signal had been arranged, but it was never given; and at about half past four, the place was raided."

"Surely some arrests were made?"

"But there was no evidence!" cried Ryman. "Every inch of the rat-burrow was searched. The Chinese gentleman who posed as the proprietor of what he claimed to be a respectable lodging-house offered every facility to the police. What could we do?"

"I take it that the place is being watched?"

"Certainly," said Ryman. "Both from the river and from the shore. Oh! they are not there! God knows where they are, but they are not *there!*"

I stood for a moment in silence, endeavoring to determine my course; then, telling Ryman that I hoped to see him later, I walked out slowly into the rain and mist, and nodding to the taxi-driver to proceed to our original destination, I re-entered the cab.

As we moved off, the lights of the River Police depôt were swallowed up in the humid murk, and again I found myself being carried through the darkness of those narrow streets, which, like a maze, hold secret within their labyrinth mysteries as great, and at least as foul, as that of Pasiphaë.

The marketing centers I had left far behind me; to my right stretched the broken range of riverside buildings, and beyond them flowed the Thames, a stream more heavily burdened with secrets than ever was Tiber or Tigris. On my left, occasional flickering lights broke through the mist, for the most part the lights of taverns; and saving these

rents in the veil, the darkness was punctuated with nothing but the faint and yellow luminance of the street lamps.

Ahead was a black mouth, which promised to swallow me up as it had swallowed up my friend.

In short, what with my lowered condition and consequent frame of mind, and what with the traditions, for me inseparable from that gloomy quarter of London, I was in the grip of a shadowy menace which at any moment might become tangible—I perceived, in the most commonplace objects, the yellow hand of Dr. Fu-Manchu.

When the cab stopped in a place of utter darkness, I aroused myself with an effort, opened the door, and stepped out into the mud of a narrow lane. A high brick wall frowned upon me from one side, and, dimly perceptible, there towered a smoke stack, beyond. On my right uprose the side of a wharf building, shadowly, and some distance ahead, almost obscured by the drizzling rain, a solitary lamp flickered.

I turned up the collar of my raincoat, shivering, as much at the prospect as from physical chill.

"You will wait here," I said to the man; and, feeling in my breast-pocket, I added: "If you hear the note of a whistle, drive on and rejoin me."

He listened attentively and with a certain eagerness. I had selected him that night for the reason that he had driven Smith and myself on previous occasions and had proved himself a man of intelligence. Transferring a Browning pistol from my hip-pocket to that of my raincoat, I trudged on into the mist.

The headlights of the taxi were swallowed up behind me, and just abreast of the street lamp I stood listening.

Save for the dismal sound of rain, and the trickling of water along the gutters, all about me was silent. Sometimes this silence would be broken by the distant, muffled note of a steam siren; and always, forming a sort of background to the near stillness, was the remote din of riverside activity.

I walked on to the corner just beyond the lamp. This was the street in which the wooden buildings were situated. I had expected to detect some evidences of surveillances, but if any were indeed being observed, the fact was effectively masked. Not a living creature was visible, peer as I could.

Plans, I had none, and perceiving that the street was empty, and that no lights showed in any of the windows, I passed on, only to find that I had entered a *cul-de-sac*.

A rickety gate gave access to a descending flight of stone steps, the bottom invisible in the denser shadows of an archway, beyond which, I doubted not, lay the river.

Still uninspired by any definite design, I tried the gate and found that it was unlocked. Like some wandering soul, as it has since seemed to me, I descended. There was a lamp over the archway, but the glass was broken, and the rain apparently had extinguished the light; as I passed under it, I could hear the gas whistling from the burner.

Continuing my way, I found myself upon a narrow wharf with the Thames flowing gloomily beneath me. A sort of fog hung over the river, shutting me in. Then came an incident.

Suddenly, quite near, there arose a weird and mournful cry—a cry indescribable, and inexpressibly uncanny!

I started back so violently that how I escaped falling into the river I do not know to this day. That cry, so eerie and so wholly unexpected, had unnerved me; and realizing the nature of my surroundings, and the folly of my presence alone in such a place, I began to edge back toward the foot of the steps, away from the thing that cried; when—a great white shape uprose like a phantom before me! . . .

There are few men, I suppose, whose lives have been crowded with so many eerie happenings as mine, but this phantom thing which grew out of the darkness, which seemed about to envelope me, takes rank in my memory amongst the most fearsome apparitions which I have witnessed.

I knew that I was frozen with a sort of supernatural terror. I stood there with hands clenched, staring—staring—at that white shape, which seemed to float.

As I stared, every nerve in my body thrilling, I distinguished the outline of the phantom. With a subdued cry, I stepped forward. A new sensation claimed me. In that one stride I passed from the horrible to the bizarre.

I found myself confronted with something tangible, certainly, but something whose presence in that place was utterly extravagant—could only be reconcilable in the dreams of an opium slave.

Was I awake, was I sane? Awake and sane beyond doubt, but surely moving, not in the purlieus of Limehouse, but in the fantastic realms of fairyland.

Swooping, with open arms, I rounded up in an angle against the building and gathered in this screaming thing which had inspired in me so keen a terror.

The great, ghostly fan was closed as I did so, and I stumbled back toward the stair with my struggling captive tucked under my arm; I mounted into one of London's darkest slums, carrying a beautiful white peacock!

Chapter XII

DARK EYES LOOKED INTO MINE

My adventure had done nothing to relieve the feeling of unreality which held me enthralled. Grasping the struggling bird firmly by the body, and having the long white tail fluttering a yard or so behind me, I returned to where the taxi waited.

"Open the door!" I said to the man—who greeted me with such a stare of amazement that I laughed outright, though my mirth was but hollow.

He jumped into the road and did as I directed. Making sure that both windows were closed, I thrust the peacock into the cab and shut the door upon it.

"For God's sake, sir!" began the driver—"It has probably escaped from some collector's place on the riverside," I explained, "but one never knows. See that it does not escape again, and if at the end of an hour, as arranged, you do not hear from me, take it back with you to the River Police Station."

"Right you are, sir," said the man, remounting his seat. "It's the first time I ever saw a peacock in Limehouse!"

It was the first time *I* had seen one, and the incident struck me as being more than odd; it gave me an idea, and a new, faint hope. I returned to the head of the steps, at the foot of which I had met with this singular experience, and gazed up at the dark building beneath which they led. Three windows were visible, but they were broken and neglected. One, immediately above the arch, had been pasted up with brown paper, and this was now peeling off in the rain, a little stream of which trickled down from the detached corner to drop, drearily, upon the stone stairs beneath.

Where were the detectives? I could only assume that they had directed their attention elsewhere, for had the place not been utterly deserted, surely I had been challenged.

In pursuit of my new idea, I again descended the steps. The persuasion (shortly to be verified) that I was close upon the secret hold of the Chinaman, grew stronger, unaccountably. I had descended some eight steps, and was at the darkest part of the archway or tunnel, when confirmation of my theories came to me.

A noose settled accurately upon my shoulders, was snatched tightly about my throat, and with a feeling of insupportable agony at the base of my skull, and a sudden supreme knowledge that I was being strangled—hanged—I lost consciousness!

How long I remained unconscious, I was unable to determine at the time, but I learned later, that it was for no more than half an hour; at any rate, recovery was slow.

The first sensation to return to me was a sort of repetition of the asphyxia. The blood seemed to be forcing itself into my eyes—I choked—I felt that my end was come. And, raising my hands to my throat, I found it to be swollen and inflamed. Then the floor upon which I lay seemed to be rocking like the deck of a ship, and I glided back again into a place of darkness and forgetfulness.

My second awakening was heralded by a returning sense of smell; for I became conscious of a faint, exquisite perfume.

It brought me to my senses as nothing else could have done, and I sat upright with a hoarse cry. I could have distinguished that perfume amid a thousand others, could have marked it apart from the rest in a scent bazaar. For me it had one meaning, and one meaning only—Kâramanèh.

She was near to me, or had been near to me!

And in the first moments of my awakening I groped about in the darkness blindly seeking her. Then my swollen throat and throbbing head, together with my utter inability to move my neck even slightly, reminded me of the facts as they were. I knew in that bitter moment that Kâramanèh was no longer my friend; but, for all her beauty and charm, was the most heartless, the most fiendish creature in the service of Dr. Fu-Manchu. I groaned aloud in my despair and misery.

Something stirred, near to me in the room, and set my nerves creeping with a new apprehension. I became fully alive to the possibilities of the darkness.

To my certain knowledge, Dr. Fu-Manchu at this time had been in England for fully three months, which meant that by now he must be equipped with all the instruments of destruction, animate and inanimate, which dread experience had taught me to associate with him.

Now, as I crouched there in that dark apartment listening for a repetition of the sound, I scarcely dared to conjecture what might have occasioned it, but my imagination peopled the place with reptiles which writhed upon the floor, with tarantulas and other deadly insects which crept upon the walls, which might drop upon me from the ceiling at any moment.

Then, since nothing stirred about me, I ventured to move, turning my shoulders, for I was unable to move my aching head; and I looked in the direction from which a faint, very faint, light proceeded.

A regular tapping sound now began to attract my attention, and, having turned about, I perceived that behind me was a broken window, in places patched with brown paper; the corner of one sheet of paper was detached, and the rain trickled down upon it with a rhythmical sound.

In a flash I realized that I lay in the room immediately above the archway; and listening intently, I perceived above the other faint sounds of the night, or thought that I perceived, the hissing of the gas from the extinguished lamp-burner.

Unsteadily I rose to my feet, but found myself swaying like a drunken man. I reached out for support, stumbling in the direction of the wall. My foot came in contact with something that lay there, and I pitched forward and fell. . . .

I anticipated a crash which would put an end to my hopes of escape, but my fall was comparatively noiseless—for I fell upon the body of a man who lay bound up with rope close against the wall!

A moment I stayed as I fell, the chest of my fellow captive rising and falling beneath me as he breathed. Knowing that my life depended upon retaining a firm hold upon myself, I succeeded in overcoming the dizziness and nausea which threatened to drown my senses, and, moving back so that I knelt upon the floor, I fumbled in my pocket for the electric lamp which I had placed there. My raincoat had been removed whilst I was unconscious, and with it my pistol, but the lamp was untouched.

I took it out, pressed the button, and directed the ray upon the face of the man beside me.

It was Nayland Smith!

Trussed up and fastened to a ring in the wall he lay, having a cork gag strapped so tightly between his teeth that I wondered how he had escaped suffocation.

But, although a grayish pallor showed through the tan of his skin, his eyes were feverishly bright, and there, as I knelt beside him, I thanked heaven, silently but fervently.

Then, in furious haste, I set to work to remove the gag. It was most ingeniously secured by means of leather straps buckled at the back of his head, but I unfastened these without much difficulty, and he spat out the gag, uttering an exclamation of disgust.

"Thank God, old man!" he said, huskily. "Thank God that you are alive! I saw them drag you in, and I thought . . ."

"I have been thinking the same about you for more than twenty-four hours," I said, reproachfully. "Why did you start without—"

"I did not want you to come, Petrie," he replied. "I had a sort of premonition. You see it was realized; and instead of being as helpless as I, Fate has made you the instrument of my release. Quick! You have a knife? Good!" The old, feverish energy was by no means extinguished in him. "Cut the ropes about my wrists and ankles, but don't otherwise disturb them—"

I set to work eagerly.

"Now," Smith continued, "put that filthy gag in place again—but you need not strap it so tightly! Directly they find that you are alive, they will treat you the same—you understand? *She* has been here three times—"

"Kâramanèh?" . . .

"Ssh!"

I heard a sound like the opening of a distant door.

"Quick! the straps of the gag!" whispered Smith—"and pretend to recover consciousness just as they enter—"

Clumsily I followed his directions, for my fingers were none too steady, replaced the lamp in my pocket, and threw myself upon the floor.

Through half-shut eyes, I saw the door open and obtained a glimpse of a desolate, empty passage beyond. On the threshold stood Kâramanèh. She held in her hand a common tin oil lamp which smoked and flickered with every movement, filling the already none too cleanly air with an odor of burning paraffin.

She personified the outré; nothing so incongruous as her presence in that place could well be imagined. She was dressed as I remembered once to have seen her two years before, in the gauzy silks of the harem. There were pearls glittering like great tears amid the cloud of her wonderful hair. She wore broad gold bangles upon her bare arms, and her fingers were laden with jewelry. A heavy girdle swung from her hips, defining the lines of her slim shape, and about one white ankle was a gold band.

As she appeared in the doorway I almost entirely closed my eyes, but my gaze rested fascinatedly upon the little red slippers which she wore.

Again I detected the exquisite, elusive perfume, which, like a breath of musk, spoke of the Orient; and, as always, it played havoc with my reason, seeming to intoxicate me as though it were the very essence of her loveliness.

But I had a part to play, and throwing out one clenched hand so that my fist struck upon the floor, I uttered a loud groan, and made as if to rise upon my knees.

One quick glimpse I had of her wonderful eyes, widely opened and turned upon me with such an enigmatical expression as set my heart leaping wildly—then, stepping back, Kâramanèh placed the lamp upon the boards of the passage and clapped her hands.

As I sank upon the floor in assumed exhaustion, a Chinaman with a perfectly impassive face, and a Burman, whose pockmarked, evil countenance was set in an apparently habitual leer, came running into the room past the girl.

With a hand which trembled violently, she held the lamp whilst the two yellow ruffians tied me. I groaned and struggled feebly, fixing my gaze upon the lamp-bearer in a silent reproach which was by no means without its effect.

She lowered her eyes, and I could see her biting her lip, whilst the color gradually faded from her cheeks. Then, glancing up again quickly, and still meeting that reproachful stare, she turned her head aside altogether, and rested one hand upon the wall, swaying slightly as she did so.

It was a singular ordeal for more than one of that incongruous group; but in order that I may not be charged with hypocrisy or with seeking to hide my own folly, I confess, here, that when again I found myself in darkness, my heart was leaping not because of the success of my strategy, but because of the success of that reproachful glance which I had directed toward the lovely, dark-eyed Kâramanèh, toward the faithless, evil Kâramanèh! So much for myself.

The door had not been closed ten seconds, ere Smith again was spitting out the gag, swearing under his breath, and stretching his cramped limbs free from their binding. Within a minute from the time of my trussing, I was a free man again; save that look where I would—to right, to left, or inward, to my own conscience—two dark eyes met mine, enigmatically.

"What now?" I whispered.

"Let me think," replied Smith. "A false move would destroy us."

"How long have you been here?"

"Since last night."

"Is Fu-Manchu—"

"Fu-Manchu is here!" replied Smith, grimly—"and not only Fu-Manchu, but—another."

"Another!"

"A higher than Fu-Manchu, apparently. I have an idea of the identity of this person, but no more than an idea. Something unusual is going on, Petrie; otherwise I should have been a dead man twenty-four hours ago. Something even more important than *my* death engages Fu-Manchu's attention—and this can only be the presence of the mysterious visitor. Your seductive friend, Kâramanèh, is arrayed in her very becoming national costume in his honor, I presume." He stopped abruptly; then added: "I would give five hundred pounds for a glimpse of that visitor's face!"

"Is Burke—"

"God knows what has become of Burke, Petrie! We were both caught napping in the establishment of the amiable Shen-Yan, where, amid a very mixed company of poker players, we were losing our money like gentlemen."

"But Weymouth—"

"Burke and I had both been neatly sandbagged, my dear Petrie, and removed elsewhere, some hours before Weymouth raided the gaming-house. Oh! I don't know how they smuggled us away with the police watching the place; but my presence here is sufficient evidence of the fact. Are you armed?"

"No; my pistol was in my raincoat, which is missing."

In the dim light from the broken window, I could see Smith tugging reflectively at the lobe of his left ear.

"I am without arms, too," he mused. "We might escape from the window—"

"It's a long drop!"

"Ah! I imagined so. If only I had a pistol, or a revolver—"

"What should you do?"

"I should present myself before the important meeting, which, I am assured, is being held somewhere in this building; and to-night would see the end of my struggle with the Fu-Manchu group—the end of the whole Yellow menace! For not only is Fu-Manchu here, Petrie, with all his gang of assassins, but he whom I believe to be the real head of the group—a certain mandarin—is here also!"

Chapter XIII

THE SACRED ORDER

Smith stepped quietly across the room and tried the door. It proved to be unlocked, and an instant later, we were both outside in the passage. Coincident with our arrival there, arose a sudden outcry from some place at the westward end. A high-pitched, grating voice, in which guttural notes alternated with a serpent-like hissing, was raised in anger.

"Dr. Fu-Manchu!" whispered Smith, grasping my arm.

Indeed, it was the unmistakable voice of the Chinaman, raised hysterically in one of those outbursts which in the past I had diagnosed as symptomatic of dangerous mania. The voice rose to a scream, the scream of some angry animal rather than anything human. Then, chokingly, it ceased. Another short sharp cry followed—but not in the voice of Fu-Manchu—a dull groan, and the sound of a fall.

With Smith still grasping my wrist, I shrank back into the doorway, as something that looked in the darkness like a great ball of fluff came rapidly along the passage toward me. Just at my feet the thing stopped and I made it out for a small animal. The tiny, gleaming eyes looked up at me, and, chattering wickedly, the creature bounded past and was lost from view.

It was Dr. Fu-Manchu's marmoset.

Smith dragged me back into the room which we had just left. As he partly reclosed the door, I heard the clapping of hands. In a condition of most dreadful suspense, we waited; until a new, ominous sound proclaimed itself. Some heavy body was being dragged into the passage. I heard the opening of a trap. Exclamations in guttural voices told of a heavy task in progress; there was a great straining and creaking—whereupon the trap was softly reclosed.

Smith bent to my ear.

"Fu-Manchu has chastised one of his servants," he whispered. "There will be food for the grappling-irons to-night!"

I shuddered violently, for, without Smith's words, I knew that a bloody deed had been done in that house within a few yards of where we stood.

In the new silence, I could hear the drip, drip, drip of the rain outside the window; then a steam siren hooted dismally upon the river, and I thought how the screw of that very vessel, even as we listened, might be tearing the body of Fu-Manchu's servant!

"Have you some one waiting?" whispered Smith, eagerly.

"How long was I insensible?"

"About half an hour."

"Then the cabman will be waiting."

"Have you a whistle with you?"

I felt in my coat pocket.

"Yes," I reported.

"Good! Then we will take a chance."

Again we slipped out into the passage and began a stealthy progress to the west. Ten paces amid absolute darkness, and we found ourselves abreast of a branch corridor. At the further end, through a kind of little window, a dim light shone.

"See if you can find the trap," whispered Smith; "light your lamp."

I directed the ray of the pocket-lamp upon the floor, and there at my feet was a square wooden trap. As I stooped to examine it, I glanced back, painfully, over my shoulder—and saw Nayland Smith tiptoeing away from me along the passage toward the light!

Inwardly I cursed his folly, but the temptation to peep in at that little window proved too strong for me, as it had proved too strong for him.

Fearful that some board would creak beneath my tread, I followed; and side by side we two crouched, looking into a small rectangular room. It was a bare and cheerless apartment with unpapered walls; and car-

petless floor. A table and a chair constituted the sole furniture.

Seated in the chair, with his back toward us, was a portly Chinaman who wore a yellow, silken robe. His face, it was impossible to see; but he was beating his fist upon the table, and pouring out a torrent of words in a thin, piping voice. So much I perceived at a glance; then, into view at the distant end of the room, paced a tall, high-shouldered figure—a figure unforgettable, at once imposing and dreadful, stately and sinister.

With the long, bony hands behind him, fingers twining and intertwining serpentinely about the handle of a little fan, and with the pointed chin resting on the breast of the yellow robe, so that the light from the lamp swinging in the center of the ceiling gleamed upon the great, domelike brow, this tall man paced somberly from left to right.

He cast a sidelong, venomous glance at the voluble speaker out of half-shut eyes; in the act they seemed to light up as with an internal luminance; momentarily they sparkled like emeralds; then their brilliance was filmed over as in the eyes of a bird when the membrane is lowered.

My blood seemed to chill, and my heart to double its pulsations; beside me Smith was breathing more rapidly than usual. I knew now the explanation of the feeling which had claimed me when first I had descended the stone stairs. I knew what it was that hung like a miasma over that house. It was the aura, the glamour, which radiated from this wonderful and evil man as light radiates from radium. It was the *vril*, the *force*, of Dr. Fu-Manchu.

I began to move away from the window. But Smith held my wrist as in a vise. He was listening raptly to the torrential speech of the Chinaman who sat in the chair; and I perceived in his eyes the light of a sudden comprehension.

As the tall figure of the Chinese doctor came pacing into view again, Smith, his head below the level of the window, pushed me gently along the passage.

Regaining the site of the trap, he whispered to me:

"We owe our lives, Petrie, to the national childishness of the Chinese! A race of ancestor worshipers is capable of anything, and Dr. Fu-Manchu, the dreadful being who has rained terror upon Europe, stands in imminent peril of disgrace for having lost a decoration."

"What do you mean, Smith?"

"I mean that this is no time for delay, Petrie! Here, unless I am greatly mistaken, lies the rope by means of which you made your entrance. It shall be the means of your exit. Open the trap!"

Handing the lamp to Smith, I stooped and carefully raised the trap-door. At which moment, a singular and dramatic thing happened.

A softly musical voice—the voice of my dreams!—spoke.

"Not that way! O God, not that way!"

In my surprise and confusion I all but let the trap fall, but I retained sufficient presence of mind to replace it gently. Standing upright, I turned . . . and there, with her little jeweled hand resting upon Smith's arm, stood Kâramanèh!

In all my experience of him, I had never seen ayland Smith so utterly perplexed. Between anger, distrust and dismay, he wavered; and each passing emotion was written legibly upon the lean bronzed features. Rigid with surprise, he stared at the beautiful face of the girl. She, although her hand still rested upon Smith's arm, had her dark eyes turned upon me with that same enigmatical expression. Her lips were slightly parted, and her breast heaved tumultuously.

This ten seconds of silence in which we three stood looking at one another encompassed the whole gamut of human emotion. The silence was broken by Kâramanèh.

"They will be coming back that way!" she whispered, bending eagerly toward me. (How, in the most desperate moments, I loved to listen to that odd, musical accent!) "Please, if you would save your life, and spare mine, trust me!"—She suddenly clasped her hands together and looked up into my face, passionately—"Trust me—just for once—and I will show you the way!"

Nayland Smith never removed his gaze from her for a moment, nor did he stir.

"Oh!" she whispered, tremulously, and stamped one little red slipper upon the floor, "Won't you heed me? Come, or it will be too late!"

I glanced anxiously at my friend; the voice of Dr. Fu-Manchu, now raised again in anger, was audible above the piping tones of the other Chinaman. And as I caught Smith's eye, in silent query—the trap at my feet began slowly to lift!

Kâramanèh stifled a little sobbing cry; but the warning came too late. A hideous yellow face with oblique squinting eyes, appeared in the aperture.

I found myself inert, useless; I could neither think nor act. Nayland Smith, however, as if instinctively, delivered a pitiless kick at the head protruding above the trap.

A sickening crushing sound, with a sort of muffled snap, spoke of a broken jaw-bone; and with no word or cry, the Chinaman fell. As the trap descended with a bang, I heard the thud of his body on the stone stairs beneath.

But we were lost. Kâramanèh fled along one of the passages lightly as a bird, and disappeared—as Dr. Fu-Manchu, his top lip drawn up above his teeth in the manner of an angry jackal, appeared from the other.

"This way!" cried Smith, in a voice that rose almost to a shriek—"this way!"—and he led toward the room overhanging the steps.

Off we dashed with panic swiftness, only to find that this retreat also was cut off. Dimly visible in the darkness was a group of yellow men, and despite the gloom, the curved blades of the knives which they carried glittered menacingly. The passage was full of dacoits!

Smith and I turned, together. The trap was raised again, and the Burman, who had helped to tie me, was just scrambling up beside Dr. Fu-Manchu, who stood there watching us, a shadowy, sinister figure.

"The game's up, Petrie!" muttered Smith. "It has been a long fight, but Fu-Manchu wins!"

"Not entirely!" I cried.

I whipped the police whistle from my pocket, and raised it to my lips; but brief as the interval had been, the dacoits were upon me.

A sinewy brown arm shot over my shoulder, and the whistle was dashed from my grip. Then came a whirl of maelstrom fighting, with Smith and myself ever sinking lower amid a whirlpool, as it seemed, of bloodlustful eyes, yellow fangs, and gleaming blades.

I had some vague idea that the rasping voice of Fu-Manchu broke once through the turmoil, and when, with my wrists tied behind me, I emerged from the strife to find myself lying beside Smith in the passage, I could only assume that the Chinaman had ordered his bloody servants to take us alive; for saving numerous bruises and a few superficial cuts, I was unwounded.

The place was utterly deserted again, and we two panting captives found ourselves alone with Dr. Fu-Manchu. The scene was unforgettable; that dimly lighted passage, its extremities masked in shadow, and the tall, yellow-robed figure of the Satanic Chinaman towering over us where we lay.

He had recovered his habitual calm, and as I peered at him through the gloom, was impressed anew with the tremendous intellectual force of the man. He had the brow of a genius, the features of a born ruler; and even in that moment I could find time to search my memory, and to discover that the face, saving the indescribable evil of its expression, was identical with that of Seti, the mighty Pharaoh who lies in the Cairo Museum.

Down the passage came leaping and gamboling the doctor's marmoset. Uttering its shrill, whistling cry, it leaped onto his shoulder, clutched with its tiny fingers at the scanty, neutral-colored hair upon his crown, and bent forward, peering grotesquely into that still, dreadful face.

Dr. Fu-Manchu stroked the little creature; and crooned to it, as a mother to her infant. Only this crooning, and the labored breathing of Smith and myself, broke that impressive stillness.

Suddenly the guttural voice began:

"You come at an opportune time, Mr. Commissioner Nayland Smith, and Dr. Petrie; at a time when the greatest man in China flatters me with a visit. In my absence from home, a tremendous honor has been conferred upon me, and, in the hour of this supreme honor, dishonor and calamity have befallen! For my services to China—the New China, the China of the future—I have been admitted by the Sublime Prince to the Sacred Order of the White Peacock."

Warming to his discourse, he threw wide his arms, hurling the chattering marmoset fully five yards along the corridor.

"O god of Cathay!" he cried, sibilantly, "in what have I sinned that this catastrophe has been visited upon my head! Learn, my two dear friends, that the sacred white peacock brought to these misty shores for my undying glory, has been lost to me! Death is the penalty of such a sacrilege; death shall be my lot, since death I deserve."

Covertly Smith nudged me with his elbow. I knew what the nudge was designed to convey; he would remind me of his words—anent the childish trifles which sway the life of intellectual China.

Personally, I was amazed. That Fu-Man-chu's anger, grief, sorrow and resignation were real, no one watching him, and hearing his voice, could doubt. He continued:

"By one deed, and one deed alone, may I win a lighter punishment. By one deed, and the resignation of all my titles, all my lands, and all my honors, may I merit to be spared to my work—which has only begun."

I knew now that we were lost, indeed; these were confidences which our graves should hold inviolate! He suddenly opened fully those blazing green eyes and directed their baneful glare upon Nayland Smith.

"The Director of the Universe," he continued, softly, "has relented toward me. To-night, you die! To-night, the arch-enemy of our caste shall be no more. This is my offering—the price of redemption . . ."

My mind was working again, and actively. I managed to grasp the stupendous truth—and the stupendous possibility.

Dr. Fu-Manchu was in the act of clapping his hands, when I spoke.

"Stop!" I cried.

He paused, and the weird film, which sometimes became visible in his eyes, now obscured their greenness, and lent him the appearance of a blind man.

"Dr. Petrie," he said, softly, "I shall always listen to you with respect."

"I have an offer to make," I continued, seeking to steady my voice. "Give us our freedom, and I will restore your shattered honor—I will restore the sacred peacock!"

Dr. Fu-Manchu bent forward until his face was so close to mine that I could see the innumerable lines which, an intricate network, covered his yellow skin.

"Speak!" he hissed. "You lift up my heart from a dark pit."

"I can restore your white peacock," I said; "I, and I alone, know where it is!"—and I strove not to shrink from the face so close to mine.

Upright shot the tall figure; high above his head Fu-Manchu threw his arms—and a light of exaltation gleamed in the now widely opened, catlike eyes.

"O god!" he screamed, frenziedly—"O god of the Golden Age! like a phœnix I arise from the ashes of myself!" He turned to me. "Quick! Quick! make your bargain! End my suspense!"

Smith stared at me like a man dazed; but, ignoring him, I went on:

"You will release me, now, immediately. In another ten minutes it will be too late; my friend will remain. One of your—servants—can accompany me, and give the signal when I return with the peacock. Mr. Nayland Smith and yourself, or another, will join me at the corner of the street where the raid took place last night. We shall then give you ten minutes' grace, after which we shall take whatever steps we choose."

"Agreed!" cried Fu-Manchu. "I ask but one thing from an Englishman; your word of honor?"

"I give it."

"I, also," said Smith, hoarsely.

. . . .

Ten minutes later, Nayland Smith and I, standing beside the cab, whose lights gleamed yellowy through the mist, exchanged a struggling, frightened bird for our lives—capitulated with the enemy of the white race.

With characteristic audacity—and characteristic trust in the British sense of honor—Dr. Fu-Manchu came in person with Nayland Smith, in response to the wailing signal of the dacoit who had accompanied me. No word was spoken, save that the cabman suppressed a curse of amazement; and the Chinaman, his sinister servant at his elbow, bowed low—and left us, surely to the mocking laughter of the gods!

Chapter XIV

THE COUGHING HORROR

I leaped up in bed with a great start.

My sleep was troubled often enough in these days, which immediately followed our almost miraculous escape from the den of Fu-Manchu; and now, as I crouched there, nerves aquiver—listening—listening—I could not be sure if this dank panic which possessed me had its origin in nightmare or in something else.

Surely a scream, a choking cry for help, had reached my ears; but now, almost holding my breath in that sort of nervous tensity peculiar to one aroused thus, I listened, and the silence seemed complete. Perhaps I had been dreaming . . .

"Help! Petrie! *Help!* . . ."

It was Nayland Smith in the room above me!

My doubts were dissolved; this was no trick of an imagination disordered. Some

dreadful menace threatened my friend. Not delaying even to snatch my dressing-gown, I rushed out on to the landing, up the stairs, bare-footed as I was, threw open the door of Smith's room and literally hurled myself in.

Those cries had been the cries of one assailed, had been uttered, I judged, in the brief interval of a life and death struggle; had been choked off . . .

A certain amount of moonlight found access to the room, without spreading so far as the bed in which my friend lay. But at the moment of my headlong entrance, and before I had switched on the light, my gaze automatically was directed to the pale moonbeam streaming through the window and down on to one corner of the sheep-skin rug beside the bed.

There came a sound of faint and muffled coughing.

What with my recent awakening and the panic at my heart, I could not claim that my vision was true; but across this moonbeam passed a sort of gray streak, for all the world as though some long thin shape had been withdrawn, snakelike, from the room, through the open window . . . From somewhere outside the house, and below, I heard the cough again, followed by a sharp cracking sound like the lashing of a whip.

I depressed the switch, flooding the room with light, and as I leaped forward to the bed a word picture of what I had seen formed in my mind; and I found that I was thinking of a gray feather boa.

"Smith!" I cried (my voice seemed to pitch itself, unwilled, in a very high key), "Smith, old man!"

He made no reply, and a sudden, sorrowful fear clutched at my heart-strings. He was lying half out of bed flat upon his back, his head at a dreadful angle with his body. As I bent over him and seized him by the shoulders, I could see the whites of his eyes. His arms hung limply, and his fingers touched the carpet.

"My God!" I whispered—"what has happened?"

I heaved him back onto the pillow, and looked anxiously into his face. Habitually gaunt, so refined away by the consuming nervous energy of the man as to reveal the cheekbones in sharp prominence, he now looked truly ghastly. His skin was so sunbaked as to have changed constitutionally; nothing could ever eradicate that tan. But tonight a fearful grayness was mingled with the brown, his lips were purple . . . and there were marks of strangulation upon the lean throat—ever darkening weals made by clutching fingers.

He began to breathe stentoriously and convulsively, inhalation being accompanied by a significant gurgling in the throat. But now my calm was restored in face of a situation which called for professional attention.

I aided my friend's labored respirations by the usual means, setting to work vigorously; so that presently he began to clutch at his inflamed throat which that murderous pressure had threatened to close.

I could hear sounds of movement about the house, showing that not I alone had been awakened by those hoarse screams.

"It's all right, old man," I said, bending over him; "brace up!"

He opened his eyes—they looked bleared and bloodshot—and gave me a quick glance of recognition.

"It's all right, Smith!" I said—"no! don't sit up; lie there for a moment."

I ran across to the dressing-table, whereon I perceived his flask to lie, and mixed him a weak stimulant with which I returned to the bed.

As I bent over him again, my housekeeper appeared in the doorway, pale and wide-eyed.

"There is no occasion for alarm," I said over my shoulder; "Mr. Smith's nerves are overwrought and he was awakened by some disturbing dream. You can return to bed, Mrs. Newsome."

Nayland Smith seemed to experience much difficulty in swallowing the contents of the tumbler which I held to his lips; and, from the way in which he fingered the swollen glands, I could see that his throat, which I had vigorously massaged, was occasioning him great pain. But the danger was past, and already that glassy look was disappearing from his eyes, nor did they protrude so unnaturally.

"God, Petrie!" he whispered, "that was a near shave! I haven't the strength of a kitten!"

"The weariness will pass off," I replied; "there will be no collapse, now. A little more fresh air . . ."

I stood up, glancing at the windows, then back at Smith, who forced a wry smile in answer to my look.

"Couldn't be done, Petrie," he said, huskily.

His words referred to the state of the windows. Although the night was oppressively hot, these were only opened some four inches at top and bottom. Further opening was impossible because of iron brackets screwed firmly into the casements which prevented the windows being raised or lowered further.

It was a precaution adopted after long experience of the servants of Dr. Fu-Manchu.

Now, as I stood looking from the half-strangled man upon the bed to those screwed-up windows, the fact came home to my mind that this precaution had proved futile. I thought of the thing which I had likened to a feather boa; and I looked at the swollen weals made by clutching fingers upon the throat of Nayland Smith.

The bed stood fully four feet from the nearest window.

I suppose the question was written in my face; for, as I turned again to Smith, who, having struggled upright, was still fingering his injured throat ruefully:

"God only knows, Petrie!" he said; "no human arm could have reached me . . ."

For us, the night was ended so far as sleep was concerned. Arrayed in his dressing-gown, Smith sat in the white cane chair in my study with a glass of brandy-and-water beside him, and (despite my official prohibition) with the cracked briar which had sent up its incense in many strange and dark places of the East and which yet survived to perfume these prosy rooms in suburban London, steaming between his teeth. I stood with my elbow resting upon the mantelpiece looking down at him where he sat.

"By God! Petrie," he said, yet again, with his fingers straying gently over the surface of his throat, "that was a narrow shave—a damned narrow shave!"

"Narrower than perhaps you appreciate, old man," I replied. "You were a most unusual shade of blue when I found you . . ."

"I managed," said Smith evenly, "to tear those clutching fingers away for a moment and to give a cry for help. It was only for a moment, though. Petrie! they were fingers of steel—of steel!"

"The bed," I began . . .

"I know that," rapped Smith. "I shouldn't have been sleeping in it, had it been within reach of the window; but, knowing that the doctor avoids noisy methods, I had thought myself fairly safe so long as I made it impossible for any one actually to enter the room . . ."

"I have always insisted, Smith," I cried, "that there was danger! What of poisoned darts? What of the damnable reptiles and insects which form part of the armory of Fu-Manchu?"

"Familiarity breeds contempt, I suppose," he replied. "But as it happened none of those agents was employed. The very menace that I sought to avoid reached me somehow. It would almost seem that Dr. Fu-Manchu deliberately accepted the challenge of those screwed-up windows! Hang it all, Petrie! one cannot sleep in a room hermetically sealed, in weather like this! It's positively Burmese; and although I can stand tropical heat, curiously enough the heat of London gets me down almost immediately."

"The humidity; that's easily understood. But you'll have to put up with it in the future. After nightfall our windows must be closed entirely, Smith."

Nayland Smith knocked out his pipe upon the side of the fireplace. The bowl sizzled furiously, but without delay he stuffed broad-cut mixture into the hot pipe, dropping a liberal quantity upon the carpet during the process. He raised his eyes to me, and his face was very grim.

"Petrie," he said, striking a match on the heel of his slipper, "the resources of Dr. Fu-Manchu are by no means exhausted. Before we quit this room it is up to us to come to a decision upon a certain point." He got his pipe well alight. "What kind of thing, what unnatural, distorted creature, laid hands upon my throat to-night? I owe my life, primarily, to you, old man, but, secondarily, to the fact that I was awakened, just before the attack—by the creature's *coughing*—by its vile, high-pitched *coughing* . . ."

I glanced around at the books upon my shelves. Often enough, following some outrage by the brilliant Chinese doctor whose genius was directed to the discovery of new and unique death agents, we had obtained a clue in those works of a scientific nature which bulk largely in the library of a medical man. There are creatures, there are drugs, which, ordinarily innocuous, may be so employed as to become inimical to human life; and in the distorting of nature, in the disturbing of balances and the diverting of beneficent forces into strange and dangerous channels, Dr. Fu-Manchu excelled. I had known him to enlarge, by artificial culture, a minute species of fungus so as to render it a powerful agent capable of attacking man; his knowledge of venomous insects has

probably never been paralleled in the history of the world; whilst, in the sphere of pure toxicology, he had, and has, no rival; the Borgias were children by comparison. But, look where I would, think how I might, no adequate explanation of this latest outrage seemed possible along normal lines.

"There's the clue," said Nayland Smith, pointing to a little ash-tray upon the table near by. "Follow it if you can."

But I could not.

"As I have explained," continued my friend, "I was awakened by a sound of coughing; then came a death grip on my throat, and instinctively my hands shot out in search of my attacker. I could not reach him; my hands came in contact with nothing palpable. Therefore I clutched at the fingers which were dug into my windpipe, and found them to be small—as the marks show—and *hairy*. I managed to give that first cry for help, then with all my strength I tried to unfasten the grip that was throttling the life out of me. At last I contrived to move one of the hands, and I called out again, though not so loudly. Then both the hands were back again; I was weakening; but I clawed like a madman at the thin, hairy arms of the strangling thing, and with a blood-red mist dancing before my eyes, I seemed to be whirling madly round and round until all became a blank. Evidently I used my nails pretty freely—and there's the trophy."

For the twentieth time, I should think, I carried the ash-tray in my hand and laid it immediately under the table-lamp in order to examine its contents. In the little brass bowl lay a blood-stained fragment of grayish hair attached to a tatter of skin. This fragment of epidermis had an odd bluish tinge, and the attached hair was much darker at the roots than elsewhere. Saving its singular color, it might have been torn from the fore-arm of a very hirsute human; but although my thoughts wandered unfettered, north, south, east and west; although, knowing the resources of Fu-Manchu, I considered all the recognized Mongolian types, and, in quest of hirsute mankind, even roamed far north among the blubber-eating Esquimo; although I glanced at Australasia, at Central Africa, and passed in mental review the dark places of the Congo, nowhere in the known world, nowhere in the history of the human species, could I come upon a type of man answering to the description suggested by our strange clue.

Nayland Smith was watching me curiously as I bent over the little brass ash-tray.

"You are puzzled," he rapped in his short way. "So am I—utterly puzzled. Fu-Manchu's gallery of monstrosities clearly has become reinforced; for even if we identified the type, we should not be in sight of our explanation."

"You mean," I began . . .

"Fully four feet from the window, Petrie, and that window but a few inches open! Look"—he bent forward, resting his chest against the table, and stretched out his hand toward me. "You have a rule there; just measure."

Setting down the ash-tray, I opened out the rule and measured the distance from the further edge of the table to the tips of Smith's fingers.

"Twenty-eight inches—and *I* have a long reach!" snapped Smith, withdrawing his arm and striking a match to relight his pipe. "There's one thing, Petrie, often proposed before, which now we must do without delay. The ivy must be stripped from the walls at the back. It's a pity, but we cannot afford to sacrifice our lives to our sense of the æsthetic. What do you make of the sound like the cracking of a whip?"

"I make nothing of it, Smith," I replied, wearily. "It might have been a thick branch of ivy breaking beneath the weight of a climber."

"Did it sound like it?"

"I must confess that the explanation does not convince me, but I have no better one."

Smith, permitting his pipe to go out, sat staring straight before him, and tugging at the lobe of his left ear.

"The old bewilderment is seizing me," I continued. "At first, when I realized that Dr. Fu-Manchu was back in England, when I realized that an elaborate murder-machine was set up somewhere in London, it seemed unreal, fantastical. Then I met—Kâramanèh! She, whom we thought to be his victim, showed herself again to be his slave. Now, with Weymouth and Scotland Yard at work, the old secret evil is established again in our midst, unaccountably—our lives are menaced—sleep is a danger—every shadow threatens death . . . oh! it is awful."

Smith remained silent; he did not seem to have heard my words. I knew these moods and had learnt that it was useless to seek to interrupt them. With his brows drawn down, and his deep-set eyes staring into space, he sat there gripping his cold pipe so tightly that my own jaw muscles ached sympathetically. No man was better equipped than this gaunt British Commissioner to stand between society and the menace of the Yellow Doctor; I respected his meditations, for, unlike my own, they were informed by an intimate knowledge of the dark and secret things of the East, of that mysterious East out of which Fu-Manchu came, of that jungle of noxious things whose miasma had been wafted Westward with the implacable Chinaman.

I walked quietly from the room, occupied with my own bitter reflections.

Chapter XV

BEWITCHMENT

"You say you have two items of news for me?" said Nayland Smith, looking across the breakfast table to where Inspector Weymouth sat sipping coffee.

"There are two points—yes," replied the Scotland Yard man, whilst Smith paused, eggspoon in hand, and fixed his keen eyes upon the speaker. "The first is this: the headquarters of the Yellow group is no longer in the East End."

"How can you be sure of that?"

"For two reasons. In the first place, that district must now be too hot to hold Dr. Fu-Manchu; in the second place, we have just completed a house-to-house inquiry which has scarcely overlooked a rathole or a rat. That place where you saw Fu-Manchu was visited by some Chinese mandarin; where you, Mr. Smith," and—glancing in my direction—"you, Doctor, were confined for a time—"

"Yes?" snapped Smith, attacking his egg.

"Well," continued the inspector, "it is all deserted, now. There is not the slightest doubt that the Chinaman has fled to some other abode. I am certain of it. My second piece of news will interest you very much, I am sure. You were taken to the establishment of the Chinaman, Shen-Yan, by a certain ex-officer of New York Police—Burke . . ."

"Good God!" cried Smith, looking up with a start; "I thought they had him!"

"So did I," replied Weymouth grimly; "but they haven't! He got away in the confusion following the raid, and has been hiding ever since with a cousin—a nurseryman up Upminster way . . ."

"Hiding?" snapped Smith.

"Exactly—hiding. He has been afraid to stir ever since, and has scarcely shown his nose outside the door. He says he is watched night and day."

"Then how . . ."

"He realized that something must be done," continued the inspector, "and made a break this morning. He is so convinced of this constant surveillance that he came away secretly, hidden under the boxes of a market-wagon. He landed at Covent Garden in the early hours of this morning and came straight away to the Yard."

"What is he afraid of exactly?"

Inspector Weymouth put down his coffee cup and bent forward slightly.

"He knows something," he said in a low voice, "and *they* are aware that he knows it!"

"And what is this he knows?"

Nayland Smith stared eagerly at the detective.

"Every man has his price," replied Weymouth with a smile, "and Burke seems to think that you are a more likely market than the police authorities."

"I see," snapped Smith. "He wants to see *me?*"

"He wants you to go and see *him,*" was the reply. "I think he anticipates that you may make a capture of the person or persons spying upon him."

"Did he give you any particulars?"

"Several. He spoke of a sort of gipsy girl with whom he had a short conversation one day, over the fence which divides his cousin's flower plantations from the lane adjoining."

"Gipsy girl!" I whispered, glancing rapidly at Smith.

"I think you are right, Doctor," said Weymouth with his slow smile; "it was Kâramanèh. She asked him the way to somewhere or other and got him to write it upon a loose page of his notebook, so that she should not forget it."

"You hear that, Petrie?" rapped Smith.

"I hear it," I replied, "but I don't see any special significance in the fact."

"I do!" rapped Smith; "I didn't sit up the greater part of last night thrashing my weary brains for nothing! But I am going to the British Museum to-day, to confirm a certain suspicion." He turned to Weymouth. "Did Burke go back?" he demanded abruptly.

"He returned hidden under the empty boxes," was the reply. "Oh! you never saw

a man in such a funk in all your life!"

"He may have good reasons," I said.

"He *has* good reasons!" replied Nayland Smith grimly; "if that man really possesses information inimical to the safety of Fu-Manchu, he can only escape doom by means of a miracle similar to that which has hitherto protected you and me."

"Burke insists," said Weymouth at this point, "that something comes almost every night after dusk, slinking about the house—it's an old farmhouse, I understand; and on two or three occasions he has been awakened (fortunately for him he is a light sleeper) by sounds of *coughing* immediately outside his window. He is a man who sleeps with a pistol under his pillow, and more than once, on running to the window, he has had a vague glimpse of some creature leaping down from the tiles of the roof, which slopes up to his room, into the flower beds below . . ."

"Creature!" said Smith, his gray eyes ablaze now—"you said *creature!*"

"I used the word deliberately," replied Weymouth, "because Burke seems to have the idea that it goes on all fours."

There was a short and rather strained silence. Then:

"In descending a sloping roof," I suggested, "a human being would probably employ his hands as well as his feet."

"Quite so," agreed the inspector. "I am merely reporting the impression of Burke."

"Has he heard no other sound?" rapped Smith; "one like the cracking of dry branches, for instance?"

"He made no mention of it," replied Weymouth, staring.

"And what is the plan?"

"One of his cousin's vans," said Weymouth, with his slight smile, "has remained behind at Covent Garden and will return late this afternoon. I propose that you and I, Mr. Smith, imitate Burke and ride down to Upminster under the empty boxes!"

Nayland Smith stood up, leaving his breakfast half finished, and began to wander up and down the room, reflectively tugging at his ear. Then he began to fumble in the pockets of his dressing-gown and finally produced the inevitable pipe, dilapidated pouch, and box of safety matches. He began to load the much-charred agent of reflection.

"Do I understand that Burke is actually too afraid to go out openly even in daylight?" he asked suddenly.

"He has not hitherto left his cousin's plantations at all," replied Weymouth. "He seems to think that openly to communicate with the authorities, or with you, would be to seal his death warrant."

"He's right," snapped Smith.

"Therefore he came and returned secretly," continued the inspector; "and if we are to do any good, obviously we must adopt similar precautions. The market wagon, loaded in such a way as to leave ample space in the interior for us, will be drawn up outside the office of Messrs. Pike and Pike, in Covent Garden, until about five o'clock this afternoon. At, say, half past four, I propose that we meet there and embark upon the journey."

The speaker glanced in my direction interrogatively.

"Include me in the program," I said. "Will there be room in the wagon?"

"Certainly," was the reply; "it is most commodious, but I cannot guarantee its comfort."

Nayland Smith promenaded the room, unceasingly, and presently he walked out altogether, only to return ere the inspector and I had had time to exchange more than a glance of surprise, carrying a brass ashtray. He placed this on a corner of the breakfast table before Weymouth.

"Ever seen anything like that?" he inquired.

The inspector examined the gruesome relic with obvious curiosity, turning it over with the tip of his little finger and manifesting considerable repugnance in touching it at all. Smith and I watched him in silence, and, finally, placing the tray again upon the table, he looked up in a puzzled way.

"It's something like the skin of a water rat," he said.

Nayland Smith stared at him fixedly.

"A water rat? Now that you come to mention it, I perceive a certain resemblance—yes. But"—he had been wearing a silk scarf about his throat and now he unwrapped it—"did you ever see a water rat that could make marks like these?"

Weymouth started to his feet with some muttered exclamation.

"What is this?" he cried. "When did it happen, and how?"

In his own terse fashion, Nayland Smith related the happenings of the night. At the conclusion of the story:

"By heaven!" whispered Weymouth, "the thing on the roof—the coughing thing that goes on all fours, seen by Burke . . ."

"My own idea exactly!" cried Smith . . .

"Fu-Manchu," I said excitedly, "has brought some new, some dreadful creature, from Burma . . ."

"No, Petrie," snapped Smith, turning upon me suddenly. "Not from Burma—from Abyssinia."

That day was destined to be an eventful one; a day never to be forgotten by any of us concerned in those happenings which I have to record. Early in the morning Nayland Smith set off for the British Museum to pursue his mysterious investigations, and having performed my brief professional round (for, as Nayland Smith had remarked on one occasion, this was a beastly healthy district), I found, having made the necessary arrangements, that, with over three hours to spare, I had nothing to occupy my time until the appointment in Covent Garden Market. My lonely lunch completed, a restless fit seized me, and I felt unable to remain longer in the house. Inspired by this restlessness, I attired myself for the adventure of the evening, not neglecting to place a pistol in my pocket, and, walking to the neighboring Tube station, I booked to Charing Cross, and presently found myself rambling aimlessly along the crowded streets. Led on by what link of memory I know not, I presently drifted into New Oxford Street, and looked up with a start—to learn that I stood before the shop of a second-hand bookseller where once two years before I had met Kâramanèh.

The thoughts conjured up at that moment were almost too bitter to be borne, and without so much as glancing at the books displayed for sale, I crossed the roadway, entered Museum Street, and, rather in order to distract my mind than because I contemplated any purchase, began to examine the Oriental pottery, Egyptian statuettes, Indian armor, and other curios, displayed in the window of an antique dealer.

But, strive as I would to concentrate my mind upon the objects in the window, my memories persistently haunted me, and haunted me to the exclusion even of the actualities. The crowds thronging the pavement, the traffic in New Oxford Street, swept past unheeded; my eyes saw nothing of pot nor statuette, but only met, in a misty imaginative world, the glance of two other eyes—the dark and beautiful eyes of Kâramanèh. In the exquisite tinting of a Chinese vase dimly perceptible in the background of the shop, I perceived only the blushing cheeks of Kâramanèh; her face rose up, a taunting phantom, from out of the darkness between a hideous, gilded idol and an Indian sandalwood screen.

I strove to dispel this obsessing thought, resolutely fixing my attention upon a tall Etruscan vase in the corner of the window, near to the shop door. Was I losing my senses indeed? A doubt of my own sanity momentarily possessed me. For, struggle as I would to dispel the illusion—there, looking out at me over that ancient piece of pottery, was the bewitching face of the slave-girl!

Probably I was glaring madly, and possibly I attracted the notice of the passers-by; but of this I cannot be certain, for all my attention was centered upon that phantasmal face, with the cloudy hair, slightly parted red lips, and the brilliant dark eyes which looked into mine out of the shadows of the shop.

It was bewildering—it was uncanny; for, delusion or verity, the glamour prevailed. I exerted a geat mental effort, stepped to the door, turned the handle, and entered the shop with as great a show of composure as I could muster.

A curtain draped in a little door at the back of one counter swayed slightly, with no greater violence than may have been occasioned by the draught. But I fixed my eyes upon this swaying curtain almost fiercely . . . as an impassive half-caste of some kind who appeared to be a strange cross between a Græco-Hebrew and a Japanese, entered and quite unemotionally faced me, with a slight bow.

So wholly unexpected was this apparition that I started back.

"Can I show you anything, sir?" inquired the new arrival, with a second slight inclination of the head.

I looked at him for a moment in silence. Then:

"I thought I saw a lady of my acquaintance here a moment ago," I said. "Was I mistaken?"

"Quite mistaken, sir," replied the shopman, raising his black eyebrows ever so slightly; "a mistake possibly due to a reflection in the window. Will you take a look around now that you are here?"

"Thank you," I replied, staring him hard in the face; "at some other time."

I turned and quitted the shop abruptly.

Either I was mad, or Kâramanèh was concealed somewhere therein.

However, realizing my helplessness in the matter, I contented myself with making a mental note of the name which appeared above the establishment—J. Salaman—and walked on, my mind in a chaotic condition and my heart beating with unusual rapidity.

Chapter XVI

THE QUESTING HANDS

Within my view, from the corner of the room where I sat in deepest shadow, through the partly opened window (it was screwed, like our own) were rows of glass-houses gleaming in the moonlight, and, beyond them, orderly ranks of flower-beds extending into a blue haze of distance. By reason of the moon's position, no light entered the room, but my eyes, from long watching, were grown familiar with the darkness, and I could see Burke quite clearly as he lay in the bed between my post and the window. I seemed to be back again in those days of the troubled past when first Nayland Smith and I had come to grips with the servants of Dr. Fu-Manchu. A more peaceful scene than this flower-planted corner of Essex it would be difficult to imagine; but, either because of my knowledge that its peace was chimerical, or because of that outflung consciousness of danger which, actually, or in my imagination, preceded the coming of the Chinaman's agents, to my seeming the silence throbbed electrically and the night was laden with stilly omens.

Already cramped by my journey in the market-cart, I found it difficult to remain very long in any one position. What information had Burke to sell? He had refused, for some reason, to discuss the matter that evening, and now, enacting the part allotted him by Nayland Smith, he feigned sleep consistently, although at intervals he would whisper to me his doubts and fears.

All the chances were in our favor to-night; for whilst I could not doubt that Dr. Fu-Manchu was set upon the removal of the ex-officer of New York police, neither could I doubt that our presence in the farm was unknown to the agents of the Chinaman. According to Burke, constant attempts had been made to achieve Fu-Manchu's purpose, and had only been frustrated by his (Burke's) wakefulness. There was every probability that another attempt would be made to-night.

Any one who has been forced by circumstance to undertake such a vigil as this will be familiar with the marked changes (corresponding with phases of the earth's movement) which take place in the atmosphere, at midnight, at two o'clock, and again at four o'clock. During those four hours falls a period wherein all life is at its lowest ebb, and every physician is aware that there is a greater likelihood of a patient's passing between midnight and four A. M., than at any other period during the cycle of the hours.

To-night I became specially aware of this lowering of vitality, and now, with the night at that darkest phase which precedes the dawn, an indescribable dread, such as I had known before in my dealings with the Chinaman, assailed me, when I was least prepared to combat it. The stillness was intense. Then:

"*Here it is!*" whispered Burke from the bed.

The chill at the very center of my being, which but corresponded with the chill of all surrounding nature at that hour, became intensified, keener, at the whispered words.

I rose stealthily out of my chair, and from my nest of shadows watched—watched intently, the bright oblong of the window . . .

Without the slightest heralding sound— a black silhouette crept up against the pane . . . the silhouette of a small, malformed head, a dog-like head, deep-set in square shoulders. Malignant eyes peered intently in. Higher it arose—that wicked head— against the window, then crouched down on the sill and became less sharply defined as the creature stooped to the opening below. There was a faint sound of sniffing.

Judging from the stark horror which I experienced, myself, I doubted, now, if Burke could sustain the rôle allotted him. In beneath the slightly raised window came a hand, perceptible to me despite the darkness of the room. It seemed to project from the black silhouette outside the pane, to be thrust forward—and forward—and forward . . . that small hand with the outstretched fingers.

The unknown possesses unique terrors; and since I was unable to conceive what manner of thing this could be, which, extending its incredibly long arms, now sought the throat of the man upon the bed, I tasted of that sort of terror which ordinarily one knows only in dreams.

"Quick, sir—*Quick!*" screamed Burke,

starting up from the pillow.

The questing hands had reached his throat!

Choking down an urgent dread that I had of touching the thing which had reached through the window to kill the sleeper, I sprang across the room and grasped the rigid, hairy forearms.

Heavens! Never have I felt such muscles, such tendons, as those beneath the hirsute skin! They seemed to be of steel wire, and with a sudden frightful sense of impotence, I realized that I was as powerless as a child to relax that strangle-hold. Burke was making the most frightful sounds and quite obviously was being asphyxiated before my eyes!

"Smith!" I cried, "Smith! Help! *help!* for God's sake!"

Despite the confusion of my mind I became aware of sounds outside and below me. Twice the thing at the window coughed; there was an incessant, lashlike cracking, then some shouted words which I was unable to make out; and finally the staccato report of a pistol.

Snarling like that of a wild beast came from the creature with the hairy arms, together with renewed coughing. But the steel grip relaxed not one iota. I realized two things: the first, that in my terror at the suddenness of the attack I had omitted to act as prearranged: the second, that I had discredited the strength of the visitant, whilst Smith had foreseen it.

Desisting in my vain endeavor to pit my strength against that of the nameless thing, I sprang back across the room and took up the weapon which had been left in my charge earlier in the night, but which I had been unable to believe it would be necessary to employ. This was a sharp and heavy axe, which Nayland Smith, when I had met him in Covent Garden, had brought with him, to the great amazement of Weymouth and myself.

As I leaped back to the window and uplifted this primitive weapon, a second shot sounded from below, and more fierce snarling, coughing, and guttural mutterings assailed my ears from beyond the pane.

Lifting the heavy blade, I brought it down with all my strength upon the nearer of those hairy arms where it crossed the window ledge, severing muscle, tendon and bone as easily as a knife might cut cheese. . . .

A shriek—a shriek neither human nor animal, but gruesomely compounded of both— followed . . . and merged into a choking cough. Like a flash the other shaggy arm was withdrawn, and some vaguely-seen body went rolling down the sloping red tiles and crashed on to the ground beneath.

With a second piercing shriek, louder than that recently uttered by Burke, wailing through the night from somewhere below, I turned desperately to the man on the bed, who now was become significantly silent. A candle, with matches, stood upon a table hard by, and, my fingers far from steady, I set about obtaining a light. This accomplished, I stood the candle upon the little chest-of-drawers and returned to Burke's side.

"Merciful God!" I cried.

Of all the pictures which remain in my memory, some of them dark enough, I can find none more horrible than that which now confronted me in the dim candle-light. Burke lay crosswise on the bed, his head thrown back and sagging; one rigid hand he held in the air, and with the other grasped the hairy forearm which I had severed with the ax; for, in a death-grip, the dead fingers were still fastened, vise-like, at his throat.

His face was nearly black, and his eyes projected from their sockets horribly. Mastering my repugnance, I seized the hideous piece of bleeding anatomy and strove to release it. It defied all my efforts; in death it was as implacable as in life. I took a knife from my pocket, and, tendon by tendon, cut away that uncanny grip from Burke's throat . . .

But my labor was in vain. Burke was dead!

I think I failed to realize this for some time. My clothes were sticking clammily to my body; I was bathed in perspiration, and, shaking furiously, I clutched at the edge of the window, avoiding the bloody patch upon the ledge, and looked out over the roofs to where, in the more distant plantations, I could hear excited voices. What had been the meaning of that scream which I had heard but to which in my frantic state of mind I had paid comparatively little attention?

There was a great stirring all about me.

"Smith!" I cried from the window; "Smith, for mercy's sake where are you?"

Footsteps came racing up the stairs. Behind me the door burst open and Nayland Smith stumbled into the room.

"God!" he said, and started back in the doorway.

"Have you got it, Smith?" I demanded hoarsely. "In sanity's name what is it—*what is it?*"

"Come downstairs," replied Smith quietly, "and see for yourself." He turned his head aside from the bed.

Very unsteadily I followed him down the stairs and through the rambling old house out into the stone-paved courtyard. There were figures moving at the end of a long alleyway between the glass houses, and one, carrying a lantern, stooped over something which lay upon the ground.

"That's Burke's cousin with the lantern," whispered Smith in my ear; "don't tell him yet."

I nodded, and we hurried up to join the group. I found myself looking down at one of those thick-set Burmans whom I always associated with Fu-Manchu's activities. He lay quite flat, face downward; but the back of his head was a shapeless blood-clotted mass, and a heavy stock-whip, the butt end ghastly because of the blood and hair which clung to it, lay beside him. I started back appalled as Smith caught my arm.

"*It* turned on its keeper!" he hissed in my ear. "I wounded it twice from below, and you severed one arm; in its insensate fury, its unreasoning malignity, it returned—and there lies its second victim . . ."

"Then . . ."

"It's gone, Petrie! It has the strength of four men even now. Look!"

He stooped, and from the clenched left hand of the dead Burman, extracted a piece of paper and opened it.

"Hold the lantern a moment," he said.

In the yellow light he glanced at the scrap of paper.

"As I expected—a leaf of Burke's note-book; it worked by *scent*." He turned to me with an odd expression in his gray eyes. "I wonder what piece of *my* personal property Fu-Manchu has pilfered," he said, "in order to enable it to sleuth *me?*"

He met the gaze of the man holding the lantern.

"Perhaps you had better return to the house," he said, looking him squarely in the eyes.

The other's face blanched.

"You don't mean, sir—you don't mean . . ."

"Brace up!" said Smith, laying his hand upon his shoulder. "Remember—he chose to play with fire!"

One wild look the man cast from Smith to me, then went off, staggering, toward the farm.

"Smith," I began . . .

He turned to me with an impatient gesture.

"Weymouth has driven into Upminster," he snapped; "and the whole district will be scoured before morning. They probably motored here, but the sounds of the shots will have enabled whoever was with the car to make good his escape. And—exhausted from loss of blood, its capture is only a matter of time, Petrie."

Chapter XVII

ONE DAY IN RANGOON

Nayland Smith returned from the telephone. Nearly twenty-four hours had elapsed since the awful death of Burke.

"No news, Petrie," he said, shortly. "It must have crept into some inaccessible hole to die."

I glanced up from my notes. Smith settled into the white cane armchair, and began to surround himself with clouds of aromatic smoke. I took up a half-sheet of foolscap covered with penciled writing in my friend's cramped characters, and transcribed the following, in order to complete my account of the latest Fu-Manchu outrage:

"The Amharûn, a Semitic tribe allied to the Falashas, who have been settled for many generations in the southern province of Shoa (Abyssinia) have been regarded as unclean and outcast, apparently since the days of Menelek—son of Suleyman and the Queen of Sheba—from whom they claim descent. Apart from their custom of eating meat cut from living beasts, they are accursed because of their alleged association with the *Cynocephalus hamadryas* (Sacred Baboon). I, myself, was taken to a hut on the banks of the Hawash and shown a creature . . . whose predominant trait was an unreasoning malignity toward . . . and a ferocious tenderness for the society of its furry brethren. Its powers of *scent* were fully equal to those of a bloodhound, whilst its abnormally long forearms possessed incredible strength . . . a *Cynocephalyte* such as this, contracts phthisis even in the more northern provinces of Abyssinia . . ."

"You have not explained to me, Smith," I said, having completed this note, "how you got in touch with Fu-Manchu; how you learnt that he was not dead, as we had supposed, but living—active."

Nayland Smith stood up and fixed his steely eyes upon me with an indefinable expression in them. Then:

"No," he replied; "I haven't. Do you wish to know?"

"Certainly," I said with surprise; "is there any reason why I should not?"

"There is no real reason," said Smith; "or"—staring at me very hard—"I hope there is no real reason."

"What do you mean?"

"Well"—he grabbed up his pipe from the table and began furiously to load it—"I blundered upon the truth one day in Rangoon. I was walking out of a house which I occupied there for a time, and as I swung around the corner into the main street, I ran into—literally ran into . . ."

Again he hesitated oddly; then closed up his pouch and tossed it into the cane chair. He struck a match.

"I ran into Kâramanèh," he continued abruptly, and began to puff away at his pipe, filling the air with clouds of tobacco smoke.

I caught my breath. This was the reason why he had kept me so long in ignorance of the story. He knew of my hopeless, uncrushable sentiments toward the gloriously beautiful but utterly hypocritical and evil Eastern girl who was perhaps the most dangerous of all Dr. Fu-Manchu's servants; for the power of her loveliness was magical, as I knew to my cost.

"What did you do?" I asked quietly, my fingers drumming upon the table.

"Naturally enough," continued Smith, "with a cry of recognition I held out both my hands to her, gladly. I welcomed her as a dear friend regained; I thought of the joy with which *you* would learn that I had found the missing one; I thought how you would be in Rangoon just as quickly as the fastest steamer could get you there . . ."

"Well?"

"Kâramanèh started back and treated me to a glance of absolute animosity. No recognition was there, and no friendliness—only a sort of scornful anger."

He shrugged his shoulders and began to walk up and down the room.

"I do not know what *you* would have done in the circumstances, Petrie, but I—"

"Yes?"

"I dealt with the situation rather promptly, I think. I simply picked her up without another word, right there in the public street, and raced back into the house, with her kicking and fighting like a little demon! She did not shriek or do anything of that kind, but fought silently like a vicious wild animal. Oh! I had some scars, I assure you; but I carried her up into my office, which fortunately was empty at the time, plumped her down in a chair, and stood looking at her."

"Go on," I said rather hollowly; "what next?"

"She glared at me with those wonderful eyes, an expression of implacable hatred in them! Remembering all that we had done for her; remembering our former friendship; above all, remembering *you*—this look of hers almost made me shiver. She was dressed very smartly in European fashion, and the whole thing had been so sudden that as I stood looking at her I half expected to wake up presently and find it all a day-dream. But it was real—as real as her enmity. I felt the need for reflection, and having vainly endeavored to draw her into conversation, and elicited no other answer than this glare of hatred—I left her there, going out and locking the door behind me."

"Very high-handed?"

"A commissioner has certain privileges, Petrie; and any action I might choose to take was not likely to be questioned. There was only one window to the office, and it was fully twenty feet above the level; it overlooked a narrow street off the main thoroughfare (I think I have explained that the house stood on a corner) so I did not fear her escaping. I had an important engagement which I had been on my way to fulfil when the encounter took place, and now, with a word to my native servant—who chanced to be downstairs—I hurried off."

Smith's pipe had gone out as usual, and he proceeded to relight it, whilst, with my eyes lowered, I continued to drum upon the table.

"This boy took her some tea later in the afternoon," he continued, "and apparently found her in a more placid frame of mind. I returned immediately after dusk, and he reported that when last he had looked in, about half an hour earlier, she had been seated in an armchair reading a newspaper (I may mention that everything of value in the office was securely locked up!) I was determined upon a certain course by this time, and I went slowly upstairs, unlocked the door, and walked into the darkened office. I turned up the light . . . the place was empty!"

"Empty!"

"The window was open, and the bird flown! Oh! it was not so simple a flight—as you would realize if you knew the place. The street, which the window overlooked, was bounded by a blank wall, on the opposite side, for thirty or forty yards along; and as we had been having heavy rains, it was full of glutinous mud. Furthermore, the boy whom I had left in charge had been sitting in the doorway immediately below the office window watching for my return ever since his last visit to the room above . . ."

"She must have bribed him," I said bitterly—"or corrupted him with her infernal blandishments."

"I'll swear she did not," rapped Smith decisively. "I know my man, and I'll swear she did not. There were no marks in the mud of the road to show that a ladder had been placed there; moreover, nothing of the kind could have been attempted whilst the boy was sitting in the doorway; that was evident. In short, she did not descend into the roadway and did not come out by the door . . ."

"Was there a gallery outside the window?"

"No; it was impossible to climb to right or left of the window or up on to the roof. I convinced myself of that."

"But, my dear man!" I cried, "you are eliminating every natural mode of egress! Nothing remains but flight."

"I am aware, Petrie, that nothing remains but flight; in other words I have never to this day understood how she quitted the room. I only know that she did."

"And then?"

"I saw in this incredible escape the cunning hand of Dr. Fu-Manchu—saw it at once. Peace was ended; and I set to work along certain channels without delay. In this manner I got on the track at last, and learned, beyond the possibility of doubt, that the Chinese doctor lived—nay! was actually on his way to Europe again!"

There followed a short silence. Then:

"I suppose it's a mystery that will be cleared up some day," concluded Smith; "but to date the riddle remains intact." He glanced at the clock. "I have an appointment with Weymouth; therefore, leaving you to the task of solving this problem which thus far has defied my own efforts, I will get along."

He read a query in my glance.

"Oh! I shall not be late," he added; "I think I may venture out alone on this occasion without personal danger."

Nayland Smith went upstairs to dress,

leaving me seated at my writing table, deep in thought. My notes upon the renewed activity of Dr. Fu-Manchu were stacked at my left hand, and, opening a new writing block, I commenced to add to them particulars of this surprising event in Rangoon which properly marked the opening of the Chinaman's second campaign. Smith looked in at the door on his way out, but seeing me thus engaged, did not disturb me.

I think I have made it sufficiently evident in these records that my practice was not an extensive one, and my hour for receiving patients arrived and passed with only two professional interruptions.

My task concluded, I glanced at the clock, and determined to devote the remainder of the evening to a little private investigation of my own. From Nayland Smith I had preserved the matter a secret, largely because I feared his ridicule; but I had by no means forgotten that I had seen, or had strongly imagined that I had seen, Kâramanèh—that beautiful anomaly, who (in modern London) asserted herself to be a slave—in the shop of an antique dealer not a hundred yards from the British Museum!

A theory was forming in my brain, which I was burningly anxious to put to the test. I remembered how, two years before, I had met Kâramanèh near to this same spot; and I had heard Inspector Weymouth assert positively that Fu-Manchu's headquarters were no longer in the East End, as of yore. There seemed to me to be a distinct probability that a suitable center had been established for his reception in this place, so much less likely to be suspected by the authorities. Perhaps I attached too great a value to what may have been a delusion; perhaps my theory rested upon no more solid foundation than the belief that I had seen Kâramanèh in the shop of the curio dealer. If her appearance there should prove to have been phantasmal, the structure of my theory would be shattered at its base. To-night I should test my premises, and upon the result of my investigations determine my future action.

Chapter XVIII

THE SILVER BUDDHA

Museum Street certainly did not seem a likely spot for Dr. Fu-Manchu to establish himself, yet, unless my imagination had strangely deceived me, from the window of the antique dealer who traded under the name of J. Salaman, those wonderful eyes of Kâramanèh, like the velvet midnight of the Orient, had looked out at me.

As I paced slowly along the pavement toward that lighted window, my heart was beating far from normally, and I cursed the folly which, in spite of all, refused to die, but lingered on, poisoning my life. Comparative quiet reigned in Museum Street, at no time a busy thoroughfare, and, excepting another shop at the Museum end, commercial activities had ceased there. The door of a block of residential chambers almost immediately opposite to the shop which was my objective, threw out a beam of light across the pavement, but not more than two or three people were visible upon either side of the street.

I turned the knob of the door and entered the shop.

The same dark and immobile individual whom I had seen before, and whose nationality defied conjecture, came out from the curtained doorway at the back to greet me.

"Good evening, sir," he said monotonously, with a slight inclination of the head; "is there anything which you desire to inspect?"

"I merely wish to take a look around," I replied. "I have no particular item in view."

The shop man inclined his head again, swept a yellow hand comprehensively about, as if to include the entire stock, and seated himself on a chair behind the counter.

I lighted a cigarette with such an air of nonchalance as I could summon to the operation, and began casually to inspect the varied objects of interest loading the shelves and tables about me. I am bound to confess that I retain no one definite impression of this tour. Vases I handled, statuettes, Egyptian scarabs, bead necklaces, illuminated missals, portfolios of old prints, jade ornaments, bronzes, fragments of rare lace, early printed books, Assyrian tablets, daggers, Roman rings, and a hundred other curiosities, leisurely, and I trust with apparent interest, yet without forming the slightest impression respecting any one of them.

Probably I employed myself in this way for half an hour or more, and whilst my hands busied themselves among the stock of J. Salaman, my mind was occupied entirely elsewhere. Furtively I was studying the shopman himself, a human presentment of a Chinese idol; I was listening and watching; especially I was watching the curtained doorway at the back of the shop.

"We close at about this time, sir," the man interrupted me, speaking in the emotionless, monotonous voice which I had noted before.

I replaced upon the glass counter a little Sekhet boat, carved in wood and highly colored, and glanced up with a start. Truly my methods were amateurish; I had learnt nothing; I was unlikely to learn anything. I wondered how Nayland Smith would have conducted such an inquiry, and I racked my brains for some means of penetrating into the recesses of the establishment. Indeed, I had been seeking such a plan for the past half an hour, but my mind had proved incapable of suggesting one.

Why I did not admit failure I cannot imagine, but, instead, I began to tax my brains anew for some means of gaining further time; and, as I looked about the place, the shopman very patiently awaiting my departure, I observed an open case at the back of the counter. The three lower shelves were empty, but upon the fourth shelf squatted a silver Buddha.

"I should like to examine the silver image yonder," I said; "what price are you asking for it?"

"It is not for sale, sir," replied the man, with a greater show of animation than he had yet exhibited.

"Not for sale!" I said, my eyes ever seeking the curtained doorway; "how's that?"

"It is sold."

"Well, even so, there can be no objection to my examining it?"

"It is not for sale, sir."

Such a rebuff from a tradesman would have been more than sufficient to call for a sharp retort at any other time, but now it excited the strangest suspicions. The street outside looked comparatively deserted, and prompted, primarily, by an emotion which I did not pause to analyze, I adopted a singular measure; without doubt I relied upon the unusual powers vested in Nayland Smith to absolve me in the event of error. I made as if to go out into the street, then turned, leaped past the shopman, ran behind the counter, and grasped at the silver Buddha!

That I was likely to be arrested for attempted larceny I cared not; the idea that Kâramanèh was concealed somewhere in the building ruled absolutely, and a theory respecting this silver image had taken possession of my mind. Exactly what I expected to happen at that moment I cannot say, but what actually happened was far more startling than anything I could have imagined.

At the instant that I grasped the figure I realized that it was attached to the woodwork; in the next I knew that it was a handle . . . as I tried to pull it toward me I became aware that this handle was the handle of a door. For that door swung open before me, and I found myself at the foot of a flight of heavily carpeted stairs.

Anxious as I had been to proceed a moment before, I was now trebly anxious to retire, and for this reason: on the bottom step of the stair, facing me, *stood Dr. Fu-Manchu!*

Chapter XIX

DR. FU-MANCHU'S LABORATORY

I cannot conceive that any ordinary mortal ever attained to anything like an intimacy with Dr. Fu-Manchu; I cannot believe that any man could ever grow used to his presence, could ever cease to fear him. I suppose I had set eyes upon Fu-Manchu some five or six times prior to this occasion, and now he was dressed in the manner which I always associated with him, probably because it was thus I first saw him. He wore a plain yellow robe, and, with his pointed chin resting upon his bosom, he looked down at me, revealing a great expanse of the marvelous brow with its sparse, neutral-colored hair.

Never in my experience have I known such *force* to dwell in the glance of any human eye as dwelt in that of this uncanny being. His singular affliction (if affliction it were), the film or slight membrane which sometimes obscured the oblique eyes, was particularly evident at the moment that I crossed the threshold, but now, as I looked up at Dr. Fu-Manchu, it lifted—revealing the eyes in all their emerald greenness.

The idea of physical attack upon this incredible being seemed childish—inadequate. But, following that first instant of stupefaction, I forced myself to advance upon him.

A dull, crushing blow descended on the top of my skull, and I became oblivious of all things.

My return to consciousness was accompanied by tremendous pains in my head, whereby, from previous experience, I knew that a sandbag had been used against me by some one in the shop, presumably by the immobile shopman. This awakening was accompanied by none of those hazy doubts respecting previous events and present surroundings which are the usual symptoms of revival from sudden unconsciousness; even before I opened my eyes, before I had more than a partial command of my senses, I knew that, with my wrists handcuffed behind me, I lay in a room which was also occupied by Dr. Fu-Manchu. This absolute certainty of the Chinaman's presence was evidenced, not by my senses, but only by an inner consciousness, and the same that always awoke into life at the approach not only of Fu-Manchu in person but of certain of his uncanny servants.

A faint perfume hung in the air about me; I do not mean that of any essence or of any incense, but rather the smell which is suffused by Oriental furniture, by Oriental draperies; the indefinable but unmistakable perfume of the East.

Thus, London has a distinct smell of its own, and so has Paris, whilst the difference between Marseilles and Suez, for instance, is even more marked. Now, the atmosphere surrounding me was Eastern, but not of the East that I knew; rather it was Far Eastern. Perhaps I do not make myself very clear, but to me there was a mysterious significance in that perfumed atmosphere. I opened my eyes.

I lay upon a long low settee, in a fairly large room which was furnished as I had anticipated in an absolutely Oriental fashion. The two windows were so screened as to have lost, from the interior point of view, all resemblance to European windows, and the whole structure of the room had been altered in conformity, bearing out my idea that the place had been prepared for Fu-Manchu's reception some time before his actual return. I doubt if, East or West, a duplicate of that singular apartment could be found.

The end in which I lay, was, as I have said, typical of an Eastern house, and a large, ornate lantern hung from the ceiling almost directly above me. The further end of the room was occupied by tall cases, some of them containing books, but the majority filled with scientific paraphernalia; rows of flasks and jars, frames of test-tubes, retorts, scales, and other objects of the laboratory. At a large and very finely carved table sat Dr. Fu-Manchu, a yellow and faded volume open before

him, and some dark red fluid, almost like blood, bubbling in a test-tube which he held over the flame of a Bunsen-burner.

The enormously long nail of his right index finger rested upon the opened page of the book to which he seemed constantly to refer, dividing his attention between the volume, the contents of the test-tube, and the progress of a second experiment, or possibly a part of the same, which was taking place upon another corner of the littered table.

A huge glass retort (the bulb was fully two feet in diameter), fitted with a Liebig's Condenser, rested in a metal frame, and within the bulb, floating in an oily substance, was a fungus some six inches high, shaped like a toadstool, but of a brilliant and venomous orange color. Three flat tubes of light were so arranged as to cast violet rays upward into the retort, and the receiver, wherein condensed the product of this strange experiment, contained some drops of a red fluid which may have been identical with that boiling in the test-tube.

These things I perceived at a glance: then the filmy eyes of Dr. Fu-Manchu were raised from the book, turned in my direction, and all else was forgotten.

"I regret," came the sibilant voice, "that unpleasant measures were necessary, but hesitation would have been fatal. I trust, Dr. Petrie, that you suffer no inconvenience?"

To this speech no reply was possible, and I attempted none.

"You have long been aware of my esteem for your acquirements," continued the Chinaman, his voice occasionally touching deep guttural notes, "and you will appreciate the pleasure which this visit affords me. I kneel at the feet of my silver Buddha. I look to you, when you shall have overcome your prejudices—due to ignorance of my true motives—to assist me in establishing that intellectual control which is destined to be the new World Force. I bear you no malice for your ancient enmity, and even now"—he waved one yellow hand toward the retort— "I am conducting an experiment designed to convert you from your misunderstanding, and to adjust your perspective."

Quite unemotionally he spoke, then turned again to his book, his test-tube and retort, in the most matter-of-fact way imaginable. I do not think the most frenzied outburst on his part, the most fiendish threats could have produced such effect upon me as those cold and carefully calculated words, spoken in that unique voice which rang about the room sibilantly. In its tones, in the glance of the green eyes, in the very pose of the gaunt, high-shouldered body, there was power—force.

I counted myself lost, and in view of the doctor's words, studied the progress of the experiment with frightful interest. But a few moments sufficed in which to realize that, for all my training, I knew as little of chemistry—of chemistry as understood by this man's genius—as a junior student in surgery knows of trephining. The process in operation was a complete mystery to me; the means and the end alike incomprehensible.

Thus, in the heavy silence of that room, a silence only broken by the regular bubbling from the test-tube, I found my attention straying from the table to the other objects surrounding it; and at one of them my gaze stopped and remained chained with horror.

It was a glass jar, some five feet in height and filled with viscous fluid of a light amber color. Out from this peered a hideous, dog-like face, low browed, with pointed ears and a nose almost hoggishly flat. By the death-grin of the face the gleaming fangs were revealed; and the body, the long yellow-gray body, rested, or seemed to rest, upon short, malformed legs, whilst one long limp arm, the right, hung down straightly in the preservative. The left arm had been severed above the elbow.

Fu-Manchu, finding his experiment to be proceeding favorably, lifted his eyes to me again.

"You are interested in my poor *Cynocephalyte?*" he said; and his eyes were filmed like the eyes of one afflicted with cataract. "He was a devoted servant, Dr. Petrie, but the lower influences in his genealogy sometimes conquered. Then he got out of hand; and at last he was so ungrateful toward those who had educated him, that, in one of those paroxysms of his, he attacked and killed a most faithful Burman, one of my oldest followers."

Fu-Manchu returned to his experiment. Not the slightest emotion had he exhibited thus far, but had chatted with me as any other scientist might chat with a friend who casually visits his laboratory. The horror of the thing was playing havoc with my own composure, however. There I lay, fettered, in the same room with this man whose existence was a menace to the entire white race, whilst placidly he pursued an experiment

designed, if his own words were believable, to cut me off from my kind—to wreak some change, psychological or physiological I knew not; to place me, it might be, upon a level with such brute-things as that which now hung, half floating, in the glass jar!

Something I knew of the history of that ghastly specimen, that thing neither man nor ape; for within my own knowledge had it not attempted the life of Nayland Smith, and was it not *I* who, with an ax, had maimed it in the instant of one of its last slayings?

Of these things Dr. Fu-Manchu was well aware, so that his placid speech was doubly, trebly horrible to my ears. I sought, furtively, to move my arms, only to realize that, as I had anticipated, the handcuffs were chained to a ring in the wall behind me. The establishments of Dr. Fu-Manchu were always well provided with such contrivances as these.

I uttered a short, harsh laugh. Fu-Manchu stood up slowly from the table, and, placing the test-tube in a rack, stood the latter carefully upon a shelf at his side.

"I am happy to find you in such good humor," he said softly. "Other affairs call me; and, in my absence, that profound knowledge of chemistry, of which I have had evidence in the past, will enable you to follow with intelligent interest the action of these violet rays upon this exceptionally fine specimen of Siberian *amanita muscaria*. At some future time, possibly when you are my guest in China—which country I am now making arrangements for you to visit—I shall discuss with you some lesser-known properties of this species; and I may say that one of your first tasks when you commence your duties as assistant in my laboratory in Kiang-su, will be to conduct a series of twelve experiments, which I have outlined, into other potentialities of this unique fungus."

He walked quietly to a curtained doorway, with his cat-like yet awkward gait, lifted the drapery, and, with a slight nod in my direction, went out of the room.

Chapter XX

THE CROSS BAR

How long I lay there alone I had no means of computing. My mind was busy with many matters, but principally concerned with my fate in the immediate future. That Dr. Fu-

Manchu entertained for me a singular kind of regard, I had had evidence before. He had formed the erroneous opinion that I was an advanced scientist who could be of use to him in his experiments and I was aware that he cherished a project of transporting me to some place in China where his principal laboratory was situated. Respecting the means which he proposed to employ, I was unlikely to forget that this man, who had penetrated further along certain by-ways of science than seemed humanly possible, undoubtedly was master of a process for producing artificial catalepsy. It was my lot, then, to be packed in a chest (to all intents and purposes a dead man for the time being) and despatched to the interior of China!

What a fool I had been. To think that I had learned nothing from my long and dreadful experience of the methods of Dr. Fu-Manchu; to think that I had come *alone* in quest of him; that, leaving no trace behind me, I had deliberately penetrated to his secret abode!

I have said that my wrists were manacled behind me, the manacles being attached to a chain fastened in the wall. I now contrived, with extreme difficulty, to reverse the position of my hands; that is to say, I climbed backward through the loop formed by my fettered arms, so that instead of their being locked behind me, they now were locked in front.

Then I began to examine the fetters, learning, as I had anticipated, that they fastened with a lock. I sat gazing at the steel bracelets in the light of the lamp which swung over my head, and it became apparent to me that I had gained little by my contortion.

A slight noise disturbed these unpleasant reveries. It was nothing less than the rattling of keys!

For a moment I wondered if I had heard aright, or if the sound portended the coming of some servant of the doctor, who was locking up the establishment for the night. The jangling sound was repeated, and in such a way that I could not suppose it to be accidental. Some one was deliberately rattling a small bunch of keys in an adjoining room.

And now my heart leaped wildly—then seemed to stand still.

With a low whistling cry a little gray shape shot through the doorway by which Fu-Manchu had retired, and rolled, like a ball of fluff blown by the wind, completely under the table which bore the weird scientific appliances of the Chinaman; the advent of the gray object was accompanied by a further rattling of keys.

My fear left me, and a mighty anxiety took its place. This creature which now crouched chattering at me from beneath the big table was Fu-Manchu's marmoset, and in the intervals of its chattering and grimacing, it nibbled, speculatively, at the keys upon the ring which it clutched in its tiny hands. Key after key it sampled in this manner, evincing a growing dissatisfaction with the uncrackable nature of its find.

One of those keys might be that of the handcuffs!

I could not believe that the tortures of Tantulus were greater than were mine at this moment. In all my hopes of rescue or release, I had included nothing so strange, so improbable as this. A sort of awe possessed me; for if by this means the key which should release me should come into my possession, how, ever again, could I doubt a beneficent Providence?

But they were not yet in my possession; moreover, the key of the handcuffs might not be amongst the bunch.

Were there no means whereby I could induce the marmoset to approach me?

Whilst I racked my brains for some scheme, the little animal took the matter out of my hands. Tossing the ring with its jangling contents a yard or so across the carpet in my direction, it leaped in pursuit, picked up the ring, whirled it over its head, and then threw a complete somersault around it. Now it snatched up the keys again, and holding them close to its ear, rattled them furiously. Finally, with an incredible spring, it leaped onto the chain supporting the lamp above my head, and with the garish shade swinging and spinning wildly, clung there looking down at me like an acrobat on a trapeze. The tiny, bluish face, completely framed in grotesque whiskers, enhanced the illusion of an acrobatic comedian. Never for a moment did it release its hold upon the key-ring.

My suspense now was intolerable. I feared to move, lest, alarming the marmoset, it should run off again, taking the keys with it. So as I lay there, looking up at the little creature swinging above me, the second wonder of the night came to pass.

A voice that I could never forget, strive how I would, a voice that haunted my dreams by night, and for which by day I was ever listening, cried out from some adjoining room. *"Ta'ala hina!"* it called. *"Ta'ala hina, Peko!"*

It was Kâramanèh!

The effect upon the marmoset was instantaneous. Down came the bunch of keys upon one side of the shade, almost falling on my head, and down leaped the ape upon the other. In two leaps it had traversed the room and had vanished through the curtained doorway.

If ever I had need of coolness it was now; the slightest mistake would be fatal. The keys had slipped from the mattress of the divan, and now lay just beyond reach of my fingers. Rapidly I changed my position, and sought, without undue noise, to move the keys with my foot.

I had actually succeeded in sliding them back on to the mattress, when, unheralded by any audible footstep, Kâramanèh came through the doorway, holding the marmoset in her arms. She wore a dress of fragile muslin material, and out from its folds protruded one silk-stockinged foot, resting in a high-heeled red shoe. . . .

For a moment she stood watching me, with a sort of enforced composure; then her glance strayed to the keys lying upon the floor. Slowly, and with her eyes fixed again upon my face, she crossed the room, stooped, and took up the key-ring.

It was one of the poignant moments of my life; for by that simple act all my hopes had been shattered!

Any poor lingering doubt that I may have had, left me now. Had the slightest spark of friendship animated the bosom of Kâramanèh, most certainly she would have overlooked the presence of the keys—of the keys which represented my one hope of escape from the clutches of the fiendish Chinaman.

There is a silence more eloquent than words. For half a minute or more, Kâramanèh stood watching me—forcing herself to watch me—and I looked up at her with a concentrated gaze in which rage and reproach must have been strangely mingled.

What eyes she had!—of that blackly lustrous sort nearly always associated with unusually dark complexions; but Kâramanèh's complexion was peachlike, or rather of an exquisite and delicate fairness which reminded me of the petal of a rose. By some I have been accused of raving about this girl's beauty, but only by those who had not met her; for indeed she was astonishingly lovely.

At last her eyes fell, the long lashes drooped upon her cheeks. She turned and walked slowly to the chair in which Fu-Manchu had sat. Placing the keys upon the table amid the scientific litter, she rested one dimpled elbow upon the yellow page of the book, and with her chin in her palm, again directed upon me that enigmatical gaze.

I dared not think of the past, of the past in which this beautiful, treacherous girl had played a part; yet, watching her, I could not believe, even now, that she was false! My state was truly a pitiable one; I could have cried out in sheer anguish. With her long lashes partly lowered, she watched me awhile, then spoke; and her voice was music which seemed to mock me; every inflection of that elusive accent reopened, lancet-like, the ancient wound.

"Why do you look at me so?" she said, almost in a whisper. "By what right do you reproach me?—Have you ever offered me friendship, that I should repay you with friendship? When first you came to the house where I was, by the river—came to save some one from" (there was the familiar hesitation which always preceded the name of Fu-Manchu) "from—*him*, you treated me as your enemy, although—I would have been your friend . . ."

There was appeal in the soft voice, but I laughed mockingly, and threw myself back upon the divan. Kâramanèh stretched out her hands toward me, and I shall never forget the expression which flashed into those glorious eyes; but, seeing me intolerant of her appeal, she drew back and quickly turned her head aside. Even in this hour of extremity, of impotent wrath, I could find no contempt in my heart for her feeble hypocrisy; with all the old wonder I watched that exquisite profile, and Kâramanèh's very deceitfulness was a salve—for had she not cared she would not have attempted it!

Suddenly she stood up, taking the keys in her hands, and approached me.

"Not by word, nor by look," she said, quietly, "have you asked for my friendship, but because I cannot bear you to think of me as you do, I will prove that I am not the hypocrite and the liar you think me. You will not trust me, but I will trust you."

I looked up into her eyes, and knew a pagan joy when they faltered before my searching gaze. She threw herself upon her knees beside me, and the faint exquisite perfume inseparable from my memories of her, became perceptible, and seemed as of old to intoxicate me. The lock clicked . . . and I was free.

Kâramanèh rose swiftly to her feet as I stood up and outstretched my cramped arms. For one delirious moment her bewitching face was close to mine, and the dictates of madness almost ruled; but I clenched my teeth and turned sharply aside. I could not trust myself to speak.

With Fu-Manchu's marmoset again gamboling before us, she walked through the curtained doorway into the room beyond. It was in darkness, but I could see the slave-girl in front of me, a slim silhouette, as she walked to a screened window, and, opening the screen in the manner of a folding door, also threw up the window.

"Look!" she whispered.

I crept forward and stood beside her. I found myself looking down into Museum Street from a first-floor window! Belated traffic still passed along New Oxford Street on the left, but not a solitary figure was visible to the right, as far as I could see, and that was nearly to the railings of the Museum. Immediately opposite, in one of the flats which I had noticed earlier in the evening, another window was opened. I turned, and in the reflected light saw that Kâramanèh held a cord in her hand. Our eyes met in the semi-darkness.

She began to haul the cord into the window, and, looking upward, I perceived that it was looped in some way over the telegraph cables which crossed the street at that point. It was a slender cord, and it appeared to be passed across a joint in the cables almost immediately above the center of the roadway. As it was hauled in, a second and stronger line attached to it was pulled, in turn, over the cables, and thence in by the window. Kâramanèh twisted a length of it around a metal bracket fastened in the wall, and placed a light wooden crossbar in my hand.

"Make sure that there is no one in the street," she said, craning out and looking to right and left, "then *swing across*. The length of the rope is just sufficient to enable you to swing through the open window opposite, and there is a mattress inside to drop upon. But release the bar immediately, or you may be dragged back. The door of the room in which you will find yourself is unlocked, and you have only to walk down the stairs and out into the street."

I peered at the crossbar in my hand, then looked hard at the girl beside me. I missed something of the old fire of her nature; she was very subdued, tonight.

"Thank you, Kâramanèh," I said, softly.

She suppressed a little cry as I spoke her name, and drew back into the shadows.

"I believe you are my friend," I said, "but I cannot understand. Won't you help me to understand?"

I took her unresisting hand, and drew her toward me. My very soul seemed to thrill at the contact of her lithe body . . .

She was trembling wildly and seemed to be trying to speak, but although her lips framed the words no sound followed. Suddenly comprehension came to me. I looked down into the street, hitherto deserted . . . and into the upturned face of Fu-Manchu.

Wearing a heavy fur-collared coat, and with his yellow, malignant countenance grotesquely horrible beneath the shade of a large tweed motor cap, he stood motionless, looking up at me. That he had seen me, I could not doubt; but had he seen my companion?

In a choking whisper Kâramanèh answered my unspoken question.

"He has not seen me! I have done much for you; do in return a small thing for me. Save my life!"

She dragged me back from the window and fled across the room to the weird laboratory where I had lain captive. Throwing herself upon the divan, she held out her white wrists and glanced significantly at the manacles.

"Lock them upon me!" she said, rapidly. "Quick! quick!"

Great as was my mental disturbance, I managed to grasp the purpose of this device. The very extremity of my danger found me cool. I fastened the manacles, which so recently had confined my own wrists, upon the slim wrists of Kâramanèh. A faint and muffled disturbance, doubly ominous because there was nothing to proclaim its nature, reached me from some place below, on the ground floor.

"Tie something around my mouth!" directed Kâramanèh with nervous rapidity. As I began to look about me:—"Tear a strip from my dress," she said; "do not hesitate—be quick! be quick!"

I seized the flimsy muslin and tore off half a yard or so from the hem of the skirt. The voice of Dr. Fu-Manchu became audible. He was speaking rapidly, sibilantly, and evidently was approaching—would be upon me in a matter of moments. I fastened the strip of fabric over the girl's mouth and tied it behind, experiencing a pang half pleasurable and half fearful as I found my hands in contact with the foamy luxuriance of her hair.

Dr. Fu-Manchu was entering the room immediately beyond.

Snatching up the bunch of keys, I turned and ran, for in another instant my retreat would be cut off. As I burst once more into the darkened room I became aware that a door on the further side of it was open; and framed in the opening was the tall, high-shouldered figure of the Chinaman, still enveloped in his fur coat and wearing the grotesque cap. As I saw him, so he perceived me; and as I sprang to the window, he advanced.

I turned desperately and hurled the bunch of keys with all my force into the dimly-seen face . . .

Either because they possessed a chatoyant quality of their own (as I had often suspected), or by reason of the light reflected through the open window, the green eyes gleamed upon me vividly like those of a giant cat. One short guttural exclamation paid tribute to the accuracy of my aim; then I had the crossbar in my hand. I threw one leg across the sill, and dire as was my extremity, hesitated for an instant ere trusting myself to the flight . . .

A vise-like grip fastened upon my left ankle.

Hazily I became aware that the dark room was become flooded with figures. The whole yellow gang were upon me—the entire murder-group composed of units recruited from the darkest place of the East!

I have never counted myself a man of resource, and have always envied Nayland Smith his possession of that quality, in him extraordinarily developed; but on this occasion the gods were kind to me, and I resorted to the only device, perhaps, which could have saved me. Without releasing my hold upon the crossbar, I clutched at the ledge with the fingers of both hands and swung back into the room my right leg, which was already across the sill. With all my strength I kicked out. My heel came in contact, in sickening contact, with a human head; beyond doubt I had split the skull of the man who held me.

The grip upon my ankle was released automatically; and now consigning all my weight to the rope I slipped forward, as a diver, across the broad ledge and found myself sweeping through the night like a winged thing . . .

The line, as Kâramanèh had assured me, was of well-judged length. Down I swept to within six or seven feet of the street level, then up, at ever decreasing speed, toward the vague oblong of the open window beyond.

I hope I have been successful, in some measure, in portraying the varied emotions which it was my lot to experience that night, and it may well seem that nothing more exquisite could remain for me. Yet it was written otherwise; for as I swept up to my goal, describing the inevitable arc which I had no power to check, I saw that *one* awaited me.

Crouching forward half out of the open window was a Burmese dacoit, a cross-eyed, leering being whom I well remembered to have encountered two years before in my dealings with Dr. Fu-Manchu. One bare, sinewy arm held rigidly at right angles before his breast, he clutched a long curved knife and waited—waited—for the critical moment when my throat should be at his mercy!

I have said that a strange coolness had come to my aid; even now it did not fail me, and so incalculably rapid are the workings of the human mind that I remember complimenting myself upon an achievement which Smith himself could not have bettered, and this in the immeasurable interval which intervened between the commencement of my upward swing and my arrival on a level with the window.

I threw my body back and thrust my feet forward. As my legs went through the opening, an acute pain in one calf told me that I was not to escape scatheless from the night's mêlée. But the dacoit went rolling over in the darkness of the room, as helpless in face of that ramrod stroke as the veriest infant . . .

Back I swept upon my trapeze, a sight to have induced any passing citizen to question his sanity. With might and main I sought to check the swing of the pendulum, for if I should come within reach of the window behind I doubted not that other knives awaited me. It was no difficult feat, and I succeeded in checking my flight. Swinging there above Museum Street I could even appreciate, so lucid was my mind, the ludicrous element of the situation.

I dropped. My wounded leg almost failed me; and greatly shaken, but with no other serious damage, I picked myself up from the dust of the roadway. It was a mockery of Fate that the problem which Nayland Smith had set me to solve, should have been solved thus; for I could not doubt that by means of the branch of a tall tree or some other suitable object situated opposite to Smith's house in Rangoon, Kâramanèh had made her escape as tonight I had made mine.

Apart from the acute pain in my calf I knew that the dacoit's knife had bitten deeply, by reason of the fact that a warm liquid was trickling down into my boot. Like any drunkard I stood there in the middle of the road looking up at the vacant window where the dacoit had been, and up at the window above the shop of J. Salaman where I knew Fu-Manchu to be. But for some reason the latter window had been closed or almost closed, and as I stood there this reason became apparent to me.

The sound of running footsteps came from the direction of New Oxford Street. I turned—to see two policemen bearing down upon me!

This was a time for quick decisions and prompt action. I weighed all the circumstances in the balance, and made the last vital choice of the night; I turned and ran toward the British Museum as though the worst of Fu-Manchu's creatures, and not my allies the police, were at my heels!

No one else was in sight, but, as I whirled into the Square, the red lamp of a slowly retreating taxi became visible some hundred yards to the left. My leg was paining me greatly, but the nature of the wound did not interfere with my progress; therefore I continued my headlong career, and ere the police had reached the end of Museum Street I had my hand upon the door handle of the cab,—for, the Fates being persistently kind to me, the vehicle was for hire.

"Dr. Cleeve's, Harley Street!" I shouted at the man. "Drive like hell! It's an urgent case."

I leaped into the cab.

Within five seconds from the time that I slammed the door and dropped back panting upon the cushions, we were speeding westward toward the house of the famous pathologist, thereby throwing the police hopelessly off the track.

Faintly to my ears came the purr of a police whistle. The taxi-man evidently did not hear the significant sound. Merciful Providence had rung down the curtain; for to-night my rôle in the yellow drama was finished.

Chapter XXI

CRAGMIRE TOWER

Less than two hours later, Inspector Weymouth and a party of men from Scotland Yard raided the house in Museum Street. They found the stock of J. Salaman practically intact, and, in the strangely appointed rooms above, every evidence of a hasty outgoing. But of the instruments, drugs and other laboratory paraphernalia not one item remained. I would gladly have given my income for a year, to have gained possession of the books, alone; for, beyond all shadow of doubt, I knew them to contain formulæ calculated to revolutionize the science of medicine.

Exhausted, physically and mentally, and with my mind a whispering-gallery of conjectures (it were needless for me to mention *whom* respecting) I turned in, gratefully, having patched up the slight wound in my calf.

I seemed scarcely to have closed my eyes, when Nayland Smith was shaking me into wakefulness.

"You are probably tired out," he said; "but your crazy expedition of last night entitles you to no sympathy. Read this; there is a train in an hour. We will reserve a compartment and you can resume your interrupted slumbers in a corner seat."

As I struggled upright in bed, rubbing my eyes sleepily, Smith handed me the *Daily Telegraph*, pointing to the following paragraph upon the literary page:

> Messrs. M—— announce that they will publish shortly the long delayed work of Kegan Van Roon, the celebrated American traveler, Orientalist and psychic investigator, dealing with his recent inquiries in China. It will be remembered that Mr. Van Roon undertook to motor from Canton to Siberia last winter, but met with unforseen difficulties in the province of Ho-Nan. He fell into the hands of a body of fanatics and was fortunate to escape with his life. His book will deal in particular with his experiences in Ho-Nan, and some sensational revelations regarding the awakening of that most mysterious race, the Chinese, are promised. For reasons of his own he has decided to remain in England until the completion of his book (which will be published simultaneously in New York and London) and has leased Cragmire Tower, Somersetshire, in which romantic and historical residence he will collate his notes and prepare for the world a work ear-marked as a classic even before it is published.

I glanced up from the paper, to find Smith's eyes fixed upon me, inquiringly.

"From what I have been able to learn," he said, evenly, "we should reach Saul, with decent luck, just before dusk."

As he turned, and quitted the room without another word, I realized, in a flash, the purport of our mission; I understood my friend's ominous calm, betokening suppressed excitement.

The Fates were with us (or so it seemed); and whereas we had not hoped to gain Saul before sunset, as a matter of fact, the autumn afternoon was in its most glorious phase as we left the little village with its oldtime hostelry behind us and set out in an easterly direction, with the Bristol Channel far away on our left and a gently sloping upland on our right.

The crooked high-street practically constituted the entire hamlet of Saul, and the inn, "The Wagoners," was the last house in the street. Now, as we followed the ribbon of moor-path to the top of the rise, we could stand and look back upon the way we had come; and although we had covered fully a mile of ground, it was possible to detect the sunlight gleaming now and then upon the gilt lettering of the inn sign as it swayed in the breeze. The day had been unpleasantly warm, but was relieved by this same sea breeze, which, although but slight, had in it the tang of the broad Atlantic. Behind us, then, the foot-path sloped down to Saul, unpeopled by any living thing; east and northeast swelled the monotony of the moor right out to the hazy distance where the sky began and the sea remotely lay hidden; west fell the gentle gradient from the top of the slope which we had mounted, and here, as far as the eye could reach, the country had an appearance suggestive of a huge and dried-up lake. This idea was borne out by an odd blotchiness, for sometimes there would be half a mile or more of seeming moorland, then a sharply defined change (or it seemed sharply defined from that bird's-eye point of view). A vivid greenness marked these changes, which merged into a dun-colored smudge and again into the brilliant green; then the moor would begin once more.

"That will be the Tor of Glastonbury, I suppose," said Smith, suddenly peering through his field-glasses in an easterly direction; "and yonder, unless I am greatly mistaken, is Cragmire Tower."

Shading my eyes with my hand, I also looked ahead, and saw the place for which we were bound; one of those round towers, more common in Ireland, which some authorities have declared to be of Phoenician origin. Ramshackle buildings clustered untidily about its base, and to it a sort of tongue of that oddly venomous green which patched the lowlands, shot out and seemed almost to reach the tower-base. The land for miles around was as flat as the palm of my hand, saving certain hummocks, lesser tors, and irregular piles of boulders which dotted its expanse. Hills and uplands there were in the hazy distance, forming a sort of mighty inland bay which I doubted not in some past age had been covered by the sea. Even in the brilliant sunlight the place had something of a mournful aspect, looking like a great dried-up pool into which the children of giants had carelessly cast stones.

We met no living soul upon the moor. With Cragmire Tower but a quarter of a mile off, Smith paused again, and raising his powerful glasses swept the visible landscape.

"Not a sign. Petrie," he said, softly; "yet . . ."

Dropping the glasses back into their case, my companion began to tug at his left ear.

"Have we been overconfident?" he said, narrowing his eyes in speculative fashion. "No less than three times I have had the idea that something, or some one, has just dropped out of sight, *behind* me, as I focused . . ."

"What do you mean, Smith?"

"Are we"—he glanced about him as though the vastness were peopled with listening Chinamen—*"followed?"*

Silently we looked into one another's eyes, each seeking for the dread which neither had named. Then:

"Come on, Petrie!" said Smith, grasping my arm; and at quick march we were off again.

Cragmire Tower stood upon a very slight eminence, and what had looked like a green tongue, from the moorland slopes above, was in fact a creek, flanked by lush land, which here found its way to the sea. The house which we were come to visit consisted in a low, two-story building, joining the ancient tower on the east with two smaller outbuildings. There was a miniature kitchen-garden, and a few stunted fruit trees in the northwest corner; the whole being surrounded by a gray stone wall.

The shadow of the tower fell sharply across the path, which ran up almost alongside of it. We were both extremely warm by reason of our long and rapid walk on that hot day, and this shade should have been grateful to us. In short, I find it difficult to account for the unwelcome chill which I experienced at the moment that I found myself at the foot of the time-worn monument. I know that we both pulled up sharply and looked at one another as though acted upon by some mutual disturbance.

But not a sound broke the stillness save a remote mumuring, until a solitary sea gull rose in the air and circled directly over the tower, uttering its mournful and unmusical cry. Automatically to my mind sprang the lines of the poem:

Far from all brother-men, in the weird of the fen,
With God's creatures I bide,'mid the birds that I ken;
Where the winds ever dree, where the hymn of the sea
Brings a message of peace from the ocean to me.

Not a soul was visible about the premises; there was no sound of human activity and no dog barked. Nayland Smith drew a long breath, glanced back along the way we had come, then went on, following the wall, I beside him, until we came to the gate. It was unfastened, and we walked up the stone path through a wilderness of weeds. Four windows of the house were visible, two on the ground floor and two above. Those on the ground floor were heavily boarded up, those above, though glazed, boasted neither blinds nor curtains. Cragmire Tower showed not the slightest evidence of tenancy.

We mounted three steps and stood before a tremendously massive oaken door. An iron bell-pull, ancient and rusty, hung on the right of the door, and Smith, giving me an odd glance, seized the ring and tugged it.

From somewhere within the building answered a mournful clangor, a cracked and toneless jangle, which, seeming to echo through empty apartments, sought and found an exit apparently by way of one of the openings in the round tower; for it was from above our heads that the noise came to us.

It died away, that eerie ringing—that clanging so dismal that it could chill my heart even then with the bright sunlight streaming down out of the blue; it awoke no other response than the mournful cry of the sea gull circling over our heads. Silence fell. We looked at one another, and we were both about to express a mutual doubt, when, unheralded by any unfastening of bolts or bars, the oaken door was opened, and a huge mulatto, dressed in white, stood there regarding us.

I started nervously, for the apparition was so unexpected, but Nayland Smith, without evidence of surprise, thrust a card into the man's hand.

"Take my card to Mr. Van Roon, and say

that I wish to see him on important business," he directed, authoritatively.

The mulatto bowed and retired. His white figure seemed to be swallowed up by the darkness within, for beyond the patch of uncarpeted floor revealed by the peeping sunlight, was a barn-like place of densest shadow. I was about to speak, but Smith laid his hand upon my arm warningly, as, out from the shadows the mulatto returned. He stood on the right of the door and bowed again.

"Be pleased to enter," he said, in his harsh, negro voice. "Mr. Van Roon will see you."

The gladness of the sun could no longer stir me; a chill and sense of foreboding bore me company, as beside Nayland Smith I entered Cragmire Tower.

Chapter XXII

THE MULATTO

The room in which Van Roon received us was roughly of the shape of an old-fashioned keyhole; one end of it occupied the base of the tower, upon which the remainder had evidently been built. In many respects it was a singular room, but the feature which caused me the greatest amazement was this:—it had no windows!

In the deep alcove formed by the tower sat Van Roon at a littered table, upon which stood an oil reading-lamp, green shaded, of the "Victoria" pattern, to furnish the entire illumination of the apartment. That bookshelves lined the rectangular portion of this strange study I divined, although that end of the place was dark as a catacomb. The walls were wood-paneled, and the ceiling was oaken beamed. A small bookshelf and tumble-down cabinet stood upon either side of the table, and the celebrated American author and traveler lay propped up in a long split-cane chair. He wore smoked glasses, and had a clean-shaven, olive face, with a profusion of jet black hair. He was garbed in a dirty red dressing-gown, and a perfect fog of cigar smoke hung in the room. He did not rise to greet us, but merely extended his right hand, between two fingers whereof he held Smith's card.

"You will excuse the seeming discourtesy of an invalid, gentlemen?" he said; "but I am suffering from undue temerity in the interior of China!"

He waved his hand vaguely, and I saw that two rough deal chairs stood near the table. Smith and I seated ourselves, and my friend, leaning his elbow upon the table, looked fixedly at the face of the man whom we had come from London to visit. Although comparatively unfamiliar to the British public, the name of Van Roon was well-known in American literary circles; for he enjoyed in the United States a reputation somewhat similar to that which had rendered the name of our mutual friend, Sir Lionel Barton, a household word in England. It was Van Roon who, following in the footsteps of Madame Blavatsky, had sought out the haunts of the fabled mahatmas in the Himalayas, and Van Roon who had essayed to explore the fever swamps of Yucatan in quest of the secret of lost Atlantis; lastly, it was Van Roon, who, with an overland car specially built for him by a celebrated American firm, had undertaken the journey across China.

I studied the olive face with curiosity. Its natural impassivity was so greatly increased by the presence of the colored spectacles that my study was as profitless as if I had scrutinized the face of a carven Buddha. The mulatto had withdrawn, and in an atmosphere of gloom and tobacco smoke, Smith and I sat staring, perhaps rather rudely, at the object of our visit to the West Country.

"Mr. Van Roon," began my friend abruptly, "you will no doubt have seen this paragaph. It appeared in this morning's *Daily Telegraph*."

He stood up, and taking out the cutting from his notebook, placed it on the table.

"I have seen this—yes," said Van Roon, revealing a row of even, white teeth in a rapid smile. "Is it to this paragraph that I owe the pleasure of seeing you here?"

"The paragraph appeared in this morning's issue," replied Smith. "An hour from the time of seeing it, my friend, Dr. Petrie, and I were entrained for Bridgewater."

"Your visit delights me, gentlemen, and I should be ungrateful to question its cause; but frankly I am at a loss to understand why you should have honored me thus. I am a poor host, God knows; for what with my tortured limb, a legacy from the Chinese devils whose secrets I surprised, and my semi-blindness, due to the same cause, I am but sorry company."

Nayland Smith held up his right hand deprecatingly. Van Roon tendered a box of cigars and clapped his hands, whereupon the mulatto entered.

"I see that you have a story to tell me, Mr. Smith," he said; "therefore I suggest whisky-and-soda—or you might prefer tea, as it is nearly tea time?"

Smith and I chose the former refreshment, and the soft-footed half-breed having departed upon his errand, my companion, leaning forward earnestly across the littered table, outlined for Van Roon the story of Dr. Fu-Manchu, the great and malign being whose mission in England at that moment was none other than the stoppage of just such information as our host was preparing to give to the world.

"There is a giant conspiracy, Mr. Van Roon," he said, "which had its birth in this very province of Ho-Nan, from which you were so fortunate to escape alive; whatever its scope or limitations, a great secret society is established among the yellow races. It means that China, which has slumbered for so many generations, now stirs in that age-long sleep. I need not tell *you* how much more it means, this seething in the pot . . ."

"In a word," interrupted Van Roon, pushing Smith's glass across the table, "you would say?—"

"That your life is not worth that!" replied Smith, snapping his fingers before the other's face.

A very impressive silence fell. I watched Van Roon curiously as he sat propped up among his cushions, his smooth face ghastly in the green light from the lamp-shade. He held the stump of a cigar between his teeth, but, apparently unnoticed by him, it had long since gone out. Smith, out of the shadows, was watching him, too. Then:

"Your information is very disturbing," said the American. "I am the more disposed to credit your statement because I am all too painfully aware of the existence of such a group as you mention, in China, but that they had an agent here in England is something I had never conjectured. In seeking out this solitary residence I have unwittingly done much to assist their designs . . . But—my dear Mr. Smith, I am very remiss! Of course you will remain to-night, and I trust for some days to come?"

Smith glanced rapidly across at me, then turned again to our host.

"It seems like forcing our company upon you," he said, "but in your own interests I think it will be best to do as you are good enough to suggest. I hope and believe that our arrival here has not been noticed by the enemy; therefore it will be well if we remain concealed as much as possible for the present, until we have settled upon some plan."

"Hagar shall go to the station for your baggage," said the American rapidly, and clapped his hands, his usual signal to the mulatto.

Whilst the latter was receiving his orders I noticed Nayland Smith watching him closely; and when he had departed:

"How long has that man been in your service?" snapped my friend.

Van Roon peered blindly through his smoked glasses.

"For some years," he replied; "he was with me in India—and in China."

"Where did you engage him?"

"Actually, in St. Kitts."

"H'm," muttered Smith, and automatically he took out and began to fill his pipe.

"I can offer you no company but my own, gentlemen," continued Van Roon, "but unless it interferes with your plans, you may find the surrounding district of interest and worthy of inspection, between now and dinner time. By the way, I think I can promise you quite a satisfactory meal, for Hagar is a model chef."

"A walk would be enjoyable," said Smith, "but dangerous."

"Ah! perhaps you are right. Evidently you apprehend some attempt upon me?"

"At any moment!"

"To one in my crippled condition, an alarming outlook! However, I place myself unreservedly in your hands. But really, you must not leave this interesting district before you have made the acquaintance of some of its historical spots. To me, steeped as I am in what I may term the lore of the odd, it·is a veritable wonderland, almost as interesting, in its way, as the caves and jungles of Hindustan depicted by Madame Blavatsky."

His high-pitched voice, with a certain labored intonation, not quite so characteristically American as was his accent, rose even higher; he spoke with the fire of the enthusiast.

"When I learned that Cragmire Tower was vacant," he continued, "I leaped at the chance (excuse the metaphor, from a lame man!). This is a ghost hunter's paradise. The tower itself is of unknown origin, though probably Phoenician, and the house traditionally sheltered Dr. Macleod, the necromancer, after his flight from the persecution of James of

Scotland. Then, to add to its interest, it borders on Sedgemoor, the scene of the bloody battle during the Monmouth rising, whereat a thousand were slain on the field. It is a local legend that the unhappy Duke and his staff may be seen, on stormy nights, crossing the path which skirts the mire, after which this building is named, with flaming torches held aloft."

"Merely marsh-lights, I take it?" interjected Smith, gripping his pipe hard between his teeth.

"Your practical mind naturally seeks a practical explanation," smiled Van Roon, "but I myself have other theories. Then in addition to the charms of Sedgemoor—haunted Sedgemoor—on a fine day it is quite possible to see the ruins of Glastonbury Abbey from here; and Glastonbury Abbey, as you may know, is closely bound up with the history of alchemy. It was in the ruins of Glastonbury Abbey that the adept Kelly, companion of Dr. Dee, discovered, in the reign of Elizabeth, the famous caskets of St. Dunstan, containing the two tinctures . . ."

So he ran on, enumerating the odd charms of his residence, charms which for my part I did not find appealing. Finally:

"We cannot presume further upon your kindness," said Nayland Smith, standing up. "No doubt we can amuse ourselves in the neighborhood of the house until the return of your servant."

"Look upon Cragmire Tower as your own, gentlemen!" cried Van Roon. "Most of the rooms are unfurnished, and the garden is a wilderness, but the structure of the brickwork in the tower may interest you archæologically, and the view across the moor is at least as fine as any in the neighborhood."

So, with his brilliant smile and a gesture of one thin yellow hand, the crippled traveler made us free of his odd dwelling. As I passed out from the room close at Smith's heels, I glanced back, I cannot say why. Van Roon already was bending over his papers, in his green shadowed sanctuary, and the light shining down upon his smoked glasses created the odd illusion that he was looking over the tops of the lenses and not down at the table as his attitude suggested. However, it was probably ascribable to the weird chiaroscuro of the scene, although it gave the seated figure an oddly malignant appearance, and I passed out through the utter darkness of the outer room to the front door.

Smith opening it, I was conscious of surprise to find dusk come—to meet darkness where I had looked for sunlight.

The silver wisps which had raced along the horizon, as we came to Cragmire Tower, had been harbingers of other and heavier banks. A stormy sunset smeared crimson streaks across the skyline, where a great range of clouds, like the oily smoke of a city burning, was banked, mountain topping mountain, and lighted from below by this angry red. As we came down the steps and out by the gate, I turned and looked across the moor behind us. A sort of reflection from this distant blaze encrimsoned the whole landscape. The inland bay glowed sullenly, as if internal fires and not reflected light were at work; a scene both wild and majestic.

Nayland Smith was staring up at the cone-like top of the ancient tower in a curious, speculative fashion. Under the influence of our host's conversation I had forgotten the reasonless dread which had touched me at the moment of our arrival, but now, with the red light blazing over Sedgemoor, as if in memory of the blood which had been shed there, and with the tower of unknown origin looming above me, I became very uncomfortable again, nor did I envy Van Roon his eerie residence. The proximity of a tower of any kind, at night, makes in some inexplicable way for awe, and to-night there were other agents, too.

"What's that?" snapped Smith suddenly, grasping my arm.

He was peering southward, toward the distant hamlet, and, starting violently at his words and the sudden grasp of his hand, I, too, stared in that direction.

"We were followed, Petrie," he almost whispered. "I never got a sight of our follower, but I'll swear we were followed. Look! there's something moving over yonder!"

Together we stood staring into the dusk; then Smith burst abruptly into one of his rare laughs, and clapped me upon the shoulder.

"It's Hagar, the mulatto!" he cried—"and our grips. That extraordinary American with his tales of witch-lights and haunted abbeys has been playing the devil with our nerves."

Together we waited by the gate until the half-caste appeared on the bend of the path with a grip in either hand. He was a great, muscular fellow with a stoic face, and, for the purpose of visiting Saul, presumably, he had doffed his white raiment and now wore a sort of livery, with a peaked cap.

Smith watched him enter the house. Then:

"I wonder where Van Roon obtains his provisions and so forth," he muttered. "It's odd they knew nothing about the new tenant of Cragmire Tower at 'The Wagoners.'"

There came a sort of sudden expectancy into his manner for which I found myself at a loss to account. He turned his gaze inland and stood there tugging at his left ear and clicking his teeth together. He stared at me, and his eyes looked very bright in the dusk, for a sort of red glow from the sunset touched them; but he spoke no word, merely taking my arm and leading me off on a rambling walk around and about the house. Neither of us spoke a word until we stood at the gate of Cragmire Tower again; then:

"I'll swear, now, that we were followed here today!" muttered Smith.

The lofty place immediately within the doorway proved, in the light of a lamp now fixed in an iron bracket, to be a square entrance hall meagerly furnished. The closed study door faced the entrance, and on the left of it ascended an open staircase up which the mulatto led the way. We found ourselves on the floor above, in a corridor traversing the house from back to front. An apartment on the immediate left was indicated by the mulatto as that allotted to Smith. It was a room of fair size, furnished quite simply but boasting a wardrobe cupboard, and Smith's grip stood beside the white enameled bed. I glanced around, and then prepared to follow the man, who had awaited me in the doorway.

He still wore his dark livery, and as I followed the lithe, broad-shouldered figure along the corridor, I found myself considering critically his breadth of shoulder and the extraordinary thickness of his neck.

I have repeatedly spoken of a sort of foreboding, an elusive stirring in the depths of my being of which I became conscious at certain times in my dealings with Dr. Fu-Manchu and his murderous servants. This sensation, or something akin to it, claimed me now, unaccountably, as I stood looking into the neat bedroom, on the same side of the corridor but at the extreme end, wherein I was to sleep. A voiceless warning urged me to return; a kind of childish panic came fluttering about my heart, a dread of entering the room, of allowing the mulatto to come *behind me.*

Doubtless this was no more than a sub-conscious product of my observations respecting his abnormal breadth of shoulder. But whatever the origin of the impulse, I found myself unable to disobey it. Therefore, I merely nodded, turned on my heel and went back to Smith's room.

I closed the door, then turned to face Smith, who stood regarding me.

"Smith," I said, "that man sends cold water trickling down my spine!"

Still regarding me fixedly, my friend nodded his head.

"You are curiously sensitive to this sort of thing," he replied slowly; "I have noticed it before as a useful capacity. I don't like the look of the man myself. The fact that he has been in Van Roon's employ for some years goes for nothing. We are neither of us likely to forget Kwee, the Chinese servant of Sir Lionel Barton, and it is quite possible that Fu-Manchu has corrupted this man as he corrupted the other. It is quite possible . . ."

His voice trailed off into silence, and he stood looking across the room with unseeing eyes, meditating deeply. It was quite dark now outside, as I could see through the uncurtained window, which opened upon the dreary expanse stretching out to haunted Sedgemoor. Two candles were burning upon the dressing table; they were but recently lighted, and so intense was the stillness that I could distinctly hear the spluttering of one of the wicks, which was damp. Without giving the slightest warning of his intention, Smith suddenly made two strides forward, stretched out his long arms, and snuffed the pair of candles in a twinkling.

The room became plunged in impenetrable darkness.

"Not a word, Petrie!" whispered my companion.

I moved cautiously to join him, but as I did so, perceived that he was moving too. Vaguely, against the window I perceived him silhouetted. He was looking out across the moor, and:

"See! see!" he hissed.

With my heart thumping furiously in my breast, I bent over him; and for the second time since our coming to Cragmire Tower, my thoughts flew to "The Fenman."

There are shades in the fen; ghosts of women and men
Who have sinned and have died, but are living again.
O'er the waters they tread, with their lanterns of dread,
And they peer in the pools—in the pools of the dead . . .

A light was dancing out upon the moor,

a witchlight that came and went unaccountably, up and down, in and out, now clearly visible, now masked in the darkness!

"Lock the door!" snapped my companion—"if there's a key."

I crept across the room and fumbled for a moment; then:

"There is no key," I reported.

"Then wedge the chair under the knob and let no one enter until I return!" he said, amazingly.

With that he opened the window to its fullest extent, threw his leg over the sill, and went creeping along a wide concrete ledge, in which ran a leaded gutter, in the direction of the tower on the right!

Not pausing to follow his instructions respecting the chair, I craned out of the window, watching his progress, and wondering with what sudden madness he was bitten. Indeed, I could not credit my senses, could not believe that I heard and saw aright. Yet there out in the darkness on the moor moved the willo'-the-wisp, and ten yards along the gutter crept my friend, like a great gaunt cat. Unknown to me he must have prospected the route by daylight, for now I saw his design. The ledge terminated only where it met the ancient wall of the tower, and it was possible for an agile climber to step from it to the edge of the unglazed window some four feet below, and to scramble from that point to the stone fence and I thence on to the path by which we had come from Saul.

This difficult operation Nayland Smith successfully performed, and, to my unbounded amazement, went racing into the darkness toward the dancing light, headlong, like a madman! The night swallowed him up, and between my wonder and my fear my hands trembled so violently that I could scarce support myself where I rested, with my full weight upon the sill.

I seemed now to be moving through the fevered phases of a nightmare. Around and below me Cragmire Tower was profoundly silent, but a faint odor of cookery was now perceptible. Outside, from the night, came a faint whispering as of the distant sea, but no moon and no stars relieved the impenetrable blackness. Only out over the moor the mysterious light still danced and moved.

One—two—three—four—five minutes passed. The light vanished and did not appear again. Five more age-long minutes elapsed in absolute silence, whilst I peered into the darkness of the night and listened, every nerve in my body tense, for the return of Nayland Smith. Yet two more minutes, which embraced an agony of suspense, passed in the same fashion; then a shadowy form grew, phantomesque, out of the gloom; a moment more, and I distinctly heard the heavy breathing of a man nearly spent, and saw my friend scrambling up toward the black embrasure in the tower. His voice came huskily, pantingly:

"Creep along and lend me a hand, Petrie! I am nearly winded."

I crept through the window, steadied my quivering nerves by an effort of the will, and reached the end of the ledge in time to take Smith's extended hand and to draw him up beside me against the wall of the tower. He was shaking with his exertions, and must have fallen, I think, without my assistance. Inside the room again:

"Quick! light the candles!" he breathed hoarsely. "Did any one come?"

"No one—nothing."

Having expended several matches in vain, for my fingers twitched nervously, I ultimately succeeded in relighting the candles.

"Get along to your room!" directed Smith. "Your apprehensions are unfounded at the moment, but you may as well leave both doors wide open!"

I looked into his face—it was very drawn and grim, and his brow was wet with perspiration, but his eyes had the fighting glint, and I knew that we were upon the eve of strange happenings.

Chapter XXIII

A CRY ON THE MOOR

Of the events intervening between this moment and that when death called to us out of the night, I have the haziest recollections. An excellent dinner was served in the bleak and gloomy dining-room by the mulatto, and the crippled author was carried to the head of the table by this same Herculean attendant, as lightly as though he had but the weight of a child.

Van Roon talked continuously, revealing a deep knowledge of all sorts of obscure matters; and in the brief intervals, Nayland Smith talked also, with almost feverish rapidity. Plans for the future were discussed. I can recall no one of them.

I could not stifle my queer sentiments in regard to the mulatto, and every time I found him behind my chair I was hard put to it to repress a shudder. In this fashion the strange evening passed; and to the accompaniment of distant, muttering thunder, we two guests retired to our chambers in Cragmire Tower. Smith had contrived to give me my instructions in a whisper, and five minutes after entering my own room, I had snuffed the candles, slipped a wedge, which he had given me, under the door, crept out through the window onto the guttered ledge, and joined Smith in his room. He, too, had extinguished his candles, and the place was in darkness. As I climbed in, he grasped my wrist to silence me, and turned me forcibly toward the window.

"Listen!" he said.

I turned and looked out upon a prospect which had been a fit setting for the witch scene in Macbeth. Thunder clouds hung low over the moor, but through them ran a sort of chasm, or rift, allowing a bar of lurid light to stretch across the drear, from east to west—a sort of lane walled by darkness. There came a remote murmuring, as of a troubled sea—a hushed and distant chorus; and sometimes in upon it broke the drums of heaven. In the west lightning flickered, though but faintly, intermittently.

Then came the *call*.

Out of the blackness of the moor it came, wild and distant—"*Help! help!*"

"Smith!" I whispered—"what is it? What . . ."

"Mr. Smith!" came the agonized cry . . . "Nayland Smith, help! for God's sake . . . ."

"Quick, Smith!" I cried, "quick, man! It's Van Roon—he's been dragged out . . . they are murdering him . . ."

Nayland Smith held me in a vise-like grip, silent, unmoved!

Louder and more agonized came the cry for aid, and I became more than ever certain that it was poor Van Roon who uttered it.

"Mr. Smith! Dr. Petrie! for God's sake come . . . or . . . it will be . . . too . . . late . . ."

"Smith!" I said, turning furiously upon my friend, "if you are going to remain here whilst murder is done, I am not!"

My blood boiled now with hot resentment. It was incredible, inhuman, that we should remain there inert whilst a fellow man, and our host to boot, was being done to death out there in the darkness. I exerted all my strength to break away; but although my efforts told upon him, as his loud breathing revealed, Nayland Smith clung to me tenaciously. Had my hands been free, in my fury, I could have struck him, for the pitiable cries, growing fainter, now, told their own tale. Then Smith spoke—shortly and angrily—breathing hard between the words.

"Be quiet, you fool!" he snapped; "it's little less than an insult, Petrie, to think me capable of refusing help where help is needed!"

Like a cold douche his words acted; in that instant I knew myself a fool.

"You remember the Call of Siva?" he said, thrusting me away irritably, "—two years ago, and what it meant to those who obeyed it?"

"You might have told me . . ."

"*Told* you! You would have been through the window before I had uttered two words!"

I realized the truth of his assertion, and the justness of his anger.

"Forgive me, old man," I said, very crestfallen, "but my impulse was a natural one, you'll admit. You must remember that I have been trained never to refuse aid when aid is asked."

"Shut up, Petrie!" he growled; "forget it."

The cries had ceased now, entirely, and a peal of thunder, louder than any yet, echoed over distant Sedgemoor. The chasm of light splitting the heavens closed in, leaving the night wholly black.

"Don't talk!" rapped Smith; "act! You wedged your door?"

"Yes."

"Good. Get into that cupboard, have your Browning ready, and keep the door very slightly ajar."

He was in that mood of repressed fever which I knew and which always communicated itself to me. I spoke no further word, but stepped into the wardrobe indicated and drew the door nearly shut. The recess just accommodated me, and through the aperture I could see the bed, vaguely, the open window, and part of the opposite wall. I saw Smith cross the floor, as a mighty clap of thunder boomed over the house.

A gleam of lightning flickered through the gloom.

I saw the bed for a moment, distinctly, and it appeared to me that Smith lay therein, with the sheets pulled up over his head. The light was gone, and I could hear big drops of rain pattering upon the leaden gutter below the open window.

My mood was strange, detached, and characterized by vagueness. That Van Roon lay dead upon the moor I was convinced; and—although I recognized that it must be a sufficient one—I could not even dimly divine the reason why we had refrained from lending him aid. To have failed to save him, knowing his peril, would have been bad enough; to have *refused*, I thought was shameful. Better to have shared his fate—yet . . .

The downpour was increasing, and beating now a regular tattoo upon the gutterway. Then, splitting the oblong of greater blackness which marked the casement, quivered dazzlingly another flash of lightning in which I saw the bed again, with that impression of Smith curled up in it. The blinding light died out; came the crash of thunder, harsh and fearsome, more imminently above the tower than ever. The building seemed to shake.

Coming as they did, horror and the wrath of heaven together, suddenly, crashingly, black and angry after the fairness of the day, these happenings and their setting must have terrorized the stoutest heart; but somehow I seemed detached, as I have said, and set apart from the whirl of events; a spectator. Even when a vague yellow light crept across the room from the direction of the door, and flickered unsteadily on the bed, I remained unmoved to a certain degree, although passively alive to the significance of the incident. I realized that the ultimate issue was at hand, but either because I was emotionally exhausted, or from some other cause, the pending climax failed to disturb me.

Going on tiptoe, in stockinged feet, across my field of vision, passed Kegan Van Roon! he was in his shirt-sleeves and held a lighted candle in one hand whilst with the other he shaded it against the draught from the window. He was a cripple no longer, and the smoked glasses were discarded; most of the light, at the moment when first I saw him, shone upon his thin, olive face, and at sight of his eyes much of the mystery of Cragmire Tower was resolved. For they were oblique, very slightly, but nevertheless unmistakably oblique. Though highly educated, and possibly an American citizen, *Van Roon was a Chinaman!*

Upon the picture of his face as I saw it then, I do not care to dwell. It lacked the unique horror of Dr. Fu-Manchu's unforgettable countenance, but possessed a sort of animal malignancy which the latter lacked . . .

He approached within three or four feet of

the bed, peering—peering. Then, with a timidity which spoke well for Nayland Smith's reputation, paused and beckoned to some one who evidently stood in the doorway behind him. As he did so I noted that the legs of his trousers were caked with greenish brown mud nearly up to the knees.

The huge mulatto, silent-footed, crossed to the bed in three strides. He was stripped to the waist, and excepting some few professional athletes, I had never seen a torso to compare with that which, brown and glistening, now bent over Nayland Smith. The muscular development was simply enormous; the man had a neck like a column, and the thews around his back and shoulders were like ivy tentacles wreathing some gnarled oak.

Whilst Van Roon, his evil gaze upon the bed, held the candle aloft, the mulatto, with a curious preparatory writhing movement of the mighty shoulders, lowered his outstretched fingers to the disordered bed linen . . .

I pushed open the cupboard door and thrust out the Browning. As I did so a dramatic thing happened. A tall, gaunt figure shot suddenly upright from *beyond* the bed. It was Nayland Smith!

Upraised in his hand he held a heavy walking cane. I knew the handle to be leaded, and I could judge of the force with which he wielded it by the fact that it cut the air with a keen *swishing* sound. It descended upon the back of the mulatto's skull with a sickening thud, and the great brown body dropped inert upon the padded bed—in which not Smith, but his grip, reposed. There was no word, no cry. Then:

"Shoot, Petrie! Shoot the fiend! *Shoot* . . ."

Van Roon, dropping the candle, in the falling gleam of which I saw the whites of the oblique eyes, turned and leaped from the room with the agility of a wild cat. The ensuing darkness was split by a streak of lightning . . . and there was Nayland Smith scrambling around the foot of the bed and making for the door in hot pursuit.

We gained it almost together. Smith had dropped the cane, and now held his pistol in his hand. Together we fired into the chasm of the corridor, and in the flash, saw Van Roon hurling himself down the stairs. He went silently in his stockinged feet, and our own clatter was drowned by the awful booming of the thunder which now burst over us again.

Crack!—crack!—crack! Three times our pistols spat venomously after the flying figure . . . then we had crossed the hall below and were in the wilderness of the night with the rain descending upon us in sheets. Vaguely I saw the white shirt-sleeves of the fugitive near the corner of the stone fence. A moment he hesitated, then darted away inland, not toward Saul, but toward the moor and the cup of the inland bay.

"Steady, Petrie! steady!" cried Nayland Smith. He ran, panting, beside me. "It is the path to the mire." He breathed sibilantly between every few words. "It was out there . . . that he hoped to lure us . . . with the cry for help."

A great blaze of lightning illuminated the landscape as far as the eye could see. Ahead of us a flying shape, hair lank and glistening in the downpour, followed a faint path skirting that green tongue of morass which we had noted from the upland. It was Kegan Van Roon. He glanced over his shoulder, showing a yellow, terror-stricken face. We were gaining upon him. Darkness fell, and the thunder cracked and boomed as though the very moor were splitting about us.

"Another fifty yards, Petrie," breathed Nayland Smith, "and after that it's unchartered ground."

On we went through the rain and the darkness; then:

"Slow up! slow up!" cried Smith. "It feels soft!"

Indeed, already I had made one false step—and the hungry mire had fastened upon my foot, almost tripping me.

"Lost the path!"

We stopped dead. The falling rain walled us in. I dared not move, for I knew that the mire, the devouring mire, stretched, eager, close about my feet. We were both waiting for the next flash of lightning, I think, but, before it came, out of the darkness ahead of us rose a cry that sometimes rings in my ears to this hour. Yet it was no more than a repetition of that which had called to us, deathfully, awhile before.

"Help! help! for God's sake help! Quick! I am sinking . . ."

Nayland Smith grasped my arm furiously.

"We dare not move, Petrie—we dare not move!" he breathed. "It's God's justice—visible for once."

Then came the lightning; and—ignoring a splitting crash behind us—we both looked ahead, over the mire.

Just on the edge of the venomous green

path, not thirty yards away, I saw the head and shoulders and upstretched, appealing arms of Van Roon. Even as the lightning flickered and we saw him, he was gone; with one last, long, drawn-out cry, horribly like the mournful wail of a sea gull, he was gone!

That eerie light died, and in the instant before the sound of the thunder came shatteringly, we turned about . . . in time to see Cragmire Tower, a blacker silhouette against the night, topple and fall! A red glow began to be perceptible above the building. The thunder came booming through the caverns of space. Nayland Smith lowered his wet face close to mine and shouted in my ear:

"Kegan Van Roon never returned from China. It was a trap. Those were two creatures of Dr. Fu-Manchu . . ."

The thunder died away, hollowly, echoing over the distant sea . . .

"That light on the moor to-night?"

"You have not learned the Morse Code, Petrie. It was a signal, and it read:— S–M–I–T–H . . . S–O–S."

"Well?"

"I took the chance, as you know. And it was Kâramanèh! She knew of the plot to bury us in the mire. She had followed from London, but could do nothing until dusk. God forgive me if I've misjudged her—for we owe her our lives to-night."

Flames were bursting up from the building beside the ruin of the ancient tower which had faced the storms of countless ages only to succumb at last. The lightning literally had cloven it in twain.

"The mulatto? . . ."

Again the lightning flashed, and we saw the path and began to retrace our steps. Nayland Smith turned to me; his face was very grim in that unearthly light, and his eyes shone like steel.

"I killed him, Petrie . . . as I meant to do."

From out over Sedgemoor it came, cracking and rolling and booming toward us, swelling in volume to a stupendous climax, that awful laughter of Jove the destroyer of Cragmire Tower.

Chapter XXIV

STORY OF THE GABLES

In looking over my notes dealing with the second phase of Dr. Fu-Manchu's activities in England, I find that one of the worst hours of my life was associated with the singular and seemingly inconsequent adventure of the fiery hand. I shall deal with it in this place, begging you to bear with me if I seem to digress.

Inspector Weymouth called one morning, shortly after the Van Roon episode, and entered upon a surprising account of a visit to a house at Hampstead which enjoyed the sinister reputation of being uninhabitable.

"But in what way does the case enter into your province?" inquired Nayland Smith, idly tapping out his pipe on a bar of the grate.

We had not long finished breakfast, but from an early hour Smith had been at his eternal smoking, which only the advent of the meal had interrupted.

"Well," replied the inspector, who occupied a big armchair near the window, "I was sent to look into it, I suppose, because I had nothing better to do at the moment."

"Ah!" jerked Smith, glancing over his shoulder.

The ejaculation had a veiled significance; for our quest of Dr. Fu-Manchu had come to an abrupt termination by reason of the fact that all trace of that malignant genius, and of the group surrounding him, had vanished with the destruction of Cragmire Tower.

"The house is called the Gables," continued the Scotland Yard man, "and I knew I was on a wild goose chase from the first—"

"Why?" snapped Smith.

"Because I was there before, six months ago or so—just before your present return to England—and I knew what to expect."

Smith looked up with some faint dawning of interest perceptible in his manner.

"I was unaware," he said with a slight smile, "that the cleaning-up of haunted houses came within the jurisdiction of Scotland Yard. I am learning something."

"In the ordinary way," replied the big man good-humoredly, "it doesn't. But a sudden death always excites suspicion, and—"

"A sudden death?" I said, glancing up; "you didn't explain that the ghost had killed any one!"

"I'm afraid I'm a poor hand at yarn-spinning, Doctor," said Weymouth, turning his blue, twinkling eyes in my direction. "Two people have died at the Gables within the last six months."

"You begin to interest me," declared Smith, and there came something of the old, eager look into his gaunt face, as, having lighted his pipe, he tossed the match-end into the hearth.

"I had hoped for some little excitement, myself," confessed the inspector. "This dead-end, with not a ghost of a clue to the whereabouts of the yellow fiend, has been getting on my nerves—"

Nayland Smith grunted sympathetically.

"Although Dr. Fu-Manchu has been in England for some months, now," continued Weymouth, "I have never set eyes upon him; the house we raided in Museum Street proved to be empty; in a word, I am wasting my time. So that I volunteered to run up to Hampstead and look into the matter of the Gables, principally as a distraction. It's a queer business, but more in the Psychical Research Society's line than mine, I'm afraid. Still, if there were no Dr. Fu-Manchu it might be of interest to you—and to you, Dr. Petrie, because it illustrates the fact, that, given the right sort of subject, death can be brought about without any elaborate mechanism—such as our Chinese friends employ."

"You interest me more and more," declared Smith, stretching himself in the long, white cane rest-chair.

"Two men, both fairly sound, except that the first one had an asthmatic heart, have died at the Gables without any one laying a little finger upon them. Oh! there was no jugglery! They weren't poisoned, or bitten by venomous insects, or suffocated, or anything like that. They just died of fear—stark fear."

With my elbows resting upon the table cover, and my chin in my hands, I was listening attentively, now, and Nayland Smith, a big cushion behind his head, was watching the speaker with a keen and speculative look in those steely eyes of his.

"You imply that Dr. Fu-Manchu has something to learn from the Gables?" he jerked.

Weymouth nodded stolidly.

"I can't work up anything like amazement in these days," continued the latter; "every other case seems stale and hackneyed alongside *the* case. But I must confess that when the Gables came on the books of the Yard the second time, I began to wonder. I thought there might be some tangible clue, some link connecting the two victims; perhaps some evidence of robbery or of revenge—of some sort of motive. In short, I hoped to find evidence of human agency at work, but, as before, I was disappointed."

"It's a legitimate case of a haunted house, then?" said Smith.

"Yes; we find them occasionally, these uninhabitable places, where there is *something*, something malignant and harmful to human life, but something that you cannot arrest, that you cannot hope to bring into court."

"Ah," replied Smith slowly; "I suppose you are right. There are historic instances, of course: Glamys Castle and Spedlins Tower in Scotland, Peel Castle, Isle of Man, with its *Maudhe Dhug*, the gray lady of Rainham Hall, the headless horses of Caistor, the Wesley ghost of Epworth Rectory, and others. But I have never come in personal contact with such a case, and if I did I should feel very humiliated to have to confess that there was *any* agency which could produce a *physical* result—death—but which was immune from physical retaliation."

Weymouth nodded his head again.

"I might feel a bit sour about it, too," he replied, "if it were not that I haven't much pride left in these days, considering the show of physical retaliation I have made against Dr. Fu-Manchu."

"A home thrust, Weymouth!" snapped Nayland Smith, with one of those rare, boyish laughs of his. "We're children to that Chinese doctor, Inspector, to that weird product of a weird people who are as old in evil as the pyramids are old in mystery. But about the Gables?"

"Well, it's an uncanny place. You mentioned Glamys Castle a moment ago, and it's possible to understand an old stronghold like that being haunted, but the Gables was only built about 1870; it's quite a modern house. It was built for a wealthy Quaker family, and they occupied it, uninterruptedly and apparently without anything unusual occurring, for over forty years. Then it was sold to a Mr. Maddison—and Mr. Maddison died there six months ago."

"Maddison?" said Smith sharply, staring across at Weymouth. "What was he? Where did he come from?"

"He was a retired tea-planter from Colombo," replied the inspector.

"Colombo?"

"There's a link with the East, certainly, if that's what you are thinking; and it was this fact which interested me at the time, and which led me to waste precious days and nights on the case. But there was no mortal connection between this liverish individual and the schemes of Dr. Fu-Manchu. I'm certain of that."

"And how did he die?" I asked, interestedly.

"He just died in his chair one evening, in the room which he used as a library. It was his custom to sit there every night, when there were no visitors, reading, until twelve o'clock or later. He was a bachelor, and his household consisted of a cook, a housemaid, and a man who had been with him for thirty years, I believe. At the time of Mr. Maddison's death, his household had recently been deprived of two of its members. The cook and housemaid both resigned one morning, giving as their reason the fact that the place was haunted."

"In what way?"

"I interviewed the precious pair at the time, and they told me absurd and various tales about dark figures wandering along the corridors and bending over them in bed at night, whispering; but their chief trouble was a continuous ringing of bells about the house."

"Bells?"

"They said that it became unbearable. Night and day there were bells ringing all over the house. At any rate, they went, and for three or four days the Gables was occupied only by Mr. Maddison and his man, whose name was Stevens. I interviewed the latter also, and he was an altogether more reliable witness; a decent, steady sort of man whose story impressed me very much at the time."

"Did he confirm the ringing?"

"He swore to it—a sort of jangle, sometimes up in the air, near the ceilings, and sometimes under the floor, like the shaking of silver bells."

Nayland Smith stood up abruptly and began to pace the room, leaving great trails of blue-gray smoke behind him.

"Your story is sufficiently interesting, Inspector," he declared, "even to divert my mind from the eternal contemplation of the Fu-Manchu problem. This would appear to be distinctly a case of an 'astral bell' such as we sometimes hear of in India."

"It was Stevens," continued Weymouth, "who found Mr. Maddison. He (Stevens) had been out on business connected with the household arrangements, and at about eleven o'clock he returned, letting himself in with a key. There was a light in the library, and getting no response to his knocking, Stevens entered. He found his master sitting bolt upright in a chair, clutching the arms with rigid fingers and staring straight before him with a look of such frightful horror on his face, that Stevens positively ran from the room and out of the house. Mr. Maddison was stone dead. When a doctor, who lives at no great distance away, came and examined him, he could find no trace of violence whatever; he had apparently died of fright, to judge from the expression on his face."

"Anything else?"

"Only this: I learnt, indirectly, that the last member of the Quaker family to occupy the house had apparently witnessed the apparition, which had led to his vacating the place. I got the story from the wife of a man who had been employed as gardener there at that time. The apparition—which he witnessed in the hallway, if I remember rightly—took the form of a sort of luminous hand clutching a long, curved knife."

"Oh, Heavens!" cried Smith, and laughed shortly; "that's quite in order!"

"This gentleman told no one of the occurrence until after he had left the house, no doubt in order that the place should not acquire an evil reputation. Most of the original furniture remained, and Mr. Maddison took the house furnished. I don't think there can be any doubt that what killed him was fear at seeing a repetition—"

"Of the fiery hand?" concluded Smith.

"Quite so. Well, I examined the Gables pretty closely, and, with another Scotland Yard man, spent a night in the empty house. We saw nothing; but once, very faintly, we heard the ringing of bells."

Smith spun around upon him rapidly.

"You can swear to that?" he snapped.

"I can swear to it," declared Weymouth stolidly. "It seemed to be over our heads. We were sitting in the dining-room. Then it was gone, and we heard nothing more whatever of an unusual nature. Following the death of Mr. Maddison, the Gables remained empty until a while ago, when a French gentleman, name Lejay, leased it—"

"Furnished?"

"Yes; nothing was removed—"

"Who kept the place in order?"

"A married couple living in the neighborhood undertook to do so. The man attended to the lawn and so forth, and the woman came once a week, I believe, to clean up the house."

"And Lejay?"

"He came in only last week, having leased

the house for six months. His family were to have joined him in a day or two, and he, with the aid of the pair I have just mentioned, and assisted by a French servant he brought over with him, was putting the place in order. At about twelve o'clock on Friday night this servant ran into a neighboring house screaming 'the fiery hand!' and when at last a constable arrived and a frightened group went up the avenue of the Gables, they found M. Lejay, dead in the avenue, near the steps just outside the hall door! He had the same face of horror . . ."

"What a tale for the press!" snapped Smith.

"The owner has managed to keep it quiet so far, but this time I think it will leak into the press—yes."

There was a short silence; then:

"And you have been down to the Gables again?"

"I was there on Saturday, but there's not a scrap of evidence. The man undoubtedly died of fright in the same way as Madison. The place ought to be pulled down; it's unholy."

"Unholy is the word," I said. "I never heard anything like it. This M. Lejay had no enemies?—there could be no possible motive?"

"None whatever. He was a business man from Marseilles, and his affairs necessitated his remaining in or near London for some considerable time; therefore, he decided to make his headquarters here, temporarily, and leased the Gables with that intention."

Nayland Smith was pacing the floor with increasing rapidity; he was tugging at the lobe of his left ear and his pipe had long since gone out.

Chapter XXV

THE BELLS

I started to my feet as a tall, bearded man swung open the door and hurled himself impetuously into the room. He wore a silk hat, which fitted him very ill, and a black frock coat which did not fit him at all.

"It's all right, Petrie!" cried the apparition; "I've leased the Gables!"

It was Nayland Smith! I stared at him in amazement.

"The first time I have employed a disguise," continued my friend rapidly, "since

the memorable episode of the false pigtail." He threw a small brown leather grip upon the floor. "In case you should care to visit the house, Petrie, I have brought these things. My tenancy commences to-night!"

Two days had elapsed, and I had entirely forgotten the strange story of the Gables which Inspector Weymouth had related to us; evidently it was otherwise with my friend, and utterly at a loss for an explanation of his singular behavior, I stooped mechanically and opened the grip. It contained an odd assortment of garments, and amongst other things several gray wigs and a pair of gold-rimmed spectacles.

Kneeling there with this strange litter about me, I looked up amazedly. Nayland Smith, with the unsuitable silk hat set right upon the back of his head, was pacing the room excitedly, his fuming pipe protruding from the tangle of factitious beard.

"You see, Petrie," he began again, rapidly, "I did not entirely trust the agent. I've leased the house in the name of Professor Maxton . . ."

"But, Smith," I cried, "what possible reason can there be for disguise?"

"There's every reason," he snapped. "Why should you interest yourself in the Gables?"

"Does no explanation occur to you?"

"None whatever; to me the whole thing smacks of stark lunacy."

"Then you won't come?"

"I've never stuck at anything, Smith," I replied, "however undignified, when it has seemed that my presence could be of the slightest use."

As I rose to my feet, Smith stepped in front of me, and the steely gray eyes shone out strangely from the altered face. He clapped his hands upon my shoulders.

"If I assure you that your presence is necessary to my safety," he said—"that if you fail me I must seek another companion—will you come?"

Intuitively, I knew that he was keeping something back, and I was conscious of some resentment, but nevertheless my reply was a foregone conclusion, and—with the borrowed appearance of an extremely untidy old man—I crept guiltily out of my house that evening and into the cab which Smith had waiting.

The Gables was a roomy and rambling place lying back a considerable distance from the road. A semi-circular drive gave access to the door, and so densely wooded was the ground, that for the most part the drive was practically a tunnel—a verdant tunnel. A high brick wall concealed the building from the point of view of any one on the roadway, but either horn of the crescent drive terminated at a heavy, wrought-iron gateway.

Smith discharged the cab at the corner of the narrow and winding road upon which the Gables fronted. It was walled in on both sides; on the left the wall being broken by tradesmen's entrances to the houses fronting upon another street, and on the right following, uninterruptedly, the grounds of the Gables. As we came to the gate:

"Nothing now," said Smith, pointing into the darkness of the road before us, "except a couple of studios, until one comes to the Heath."

He inserted the key in the lock of the gate and swung it creakingly open. I looked into the black arch of the avenue, thought of the haunted residence that lay hidden somewhere beyond, of those who had died in it—especially of the one who had died there under the trees—and found myself out of love with the business of the night.

"Come on!" said Nayland Smith briskly, holding the gate open; "there should be a fire in the library and refreshments, if the charwoman has followed instructions."

I heard the great gate clang to behind us. Even had there been any moon (and there was none) I doubted if more than a patch or two of light could have penetrated there. The darkness was extraordinary. Nothing broke it, and I think Smith must have found his way by the aid of some sixth sense. At any rate, I saw nothing of the house until I stood some five paces from the steps leading up to the porch. A light was burning in the hallway, but dimly and inhospitably; of the façade of the building I could perceive little.

When we entered the hall and the door was closed behind us, I began wondering anew what purpose my friend hoped to serve by a vigil in this haunted place. There was a light in the library, the door of which was ajar, and on the large table were decanters, a siphon, and some biscuits and sandwiches. A large grip stood upon the floor, also. For some reason which was a mystery to me, Smith had decided that we must assume false names whilst under the roof of the Gables; and:

"Now, Pearce," he said, "a whisky-and-soda before we look around?"

The proposal was welcome enough, for I felt strangely dispirited, and, to tell the truth, in my strange disguise, not a little ridiculous.

All my nerves, no doubt, were highly strung, and my sense of hearing unusually acute, for I went in momentary expectation of some uncanny happening. I had not long to wait. As I raised the glass to my lips and glanced across the table at my friend, I heard the first faint sound heralding the coming of the bells.

It did not seem to proceed from anywhere within the library, but from some distant room, far away overhead. A musical sound it was, but breaking in upon the silence of that ill-omened house, its music was the music of terror. In a faint and very sweet cascade it rippled; a ringing as of tiny silver bells.

I set down my glass upon the table, and rising slowly from the chair in which I had been seated, stared fixedly at my companion, who was staring with equal fixity at me. I could see that I had not been deluded; Nayland Smith had heard the ringing, too.

"The ghosts waste no time!" he said softly. "This is not new to me; I spent an hour here last night—and heard the same sound . . ."

I glanced hastily around the room. It was furnished as a library, and contained a considerable collection of works, principally novels. I was unable to judge of the outlook, for the two lofty windows were draped with heavy purple curtains which were drawn close. A silk shaded lamp swung from the center of the ceiling, and immediately over the table by which I stood. There was much shadow about the room; and now I glanced apprehensively about me, but especially toward the open door.

In that breathless suspense of listening we stood awhile; then:

"There it is again!" whispered Smith, tensely.

The ringing of bells was repeated, and seemingly much nearer to us; in fact it appeared to come from somewhere above, up near the ceiling of the room in which we stood. Simultaneously, we looked up, then Smith laughed, shortly.

"Instinctive, I suppose," he snapped; "but what do we expect to see in the air?"

The musical sound now grew in volume; the first tiny peal seemed to be reinforced by others and by others again, until the air around about us was filled with the pealings of these invisible bell-ringers.

Although, as I have said, the sound was

rather musical than horrible, it was, on the other hand, so utterly unaccountable as to touch the supreme heights of the uncanny. I could not doubt that our presence had attracted these unseen ringers to the room in which we stood, and I knew quite well that I was growing pale. This was the room in which at least one unhappy occupant of the Gables had died of fear. I recognized the fact that if this mere overture were going to affect my nerves to such an extent, I could not hope to survive the ordeal of the night; a great effort was called for. I emptied my glass at a gulp, and stared across the table at Nayland Smith with a sort of defiance. He was standing very upright and motionless, but his eyes were turning right and left, searching every visible corner of the big room.

"Good!" he said in a very low voice. "The terrorizing power of the Unknown is boundless, but we must not get in the grip of panic, or we could not hope to remain in this house ten minutes."

I nodded without speaking. Then Smith, to my amazement, suddenly began to speak in a loud voice, a marked contrast to that, almost a whisper, in which he had spoken formerly.

"My dear Pearce," he cried, "do you hear the ringing of bells?"

Clearly the latter words were spoken for the benefit of the unseen intelligence controlling these manifestations; and although I regarded such finesse as somewhat wasted, I followed my friend's lead and replied in a voice as loud as his own:

"Distinctly, Professor!"

Silence followed my words, a silence in which both stood watchful and listening. Then, very faintly, I seemed to detect the silvern ringing receding away through distant rooms. Finally it became inaudible, and in the stillness of the Gables I could distinctly hear my companion breathing. For fully ten minutes we two remained thus, each momentarily expecting a repetition of the ringing, or the coming of some new and more sinister manifestation. But we heard nothing and saw nothing.

"Hand me that grip, and don't stir until I come back!" hissed Smith in my ear.

He turned and walked out of the library, his boots creaking very loudly in that awe-inspiring silence.

Standing beside the table, I watched the open door for his return, crushing down a dread that *another* form than his might suddenly appear there.

I could hear him moving from room to room, and presently, as I waited in hushed, tense watchfulness, he came in, depositing the grip upon the table. His eyes were gleaming feverishly.

"The house is haunted, Pearce!" he cried. "But no ghost ever frightened *me!* Come, I will show you your room."

Chapter XXVI

THE FIERY HAND

Smith walked ahead of me upstairs; he had snapped up the light in the hallway, and now he turned and cried back loudly:

"I fear we should never get servants to stay here."

Again I detected the appeal to a hidden Audience; and there was something very uncanny in the idea. The house now was deathly still; the ringing had entirely subsided. In the upper corridor my companion, who seemed to be well acquainted with the position of the switches, again turned up all the lights, and in pursuit of the strange comedy which he saw fit to enact, addressed me continuously in the loud and unnatural voice which he had adopted as part of his disguise.

We looked into a number of rooms all well and comfortably furnished, but although my imagination may have been responsible for the idea, they all seemed to possess a chilly and repellent atmosphere. I felt that to essay sleep in any one of them would be the merest farce, that the place to all intents and purposes was uninhabitable, that something incalculably evil presided over the house.

And through it all, so obtuse was I, that no glimmer of the truth entered my mind. Outside again in the long, brightly lighted corridor, we stood for a moment as if a mutual anticipation of some new event pending had come to us. It was curious—that sudden pulling up and silent questioning of one another; because, although we acted thus, no sound had reached us. A few seconds later our anticipation was realized. From the direction of the stairs it came—a low wailing in a woman's voice; and the sweetness of the tones added to the terror of the sound. I clutched at Smith's arm convulsively whilst that uncanny cry rose and fell—rose and fell—and died away.

Neither of us moved immediately. My mind was working with feverish rapidity and seeking to run down a memory which the sound had stirred into faint quickness. My heart was still leaping wildly when the wailing began again, rising and falling in regular cadence. At that instant I identified it.

During the time Smith and I had spent together in Egypt, two years before, searching for Kâramanèh, I had found myself on one occasion in the neighborhood of a native cemetery near to Bedrasheen. Now, the scene which I had witnessed there rose up again vividly before me, and I seemed to see a little group of black-robed women clustered together about a native grave; for the wailing which now was dying away again in the Gables was the same, or almost the same, as the wailing of those Egyptian mourners.

The house was very silent again, now. My forehead was damp with perspiration, and I became more and more convinced that the uncanny ordeal must prove too much for my nerves. Hitherto, I had accorded little credence to tales of the supernatural, but face to face with such manifestations as these, I realized that I would have faced rather a group of armed dacoits, nay! Dr. Fu-Manchu himself, than have remained another hour in that ill-omened house.

My companion must have read as much in my face. But he kept up the strange, and to me, purposeless comedy, when presently he spoke.

"I feel it to be incumbent upon me to suggest," he said, "that we spend the night at a hotel after all."

He walked rapidly downstairs and into the library and began to strap up the grip.

"After all," he said, "there may be a natural explanation of what we've heard; for it is noteworthy that we have actually *seen* nothing. It might even be possible to get used to the ringing and the wailing after a time. Frankly, I am loath to go back on my bargain!"

Whilst I stared at him in amazement, he stood there indeterminate as it seemed. Then:

"Come, Pearce!" he cried loudly, "I can see that you do not share my views; but for my own part I shall return to-morrow and devote further attention to the phenomena."

Extinguishing the light, he walked out into the hallway, carrying the grip in his hand. I was not far behind him. We walked toward the door together, and:

"Turn the light out, Pearce," directed Smith; "the switch is at your elbow. We can see our way to the door well enough, now."

In order to carry out these instructions, it became necessary for me to remain a few paces in the rear of my companion, and I think I have never experienced such a pang of nameless terror as pierced me at the moment of extinguishing the light; for Smith had not yet opened the door, and the utter darkness of the Gables was horrible beyond expression. Surely darkness is the most potent weapon of the Unknown. I know that at the moment my hand left the switch, I made for the door as though the hosts of hell pursued me. I collided violently with Smith. He was evidently facing toward me in the darkness, for at the moment of our collision, he grasped my shoulder as in a vise.

"My God, Petrie! look behind you!" he whispered.

I was enabled to judge of the extent and reality of his fear by the fact that the strange subterfuge of addressing me always as Pearce was forgotten. I turned, in a flash. . . .

Never can I forget what I saw. Many strange and terrible memories are mine, memories stranger and more terrible than those of the average man; but this *thing* which now moved slowly down upon us through the impenetrable gloom of that haunted place, was (if the term be understood) almost absurdly horrible. It was a medieval legend come to life in modern London; it was as though some horrible chimera of the black and ignorant past was become create and potent in the present.

A luminous hand—a hand in the veins of which fire seemed to run so that the texture of the skin and the shape of the bones within were perceptible—in short a hand of glowing, fiery flesh clutching a short knife or dagger which also glowed with the same hellish, internal luminance, was advancing upon us where we stood—was not three paces removed!

What I did or how I came to do it, I can never recall. In all my years I have experienced nothing to equal the stark panic which seized upon me then. I know that I uttered a loud and frenzied cry; I know that I tore myself like a madman from Smith's restraining grip . . .

"Don't touch it! Keep away, for your life!" I heard . . .

But, dimly I recollect that, finding the thing approaching yet nearer, I lashed out with my fists—madly, blindly—and struck something palpable . . .

What was the result, I cannot say. At that

point my recollections merge into confusion. Something or some one (Smith, as I afterwards discovered) was hauling me by main force through the darkness; I fell a considerable distance onto gravel which lacerated my hands and gashed my knees. Then, with the cool night air fanning my brow, I was running—running—my breath coming in hysterical sobs. Beside me fled another figure. . . . And my definite recollections commence again at that point. For this companion of my flight from the Gables threw himself roughly against me to alter my course.

"Not that way! not that way!" came pantingly. "Not on to the Heath . . . we must keep to the roads . . ."

It was Nayland Smith. That healing realization came to me, bringing such a gladness as no words of mine can express nor convey. Still we ran on.

"There's a policeman's lantern," panted my companion. "They'll attempt nothing, now!"

I gulped down the stiff brandy-and-soda, then glanced across to where Nayland Smith lay extended in the long, cane chair.

"Perhaps you will explain," I said, "for what purpose you submitted me to that ordeal. If you proposed to correct my skepticism concerning supernatural manifestations, you have succeeded."

"Yes," said my companion, musingly, "they are devilishly clever; but we knew that already."

I stared at him, fatuously.

"Have you ever known me to waste my time when there was important work to do?" he continued. "Do you seriously believe that my ghost-hunting was undertaken for amusement? Really, Petrie, although you are very fond of assuring me that I need a holiday, I think the shoe is on the other foot!"

From the pocket of his dressing-gown, he took out a piece of silk fringe which had apparently been torn from a scarf, and rolling it into a ball, tossed it across to me.

"Smell!" he snapped.

I did as he directed—and gave a great start. The silk exhaled a faint perfume, but its effect upon me was as though some one

had cried aloud:—"Kâramanèh!"

Beyond doubt the silken fragment had belonged to the beautiful servant of Dr. Fu-Manchu, to the dark-eyed, seductive Kâramanèh. Nayland Smith was watching me keenly.

"You recognize it—yes?"

I placed the piece of silk upon the table, slightly shrugging my shoulders.

"It was sufficient evidence in itself," continued my friend, "but I thought it better to seek confirmation, and the obvious way was to pose as a new lessee of the Gables . . ."

"But, Smith," I began . . .

"Let me explain, Petrie. The history of the Gables seemed to be susceptible of only one explanation; in short it was fairly evident to me that the object of the manifestations was to insure the place being kept empty. This idea suggested another, and with them both in mind, I set out to make my inquiries, first taking the precaution to disguise my identity, to which end Weymouth gave me the freedom of Scotland Yard's fancy wardrobe. I did not take the agent into my confidence, but posed as a stranger who had heard that the house was to let furnished and thought it might suit his purpose. My inquiries were directed to a particular end, but I failed to achieve it at the time. I had theories, as I have said, and when, having paid the deposit and secured possession of the keys, I was enabled to visit the place alone, I was fortunate enough to obtain evidence to show that my imagination had not misled me.

"You were very curious the other morning, I recall, respecting my object in borrowing a large brace and bit. My object, Petrie, was to bore a series of holes in the wainscoting of various rooms at the Gables—in inconspicuous positions, of course . . ."

"But, my dear Smith!" I cried, "you are merely adding to my mystification."

He stood up and began to pace the room in his restless fashion.

"I had cross-examined Weymouth closely regarding the phenomenon of the bell-ringing, and an exhaustive search of the premises led to the discovery that the house was in such excellent condition that, from ground-floor to attic, there was not a solitary crevice large enough to admit of the passage of a mouse."

I suppose I must have been staring very foolishly indeed, for Nayland Smith burst into one of his sudden laughs.

"A mouse, I said, Petrie!" he cried. "With the brace-and-bit I rectified that matter. I made the holes I have mentioned, and before each set a trap baited with a piece of succulent, toasted cheese. Just open that grip!"

The light at last was dawning upon my mental darkness, and I pounced upon the grip, which stood upon a chair near the window, and opened it. A sickly smell of cooked cheese assailed my nostrils.

"Mind your fingers!" cried Smith; "some of them are still set, possibly."

Out from the grip I began to take *mousetraps!* Two or three of them were still set, but in the case of the greater number the catches had slipped. Nine I took out and placed upon the table, and all were empty. In the tenth there crouched, panting, its soft furry body dank with perspiration, a little white mouse!

"Only one capture!" cried my companion, "showing how well-fed the creatures were. Examine his tail!"

But already I had perceived that to which Smith would draw my attention, and the mystery of the "astral bells" was a mystery no longer. Bound to the little creature's tail, close to the root, with fine soft wire such as is used for making up bouquets, were three tiny silver bells, I looked across at my companion in speechless surprise.

"Almost childish, is it not?" he said; "yet by means of this simple device the Gables has been emptied of occupant after occupant. There was small chance of the trick being detected, for, as I have said, there was absolutely no aperture from roof to basement by means of which one of them could have escaped into the building."

"Then . . ."

"They were admitted into the wall cavities and the rafters, from some cellar underneath, Petrie, to which, after a brief scamper under the floors and over the ceilings, they instinctively returned for the food they were accustomed to receive, and for which, even had it been possible (which it was not) they had no occasion to forage."

I, too, stood up; for excitement was growing within me. I took up the piece of silk from the table.

"Where did you find this?" I asked, my eyes upon Smith's keen face.

"In a sort of wine cellar, Petrie," he replied, "under the stair. There is no cellar proper to the Gables—at least no such cellar appears in the plans."

"But . . ."

"But there *is* one beyond doubt—yes! It must be part of some older building which occupied the site before the Gables was built.

One can only surmise that it exists, although such a surmise is a fairly safe one, and the entrance to the subterranean portion of the building is situated beyond doubt in the wine cellar. Of this we have at least two evidences:—the finding of the fragment of silk there, and the fact that in one case at least— as I learned—the light was extinguished in the library unaccountably. This could only have been done in one way: by manipulating the main switch, which is also in the wine cellar."

"But Smith!" I cried, "do you mean that *Fu-Manchu* . . ."

Nayland Smith turned in his promenade of the floor, and stared into my eyes.

"I mean that Dr. Fu-Manchu has had a hiding-place under the Gables for an indefinite period!" he replied. "I always suspected that a man of his genius would have a second retreat prepared for him, anticipating the event of the first being discovered. Oh! I don't doubt it! The place probably is extensive, and I am almost certain—though the point has to be confirmed—that there is another entrance from the studio further along the road. We know, now, why our recent searchings in the East End have proved futile; why the house in Museum Street was deserted; he has been lying low in this burrow at Hampstead!"

"But the hand, Smith, the luminous hand . . ."

Nayland Smith laughed shortly.

"Your superstitious fears overcame you to such an extent, Petrie—and I don't wonder at it; the sight was a ghastly one—that probably you don't remember what occurred when you struck out at that same ghostly hand?"

"I seemed to hit something."

"That was why we ran. But I think our retreat had all the appearance of a rout, as I intended that it should. Pardon my playing upon your very natural fears, old man, but you could not have *simulated* panic half so naturally! And if they had suspected that the device was discovered, we might never have quitted the Gables alive. It was touch-and-go for a moment."

"But . . ."

"Turn out the light!" snapped my companion.

Wondering greatly, I did as he desired. I turned out the light . . . and in the darkness of my own study I saw a fiery fist being shaken at me threateningly! . . . The bones were distinctly visible, and the luminosity of the flesh was truly ghastly.

"Turn on the light, again!" cried Smith.

Deeply mystified, I did so . . . and my friend tossed a little electric pocket-lamp on to the writing-table.

"They used merely a small electric lamp fitted into the handle of a glass dagger," he said with a sort of contempt. "It was very effective, but the luminous hand is a phenomenon producible by any one who possesses an electric torch."

"The Gables will be watched?"

"At last, Petrie, I think we have Fu-Manchu—in his own trap!"

Chapter XXVII

THE NIGHT OF THE RAID

"Dash it all, Petrie!" cried Smith, "this is most annoying!"

The bell was ringing furiously, although midnight was long past. Whom could my late visitor be? Almost certainly this ringing portended an urgent case. In other words, I was not fated to take part in what I anticipated would prove to be the closing scene of the Fu-Manchu drama.

"Every one is in bed," I said, ruefully; "and how can I possibly see a patient—in this costume?"

Smith and I were both arrayed in rough tweeds, and anticipating the labors before us, had dispensed with collars and wore soft mufflers. It was hard to be called upon to face a professional interview dressed thus, and having a big tweed cap pulled down over my eyes.

Across the writing-table we confronted one another in dismayed silence, whilst, below, the bell sent up its ceaseless clangor.

"It has to be done, Smith," I said, regretfully. "Almost certainly it means a journey and probably an absence of some hours."

I threw my cap upon the table, turned up my coat to hide the absence of collar, and started for the door. My last sight of Smith showed him standing looking after me, tugging at the lobe of his ear and clicking his teeth together with suppressed irritability. I stumbled down the dark stairs, along the hall, and opened the front door. Vaguely visible in the light of a street lamp which stood at no great distance away, I saw a slender

man of medium height confronting me. From the shadowed face two large and luminous eyes looked out into mine. My visitor, who, despite the warmth of the evening, wore a heavy greatcoat, was an Oriental!

I drew back, apprehensively; then:

"Ah! Dr. Petrie!" he said in a softly musical voice which made me start again, "to God be all praise that I have found you!"

Some emotion, which at present I could not define, was stirring within me. Where had I seen this graceful Eastern youth before? Where had I heard that soft voice?

"Do you wish to see me professionally?" I asked—yet even as I put the question, I seemed to know it unnecessary.

"So you know me no more?" said the stranger—and his teeth gleamed in a slight smile.

Heavens! I knew now what had struck that vibrant chord within me! The voice, though infinitely deeper, yet had an unmistakable resemblance to the dulcet tones of Kâramanèh—of Kâramanèh, whose eyes haunted my dreams, whose beauty had done much to embitter my years.

The Oriental youth stepped forward, with outstretched hand.

"So you know me no more?" he repeated; "but I know *you*, and give praise to Allah that I have found you!"

I stepped back, pressed the electric switch, and turned, with leaping heart, to look into the face of my visitor. It was a face of the purest Greek beauty, a face that might have served as a model for Praxiteles; the skin had a golden pallor, which, with the crisp black hair and magnetic yet velvety eyes, suggested to my fancy that this was the young Antinöus risen from the Nile, whose wraith now appeared to me out of the night. I stifled a cry of surprise, not unmingled with gladness.

It was Azîz—the brother of Kâramanèh!

Never could the entrance of a figure upon the stage of a drama have been more dramatic than the coming of Azîz upon this night of all nights. I seized the outstretched hand and drew him forward, then reclosed the door and stood before him a moment in doubt.

A vaguely troubled look momentarily crossed the handsome face; with the Oriental's unerring instinct, he had detected the reserve of my greeting. Yet, when I thought of the treachery of Kâramanèh, when I remember how she, whom we had befriended, whom we had rescued from the house of Fu-

Manchu, now had turned like the beautiful viper that she was to strike at the hand that caressed her; when I thought how to-night we were set upon raiding the place where the evil Chinese doctor lurked in hiding, were set upon the arrest of that malignant genius and of all his creatures, Kâramanèh amongst them, is it strange that I hesitated? Yet, again, when I thought of my last meeting with her, and of how, twice, she had risked her life to save me . . .

So, avoiding the gaze of the lad, I took his arm, and in silence we two ascended the stairs and entered my study . . . where Nayland Smith stood bolt upright beside the table, his steely eyes fixed upon the face of the new arrival.

No look of recognition crossed the bronzed features, and Azîz, who had started forward with outstretched hands, fell back a step and looked pathetically from me to Nayland Smith, and from the grim commissioner back again to me. The appeal in the velvet eyes was more than I could tolerate, unmoved.

"Smith," I said shortly, "you remember Azîz?"

Not a muscle visibly moved in Smith's face, as he snapped back:

"I remember him perfectly."

"He has come, I think, to seek our assistance."

"Yes, yes!" cried Azîz, laying his hand upon my arm with a gesture painfully reminiscent of Kâramanèh—"I came only to-night to London. Oh, my gentlemen! I have searched, and searched, and searched, until I am weary. Often I have wished to die. And then at last I come to Rangoon . . ."

"To Rangoon!" snapped Smith, still with the gray eyes fixed almost fiercely upon the lad's face.

"To Rangoon—yes; and there I heard news at last. I hear that you have seen her—have seen Kâramanèh—that you are back in London." He was not entirely at home with his English. "I know then that she must be here, too. I ask them everywhere, and they answer 'yes.' Oh, Smith Pasha!"—he stepped forward and impulsively seized both Smith's hands—"You know where she is—take me to her!"

Smith's face was a study in perplexity, now. In the past we had befriended the young Azîz, and it was hard to look upon him in the light of an enemy. Yet had we not equally befriended his sister?—and she . . .

At last Smith glanced across at me where I stood just within the doorway.

"What do you make of it, Petrie?" he said harshly. "Personally I take it to mean that our plans have leaked out." He sprang suddenly back from Azîz, and I saw his glance traveling rapidly over the slight figure as if in quest of concealed arms. "I take it to be a trap!"

A moment he stood so, regarding him, and despite my well-grounded distrust of the Oriental character, I could have sworn that the expression of pained surprise upon the youth's face was not simulated but real. Even Smith, I think, began to share my view; for suddenly he threw himself into the white cane rest-chair, and, still fixedly regarding Azîz:

"Perhaps I have wronged you," he said. "If I have, you shall know the reason presently. Tell your own story!"

There was a pathetic humidity in the velvet eyes of Azîz—eyes so like those others that were ever looking into mine in dreams—as glancing from Smith to me he began, hands outstretched, characteristically, palms upward and fingers curling, to tell in broken English the story of his search for Kâramanèh . . .

"It was Fu-Manchu, my kind gentlemen—it was the *hâkîm* who is really not a man at all, but an *efreet*. He found us again less than four days after you had left us, Smith Pasha! . . . He found us in Cairo, and to Kâramanèh he made the forgetting of all things—even of me—even of me . . ."

Nayland Smith snapped his teeth together sharply; then:

"What do you mean by that?" he demanded.

For my own part I understood well enough, remembering how the brilliant Chinese doctor once had performed such an operation as this upon poor Inspector Weymouth; how, by means of an injection of some serum prepared (as Kâramanèh afterwards told us) from the venom of a swamp adder or similar reptile, he had induced *amnesia*, or complete loss of memory. I felt every drop of blood recede from my cheeks.

"Smith!" I began . . .

"Let him speak for himself," interrupted my friend sharply.

"They tried to take us both," continued Azîz, still speaking in that soft, melodious manner, but with deep seriousness. "I escaped, I, who am swift of foot, hoping to bring help."—He shook his head sadly—"But, except the All Powerful, who is so powerful as the *Hâkîm* Fu-Manchu? I hid, my gentlemen, and watched and waited, one—two—three weeks. At last I saw her again, my sister, Kâramanèh; but ah! she did not know me, did not know *me*, Azîz, her brother! She was in an *arabeeyeh*, and passed me quickly along the Sharia en-Nahhâsin. I ran, and ran, and ran, crying her name, but although she looked back, she did not know me—she did not know me! I felt that I was dying, and presently I fell—upon the steps of the Mosque of Abu."

He dropped the expressive hands wearily to his sides and sank his chin upon his breast.

"And then?" I said, huskily—for my heart was fluttering like a captive bird.

"Alas! from that day to this I see her no more, my gentlemen. I travel, not only in Egypt, but near and far, and still I see her no more until in Rangoon I hear that which brings me to England again"—he extended his palms naïvely—"and here I am—Smith Pasha."

Smith sprang upright again and turned to me.

"Either I am growing over-credulous," he said, "or Azîz speaks the truth. But"—he held up his hand—"you can tell me all that at some other time, Petrie! We must take no chances. Sergeant Carter is downstairs with the cab; you might ask him to step up. He and Azîz can remain here until our return."

Chapter XXVIII

THE SAMURAI'S SWORD

The muffled drumming of sleepless London seemed very remote from us, as side by side we crept up the narrow path to the studio. This was a starry but moonless night, and the little dingy white building with a solitary tree peeping, in silhouette, above the glazed roof, bore an odd resemblance to one of those tombs which form a city of the dead so near to the city of feverish life on the slopes of the Mokattam Hills. This line of reflection proved unpleasant, and I dismissed it sternly from my mind.

The shriek of a train-whistle reached me, a sound which breaks the stillness of the most silent London night, telling of the ceaseless, febrile life of the great world-capital whose activity ceases not with the coming of dark-

ness. Around and about us a very great stillness reigned, however, and the velvet dusk—which, with the star-jeweled sky, was strongly suggestive of an Eastern night—gave up no sign to show that it masked the presence of more than twenty men. Some distance away on our right was the Gables, that sinister and deserted mansion which we assumed, and with good reason, to be nothing less than the gateway to the subterranean abode of Dr. Fu-Manchu; before us was the studio, which, if Nayland Smith's deductions were accurate, concealed a second entrance to the same mysterious dwelling.

As my friend, glancing cautiously all about him, inserted the key in the lock, an owl hooted dismally almost immediately above our heads. I caught my breath sharply, for it might be a signal; but, looking upward, I saw a great black shape float slantingly from the tree beyond the studio into the coppice on the right which hemmed in the Gables. Silently the owl winged its uncanny flight into the greater darkness of the trees, and was gone. Smith opened the door and we stepped into the studio. Our plans had been well considered, and in accordance with these, I now moved up beside my friend, who was dimly perceptible to me in the starlight which found access through the glass roof, and pressed the catch of my electric pocket-lamp . . .

I suppose that by virtue of my self-imposed duty as chronicler of the deeds of Dr. Fu-Manchu—the greatest and most evil genius whom the later centuries have produced, the man who dreamt of an universal Yellow Empire—I should have acquired a certain facility in describing bizarre happenings. But I confess that it fails me now as I attempt in cold English to portray my emotions when the white beam from the little lamp cut through the darkness of the studio, and shone fully upon the beautiful face of *Kâramanèh!*

Less than six feet away from me she stood, arrayed in the gauzy dress of the harem, her fingers and slim white arms laden with barbaric jewelry! The light wavered in my suddenly nerveless hand, gleaming momentarily upon bare ankles and golden anklets, upon little red leather shoes.

I spoke no word, and Smith was as silent as I; both of us, I think, were speechless rather from amazement than in obedience to the evident wishes of Fu-Manchu's slave-girl. Yet I have only to close my eyes at this moment to see her as she stood, one finger raised to her lips, enjoining us to silence. She looked ghastly pale in the light of the lamp, but so lovely that my rebellious heart threatened already to make a fool of me.

So we stood in that untidy studio, with canvases and easels heaped against the wall and with all sorts of litter about us, a trio strangely met, and one to have amused the high gods watching through the windows of the stars.

"Go back!" came in a whisper from Kâramanèh.

I saw the red lips moving and read a dreadful horror in the widely opened eyes, in those eyes like pools of mystery to taunt the thirsty soul. The world of realities was slipping past me; I seemed to be losing my hold on things actual; I had built up an Eastern palace about myself and Kâramanèh, wherein, the world shut out, I might pass the hours in reading the mystery of those dark eyes. Nayland Smith brought me sharply to my senses.

"Steady with the light, Petrie!" he hissed in my ear. "My skepticism has been shaken, to-night, but I am taking no chances."

He moved from my side and forward toward that lovely, unreal figure which stood immediately before the model's throne and its background of plush curtains. Kâramanèh started forward to meet him, suppressing a little cry, whose real anguish could not have been simulated.

"Go back! go back!" she whispered urgently, and thrust out her hands against Smith's breast. "For God's sake, go back! I have risked my life to come here to-night. *He knows*, and is ready!" . . .

The words were spoken with passionate intensity, and Nayland Smith hesitated. To my nostrils was wafted that faint, delightful perfume which, since one night, two years ago, it had come to disturb my senses, had taunted me many times as the mirage taunts the parched Sahara traveler. I took a step forward.

"Don't move!" snapped Smith.

Kâramanèh clutched frenziedly at the lapels of his coat.

"Listen to me!" she said, beseechingly, and stamped one little foot upon the floor— "listen to me! You are a clever man, but you know nothing of a woman's heart—nothing—*nothing*—if seeing me, hearing me, knowing, as you do know, what I risk, you can doubt that I speak the truth. And I tell

you that it is death to go behind those curtains—that *he* . . ."

"That's what I wanted to know!" snapped Smith. His voice quivered with excitement.

Suddenly grasping Kâramanèh by the waist, he lifted her and set her aside; then in three bounds he was on to the model's throne and had torn the plush curtains bodily from their fastenings.

How it occurred I cannot hope to make clear, for here my recollections merge into a chaos. I know that Smith seemed to topple forward amid the purple billows of velvet, and his muffled cry came to me:

"Petrie! My God, Petrie!" . . .

The pale face of Kâramanèh looked up into mine and her hands were clutching me, but the glamour of her personality had lost its hold, for I knew—heavens, how poignantly it struck home to me!—that Nayland Smith was gone to his death. What I hoped to achieve, I know not, but hurling the trembling girl aside, I snatched the Browning pistol from my coat pocket, and with the ray of the lamp directed upon the purple mound of velvet, I leaped forward.

I think I realized that the curtains had masked a collapsible trap, a sheer pit of blackness, an instant before I was precipitated into it, but certainly the knowledge came too late. With the sound of a soft, shuddering cry in my ears, I fell, dropping lamp and pistol, and clutching at the fallen hangings. But they offered me no support. My head seemed to be bursting; I could utter only a hoarse groan, as I fell—fell—fell . . .

When my mind began to work again, in returning consciousness, I found it to be laden with reproach. How often in the past had we blindly hurled ourselves into just such a trap as this? Should we never learn that where Fu-Manchu was, impetuosity must prove fatal? On two distinct occasions in the past we had been made the victims of this device, yet even although we had had practically conclusive evidence that this studio was used by Dr. Fu-Manchu, we had relied upon its floor being as secure as that of any other studio, we had failed to sound every foot of it ere trusting our weight to its support. . . .

"There is such a divine simplicity in the English mind that one may lay one's plans with mathematical precision, and rely upon the Nayland Smiths and Dr. Petries to play their allotted parts. Excepting two faithful followers, my friends are long since departed. But here, in these vaults which time has overlooked and which are as secret and as serviceable to-day as they were two hundred years ago, I wait patiently, with my trap set, like the spider for the fly! . . ."

To the sound of that taunting voice, I opened my eyes. As I did so I strove to spring upright—only to realize that I was tied fast to a heavy ebony chair inlaid with ivory, and attached by means of two iron brackets to the floor.

"Even children learn from experience," continued the unforgettable voice, alternately guttural and sibilant, but always as deliberate as though the speaker were choosing with care words which should perfectly clothe his thoughts. "For 'a burnt child fears the fire,' says your English adage. But Mr. Commissioner Nayland Smith, who enjoys the confidence of the India Office, and who is empowered to control the movements of the Criminal Investigation Department, learns nothing from experience. He is less than a child, since he has twice rashly precipitated himself into a chamber charged with an anesthetic prepared, by a process of my own, from the *lycoperdon* or Common Puff-ball."

I became fully master of my senses, and I became fully alive to a stupendous fact. At last it was ended; we were utterly in the power of Dr. Fu-Manchu; our race was run.

I sat in a low vaulted room. The roof was of ancient brickwork, but the walls were draped with exquisite Chinese fabric having a green ground whereon was a design representing a grotesque procession of white peacocks. A green carpet covered the floor, and the whole of the furniture was of the same material as the chair to which I was strapped, viz:—ebony inlaid with ivory. This furniture was scanty. There was a heavy table in one corner of the dungeonesque place, on which were a number of books and papers. Before this table was a high-backed, heavily carven chair. A smaller table stood upon the right of the only visible opening, a low door partially draped with beadwork curtains, above which hung a silver lamp. On this smaller table, a stick of incense, in a silver holder, sent up a pencil of vapor into the air, and the chamber was loaded with the sickly sweet fumes. A faint haze from the incense-stick hovered up under the roof.

In the high-backed chair sat Dr. Fu-Manchu, wearing a green robe upon which was embroidered a design, the subject of which at first glance was not perceptible, but which

presently I made out to be a huge white peacock. He wore a little cap perched upon the dome of his amazing skull, and with one clawish hand resting upon the ebony of the table, he sat slightly turned toward me, his emotionless face a mask of incredible evil. In spite of, or because of, the high intellect written upon it, the face of Dr. Fu-Manchu was more utterly repellent than any I have ever known, and the green eyes, eyes green as those of a cat in the darkness, which sometimes burned like witch lamps, and sometimes were horribly filmed like nothing human or imaginable, might have mirrored not a soul, but an emanation of hell, incarnate in this gaunt, high-shouldered body.

Stretched flat upon the floor lay Nayland Smith, partially stripped, his arms thrown back over his head and his wrists chained to a stout iron staple attached to the wall; he was fully conscious and staring intently at the Chinese doctor. His bare ankles also were manacled, and fixed to a second chain, which quivered tautly across the green carpet and passed out through the doorway, being attached to something beyond the curtain, and invisible to me from where I sat.

Fu-Manchu was now silent. I could hear Smith's heavy breathing and hear my watch ticking in my pocket. I suddenly realized that although my body was lashed to the ebony chair, my hands and arms were free. Next, looking dazedly about me, my attention was drawn to a heavy sword which stood hilt upward against the wall within reach of my hand. It was a magnificent piece, of Japanese workmanship; a long, curved Damascened blade having a double-handed hilt of steel, inlaid with gold, and resembling fine Kuft work. A host of possibilities swept through my mind. Then I perceived that the sword was attached to the wall by a thin steel chain some five feet in length.

"Even if you had the dexterity of a Mexican knife-thrower," came the guttural voice of Fu-Manchu, "you would be unable to reach me, dear Dr. Petrie."

The Chinaman had read my thoughts.

Smith turned his eyes upon me momentarily, only to look away again in the direction of Fu-Manchu. My friend's face was slightly pale beneath the tan, and his jaw muscles stood out with unusual prominence. By this fact alone did he reveal his knowledge that he lay at the mercy of this enemy of the white race, of this inhuman being who himself knew no mercy, of this man whose

very genius was inspired by the cool, calculated cruelty of his race, of that race which
to this day disposes of hundreds, nay! thousands, of its unwanted girl-children by the
simple measure of throwing them down a
well specially dedicated to the purpose.

"The weapon near your hand," continued the Chinaman, imperturbably, "is a
product of the civilization of our near neighbors, the Japanese, a race to whose courage
I prostrate myself in meekness. It is the sword
of a *samurai*, Dr. Petrie. It is of very great
age, and was, until an unfortunate misunderstanding with myself led to the extinction
of the family, a treasured possession of a
noble Japanese house . . ."

The soft voice, into which an occasional
sibilance crept, but which never rose above
a cool monotone, gradually was lashing me
into fury, and I could see the muscles moving
in Smith's jaws as he convulsively clenched
his teeth; whereby I knew that, impotent, he
burned with a rage at least as great as mine.
But I did not speak, and did not move.

"The ancient tradition of *seppuku*," continued the Chinaman, "or *hara-kiri*, still rules,
as you know, in the great families of Japan.
There is a sacred ritual, and the *samurai* who
dedicates himself to this honorable end, must
follow strictly the ritual. As a physician, the
exact nature of the ceremony might possibly
interest you, Dr. Petrie, but a technical account of the two incisions which the sacri-
ficant employs in his self-dismissal, might,
on the other hand, bore Mr. Nayland Smith.
Therefore I will merely enlighten you upon
one little point, a minor one, but interesting
to the student of human nature. In short,
even a *samurai*—and no braver race has ever
honored the world—sometimes hesitates to
complete the operation. The weapon near to
your hand, my dear Dr. Petrie, is known as
the Friend's Sword. On such occasions as we
are discussing, a trusty friend is given the
post—an honored one—of standing behind
the brave man who offers himself to his gods,
and should the latter's courage momentarily
fail him, the friend with the trusty blade (to
which now I especially direct your attention)
diverts the hierophant's mind from his di-
gression, and rectifies his temporary breach
of etiquette by severing the cervical vertebræ
of the spinal column with the friendly blade—
which you can reach quite easily, Dr. Petrie,
if you care to extend your hand."

Some dim perception of the truth was beginning to creep into my mind. When I say

a perception of the truth, I mean rather of
some part of the purpose of Dr. Fu-Manchu;
of the whole horrible truth, of the scheme
which had been conceived by that mighty,
evil man, I had no glimmering, but I foresaw
that a frightful ordeal was before us both.

"That I hold you in high esteem," continued Fu-Manchu, "is a fact which must be
apparent to you by this time, but in regard
to your companion, I entertain very different
sentiments. . . ."

Always underlying the deliberate calm of
the speaker, sometimes showing itself in an
unusually deep guttural, sometimes in an
unusually serpentine sibilance, lurked the
frenzy of hatred which in the past had revealed itself occasionally in wild outbursts.
Momentarily I expected such an outburst now,
but it did not come.

"One quality possessed by Mr. Nayland
Smith," resumed the Chinaman, "I admire;
I refer to his courage. I would wish that so
courageous a man should seek his own end,
should voluntarily efface himself from the
path of that world-movement which he is
powerless to check. In short, I would have
him show himself a *samurai*. Always his
friend, you shall remain so to the end, Dr.
Petrie. I have arranged for this."

He struck lightly a little silver gong, dependent from the corner of the table, whereupon, from the curtained doorway, there
entered a short, thickly built Burman whom
I recognized for a dacoit. He wore a shoddy
blue suit, which had been made for a much
larger man; but these things claimed little of
my attention, which automatically was directed to the load beneath which the Burman
labored.

Upon his back he carried a sort of wire
box rather less than six feet long, some two
feet high, and about two feet wide. In short,
it was a stout framework covered with fine
wire-netting on the top, sides and ends, but
being open at the bottom. It seemed to be
made in five sections or to contain four sliding partitions which could be raised or lowered at will. These were of wood, and in the
bottom of each was cut a little arch. The arches
in the four partitions varied in size, so that
whereas the first was not more than five inches
high, the fourth opened almost to the wire
roof of the box or cage; and a fifth, which
was but little higher than the first, was cut
in the actual end of the contrivance.

So intent was I upon this device, the purpose of which I was wholly unable to divine,

that I directed the whole of my attention upon it. Then, as the Burman paused in the doorway, resting a corner of the cage upon the brilliant carpet, I glanced toward Fu-Manchu. He was watching Nayland Smith, and revealing his irregular yellow teeth—the teeth of an opium smoker—in the awful mirthless smile which I knew.

"God!" whispered Smith—"the Six Gates!"

"The knowledge of my beautiful country serves you well," replied Fu-Manchu gently.

Instantly I looked to my friend . . . and every drop of blood seemed to recede from my heart, leaving it cold in my breast. If I did not know the purpose of the cage, obviously Smith knew it all too well. His pallor had grown more marked, and although his gray eyes stared defiantly at the Chinaman, I, who knew him, could read a deathly horror in their depths.

The dacoit, in obedience to a guttural order from Dr. Fu-Manchu, placed the cage upon the carpet, completely covering Smith's body, but leaving his neck and head exposed. The seared and pock-marked face set in a sort of placid leer, the dacoit adjusted the sliding partitions to Smith's recumbent form, and I saw the purpose of the graduated arches. They were intended to divide a human body in just such fashion, and, as I realized, were most cunningly shaped to that end. The whole of Smith's body lay now in the wire cage, each of the five compartments whereof was shut off from its neighbor.

The Burman stepped back and stood waiting in the doorway. Dr. Fu-Manchu, removing his gaze from the face of my friend, directed it now upon me.

"Mr. Commissioner Nayland Smith shall have the honor of acting as hierophant, admitting himself to the Mysteries," said Fu-Manchu softly, "and you, Dr. Petrie, shall be the Friend."

Chapter XXIX

THE SIX GATES

He glanced toward the Burman, who retired immediately, to re-enter a moment later carrying a curious leather sack, in shape not unlike that of a *sakka* or Arab water-carrier. Opening a little trap in the top of the first compartment of the cage (that is, the compartment which covered Smith's bare feet

and ankles) he inserted the neck of the sack, then suddenly seized it by the bottom and shook it vigorously. Before my horrified gaze, four huge rats came tumbling out from the bag into the cage!

The dacoit snatched away the sack and snapped the shutter fast. A moving mist obscured my sight, a mist through which I saw the green eyes of Dr. Fu-Manchu fixed upon me, and through which, as from a great distance, his voice, sunk to a snake-like hiss, came to my ears.

"Cantonese rats, Dr. Petrie . . . the most ravenous in the world . . . they have eaten nothing for nearly a week!"

Then all became blurred as though a painter with a brush steeped in red had smudged out the details of the picture. For an indefinite period, which seemed like many minutes yet probably was only a few seconds, I saw nothing and heard nothing; my sensory nerves were dulled entirely. From this state I was awakened and brought back to the realities by a sound which ever afterward I was doomed to associate with that ghastly scene.

This was the squealing of the rats.

The red mist seemed to disperse at that, and with frightfully intense interest, I began to study the awful torture to which Nayland Smith was being subjected. The dacoit had disappeared, and Fu-Manchu placidly was watching the four lean and hideous animals in the cage. As I also turned my eyes in that direction, the rats overcame their temporary fear, and began . . .

"You have been good enough to notice," said the Chinaman, his voice still sunk in that sibilant whisper, "my partiality for dumb allies. You have met my scorpions, my death-adders, my baboon-man. The uses of such a playful little animal as a marmoset have never been fully appreciated before, I think, but to an indiscretion of this last-named pet of mine, I seem to remember that you owed something in the past, Dr. Petrie . . ."

Nayland Smith stifled a deep groan. One rapid glance I ventured at his face. It was a grayish hue, now, and dank with perspiration. His gaze met mine.

The rats had almost ceased squealing.

"Much depends upon yourself, Doctor," continued Fu-Manchu, slightly raising his voice. "I credit Mr. Commissioner Nayland Smith with courage high enough to sustain the raising of all the gates; but I estimate the strength of your friendship highly, also, and predict that you will use the sword of the *samurai* certainly not later than the time when I shall raise the third gate. . . ."

A low shuddering sound, which I cannot hope to describe, but alas! can never forget, broke from the lips of the tortured man.

"In China," resumed Fu-Manchu, "we call this quaint fancy the Six Gates of Joyful Wisdom. The first gate, by which the rats are admitted, is called the Gate of Joyous Hope; the second, the Gate of Mirthful Doubt. The third gate is poetically named the Gate of True Rapture, and the fourth, the Gate of Gentle Sorrow. I once was honored in the friendship of an exalted mandarin who sustained the course of Joyful Wisdom to the raising of the Fifth Gate (called the Gate of Sweet Desires) and the admission of the twentieth rat. I esteem him almost equally with my ancestors. The Sixth, or Gate Celestial—whereby a man enters into the Joy of Complete Understanding—I have dispensed with, here, substituting a Japanese fancy of an antiquity nearly as great and honorable. The introduction of this element of speculation, I count a happy thought, and accordingly take pride to myself."

"The sword, Petrie!" whispered Smith. I should not have recognized his voice, but he spoke quite evenly and steadily. "I rely upon you, old man, to spare me the humiliation of asking mercy from that yellow fiend!"

My mind throughout this time had been gaining a sort of dreadful clarity. I had avoided looking at the sword of *hara-kiri*, but my thoughts had been leading me mercilessly up to the point at which we were now arrived. No vestige of anger, of condemnation of the inhuman being seated in the ebony chair, remained; that was past. Of all that had gone before, and of what was to come in the future, I thought nothing, knew nothing. Our long fight against the yellow group, our encounters with the numberless creatures of Fu-Manchu, the dacoits—even Kâramanèh—were forgotten, blotted out. I saw nothing of the strange appointments of that subterranean chamber; but face to face with the supreme moment of a lifetime, I was alone with my poor friend—and God.

The rats began squealing again. They were fighting . . .

"Quick, Petrie! Quick, man! I am weakening. . . ."

I turned and took up the *samurai* sword. My hands were very hot and dry, but perfectly steady, and I tested the edge of the heavy weapon upon my left thumb-nail as

quietly as one might test a razor blade. It was as keen, this blade of ghastly history, as any razor ever wrought in Sheffield. I seized the graven hilt, bent forward in my chair, and raised the Friend's Sword high above my head. With the heavy weapon poised there, I looked into my friend's eyes. They were feverishly bright, but never in all my days, nor upon the many beds of suffering which it had been my lot to visit, had I seen an expression like that within them.

"The raising of the First Gate is always a crucial moment," came the guttural voice of the Chinaman.

Although I did not see him, and barely heard his words, I was aware that he had stood up and was bending forward over the lower end of the cage.

"Now, Petrie! now! God bless you . . . and good-by . . ."

From somewhere—somewhere remote—I heard a hoarse and animal-like cry, followed by the sound of a heavy fall. I can scarcely bear to write of that moment, for I had actually begun the downward sweep of the great sword when that sound came—a faint Hope, speaking of aid where I had thought no aid possible.

How I contrived to divert the blade, I do not know to this day; but I do know that its mighty sweep sheared a lock from Smith's head and laid bare the scalp. With the hilt in my quivering hands I saw the blade bite deeply through the carpet and floor above Nayland Smith's skull. There, buried fully two inches in the woodwork, it stuck, and still clutching the hilt, I looked to the right and across the room—I looked to the curtained doorway.

Fu-Manchu, with one long, claw-like hand upon the top of the First Gate, was bending over the trap, but his brilliant green eyes were turned in the same direction as my own—upon the curtained doorway.

Upright within it, her beautiful face as pale as death, but her great eyes blazing with a sort of splendid madness, stood Kâramanèh!

She looked, not at the tortured man, not at me, but fully at Dr. Fu-Manchu. One hand clutched the trembling draperies; now she suddenly raised the other, so that the jewels on her white arm glittered in the light of the lamp above the door. She held my Browning pistol! Fu-Manchu sprang upright, inhaling sibilantly, as Kâramanèh pointed the pistol point blank at his high skull and fired. . . .

I saw a little red streak appear, up by the

neutral colored hair, under the black cap. I became as a detached intelligence, unlinked with the corporeal, looking down upon a thing which for some reason I had never thought to witness.

Fu-Manchu threw up both arms, so that the sleeves of the green robe fell back to the elbows. He clutched at his head, and the black cap fell behind him. He began to utter short, guttural cries; he swayed backward—to the right—to the left—then lurched forward right across the cage. There he lay, writhing, for a moment, his baneful eyes turned up, revealing the whites; and the great gray rats, released, began leaping about the room. Two shot like gray streaks past the slim figure in the doorway, one darted behind the chair to which I was lashed, and the fourth ran all around against the wall . . . Fu-Manchu, prostrate across the overturned cage, lay still, his massive head sagging downward.

I experienced a mental repetition of my adventure in the earlier evening—I was dropping, dropping, dropping into some bottomless pit . . . warm arms were about my neck; and burning kisses upon my lips.

Chapter XXX

THE CALL OF THE EAST

I seemed to haul myself back out of the pit of unconsciousness by the aid of two little hands which clasped my own. I uttered a sigh that was almost a sob, and opened my eyes.

I was sitting in the big red-leathern arm-chair in my own study . . . and a lovely but truly bizarre figure, in a harem dress, was kneeling on the carpet at my feet; so that my first sight of the world was the sweetest sight that the world had to offer me, the dark eyes of Kâramanèh, with tears trembling like jewels upon her lashes!

I looked no further than that, heeded not if there were others in the room beside we two, but, gripping the jewel laden fingers in what must have been a cruel clasp, I searched the depths of the glorious eyes in ever growing wonder. What change had taken place in those limpid, mysterious pools? Why was a wild madness growing up within me like a flame? Why was the old longing returned, ten-thousandfold, to snatch that pliant, exquisite shape to my breast?

No word was spoken, but the spoken words of a thousand ages could not have expressed one tithe what was held in that silent communion. A hand was laid hesitatingly on my shoulder. I tore my gaze away from the lovely face so near to mine, and glanced up.

Azîz stood at the back of my chair.

"God is all merciful," he said. "My sister is restored to us" (I loved him for the plural); "and she *remembers*."

Those few words were enough; I understood now that this lovely girl, who half knelt, half lay, at my feet, was not the evil, perverted creature of Fu-Manchu whom we had gone out to arrest with the other vile servants of the Chinese doctor, but was the old, beloved companion of two years ago, the Kâramanèh for whom I had sought long and wearily in Egypt, who had been swallowed up and lost to me in that land of mystery.

The loss of memory which Fu-Manchu had artificially induced was subject to the same inexplicable laws which ordinarily rule in cases of *amnesia*. The shock of her brave action that night had begun to effect a cure; the sight of Azîz had completed it.

Inspector Weymouth was standing by the writing-table. My mind cleared rapidly now, and standing up, but without releasing the girl's hands, so that I drew her up beside me, I said:

"Weymouth—where is—?"

"He's waiting to see you, Doctor," replied the inspector.

A pang, almost physical, struck at my heart.

"Poor, dear old Smith!" I cried, with a break in my voice.

Dr. Gray, a neighboring practitioner, appeared in the doorway at the moment that I spoke the words.

"It's all right, Petrie," he said, reassuringly; "I think we took it in time. I have thoroughly cauterized the wounds, and granted that no complication sets in, he'll be on his feet again in a week or two."

I suppose I was in a condition closely bordering upon the hysterical. At any rate, my behavior was extraordinary. I raised both my hands above my head.

"Thank God!" I cried at the top of my voice, "thank God!—thank God!"

"Thank Him, indeed," responded the musical voice of Azîz. He spoke with all the passionate devoutness of the true Môslem.

Everything, even Kâramanèh, was forgotten, and I started for the door as though my life depended upon my speed. With one foot upon the landing, I turned, looked back, and met the glance of Inspector Weymouth.

"What have you done with—the body?" I asked.

"We haven't been able to get to it. That end of the vault collapsed two minutes after we hauled you out!"

As I write, now, of those strange days, already they seem remote and unreal. But, where other and more dreadful memories already are grown misty, the memory of that evening in my rooms remains clear-cut and intimate. It marked a crisis in my life.

During the days that immediately followed, whilst Smith was slowly recovering from his hurts, I made my plans deliberately; I prepared to cut myself off from old associations—prepared to exile myself, gladly; how gladly I cannot hope to express in mere cold words.

That my friend approved of my projects, I cannot truthfully state, but his disapproval at least was not openly expressed. To Kâramanèh I said nothing of my plans, but her complete reliance in my powers to protect her, now, from all harm, was at once pathetic and exquisite.

Since, always, I have sought in these chronicles to confine myself to the facts directly relating to the malignant activity of Dr. Fu-Manchu, I shall abstain from burdening you with details of my private affairs. As an instrument of the Chinese doctor, it has sometimes been my duty to write of the beautiful Eastern girl; I cannot suppose that my readers have any further curiosity respecting her from the moment that Fate freed her from that awful servitude. Therefore, when I shall have dealt with the episodes which marked our voyage to Egypt—I had opened negotiations in regard to a practice in Cairo—I may honorably lay down my pen.

These episodes opened, dramatically, upon the second night of the voyage from Marseilles.

Chapter XXXI

"MY SHADOW LIES UPON YOU"

I suppose I did not awake very readily. Following the nervous vigilance of the past six months, my tired nerves, in the enjoyment of this relaxation, were rapidly recuperating. I no longer feared to awake to find a knife at my throat, no longer dreaded the darkness as a foe.

So that the voice may have been calling (indeed, *had* been calling) for some time, and of this I had been hazily conscious before finally I awoke. Then, ere the new sense of security came to reassure me, the old sense of impending harm set my heart leaping nervously. There is always a certain physical panic attendant upon such awakening in the still of night, especially in novel surroundings. Now, I sat up abruptly, clutching at the rail of my berth and listening.

There was a soft thudding on my cabin door, and a voice, low and urgent, was crying my name.

Through the open porthole the moonlight streamed into my room, and save for a remote and soothing throb, inseparable from the progress of a great steamship, nothing else disturbed the stillness; I might have floated lonely upon the bosom of the Mediterranean. But there was the drumming on the door again, and the urgent appeal:

"Dr. Petrie! Dr. Petrie!"

I threw off the bedclothes and stepped on to the floor of the cabin, fumbling hastily for my slippers. A fear that something was amiss, that some aftermath, some wraith of the dread Chinaman, was yet to come to disturb our premature peace, began to haunt me. I threw open the door.

Upon the gleaming deck, blackly outlined against a wondrous sky, stood a man who wore a blue greatcoat over his pyjamas, and whose unstockinged feet were thrust into red slippers. It was Platts, the Marconi operator.

"I'm awfully sorry to disturb you, Dr. Petrie," he said, "and I was even less anxious to arouse your neighbor; but somebody seems to be trying to get a message, presumably urgent, through to you."

"To me!" I cried.

"I cannot make it out," admitted Platts, running his fingers through disheveled hair, "but I thought it better to arouse you. Will you come up?"

I turned without a word, slipped into my dressing-gown, and with Platts passed aft along the deserted deck. The sea was as calm as a great lake. Ahead, on the port bow, an angry flambeau burned redly beneath the peaceful vault of the heavens. Platts nodded absently in the direction of the weird flames.

"Stromboli," he said; "we shall be nearly

through the Straits by breakfast-time."

We mounted the narrow stair to the Marconi deck. At the table sat Platts' assistant with the Marconi attachment upon his head— an apparatus which always set me thinking of the electric chair.

"Have you got it?" demanded my companion as we entered the room.

"It's still coming through," replied the other without moving, "but in the same jerky fashion. Every time I get it, it seems to have gone back to the beginning—just *Dr. Petrie—Dr. Petrie.*"

He began to listen again for the elusive message. I turned to Platts.

"Where is it being sent from?" I asked.

Platts shook his head.

"That's the mystery," he declared. "Look!"—he pointed to the table; "according to the Marconi chart, there's a Messagerie boat due west between us and Marseilles, and the homeward-bound P. & O. which we passed this morning must be getting on that way also, by now. The *Isis* is somewhere ahead, but I've spoken all these, and the message comes from none of them."

"Then it may come from Messina."

"It doesn't come from Messina," replied the man at the table, beginning to write rapidly.

Platts stepped forward and bent over the message which the other was writing.

"Here it is!" he cried, excitedly; "we're getting it."

Stepping in turn to the table, I leaned over between the two and read these words as the operator wrote them down:

Dr. Petrie—my shadow . . .

I drew a quick breath and gripped Platts' shoulder harshly. His assistant began fingering the instrument with irritation.

"Lost it again!" he muttered.

"This message," I began . . .

But again the pencil was traveling over the paper:—*lies upon you all . . . end of message.*

The operator stood up and unclasped the receivers from his ears. There, high above the sleeping ship's company, with the carpet of the blue Mediterranean stretched indefinitely about us, we three stood looking at one another. By virtue of a miracle of modern science, some one, divided from me by mile upon mile of boundless ocean, had spoken— and had been heard.

"Is there no means of learning," I said, "from whence this message emanated?"

Platts shook his head, perplexedly.

"They gave no code word," he said. "God knows who they were. It's a strange business and a strange message. Have you any sort of idea, Dr. Petrie, respecting the identity of the sender?"

I stared him hard in the face; an idea had mechanically entered my mind, but one of which I did not choose to speak, since it was opposed to human possibility.

But, had I not seen with my own eyes the bloody streak across his forehead as the shot fired by Kâramanèh entered his high skull, had I not known, so certainly as it is given to man to know, that the giant intellect was no more, the mighty will impotent, I should have replied:

"The message is from Dr. Fu-Manchu!"

My reflections were rudely terminated and my sinister thoughts given new stimulus, by a loud though muffled cry which reached me from somewhere in the ship, below. Both my companions started as violently as I, whereby I knew that the mystery of the wireless message had not been without its effect upon their minds also. But whereas they paused in doubt, I leaped from the room and almost threw myself down the ladder.

It was Kâramanèh who had uttered that cry of fear and horror!

Although I could perceive no connection betwixt the strange message and the cry in the night, intuitively I linked them, intuitively I knew that my fears had been well-grounded; that the shadow of Fu-Manchu still lay upon us.

Kâramanèh occupied a large stateroom aft on the main deck; so that I had to descend from the upper deck on which my own room was situated to the promenade deck, again to the main deck and thence proceed nearly the whole length of the alleyway.

Kâramanèh and her brother, Azîz, who occupied a neighboring room, met me, near the library. Kâramanèh's eyes were wide with fear; her peerless coloring had fled, and she was white to the lips. Azîz, who wore a dressing-gown thrown hastily over his night attire, had his arm protectively about the girl's shoulders.

"The mummy!" she whispered tremulously—"the mummy!"

There came a sound of opening doors, and several passengers, whom Kâramanèh's cries had alarmed, appeared in various stages of undress. A stewardess came running from the far end of the alleyway, and I found time to wonder at my own speed; for, starting from the distant Marconi deck, yet I had been the first to arrive upon the scene.

Stacey, the ship's doctor, was quartered at no great distance from the spot, and he now joined the group. Anticipating the question which trembled upon the lips of several of those about me:

"Come to Dr. Stacey's room," I said, taking Kâramanèh's arm; "we will give you something to enable you to sleep." I turned to the group. "My patient has had severe nerve trouble," I explained, "and has developed somnambulistic tendencies."

I declined the stewardess' offer of assistance, with a slight shake of the head, and shortly the four of us entered the doctor's cabin, on the deck above. Stacey carefully closed the door. He was an old fellow student of mine, and already he knew much of the history of the beautiful Eastern girl and her brother Azîz.

"I fear there's mischief afoot, Petrie," he said. "Thanks to your presence of mind, the ship's gossips need know nothing of it."

I glanced at Kâramanèh, who, since the moment of my arrival had never once removed her gaze from me; she remained in that state of passive fear in which I had found her, the lovely face pallid; and she stared at me fixedly in a childish, expressionless way which made me fear that the shock to which she had been subjected, whatever its nature, had caused a relapse into that strange condition of forgetfulness from which a previous shock had aroused her. I could see that Stacey shared my view, for:

"Something has frightened you," he said gently, seating himself on the arm of Kâramanèh's chair and patting her hand as if to reassure her. "Tell us all about it."

For the first time since our meeting that night, the girl turned her eyes from me and glanced up at Stacey, a sudden warm blush stealing over her face and throat and as quickly departing, to leave her even more pale than before. She grasped Stacey's hand in both her own—and looked again at me.

"Send for Mr. Nayland Smith without delay!" she said, and her sweet voice was slightly tremulous. "He must be put on his guard!"

I started up.

"Why?" I said. "For God's sake tell us what has happened!"

Azîz, who evidently was as anxious as myself for information, and who now knelt at his sister's feet looking at her with that strange love, which was almost adoration, in his eyes, glanced back at me and nodded his head rapidly.

"Something"—Kâramanèh paused, shuddering violently—"some dreadful thing, like a mummy escaped from its tomb, came into my room to-night through the porthole . . ."

"Through the porthole?" echoed Stacey, amazedly.

"Yes, yes, through the porthole! A creature tall and very, very thin. He wore wrappings—yellow wrappings—swathed about his head, so that only his eyes, his evil gleaming eyes, were visible. . . . From waist to knees he was covered, also, but his body, his feet, and his legs were bare . . ."

"Was he—?" I began . . .

"He was a brown man, yes"—Kâramanèh, divining my question, nodded, and the shimmering cloud of her wonderful hair, hastily confined, burst free and rippled about her shoulders. "A gaunt, fleshless brown man, who bent, and writhed bony fingers—so!"

"A thug!" I cried.

"He—it—the mummy thing—would have strangled me if I had slept, for he crouched over the berth—seeking—seeking . . ."

I clenched my teeth convulsively.

"But I was sitting up—"

"With the light on?" interrupted Stacey in surprise.

"No," added Kâramanèh; "the light was out." She turned her eyes toward me, as the wonderful blush overspread her face once more. "I was sitting thinking. It all happened within a few seconds, and quite silently. As the mummy crouched over the berth, I unlocked the door and leaped out into the passage. I think I screamed; I did not mean to. Oh, Dr. Stacey, there is not a moment to spare! Mr. Nayland Smith must be warned immediately. Some horrible servant of Dr. Fu-Manchu is on the ship!"

Chapter XXXII

THE TRAGEDY

Nayland Smith leaned against the edge of the dressing-table, attired in pyjamas. The little stateroom was hazy with smoke, and my friend gripped the charred briar between his teeth and watched the blue-gray clouds arising from the bowl, in an abstracted way. I knew that he was thinking hard, and from the fact that he had exhibited no surprise when I had related to him the particulars of the attack upon Kâramanèh, I judged that he had half anticipated something of the kind. Suddenly he stood up, staring at me fixedly.

"Your tact has saved the situation, Petrie," he snapped. "It failed you momentarily, though, when you proposed to me just now that we should muster the lascars for inspection. Our game is to pretend that we know nothing—that we believe Kâramanèh to have had a bad dream."

"But, Smith," I began—

"It would be useless, Petrie," he interrupted me. "You cannot suppose that I overlooked the possibility of some creature of the doctor's being among the lascars. I can assure you that not one of them answers to the description of the midnight assailant. From the girl's account we have to look (discarding the idea of a revivified mummy) for a man of unusual height—and there's no lascar of unusual height on board; and from the visible evidence, that he entered the stateroom through the porthole, we have to look for a man more than normally thin. In a word, the servant of Dr. Fu-Manchu who attempted the life of Kâramanèh is either in hiding on the ship, or, if visible, is disguised."

With his usual clarity of vision, Nayland Smith had visualized the facts of the case; I passed in mental survey each one of the passengers, and those of the crew whose appearances were familar to me, with the result that I had to admit the justice of my friend's conclusions. Smith began to pace the narrow strip of carpet between the dressing-table and the door. Suddenly he began again.

"From our knowledge of Fu-Manchu—and of the group surrounding him (and, don't forget, *surviving* him)—we may further assume that the wireless message was no gratuitous piece of melodrama, but that it was directed to a definite end. Let us endeavor to link up the chain a little. You occupy an upper deck berth; so do I. Experience of the Chinaman has formed a habit in both of us; that of sleeping with closed windows. Your port was fastened and so was my own. Kâramanèh is quartered on the main deck, and her brother's stateroom opens into the same alleyway. Since the ship is in the Straits of

Messina, and the glass set fair, the stewards have not closed the portholes nightly at present. We know that that of Kâramanèh's stateroom was open. Therefore, in any attempt upon our quartet, Kâramanèh would automatically be selected for the victim, since failing you or myself she may be regarded as being the most obnoxious to Dr. Fu-Manchu."

I nodded comprehendingly. Smith's capacity for throwing the white light of reason into the darkest places often amazed me.

"You may have noticed," he continued, "that Kâramanèh's room is directly below your own. In the event of any outcry, you would be sooner upon the scene than I should, for instance, because I sleep on the opposite side of the ship. This circumstance I take to be the explanation of the wireless message, which, because of its hesitancy (a piece of ingenuity very characteristic of the group), led to your being awakened and invited up to the Marconi deck; in short, it gave the would-be assassin a better chance of escaping before your arrival."

I watched my friend in growing wonder. The strange events, seemingly having no link, took their places in the drama, and became well-ordered episodes in a plot that only a criminal genius could have devised. As I studied the keen, bronzed face, I realized to the full the stupendous mental power of Dr. Fu-Manchu, measuring it by the criterion of Nayland Smith's. For the cunning Chinaman, in a sense, had foiled this brilliant man before me, whereby, if by nought else, I might know him a master of his evil art.

"I regard the episode," continued Smith, "as a posthumous attempt of the doctor's; a legacy of hate which may prove more disastrous than any attempt made upon us by Fu-Manchu in life. Some fiendish member of the murder group is on board the ship. We must, as always, meet guile with guile. There must be no appeal to the captain, no public examination of passengers and crew. One attempt has failed; I do not doubt that others will be made. At present, you will enact the rôle of physician-in-attendance upon Kâramanèh, and will put it about for whom it may interest that a slight return of her nervous trouble is causing her to pass uneasy nights. I can safely leave this part of the case to you, I think?"

I nodded rapidly.

"I haven't troubled to make inquiries,"

added Smith, "but I think it probable that the regulation respecting closed ports will come into operation immediately we have passed the Straits, or at any rate immediately there is any likelihood of bad weather."

"You mean—"

"I mean that no alteration should be made in our habits. A second attempt along similar lines is to be apprehended—to-night. After that we may begin to look out for a new danger."

"I pray we may avoid it," I said fervently.

As I entered the saloon for breakfast in the morning, I was subjected to solicitous inquiries from Mrs. Prior, the gossip of the ship. Her room adjoined Kâramanèh's and she had been one of the passengers aroused by the girl's cries in the night. Strictly adhering to my rôle, I explained that my patient was threatened with a second nervous breakdown, and was subject to vivid and disturbing dreams. One or two other inquiries I met in the same way, ere escaping to the corner table reserved to us.

That iron-bound code of conduct which rules the Anglo-Indian, in the first days of the voyage had threatened to ostracize Kâramanèh and Azîz, by reason of the Eastern blood to which their brilliant but peculiar type of beauty bore witness. Smith's attitude, however—and, in a Burmese commissioner, it constituted something of a law—had done much to break down the barriers; the extraordinary beauty of the girl had done the rest. So that now, far from finding themselves shunned, the society of Kâramanèh and her romantic-looking brother was universally courted. The last inquiry that morning, respecting my interesting patient, came from the bishop of Damascus, a benevolent old gentleman whose ancestry was not wholly innocent of Oriental strains, and who sat at a table immediately behind me. As I settled down to my porridge, he turned his chair slightly and bent to my ear.

"Mrs. Prior tells me that your charming friend was disturbed last night," he whispered. "She seems rather pale this morning; I sincerely trust that she is suffering no ill-effect."

I swung around, with a smile. Owing to my carelessness, there was a slight collision, and the poor bishop, who had been invalided to England after typhoid, in order to undergo special treatment, suppressed an exclamation of pain, although his fine dark eyes gleamed kindly upon me through the pebbles of his gold-rimmed pince-nez.

Indeed, despite his Eastern blood, he might have posed for a Sadler picture, his small and refined features seeming out of place above the bulky body.

"Can you forgive my clumsiness," I began—

But the bishop raised his small, slim fingered hand of old ivory hue, deprecatingly.

His system was supercharged with typhoid bacilli, and, as sometimes occurs, the superfluous "bugs" had sought exit. He could only walk with the aid of two stout sticks, and bent very much at that. His left leg had been surgically scraped to the bone, and I appreciated the exquisite torture to which my awkwardness had subjected him. But he would entertain no apologies, pressing his inquiry respecting Kâramanèh, in the kindly manner which had made him so deservedly popular on board.

"Many thanks for your solicitude," I said; "I have promised her sound repose to-night, and since my professional reputation is at stake, I shall see that she secures it."

In short, we were in pleasant company, and the day passed happily enough and without notable event. Smith spent some considerable time with the chief officer, wandering about unfrequented parts of the ship. I learned later that he had explored the lascars' quarters, the forecastle, the engine-room, and had even descended to the stoke-hold; but this was done so unostentatiously that it occasioned no comment.

With the approach of evening, in place of that physical contentment which usually heralds the dinner-hour, at sea, I experienced a fit of the seemingly causeless apprehension which too often in the past had harbingered the coming of grim events; which I had learnt to associate with the nearing presence of one of Fu-Manchu's death-agents. In view of the facts, as I afterwards knew them to be, I cannot account for this.

Yet, in an unexpected manner, my forebodings were realized. That night I was destined to meet a sorrow surpassing any which my troubled life had known. Even now I experience great difficulty in relating the matters which befell, in speaking of the sense of irrevocable loss which came to me. Briefly, then, at about ten minutes before the dining hour, whilst all the passengers, myself included, were below, dressing, a faint cry arose from somewhere aft on the upper deck—a cry which was swiftly taken up by other

THE RETURN OF DR. FU-MANCHU

voices, so that presently a deck steward echoed it immediately outside my own stateroom:

"Man overboard! Man overboard!"

All my premonitions rallying in that one sickening moment, I sprang out on the deck, half dressed as I was, and leaping past the boat which swung nearly opposite my door, craned over the rail, looking astern.

For a long time I could detect nothing unusual. The engine-room telegraph was ringing—and the motion of the screws momentarily ceased; then, in response to further ringing, recommenced, but so as to jar the whole structure of the vessel; whereby I knew that the engines were reversed. Peering intently into the wake of the ship, I was but dimly aware of the ever growing turmoil around me, of the swift mustering of a boat's crew, of the shouted orders of the third-officer. Suddenly I saw it—the sight which was to haunt me for succeeding days and nights.

Half in the streak of the wake and half out of it, I perceived the sleeve of a white jacket, and, near to it, a soft felt hat. The sleeve rose up once into clear view, seemed to describe a half-circle in the air then sink back again into the glassy swell of the water. Only the hat remained floating upon the surface.

By the evidence of the white sleeve alone I might have remained unconvinced, although upon the voyage I had become familiar enough with the drill shooting-jacket, but the presence of the gray felt hat was almost conclusive.

The man overboard was Nayland Smith!

I cannot hope, writing now, to convey in any words at my command, a sense, even remote, of the utter loneliness which in that dreadful moment closed coldly down upon me.

To spring overboard to the rescue was a natural impulse, but to have obeyed it would have been worse than quixotic. In the first place, the drowning man was close upon half a mile astern; in the second place, others had seen the hat and the white coat as clearly as I; among them the third-officer, standing upright in the stern of the boat—which, with commendable promptitude had already been swung into the water. The steamer was being put about, describing a wide arc around the little boat dancing on the deep blue rollers. . . .

Of the next hour, I cannot bear to write at all. Long as I had known him, I was ig-

norant of my friend's powers as a swimmer, but I judged that he must have been a poor one from the fact that he had sunk so rapidly in a calm sea. Except the hat, no trace of Nayland Smith remained when the boat got to the spot.

Chapter XXXIII

THE MUMMY

Dinner was out of the question that night for all of us. Kâramanèh, who had spoken no word, but, grasping my hands, had looked into my eyes—her own glassy with unshed tears—and then stolen away to her cabin, had not since reappeared. Seated upon my berth, I stared unseeingly before me, upon a changed ship, a changed sea and sky— upon another world. The poor old bishop, my neighbor, had glanced in several times, as he hobbled by, and his spectacles were unmistakably humid; but even he had vouchsafed no word, realizing that my sorrow was too deep for such consolation.

When at last I became capable of connected thought, I found myself faced by a big problem. Should I place the facts of the matter, as I knew them to be, before the captain? or could I hope to apprehend Fu-Manchu's servant by the methods suggested by my poor friend? That Smith's death was an accident, I did not believe for a moment; it was impossible not to link it with the attempt upon Kâramanèh. In my misery and doubt, I determined to take counsel with Dr. Stacey. I stood up, and passed out on to the deck.

Those passengers whom I met on my way to his room regarded me in respectful silence. By contrast, Stacey's attitude surprised and even annoyed me.

"I'd be prepared to stake all I possess— although it's not much," he said, "that this was not the work of your hidden enemy."

He blankly refused to give me his reasons for the statement and strongly advised me to watch and wait but to make no communication to the captain.

At this hour I can look back and savor again something of the profound dejection of that time. I could not face the passengers; I even avoided Kâramanèh and Azîz. I shut myself in my cabin and sat staring aimlessly into the growing darkness. The steward knocked, once, inquiring if I needed anything, but I dismissed him abruptly. So I passed the evening and the greater part of the night.

Those groups of promenaders who passed my door, invariably were discussing my poor friend's tragic end; but as the night wore on, the deck grew empty, and I sat amid a silence that in my miserable state I welcomed more than the presence of any friend, saving only the one whom I should never welcome again.

Since I had not counted the bells, to this day I have only the vaguest idea respecting the time whereat the next incident occurred which it is my duty to chronicle. Perhaps I was on the verge of falling asleep, seated there as I was; at any rate, I could scarcely believe myself awake, when, unheralded by any footsteps to indicate his coming, some one who seemed to be crouching outside my stateroom, slightly raised himself and peered in through the porthole—which I had not troubled to close.

He must have been a fairly tall man to have looked in at all, and although his features were indistinguishable in the darkness, his outline, which was clearly perceptible against the white boat beyond, was unfamiliar to me. He seemed to have a small, and oddly swathed head, and what I could make out of the gaunt neck and square shoulders in some way suggested an unnatural thinness; in short, the smudgy silhouette in the porthole was weirdly like that of a *mummy!*

For some moments I stared at the apparition; then, rousing myself from the apathy into which I had sunk, I stood up very quickly and stepped across the room. As I did so the figure vanished, and when I threw open the door and looked out upon the deck . . . the deck was wholly untenanted!

I realized at once that it would be useless, even had I chosen the course, to seek confirmation of what I had seen from the officer on the bridge: my own berth, together with the one adjoining—that of the bishop—was not visible from the bridge.

For some time I stood in my doorway, wondering in a disinterested fashion which now I cannot explain, if the hidden enemy had revealed himself to me, or if disordered imagination had played me a trick. Later, I was destined to know the truth of the matter, but when at last I fell into a troubled sleep, that night, I was still in some doubt upon the point.

My state of mind when I awakened on the following day was indescribable; I found it difficult to doubt that Nayland Smith would meet me on the way to the bathroom as usual, with the cracked briar fuming between his teeth. I felt myself almost compelled to pass around to his stateroom in order to convince myself that he was not really there. The catastrophe was still unreal to me, and the world a dream-world. Indeed I retain scarcely any recollections of the traffic of that day, or of the days that followed it until we reached Port Said.

Two things only made any striking appeal to my dulled intelligence at that time. These were: the aloof attitude of Dr. Stacey, who seemed carefully to avoid me; and a curious circumstance which the second officer mentioned in conversation one evening as we strolled up and down the main deck together.

"Either I was fast asleep at my post, Dr. Petrie," he said, "or last night, in the middle watch, some one or something came over the side of the ship just aft the bridge, slipped across the deck, and disappeared."

I stared at him wonderingly.

"Do you mean something that came up out of the sea?" I said.

"Nothing could very well have come up out of the sea," he replied, smiling slightly, "so that it must have come up from the deck below."

"Was it a man?"

"It looked like a man, and a fairly tall one, but he came and was gone like a flash, and I saw no more of him up to the time I was relieved. To tell you the truth, I did not report it because I thought I must have been dozing; it's a dead slow watch, and the navigation on this part of the run is child's play."

I was on the point of telling him what I had seen myself, two evenings before, but for some reason I refrained from doing so, although I think had I confided in him he would have abandoned the idea that what he had seen was phantasmal; for the pair of us could not very well have been dreaming. Some malignant presence haunted the ship; I could not doubt this; yet I remained passive, sunk in a lethargy of sorrow.

We were scheduled to reach Port Said at about eight o'clock in the evening, but by reason of the delay occasioned so tragically, I learned that in all probability we should not arrive earlier than midnight, whilst passengers would not go ashore until the following morning. Kâramanèh, who had been staring ahead all day, seeking a first glimpse of her native land, was determined to remain up until the hour of our arrival, but after dinner a notice was posted up stating that we should not be in before two A.M. Even those passengers who were the most enthusiastic thereupon determined to postpone, for a few hours, their first glimpse of the land of the Pharaohs and even to forego the sight—one of the strangest and most interesting in the world—of Port Said by night.

For my own part, I confess that all the interest and hope with which I had looked forward to our arrival, had left me, and often I detected tears in the eyes of Kâramanèh; whereby I knew that the coldness in my heart had manifested itself even to her. I had sustained the greatest blow of my life, and not even the presence of so lovely a companion could entirely recompense me for the loss of my dearest friend.

The lights on the Egyptian shore were faintly visible when the last group of stragglers on deck broke up. I had long since prevailed upon Kâramanèh to retire, and now, utterly sick at heart, I sought my own stateroom, mechanically undressed, and turned in.

It may, or may not be singular that I had neglected all precautions since the night of the tragedy; I was not even conscious of a desire to visit retribution upon our hidden enemy; in some strange fashion I took it for granted that there would be no further attempts upon Kâramanèh, Azîz, or myself. I had not troubled to confirm Smith's surmise respecting the closing of the portholes; but I know now for a fact that, whereas they had been closed from the time of our leaving the Straits of Messina, to-night, in sight of the Egyptian coast, the regulation was relaxed again. I cannot say if this is usual, but that it occurred on this ship is a fact to which I can testify—a fact to which my attention was to be drawn dramatically.

The night was steamingly hot, and because I welcomed the circumstance that my own port was widely opened, I reflected that those on the lower decks might be open also. A faint sense of danger stirred within me; indeed, I sat upright and was about to spring out of my berth when that occurred which induced me to change my mind.

All passengers had long since retired, and a midnight silence descended upon the ship, for we were not yet close enough to port for any unusual activities to have commenced.

Clearly outlined in the open porthole there suddenly arose that same grotesque silhouette which I had seen once before.

Prompted by I know not what, I lay still and simulated heavy breathing; for it was evident to me that I must be partly visible to the watcher, so bright was the night. For ten—twenty—thirty seconds he studied me in absolute silence, that gaunt thing so like a mummy; and, with my eyes partly closed, I watched him, breathing heavily all the time. Then, making no more noise than a cat, he moved away across the deck, and I could judge of his height by the fact that his small, swathed head remained visible almost to the time that he passed to the end of the white boat which swung opposite my stateroom.

In a moment I slipped quietly to the floor, crossed, and peered out of the porthole; so that at last I had a clear view of the sinister mummy-man. He was crouching under the bow of the boat, and attaching to the white rails, below, a contrivance of a kind with which I was not entirely unfamiliar. This was a thin ladder of silken rope, having bamboo rungs, with two metal hooks for attaching it to any suitable object.

The one thus engaged was, as Kâramanèh had declared, almost superhumanly thin. His loins were swathed in a sort of linen garment, and his head so bound about, turban fashion, that only his gleaming eyes remained visible. The bare limbs and body were of a dusky yellow color, and, at sight of him, I experienced a sudden nausea.

My pistol was in my cabin-trunk, and to have found it in the dark, without making a good deal of noise, would have been impossible. Doubting how I should act, I stood watching the man with the swathed head whilst he threw the end of the ladder over the side, crept past the bow of the boat, and swung his gaunt body over the rail, exhibiting the agility of an ape. One quick glance fore and aft he gave, then began to swarm down the ladder: in which instant I knew his mission.

With a choking cry, which forced itself unwilled from my lips, I tore at the door, threw it open, and sprang across the deck. Plans, I had none, and since I carried no instrument wherewith to sever the ladder, the murderer might indeed have carried out his design for all that I could have done to prevent him, were it not that another took a hand in the game. . . .

At the moment that the mummy-man—his head now on a level with the deck—perceived me, he stopped dead. Coincident with his stopping, the crack of a pistol shot sounded—from immediately beyond the boat.

Uttering a sort of sobbing sound, the creature fell—then clutched, with straining yellow fingers, at the rails, and, seemingly by dint of a great effort, swarmed along aft some twenty feet, with incredible swiftness and agility, and clambered onto the deck.

A second shot cracked sharply; and a voice (God! was I mad!) cried: "Hold him, Petrie!"

Rigid with fearful astonishment I stood, as out from the boat above me leaped a figure attired solely in shirt and trousers. The newcomer leaped away in the wake of the mummy-man—who had vanished around the corner by the smoke-room. Over his shoulder he cried back at me:

"The bishop's stateroom! See that no one enters!"

I clutched at my head—which seemed to be fiery hot; I realized in my own person the sensation of one who knows himself mad.

For the man who pursued the mummy was *Nayland Smith!*

.   .   .   .

I stood in the bishop's state-room, Nayland Smith, his gaunt face wet with perspiration, beside me, handling certain odd looking objects which littered the place, and lay amid the discarded garments of the absent cleric.

"Pneumatic pads!" he snapped. "The man was a walking air-cushion!" He gingerly fingered two strange rubber appliances. "For distending the cheeks," he muttered, dropping them disgustedly on the floor. "His hands and wrists betrayed him, Petrie. He wore his cuffs unusually long but he could not entirely hide his bony wrists. To have watched him, whilst remaining myself unseen, was next to impossible; hence my device of tossing a dummy overboard, calculated to float for less than ten minutes! It actually floated nearly fifteen, as a matter of fact, and I had some horrible moments!"

"Smith!" I said—"how could you submit me . . ."

He clapped his hands on my shoulders.

"My dear old chap—there was no other way, believe me. From that boat I could see right into his stateroom, but, once in, I dare not leave it—except late at night, stealthily! The second spotted me one night and I thought the game was up, but evidently he didn't report it."

"But you might have confided . . ."

"Impossible! I'll admit I nearly fell to the temptation that first night; for I could see into your room as well as into his!" He slapped me boisterously on the back, but his gray eyes were suspiciously moist. "Dear old Petrie! Thank God for our friends! But you'd be the first to admit, old man, that you're a dead rotten actor! Your portrayal of grief for the loss of a valued chum would not have convinced a soul on board!

"Therefore I made use of Stacey, whose callous attitude was less remarkable. Gad, Petrie! I nearly bagged our man the first night! The elaborate plan—Marconi message to get you out of the way, and so forth—had miscarried, and he knew the porthole trick would be useless once we got into the open sea. He took a big chance. He discarded his clerical guise and peeped into your room—you remember?—but you were awake, and I made no move when he slipped back to his own cabin; I wanted to take him red-handed."

"Have you any idea . . ."

"Who he is? No more than *where* he is! Probably some creature of Dr. Fu-Manchu specially chosen for the purpose; obviously a man of culture, and probably of thug ancestry. I hit him—in the shoulder; but even then he ran like a hare. We've searched the ship, without result. He may have gone overboard and chanced the swim to shore . . ."

We stepped out onto the deck. Around us was that unforgettable scene—Port Said by night. The ship was barely moving through the glassy water, now. Smith took my arm and we walked forward. Above us was the mighty peace of Egypt's sky ablaze with splendor; around and about us moved the unique turmoil of the clearing-house of the Near East.

"I would give much to know the real identity of the bishop of Damascus," muttered Smith.

He stopped abruptly, snapping his teeth together and grasping my arm as in a vise. Hard upon his words had followed the rattling clangor as the great anchor was let go; but horribly intermingled with the metallic roar there came to us such a fearful, inarticulate shrieking as to chill one's heart.

The anchor plunged into the water of the harbor; the shrieking ceased. Smith turned to me, and his face was tragic in the light of the arc lamp swung hard by.

"We shall never know," he whispered.

"God forgive him—he must be in bloody tatters now. Petrie, the poor fool was hiding in the *chain-locker!*"

A little hand stole into mine. I turned quickly. Kâramanèh stood beside me. I placed my arm about her shoulders, drawing her close; and I blush to relate that all else was forgotten.

For a moment, heedless of the fearful turmoil forward, Nayland Smith stood looking at us. Then he turned, with his rare smile, and walked aft.

"Perhaps you're right, Petrie!" he said.

The Yellow Claw

" You have no right to refuse," she said softly

I

THE LADY OF THE CIVET FURS

Henry Leroux wrote busily on. The light of the table-lamp, softened and enriched by its mosaic shade, gave an appearance of added opulence to the already handsome appointments of the room. The little table-clock ticked merrily from half-past eleven to a quarter to twelve.

Into the cozy, bookish atmosphere of the novelist's study penetrated the muffled chime of Big Ben; it chimed the three-quarters. But, with his mind centered upon his work, Leroux wrote on ceaselessly.

An odd figure of a man was this popular novelist, with patchy and untidy hair which lessened the otherwise striking contour of his brow. A neglected and unpicturesque figure, in a baggy, neutral-colored dressing-gown; a figure more fitted to a garret than to this spacious, luxurious workroom, with the soft light playing upon rank after rank of rare and costly editions, deepening the tones in the Persian carpet, making red morocco more red, purifying the vellum and regilding the gold of the choice bindings, caressing lovingly the busts and statuettes surmounting the book-shelves, and twinkling upon the scantily-covered crown of Henry Leroux. The door bell rang.

Leroux, heedless of external matters, pursued his work. But the door bell rang again and continued to ring.

"Soames! Soames!" Leroux raised his voice irascibly, continuing to write the while. "Where the devil are you! Can't you hear the door bell?"

Soames did not reveal himself; and to the ringing of the bell was added the unmistakable rattling of a letter-box.

"Soames!" Leroux put down his pen and stood up. "Damn it! he's out! I have no memory!"

He retied the girdle of his dressing-gown, which had become unfastened, and opened the study door. Opposite, across the entrance lobby, was the outer door; and in the light from the lobby lamp he perceived two laughing eyes peering in under the upraised flap of the letter-box. The ringing ceased.

"Are you *very* angry with me for interrupting you?" cried a girl's voice.

"My dear Miss Cumberly!" said Leroux without irritation; "on the contrary—er—I am delighted to see you—or rather to hear you.

There is nobody at home, you know." . . .

"I *do* know," replied the girl firmly, "and I know something else, also. Father assures me that you simply *starve* yourself when Mrs. Leroux is away! So I have brought down an omelette!"

"Omelette!" muttered Leroux, advancing toward the door; "you have—er—brought an omelette! I understand—yes; you have brought an omelette? Er—that is very good of you."

He hesitated when about to open the outer door, raising his hands to his dishevelled hair and unshaven chin. The flap of the letter-box dropped; and the girl outside could be heard stifling her laughter.

"You must think me—er—very rude," began Leroux; "I mean—not to open the door. But" . . .

"I quite understand," concluded the voice of the unseen one. "You are a most untidy object! And I shall tell Mira *directly* she returns that she has no right to leave you alone like this! Now I am going to hurry back upstairs; so you may appear safely. Don't let the omelette get cold. Good night!"

"No, certainly I shall not!" cried Leroux. "So good of you—I—er—do like omelette. . . . Good night!"

Calmly he returned to his writing-table, where, in the pursuit of the elusive character whose exploits he was chronicling and who had brought him fame and wealth, he forgot in the same moment Helen Cumberly and the omelette.

The table-clock ticked merrily on; *scratch—scratch—splutter—scratch*—went Henry Leroux's pen; for this up-to-date litterateur, essayist by inclination, creator of "Martin Zeda, Criminal Scientist" by popular clamor, was yet old-fashioned enough, and sufficient of an enthusiast, to pen his work, while lesser men dictated.

So, amidst that classic company, smiling or frowning upon him from the oaken shelves, where Petronius Arbiter, exquisite, rubbed shoulders with Balzac, plebeian; where Omar Khayyam leaned confidentially toward Philostratus; where Mark Twain, standing squarely beside Thomas Carlyle, glared across the room at George Meredith, Henry Leroux pursued the amazing career of "Martin Zeda."

It wanted but five minutes to the hour of midnight, when again the door bell clamored in the silence.

Leroux wrote steadily on. The bell continued to ring, and, furthermore, the ringer could be heard beating upon the outer door.

"Soames!" cried Leroux irritably, "Soames! Why the hell don't you go to the door!"

Leroux stood up, dashing his pen upon the table.

"I shall have to sack that damned man!" he cried; "he takes too many liberties—stopping out until this hour of the night!"

He pulled open the study door, crossed the hallway, and opened the door beyond.

In, out of the darkness—for the stair lights had been extinguished—staggered a woman; a woman whose pale face exhibited, despite the ravages of sorrow or illness, signs of quite unusual beauty. Her eyes were wide opened, and terror-stricken, the pupils contracted almost to vanishing point. She wore a magnificent cloak of civet fur wrapped tightly about her, and, as Leroux opened the door, she tottered past him into the lobby, glancing back over her shoulder.

With his upraised hands plunged pathetically into the mop of his hair, Leroux turned and stared at the intruder. She groped as if a darkness had descended, clutched at the sides of the study doorway, and then, unsteadily, entered—and sank down upon the big chesterfield in utter exhaustion.

Leroux, rubbing his chin, perplexedly, walked in after her. He scarcely had his foot upon the study carpet, ere the woman started up, tremulously, and shot out from the enveloping furs a bare arm and a pointing, quivering finger.

"Close the door!" she cried hoarsely—"close the door! . . . He has . . . followed me!". . .

The disturbed novelist, as a man in a dream, turned, retraced his steps, and closed the outer door of the flat. Then, rubbing his chin more vigorously than ever and only desisting from this exercise to fumble in his dishevelled hair, he walked back into the study, whose Athenean calm had thus mysteriously been violated.

Two minutes to midnight; the most respectable flat in respectable Westminster; a lonely and very abstracted novelist—and a pale-faced, beautiful woman, enveloped in costly furs, sitting staring with fearful eyes straight before her. This was such a scene as his sense of the proprieties and of the probabilities could never have permitted Henry Leroux to create.

His visitor kept moistening her dry lips and swallowing, emotionally.

Standing at a discreet distance from her:—

"Madam," began Leroux, nervously.

She waved her hand, enjoining him to silence, and at the same time intimating that she would explain herself directly speech became possible. Whilst she sought to recover her composure, Leroux, gradually forcing himself out of the dreamlike state, studied her with a sort of anxious curiosity.

It now became apparent to him that his visitor was no more than twenty-five or twenty-six years of age, but illness or trouble, or both together, had seared and marred her beauty. Amid the auburn masses of her hair, gleamed streaks, not of gray, but of purest white. The low brow was faintly wrinkled, and the big—unnaturally big—eyes were purple shaded; whilst two heavy lines traced their way from the corner of the nostrils to the corner of the mouth—of the drooping mouth with the bloodless lips.

Her pallor became more strange and interesting the longer he studied it; for, underlying the skin was a yellow tinge which he found inexplicable, but which he linked in his mind with the contracted pupils of her eyes, seeking vainly for a common cause.

He had a hazy impression that his visitor, beneath her furs, was most inadequately clothed; and seeking confirmation of this, his gaze strayed downward to where one little slippered foot peeped out from the civet furs.

Leroux suppressed a gasp. He had caught a glimpse of a bare ankle!

He crossed to his writing-table, and seated himself, glancing sideways at this living mystery. Suddenly she began, in a voice tremulous and scarcely audible:—

"Mr. Leroux, at a great—at a very great personal risk, I have come to-night. What I have to ask of you—to entreat of you, will . . . will" . . .

Two bare arms emerged from the fur, and she began clutching at her throat and bosom as though choking—dying.

Leroux leapt up and would have run to her; but forcing a ghastly smile, she waved him away again.

"It is all right," she muttered, swallowing noisily.

But frightful spasms of pain convulsed her, contorting her pale face.

"Some brandy—!" cried Leroux, anxiously.

"If you please," whispered the visitor.

She dropped her arms and fell back upon the chesterfield, insensible.

II

MIDNIGHT AND MR. KING

Leroux clutched at the corner of the writing-table to steady himself and stood there looking at the deathly face. Under the most favorable circumstances, he was no man of action, although in common with the rest of his kind he prided himself upon the possession of that presence of mind which he lacked. It was a situation which could not have alarmed "Martin Zeda," but it alarmed, immeasurably, nay, struck inert with horror, Martin Zeda's creator.

Then, in upon Leroux's mental turmoil, a sensible idea intruded itself.

"Dr. Cumberly!" he muttered. "I hope to God he is in!"

Without touching the recumbent form upon the chesterfield, without seeking to learn, without daring to learn, if she lived or had died, Leroux, the *tempo* of his life changed to a breathless gallop, rushed out of the study, across the entrance hall, and, throwing wide the flat door, leapt up the stairs to the flat above—that of his old friend, Dr. Cumberly.

The patter of the slippered feet grew faint upon the stair; then, as Leroux reached the landing above, became inaudible altogether.

In Leroux's study, the table-clock ticked merrily on, seeming to hasten its ticking as the hand crept around closer and closer to midnight. The mosaic shade of the lamp mingled reds and blues and greens upon the white ceiling above and poured golden light upon the pages of manuscript strewn about beneath it. This was a typical work-room of a literary man having the ear of the public—typical in every respect, save for the fur-clad figure outstretched upon the settee.

And now the peeping light indiscreetly penetrated to the hem of a silken garment revealed by some disarrangement of the civet fur. To the eye of an experienced observer, had such an observer been present in Henry Leroux's study, this billow of silk and lace behind the sheltering fur must have proclaimed itself the edge of a night-robe, just as the ankle beneath had proclaimed itself to Henry Leroux's shocked susceptibilities to be innocent of stocking.

Thirty seconds were wanted to complete the cycle of the day, when one of the listless hands thrown across the back of the chesterfield opened and closed spasmodically. The fur at the bosom of the midnight visitor began to rapidly rise and fall.

Then, with a choking cry, the woman struggled upright; her hair, hastily dressed, burst free of its bindings and poured in gleaming cascade down about her shoulders.

Clutching with one hand at her cloak in order to keep it wrapped about her, and holding the other blindly before her, she rose, and with that same odd, groping movement, began to approach the writing-table. The pupils of her eyes were mere pin-points now; she shuddered convulsively, and her skin was dewed with perspiration. Her breath came in agonized gasps.

"God!—I . . . am dying . . . and I cannot—tell him!" she breathed.

Feverishly, weakly, she took up a pen, and upon a quarto page, already half filled with Leroux's small, neat, illegible writing, began to scrawl a message, bending down, one hand upon the table, and with her whole body shaking.

Some three or four wavering lines she had written, when intimately, for the flat of Henry Leroux in Palace Mansions lay within sight of the clock-face—Big Ben began to chime midnight.

The writer started back and dropped a great blot of ink upon the paper; then, realizing the cause of the disturbance, forced herself to continue her task.

The chime being completed: *One!* boomed the clock; *two! . . . three! . . . four! . . .*

The light in the entrance-hall went out!

Five! boomed Big Ben;—*six! . . . seven! . . .*

A hand, of old ivory hue, a long, yellow, clawish hand, with part of a sinewy forearm, crept in from the black lobby through the study doorway and touched the electric switch!

Eight! . . .

The study was plunged in darkness!

Uttering a sob—a cry of agony and horror that came from her very soul—the woman stood upright and turned to face toward the door, clutching the sheet of paper in one rigid hand.

Through the leaded panes of the window above the writing-table swept a silvern beam of moonlight. It poured, searchingly, upon the fur-clad figure swaying by the table; cutting through the darkness of the room like some huge scimitar, to end in a pallid pool about the woman's shadow on the center of the Persian carpet.

Coincident with her sobbing cry—*Nine!* boomed Big Ben; *ten! . . .*

Two hands—with outstretched, crooked, clutching fingers—leapt from the darkness into the light of the moonbeam.

"God! Oh, God!" came a frenzied, rasping shriek—"Mr. King!"

Straight at the bare throat leapt the yellow hands; a gurgling cry rose—fell—and died away.

Gently, noiselessly, the lady of the civet fur sank upon the carpet by the table; as she fell, a dim black figure bent over her. The tearing of paper told of the note being snatched from her frozen grip; but never for a moment did the face or the form of her assailant encroach upon the moonbeam.

Batlike, this second and terrible visitant avoided the light.

The deed had occupied so brief a time that but one note of the great bell had accompanied it.

Twelve! rang out the final stroke from the clock-tower. A low, eerie whistle, minor, rising in three irregular notes and falling in weird, unusual cadence to silence again, came from somewhere outside the room.

Then darkness—stillness—with the moon a witness of one more ghastly crime.

Presently, confused and intermingled voices from above proclaimed the return of Leroux with the doctor. They were talking in an excited key, the voice of Leroux, especially, sounding almost hysterical. They created such a disturbance that they attracted the attention of Mr. John Exel, M. P., occupant of the flat below, who at that very moment had returned from the House and was about to insert the key in the lock of his door. He looked up the stairway but, all being in darkness, was unable to detect anything. Therefore he called out:—

"Is that you, Leroux? Is anything the matter?"

"Matter, Exel!" cried Leroux; "there's a devil of a business! For mercy's sake, come up!"

His curiosity greatly excited, Mr. Exel mounted the stairs, entering the lobby of Leroux's flat immediately behind the owner and Dr. Cumberly—who, like Leroux, was arrayed in a dressing-gown; for he had been in bed when summoned by his friend.

"You are all in the dark, here," muttered Dr. Cumberly, fumbling for the switch.

"Some one has turned the light out!" whispered Leroux, nervously; "*I* left it on."

Dr. Cumberly pressed the switch, turning up the lobby light as Exel entered from the landing. Then Leroux, entering the study first of the three, switched on the light there, also.

One glance he threw about the room, then started like a man physically stricken.

"Cumberly!" he gasped, "Cumberly"—and he pointed to the furry heap by the writing-table.

"You said she lay on the chesterfield," muttered Cumberly.

"I left her there." . . .

Dr. Cumberly crossed the room and dropped upon his knees. He turned the white face toward the light, gently parted the civet fur, and pressed his ear to the silken covering of the breast. He started slightly and looked into the glazing eyes.

Replacing the fur which he had disarranged, the physician stood up and fixed a keen gaze upon the face of Henry Leroux. The latter swallowed noisily, moistening his parched lips.

"Is she" . . . he muttered; "is she" . . .

"God's mercy, Leroux!" whispered Mr. Exel—"what does this mean?"

"The woman is dead," said Dr. Cumberly.

In common with all medical men, Dr. Cumberly was a physiognomist; he was a great physician and a proportionately great physiognomist. Therefore, when he looked into Henry Leroux's eyes, he saw there, and recognized, horror and consternation. With no further evidence than that furnished by his own powers of perception, he knew that the mystery of this woman's death was as inexplicable to Henry Leroux as it was inexplicable to himself.

He was a masterful man, with the gray eyes of a diplomat, and he knew Leroux as did few men. He laid both hands upon the novelist's shoulders.

"Brace up, old chap!" he said; "you will want all your wits about you."

"I left her," began Leroux, hesitatingly—"I left" . . .

"We know all about where you left her, Leroux," interrupted Cumberly; "but what we want to get at is this: what occurred between the time you left her, and the time of our return?"

Exel, who had walked across to the table, and with a horror-stricken face was gingerly examining the victim, now exclaimed:—

"Why! Leroux! she is—she is . . . *undressed!*"

Leroux clutched at his dishevelled hair with both hands.

"My dear Exel!" he cried—"my dear, good man! Why do you use that tone? You say 'she is undressed!' as though *I* were responsible for the poor soul's condition!"

"On the contrary, Leroux!" retorted Exel, standing very upright, and staring through his monocle; "on the contrary, *you* misconstrue *me*! I did not intend to imply—to insinuate—"

"My dear Exel!" broke in Dr. Cumberly—"Leroux is perfectly well aware that you intended nothing unkindly. But the poor chap, quite naturally, is distraught at the moment. You *must* understand that, man!"

"I understand; and I am sorry," said Exel, casting a sidelong glance at the body. "Of course, it is a delicate subject. No doubt Leroux can explain." . . .

"Damn your explanation!" shrieked Leroux hysterically. "I *cannot* explain! If I could explain, I" . . .

"Leroux!" said Cumberly, placing his arm paternally about the shaking man—"you are such a nervous subject. *Do* make an effort, old fellow. Pull yourself together. Exel does not know the circumstances—"

"I am curious to learn them," said the M. P. icily.

Leroux was about to launch some angry retort, but Cumberly forced him to the chesterfield, and crossing to the bureau, poured out a stiff peg of brandy from a decanter which stood there. Leroux sank upon the chesterfield, rubbing his fingers up and down his palms with a curious nervous movement and glancing at the dead woman, and at Exel, alternately, in a mechanical, regular fashion, pathetic to behold.

Mr. Exel, tapping his boot with the head of his inverted cane, was staring fixedly at the doctor.

"Here you are, Leroux," said Cumberly; "drink this up, and let us arrange our facts in decent order before we—"

" 'Phone for the police?" concluded Exel, his gaze upon the last speaker.

Leroux drank the brandy at a gulp and put down the glass upon the little Persian coffee table with a hand which he had somehow contrived to steady.

"You are keen on the official forms, Exel?" he said, with a wry smile. "Please accept my apology for my recent—er—outburst, but picture this thing happening in your place!"

"I cannot," declared Exel, bluntly.

"You lack imagination," said Cumberly. "Take a whisky and soda, and help me to search the flat."

"Search the flat!"

The physician raised a forefinger, forensically.

"Since you, Exel, if not actually in the building, must certainly have been within sight of the street entrance at the moment of the crime, and since Leroux and I descended the stair and met you on the landing, it is reasonable to suppose that the assassin can only be in one place: *here!*"

"*Here!*" cried Exel and Leroux, together.

"Did you see anyone leave the lower hall as you entered?"

"No one; emphatically, there was no one there!"

"Then I am right."

"Good God!" whispered Exel, glancing about him, with a new, and keen apprehensiveness.

"Take your drink," concluded Cumberly, "and join me in my search."

"Thanks," replied Exel, nervously proffering a cigar-case; "but I won't drink."

"As you wish," said the doctor, who thus, in his masterful way, acted the host; "and I won't smoke. But do you light up."

"Later," muttered Exel; "later. Let us search, first."

Leroux stood up; Cumberly forced him back.

"Stay where you are, Leroux; it is elementary strategy to operate from a fixed base. This study shall be the base. Ready, Exel?"

Exel nodded, and the search commenced. Leroux sat rigidly upon the settee, his hands resting upon his knees, watching and listening. Save for the merry ticking of the table-clock, and the movements of the searchers from room to room, nothing disturbed the silence. From the table, and that which lay near to it, he kept his gaze obstinately averted.

Five or six minutes passed in this fashion, Leroux expecting each to bring a sudden outcry. He was disappointed. The searchers returned, Exel noticeably holding himself aloof and Cumberly very stern.

Exel, a cigar between his teeth, walked to the writing-table, carefully circling around the dreadful obstacle which lay in his path, to help himself to a match. As he stooped to do so, he perceived that in the closed right hand of the dead woman was a torn scrap of paper.

"Leroux! Cumberly!" he exclaimed; "come here!"

He pointed with the match as Cumberly

hurriedly crossed to his side. Leroux, inert, remained where he sat, but watched with haggard eyes. Dr. Cumberly bent down and sought to detach the paper from the grip of the poor cold fingers, without tearing it. Finally he contrived to release the fragment, and, perceiving it to bear some written words, he spread it out beneath the lamp, on the table, and eagerly scanned it, lowering his massive gray head close to the writing.

He inhaled, sibilantly.

"Do you see, Exel?" he jerked—for Exel was bending over his shoulder.

"I do—but I don't understand."

"What is it?" came hollowly from Leroux.

"It is the bottom part of an unfinished note," said Cumberly, slowly. "It is written shakily in a woman's hand, and it reads:— 'Your wife' " . . .

Leroux sprang to his feet and crossed the room in three strides.

"Wife!" he muttered. His voice seemed to be choked in his throat; "my wife! It says something about my wife?"

"It says," resumed the doctor, quietly, " 'your wife.' Then there's a piece torn out, and the two words 'Mr. King.' No stop follows, and the line is evidently incomplete."

"My wife!" mumbled Leroux, staring unseeingly at the fragment of paper. *"My wife! Mr. King!* Oh! God! I shall go mad!"

"Sit down!" snapped Dr. Cumberly, turning to him; "damn it, Leroux, you are worse than a woman!"

In a manner almost childlike, the novelist obeyed the will of the stronger man, throwing himself into an armchair, and burying his face in his hands.

"My wife!" he kept muttering—"my wife!" . . .

Exel and the doctor stood staring at one another; when suddenly, from outside the flat, came a metallic clattering, followed by a little suppressed cry. Helen Cumberly, in daintiest deshabille, appeared in the lobby, carrying, in one hand, a chafing-dish, and, in the other, the lid. As she advanced toward the study, from whence she had heard her father's voice:—

"Why, Mr. Leroux!" she cried, "I shall *certainly* report you to Mira, now! You have not even touched the omelette!"

"Good God! Cumberly! stop her!" muttered Exel, uneasily. "The door was not latched!" . . .

But it was too late. Even as the physician turned to intercept his daughter, she crossed the threshold of the study. She stopped short at perceiving Exel; then, with a woman's unerring intuition, divined a tragedy, and, in the instant of divination, sought for, and found, the hub of the tragic wheel.

One swift glance she cast at the fur-clad form, prostrate.

The chafing-dish fell from her hand, and the omelette rolled, a grotesque mass, upon the carpet. She swayed, dizzily, raising one hand to her brow, but had recovered herself even as Leroux sprang forward to support her.

"All right, Leroux!" cried Cumberly; "I will take her upstairs again. Wait for me, Exel."

Exel nodded, lighted his cigar, and sat down in a chair, remote from the writing-table.

"Mira—my wife!" muttered Leroux, standing, looking after Dr. Cumberly and his daughter as they crossed the lobby. "She will report to—my wife." . . .

In the outer doorway, Helen Cumberly looked back over her shoulder, and her glance met that of Leroux. Hers was a healing glance and a strengthening glance; it braced him up as nothing else could have done. He turned to Exel.

"For Heaven's sake, Exel!" he said, evenly, "give me your advice—give me your help; I am going to 'phone for the police."

Exel looked up with an odd expression.

"I am entirely at your service, Leroux," he said. "I can quite understand how this ghastly affair has shaken you up."

"It was so sudden," said the other, plaintively. "It is incredible that so much emotion can be crowded into so short a period of a man's life." . . .

Big Ben chimed the quarter after midnight. Leroux, eyes averted, walked to the writing-table, and took up the telephone.

III

INSPECTOR DUNBAR TAKES CHARGE

Detective-Inspector Dunbar was admitted by Dr. Cumberly. He was a man of notable height, large-boned, and built gauntly and squarely. His clothes fitted him ill, and through them one seemed to perceive the massive scaffolding of his frame. He had gray hair retiring above a high brow, but worn long and untidy at the back; a wire-like straight-cut mustache, also streaked with gray, which served to accentuate the grimness of his mouth and slightly undershot jaw. A massive head, with tawny, leonine eyes; indeed, altogether a leonine face, and a frame indicative of tremendous nervous energy.

In the entrance lobby he stood for a moment.

"My name is Cumberly," said the doctor, glancing at the card which the Scotland Yard man proffered. "I occupy the flat above."

"Glad to know you, Dr. Cumberly," replied the detective in a light and not unpleasant voice—and the fierce eyes momentarily grew kindly.

"This—" continued Cumberly, drawing Dunbar forward into the study, "is my friend, Leroux—Henry Leroux, whose name you will know?"

"I have not that pleasure," replied Dunbar.

"Well," added Cumberly, "he is a famous novelist, and his flat, unfortunately, has been made the scene of a crime. This is Detective-Inspector Dunbar, who has come to solve our difficulties, Leroux." He turned to where Exel stood upon the hearth-rug—toying with his monocle. "Mr. John Exel, M. P."

"Glad to know you, gentlemen," said Dunbar.

Leroux rose from the armchair in which he had been sitting and stared, drearily, at the newcomer. Exel screwed the monocle into his right eye, and likewise surveyed the detective. Cumberly, taking a tumbler from the bureau, said:—

"A scotch-and-soda, Inspector?"

"It is a suggestion," said Dunbar, "that, coming from a medical man, appeals."

Whilst the doctor poured out the whiskey and squirted the soda into the glass, Inspector Dunbar, standing squarely in the middle of the room, fixed his eyes upon the still form lying in the shadow of the writing-table.

"You will have been called in, doctor," he said, taking the proffered tumbler, "at the time of the crime?"

"Exactly!" replied Cumberly. "Mr. Leroux ran up to my flat and summoned me to see the woman."

"What time would that be?"

"Big Ben had just struck the final stroke of twelve when I came out on to the landing."

"Mr. Leroux would be waiting there for you?"

"He stood in my entrance-lobby whilst I slipped on my dressing-gown, and we came down together."

"I was entering from the street," interrupted Exel, "as they were descending from above" . . .

"You can enter from the street, sir, in a moment," said Dunbar, holding up his hand. "One witness at a time, if you please."

Exel shrugged his shoulders and turned slightly, leaning his elbow upon the mantelpiece and flicking off the ash from his cigar.

"I take it you were in bed?" questioned Dunbar, turning again to the doctor.

"I had been in bed about a quarter of an hour when I was aroused by the ringing of the door-bell. This ringing struck me as so urgent that I ran out in my pajamas, and found there Mr. Leroux, in a very disturbed state—"

"What did he say? Give his own words as nearly as you remember them."

Leroux, who had been standing, sank slowly back into the armchair, with his eyes upon Dr. Cumberly as the latter replied:—

"He said 'Cumberly! Cumberly! For God's sake, come down at once; there is a strange woman in my flat, apparently in a dying condition!' "

"What did you do?"

"I ran into my bedroom and slipped on my dressing-gown, leaving Mr. Leroux in the entrance-hall. Then, with the clock chiming the last stroke of midnight, we came out together and I closed my door behind me. There was no light on the stair; but our conversation—Mr. Leroux was speaking in a very high-pitched voice" . . .

"What was he saying?"

"He was explaining to me how some woman, unknown to him, had interrupted his work a few minutes before by ringing his door-bell." . . .

Inspector Dunbar held up his hand.

"I won't ask you to repeat what he said, doctor; Mr. Leroux, presently, can give me his own words."

"We had descended to this floor, then," resumed Cumberly, "when Mr. Exel, entering below, called up to us, asking if anything was the matter. Leroux replied, 'Matter Exel! There's a devil of a business! For mercy's sake, come up!' "

"Well?"

"Mr. Exel thereupon joined us at the door

of this flat."

"Was it open?"

"Yes. Mr. Leroux had rushed up to me, leaving the door open behind him. The light was out, both in the lobby and in the study, a fact upon which I commented at the time. It was all the more curious as Mr. Leroux had left both lights on!" . . .

"Did he say so?"

"He did. The circumstances surprised him to a marked degree. We came in and I turned up the light in the lobby. Then Leroux, entering the study, turned up the light there, too. I entered next, followed by Mr. Exel— and we saw the body lying where you see it now.

"Who saw it first?"

"Mr. Leroux; he drew my attention to it, saying that he had left her lying on the chesterfield and *not* upon the floor."

"You examined her?"

"I did. She was dead, but still warm. She exhibited signs of recent illness, and of being addicted to some drug habit; probably morphine. This, beyond doubt, contributed to her death, but the direct cause was asphyxiation. She had been strangled!"

"My God!" groaned Leroux, dropping his face into his hands.

"You found marks on her throat?"

"The marks were very slight. No great pressure was required in her weak condition."

"You did not move the body?"

"Certainly not; a more complete examination must be made, of course. But I extracted a piece of torn paper from her clenched right hand."

Inspector Dunbar lowered his tufted brows.

"I'm not glad to know you did that," he said. "It should have been left."

"It was done on the spur of the moment, but without altering the position of the hand or arm. The paper lies upon the table, yonder."

Inspector Dunbar took a long drink. Thus far he had made no attempt to examine the victim. Pulling out a bulging note-case from the inside pocket of his blue serge coat, he unscrewed a fountain-pèn, carefully tested the nib upon his thumb nail, and made three or four brief entries. Then, stretching out one long arm, he laid the wallet and the pen beside his glass upon the top of a bookcase, without otherwise changing his position, and

glancing aside at Exel, said:—

"Now, Mr. Exel, what help can you give us?"

"I have little to add to Dr. Cumberly's account," answered Exel, offhandedly. "The whole thing seemed to me" . . .

"What it seemed," interrupted Dunbar, "does not interest Scotland Yard, Mr. Exel, and won't interest the jury."

Leroux glanced up for a moment, then set his teeth hard, so that his jaw muscles stood out prominently under the pallid skin.

"What do you want to know, then?" asked Exel.

"I will be wanting to know," said Dunbar, "where you were coming from, to-night?"

"From the House of Commons."

"You came direct?"

"I left Sir Brian Malpas at the corner of Victoria Street at four minutes to twelve by Big Ben, and walked straight home, actually entering here, from the street, as the clock was chiming the last stroke of midnight."

"Then you would have walked up the street from an easterly direction?"

"Certainly."

"Did you meet any one or anything?"

"A taxi-cab, empty—for the hood was lowered—passed me as I turned the corner. There was no other vehicle in the street, and no person."

"You don't know from which door the cab came?"

"As I turned the corner," replied Exel, "I heard the man starting his engine, although when I actually saw the cab, it was in motion; but judging by the sound to which I refer, the cab had been stationary, if not at the door of Palace Mansions, certainly at that of the next block—St. Andrew's Mansions."

"Did you hear, or see anything else?"

"I saw nothing whatever. But just as I approached the street door, I heard a peculiar whistle, apparently proceeding from the gardens in the center of the square. I attached no importance to it at the time."

"What kind of whistle?"

"I have forgotten the actual notes, but the effect was very odd in some way."

"In what way?"

"An impression of this sort is not entirely reliable, Inspector; but it struck me as Oriental."

"Ah!" said Dunbar, and reached out the long arm for his notebook.

"Can I be of any further assistance?" said

Exel—glancing at his watch.

"You had entered the hall-way and were about to enter your own flat when the voices of Dr. Cumberly and Mr. Leroux attracted your attention?"

"I actually had the key in my hands," replied Exel.

"Did you actually have the key in the lock?"

"Let me think," mused Exel, and he took out a bunch of keys and dangled them, reflectively, before his eyes. "No! I was fumbling for the right key when I heard the voices above me."

"But were you facing your door?"

"No," averred Exel, perceiving the drift of the inspector's inquiries; "I was facing the stairway the whole time, and although it was in darkness, there is a street lamp immediately outside on the pavement, and I can swear, positively, that no one descended; that there was no one in the hall nor on the stair, except Mr. Leroux and Dr. Cumberly."

"Ah!" said Dunbar again, and made further entries in his book. "I need not trouble you further, sir. Good night!"

Exel, despite his earlier attitude of boredom, now ignored this official dismissal, and, tossing the stump of his cigar into the grate, lighted a cigarette, and with both hands thrust deep in his pockets, stood leaning back against the mantelpiece. The detective turned to Leroux.

"Have a brandy-and-soda?" suggested Dr. Cumberly, his eyes turned upon the pathetic face of the novelist.

But Leroux shook his head, wearily.

"Go ahead, Inspector!" he said. "I am anxious to tell you all I know. God knows I am anxious to tell you."

A sound was heard of a key being inserted in the lock of a door.

Four pairs of curious eyes were turned toward the entrance lobby, when the door opened, and a sleek man of medium height, clean shaven, but with his hair cut low upon the cheek bones, so as to give the impression of short side-whiskers, entered in a manner at once furtive and servile.

He wore a black overcoat and a bowler hat. Reclosing the door, he turned, perceived the group in the study, and fell back as though someone had struck him a fierce blow.

Abject terror was written upon his features, and, for a moment, the idea of flight appeared to suggest itself urgently to him; but finally, he took a step forward toward

the study.

"Who's this?" snapped Dunbar, without removing his leonine eyes from the new-comer.

"It is Soames," came the weary voice of Leroux.

"Butler?"

"Yes."

"Where's he been?"

"I don't know. He remained out without my permission."

"He did, eh?"

Inspector Dunbar thrust forth a long finger at the shrinking form in the doorway.

"Mr. Soames," he said, "you will be going to your own room and waiting there until I ring for you."

"Yes, sir," said Soames, holding his hat in both hands, and speaking huskily. "Yes, sir: certainly, sir."

He crossed the lobby and disappeared.

"There is no other way out, is there?" inquired the detective, glancing at Dr. Cumberly.

"There is no other way," was the reply; "but surely you don't suspect" . . .

"I would suspect the Archbishop of Westminster," snapped Dunbar, "if he came in like that! Now, sir,"—he turned to Leroux—"you were alone, here, to-night?"

"Quite alone, Inspector. The truth is, I fear, that my servants take liberties in the absence of my wife."

"In the absence of your wife? Where is your wife?"

"She is in Paris."

"Is she a Frenchwoman?"

"No! oh, no! But my wife is a painter, you understand, and—er—I met her in Paris—er— . . . Must you insist upon these—domestic particulars, Inspector?"

"If Mr. Exel is anxious to turn in," replied the inspector, "after his no doubt exhausting duties at the House, and if Dr. Cumberly—"

"I have no secrets from Cumberly!" interjected Leroux. "The doctor has known me almost from boyhood, but—er—" turning to the politician—"don't you know, Exel—no offense, no offense" . . .

"My dear Leroux," responded Exel hastily, "I am the offender! Permit me to wish you all good night."

He crossed the study, and, at the door, paused and turned.

"Rely upon me, Leroux," he said, "to help in any way within my power."

He crossed the lobby, opened the outer door, and departed.

"Now, Mr. Leroux," resumed Dunbar, "about this matter of your wife's absence."

IV

A WINDOW IS OPENED

Whilst Henry Leroux collected his thoughts, Dr. Cumberly glanced across at the writing-table where lay the fragment of paper which had been clutched in the dead woman's hand, then turned his head again toward the inspector, staring at him curiously. Since Dunbar had not yet attempted even to glance at the strange message, he wondered what had prompted the present line of inquiry.

"My wife," began Leroux, "shared a studio in Paris, at the time that I met her, with an American lady—a very talented portrait painter—er—a Miss Denise Ryland. You may know her name?—but of course, you don't, no! Well, my wife is, herself, quite clever with her brush; in fact she has exhibited more than once at the Paris Salon. We agreed at—er—the time of our—of our—engagement, that she should be free to visit her old artistic friends in Paris at any time. You understand? There was to be no let or hindrance. . . . Is this really necessary, Inspector?"

"Pray go on, Mr. Leroux."

"Well, you understand, it was a give-and-take arrangement; because I am afraid that I, myself, demand certain—sacrifices from my wife—and—er—I did not feel entitled to—interfere" . . .

"You see, Inspector," interrupted Dr. Cumberly, "they are a Bohemian pair, and Bohemians, inevitably, bore one another at times! This little arrangement was intended as a safety-valve. Whenever ennui attacked Mrs. Leroux, she was at liberty to depart for a week to her own friends in Paris, leaving Leroux to the bachelor's existence which is really his proper state; to go unshaven and unshorn, to dine upon bread and cheese and onions, to work until all hours of the morning, and generally to enjoy himself!"

"Does she usually stay long?" inquired Dunbar.

"Not more than a week, as a rule," answered Leroux.

"You must excuse me," continued the detective, "if I seem to pry into intimate matters; but on these occasions, how does Mrs. Leroux get on for money?"

"I have opened a credit for her," explained the novelist, wearily, "at the Credit Lyonnais, in Paris."

Dunbar scribbled busily in his notebook.

"Does she take her maid with her?" he jerked, suddenly.

"She has no maid at the moment," replied Leroux; "she has been without one for twelve months or more, now."

"When did you last hear from her?"

"Three days ago."

"Did you answer the letter?"

"Yes; my answer was amongst the mail which Soames took to the post, to-night."

"You said, though, if I remember rightly, that he was out without permission?"

Leroux ran his fingers through his hair.

"I meant that he should only have been absent five minutes or so; whilst he remained out for more than an hour."

Inspector Dunbar nodded, comprehendingly, tapping his teeth with the head of the fountain-pen.

"And the other servants?"

"There are only two: a cook and a maid. I released them for the evening—glad to get rid of them—wanted to work."

"They are late?"

"They take liberties, damnable liberties, because I am easy-going."

"I see," said Dunbar. "So that you were quite alone this evening, when"—he nodded in the direction of the writing-table—"your visitor came?"

"Quite alone."

"Was her arrival the first interruption?"

"No—er—not exactly. Miss Cumberly . . ."

"My daughter," explained Dr. Cumberly, "knowing that Mr. Leroux, at these times, was very neglectful in regard to meals, prepared him an omelette, and brought it down in a chafing-dish."

"How long did she remain?" asked the inspector of Leroux.

"I—er—did not exactly open the door. We chatted, through—er—through the letter-box, and she left the omelette outside on the landing."

"What time would that be?"

"It was a quarter to twelve," declared Cumberly. "I had been supping with some friends, and returned to find Helen, my daughter, engaged in preparing the omelette. I congratulated her upon the happy thought, knowing that Leroux was probably starving himself."

"I see. The omelette, though, seems to be upset here on the floor?" said the inspector.

Cumberly briefly explained how it came to be there, Leroux punctuating his friend's story with affirmative nods.

"Then the door of the flat was open all the time?" cried Dunbar.

"Yes," replied Cumberly; "but whilst Exel and I searched the other rooms—and our search was exhaustive—Mr. Leroux remained here in the study, and in full view of the lobby—as you see for yourself."

"No living thing," said Leroux, monotonously, "left this flat from the time that the three of us, Exel, Cumberly, and I, entered, up to the time that Miss Cumberly came, and, with the doctor, went out again."

"H'm!" said the inspector, making notes; "it appears so, certainly. I will ask you then, for your own account, Mr. Leroux, of the arrival of the woman in the civet furs. Pay special attention"—he pointed with his fountain-pen—"to the *time* at which the various incidents occurred."

Leroux, growing calmer as he proceeded with the strange story, complied with the inspector's request. He had practically completed his account when the door-bell rang.

"It's the servants," said Dr. Cumberly. "Soames will open the door."

But Soames did not appear.

The ringing being repeated:—

"I told him to remain in his room," said Dunbar, "until I rang for him, I remember—"

"I will open the door," said Cumberly.

"And tell the servants to stay in the kitchen," snapped Dunbar.

Dr. Cumberly opened the door, admitting the cook and housemaid.

"There has been an unfortunate accident," he said—"but not to your master; you need not be afraid. But be good enough to remain in the kitchen for the present."

Peeping in furtively as they passed, the two women crossed the lobby and went to their own quarters.

"Mr. Soames next," muttered Dunbar, and glancing at Cumberly as he returned from the lobby:—"Will you ring for him?" he requested.

Dr. Cumberly nodded, and pressed a bell beside the mantelpiece. An interval followed, in which the inspector made notes and Cumberly stood looking at Leroux, who was beating his palms upon his knees, and staring unseeingly before him.

Cumberly rang again; and in response to the second ring, the housemaid appeared at the door.

"I rang for Soames," said Dr. Cumberly.

"He is not in, sir," answered the girl.

Inspector Dunbar started as though he had been bitten.

"What!" he cried; "not in?"

"No, sir," said the girl, with wide-open, frightened eyes.

Dunbar turned to Cumberly.

"You said there was no other way out!"

"There *is* no other way, to my knowledge."

"Where's his room?"

Cumberly led the way to a room at the end of a short corridor, and Inspector Dunbar, entering, and turning up the light, glanced about the little apartment. It was a very neat servants' bedroom; with comfortable, quite simple, furniture; but the chest-of-drawers had been hastily ransacked, and the contents of a trunk—or some of its contents—lay strewn about the floor.

"He has packed his grip!" came Leroux's voice from the doorway. "It's gone!"

The window was wide open. Dunbar sprang forward and leaned over the ledge, looking to the right and left, above and below.

A sort of square courtyard was beneath, and for the convenience of tradesmen, a hand-lift was constructed outside the kitchens of the three flats comprising the house; i.e.:— Mr. Exel's, ground floor, Henry Leroux's second floor, and Dr. Cumberly's, top. It worked in a skeleton shaft which passed close to the left of Soames' window.

For an active man, this was a good enough ladder, and the inspector withdrew his head shrugging his square shoulders, irritably.

"My fault entirely!" he muttered, biting his wiry mustache. "I should have come and seen for myself if there was another way out."

Leroux, in a new flutter of excitement, now craned from the window.

"It might be possible to climb down the shaft," he cried, after a brief survey "but not if one were carrying a heavy grip, such as that which he has taken!"

"H'm!" said Dunbar. "You are a writing gentleman, I understand, and yet it does not occur to you that he could have lowered the bag on a cord, if he wanted to avoid the noise of dropping it!"

"Yes—er—of course!" muttered Leroux. "But really—but really—oh, good God! I am bewildered! What in Heaven's name does it all mean!"

"It means trouble," replied Dunbar, grimly; "bad trouble."

They returned to the study, and Inspector Dunbar, for the first time since his arrival, walked across and examined the fragmentary message, raising his eyebrows when he discovered that it was written upon the same paper as Leroux's MSS. He glanced, too, at the pen lying on a page of "Martin Zeda" near the lamp and at the inky splash which told how hastily the pen had been dropped.

Then—his brows drawn together—he stooped to the body of the murdered woman. Partially raising the fur cloak, he suppressed a gasp of astonishment.

"Why! she only wears a silk night-dress, and a pair of suede slippers!"

He glanced back over his shoulder.

"I had noted that," said Cumberly. "The whole business is utterly extraordinary."

"Extraordinary is no word for it!" growled the inspector, pursuing his examination. . . . "Marks of pressure at the throat—yes; and generally unhealthy appearance."

"Due to the drug habit," interjected Dr. Cumberly.

"What drug?"

"I should not like to say out of hand; possibly morphine."

"No jewelry," continued the detective, musingly; "wedding ring—not a new one. Finger nails well cared for, but recently neglected. Hair dyed to hide gray patches; dye wanted renewing. Shoes, French. Night-robe, silk; good lace; probably French, also. Faint perfume—don't know what it is—apparently proceeding from civet fur. Furs, magnificent; very costly." . . .

He slightly moved the table-lamp in order to direct its light upon the white face. The bloodless lips were parted and the detective bent, closely peering at the teeth thus revealed.

"Her teeth were oddly discolored, doctor" he said, taking out a magnifying glass and examining them closely. "They had been recently scaled, too; so that she was not in the habit of neglecting them."

Dr. Cumberly nodded.

"The drug habit, again," he said guardedly; "a proper examination will establish the full facts."

The inspector added brief notes to those

already made, ere he rose from beside the body. Then:—

"You are absolutely certain," he said, deliberately, facing Leroux, "that you had never set eyes on this woman prior to her coming here, to-night?"

"I can swear it!" said Leroux.

"Good!" replied the detective, and closed his notebook with a snap. "Usual formalities will have to be gone through, but I don't think I need trouble you, gentlemen, any further, to-night."

V

DOCTORS DIFFER

Dr. Cumberly walked slowly upstairs to his own flat, a picture etched indelibly upon his mind, of Henry Leroux, with a face of despair, sitting below in his dining-room and listening to the ominous sounds proceeding from the study, where the police were now busily engaged. In the lobby he met his daughter Helen, who was waiting for him in a state of nervous suspense.

"Father!" she began, whilst rebuke died upon the doctor's lips—"tell me quickly what has happened."

Perceiving that an explanation was unavoidable, Dr. Cumberly outlined the story of the night's gruesome happenings, whilst Big Ben began to chime the hour of one.

Helen, eager-eyed, and with her charming face rather pale, hung upon every word of the narrative.

"And now," concluded her father, "you must go to bed. I insist."

"But father!" cried the girl—"there is something" . . .

She hesitated, uneasily.

"Well, Helen, go on," said the doctor.

"I am afraid you will refuse."

"At least give me the opportunity."

"Well—in the glimpse, the half-glimpse, which I had of her, I seemed" . . .

Dr. Cumberly rested his hands upon his daughter's shoulders characteristically, looking into the troubled gray eyes.

"You don't mean," he began . . .

"I thought I recognized her!" whispered the girl.

"Good God! can it be possible?"

"I have been trying ever since, to recall where we had met, but without result. It might mean so much" . . .

Dr. Cumberly regarded her, fixedly.

"It might mean so much to—Mr. Leroux. But I suppose you will say it is impossible?"

"It *is* impossible," said Dr. Cumberly firmly; "dismiss the idea, Helen."

"But father," pleaded the girl, placing her hands over his own, "consider what is at stake" . . .

"I am anxious that you should not become involved in this morbid business."

"But surely you know me better than to expect me to faint or become hysterical, or anything silly like that! I was certainly shocked when I came down to-night, because—well, it was all so frightfully unexpected" . . .

Dr. Cumberly shook his head. Helen put her arms about his neck and raised her eyes to his.

"You have no right to refuse," she said, softly: "don't you see that?"

Dr. Cumberly frowned. Then:—

"You are right, Helen," he agreed. "I should know your pluck well enough. But if Inspector Dunbar is gone, the police may refuse to admit us" . . .

"Then let us hurry!" cried Helen. "I am afraid they will take away" . . .

Side by side they descended to Henry Leroux's flat, ringing the bell, which, an hour earlier, the lady of the civet furs had rung.

"Is Detective-Inspector Dunbar here?" inquired the physician.

"Yes, sir."

"Say that Dr. Cumberly wishes to speak to him. And"—as the man was about to depart—"request him not to arouse Mr. Leroux."

Almost immediately the inspector appeared, a look of surprise upon his face, which increased on perceiving the girl beside her father.

"This is my daughter, Inspector," explained Cumberly; "she is a contributor to the *Planet*, and to various magazines, and in this journalistic capacity, meets many people in many walks of life. She thinks she may be of use to you in preparing your case."

Dunbar bowed rather awkwardly.

"Glad to meet you, Miss Cumberly," came the inevitable formula. "Entirely at your service."

"I had an idea, Inspector," said the girl, laying her hand confidentially upon Dunbar's arm, "that I recognized, when I entered Mr. Leroux's study, to-night"—Dunbar nodded—"that I recognized—the—victim!"

"Good!" said the inspector, rubbing his palms briskly together. His tawny eyes sparkled. "And you would wish to see her again before we take her away. Very plucky of you, Miss Cumberly! But then, you are a doctor's daughter."

They entered, and the inspector closed the door behind them.

"Don't arouse poor Leroux," whispered Cumberly to the detective. "I left him on a couch in the dining-room." . . .

"He is still there," replied Dunbar; "poor chap! It is" . . .

He met Helen's glance, and broke off shortly.

In the study two uniformed constables, and an officer in plain clothes, were apparently engaged in making an inventory—or such was the impression conveyed. The clock ticked merrily on; its ticking a desecration, where all else was hushed in deference to the grim visitor. The body of the murdered woman had been laid upon the chesterfield, and a little, dark, bearded man was conducting an elaborate examination; when, seeing the trio enter, he hastily threw the coat of civet fur over the body, and stood up, facing the intruders.

"It's all right, doctor," said the inspector; "and we shan't detain you a moment." He glanced over his shoulder. "Mr. Hilton, M. R. C. S." he said, indicating the dark man—"Dr. Cumberly and Miss Cumberly."

The divisional surgeon bowed to Helen and eagerly grasped the hand of the celebrated physician.

"I am fortunate in being able to ask your opinion," he began. . . .

Dr. Cumberly nodded shortly, and with upraised hand, cut him short.

"I shall willingly give you any assistance in my power," he said; "but my daughter has voluntarily committed herself to a rather painful ordeal, and I am anxious to get it over."

He stooped and raised the fur from the ghastly face.

Helen, her hand resting upon her father's shoulder, ventured one rapid glance and then looked away, shuddering slightly. Dr. Cumberly replaced the coat and gazed anxiously at his daughter. But Helen, with admirable courage, having closed her eyes for a moment, reopened them, and smiled at her father's anxiety. She was pale, but perfectly composed.

"Well, Miss Cumberly?" inquired the inspector, eagerly; whilst all in the room watched this slim girl in her charming deshabille, this dainty figure so utterly out of place in that scene of morbid crime.

She raised her gray eyes to the detective.

"I still believe that I have seen the face, somewhere, before. But I shall have to reflect a while—I meet so many folks, you know, in a casual way—before I can commit myself to any statement."

In the leonine eyes looking into hers gleamed the light of admiration and approval. The canny Scotsman admired the girl for her beauty, as a matter of course, for her courage, because courage was a quality standing high in his estimation, but, above all, for her admirable discretion.

"Very proper, Miss Cumberly," he said; "very proper and wise on your part. I don't wish to hurry you in any way, but"—he hesitated, glancing at the man in the plain clothes, who had now resumed a careful perusal of a newspaper—"but her name doesn't happen to be Vernon—"

"Vernon!" cried the girl, her eyes lighting up at the sound of the name. "Mrs. Vernon! it is! it is! She was pointed out to me at the last Arts Ball—where she appeared in a most monstrous Chinese costume—"

"Chinese?" inquired Dunbar, producing the bulky notebook.

"Yes. Oh! poor, poor soul!"

"You know nothing further about her, Miss Cumberly?"

"Nothing, Inspector. She was merely pointed out to me as one of the strangest figures in the hall. Her husband, I understand, is an art expert—"

"He was!" said Dunbar, closing the book sharply. "He died this afternoon; and a paragraph announcing his death appears in the newspaper which we found in the victim's fur coat!"

"But how—"

"It was the only paragraph on the half-page folded outwards which was in any sense personal. I am greatly indebted to you, Miss Cumberly; every hour wasted on a case like this means a fresh plait in the rope around the neck of the wrong man!"

Helen Cumberly grew slowly quite pallid.

"Good night," she said; and bowing to the detective and to the surgeon, she prepared to depart.

Mr. Hilton touched Dr. Cumberly's arm, as he, too, was about to retire.

"May I hope," he whispered, "that you will return and give me the benefit of your opinion in making out my report?"

Dr. Cumberly glanced at his daughter; and seeing her to be perfectly composed:—"For the moment, I have formed no opinion, Mr. Hilton," he said, quietly, "not having had an opportunity to conduct a proper examination."

Hilton bent and whispered, confidentially, in the other's ear:—

"She was drugged!"

The innuendo underlying the words struck Dr. Cumberly forcibly, and he started back with his brows drawn together in a frown.

"Do you mean that she was addicted to the use of drugs?" he asked, sharply; "or that the drugging took place to-night."

"The drugging did take place to-night!" whispered the other. "An injection was made in the left shoulder with a hypodermic syringe; the mark is quite fresh."

Dr. Cumberly glared at his fellow practitioner, angrily.

"Are there no other marks of injection?" he asked.

"On the left forearm, yes. Obviously self-administered. Oh, I don't deny the habit! But my point is this: the injection in the shoulder was not self-administered."

"Come, Helen," said Cumberly, taking his daughter's arm; for she had drawn near, during the coloquy—"you must get to bed."

His face was very stern when he turned again to Mr. Hilton.

"I shall return in a few minutes," he said, and escorted his daughter from the room.

VI

AT SCOTLAND YARD

Matters of vital importance to some people whom already we have met, and to others whom thus far we have not met, were transacted in a lofty and rather bleak looking room at Scotland Yard between the hours of nine and ten A.M.; that is, later in the morning of the fateful day whose advent we have heard acclaimed from the Tower of Westminster.

The room, which was lighted by a large French window opening upon a balcony, commanded an excellent view of the Thames Embankment. The floor was polished to a degree of brightness, almost painful. The distempered walls, save for a severe and solitary etching of a former Commissioner, were nude in all their unloveliness. A heavy deal table (upon which rested a blotting-pad, a pewter ink-pot, several newspapers and two pens) together with three deal chairs, built rather as monuments of durability than as examples of art, constituted the only furniture, if we except an electric lamp with a green glass shade, above the table.

This was the room of Detective-Inspector Dunbar; and Detective-Inspector Dunbar, at the hour of our entrance, will be found seated in the chair, placed behind the table, his elbows resting upon the blotting-pad.

At ten minutes past nine, exactly, the door opened, and a thick-set, florid man, buttoned up in a fawn colored raincoat and wearing a bowler hat of obsolete build, entered. He possessed a black mustache, a breezy, bustling manner, and humorous blue eyes; furthermore, when he took off his hat, he revealed the possession of a head of very bristly, upstanding, black hair. This was Detective-Sergeant Sowerby, and the same who was engaged in examining a newspaper in the study of Henry Leroux when Dr. Cumberly and his daughter had paid their second visit to that scene of an unhappy soul's dismissal.

"Well?" said Dunbar, glancing up at his subordinate, inquiringly.

"I have done all the cab depots," reported Sergeant Sowerby, "and a good many of the private owners; but so far the man seen by Mr. Exel has not turned up."

"The word will be passed round now, though," said Dunbar, "and we shall probably have him here during the day."

"I hope so," said the other good-humoredly, seating himself upon one of the two chairs ranged beside the wall. "If he doesn't show up." . . .

"Well?" jerked Dunbar—"if he doesn't?"

"It will look very black against Leroux."

Dunbar drummed upon the blotting-pad with the fingers of his left hand.

"It beats anything of the kind that has ever come my way," he confessed. "You get pretty cautious at weighing people up, in this business; but I certainly don't think— mind you, I go no further—but I certainly don't think Mr. Henry Leroux would willingly kill a fly; yet there is circumstantial evidence enough to hang him."

Sergeant Sowerby nodded, gazing speculatively at the floor.

"I wonder," he said, slowly, "why the girl—Miss Cumberly—hesitated about telling us the woman's name?"

"I am not wondering about that at all," replied Dunbar, bluntly. "She must meet thousands in the same way. The wonder to me is that she remembered at all. I am half open to bet half-a-crown that *you* couldn't remember the name of every woman you happened to have pointed out to you at an Arts Ball?"

"Maybe not," agreed Sowerby; "she's a smart girl, I'll allow. I see you have last night's papers there?"

"I have," replied Dunbar; "and I'm wondering" . . .

"If there's any connection?"

"Well," continued the inspector, "it looks on the face of it as though the news of her husband's death had something to do with Mrs. Vernon's presence at Leroux's flat. It's not a natural thing for a woman, on the evening of her husband's death, to rush straight away to another man's place" . . .

"It's strange we couldn't find her clothes" . . .

"It's not strange at all! You're simply obsessed with the idea that this was a love intrigue! Think, man! the most abandoned woman wouldn't run to keep an appointment with a lover at a time like that! And remember she had the news in her pocket! She came to that flat dressed—or undressed—just as we found her; I'm sure of it. And a point like that sometimes means the difference between hanging and acquittal."

Sergeant Sowerby digested these words, composing his jovial countenance in an expression of unnatural profundity. Then:—

"*The* point to my mind," he said, "is the one raised by Mr. Hilton. By gum! didn't Dr. Cumberly tell him off!"

"Dr. Cumberly," replied Dunbar, "is entitled to his opinion, that the injection in the woman's shoulder was at least eight hours old; whilst Mr. Hilton is equally entitled to maintain that it was less than *one* hour old. Neither of them can hope to prove his case."

"If either of them could?" . . .

"It might make a difference to the evidence—but I'm not sure."

"What time is your appointment?"

"Ten o'clock," replied Dunbar. "I am

meeting Mr. Debnam—the late Mr. Vernon's solicitor. There is something in it. Damme! I am sure of it!"

"Something in what?"

The fact that Mr. Vernon died yesterday evening, and that his wife was murdered at midnight."

"What have you told the press?"

"As little as possible, but you will see that the early editions will be screaming for the arrest of Soames."

"I shouldn't wonder. He would be a useful man to have; but he's probably out of London now."

"I think not. He's more likely to wait for instructions from his principal."

"His principal?"

"Certainly. You don't think Soames did the murder, do you?"

"No; but he's obviously an accessory."

"I'm not so sure even of that."

"Then why did he bolt?"

"Because he had a guilty conscience."

"Yes," agreed Sowerby; "it does turn out that way sometimes. At any rate, Stringer is after him, but he's got next to nothing to go upon. Has any reply been received from Mrs. Leroux in Paris?"

"No," answered Dunbar, frowning thoughtfully. "Her husband's wire would reach her first thing this morning; I am expecting to hear of a reply at any moment."

"They're a funny couple, altogether," said Sowerby. "I can't imagine myself standing for Mrs. Sowerby spending all her week-ends in Paris. Asking for trouble, *I* call it!"

"It does seem a daft arrangement," agreed Dunbar; "but then, as you say, they're a funny couple."

"I never saw such a bundle of nerves in all my life!" . . .

"Leroux?"

Sowerby nodded.

"I suppose," he said, "it's the artistic temperament! If Mrs. Leroux has got it, too, I don't wonder that they get fed up with one another's company."

"That's about the secret of it. And now, I shall be glad, Sowerby, if you will be after that taxi-man again. Report at one o'clock. I shall be here."

With his hand on the door-knob: "By the way," said Sowerby, "who the blazes is Mr. King?"

Inspector Dunbar looked up.

"Mr. King," he replied slowly, "is the solution of the mystery."

VII

THE MAN IN THE LIMOUSINE

The house of the late Horace Vernon was a modern villa of prosperous appearance; but, on this sunny September morning, a palpable atmosphere of gloom seemed to overlie it. This made itself perceptible even to the toughened and unimpressionable nerves of Inspector Dunbar. As he mounted the five steps leading up to the door, glancing meanwhile at the lowered blinds at the windows, he wondered if, failing these evidences and his own private knowledge of the facts, he should have recognized that the hand of tragedy had placed its mark upon this house. But when the door was opened by a white-faced servant, he told himself that he should, for a veritable miasma of death seemed to come out to meet him, to envelope him.

Within, proceeded a subdued activity: somber figures moved upon the staircase; and Inspector Dunbar, having presented his card, presently found himself in a well-appointed library.

At the table, whereon were spread a number of documents, sat a lean, clean-shaven, sallow-faced man, wearing gold-rimmed pince-nez; a man whose demeanor of business-like gloom was most admirably adapted to that place and occasion. This was Mr. Debnam, the solicitor. He gravely waved the detective to an armchair, adjusted his pince-nez, and coughed, introductorily.

"Your communication, Inspector," he began (he had the kind of voice which seems to be buried in sawdust packing), "was brought to me this morning, and disturbed me immeasurably, unspeakably."

"You have been to view the body, sir?"

"One of my clerks, who knew Mrs. Vernon, has just returned to this house to report that he has identified her."

"I should have preferred you to have gone yourself, sir," began Dunbar, taking out his notebook.

"My state of health, Inspector," said the solicitor, "renders it undesirable that I should submit myself to an ordeal so unnecessary—so wholly unnecessary."

"Very good!" muttered Dunbar, making an entry in his book; "your clerk, then, whom I can see in a moment, identifies the murdered woman as Mrs. Vernon. What was her Christian name?"

"Iris—Iris Mary Vernon."

Inspector Dunbar made a note of the fact.

"And now," he said, "you will have read the copy of that portion of my report which I submitted to you this morning—acting upon information supplied by Miss Helen Cumberly?"

"Yes, yes, Inspector, I have read it—but, by the way, I do not know Miss Cumberly."

"Miss Cumberly," explained the detective, "is the daughter of Dr. Cumberly, the Harley Street physician. She lives with her father in the flat above that of Mr. Leroux. She saw the body by accident—and recognized it as that of a lady who had been named to her at the last Arts Ball."

"Ah!" said Debnam, "yes—I see—at the Arts Ball, Inspector. This is a mysterious and a very ghastly case."

"It is indeed, sir," agreed Dunbar. "Can you throw any light upon the presence of Mrs. Vernon at Mr. Leroux's flat on the very night of her husband's death?"

"I can—and I cannot," answered the solicitor, leaning back in the chair and again adjusting his pince-nez, in the manner of a man having important matters—and gloomy, very gloomy matters—to communicate.

"Good!" said the inspector, and prepared to listen.

"You see," continued Debnam, "the late Mrs. Vernon was not actually residing with her husband at the date of his death."

"Indeed!"

"Ostensibly"—the solicitor shook a lean forefinger at his vis-a-vis—"ostensibly, Inspector, she was visiting her sister in Scotland."

Inspector Dunbar sat up very straight, his brows drawn down over the tawny eyes.

"These visits were of frequent occurrence, and usually of about a week's duration. Mr. Vernon, my late client, a man—I'll not deny it—of inconstant affections (you understand me, Inspector?), did not greatly concern himself with his wife's movements. She belonged to a smart Bohemian set, and—to use a popular figure of speech—burnt the candle at both ends; late dances, night clubs, bridge parties, and other feverish pursuits, possibly taken up as a result of the—shall I say cooling?—of her husband's affections" . . .

"There was another woman in the case?"

"I fear so, Inspector; in fact, I am sure of it: but to return to Mrs. Vernon. My client provided her with ample funds; and I, myself, have expressed to him astonishment respecting her expenditures in Scotland. I

understand that her sister was in comparatively poor circumstances, and I went so far as to point out to Mr. Vernon that one hundred pounds was—shall I say an excessive?—outlay upon a week's sojourn in Auchterander, Perth."

"A hundred pounds!"

"One hundred pounds!"

"Was it queried by Mr. Vernon?"

"Not at all."

"Was Mr. Vernon personally acquainted with this sister in Perth?"

"He was not, Inspector. Mrs. Vernon, at the time of her marriage, did not enjoy that social status to which my late client elevated her. For many years she held no open communication with any member of her family, but latterly, as I have explained, she acquired the habit of recuperating—recuperating from the effects of her febrile pleasures—at this obscure place in Scotland. And Mr. Vernon, his interest in her movements having considerably—shall I say abated?—offered no objection: even suffered it gladly, counting the cost but little against" . . .

"Freedom?" suggested Dunbar, scribbling in his notebook.

"Rather crudely expressed, perhaps," said the solicitor, peering over the top of his glasses, "but you have the idea. I come now to my client's awakening. Four days ago, he learned the truth; he learned that he was being deceived!"

"Deceived!"

"Mrs. Vernon, thoroughly exhausted with irregular living, announced that she was about to resort once more to the healing breezes of the heatherland"—Mr. Debnam was thoroughly warming to his discourse and thoroughly enjoying his own dusty phrases.

"Interrupting you for a moment," said the inspector, "at what intervals did these visits take place?"

"At remarkably regular intervals, Inspector: something like six times a year."

"For how long had Mrs. Vernon made a custom of these visits?"

"Roughly, for two years."

"Thank you. Will you go on, sir?"

"She requested Mr. Vernon, then, on the last occasion to give her a check for eighty pounds; and this he did, unquestioningly. On Thursday, the second of September, she left for Scotland" . . .

"Did she take her maid?"

"Her maid always received a holiday on these occasions; Mrs. Vernon wired her respecting the date of her return."

"Did anyone actually see her off?"

"No, not that I am aware of, Inspector."

"To put the whole thing quite bluntly, Mr. Debnam," said Dunbar, fixing his tawny eyes upon the solicitor, "Mr. Vernon was thoroughly glad to get rid of her for a week?"

Mr. Debnam shifted uneasily in his chair; the truculent directness of the detective was unpleasing to his tortuous mind. However:—

"I fear you have hit upon the truth," he confessed, "and I must admit that we have no legal evidence of her leaving for Scotland on this, or on any other occasion. Letters were received from Perth, and letters sent to Auchterander from London were answered. But the truth, the painful truth came to light, unexpectedly, dramatically, on Monday last" . . .

"Four days ago?"

"Exactly; three days before the death of my client." Mr. Debnam wagged his finger at the inspector again. "I maintain," he said, "that this painful discovery, which I am about to mention, precipitated my client's end; although it is a fact that there was—hereditary heart trouble. But I admit that his neglect of his wife (to give it no harsher name) contributed to the catastrophe."

He paused to give dramatic point to the revelation.

"Walking homeward at a late hour on Monday evening from a flat in Victoria Street—the flat of—shall I employ the term a particular friend?—Mr. Vernon was horrified—horrified beyond measure, to perceive, in a large and well-appointed car—a limousine—his wife!" . . .

"The inside lights of the car were on, then?"

"No; but the light from a street lamp shone directly into the car. A temporary block in the traffic compelled the driver of the car, whom my client described to me as Asiatic—to pull up for a moment. There, within a few yards of her husband, Mrs. Vernon reclined in the car—or rather in the arms of a male companion!"

"What!"

"Positively!" Mr. Debnam was sedately enjoying himself. "Positively, my dear Inspector, in the arms of a man of extremely dark complexion. Mr. Vernon was unable to perceive more than this, for the man had his back toward him. But the light shone fully upon the face of Mrs. Vernon, who appeared pale and exhausted. She wore a conspicuous motor-coat of civet fur, and it was this which first attracted Mr. Vernon's attention. The blow was a very severe one to a man in my client's state of health; and although I cannot claim that his own conscience was clear, this open violation of the marriage vows outraged the husband—outraged him. In fact he was so perturbed, that he stood there shaking, quivering, unable to speak or act, and the car drove away before he had recovered sufficient presence of mind to note the number."

"In which direction did the car proceed?"

"Toward Victoria Station."

"Any other particulars?"

"Not regarding the car, its driver, or its occupants; but early on the following morning, Mr. Vernon, very much shaken, called upon me and instructed me to dispatch an agent to Perth immediately. My agent's report reached me at practically the same time as the news of my client's death" . . .

"And his report was?" . . .

"His report, Inspector, telegraphic, of course, was this: that no sister of Mrs. Vernon resided at the address; that the place was a cottage occupied by a certain Mrs. Fry and her husband; that the husband was of no occupation, and had no visible means of support"—he ticked off the points on the long forefinger—"that the Frys lived better than any of their neighbors; and—most important of all—that Mrs. Fry's maiden name, which my agent discovered by recourse to the parish register of marriages—was Ann Fairchild."

"What of that?"

"Ann Fairchild was a former maid of Mrs. Vernon!"

"In short, it amounts to this, then: Mrs. Vernon, during these various absences, never went to Scotland at all? It was a conspiracy?"

"Exactly—exactly, Inspector! I wired instructing my agent to extort from the woman, Fry, the address to which she forwarded letters received by her for Mrs. Vernon. The lady's death, news of which will now have reached him, will no doubt be a lever, enabling my representative to obtain the desired information."

"When do you expect to hear from him?"

"At any moment. Failing a full confession by the Frys, you will of course know how to act, Inspector?"

"Damme!" cried Dunbar, "can your man be relied upon to watch them? They mustn't slip away! Shall I instruct Perth to arrest the couple?"

"I wired my agent this morning, Inspector, to communicate with the local police respecting the Frys."

Inspector Dunbar tapped his small, widely-separated teeth with the end of his fountain-pen.

"I have had one priceless witness slip through my fingers," he muttered. "I'll hand in my resignation if the Frys go!"

"To whom do you refer?"

Inspector Dunbar rose.

"It is a point with which I need not trouble you, sir," he said. "It was not included in the extract of report sent to you. This is going to be the biggest case of my professional career, or my name is not Robert Dunbar!"

Closing his notebook, he thrust it into his pocket, and replaced his fountain-pen in the little leather wallet.

"Of course," said the solicitor, rising in turn, and adjusting the troublesome pince-nez, "there was some intrigue with Leroux? So much is evident."

"You will be thinking that, eh?"

"My dear Inspector"—Mr. Debnam, the wily, was seeking information—"my dear Inspector, Leroux's own wife was absent in Paris—quite a safe distance; and Mrs. Vernon (now proven to be a woman conducting a love intrigue) is found dead under most compromising circumstances—*most* compromising circumstances—in his flat! His servants, even, are got safely out of the way for the evening" . . .

"Quite so," said Dunbar, shortly, "quite so, Mr. Debnam." He opened the door. "Might I see the late Mrs. Vernon's maid?"

"She is at her home. As I told you, Mrs. Vernon habitually released her for the period of these absences."

The notebook reappeared.

"The young woman's address?"

"You can get it from the housekeeper. Is there anything else you wish to know?"

"Nothing beyond that, thank you."

Three minutes later, Inspector Dunbar had written in his book:—Clarice Goodstone, c/o Mrs. Herne, 134a Robert Street, Hampstead Road, N. W.

He departed from the house whereat Death the Gleaner had twice knocked with his Scythe.

VIII

CABMAN TWO

Returning to Scotland Yard, Inspector Dunbar walked straight up to his room. There he found Sowerby, very red faced and humid, and a taximan who sat stolidly surveying the Embankment from the window.

"Hello!" cried Dunbar; "he's turned up, then?"

"No, he hasn't," replied Sowerby with a mild irritation. "But we know where to find him, and he ought to lose his license."

The taximan turned hurriedly. He wore a muffler so tightly packed between his neck and the collar of his uniform jacket, that it appeared materially to impair his respiration. His face possessed a bluish tinge, suggestive of asphyxia, and his watery eyes protruded remarkably; his breathing was noisily audible.

"No, chuck it, mister!" he exclaimed. "I'm only tellin' you 'cause it ain't my line to play tricks on the police. You'll find my name in the books downstairs more'n any other driver in London! I reckon I've brought enough umbrellas, cameras, walkin' sticks, hopera cloaks, watches and sicklike in 'ere, to set up a blarsted pawnbroker's!"

"That's all right, my lad!" said Dunbar, holding up his hand to silence the voluble speaker. "There's going to be no license-losing. You did not hear that you were wanted before?"

The watery eyes of the cabman protruded painfully; he respired like a horse.

"*Me*, guv'nor!" he exclaimed. "Gor'blimë! I ain't the bloke! I was drivin' back from takin' the Honorable 'Erbert 'Arding 'ome—same as I does almost every night, when the 'ouse is a-sittin'—when I see old Tom Brian drawin' away from the door o' Palace Man—"

Again Dunbar held up his hand.

"No doubt you mean well," he said; "but damme! begin at the beginning! Who are you, and what have you come to tell us?"

" 'Oo are I?—'Ere's 'oo I ham!" wheezed the cabman, proffering a greasy license. "Richard 'Amper, number 3 Breams Mews, Dulwich Village" . . .

"That's all right," said Dunbar, thrusting back the proffered document; "and last night you had taken Mr. Harding the member of Parliament, to his residence in?"—

"In Peers' Chambers, Westminister—that's

it, guv'nor! Comin' back I 'ave to pass along the north side o' the Square, an' just a'ead o' me I see old Tom Brian a-pullin' round the Johnny 'Orner,—'im comin' from Palace Mansions."

"Mr. Exel only mentioned seeing *one* cab," muttered Dunbar, glancing keenly aside at Sowerby.

"Wotcher say, guv'nor?" asked the cabman.

"I say—did you see a gentleman approaching from the corner?" asked Dunbar.

"Yus," declared the man; "I see 'im, but 'e 'adn't got as far as the Johnny 'Orner. As I passed outside old Tom Brian, wot's changin' 'is gear, I see a bloke blowin' along on the pavement—a bloke in a high 'at, an' wearin' a heye-glass."

"At this time, then," pursued Dunbar, "you had actually passed the other cab, and the gentleman on the pavement had not come up with it?"

" 'E couldn't see it, guv'nor! I'm tellin' you 'e 'adn't got to the Johnny 'Orner!"

"I see," muttered Sowerby. "It's possible that Mr. Exel took no notice of the first cab—especially as it did not come out of the Square."

"Wotcher say, guv'nor?" queried the cabman again, turning his bleared eyes upon Sergeant Sowerby.

"He said," interrupted Dunbar, "was Brian's cab empty?"

" 'Course it was," rapped Mr. Hamper, " 'e'd just dropped 'is fare at Palace Mansions." . . .

"How do you know?" snapped Dunbar, suddenly fixing his fierce eyes upon the face of the speaker.

The cabman glared in beery truculence.

"I got me blarsted senses, ain't I?" he inquired. "There's only two lots o' flats on that side o' the Square—Palace Mansions, an' St. Andrew's Mansions."

"Well?"

"St. Andrew's Mansions," continued Hamper, "is all away!"

"All away?"

"All away! I know, 'cause I used to have a reg'lar fare there. 'E's in Egyp'; flat shut up. Top floor's to let. Bottom floor's two old unmarried maiden ladies what always travels by 'bus. So does all their blarsted friends an' relations. Where can old Tom Brian 'ave been comin' from, if it wasn't Palace Mansions?"

"H'm!" said Dunbar, "you are a loss to

the detective service, my lad! And how do you account for the fact that Brian has not got to hear of the inquiry?"

Hamper bent to Dunbar and whispered, beerily, in his ear: "P'r'aps 'e don't want to 'ear, guv'nor!"

"Oh! Why not?"

"Well, 'e knows there's something up there!"

"Therefore it's his plain duty to assist the police."

"Same as what I does?" cried Hamper, raising his eyebrows. "Course it is! but 'ow d'you know 'e ain't been got at?"

"Our friend, here, evidently has one up against Mr. Tom Brian!" muttered Dunbar aside to Sowerby.

"Wotcher say, guv'nor?" inquired the cabman, looking from one to the other.

"I say, no doubt you can save us the trouble of looking out Brian's license, and give us his private address?" replied Dunbar.

"Course I can. 'E lives hat num'er 36 Forth Street, Brixton, and 'e's out o' the big Brixton depot."

"Oh!" said Dunbar, dryly. "Does he owe you anything?"

"Wotcher say, guv'nor?"

"I say, it's very good of you to take all this trouble and whatever it has cost you in time, we shall be pleased to put right."

Mr. Hamper spat in his right palm, and rubbed his hands together appreciatively.

"Make it five bob!" he said.

"Wait downstairs," directed Dunbar, pressing a bell-push beside the door. "I'll get it put through for you."

"Right'o!" rumbled the cabman, and went lurching from the room as a constable in uniform appeared at the door. "Good mornin', guv'nor. Good mornin'!"

The cabman having departed, leaving in his wake a fragrant odor of fourpenny ale:—

"Here you are, Sowerby!" cried Dunbar. "We are moving at last! This is the address of the late Mrs. Vernon's maid. See her; feel your ground, carefully, of course; get to know what clothes Mrs. Vernon took with her on her periodical visits to Scotland."

"What clothes?"

"That's the idea; it is important. I don't think the girl was in her mistress's confidence, but I leave it to you to find out. If circumstances point to my surmise being inaccurate—you know how to act."

"Just let me glance over your notes, bearing on the matter," said Sowerby, "and I'll be off."

Dunbar handed him the bulging note-book, and Sergeant Sowerby lowered his in-adequate eyebrows, thoughtfully, whilst he scanned the evidence of Mr. Debnam. Then, returning the book to his superior, and ad-justing the peculiar bowler firmly upon his head, he set out.

Dunbar glanced through some papers—apparently reports—which lay upon the ta-ble, penciled comments upon two of them, and then, consulting his notebook once more in order to refresh his memory, started off for Forth Street, Brixton.

Forth Street, Brixton, is a depressing thor-oughfare. It contains small, cheap flats, and a number of frowsy looking houses which give one the impression of having run to seed. A hostelry of sad aspect occupies a commanding position midway along the street, but inspires the traveler not with cheer, but with lugubrious reflections upon the hor-rors of inebriety. The odors, unpleasantly mingled, of fried bacon and paraffin oil, are wafted to the wayfarer from the porches of these family residences.

Number 36 proved to be such a villa, and Inspector Dunbar contemplated it from a dis-tance, thoughtfully. As he stood by the door of the public house, gazing across the street, a tired looking woman, lean and anxious-eyed, a poor, dried up bean-pod of a woman, appeared from the door of number 36, car-rying a basket. She walked along in the di-rection of the neighboring highroad, and Dunbar casually followed her.

For some ten minutes he studied her ac-tivities, noting that she went from shop to shop until her basket was laden with pro-visions of all sorts. When she entered a wine-and-spirit merchant's, the detective entered close behind her, for the place was also a post-office. Whilst he purchased a penny stamp and fumbled in his pocket for an imag-inary letter, he observed, with interest, that the woman had purchased, and was loading into the hospitable basket, a bottle of whisky, a bottle of rum, and a bottle of gin.

He left the shop ahead of her, sure, now, of his ground, always provided that the woman proved to be Mrs. Brian. Dunbar walked along Forth Street slowly enough to enable the woman to overtake him. At the door of number 36, he glanced up at the number, questioningly, and turned in at the gate as she was about to enter.

He raised his hat.

"Have I the pleasure of addressing Mrs. Brian?"

Momentarily, a hard look came to the tired eyes, but Dunbar's gentleness of manner and voice, together with the kindly expression upon his face, turned the scales favorably.

"I am Mrs. Brian," she said; "yes. Did you want to see me?"

"On a matter of some importance. May I come in?"

She nodded and led the way into the house; the door was not closed.

In a living-room whereon was written a pathetic history—a history of decline from easy circumstance and respectability to pov-erty and utter disregard of appearances—she confronted him, setting down her basket on a table from which the remains of a fish breakfast were not yet removed.

"Is your husband in?" inquired Dunbar with a subtle change of manner.

"He's lying down."

The hard look was creeping again into the woman's eyes.

"Will you please awake him, and tell him that I have called in regard to his license?"

He thrust a card into her hand:—

DETECTIVE-INSPECTOR DUNBAR,

C. I. D.

New Scotland Yard. S. W.

IX

THE MAN IN BLACK

Mrs. Brian started back, with a wild look, a trapped look, in her eyes.

"What's he done?" she inquired. "What's he done? Tom's not done anything!"

"Be good enough to waken him," per-sisted the inspector. "I wish to speak to him."

Mrs. Brian walked slowly from the room and could be heard entering one further along the passage. An angry snarling, suggesting that of a wild animal disturbed in its lair, proclaimed the arousing of Taximan Thomas

Brian. A thick voice inquired, brutally, why the sanguinary hell he (Mr. Brian) had had his bloodstained slumbers disturbed in this gory manner and who was the vermilion blighter responsible.

Then Mrs. Brian's voice mingled with that of her husband, and both became subdued. Finally, a slim man, who wore a short beard, or had omitted to shave for some days, appeared at the door of the living-room. His face was another history upon the same subject as that which might be studied from the walls, the floor, and the appointments of the room. Inspector Dunbar perceived that the shadow of the neighboring hostelry overlay this home.

"What's up?" inquired the new arrival.

The tone of his voice, thickened by excess, was yet eloquent of the gentleman. The barriers passed, your parish gentleman can be the completest blackguard of them all. He spoke coarsely, and the infectious Cockney accent showed itself in his vowels; but Dunbar, a trained observer, summed up his man in a moment and acted accordingly.

"Come in and shut the door!" he directed.

"No"—as Mrs. Brian sought to enter behind her husband—"I wish to speak with you, privately."

"Hop it!" instructed Brian, jerking his thumb over his shoulder—and Mrs. Brian obediently disappeared, closing the door.

"Now," said Dunbar, looking the man up and down, "have you been into the depot, to-day?"

"No."

"But you have heard that there's an inquiry?"

"I've heard nothing. I've been in bed."

"We won't argue about that. I'll simply put a question to you: Where did you pick up the fare that you dropped at Palace Mansions at twelve o'clock last night?"

"Palace Mansions!" muttered Brian, shifting uneasily beneath the unflinching stare of the tawny eyes. "What d'you mean? What Palace Mansions?"

"Don't quibble!" warned Dunbar, thrusting out a finger at him. "This is not a matter of a loss of license; it's a life job!"

"Life job!" whispered the man, and his weak face suddenly relaxed, so that, oddly, the old refinement shone out through the new, vulgar veneer.

"Answer my questions straight and square and I'll take your word that you have not seen the inquiry!" said Dunbar.

"Dick Hamper's done this for me!" muttered Brian. "He's a dirty, low swine! Somebody'll do for him one night!"

"Leave Hamper out of the question," snapped Dunbar. "You put down a fare at Palace Mansions at twelve o'clock last night?"

For one tremendous moment, Brian hesitated, but the good that was in him, or the evil—a consciousness of wrongdoing, or of retribution pending—respect for the law, or fear of its might—decided his course.

"I did."

"It was a man?"

Again Brian, with furtive glance, sought to test his opponent; but his opponent was too strong for him. With Dunbar's eyes upon his face, he chose not to lie.

"It was a woman."

"How was she dressed?"

"In a fur motor-coat—civet fur."

The man of culture spoke in those two words, "civet fur"; and Dunbar nodded quickly, his eyes ablaze at the importance of the evidence.

"Was she alone?"

"She was."

"What fare did she pay you?"

"The meter only registered eightpence, but she gave me half-a-crown."

"Did she appear to be ill?"

"Very ill. She wore no hat, and I supposed her to be in evening dress. She almost fell as she got out of the cab, but managed to get into the hall of Palace Mansions quickly enough, looking behind her all the time."

Inspector Dunbar shot out the hypnotic finger again.

"She told you to wait!" he asserted, positively.

Brian looked to right and left, up and down, thrusting his hands into his coat pockets, and taking them out again to stroke his collarless neck. Then:—

"She did—yes," he admitted.

"But you were bribed to drive away? Don't deny it! Don't dare to trifle with me, or by God! you'll spend the night in Brixton Jail!"

"It was made worth my while," muttered Brian, his voice beginning to break, "to hop it."

"Who paid you to do it?"

"A man who had followed all the way in a big car."

"That's it! Describe him!"

"I can't! No, no! you can threaten as much as you like, but I can't describe him. I never saw his face. He stood behind me on the near side of the cab, and just reached forward and pushed a fiver under my nose."

Inspector Dunbar searched the speaker's face closely—and concluded that he was respecting the verity.

"How was he dressed?"

"In black, and that's all I can tell you about him."

"You took the money?"

"I took the money, yes" . . .

"What did he say to you?"

"Simply: 'Drive off.' "

"Did you take him to be an Englishman from his speech?"

"No; he was not an Englishman. He had a foreign accent."

"French? German?"

"No," said Brian, looking up and meeting the glance of the fierce eyes. "Asiatic!"

Inspector Dunbar, closely as he held himself in hand, started slightly.

"Are you sure?"

"Certainly. Before I—when I was younger—I traveled in the East, and I know the voice and intonation of the cultured Oriental."

"Can you place him any closer than that?"

"No, I can't venture to do so." Brian's manner was becoming, momentarily, more nearly that of a gentleman. "I might be leading you astray if I ventured a guess, but if you asked me to do so, I should say he was a Chinaman."

"A *Chinaman?*" Dunbar's voice rose excitedly.

"I think so."

"What occurred next?"

"I turned my cab and drove off out of the Square."

"Did you see where the man went?"

"I didn't. I saw nothing of him beyond his hand."

"And his hand?"

"He wore a glove."

"And now," said Dunbar, speaking very slowly, "where did you pick up your fare?"

"In Gillingham Street, near Victoria Station."

"From a house?"

"Yes, from Nurse Proctor's."

"Nurse Proctor's! Who is Nurse Proctor?"

Brian shrugged his shoulders in a nonchalant manner, which obviously belonged to an earlier phase of existence.

"She keeps a nursing home," he said— "for ladies."

"Do you mean a maternity home?"

"Not exactly; at least I don't think so. Most of her clients are society ladies, who stay there periodically."

"What are you driving at?" demanded Dunbar. "I have asked you if it is a maternity home."

"And I have replied that it isn't. I am only giving you facts; you don't want my surmises."

"Who hailed you?"

"The woman did—the woman in the fur coat. I was just passing the door very slowly when it was flung open with a bang, and she rushed out as though hell were after her. Before I had time to pull up, she threw herself into my cab and screamed: 'Palace Mansions! Westminster!' I reached back and shut the door, and drove right away."

"When did you see that you were followed?"

"We were held up just outside the music hall, and looking back, I saw that my fare was dreadfully excited. It didn't take me long to find out that the cause of her excitement was a big limousine, three or four back in the block of traffic. The driver was some kind of an Oriental, too, although I couldn't make him out very clearly."

"Good!" snapped Dunbar; "that's important! But you saw nothing more of this car?" . . .

"I saw it follow me into the Square."

"Then where did it wait?"

"I don't know; I didn't see it again."

Inspector Dunbar nodded rapidly.

"Have you ever driven women to or from this Nurse Proctor's before?"

"On two other occasions, I have driven ladies who came from there. I knew they came from there, because it got about amongst us that the tall woman in nurse's uniform who accompanied them was Nurse Proctor."

"You mean that you didn't take these women actually from the door of the house in Gillingham Street, but from somewhere adjacent?"

"Yes; they never take a cab from the door. They always walk to the corner of the street with a nurse, and a porter belonging to the house brings their luggage along."

"The idea is secrecy?"

"No doubt. But as I have said, the word was passed round."

"Did you know either of these women?"

"No; but they were obviously members of good society."

"And you drove them?"

"One to St. Pancras, and one to Waterloo," said Brian, dropping back somewhat into his coarser style, and permitting a slow grin to overspread his countenance.

"To catch trains, no doubt?"

"Not a bit of it! To *meet* trains!"

"You mean?"

"I mean that their own private cars were waiting for them at the *arrival* platform as I drove 'em up to the *departure* platform, and that they simply marched through the station and pretended to have arrived by train!"

Inspector Dunbar took out his notebook and fountain-pen, and began to tap his teeth with the latter, nodding his head at the same time.

"You are sure of the accuracy of your last statement?" he said, raising his eyes to the other.

"I followed one of them," was the reply, "and saw her footman gravely take charge of the luggage which I had just brought from Victoria; and a pal of mine followed the other—the Waterloo one, that was."

Inspector Dunbar scribbled busily. Then:—

"You have done well to make a clean breast of it," he said. "Take a straight tip from me. Keep off the drink!"

X

THE GREAT UNDERSTANDING

It was in the afternoon of this same day—a day so momentous in the lives of more than one of London's millions—that two travelers might have been seen to descend from a first-class compartment of the Dover boat-train at Charing Cross.

They had been the sole occupants of the compartment, and, despite the wide dissimilarity of character to be read upon their countenances, seemed to have struck up an acquaintance based upon mutual amiability and worldly common sense. The traveler first to descend and gallantly to offer his hand to his companion in order to assist her to the platform, was the one whom a casual observer would first have noted.

He was a man built largely, but on good lines; a man past his youth, and somewhat too fleshy; but for all his bulk, there was nothing unwieldy, and nothing ungraceful in his bearing or carriage. He wore a French traveling-coat, conceived in a style violently Parisian, and composed of a wonderful check calculated to have blinded any cutter in Savile Row. From beneath its gorgeous folds protruded the extremities of severely creased cashmere trousers, turned up over white spats which nestled coyly about a pair of glossy black boots. The traveler's hat was of velour, silver gray and boasting a partridge feather thrust in its silken band. One glimpse of the outfit must have brought the entire staff of the *Tailor and Cutter* to an untimely grave.

But if ever man was born who could carry such a make-up, this traveler was he. The face was cut on massive lines, on fleshy lines, clean-shaven, and inclined to pallor. The hirsute blue tinge about the jaw and lips helped to accentuate the virile strength of the long, flexible mouth, which could be humorous, which could be sorrowful, which could be grim. In the dark eyes of the man lay a wealth of experience, acquired in a lifelong pilgrimage among many peoples, and to many lands. His dark brows were heavily marked, and his close-cut hair was splashed with gray.

Let us glance at the lady who accepted his white-gloved hand, and who sprang alertly onto the platform beside him.

She was a woman bordering on the forties, with a face of masculine vigor, redeemed and effeminized, by splendid hazel eyes, the kindliest imaginable. Obviously, the lady was one who had never married, who despised, or affected to despise, members of the other sex, but who had never learned to hate them; who had never grown soured, but who found the world a garden of heedless children—of children who called for mothering. Her athletic figure was clothed in a "sensible" tweed traveling dress, and she wore a tweed hat pressed well on to her head, and brown boots with the flattest heels conceivable. Add to this a Scotch woolen muffler, and a pair of woolen gloves, and you have a mental picture of the second traveler—a truly incongruous companion for the first.

Joining the crowd pouring in the direction the exit gates, the two chatted together animatedly, both speaking English, and the man employing that language with a perfect ease and command of words which nevertheless failed to disguise his French nationality. He spoke with an American accent; a phenomenon sometimes observable in one who has learned his English in Paris.

The irritating formalities which beset the returning traveler—and the lady distinctly was of the readily irritated type—were smoothed away by the magic personality of her companion. Porters came at the beck of his gloved hand; guards, catching his eye, saluted and were completely his servants; ticket inspectors yielded to him the deference ordinarily reserved for directors of the line.

Outside the station, then, her luggage having been stacked upon a cab, the lady parted from her companion with assurances, which were returned, that she should hope to improve the acquaintance.

The address to which the French gentleman politely requested the cabman to drive, was that of a sound and old-established hotel in the neighborhood of the Strand, and at no great distance from the station.

Then, having stood bareheaded until the cab turned out into the traffic stream of that busy thoroughfare, the first traveler, whose luggage consisted of a large suitcase, hailed a second cab and drove to the Hotel Astoria—the usual objective of Americans.

Taking leave of him for the moment, let us follow the lady.

Her arrangements were very soon made at the hotel, and having removed some of the travel-stains from her person and partaken of one cup of China tea, respecting the quality whereof she delivered herself of some caustic comments, she walked down into the Strand and mounted to the top of a Victoria bound 'bus.

That she was not intimately acquainted with London, was a fact readily observable by her fellow passengers; for as the 'bus went rolling westward, from the large pocket of her Norfolk jacket she took out a guide-book provided with numerous maps, and began composedly to consult its complexities.

When the conductor came to collect her fare, she had made up her mind, and was replacing the guide-book in her pocket.

"Put me down by the Storis, Victoria Street, conductor," she directed, and handed him a penny—the correct fare.

It chanced that about that time, within a minute or so, of the American lady's leaving the hotel, and just as red rays, the harbingers of dusk, came creeping in at the latticed window of her cozy work-room, Helen Cumberly laid down her pen with a sigh. She stood up, mechanically rearranging her hair as she did so, and crossed the corridor to her bedroom, the window whereof overlooked the Square.

She peered down into the central garden.

A common-looking man sat upon a bench, apparently watching the labors of the gardener, which consisted at the moment of the spiking of scraps of paper which disfigured the green carpet of the lawn.

Helen returned to her writing-table and reseated herself. Kindly twilight veiled her, and a chatty sparrow who perched upon the window-ledge pretended that he had not noticed two tears which trembled, quivering, upon the girl's lashes. Almost unconsciously, for it was an established custom, she sprinkled crumbs from the tea-tray beside her upon the ledge, whilst the tears dropped upon a written page and two more appeared in turn upon her lashes.

The sparrow supped enthusiastically, being joined in his repast by two talkative companions. As the last fragments dropped from the girl's white fingers, she withdrew her hand, and slowly—very slowly—her head sank down, pillowed upon her arms.

For some five minutes she cried silently; the sparrows, unheeded, bade her good night, and flew to their nests in the trees of the Square. Then, very resolutely, as if inspired by a settled purpose, she stood up and re-crossed the corridor to her bedroom.

She turned on the lamp above the dressing-table and rapidly removed the traces of her tears, contemplating in dismay a redness of her pretty nose which did not prove entirely amenable to treatment with the powder-puff. Finally, however, she switched off the light, and, going out onto the landing, descended to the door of Henry Leroux's flat.

In reply to her ring, the maid, Ferris, opened the door. She wore her hat and coat, and beside her on the floor stood a tin trunk.

"Why, Ferris!" cried Helen—"are you leaving?"

"I am indeed, miss!" said the girl, independently.

"But why? whatever will Mr. Leroux do?"

"He'll have to do the best he can. Cook's goin' too!"

"What! Cook is going?"

"I am!" announced a deep, female voice. And the cook appeared beside the maid.

"But whatever—" began Helen; then, realizing that she could achieve no good end by such an attitude: "Tell Mr. Leroux," she instructed the maid, quietly, "that I wish to see him."

Ferris glanced rapidly at her companion, as a man appeared on the landing, to inquire in an abysmal tone, if "them boxes was ready to be took." Helen Cumberly forestalled an insolent refusal which the cook, by a furtive wink, counseled to the housemaid.

"Don't trouble," she said, with an easy dignity reminiscent of her father. "I will announce myself."

She passed the servants, crossed the lobby, and rapped upon the study door.

"Come in," said the voice of Henry Leroux.

Helen opened the door. The place was in semidarkness, objects being but dimly discernible. Leroux sat in his usual seat at the dressing-table. The room was in the utmost disorder, evidently having received no attention since its overhauling by the police. Helen pressed the switch, lighting the two lamps.

Leroux, at last, seemed in his proper element: he exhibited an unhealthy pallor, and it was obvious that no razor had touched his chin for at least three days. His dark blue eyes—the eyes of a dreamer—were heavy and dull, with shadows pooled below them. A biscuit-jar, a decanter and a syphon stood half buried in papers on the table.

"Why, Mr. Leroux!" said Helen, with a deep note of sympathy in her voice—"you don't mean to say" . . .

Leroux rose, forcing a smile to his haggard face.

"You see—much too good," he said. "Altogether—too good." . . .

"I thought I should find you here," continued the girl, firmly; "but I did not anticipate—" she indicated the chaos about—"this! The insolence, the disgraceful, ungrateful insolence, of those women!"

"Dear, dear, dear!" murmured Leroux, waving his hand vaguely; "never mind—never mind! They—er—they . . . I don't want them to stop . . . and, believe me, I am—er—perfectly comfortable!"

"You should not be in—this room, at all. In fact, you should go right away." . . .

"I cannot . . . my wife may—return—at any moment." His voice shook. "I—am expecting her return—hourly." . . .

His gaze sought the table-clock; and he drew his lips very tightly together when the pitiless hands forced upon his mind the fact that the day was marching to its end.

Helen turned her head aside, inhaling deeply, and striving for composure.

"Garnham shall come down and tidy up for you," she said, quietly; "and you must dine with us."

The outer door was noisily closed by the departing servants.

"You are much too good," whispered Leroux, again; and the weary eyes glistened with a sudden moisture. "Thank you! Thank you! But—er—I could not dream of disturbing" . . .

"Mr. Leroux," said Helen, with all her old firmness—"Garnham is coming down *immediately* to put the place in order! And, whilst he is doing so, you are going to prepare yourself for a decent, Christian dinner!"

Henry Leroux rested one hand upon the table, looking down at the carpet. He had known for a long time, in a vague fashion, that he lacked something; that his success—a wholly inartistic one—had yielded him little gratification; that the comfort of his home was a purely monetary product and not in any sense atmospheric. He had schooled himself to believe that he liked loneliness—loneliness physical and mental, and that in marrying a pretty, but pleasure-loving girl, he had insured an ideal ménage. Furthermore, he honestly believed that he worshiped his wife; and with his present grief at her unaccountable silence was mingled no atom of reproach.

But latterly he had begun to wonder—in his peculiarly indefinite way he had begun to doubt his own philosophy. Was the void in his soul a product of thwarted ambition?—for, whilst he slaved, scrupulously, upon "Martin Zeda," he loathed every deed and every word of that Old Man of the Sea. Or could it be that his own being—his nature of Adam—lacked something which wealth, social position, and Mira, his wife, could not yield to him?

Now, a new tone in the voice of Helen Cumberly—a tone different from that compound of good-fellowship and raillery, which he knew—a tone which had entered into it when she had exclaimed upon the state of the room—set his poor, anxious heart thrumming like a lute. He felt a hot flush creeping upon him; his forehead grew damp. He feared to raise his eyes.

"Is that a bargain?" asked Helen, sweetly.

Henry Leroux found a lump in his throat; but he lifted his untidy head and took the hand which the girl had extended to him. She smiled a bit unnaturally; then every tinge of color faded from her cheeks, and Henry Leroux, unconsciously holding the white hand in a vice-like grip, looked hungrily into the eyes grown suddenly tragic whilst into his own came the light of a great and sorrowful understanding.

"God bless you," he said. "I will do anything you wish."

Helen released her hand, turned, and ran from the study. Not until she was on the landing did she dare to speak. Then:—

"Garnham shall come down immediately. Don't be late for dinner!" she called—and there was a hint of laughter and of tears in her voice, of the restraint of culture struggling with rebellious womanhood.

XI

PRESENTING M. GASTON

Not venturing to turn on the light, not daring to look upon her own face in the mirror, Helen Cumberly sat before her dressing-table, trembling wildly. She wanted to laugh, and wanted to cry; but the daughter of Seton Cumberly knew what those symptoms meant and knew how to deal with them. At the end of an interval of some four or five minutes, she rang.

The maid opened the door.

"Don't light up, Merton," she said, composedly. "I want you to tell Garnham to go down to Mr. Leroux's and put the place in order. Mr. Leroux is dining with us."

The girl withdrew; and Helen, as the door closed, pressed the electric switch. She stared at her reflection in the mirror as if it were the face of an enemy, then, turning her head aside, sat deep in reflection, biting her lip and toying with the edge of the white doily.

"You little traitor!" she whispered, through clenched teeth. "You little traitor—and hypocrite"—sobs began to rise in her throat—"and fool!"

Five more minutes passed in a silent conflict. A knock announced the return of the maid; and the girl reentered, placing upon the table a visiting-card:—

DENISE RYLAND

Atelier 4, Rue Du Coq D'or,

Montmartre,

Paris.

Helen Cumberly started to her feet with a stifled exclamation and turned to the maid; her face, to which the color slowly had been returning, suddenly blanched anew.

"Denise Ryland!" she muttered, still holding the card in her hand, "why—that's Mrs. Leroux's friend, with whom she had been staying in Paris! Whatever can it mean?"

"Shall I show her in here, please?" asked the maid.

"Yes, in here," replied Helen, absently; and, scarcely aware that she had given instructions to that effect, she presently found herself confronted by the lady of the boat-train!

"Miss Cumberly?" said the new arrival in a pleasant American voice.

"Yes—I am Helen Cumberly. Oh! I am so glad to know you at last! I have often pictured you; for Mira—Mrs. Leroux—is always talking about you, and about the glorious times you have together! I have sometimes longed to join you in beautiful Paris. How good of you to come back with her!"

Miss Ryland unrolled the Scotch muffler from her throat, swinging her head from side to side in a sort of spuriously truculent manner, quite peculiarly her own. Her keen hazel eyes were fixed upon the face of the girl before her. Instinctively and immediately she liked Helen Cumberly; and Helen felt that this strong-looking, vaguely masculine woman, was an old, intimate friend, although she had never before set eyes upon her.

"H'm!" said Miss Ryland. "I have come from Paris"—she punctuated many of her sentences with wags of the head as if carefully weighing her words—"especially" (pause) "to see you" (pause and wag of head) "I am glad . . . to find that . . . you are the thoroughly sensible . . . kind of girl that I . . . had imagined, from the accounts which . . . I have had of you." . . .

She seated herself in an armchair.

"Had of me from Mira?" asked Helen.

"Yes . . . from Mrs. Leroux."

"How delightful it must be for you to have her with you so often! Marriage, as a rule, puts an end to that particular sort of good-time, doesn't it?"

"It does . . . very properly . . . too. No *man* . . . no *man* in his . . . right senses . . . would permit . . . his wife . . . to gad about in . . . Paris with another . . . girl" (she presumably referred to herself) whom *he* had only met . . . casually . . . and did not like" . . .

"What! do you mean that Mr. Leroux doesn't like you? I can't believe that!"

"Then the sooner . . . you believe it . . . the better."

"It can only be that he does not know you, properly?"

"He has no wish . . . to know me . . . properly; and I have no desire . . . to cultivate . . . the . . . friendship of such . . . a silly being."

Helen Cumberly was conscious that a flush was rising from her face to her brow, and tingling in the very roots of her hair. She was indignant with herself and turned aside, bending over her table in order to conceal this ill-timed embarrassment from her visitor.

"Poor Mr. Leroux!" she said, speaking very rapidly; "I think it awfully good of him, and sporty, to allow his wife so much liberty."

"Sporty!" said Miss Ryland, head wagging and nostrils distended in scorn. "Idiotic . . . I should call it."

"Why?"

Helen Cumberly, perfectly composed again, raised her clear eyes to her visitor.

"You seem so . . . thoroughly sensible, except in regard to . . . Harry Leroux;—and all women, with a few . . . exceptions, are fools where the true . . . character of a man is concerned—that I will take you right into my confidence."

Her speech lost its quality of syncopation; the whole expression of her face changed; and in the hazel eyes a deep concern might be read.

"My dear," she stood up, crossed to Helen's side, and rested her artistic looking hands upon the girl's shoulder. "Harry Leroux stands upon the brink of a great tragedy—a life's tragedy!"

Helen was trembling slightly again.

"Oh, I know!" she whispered—"I know—"

"You know?"

There was surprise in Miss Ryland's voice.

"Yes, I have seen them—watched them—and I know that the police think" . . .

"Police! What are you talking about—the police?"

Helen looked up with a troubled face.

"The murder!" she began . . .

Miss Ryland dropped into a chair which, fortunately, stood close behind her, with a face suddenly set in an expression of horror. She began to understand, now, a certain restraint, a certain ominous shadow, which she

had perceived, or thought she had perceived, in the atmosphere of this home, and in the manner of its occupants.

"My dear girl," she began, and the old nervous jerky manner showed itself again, momentarily,—"remember that . . . I left Paris by . . . the first train, this morning, and have simply been . . . traveling right up to the present moment." . . .

"Then you have not heard? You don't know that a—murder—has been committed?"

"Murder! Not—not" . . .

"Not any one connected with Mr. Leroux; no, thank God! but it was done in his flat." . . .

Miss Ryland brushed a whisk of straight hair back from her brow with a rough and ungraceful movement.

"My dear," she began, taking a French telegraphic form from her pocket, "you see this message? It's one which reached me at an unearthly hour this morning from Harry Leroux. It was addressed to his wife at my studio; therefore, as her friend, I opened it. Mira Leroux has actually visited me there twice since her marriage—"

"Twice!" Helen rose slowly to her feet, with horrified eyes fixed upon the speaker.

"Twice I said! I have not seen her, and have rarely heard from her, for nearly twelve months, now! Therefore I packed up posthaste and here I am! I came to you, because, from what little I have heard of you, and of your father, I judged you to be the right kind of friends to consult." . . .

"You have not seen her for twelve months?"

Helen's voice was almost inaudible, and she was trembling dreadfully.

"That's a fact, my dear. And now, what are we going to tell Harry Leroux?"

It was a question, the answer to which was by no means evident at a glance; and leaving Helen Cumberly face to face with this new and horrible truth which had brought Denise Ryland hotfoot from Paris to London, let us glance, for a moment, into the now familiar room of Detective-Inspector Dunbar at Scotland Yard.

He had returned from his interrogation of Brian; and he received the report of Sowerby, respecting the late Mrs. Vernon's maid. The girl, Sergeant Sowerby declared, was innocent of complicity, and could only depose to the fact that her late mistress took very little luggage with her on the occasions of her trips to Scotland. With his notebook open before him upon the table, Dunbar was adding this slight item to his notes upon the case, when the door opened, and the uniformed constable entered, saluted, and placed an envelope in the Inspector's hand.

"From the commissioner!" said Sowerby, significantly.

With puzzled face, Dunbar opened the envelope and withdrew the commissioner's note. It was very brief:—

"M. Gaston Max, of the Paris Police, is joining you in the Palace Mansions murder case. You will cooperate with him from date above."

"*Max!*" said Dunbar, gazing astoundedly at his subordinate.

Certainly it was a name which might well account for the amazement written upon the inspector's face; for it was the name of admittedly the greatest criminal investigator in Europe!

"What the devil has the case to do with the French police?" muttered Sowerby, his ruddy countenance exhibiting a whole history of wonderment.

The constable, who had withdrawn, now reappeared, knocking deferentially upon the door, throwing it open, and announcing:

"Mr. Gaston Max, to see Detective-Inspector Dunbar."

Bowing courteously upon the threshold, appeared a figure in a dazzling check traveling-coat—a figure very novel, and wholly unforgettable.

"I am honored to meet a distinguished London colleague," he said in perfect English, with a faint American accent.

Dunbar stepped across the room with outstretched hand, and cordially shook that of the famous Frenchman.

"I am the more honored," he declared, gallantly playing up to the other's courtesy. "This is Detective-Sergeant Sowerby, who is acting with me in the case."

M. Gaston Max bowed low in acknowledgment of the introduction.

"It is a pleasure to meet Detective-Sergeant Sowerby," he declared.

These polite overtures being concluded then, and the door being closed, the three detectives stood looking at one another in momentary silence. Then Dunbar spoke with blunt directness:

"I am very pleased to have you with us, Mr. Max," he said; "but might I ask what your presence in London means?"

M. Gaston Max shrugged in true Gallic fashion.

"It means, monsieur," he said, "—murder—and *Mr. King!*"

XII

MR. GIANAPOLIS

It will prove of interest at this place to avail ourselves of an opportunity denied to the police, and to inquire into the activities of Mr. Soames, whilom employee of Henry Leroux.

Luke Soames was a man of unpleasant character; a man ever seeking advancement—advancement to what he believed to be an ideal state, viz.: the possession of a competency; and to this ambition he subjugated all conflicting interests—especially the interests of others. From narrow but honest beginnings, he had developed along lines ever growing narrower until gradually honesty became squeezed out. He formed the opinion that wealth was unobtainable by dint of hard work; and indeed in a man of his limited intellectual attainments, this was no more than true.

At the period when he becomes of interest, he had just discovered himself a gentleman-at-large by reason of his dismissal from the services of a wealthy bachelor, to whose establishment in Piccadilly he had been attached in the capacity of valet. There was nothing definite against his character at this time, save that he had never remained for long in any one situation.

His experience was varied, if his references were limited; he had served not only as a valet, but also as chauffeur, as steward on an ocean liner, and, for a limited period, as temporary butler in an American household at Nice.

Soames' banking account had increased steadily, but not at a rate commensurate with his ambitions; therefore, when entering his name and qualifications in the books of a certain exclusive employment agency in Mayfair he determined to avail himself, upon this occasion, of his comparative independence by waiting until kindly Fate should cast something really satisfactory in his path.

Such an opening occurred very shortly after his first visit to the agent. He received a card instructing him to call at the office in order to meet a certain Mr. Gianapolis. Quitting his rooms in Kennington, Mr. Soames, attired in discreet black, set out to make the acquaintance of his hypothetical employer.

He found Mr. Gianapolis to be a little and very swarthy man, who held his head so low as to convey the impression of having a pronounced stoop; a man whose well-cut clothes and immaculate linen could not redeem his appearance from a constitutional dirtiness. A jet black mustache, small, aquiline features, an engaging smile, and very dark brown eyes, viciously crossed, made up a personality incongruous with his sheltering silk hat, and calling aloud for a tarboosh and a linen suit, a shop in a bazaar, or a part in the campaign of commercial brigandage which, based in the Levant, spreads its ramifications throughout the Orient, Near and Far.

Mr. Gianapolis had the suave speech and smiling manner. He greeted Soames not as one greets a prospective servant, but as one welcomes as esteemed acquaintance. Following a brief chat, he proposed an adjournment to a neighboring saloon bar; and there, over cocktails, he conversed with Mr. Soames as one crook with another.

Soames was charmed, fascinated, yet vaguely horrified; for this man smilingly threw off the cloak of hypocrisy from his companion's shoulders, and pretended, with the skill of his race, equally to nullify his own villainy.

"My dear Mr. Soames!" he said, speaking almost perfect English, but with the singsong intonation of the Greek, and giving all his syllables an equal value—"you are the man I am looking for; and I can make your fortune."

This was entirely in accordance with Mr. Soames' own views, and he nodded, respectfully.

"I know," continued Gianapolis, proffering an excellent Egyptian cigarette, "that you were cramped in your last situation—that you were misunderstood" . . .

Soames, cigarette in hand, suppressed a start, and wondered if he were turning pale. He selected a match with nervous care.

"The little matter of the silver spoons," continued Gianapolis, smiling fraternally, "was perhaps an error of judgment. Although"—patting the startled Soames upon the shoulder—"they were a legitimate perquisite; I am not blaming you. But it takes so long to accumulate a really useful balance in that petty way. Now"—he glanced cautiously about him—"I can offer you a post under conditions which will place you above the consideration of silver spoons!"

Soames, hastily finishing his cocktail, sought for words; but Gianapolis, finishing his own, blandly ordered two more, and tapping Soames upon the knee, continued:

"Then that matter of the petty cash, and those trifling irregularities in the wine-bill, you remember?—when you were with Colonel Hewett in Nice?" . . .

Soames gripped the counter hard, staring at the newly arrived cocktail as though it were hypnotizing him.

"These little matters," added Gianapolis, appreciatively sipping from his own glass, "which would weigh heavily against your other references, in the event of their being mentioned to any prospective employer" . . .

Soames knew beyond doubt that his face was very pale indeed.

"These little matters, then," pursued Gianapolis, "all go to prove to *me* that you are a man of enterprise and spirit—that you are the very man I require. Now I can offer you a post in the establishment of Mr. Henry Leroux, the novelist. The service will be easy. You will be required to attend to callers and to wait at table upon special occasions. There will be no valeting, and you will have undisputed charge of the pantry and wine-cellar. In short, you will enjoy unusual liberty. The salary, you would say? It will be the same as that which you received from Mr. Mapleson" . . .

Soames raised his head drearily; he felt himself in the toils; he felt himself a ruined man.

"It isn't a salary," he began, "which" . . .

"My dear Mr. Soames," said Gianapolis, tapping him confidentially upon the knee again—"my dear Soames, it isn't the salary, I admit, which you enjoyed whilst in the services of Colonel Hewett in a similar capacity. But this is not a large establishment, and the duties are light. Furthermore, there will be—extras."

"Extras?"

Mr. Soames' eye brightened, and under the benignant influence of the cocktails his courage began to return.

"I do not refer," smiled Mr. Gianapolis, "to perquisites! The extras will be monetary. Another two pounds per week" . . .

"Two pounds!"

"Bringing your salary up to a nice round figure; the additional amount will be paid to you from another source. You will receive the latter payment quarterly" . . .

"From—from" . . .

"From me!" said Mr. Gianapolis, smiling radiantly. "Now, I know you are going to accept; that is understood between us. I will give you the address—Palace Mansions, Westminster—at which you must apply; and I will tell you what little services will be required from you in return for this additional emolument."

Mr. Soames hurriedly finished his second cocktail. Mr. Gianapolis, in true sporting fashion, kept pace with him and repeated the order.

"You will take charge of the mail!" he whispered softly, one irregular eye following the movements of the barmaid, and the other fixed almost fiercely upon the face of Soames. "At certain times—of which you will be notified in advance—Mrs. Leroux will pay visits to Paris. At such times, all letters addressed to her, or re-addressed to her, will not be posted! You will ring me up when such letters come into your possession—they must *all* come into your possession!—and I will arrange to meet you, say at the corner of Victoria Street, to receive them. You understand?"

Mr. Soames understood, and thus far found his plastic conscience marching in step with his inclinations.

"Then," resumed Gianapolis, "prior to her departure on these occasions, Mrs. Leroux will hand you a parcel. This also you will bring to me at the place arranged. Do you find anything onerous in these conditions?"

"Not at all," muttered Soames, a trifle unsteadily; "it seems all right"—the cocktails were beginning to speak now, and his voice was a duet—"simply perfectly all right—all square."

"Good!" said Mr. Gianapolis with his radiant smile; and the gaze of his left eye, crossing that of its neighbor, observed the entrance of a stranger into the bar. He drew his stool closer and lowered his voice:

"Mrs. Leroux," he continued, "will be in your confidence. Mr. Leroux and every one else—*every one* else—must not suspect the arrangement" . . .

"Certainly—I quite understand" . . .

"Mrs. Leroux will engage you this afternoon—her husband is a mere cipher in the household—and you will commence your duties on Monday. Later in the week, Wednesday or Thursday, we will meet by appointment, and discuss further details."

"Where can I see you?"

"Ring up this number: 18642 East, and ask for Mr. King. No! don't write it down; remember it! I will come to the telephone, and arrange a meeting."

Shortly after this, then, the interview concluded; and later in the afternoon of that day Mr. Soames presented himself at Palace Mansions.

He was received by Mrs. Leroux—a pretty woman with a pathetically weak mouth. She had fair hair, not very abundant, and large eyes; which, since they exhibited the unusual phenomenon, in a blonde, of long dark lashes (Mr. Soames judged their blackness to be natural), would have been beautiful had they not been of too light a color, too small in the pupils, and utterly expressionless. Indeed, her whole face lacked color, as did her personality, and the exquisite tea-gown which she wore conveyed that odd impression of slovenliness, which is often an indication of secret vice. She was quite young and indisputably pretty, but this *malpropreté*, together with a certain aimlessness of manner, struck an incongruous note; for essentially she was of a type which for its complement needs vivacity.

Mr. Soames, a man of experience, scented an intrigue and a neglectful husband. Since he was engaged on the spot without reference to the invisible Leroux, he was immediately confirmed in the latter part of his surmise. He departed well satisfied with his affairs, and with the promise of the future, over which Mr. Gianapolis, the cherubic, radiantly presided.

XIII

THE DRAFT ON PARIS

For close upon a month Soames performed the duties imposed upon him in the household of Henry Leroux. He was unable to discover, despite a careful course of inquiry from the cook and the housemaid, that Mrs. Leroux frequently absented herself. But the servants were newly engaged, for the flat in Palace Mansions had only recently been leased by the Leroux. He gathered that they had formerly lived much abroad, and that their marriage had taken place in Paris. Mrs. Leroux had been to visit a friend in the French capital once, he understood, since the housemaid had been in her employ.

The mistress (said the housemaid) did not care twopence-ha'penny for her husband; she had married him for his money, and for nothing else. She had had an earlier love (declared the cook) and was pining away to a mere shadow because of her painful memories. During the last six months (the period of the cook's service) Mrs. Leroux had altered out of all recognition. The cook was of opinion that she drank secretly.

Of Mr. Leroux, Soames formed the poorest opinion. He counted him a spiritless being, whose world was bounded by his bookshelves, and whose wife would be a fool if she did not avail herself of the liberty which his neglect invited her to enjoy. Soames felt himself, not a snake in the grass, but a benefactor—a friend in need—a champion come to the defense of an unhappy and persecuted woman.

He wondered when an opportunity should arise which would enable him to commence his chivalrous operations; almost daily he anticipated instructions to the effect that Mrs. Leroux would be leaving for Paris immediately. But the days glided by and the weeks glided by, without anything occurring to break the monotony of the Leroux household.

Mr. Soames sought an opportunity to express his respectful readiness to Mrs. Leroux; but the lady was rarely visible outside her own apartments until late in the day, when she would be engaged in preparing for the serious business of the evening: one night a dance, another, a bridge-party; so it went. Mr. Leroux rarely joined her upon these festive expeditions, but clung to his study like Diogenes to his tub.

Great was Mr. Soames' contempt; bitter were the reproaches of the cook; dark were the predictions of the housemaid.

At last, however, Soames, feeling himself neglected, seized an opportunity which offered to cement the secret bond (the *too* secret bond) existing between himself and the mistress of the house.

Meeting her one afternoon in the lobby, which she was crossing on the way from her bedroom to the drawing-room, he stood aside to let her pass, whispering:

"At your service, whenever you are ready, madam!"

It was a non-committal remark, which, if she chose to keep up the comedy, he could explain away by claiming it to refer to the summoning of the car from the garage—for Mrs. Leroux was driving out that afternoon.

She did not endeavor to evade the occult meaning of the words, however. In the wearily dreamy manner which, when first he had seen her, had aroused Soames' respectful interest, she raised her thin hand to her hair, slowly pressing it back from her brow, and directed her big eyes vacantly upon him.

"Yes, Soames," she said (her voice had a faraway quality in keeping with the rest of her personality), "Mr. King speaks well of you. But please do not refer again to"—she glanced in a manner at once furtive and sorrowful, in the direction of the study-door—"to the . . . little arrangement of" . . .

She passed on, with the slow, gliding gait, which, together with her fragility, sometimes lent her an almost phantomesque appearance.

This was comforting, in its degree; since it proved that the smiling Gianapolis had in no way misled him (Soames). But as a man of business, Mr. Soames was not fully satisfied. He selected an evening when Mrs. Leroux was absent—and indeed she was absent almost every evening, for Leroux entertained but little. The cook and the housemaid were absent, also; therefore, to all intents and purposes, Soames had the flat to himself; since Henry Leroux counted in that establishment, not as an entity, but rather as a necessary, if unornamental, portion of the fittings.

Standing in the lobby, Soames raised the telephone receiver, and having paused with closed eyes preparing the exact form of words in which he should address his invisible employer, he gave the number: East 18642.

Following a brief delay:—

"Yes," came a nasal voice, "who is it?"

"Soames! I want to speak to Mr. King!"

The words apparently surprised the man at the other end of the wire, for he hesitated ere inquiring:—

"What did you say your name was?"

"Soames—Luke Soames."

"Hold on!"

Soames, with closed eyes, and holding the receiver to his ear, silently rehearsed again the exact wording of his speech. Then:—

"Hullo!" came another voice—"is that Mr. Soames?"

"Yes! Is that Mr. Gianapolis speaking?"

"It is, my dear Soames!" replied the sing-song voice; and Soames, closing his eyes again, had before him a mental picture of the radiantly smiling Greek.

"Yes, my dear Soames," continued Gianapolis; "here I am. I hope you are quite well—perfectly well?"

"I am perfectly well, thank you; but as a

man of business, it has occurred to me that failing a proper agreement—which in this case I know would be impossible—a trifling advance on the first quarter's" . . .

"On your salary, my dear Soames! On your salary? Payment for the first quarter shall be made to you to-morrow, my dear Soames! Why ever did you not express the wish before? Certainly, certainly!" . . .

"Will it be sent to me?"

"My dear fellow! How absurd you are! Can you get out to-morrow evening about nine o'clock?"

"Yes, easily."

"Then I will meet you at the corner of Victoria Street, by the hotel, and hand you your first quarter's salary. Will that be satisfactory?"

"Perfectly," said Soames, his small eyes sparkling with avarice. "Most decidedly, Mr. Gianapolis. Many thanks." . . .

"And by the way," continued the other, "it is rather fortunate that you rang me up this evening, because it has saved me the trouble of ringing you up."

"What?"—Soames' eyes half closed, from the bottom lids upwards:—"there is something" . . .

"There is a trifling service which I require of you—yes, my dear Soames."

"Is it?" . . .

"We will discuss the matter to-morrow evening. Oh! it is a mere trifle. So good-by for the present."

Soames, with the fingers of his two hands interlocked before him, and his thumbs twirling rapidly around one another, stood in the lobby, gazing reflectively at the rug-strewn floor. He was working out in his mind how handsomely this first payment would show up on the welcome side of his pass-book. Truly, he was fortunate in having met the generous Gianapolis. . . .

He thought of a trifling indiscretion committed at the expense of one Mr. Mapleson, and of the wine-bill of Colonel Hewett; and he thought of the apparently clairvoyant knowledge of the Greek. A cloud momentarily came between his perceptive and the rosy horizon.

But nearer to the foreground of the mental picture, uprose a left-hand page of his pass-book; and its tidings of great joy, written in clerkly hand, served to dispel the cloud.

Soames sighed in gentle rapture, and, soft-footed, passed into his own room.

Certainly his duties were neither difficult nor unpleasant. The mistress of the house lived apparently in a hazy dream-world of her own, and Mr. Leroux was the ultimate expression of the non-commercial. Mr. Soames could have robbed him every day had he desired to do so; but he had refrained from availing himself even of those perquisites which he considered justly his; for it was evident, to his limited intelligence, that greater profit was to be gained by establishing himself in this household than by weeding-out five shillings here, and half-a-sovereign there, at the risk of untimely dismissal.

Yet—it was a struggle! All Mr. Soames' commercial instincts were up in arms against this voice of a greater avarice which counseled abstention. For instance: he could have added half-a-sovereign a week to his earnings by means of a simple arrangement with the local wine merchant. Leroux's cigars he could have sold by the hundreds; for Leroux, when a friend called, would absently open a new box, entirely forgetful of the fact that a box from which but two—or at most three cigars had been taken, lay already on the bureau.

Mr. Soames, in order to put his theories to the test, had temporarily abstracted half-a-dozen such boxes from the study and the dining-room and had hidden them. Leroux, finding, as he supposed, that he was out of cigars, had simply ordered Soames to get him some more.

"Er—about a dozen boxes—er—Soames," he had said; "of the same sort!"

Was ever a man of business submitted to such an ordeal? After receiving those instructions, Soames had sat for close upon an hour in his own room, contemplating the six broken boxes, containing in all some five hundred and ninety cigars; but the voice within prevailed; he must court no chance of losing his situation; therefore, he "discovered" those six boxes in a cupboard—much to Henry Leroux's surprise!

Then, Leroux regularly sent him to the Charing Cross branch of the London County and Suburban Bank with open checks! Sometimes, he would be sent to pay in, at other times to withdraw; the amounts involved varying from one guinea to £150! But, as he told himself, on almost every occasion that he went to Leroux's bank, he was deliberately throwing money away, deliberately closing his eyes to the good fortune which this careless and gullible man cast in his path.

He observed a scrupulous honesty in all these dealings, with the result that the bank manager came to regard him as a valuable and trustworthy servant, and said as much to the assistant manager, expressing his wonder that Leroux—whose account occasioned the bank more anxiety, and gave it more work, than that of any other two depositors—had at last engaged a man who would keep his business affairs in order!

And these were but a few of the golden apples which Mr. Soames permitted to slip through his fingers, so steadfast was he in his belief that Gianapolis would be as good as his word, and make his fortune.

Leroux employed no secretary; and his MSS. were typed at his agent's office. A most slovenly man in all things, and in business matters especially, he was the despair, not only of his banker, but of his broker; he was a man who, in professional parlance, "deserved to be robbed." It is improbable that he had any but the haziest ideas, at any particular time, respecting the state of his bank balance and investments. He detested the writing of business letters, and was always at great pains to avoid anything in the nature of a commercial rendezvous. He would sign any document which his lawyer or his broker cared to send him, with simple, unquestioned faith.

His bank he never visited, and his appearance was entirely unfamiliar to the staff. True, the manager knew him slightly, having had two interviews with him: one when the account was opened, and the second when Leroux introduced his solicitor and broker—in order that in the future he might not be troubled in any way with business affairs.

Mr. Soames perceived more and more clearly that the mild deception projected was unlikely to be discovered by its victim; and, at the appointed time, he hastened to the corner of Victoria Street, to his appointment with Gianapolis. The latter was prompt, for Soames perceived his radiant smile afar off.

The saloon bar of the Red Lion was affably proposed by Mr. Gianapolis as a suitable spot to discuss the business. Soames agreed, not without certain inward qualms; for the proximity of the hostelry to New Scotland Yard was a disquieting circumstance.

However, since Gianapolis affected to treat their negotiations in the light of perfectly legitimate business, he put up no protest, and presently found himself seated in a very cozy corner of the saloon bar, with a glass of whisky-and-soda on a little table before him, bubbling in a manner which rendered it an agreeable and refreshing sight in the eyes of Mr. Soames.

"You know," said Gianapolis, the gaze of his left eye bisecting that of his right in a most bewildering manner, "they call this 'the 'tec's tabernacle!' "

"Indeed," said Soames, without enthusiasm; "I suppose some of the Scotland Yard men do drop in now and then?"

"Beyond doubt, my dear Soames."

Soames responded to his companion's radiant smile with a smile of his own by no means so pleasant to look upon. Soames had the type of face which, in repose, might be the face of an honest man; but his smile would have led to his instant arrest on any racecourse in Europe: it was the smile of a pickpocket.

"Now," continued Gianapolis, "here is a quarter's salary in advance."

From a pocket-book, he took a little brown paper envelope and from the brown paper envelope counted out four five-pound notes, five golden sovereigns, one half-sovereign, and ten shillings' worth of silver. Soames' eyes glittered, delightedly.

"A little informal receipt?" smiled Gianapolis, raising his eyebrows, satanically. "Here on this page of my notebook I have written: 'Received from Mr. King for service rendered, £26, being payment, in advance, of amount due on 31st October 19—' I have attached a stamp to the page, as you will see," continued Gianapolis, "and here is a fountain-pen. Just sign across the stamp, adding to-day's date."

Soames complied with willing alacrity; and Gianapolis having carefully blotted the signature, replaced the notebook in his pocket, and politely acknowledged the return of the fountain-pen. Soames, glancing furtively about him, replaced the money in the envelope, and thrust the latter carefully into a trouser pocket.

"Now," resumed Gianapolis, "we must not permit our affairs of business to interfere with our amusements."

He stepped up to the bar and ordered two more whiskies with soda. These being sampled, business was resumed.

"To-morrow," said Gianapolis, leaning forward across the table so that his face almost touched that of his companion, "you will be entrusted by Mr. Leroux with a commission." . . .

Soames nodded eagerly, his eyes upon the speaker's face.

"You will accompany Mrs. Leroux to the bank," continued Gianapolis, "in order that she may write a specimen signature, in the presence of the manager, for transmission to the Crédit Lyonnais in Paris." . . .

Soames nearly closed his little eyes in his effort to comprehend.

"A draft in her favor," continued the Greek, "has been purchased by Mr. Leroux's bank from the Paris bank, and, on presentation of this, a checkbook will be issued to Mrs. Leroux by the Crédit Lyonnais in Paris to enable her to draw at her convenience upon that establishment against the said order. Do you follow me?"

Soames nodded rapidly, eager to exhibit an intelligent grasp of the situation.

"Now"—Gianapolis lowered his voice impressively—"no one at the Charing Cross branch of the London County and Suburban Bank has ever seen Mrs. Leroux!—Oh! we have been careful of that, and we shall be careful in the future. You are known already as an accredited agent of Leroux; therefore"—he bent yet closer to Soames' ear—"you will direct the chauffeur to drop you, not at the Strand entrance, but at the side entrance. You follow?"

Soames, almost holding his breath, nodded again.

"At the end of the court, in which the latter entrance is situated, a lady dressed in the same manner as Mrs. Leroux (this is arranged) will be waiting. Mrs. Leroux will walk straight up the court, into the corridor of Bank Chambers by the back entrance, and from thence out into the Strand. You will escort the second lady into the manager's office, and she will sign 'Mira Leroux' instead of the real Mira Leroux." . . .

Soames became aware that he was changing color. This was a superior felony, and as such it awed his little mind. It was tantamount to burning his boats. Missing silver spoons and cooked petty cash were trivialities usually expiable at the price of a boot-assisted dismissal; but this—!

"You understand?" Gianapolis was not smiling, now. "There is not the slightest danger. The signature of the lady whom you will meet will be an exact duplicate of the real one; that is, exact enough to deceive a man who is not looking for a forgery. But it would not be exact enough to deceive the French banker—he *will* be looking for a forgery. You

follow me? The signature on the checks drawn against the Crédit Lyonnais will be the *same* as the specimen forwarded by the London County and Suburban, since they will be written by the same lady—the duplicate Mrs. Leroux. Therefore, the French bank will have no means of detecting the harmless little deception practised upon them, and the English bank, if it should ever see those checks, will raise no question, since the checks will have been honored by the Crédit Lyonnais."

Soames finished his whisky-and-soda at a gulp.

"Finally," concluded Gianapolis, "you will escort the lady out by the front entrance to the Strand. She will leave you and walk in an easterly direction—making some suitable excuse if the manager should insist upon seeing her to the door; and the real Mrs. Leroux will come out by the Strand end of Bank Chambers' corridor, and walk back with you around the corner to where the car will be waiting. Perfect?"

"Quite," said Soames, huskily. . . .

But when, some twenty minutes later, he returned to Palace Mansions, he was a man lost in thought; and he did not entirely regain his wonted composure, and did not entirely shake off the incubus, Doubt, until in his own room he had re-counted the contents of the brown paper envelope. Then:—

"It's safe enough," he muttered; "and it's worth it!"

Thus it came about that, on the following morning, Leroux called him into the study and gave him just such instructions as Gianapolis had outlined the evening before.

"I am—er—too busy to go myself, Soames," said Leroux, "and—er—Mrs. Leroux will shortly be paying a visit to friends in—er—in Paris. So that I am opening a credit there for her. Save so much trouble—and—such a lot of—correspondence—international money orders—and such worrying things. Mr. Smith, the manager, knows you and you will take this letter of authority. The draft I understand has already been purchased."

Mr. Soames was bursting with anxiety to learn the amount of this draft, but could find no suitable opportunity to inquire. The astonishing deception, then, was carried out without anything resembling a hitch. Mrs. Leroux went through with her part in the comedy, in the dreamy manner of a somnambulist; and the duplicate Mrs. Leroux, who waited at the appointed spot, had achieved so startling a resemblance to her prototype, that Mr. Soames became conscious of a craving for a peg of brandy at the moment of setting eyes upon her. However, he braced himself up and saw the business through.

As was to be expected, no questions were raised and no doubts entertained. The bank manager was very courteous and very reserved, and the fictitious Mrs. Leroux equally reserved, indeed, cold. She avoided raising her motor veil, and, immediately the business was concluded, took her departure, Mr. Smith escorting her as far as the door.

She walked away toward Fleet Street, and the respectful attendant, Soames, toward Charing Cross; he rejoined Mrs. Leroux at the door of Bank Chambers, and the two turned the corner and entered the waiting car. Soames was rather nervous; Mrs. Leroux quite apathetic.

Shortly after this event, Soames learnt that the date of Mrs. Leroux's departure to Paris was definitely fixed. He received from her hands a large envelope.

"For Mr. King," she said, in her dreamy fashion; and he noticed that she seemed to be in poorer health than usual. Her mouth twitched strangely; she was a nervous wreck.

Then came her departure, attended by a certain bustle, an appointment with Mr. Gianapolis; and the delivery of the parcel into that gentleman's keeping.

Mrs. Leroux was away for six days on this occasion. Leroux sent her three postcards during that time, and re-addressed some ten or twelve letters which arrived for her. The address in all cases was:

c/o *Miss Denise Ryland,*
Atelier 4, Rue du Coq d'Or,
Montmartre,
Paris.

East 18642 was much in demand that week; and there were numerous meetings between Soames and Gianapolis at the corner of Victoria Street, and numerous whiskies-and-sodas in the Red Lion; for Gianapolis persisted in his patronage of that establishment, apparently for no other reason than because it was dangerously near to Scotland Yard, and an occasional house of call for members of the Criminal Investigation Department.

Thus did Mr. Soames commence his career of duplicity at the flat of Henry Leroux; and for some twelve months before the events which so dramatically interfered with the de-

lightful scheme, he drew his double salary and performed his perfidious work with great efficiency and contentment. Mrs. Leroux paid four other visits to Paris during that time, and always returned in much better spirits, although pale and somewhat haggard looking. It fell to the lot of Soames always to meet her at Charing Cross; but never once, by look or by word, did she proffer, or invite, the slightest exchange of confidence. She apathetically accepted his aid in conducting this intrigue as she would have accepted his aid in putting on her opera-cloak.

The curious Soames had read right through the telephone directory from A to Z in quest of East 18642—only to learn that no such number was published. His ingenuity not being great, he could think of no means to learn the address of the mysterious Mr. King. So keenly had he been impressed with the omniscience of that shadowy being who knew all his past, that he feared to inquire of the Eastern Exchange. His banking account was growing handsomely, and, above all things, he dreaded to kill the goose that laid the golden eggs.

Then came the night which shattered all. Having rung up East 18642 and made an appointment with Gianapolis in regard to some letters for Mrs. Leroux, he had been surprised, on reaching the corner of Victoria Street, to find that Gianapolis was not there! He glanced up at the face of Big Ben. Yes—for the first time during their business acquaintance, Mr. Gianapolis was late!

For close upon twenty minutes, Soames waited, walking slowly up and down. When, at last, coming from the direction of Westminster, he saw the familiar spruce figure.

Eagerly he hurried forward to meet the Greek; but Gianapolis—to the horror and amazement of Soames—affected not to know him! He stepped aside to avoid the stupefied butler, and passed. But in passing, he hissed these words at Soames:—

"Follow to Victoria Street Post Office! Pretend to post letters at next box to me and put them in my hand!"

He was gone!

Soames, dazed at this new state of affairs, followed him at a discreet distance. Gianapolis ran up the Post Office steps briskly, and Soames, immediately afterwards, ascended also—furtively. Gianapolis was taking out a number of letters from his pocket.

Soames walked across to the "Country" box on his right, and affected to scrutinize the addresses on the envelopes of Mrs. Leroux's correspondence.

Gianapolis, on the pretense of posting a country letter, reached out and snatched the correspondence from Soames' hand. The gaze of his left eye crookedly sought the face of the butler.

"Go home!" whispered Gianapolis; "be cautious!"

XIV

EAST 18642

In a pitiable state of mind, Soames walked away from the Post Office. Gianapolis had hurried off in the direction of Victoria Station. Something was wrong! Some part of the machine, of the dimly divined machine whereof he formed a cog, was out of gear. Since the very nature of this machine—its construction and purpose, alike—was unknown to Soames, he had no basis upon which to erect surmises for good or ill.

His timid inquiries into the identity of East 18642 had begun and terminated with his labored perusal of the telephone book, a profitless task which had occupied him for the greater part of an evening.

The name, Gianapolis, did not appear at all; whereas there proved to be some two hundred and ninety Kings. But, oddly, only four of these were on the Eastern Exchange; one was a veterinary surgeon; one a boat-builder; and a third a teacher of dancing. The fourth, an engineer, seemed a "possible" to Soames, although his published number was not 18642; but a brief—a very brief—conversation, convinced the butler that this was not his man.

He had been away from the flat for over an hour, and he doubted if even the lax sense of discipline possessed by Mr. Leroux would enable that gentleman to overlook this irregularity. Soames had a key of the outer door, and he built his hopes upon the possibility that Leroux had not noticed his absence and would not hear his return.

He opened the door very quietly, but had scarcely set his foot in the lobby ere the dreadful, unforgettable scene met his gaze.

For more years than he could remember, he had lived in dread of the law; and, in Luke Soames' philosophy, the words Satan and Detective were interchangeable. Now, before his eyes, was a palpable, unmistakable police officer; and on the floor . . .

Just one glimpse he permitted himself—and, in a voice that seemed to reach him from a vast distance, the detective was addressing *him!* . . .

Slinking to his room, with his craven heart missing every fourth beat, and his mind in chaos, Soames sank down upon the bed, locked his hands together and hugged them, convulsively, between his knees.

It was come! He had overstepped that almost invisible boundary-line which divides indiscretion from crime. He knew now that the voice within him, the voice which had warned him against Gianapolis and against becoming involved in what dimly he had perceived to be an elaborate scheme, had been, not the voice of cowardice (as he had supposed) but that of prudence.

And it was too late. The dead woman, he told himself—he had been unable to see her very clearly—undoubtedly was Mrs. Leroux. What in God's name had happened! Probably her husband had killed her . . . which meant? It meant that proofs—*proofs*—were come into his possession; and who should be involved, entangled in the meshes of this fallen conspiracy, but himself, Luke Soames!

As must be abundantly evident, Soames was not a criminal of the daring type; he did not believe in reaching out for anything until he was well assured that he could, if necessary, draw back his hand. This last venture, this regrettable venture—this ruinous venture—had been a mistake. He had entered into it under the glamour of Gianapolis' personality. Of what use, now, to him was his swelling bank balance?

But in justice to the mental capacity of Soames, it must be admitted that he had not entirely overlooked such a possibility as this; he had simply refrained, for the good of his health, from contemplating it.

Long before, he had observed, with interest, that, should an emergency arise (such as a fire), a means of egress had been placed by the kindly architect adjacent to his bedroom window. Thus, his departure on the night of the murder was not the fruit of a sudden scheme, but of one well matured.

Closing and locking his bedroom door, Soames threw out upon the bed the entire contents of his trunk; selected those things which he considered indispensable, and those which might constitute clues. He hastily packed his grip, and, with a last glance about the room and some seconds of breathless listening at the door, he attached to the handle a long piece of cord, which at some time had been tied about his trunk, and, gently opening the window, lowered the grip into the courtyard beneath. The light he had already extinguished, and with the conviction dwelling in his bosom that in some way he was become accessory to a murder—that he was a man shortly to be pursued by the police of the civilized world—he descended the skeleton lift-shaft, picked up his grip, and passed out under the archway into the lane at the back of Palace Mansions and St. Andrew's Mansions.

He did not proceed in the direction which would have brought him out into the Square, but elected to emerge through the other end. At exactly the moment that Inspector Dunbar rushed into his vacated room, Mr. Soames, grip in hand, was mounting to the top of a southward bound 'bus at the corner of Parliament Street!

He was conscious of a need for reflection. He longed to sit in some secluded spot in order to think. At present, his brain was a mere whirligig, and all things about him seemingly danced to the same tune. Stationary objects were become unstable in the eyes of Soames, and the solid earth, burst free of its moorings, no longer afforded him a safe foothold. There was a humming in his ears; and a mist floated before his eyes. By the time that the motor-'bus was come to the south side of the bridge, Soames had succeeded in slowing down his mental roundabout in some degree; and now he began grasping at the flying ideas which the diminishing violence of his brain storm enabled him, vaguely, to perceive.

The first fruits of his reflections were bitter. He viewed the events of the night in truer focus; he saw that by his flight he had sealed his fate—had voluntarily outlawed himself. It became frightfully evident to him that he dared not seek to draw from his bank, that he dared not touch even his modest Post Office account. With the exception of some twenty-five shillings in his pocket, he was penniless!

How could he hope to fly the country, or even to hide himself, without money?

He glanced suspiciously about the 'bus; for he perceived that an old instinct had prompted him to mount one which passed the Oval—a former point of debarkation when he lived in rooms near Kennington Park. Someone might recognize him!

Furtively, he scanned his fellow passengers, but perceived no acquaintance.

What should he do—where should he go? It was a desperate situation.

The inspector who had cared to study that furtive, isolated figure, could not have failed to mark it for that of a hunted man.

At Kennington Gate the 'bus made a halt. Soames glanced at the clock on the corner. It was close upon one A.M. Where in heaven's name should he go? What a fool he had been to come to this district where he was known!

Stay! There was one man in London, surely, who must be almost as keenly interested in the fate of Luke Soames as Luke Soames himself . . . Gianapolis!

Soames sprang up and hurried off the 'bus. No public telephone box would be available at that hour, but dire need spurred his slow mind and also lent him assurance. He entered the office of the taxicab depot on the next corner, and, from the man whom he found in charge, solicited and obtained the favor of using the telephone. Lifting the receiver, he asked for East 18642.

The seconds that elapsed, now, were as hours of deathly suspense to the man at the telephone. If the number should be engaged! . . . If the exchange could get no reply! . . .

"Hullo!" said a nasal voice—"who is it?"

"It is Soames—and I want to speak to Mr. King!"

He lowered his tone as much as possible, almost whispering his own name. He knew the voice which had answered him; it was the same that he always heard when ringing up East 18642. But would Gianapolis come to the telephone? Suddenly—

"Is that Soames?" spoke the sing-song voice of the Greek.

"Yes, yes!"

"Where are you?"

"At Kennington."

"Are they following you?"

"No—I don't think so, at least; what am I to do? Where am I to go?"

"Get to Globe Road—near Stratford Bridge, East, without delay. But whatever you do, see that you are not followed! Globe Road is the turning immediately beyond the Railway Station. It is not too late, perhaps, to get a 'bus or tram, for some part of the way, at any rate. But even if the last is gone, don't take a cab; walk. When you get to Globe Road, pass down on the left-hand side, and, if necessary, right to the end. Make sure you are not followed, then walk back again. You will receive a signal from an open door. Come right in. Good-by."

Soames replaced the receiver on the hook, uttering a long-drawn sigh of relief. The arbiter of his fortunes had not failed him!

"Thank you very much!" he said to the man in charge of the office, who had been bending over his books and apparently taking not the slightest interest in the telephone conversation. Soames placed twopence, the price of the call, on the desk. "Good night."

"Good night."

He hastened out of the gate and across the road. An electric tramcar which would bear him as far as the Elephant-and-Castle was on the point of starting from the corner. Grip in hand, Soames boarded the car and mounted to the top deck. He was in some doubt respecting his mode of travel from the next point onward, but the night was fine, even if he had to walk, and his reviving spirits would cheer him with visions of a golden future!

His money!—That indeed was a bitter draught; the loss of his hardly earned savings! But he was now established—linked by a common secret—in partnership with Gianapolis; he was one of that mysterious, obviously wealthy group which arranged drafts on Paris—which could afford to pay him some hundreds of pounds per annum for such a trifling service as juggling the mail!

Mr. King!—If Gianapolis were only the servant, what a magnificent man of business must be hidden beneath the cognomen, Mr. King! And he was about to meet that lord of mystery. Fear and curiosity were oddly blended in the anticipation.

By great good fortune, Soames arrived at the Elephant-and-Castle in time to catch an eastward bound motor-'bus, a 'bus which would actually carry him to the end of Globe Road. He took his seat on top, and with greater composure than he had known since his dramatic meeting with Gianapolis in Victoria Street, lighted one of Mr. Leroux's cabanas (with which he invariably kept his case filled) and settled down to think about the future.

His reflections served apparently to shorten the journey; and Soames found himself proceeding along Globe Road—a dark and uninviting highway—almost before he realized that London Bridge had been traversed. It was now long past one o'clock; and that part of the east-end showed dreary and deserted. Public houses had long since ejected their late guests, and even those argumentative groups, which, after closing-time, linger on the pavements, within the odor Bacchanalian, were dispersed. The jauntiness was gone, now, from Soames' manner, and aware of a marked internal depression, he passed furtively along the pavement with its long shadowy reaches between the islands of light formed by the street lamps. From patch to patch he passed, and each successive lamp that looked down upon him found him more furtive, more bent in his carriage.

Not a shop nor a house exhibited any light. Sleeping Globe Road, East, served to extinguish the last poor spark of courage within Soames' bosom. He came to the extreme end of the road without having perceived a beckoning hand, without having detected a sound to reveal that his advent was observed. In the shadow of a wall he stopped, resting his grip upon the pavement and looking back upon his tracks.

No living thing moved from end to end of Globe Road.

Shivering slightly, Soames picked up the bag and began to walk back. Less than halfway along, an icy chill entered into his veins, and his nerves quivered like piano wires, for a soft crying of his name came, eerie, through the silence, and terrified the hearer.

"Soames! . . . Soames!" . . .

Soames stopped dead, breathing very rapidly, and looking about him right and left. He could hear the muted pulse of sleeping London. Then, in the dark doorway of the house before which he stood, he perceived, dimly, a motionless figure. His first sensation was not of relief, but of fear. The figure raised a beckoning hand. Soames, conscious that his course was set and that he must navigate it accordingly, opened the iron gate, passed up the path and entered the house to which he thus had been summoned. . . .

He found himself surrounded by absolute darkness, and the door was closed behind him.

"Straight ahead, Soames!" said the familiar voice of Gianapolis out of the darkness.

Soames, with a gasp of relief, staggered on. A hand rested upon his shoulder, and he was guided into a room on the right of the passage. Then an electric lamp was lighted, and he found himself confronting the Greek.

But Gianapolis was no longer radiant; all the innate evil of the man shone out through the smirking mask.

"Sit down, Soames!" he directed.

Soames, placing his bag upon the floor, seated himself in a cane armchair. The room was cheaply furnished as an office, with a roll-top desk, a revolving chair, and a filing cabinet. On a side-table stood a typewriter, and about the room were several other chairs, whilst the floor was covered with cheap linoleum. Gianapolis sat in the revolving chair, staring at the lowered blinds of the window, and brushing up the points of his black mustache.

With a fine white silk handkerchief Soames gently wiped the perspiration from his forehead and from the lining of his hat-band. Gianapolis began abruptly:—

"There has been an—accident" (he continued to brush his mustache, with increasing rapidity). "Tell me all that took place after you left the Post Office."

Soames nervously related his painful experiences of the evening, whilst Gianapolis drilled his mustache to a satanic angle. The story being concluded:

"Whatever has happened?" groaned Soames; "and what am I to do?"

"What you are to do," replied Gianapolis, "will be arranged, my dear Soames, by—Mr. King. Where you are to go, is a problem shortly settled: you are to go nowhere; you are to stay here." . . .

"Here!"

Soames gazed drearily about the room.

"Not exactly here—this is merely the office; but our establishment proper in Limehouse." . . .

"Limehouse!"

"Certainly. Although you seem to be unaware of the fact, Soames, there are some charming resorts in Limehouse; and your duties, for the present, will confine you to one of them."

"But—but," hesitated Soames, "the police" . . .

"Unless my information is at fault," said Gianapolis, "the police have no greater chance of paying us a visit, now, than they had formerly." . . .

"But Mrs. Leroux" . . .

"Mrs. Leroux!"

Gianapolis twirled around in the chair, his eyes squinting demoniacally:—"Mrs. Leroux!"

"She—she" . . .

"What about Mrs. Leroux?"

"Isn't she dead?"

"Dead? Mrs. Leroux! You are laboring un-

der a strange delusion, Soames. The lady whom you saw was not Mrs. Leroux."

Soames' brain began to fail him again.

"Then who," he began. . . .

"That doesn't concern you in the least, Soames. But what does concern you is this: your connection, and my connection, with the matter cannot possibly be established by the police. The incident is regrettable, but the emergency was dealt with—in time. It represents a serious deficit, unfortunately, and your own usefulness, for the moment, becomes nil; but we shall have to look after you, I suppose, and hope for better things in the future."

He took up the telephone.

"East 39951," he said, whilst Soames listened, attentively. Then:—

"Is that Kan-Suh Concessions?" he asked. "Yes—good! Tell Said to bring the car past the end of the road at a quarter-to-two. That's all."

He hung up the receiver.

"Now, my dear Soames," he said, with a faint return to his old manner, "you are about to enter upon new duties. I will make your position clear to you. Whilst you do your work, and keep yourself to yourself, you are in no danger; but one indiscretion—just one— apart from what it may mean for others, will mean, for *you*, immediate arrest as accessory to a murder!"

Soames shuddered, coldly.

"You can rely upon me, Mr. Gianapolis," he protested, "to do absolutely what you wish—absolutely. I am a ruined man, and I know it—I know it. My only hope is that you will give me a chance." . . .

"You shall have every chance, Soames," replied Gianapolis—"every chance."

XV

CAVE OF THE GOLDEN DRAGON

When the car stopped at the end of a short drive, Soames had not the slightest idea of his whereabouts. The blinds at the window of the limousine had been lowered during the whole journey, and now he descended from the step of the car on to the step of a doorway. He was in some kind of roofed-in courtyard, only illuminated by the headlamps of the car. Mr. Gianapolis pushed him forward, and, as the door was closed, he heard the gear of the car reversed; then— silence fell.

"My grip!" he began, nervously. . . .

"It will be placed in your room, Soames."

The voice of the Greek answered him from the darkness.

Guided by the hand of Gianapolis, he passed on and descended a flight of stone steps. Ahead of him a light shone out beneath a door, and, as he stumbled on the steps, the door was thrown suddenly open.

He found himself looking into a long, narrow apartment. . . . He pulled up short with a smothered, gasping cry.

It was a cavern!—but a cavern the like of which he had never seen, never imagined. The walls had the appearance of being rough-hewn from virgin rock—from black rock— from rock black as the rocks of Shellal—black as the gates of Erebus.

Placed at regular intervals along the frowning walls, to right and left, were spiral, slender pillars, gilded and gleaming. They supported an archwork of fancifully carven wood, which curved gently outward to the center of the ceiling, forming, by conjunction with a similar, opposite curve, a pointed arch.

In niches of the wall were a number of grotesque Chinese idols. The floor was jet black and polished like ebony. Several tiger-skin rugs were strewn about it. But, dominating the strange place, in the center of the floor stood an ivory pedestal, supporting a golden dragon of exquisite workmanship; and before it, as before a shrine, an enormous Chinese vase was placed, of the hue, at its base, of deepest violet, fading, upward, through all the shades of rose pink seen in an Egyptian sunset, to a tint more elusive than a maiden's blush. It contained a mass of exotic poppies of every shade conceivable, from purple so dark as to seem black, to poppies of the whiteness of snow.

Just within the door, and immediately in front of Soames, stood a slim man of about his own height, dressed with great nicety in a perfectly fitting morning-coat, his well-cut cashmere trousers falling accurately over glossy boots having gray suede uppers. His linen was immaculate, and he wore a fine pearl in his black poplin cravat. Between two yellow fingers smoldered a cigarette.

Soames, unconsciously, clenched his fists: this slim man embodied the very spirit of the outré. The fantastic surroundings melted from the ken of Soames, and he seemed to stand in a shadow-world, alone with an incarnate shadow.

For this was a Chinaman! His jet black lusterless hair was not shaven in the national manner, but worn long, and brushed back from his slanting brow with no parting, so that it fell about his, white collar behind, lankly. He wore gold-rimmed spectacles, which magnified his oblique eyes and lent him a terrifying beetle-like appearance. His mephistophelean eyebrows were raised interrogatively, and he was smiling so as to exhibit a row of uneven yellow teeth.

Soames, his amazement giving place to reasonless terror, fell back a step—into the arms of Gianapolis.

"This is our friend from Palace Mansions," said the Greek. He squeezed Soames' arm, reassuringly. "Your new principal, Soames, Mr. Ho-Pin, from whom you will take your instructions."

"I have these instructions for Mr. Soames," said Ho-Pin, in a metallic, monotonous voice. (He gave to r half the value of w, with a hint of the presence of l). "He will wremain here as valet until the search fowr him becomes less wrigowrous."

Soames, scarce believing that he was awake, made no reply. He found himself unable to meet the glittering eyes of the Chinaman; he glanced furtively about the room, prepared at any moment to wake up from what seemed to him an absurd, a ghostly dream.

"Said will change his appeawrance," continued Ho-Pin, smoothly, "so that he will not wreadily be wrecognized. Said will come now."

Ho-Pin clapped his hands three times.

The door at the end of the room immediately opened, and a thick-set man of a pronounced Arabian type, entered. He wore a chauffeur's livery of dark blue; and Soames recognized him for the man who had driven the car.

"Said," said Ho-Pin very deliberately, turning to face the new arrival, "âhu hína— Lucas Effendi—Mr. Lucas. Waddî el—shenta ila betâ ôda. Fehimt?"

Said bowed his head.

"Fâhim, effendi," he muttered rapidly. "Ma fîhsh." . . .

Again Said bowed his head, then, glancing at Soames:—

"Ta'ala wayaya!" he said.

Soames, looking helplessly at Gianapolis—who merely pointed to the door—followed Said from the room.

He was conducted along a wide passage, thickly carpeted and having its walls covered with a kind of matting kept in place by strips of bamboo. Its roof was similarly concealed. A door near to the end, and on the right, proved to open into a square room quite simply furnished in the manner of a bed-sitting room. A little bathroom opened out of it in one corner. The walls were distempered white, and there was no window. Light was furnished by an electric lamp, hanging from the center of the ceiling.

Soames, glancing at his bag, which Said had just placed beside the white-enameled bedstead, turned to his impassive guide.

"This is a funny go!" he began, with forced geniality. "Am I to live here?"

"Ma'lêsh!" muttered Said—"ma'lêsh!"

He indicated, by gestures, that Soames should remove his collar; he was markedly unemotional. He crossed to the bathroom, and could be heard filling the hand-basin with water.

"Kûrsi!" he called from within.

Soames, seriously doubting his own sanity, and so obsessed with a sense of the unreal that his senses were benumbed, began to take off his collar; he could not feel the contact of his fingers with his neck in the act. Collarless, he entered the little bathroom. . . .

"Kûrsi!" repeated Said; then: "Ah! ana nesît! ma'lêsh!"

Said—whilst Soames, docile in his stupor, watched him—went back, picked up the solitary cane chair which the apartment boasted, and brought it into the bathroom. Soames perceived that he was to be treated to something in the nature of a shampoo; for Said had ranged a number of bottles, a cake of soap, and several towels, along a shelf over the bath.

In a curious state of passivity, Soames submitted to the operation. His hair was vigorously toweled, then fanned in the most approved fashion; but this was no more than the beginning of the operation. As he leaned back in the chair:

"Am I dreaming?" he said aloud. "What's all this about?"

"Uskut!" muttered Said—"Uskut!"

Soames, at no time an aggressive character, resigned himself to the incredible.

Some lotion, which tingled slightly upon the scalp, was next applied by Said from a long-necked bottle. Then, fresh water having been poured into the basin, a dark purple liquid was added, and Soames' head dipped therein by the operating Eastern. This time no rubbing followed, but after some minutes of vigorous fanning, he was thrust back into the chair, and a dry towel tucked firmly into his collar-band. He anticipated that he was about to be shaved, and in this was not disappointed.

Said, filling a shaving-mug from the hot-water tap, lathered Soames' chin and the abbreviated whiskers upon which he had prided himself. Then the razor was skilfully handled, and Soames' face shaved until his chin was as smooth as satin.

Next, a dark brown solution was rubbed over the skin, and even upon his forehead and right into the roots of the hair; upon his throat, his ears, and the back of his neck. He was now past the putting of questions or the raising of protest; he was as clay in the hands of the silent Oriental. Having fanned his wet face again for some time, Said, breaking the long silence, muttered:

"Ikfil'iyyun!"

Soames stared. Said indicated, by pantomime, that he desired him to close his eyes, and Soames obeyed mechanically. Thereupon the Oriental busied himself with the ex-butler's not very abundant lashes for five minutes or more. Then the busy fingers were at work with his inadequate eyebrows: finally:—

"Khalâs!" muttered Said, tapping him on the shoulder.

Soames wearily opened his eyes, wondering if his strange martyrdom were nearly at its end. He discovered his hair to be still rather damp, but, since it was sparse, it was rapidly drying. His eyes smarted painfully.

Removing all traces of his operations, Said, with no word of farewell, took up his towels, bottles, and other paraphernalia and departed.

Soames watched the retreating figure crossing the outer room, but did not rise from the chair until the door had closed behind Said. Then, feeling strangely like a man who has drunk too heavily, he stood up and walked into the bedroom. There was a small shaving-glass upon the chest-of-drawers, and to this he advanced, filled with the wildest apprehensions.

One glance he ventured, and started back with a groan.

His apprehensions had fallen short of the reality. With one hand clutching the bedrail, he stood there swaying from side to side, and striving to screw up his courage to the point whereat he might venture upon a second glance in the mirror. At last he succeeded, looking long and pitifully.

"Oh, Lord!" he groaned, "what a guy!"

Beyond doubt he was strangely changed. By nature, Luke Soames had hair of a sandy color; now it was of so dark a brown as to seem black in the lamplight. His thin eyebrows and scanty lashes were naturally almost colorless; but they were become those of a pronounced brunette. He was of pale complexion, but to-night had the face of a mulatto, or of one long in tropical regions. In short, he was another man—a man whom he detested at first sight!

This was the price, or perhaps only part of the price, of his indiscretion. Mr. Soames was become Mr. Lucas. Clutching the top of the chest-of-drawers with both hands, he glared at his own reflection, dazedly.

In that pose, he was interrupted. Said, silently opening the door behind him, muttered:

"Ta'ala wayyaya!"

Soames whirled around in a sudden panic, his heart leaping madly. The immobile brown face peered in at the door.

"Ta'ala wayyaya!" repeated Said, his face expressionless as a mask. He pointed along the corridor. "Ho-Pin Effendi!" he explained.

Soames, raising his hands to his collarless neck, made a swallowing noise, and would have spoken; but:

"Ta'ala wayyaya!" reiterated the Oriental.

Soames hesitated no more. Reentering the corridor, with its straw-matting walls, he made a curious discovery. Away to the left it terminated in a blank, matting-covered wall. There was no indication of the door by which he had entered it. Glancing hurriedly to the right, he failed also to perceive any door there. The bespectacled Ho-Pin stood halfway along the passage, awaiting him. Following Said in that direction, Soames was greeted with the announcement:

"Mr. King will see you."

The words taught Soames that his capacity for emotion was by no means exhausted. His endless conjectures respecting the mysterious Mr. King were at last to be replaced by facts; he was to see him, to speak with him. He knew now that it was a fearful privilege which gladly he would have denied himself.

Ho-Pin opened a door almost immediately behind him, a door the existence of which had not hitherto been evident to Soames. Beyond, was a dark passage.

"You will follow me, closely," said Ho-Pin with one of his piercing glances.

Soames, finding his legs none too steady, entered the passage behind Ho-Pin. As he did so, the door was closed by Said, and he found himself in absolute darkness.

"Keep close behind me," directed the metallic voice.

Soames could not see the speaker, since no ray of light penetrated into the passage. He stretched out a groping hand, and, although he was conscious of an odd revulsion, touched the shoulder of the man in front of him and maintained that unpleasant contact whilst they walked on and on through apparently endless passages, extensive as a catacomb. Many corners they turned; they turned to the right, they turned to the left. Soames was hopelessly bewildered. Then, suddenly, Ho-Pin stopped.

"Stand still," he said.

Soames became vaguely aware that a door was being closed somewhere near to him. A lamp lighted up directly over his head . . . he found himself in a small library!

Its four walls were covered with bookshelves from floor to ceiling, and the shelves were packed to overflowing with books in most unusual and bizarre bindings. A red carpet was on the floor and a red-shaded lamp hung from the ceiling, which was conventionally white-washed. Although there was no fireplace, the room was immoderately hot, and heavy with the perfume of roses. On three little tables were great bowls filled with roses, and there were other bowls containing roses in gaps between the books on the open shelves.

A tall screen of beautifully carved sandalwood masked one corner of the room, but beyond it protruded the end of a heavy writing-table upon which lay some loose papers, and, standing amid them, an enormous silver rose-bowl, brimming with sulphur-colored blooms.

Soames, obeying a primary instinct, turned, as the light leaped into being, to seek the door by which he had entered. As he did so, the former doubts of his own sanity returned with renewed vigor.

The book-lined wall behind him was unbroken by any opening.

Slowly, as a man awaking from a stupor, Soames gazed around the library.

It contained no door.

He rested his hand upon one of the shelves and closed his eyes. Beyond doubt he was going mad! The tragic events of that night had proved too much for him; he had never disguised from himself the fact that his mental capacity was not of the greatest. He was assured, now, that his brain had lost its balance shortly after his flight from Palace Mansions, and that the events of the past two hours had been phantasmal. He would presently return to sanity (or, blasphemously, he dared to petition heaven that he would) and find himself . . . ? Perhaps in the hands of the police!

"Oh, God!" he groaned—"Oh, God!"

He opened his eyes . . .

A woman stood before the sandalwood screen! She had the pallidly dusky skin of a Eurasian, but, by virtue of nature or artifice, her cheeks wore a peachlike bloom. Her features were flawless in their chiseling, save for the slightly distended nostrils, and her black eyes were magnificent.

She was divinely petite, slender and girlish; but there was that in the lines of her figure, so seductively defined by her clinging Chinese dress, in the poise of her small head, with the blush rose nestling amid the black hair—above all in the smile of her full red lips which discounted the youth of her body; which whispered "Mine is a soul old in strange sins—a soul for whom dead Alexandria had no secrets, that learnt nothing of Athenean Thais and might have tutored Messalina" . . .

In her fanciful robe of old gold, with her tiny feet shod in ridiculously small, gilt slippers, she stood by the screen watching the stupefied man—an exquisite, fragrantly youthful casket of ancient, unnameable evils.

"Good evening, Soames!" she said, stumbling quaintly with her English, but speaking in a voice musical as a silver bell. "You will here be known as Lucas. Mr. King he wishing me to say that you to receive two pounds, at each week." . . .

Soames, glassy-eyed, stood watching her. A horror, the horror of insanity, had descended upon him—a clammy, rose-scented mantle. The room, the incredible, booklined room, was a red blur, surrounding the black, taunting eyes of the Eurasian. Everything was out of focus; past, present, and future were merged into a red, rose-haunted nothingness . . .

"You will attend to Block A," resumed the girl, pointing at him with a little fan.

"You will also attend to the gentlemen." . . .

She laughed softly, revealing tiny white teeth; then paused, head tilted coquettishly, and appeared to be listening to someone's conversation—to the words of some person seated behind the screen. This fact broke in upon Soames' disordered mind and confirmed him in his opinion that he was a man demented. For only one slight sound broke the silence of the room. The red carpet below the little tables was littered with rose petals, and, in the superheated atmosphere, other petals kept falling—softly, with a gentle rustling. Just that sound there was . . . and no other. Then:

"Mr. King he wishing to point out to you," said the girl, "that he hold receipts of you, which bind you to him. So you will be free man, and have liberty to go out sometimes for your own business. Mr. King he wishing to hear you say you thinking to agree with the conditions and be satisfied."

She ceased speaking, but continued to smile; and so complete was the stillness, that Soames, whose sense of hearing had become nervously stimulated, heard a solitary rose petal fall upon the corner of the writing-table.

"I . . . agree," he whispered huskily; "and . . . I am . . . satisfied."

He looked at the carven screen as a lost soul might look at the gate of Hades; he felt now that if a sound should come from beyond it he would shriek out, he would stop up his ears; that if the figure of the Unseen should become visible, he must die at first glimpse of it.

The little brown girl was repeating the uncanny business of listening to that voice of silence; and Soames knew that he could not sustain his part in this eerie comedy for another half-minute without breaking out into hysterical laughter. Then:

"Mr. King he releasing you for to-night," announced the silver-bell voice.

The light went out.

Soames uttered a groan of terror, followed by a short, bubbling laugh, but was seized firmly by the arm and led on into the blackness—on through the solid, book-laden walls, presumably; and on—on—on, along those interminable passages by which he had come. Here the air was cooler, and the odor of roses no longer perceptible, no longer stifling him, no longer assailing his nostrils, not as an odor of sweetness, but as a perfume utterly damnable and unholy.

With his knees trembling at every step,

he marched on, firmly supported by his un-seen companion.

"Stop!" directed a metallic, guttural voice.

Soames pulled up, and leaned weakly against the wall. He heard the clap of hands close behind him; and a door opened within twelve inches of the spot whereat he stood.

He tottered out into the matting-lined corridor from which he had started upon that nightmare journey; Ho-Pin appeared at his elbow, but no door appeared behind Ho-Pin!

"This is your wroom," said the China-man, revealing his yellow teeth in a mirthless smile.

He walked across the corridor, threw open a door—a real, palpable door . . . and there was Soames' little white room!

Soames staggered across, for it seemed a veritable haven of refuge—entered, and dropped upon the bed. He seemed to see the rose-petals fall-fall—falling in that red room in the labyrinth—the room that had no door; he seemed to see the laughing eyes of the beautiful Eurasian.

"Good night!" came the metallic voice of Ho-Pin.

The light in the corridor went out.

XVI

HO-PIN'S CATACOMBS

The newly-created Mr. Lucas entered upon a sort of cave-man existence in this fantastic abode where night was day and day was night; where the sun never shone.

He was awakened on the first morning of his sojourn in the establishment of Ho-Pin by the loud ringing of an electric bell immediately beside his bed. He sprang upright with a catching of the breath, peering about him at the unfamiliar surroundings and wondering, in the hazy manner of a sleeper newly awakened, where he was, and how come there. He was fully dressed, and his strapped-up grip lay beside him on the floor; for he had not dared to remove his clothes, had not dared to seek slumber after that ter-rifying interview with Mr. King. But out-raged nature had prevailed, and sleep had come unbeckoned, unbidden.

The electric light was still burning in the room, as he had left it, and as he sat up, looking about him, a purring whistle drew his attention to a speaking-tube which pro-truded below the bell.

Soames rolled from the bed, head throb-bing, and an acrid taste in his mouth, and spoke into the tube:

"Hullo!"

"You will pwrepare for youwr duties," came the metallic gutturals of Ho-Pin. "Bwreakfast will be bwrought to you in a quawrter-of-an-hour."

He made no reply, but stood looking about him dully. It had not been a dream, then, nor was he mad. It was a horrible reality; here, in London, in modern, civilized London, he was actually buried in some incred-ible catacomb; somewhere near to him, very near to him, was the cave of the golden dragon, and, also adjacent—terrifying thought—was the doorless library, the rose-scented haunt where the beautiful Eurasian spoke, oracularly, the responses of Mr. King!

Soames could not understand it all; he felt that such things could not be; that there must exist an explanation of those seeming im-possibilities other than that they actually ex-isted. But the instructions were veritable enough, and would not be denied.

Rapidly he began to unpack his grip. His watch had stopped, since he had neglected to wind it, and he hurried with his toilet, fearful of incurring the anger of Ho-Pin—of Ho-Pin, the beetlesque.

He observed, with passive interest, that the operation of shaving did not appreciably lighten the stain upon his skin, and, by the time he was shaved, he had begun to know the dark-haired, yellow-faced man grimac-ing in the mirror for himself; but he was far from being reconciled to his new appear-ance.

Said peeped in at the door. He no longer wore his chauffeur's livery, but was arrayed in a white linen robe, red-sashed, and wore loose, red slippers; a tarboosh perched upon his shaven skull.

Pushing the door widely open, he entered with a tray upon which was spread a sub-stantial breakfast.

"Hurryup!" he muttered, as one word; wherewith he departed again.

Soames seated himself at the little table upon which the tray rested, and endeavored to eat. His usual appetite had departed with his identity; Mr. Lucas was a poor, twitching being of raw nerves and internal qualms. He emptied the coffee-pot, however, and smoked a cigarette which he found in his case.

Said reappeared.

"Ta'ala!" he directed.

Soames having learnt that that term was evidently intended as an invitation to follow Said, rose and followed, dumbly.

He was conducted along the matting-lined corridor to the left; and now, where formerly he had seen a blank wall, he saw an open door! Passing this, he discovered himself in the cave of the golden dragon. Ho-Pin, dressed in a perfectly fitting morning coat and its usual accompaniments, received him with a mirthless smile.

"Good mowrning!" he said; "I twrust your bwreakfast was satisfactowry?"

"Quite, sir," replied Soames, mechanically, and as he might have replied to Mr. Leroux.

"Said will show you to a wroom," continued Ho-Pin, "where you will find a gentleman awaiting you. You will valet him and perfowrm any other services which he may wrequire of you. When he departs, you will clean the wroom and adjoining bathwroom, and put it into thowrough order for an incoming tenant. In short, your duties in this wrespect will be identical to those which formerly you perfowrmed at sea. There is one important diffewrence: your name is Lucas, and you will answer no questions."

The metallic voice seemed to reach Soames' comprehension from some place other than the room of the golden dragon—from a great distance, or as though he were fastened up in a box and were being addressed by someone outside it.

"Yes, sir," he replied.

Said opened the yellow door upon the right of the room, and Soames followed him into another of the matting-lined corridors, this one running right and left and parallel with the wall of the apartment which he had just quitted. Six doors opened out of this corridor; four of them upon the side opposite to that by which he had entered, and one at either end.

These doors were not readily to be detected; and the wall, at first glance, presented an unbroken appearance. But from experience, he had learned that where the strips of bamboo which overlay the straw matting formed a rectangular panel, there was a door, and by the light of the electric lamp hung in the center of the corridor, he counted six of these.

Said, selecting a key from a bunch which he carried, opened one of the doors, held it ajar for Soames to enter, and permitted it to reclose behind him.

Soames entered nervously. He found himself in a room identical in size with his own private apartment; a bathroom, etc., opened out of it in one corner after the same fashion. But there similarity ended.

The bed in this apartment was constructed more on the lines of a modern steamer bunk; that is, it was surrounded by a rail, and was raised no more than a foot from the floor. The latter was covered with a rich carpet, worked in many colors, and the wall was hung with such paper as Soames had never seen hitherto in his life. The scheme of this mural decoration was distinctly Chinese, and consisted in an intricate design of human and animal figures, bewilderingly mingled; its coloring was brilliant, and the scheme extended, unbroken, over the entire ceiling. Cushions, most fancifully embroidered, were strewn about the floor, and the bed coverlet was a piece of heavy Chinese tapestry. A lamp, shaded with silk of a dull purple, swung in the center of the apartment, and an ebony table, inlaid with ivory, stood on one side of the bed; on the other was a cushioned armchair figured with the eternal, chaotic Chinese design, and being littered, at the moment, with the garments of the man in the bed. The air of the room was disgusting, unbreathable; it caught Soames by the throat and sickened him. It was laden with some kind of fumes, entirely unfamiliar to his nostrils. A dainty Chinese tea-service stood upon the ebony table.

For fully thirty seconds Soames, with his back to the door, gazed at the man in the bed, and fought down the nausea which the air of the place had induced in him.

This sleeper was a man of middle age, thin to emaciation and having lank, dark hair. His face was ghastly white, and he lay with his head thrown back and with his arms hanging out upon either side of the bunk, so that his listless hands rested upon the carpet. It was a tragic face; a high, intellectual brow and finely chiseled features; but it presented an indescribable aspect of decay; it was as the face of some classic statue which has long lain buried in humid ruins.

Soames shook himself into activity, and ventured to approach the bed. He moistened his dry lips and spoke:

"Good morning, sir"—the words sounded wildly, fantastically out of place. "Shall I prepare your bath?"

The sleeper showed no signs of awakening.

Soames forced himself to touch one of the

thrown-back shoulders. He shook it gently.

The man on the bed raised his arms and dropped them back into their original position, without opening his eyes.

"They . . . are hiding," he murmured thickly . . . "in the . . . orange grove. . . . If the felucca sails . . . closer . . . they will" . . .

Soames, finding something very horrifying in the broken words, shook the sleeper more urgently.

"Wake up, sir!" he cried; "I am going to prepare your bath."

"Don't let them . . . escape," murmured the man, slowly opening his eyes—"I have not" . . .

He struggled upright, glaring madly at the intruder. His light gray eyes had a glassiness as of long sickness, and his pupils, which were unnaturally dilated, began rapidly to contract; became almost invisible. Then they expanded again—and again contracted.

"Who—the deuce are you?" he murmured, passing his hand across his unshaven face.

"My name is—Lucas, sir," said Soames, conscious that if he remained much longer in the place he should be physically sick. "At your service—shall I prepare the bath?"

"The bath?" said the man, sitting up more straightly—"certainly, yes—of course" . . .

He looked at Soames, with a light of growing sanity creeping into his eyes; a faint flush tinged the pallid face, and his loose mouth twitched sensitively.

"Then, Said," he began, looking Soames up and down . . . "let me see, whom did you say you were?"

"Lucas, sir—at your service."

"Ah," muttered the man, lowering his eyes in unmistakable shame—"yes, yes, of course. You are new here?"

"Yes, sir. Shall I prepare your bath?"

"Yes, please. This is Wednesday morning?"

"Wednesday morning, sir; yes."

"Of course—it is Wednesday. You said your name was?"

"Lucas, sir," reiterated Soames, and, crossing the fantastic apartment, he entered the bath-room beyond.

This contained the most modern appointments and was on an altogether more luxurious scale than that attached to his own quarters. He noted, without drawing any deduction from the circumstance, that the fittings were of American manufacture. Here, as in the outer room, there was no window; an electric light hung from the center of the ceiling. Soames busied himself in filling the bath, and laying out the towels upon the rack.

"Fairly warm, sir?" he asked.

"Not too warm, thank you," replied the other, now stumbling out of bed and falling into the armchair—"not too warm."

"If you will take your bath, sir," said Soames, returning to the outer room, "I will brush your clothes and be ready to shave you."

"Yes, yes," said the man, rubbing his hands over his face wearily. "You are new here?"

Soames, who was becoming used to answering this question, answered it once more without irritation.

"Yes, sir, will you take your bath now? It is nearly full, I think."

The man stood up unsteadily and passed into the bath-room, closing the door behind him. Soames, seeking to forget his surroundings, took out from a small hand-bag which he found beneath the bed, a razor-case and a shaving stick. The clothes-brush he had discovered in the bathroom; and now he set to work to brush the creased garments stacked in the armchair. He noted that they were of excellent make, and that the linen was of the highest quality. He was thus employed when the outer door silently opened and the face of Said looked in.

"*Gazm*," said the Oriental; and he placed inside, upon the carpet, a pair of highly polished boots.

The door was reclosed.

Soames had all the garments in readiness by the time that the man emerged from the bathroom, looking slightly less ill, and not quite so pallid. He wore a yellow silk kimono; and, with greater composure than he had yet revealed, he seated himself in the armchair that Soames might shave him.

This operation Soames accomplished, and the subject, having partially dressed, returned to the bath-room to brush his hair. When his toilet was practically completed:

"Shall I pack the rest of the things in the bag, sir?" asked Soames.

The man nodded affirmatively.

Five minutes later he was ready to depart, and stood before the ex-butler a well-dressed, intellectual, but very debauched-looking gentleman. Being evidently well acquainted with the régime of the establishment, he pressed an electric bell beside the door, presented Soames with half-a-sovereign, and, as Said reappeared, took his departure, leaving Soames more reconciled to his lot than he could ever have supposed possible.

The task of cleaning the room was now commenced by Soames. Said returned, bringing him the necessary utensils; and for fifteen minutes or so he busied himself between the outer apartment and the bathroom. During this time he found leisure to study the extraordinary mural decorations; and, as he looked at them, he learned that they possessed a singular property.

If one gazed continuously at any portion of the wall, the intertwined figures thereon took shape—nay, took life; the intricate, elaborate design ceased to be a design, and became a procession, a saturnalia; became a sinister comedy, which, when first visualized, shocked Soames immoderately. The horrors presented by these devices of evil cunning, crowding the walls, appalled the narrow mind of the beholder, revolted him in an even greater degree than they must have revolted a man of broader and cleaner mind. He became conscious of a quality of evil which pervaded the room; the entire place seemed to lie beneath a spell, beneath the spell of an invisible, immeasurably wicked intelligence.

His reflections began to terrify him, and he hastened to complete his duties. The stench of the place was sickening him anew, and when at last Said opened the door, Soames came out as a man escaping from some imminent harm.

"Di," muttered Said.

He pointed to the opened door of a second room, identical in every respect with the first; and Soames started back with a smothered groan. Had his education been classical he might have likened himself to Hercules laboring for Augeus; but his mind tending scripturally, he wondered if he had sold his soul to Satan in the person of the invisible Mr. King!

XVII

KAN-SUH CONCESSIONS

Soames' character was of a pliable sort, and ere many days had passed he had grown accustomed to this unnatural existence among the living corpses in the catacombs of Ho-Pin.

He rarely saw Ho-Pin, and desired not to see him at all; as for Mr. King, he even endeavored to banish from his memory the name of that shadowy being. The memory of the Eurasian he could not banish, and was ever listening for the silvery voice, but in vain. He had no particular duties, apart from the care of the six rooms known as Block A, and situated in the corridor to the left of the cave of the golden dragon; this, and the valeting of departing occupants. But the hours at which he was called upon to perform these duties varied very greatly. Sometimes he would attend to four human wrecks in the same morning; whilst, perhaps on the following day, he would not be called upon to officiate until late in the evening. One fact early became evident to him. There was a ceaseless stream of these living dead men pouring into the catacombs of Ho-Pin, coming he knew not whence, and issuing forth again, he knew not whither.

Twice in the first week of his new and strange service he recognized the occupants of the rooms as men whom he had seen in the upper world. On entering the room of one of these (at ten o'clock at night) he almost cried out in his surprise; for the limp, sallow-faced creature extended upon the bed before him was none other than Sir Brian Malpas—the brilliant politician whom his leaders had earmarked for office in the next Cabinet!

As Soames stood contemplating him stretched there in his stupor, he found it hard to credit the fact that this was the same man whom political rivals feared for his hard brilliance, whom society courted, and whose engagement to the daughter of a peer had been announced only a few months before.

Throughout this time, Soames had made no attempt to seek the light of day: he had not seen a newspaper; he knew nothing of the hue and cry raised throughout England, of the hunt for the murderer of Mrs. Vernon. He suffered principally from lack of companionship. The only human being with whom he ever came in contact was Said, the Egyptian; and Said, at best, was uncommunicative. A man of very limited intellect, Luke Soames had been at a loss for many days to reconcile Block A and its temporary occupants with any comprehensible scheme of things. Whereas some of the rooms would be laden with nauseating fumes, others would be free of these; the occupants, again, exhibited various symptoms.

That he was a servant of an opium-den

de luxe did not for some time become apparent to him; then, when first the theory presented itself, he was staggered by a discovery so momentous.

But it satisfied his mind only partially. Some men whom he valeted might have been doped with opium, certainly, but all did not exhibit those indications which, from hearsay, he associated with the resin of the white poppy.

Knowing nothing of the numerous and exotic vices which have sprung from the soil of the Orient, he was at a loss for a full explanation of the facts as he saw them.

Finding himself unmolested, and noting, in the privacy of his own apartment, how handsomely his tips were accumulating, Soames was rapidly becoming reconciled to his underground existence, more especially as it spelt safety to a man wanted by the police. His duties thus far had never taken him beyond the corridor known as Block A; what might lie on the other side of the cave of the golden dragon he knew not. He never saw any of the habitués arrive, or actually leave; he did not know whether the staff of the place consisted of himself, Said, Ho-Pin, the Eurasian girl—and . . . the other, or if there were more servants of this unseen master. But never a day passed by that the clearance of at least one apartment did not fall to his lot, and never an occupant quitted those cells without placing a golden gratuity in the valet's palm.

His appetite returned, and he slept soundly enough in his clean white bedroom, content to lose the upper world, temporarily, and to become a dweller in the catacombs—where tips were large and plentiful. His was the mind of a domestic animal, neither learning from the past nor questioning the future; but dwelling only in the well-fed present.

No other type of European, however lowly, could have supported existence in such a place.

Thus the days passed, and the nights passed, the one merged imperceptibly in the other. At the end of the first week, two sovereigns appeared upon the breakfast tray which Said brought to Soames' room; and, some little time later, Said reappeared with his bottles and paraphernalia to renew the ex-butler's make-up. As he was leaving the room:

"Ahu hina—G'nap'lis effendi!" he muttered, and went out as Mr. Gianapolis entered.

At sight of the Greek, Soames realized, in one emotional moment, how really lonely he had been and how in his inmost heart he longed for a sight of the sun, for a breath of unpolluted air, for a glimpse of gray, homely London.

All the old radiance had returned to Gianapolis; his eyes were crossed in an amiable smile.

"My dear Soames!" he cried, greeting the really delighted man. "How well your new complexion suits you! Sit down, Soames, sit down, and let us talk."

Soames placed a chair for Gianapolis, and seated himself upon the bed, twirling his thumbs in the manner which was his when under the influence of excitement.

"Now, Soames," continued Gianapolis—"I mean Lucas!—my anticipations, which I mentioned to you on the night of—the accident . . . you remember?"

"Yes," said Soames rapidly, "yes."

"Well, they have been realized. Our establishment, here, continues to flourish as of yore. Nothing has come to light in the press calculated to prejudice us in the eyes of our patrons, and although your own name, Soames" . . .

Soames started and clutched at the bedcover.

"Although your own name has been freely mentioned on all sides, it is not generally accepted that you perpetrated the deed."

Soames discovered his hair to be bristling; his skin tingled with a nervous apprehension.

"That I," he began dryly, paused and swallowed—"that *I* perpetrated. . . . Has it been" . . .

"It has been hinted at by one or two Fleet Street theorists—yes, Soames! But the postmortem examination of—the victim, revealed the fact that she was addicted to drugs" . . .

"Opium?" asked Soames, eagerly.

Gianapolis smiled.

"What an observant mind you have, Soames!" he said. "So you have perceived that these groves are sacred to our Lady of the Poppies? Well, in part that is true. Here, under the auspices of Mr. Ho-Pin, fretful society seeks the solace of the brass pipe; yes, Soames, that is true. Have you ever tried opium?"

"Never!" declared Soames, with emphasis, "never!"

"Well, it is a delight in store for you! But

the reason of our existence as an institution, Soames, is not far to seek. Once the joys of *Chandu* become perceptible to the neophyte, a great need is felt—a crying need. One may drink opium or inject morphine; these, and other crude measures, may satisfy temporarily, but if one would enjoy the delights of that fairyland, of that enchanted realm which bountiful nature has concealed in the heart of the poppy, one must retire from the ken of goths and vandals who do not appreciate such exquisite delights; one must dedicate, not an hour snatched from grasping society, but successive days and nights to the goddess" . . .

Soames, barely understanding this discourse, listened eagerly to every word of it, whilst Gianapolis, waxing eloquent upon his strange thesis, seemed to be addressing, not his solitary auditor, but an invisible concourse.

"In common with the lesser deities," he continued, "our Lady of the Poppies is exacting. After a protracted sojourn at her shrine, so keen are the delights which she opens up to her worshipers, that a period of lassitude, of exhaustion, inevitably ensues. This precludes the proper worship of the goddess in the home, and necessitates—I say *necessitates*—the presence, in such a capital as London, of a suitable Temple. You have the honor, Soames, to be a minor priest of that Temple!

Soames brushed his dyed hair with his fingers and endeavored to look intelligent.

"A branch establishment—merely a sacred caravanserai where votaries might repose ere reentering the ruder world," continued Gianapolis—"has unfortunately been raided by the police!"

With that word, *police*, he seemed to come to earth again.

"Our arrangements, I am happy to say, were such that not one of the staff was found on the premises and no visible link existed between that establishment and this. But now let us talk about yourself. You may safely take an evening off, I think" . . .

He scrutinized Soames attentively.

"You will be discreet as a matter of course, and I should not recommend your visiting any of your former haunts. I make this proposal, of course, with the full sanction of Mr. King."

The muscles of Soames' jaw tightened at sound of the name, and he avoided the gaze of the crossed eyes.

"And the real purpose of my visit here this morning is to acquaint you with the little contrivance by which we ensure our privacy here. Once you are acquainted with it you can take the air every evening at suitable hours, on application to Mr. Ho-Pin."

Soames coughed dryly.

"Very good," he said in a strained voice; "I am glad of that."

"I knew you would be glad, Soames," declared the smiling Gianapolis; "and now, if you will step this way, I will show you the door by which you must come and go." He stood up, then bent confidentially to Soames' ear. "Mr. King, very wisely," he whispered, "has retained you on the premises hitherto, because some doubt, some little doubt, remained respecting the information which had come into the possession of the police."

Again that ominous word! But ere Soames had time to reflect, Gianapolis led the way out of the room and along the matting-lined corridor into the apartment of the golden dragon. Soames observed, with a nervous tremor, that Mr. Ho-Pin sat upon one of the lounges, smoking a cigarette, and arrayed in his usual faultless manner. He did not attempt to rise, however, as the pair entered, but merely nodded to Gianapolis and smiled mirthlessly at Soames.

They quitted the room by the door opening on the stone steps—the door by which Soames had first entered into that evil Aladdin's cave. Gianapolis went ahead, and Soames, following him, presently emerged through a low doorway into a concrete-paved apartment, having walls of Portland stone and a white-washed ceiling. One end consisted solely of a folding gate, evidently designed to admit the limousine.

Gianapolis turned, as Soames stepped up beside him.

"If you will glance back," he said. "you will see exactly where the door is situated."

Soames did as directed, and suppressed a cry of surprise. Four of the stone blocks were fictitious—were, in verity, a heavy wooden door, faced in some way with real, or imitation granite—a door communicating with the steps of the catacombs.

"Observe!" said Gianapolis.

He closed the door, which opened outward, and there remained nothing to show the keenest observer—unless he had resorted to sounding—that these four blocks differed in any way from their fellows.

"Ingenious, is it not?" said Gianapolis,

genially. "And now, my dear Soames, observe again!"

He rolled back the folding gates; and beyond was a garage, wherein stood the big limousine.

"I keep my car here, Soames, for the sake of—convenience! And now, my dear Soames, when you go out this evening, Said will close this entrance after you. When you return, which, I understand, you must do at ten o'clock, you will enter the garage by the side door yonder, which will not be locked, and you will press the electric button at the back of the petrol cans here—look! you can see it!—the inner door will then be opened for you. Step this way."

He passed between the car and the wall of the garage, opened the door at the left of the entrance gates, and, Soames following, came out into a narrow lane. For the first time in many days Soames scented the cleaner air of the upper world, and with it he filled his lungs gratefully.

Behind him was the garage, before him the high wall of a yard, and, on his right, for a considerable distance, extended a similar wall; in the latter case evidently that of a wharf—for beyond it flowed the Thames.

Proceeding along beside this wall, the two came to the gates of a warehouse. They passed these, however, and entered a small office. Crossing the office, they gained the interior of the warehouse, where chests bearing Chinese labels were stacked in great profusion.

"Then this place," began Soames . . .

"Is a ginger warehouse, Soames! There is a very small office staff, but sufficiently large to cope with the limited business done—in the import and export of ginger! The firm is known as Kan-Suh Concessions and imports preserved Chinese ginger from its own plantations in that province of the Celestial Empire. There is a small wharf attached, as you may have noted. Oh! it is a going concern and perfectly respectable!"

Soames looked about him with wide-opened eyes.

"The ginger staff," said Gianapolis, "is not yet arrived. Mr. Ho-Pin is the manager. The lane, in which the establishment is situated, communicates with Limehouse Causeway, and, being a cul-de-sac, is little frequented. Only this one firm has premises actually opening into it and I have converted the small corner building at the extremity of the wharf into a garage for my car. There are

no means of communication between the premises of Kan-Suh Concessions and those of the more important enterprise below—and I, myself, am not officially associated with the ginger trade. It is a precaution which we all adopt, however, never to enter or leave the garage if anyone is in sight." . . .

Soames became conscious of a new security. He set about his duties that morning with a greater alacrity than usual, valeting one of the living dead men—a promising young painter whom he chanced to know by sight—with a return to the old affable manner which had rendered him so popular during his career as cabin steward.

He felt that he was now part and parcel of Kan-Suh Concessions; that Kan-Suh Concessions and he were at one. He had yet to learn that his sense of security was premature, and that his added knowledge might be an added danger.

When Said brought his lunch into his room, he delivered also a slip of paper bearing the brief message:

"Go out 6:30—return 10."

Mr. Soames uncorked his daily bottle of Bass almost gaily, and attacked his lunch with avidity.

XVIII

THE WORLD ABOVE

The night had set in grayly, and a drizzle of fine rain was falling. West India Dock Road presented a prospect so uninviting that it must have damped the spirits of anyone but a cave-dweller.

Soames, buttoned up in a raincoat kindly lent by Mr. Gianapolis, and of a somewhat refined fit, with a little lagoon of rainwater forming within the reef of his hat-brim, trudged briskly along. The necessary ingredients for the manufacture of mud are always present (if invisible during dry weather) in the streets of East-end London, and already Soames' neat black boots were liberally bedaubed with it. But what cared Soames? He inhaled the soot-laden air rapturously; he was glad to feel the rain beating upon his face, and took a childish pleasure in ducking his head suddenly and seeing the little stream of water spouting from his hat-brim. How healthy they looked, these East-end workers, these Italian dock-hands, these Jewish tailors, these nondescript, greasy beings who sometimes saw the sun. Many of them, he knew well, labored in cellars; but he had learnt that there are cellars and cellars. Ah! it was glorious, this gray, murky London!

Yet, now that temporarily he was free of it, he realized that there was that within him which responded to the call of the catacombs; there was a fascination in the fume-laden air of those underground passages; there was a charm, a mysterious charm, in the cave of the golden dragon, in that unforgettable place which he assumed to mark the center of the labyrinth; in the wicked, black eyes of the Eurasian. He realized that between the abstraction of silver spoons and deliberate, organized money-making at the expense of society, a great chasm yawned; that there may be romance even in felony.

Soames at last felt himself to be a traveler on the highroad to fortune; he had become almost reconciled to the loss of his bank balance, to the loss of his place in the upper world. His was the constitution of a born criminal, and, had he been capable of subtle self-analysis, he must have known now that fear, and fear only, hitherto had held him back, had confined him to the ranks of the amateurs. Well, the plunge was taken.

Deep in such reflections, he trudged along through the rain, scarce noting where his steps were leading him, for all roads were alike to-night. His natural inclinations presently dictated a halt at a brilliantly-lighted public house; and, taking off his hat to shake some of the moisture from it, he replaced it on his head and entered the saloon lounge.

The place proved to be fairly crowded, principally with local tradesmen whose forefathers had toiled for Pharaoh; and conveying his glass of whisky to a marble-topped table in a corner comparatively secluded, Soames sat down for a consideration of past, present, and future; an unusual mental exercise. Curiously enough, he had lost some of his old furtiveness; he no longer examined, suspiciously, every stranger who approached his neighborhood; for as the worshipers of old came by the gate of Fear into the invisible presence of Moloch, so he—of equally untutored mind—had entered the presence of Mr. King! And no devotee of the Ammonite god had had greater faith in his potent protection than Soames had in that of his unseen master. What should a servant of Mr. King fear from the officers of the law?

How puny a thing was the law in comparison with the director of that secret, powerful, invulnerable organization whereof to-day he (Soames) formed an unit!

Then, oddly, the old dormant cowardice of the man received a sudden spurring, and leaped into quickness. An evening paper lay upon the marble top of the table, and carelessly taking it up, Soames, hitherto lost in imaginings, was now reminded that for more than a week he had lain in ignorance of the world's doings. Good Heavens! how forgetful he had been! It was the nepenthe of the catacombs. He must make up for lost time and get in touch again with passing events: especially he must post himself up on the subject of . . . the murder. . . .

The paper dropped from his hands, and, feeling himself blanch beneath his artificial tan, Soames, in his old furtive manner, glanced around the saloon to learn if he were watched. Apparently no one was taking the slightest notice of him, and, with an unsteady hand, he raised his glass and drained its contents. There, at the bottom of the page before him, was the cause of this sudden panic; a short paragraph conceived as follows:—

REPORTED ARREST OF SOAMES

It is reported that a man answering to the description of Soames, the butler wanted in connection with the Palace Mansions outrage, has been arrested in Birmingham. He was found sleeping in an outhouse belonging to Major Jennings, of Olton, and as he refused to give any account of himself, was handed over, by the gentleman's gardener, to the local police. His resemblance to the published photograph being observed, he was closely questioned, and although he denies being Luke Soames, he is being held for further inquiry.

Soames laid down the paper, and, walking across to the bar, ordered a second glass of whisky. With this he returned to the table and began more calmly to re-read the paragraph. From it he passed to the other news. He noted that little publicity was given to the Palace Mansions affair, from which he judged that public interest in the matter was already growing cold. A short summary appeared on the front page, and this he eagerly devoured. It read as follows:—

PALACE MANSIONS MYSTERY

The police are following up an important clue to the murderer of Mrs. Vernon, and it is significant in this connection that a man answering to the description of

Soames was apprehended at Olton (Birmingham) late last night. (See Page 6). The police are very reticent in regard to the new information which they hold, but it is evident that at last they are confident of establishing a case. Mr. Henry Leroux, the famous novelist, in whose flat the mysterious outrage took place, is suffering from a nervous breakdown, but is reported to be progressing favorably by Dr. Cumberly, who is attending him. Dr. Cumberly, it will be remembered, was with Mr. Leroux, and Mr. John Exel, M.P., at the time that the murder was discovered. The executors of the late Mr. Horace Vernon are faced with extraordinary difficulties in administering the will of the deceased, owing to the tragic coincidence of his wife's murder within twenty-four hours of his own demise.

Public curiosity respecting the nursing home in Gillingham Street, with its electric baths and other modern appliances, has by no means diminished, and groups of curious spectators regularly gather outside the former establishment of Nurse Proctor, and apparently derive some form of entertainment from staring at the windows and questioning the constable on duty. The fact that Mrs. Vernon undoubtedly came from this establishment on the night of the crime, and that the proprietors of the nursing home fled immediately, leaving absolutely no clue behind them, complicates the mystery which Scotland Yard is engaged in unraveling.

It is generally believed that the woman, Proctor, and her associates had actually no connection with the crime, and that realizing that the inquiry might turn in their direction, they decamped. The obvious inference, of course, is that the nursing home was conducted on lines which would not bear official scrutiny.

The flight of the butler, Soames, presents a totally different aspect, and in this direction the police are very active.

Soames searched the remainder of the paper scrupulously, but failed to find any further reference to the case. The second Scottish stimulant had served somewhat to restore his courage; he congratulated himself upon taking the only move which could have saved him from arrest; he perceived that he owed his immunity entirely to the protective wings of Mr. King. He trembled to think that his fate might indeed have been that of the man arrested at Olton; for, without money and without friends, he would have become, ere this, just such an outcast and natural object of suspicion.

He noted, as a curious circumstance, that throughout the report there was no reference to the absence of Mrs. Leroux; therefore—a primitive reasoner—he assumed that she was back again at Palace Mansions. He was mentally incapable of fitting Mrs. Leroux into the secret machine engineered by Mr. King through the visible agency of Ho-Pin. On the whole, he was disposed to believe that her several absences—ostensibly on visits to Paris—had nothing to do with the catacombs of Ho-Pin, but were to be traced to the amours of the radiant Gianapolis. Taking into consideration his reception by the Chinaman in the cave of the golden dragon, he determined, to his own satisfaction, that this had been dictated by prudence, and by Mr. Gianapolis. In short he believed that the untimely murder of Mrs. Vernon had threatened to direct attention to the commercial enterprise of the Greek, and that he, Soames, had become incorporated in the latter in this accidental fashion. He believed himself to have been employed in a private intrigue during the time that he was at Palace Mansions, and counted it a freak of fate that Mr. Gianapolis' affairs of the pocket had intruded upon his affairs of the heart.

It was all very confusing, and entirely beyond Soames' mental capacity to unravel.

He treated himself to a third scotch whisky, and sallied out into the rain. A brilliantly lighted music hall upon the opposite side of the road attracted his attention. The novelty of freedom having worn off, he felt no disposition to spend the remainder of the evening in the street, for the rain was now falling heavily, but determined to sample the remainder of the program offered by the "first house," and presently was reclining in a plush-covered, tip-up seat in the back row of the stalls.

The program was not of sufficient interest wholly to distract his mind, and during the performance of a very tragic comedian, Soames found his thoughts wandering far from the stage. His seat was at the extreme end of the back row, and, quite unintentionally, he began to listen to the conversation of two men, who, standing just inside the entrance door and immediately behind him to the right, were talking in subdued voices.

"There are thousands of Kings in London," said one . . .

Soames slowly lowered his hands to the chair-arms on either side of him and clutched them tightly. Every nerve in his body seemed to be strung up to the ultimate pitch of tensity. He was listening, now, as a man arraigned might listen for the pronouncement of a judgment.

"That's the trouble," replied a second voice; "but you know Max's ideas on the subject? He has his own way of going to work; but my idea, Sowerby, is that if we can find the one Mr. Soames—and I am open to bet he hasn't left London—we shall find the right Mr. King."

The comedian finished, and the orchestra noisily chorded him off. Soames, his forehead wet with perspiration, began to turn his head, inch by inch. The lights in the auditorium were partially lowered, and he prayed, devoutly, that they would remain so; for now, glancing out of the corner of his right eye, he saw the speakers.

The taller of the two, a man wearing a glistening brown overall and rain-drenched tweed cap, was the detective who had been in Leroux's study and who had ordered him to his room on the night of the murder!

Then commenced for Soames such an ordeal as all his previous life had not offered him; an ordeal beside which even the interview with Mr. King sank into insignificance. His one hope was in the cunning of Said's disguise; but he knew that Scotland Yard men judged likenesses, not by complexions, which are alterable, not by the color of the hair, which can be dyed, but by certain features which are measurable, and which may be memorized because nature has fashioned them immutable.

What should he do?—What should he do? In the silence:

"No good stopping any longer," came the whispered voice of the shorter detective; "I have had a good look around the house, and there is nobody here." . . .

Soames literally held his breath.

"We'll get along down to the Dock Gate," was the almost inaudible reply; "I am meeting Stringer there at nine o'clock."

Walking softly, the Scotland Yard men passed out of the theater.

XIX

THE LIVING DEAD

The night held yet another adventure in store for Soames. His encounter with the two Scotland Yard men had finally expelled all thoughts of pleasure from his mind. The upper world, the free world, was beset with pitfalls; he realized that for the present, at any rate, there could be no security for him, save in the catacombs of Ho-Pin. He came out of the music-hall and stood for a moment just outside the foyer, glancing fearfully up and down the rain-swept street. Then, re-

suming the drenched raincoat which he had taken off in the theater, and turning up its collar about his ears, he set out to return to the garage adjoining the warehouse of Kan-Suh Concessions.

He had fully another hour of leave if he cared to avail himself of it, but, whilst every pedestrian assumed, in his eyes, the form of a detective, whilst every dark corner seemed to conceal an ambush, whilst every passing instant he anticipated feeling a heavy hand upon his shoulder, and almost heard the words:—"Luke Soames, I arrest you" . . . Whilst this was his case, freedom had no joys for him.

No light guided him to the garage door, and he was forced to seek for the handle by groping along the wall. Presently, his hand came in contact with it, he turned it—and the way was open before him.

Being far from familiar with the geography of the place, he took out a box of matches, and struck one to light him to the shelf above which the bell-push was concealed.

Its feeble light revealed, not only the big limousine near which he was standing and the usual fixtures of a garage, but, dimly penetrating beyond into the black places, it also revealed something else. . . .

The door in the false granite blocks was open!

Soames, who had advanced to seek the bell-push, stopped short. The match burnt down almost to his fingers, whereupon he blew it out and carefully crushed it under his foot. A faint reflected light rendered perceptible the stone steps below. At the top, Soames stood looking down. Nothing stirred above, below, or around him. What did it mean? Dimly to his ears came the hooting of some siren from the river—evidently that of a large vessel. Still he hesitated; why he did so, he scarce knew, save that he was afraid—vaguely afraid.

Then, he asked himself what he had to fear, and conjuring up a mental picture of his white bedroom below, he planted his foot firmly upon the first step, and from thence, descended to the bottom, guided by the faint light which shone out from the doorway beneath.

But the door proved to be only partly opened, and Soames knocked deferentially. No response came to his knocking, and he so greatly ventured as to push the door fully open.

The cave of the golden dragon was empty. Half frightfully, Soames glanced about the singular apartment, in amid the mountainous cushions of the lee-wans, behind the pedestal of the dragon; to the right and to the left of the doorway wherein he stood.

There was no one there; but the door on the right—the door inlaid with ebony and green stone, which he had never yet seen open was open now, widely opened. He glided across the floor, his wet boots creaking unmusically, and peeped through. He saw a matting-lined corridor identical with that known as Block A. The door of one apartment, that on the extreme left, was opened. Sickly fumes were wafted out to him, and these mingled with the incense-like odor which characterized the temple of the dragon.

A moment he stood so, then started back, appalled.

An outcry—the outcry of a woman, of a woman whose very soul is assailed—split the stillness. Not from the passageway before him, but from somewhere behind him—from the direction of Block A—it came.

"For God's sake—oh! for God's sake, have mercy! Let me go! . . . let me go!" Higher, shriller, more fearful and urgent, grew the voice—"*Let me go!*" . . .

Soames' knees began to tremble beneath him; he clutched at the black wall for support; then turned, and with unsteady footsteps crossed to the door communicating with the corridor which contained his room. It had a lever handle of the Continental pattern, and, trembling with apprehension that it might prove to be locked, Soames pressed down this handle.

The door opened . . .

"*Hina, effendi!—hina!*"

The voice sounded like that of Said. . . .

"Oh! God in Heaven help me! . . . Help!—help!" . . .

"*Imsik!*" . . .

Footsteps were pattering upon the stone stairs; someone was descending from the warehouse! The frenzied shrieks of the woman continued. Soames broke into a cold perspiration; his heart, which had leaped wildly, seemed now to have changed to a cold stone in his breast. Just at the entrance to the corridor he stood, frozen with horror at those cries.

"*Ikfil el-bâb!*" came now, in the voice of Ho-Pin,—and nearer.

"Let me go! . . . only let me go, and I will never breathe a word. . . . Ah! Ah! Oh! God of mercy! not the needle again! You are killing me! . . . not the needle!" . . .

Soames staggered on to his own room and literally fell within—as across the cave of the golden dragon, behind him, *someone*—one whom he did not see but only heard, one whom with all his soul he hoped had not seen *him*—passed rapidly.

Another shriek, more frightful than any which had preceded it, struck the trembling man as an arrow might have struck him. He dropped upon his knees at the side of the bed and thrust his fingers firmly into his ears. He had never swooned in his life, and was unfamiliar with the symptoms, but now he experienced a sensation of overpowering nausea; a blood-red mist floated before his eyes, and the floor seemed to rock beneath him like the deck of a ship. . . .

That soul-appalling outcry died away, merged into a sobbing, moaning sound which defied Soames' efforts to exclude it. . . . He rose to his feet, feeling physically ill, and turned to close his door. . . .

They were dragging someone—someone who sighed, shudderingly, and whose sighs sank to moans, and sometimes rose to sobs,—across the apartment of the dragon. In a faint, dying voice, the woman spoke again:—

"Not Mr. King! . . . *not Mr. King!* . . . Is there no God in Heaven! . . . *Ah!* spare me . . . spare" . . .

Soames closed the door and stood propped up against it, striving to fight down the deathly sickness which assailed him. His clothes were sticking to his clammy body, and a cold perspiration was trickling down his forehead and into his eyes. The sensation at his heart was unlike anything that he had ever known; he thought that he must be dying.

The awful sounds died away . . . then a muffled disturbance drew his attention to a sort of square trap which existed high up on one wall of the room, but which admitted no light, and which hitherto had never admitted any sound. Now, in the utter darkness, he found himself listening—listening . . .

He had learnt, during his duties in Block A, that each of the minute suites was rendered sound-proof in some way, so that what took place in one would be inaudible to the occupant of the next, provided that both doors were closed. He perceived, now, that some precaution hitherto exercised continuously had been omitted to-night, and that the sounds which he could hear came from the room next to his own—the room which

opened upon the corridor that he had never
entered, and which now he classified, mentally, as Block B.

What did it mean?

Obviously there had been some mishap
in the usually smooth conduct of Ho-Pin's
catacombs. There had been a hurried outgoing in several directions . . . a search?

And by the accident of his returning an
hour earlier than he was expected, he was
become a witness of this incident, or of its
dreadful, concluding phases. He had begun
to move away from the door, but now he
returned, and stood leaning against it.

That stifling room where roses shed their
petals, had been opened to-night; a chill
touched the very center of his being and told
him so. The occupant of that room—the Min-
otaur of this hideous labyrinth—was at large
to-night, was roaming the passages about
him, was perhaps outside his very door. . . .

Dull moaning sounds reached him through
the trap. He realized that if he had the courage to cross the room, stand upon a chair
and place his ear to the wall, he might be
able to detect more of what was passing in
the next apartment. But craven fear held him
in its grip, and in vain he strove to shake it
off. Trembling wildly, he stood with his back
to the door, whilst muttered words, and
moans, ever growing fainter, reached him
from beyond. A voice, a harsh, guttural
voice—surely not that of Ho-Pin—was audible, above the moaning.

For two minutes—three minutes—four
minutes—he stood there, tottering on the
brink of insensibility, then . . . a faint sound—
a new sound,—drew his gaze across the room,
and up to the corner where the trap was
situated.

A very dim light was dawning there; he
could just detect the outline of an opening—
a half-light breaking the otherwise impenetrable darkness.

He felt that his capacity for fear was
strained to its utmost; that he could support
nothing more, yet a new horror was in store
for him; for, as he watched that gray patch,
in it, as in a frame, a black silhouette appeared—the silhouette of a human head . . .
a woman's head!

Soames convulsively clenched his jaws,
for his teeth were beginning to chatter.

A whistle, an eerie, minor whistle, sub-
scribed the ultimate touch of terror to the
night. The silhouette disappeared, and,
shortly afterwards, the gray luminance. A

faint click told of some shutter being fastened; complete silence reigned.

Soames groped his way to the bed and
fell weakly upon it, half lying down and
burying his face in the pillow. For how long,
he had no idea, but for some considerable
time, he remained so, fighting to regain sufficient self-possession to lie to Ho-Pin, who
sooner or later must learn of his return.

At last he managed to sit up. He was not
trembling quite so wildly, but he still suffered from a deathly sickness. A faint streak
of light from the corridor outside shone under his door. As he noted it, it was joined
by a second streak, forming a triangle.

There was a very soft rasping of metal.
Someone was opening the door!

Soames lay back upon the bed. This time
he was past further panic and come to a stage
of sickly apathy. He lay, now, because he
could not sit upright, because stark horror
had robbed him of physical strength, and
had drained the well of his emotions dry.

Gradually—so that the operation seemed
to occupy an interminable time, the door
opened, and in the opening a figure appeared.

The switch clicked, and the room was
flooded with electric light.

Ho-Pin stood watching him.

Soames—in his eyes that indescribable
expression seen in the eyes of a bird placed
in a cobra's den—met the Chinaman's gaze.
This gaze was no different from that which
habitually he directed upon the people of the
catacombs. His yellow face was set in the
same mirthless smile, and his eyebrows were
raised interrogatively. For the space of ten
seconds he stood watching the man on the
bed. Then:—

"You wreturn vewry soon, Mr. Soames?"
he said, softly.

Soames groaned like a dying man, whispering:

"I was . . . taken ill—very ill." . . .

"So you wreturn befowre the time a-
wranged for you?"

His metallic voice was sunk in a soothing
hiss. He smiled steadily: he betrayed no
emotion.

"Yes . . . sir," whispered Soames, his hair
clammily adhering to his brow and beads of
perspiration trickling slowly down his nose.

"And when you wreturn, you see and
you hear—stwrange things, Mr. Soames?"

Soames, who was in imminent danger of
becoming physically ill, gulped noisily.

"No, sir," he whispered,—tremulously, "I've been—in here all the time."

Ho-Pin nodded, slowly and sympathetically, but never removed the glittering eyes from the face of the man on the bed.

"So you hear nothing, and see nothing?"

The words were spoken even more softly than he had spoken hitherto.

"Nothing," protested Soames. He suddenly began to tremble anew, and his trembling rattled the bed. "I have been—very ill indeed, sir."

Ho-Pin nodded again slowly, and with deep sympathy.

"Some medicine shall be sent to you, Mr. Soames," he said.

He turned and went out slowly, closing the door behind him.

XX

ABRAHAM LEVINSKY BUTTS IN

At about the time that this conversation was taking place in Ho-Pin's catacombs, Detective-Inspector Dunbar and Detective-Sergeant Sowerby were joined by a third representative of New Scotland Yard at the appointed spot by the dock gates. This was Stringer, the detective to whom was assigned the tracing of the missing Soames; and he loomed up through the rain-mist, a glistening but dejected figure.

"Any luck?" inquired Sowerby, sepulchrally.

Stringer, a dark and morose looking man, shook his head.

"I've beaten up every 'Chink' in Wapping and Limehouse, I should reckon," he said, plaintively. "They're all as innocent as babes unborn. You can take it from me: Chinatown hasn't got a murder on its conscience at present. Brr! it's a beastly night. Suppose we have one?"

Dunbar nodded, and the three wet investigators walked back for some little distance in silence, presently emerging via a narrow, dark, uninviting alleyway into West India Dock Road. A brilliantly lighted hostelry proved to be their objective, and there, in a quiet corner of the deserted billiard room, over their glasses, they discussed this mysterious case, which at first had looked so simple of solution if only because it offered so many unusual features, but which, the

deeper they probed, merely revealed fresh complications.

"The business of those Fry people, in Scotland, was a rotten disappointment," said Dunbar, suddenly. "They were merely paid by the late Mrs. Vernon to re-address letters to a little newspaper shop in Knightsbridge, where an untraceable boy used to call for them! Martin has just reported this evening. Perth wires for instructions, but it's a dead-end, I'm afraid."

"You know," said Sowerby, fishing a piece of cork from the brown froth of a fine example by Guinness, "to my mind our hope's in Soames; and if we want to find Soames, to my mind we want to look, not east, but west."

"Hear, hear!" concorded Stringer, gloomily sipping hot rum.

"It seems to me," continued Sowerby, "that Limehouse is about the last place in the world a man like Soames would think of hiding in."

"It isn't where he'll be *thinking* of hiding," snapped Dunbar, turning his fierce eyes upon the last speaker. "You can't seem to get the idea out of your head, Sowerby, that Soames is an independent agent. He *isn't* an independent agent. He's only the servant; and through the servant we hope to find the master."

"But why in the east-end?" came the plaintive voice of Stringer; "for only one reason, that I can see—because Max says that there's a Chinaman in the case."

"There's opium in the case, isn't there?" said Dunbar, adding more water to his whisky, "and where there's opium there is pretty frequently a Chinaman."

"But to my mind," persisted Sowerby, his eyebrows drawn together in a frown of concentration, "the place where Mrs. Vernon used to get the opium was the place we raided in Gillingham Street."

"Nurse Proctor's!" cried Stringer, banging his fist on the table. "Exactly my idea! There may have been a Chinaman concerned in the management of the Gillingham Street stunt, or there may not, but I'll swear that was where the opium was supplied. In fact I don't think that there's any doubt about it. Medical evidence (opinions differed a bit, certainly) went to show that she had been addicted to opium for some years. Other evidence—you got it yourself, Inspector—went to show that she came from Gillingham Street on the night of the murder. Gillingham Street crowd vanished like a beautiful dream before we had time to nab them! What more do you want? What are we up to, messing about in Limehouse and Wapping?''

Sowerby partook of a long drink and turned his eyes upon Dunbar, awaiting the inspector's reply.

''You both have the wrong idea!'' said Dunbar, deliberately; ''you are all wrong! You seem to be under the impression that if we could lay our hands upon the missing staff of the so-called Nursing Home, we should find the assassin to be one of the crowd. It doesn't follow at all. For a long time, you, Sowerby,''—he turned his tawny eyes upon the sergeant—''had the idea that Soames was the murderer, and I'm not sure that you have got rid of it yet! You, Stringer, appear to think that Nurse Proctor is responsible. Upon my word, you are a hopeless pair! Suppose Soames had nothing whatever to do with the matter, but merely realized that he could not prove an alibi? Wouldn't *you* bolt? I put it to you.''

Sowerby stared hard, and Stringer scratched his chin, reflectively.

''The same reasoning applies to the Gillingham Street people,'' continued Dunbar. ''We haven't the slightest idea of *their* whereabouts because we don't even know who they were; but we do know something about Soames, and we're looking for him, not because we think he did the murder, but because we think he can tell us who did.''

''Which brings us back to the old point,'' interrupted Stringer, softly beating his fist upon the table at every word; ''why are we looking for Soames in the east-end?''

''Because,'' replied Dunbar, ''we're working on the theory that Soames, though actually not accessory to the crime, was in the pay of those who were'' . . .

''Well?''—Stringer spoke the word eagerly, his eyes upon the inspector's face.

''And those who *were* accessory,''—continued Dunbar, ''were servants of Mr. King.''

''Ah!'' Stringer brought his fist down with a bang—''Mr. King! That's where I am in the dark, and where Sowerby, here, is in the dark.'' He bent forward over the table. ''Who the devil is Mr. King?''

Dunbar twirled his whisky glass between his fingers.

''We don't know,'' he replied quietly, ''but Soames does, in all probability; and that's why we're looking for Soames.''

''Is it why we're looking in Limehouse?'' persisted Stringer, the argumentative.

''It is,'' snapped Dunbar. ''We have only got one Chinatown worthy of the name, in London, and that's not ten minutes' walk from here.''

''Chinatown—yes,'' said Sowerby, his red face glistening with excitement; ''but why look for Mr. King in Chinatown?''

''Because,'' replied Dunbar, lowering his voice, ''Mr. King in all probability is a Chinaman.''

''Who says so?'' demanded Stringer.

''Max says so . . .''

''*Max!*''—again Stringer beat his fist upon the table. ''Now we have got to it! We're working, then, not on our own theories, but on those of Max?''

Dunbar's sallow face flushed slightly, and his eyes seemed to grow brighter.

''Mr. Gaston Max obtained information in Paris,'' he said, ''which he placed, unreservedly, at my disposal. We went into the matter thoroughly, with the result that our conclusions were identical. A certain Mr. King is at the bottom of this mystery, and, in all probability, Mr. King is a Chinaman. Do I make myself clear?''

Sowerby and Stringer looked at one another, perplexedly. Each man finished his drink in silence. Then:

''What took place in Paris?'' began Sowerby.

There was an interruption. A stooping figure in a shabby, black frock-coat, the figure of a man who wore a dilapidated bowler pressed down upon his ears, who had a greasy, Semitic countenance, with a scrubby, curling, sandy colored beard, sparse as the vegetation of a desert, appeared at Sowerby's elbow.

He carried a brimming pewter pot. This he set down upon a corner of the table, depositing himself in a convenient chair and pulling out a very dirty looking letter from an inside pocket. He smoothed it carefully. He peered, little-eyed, from the frowning face of Dunbar to the surprised countenance of Sowerby, and smiled with native amiability at the dangerous-looking Stringer.

''Excuthe me,'' he said, and his propitiatory smile was expansive and dazzling, ''excuthe me buttin' in like thith. It theemth rude, I know—it doth theem rude; but the fact of the matter ith I'm a tailor—thath's my pithneth, a tailor. When I thay a tailor, I really mean a breecheth-maker—tha'th what I mean, a breecheth-maker. Now thethe timeth ith very hard timeth for breecheth-maketh.'' . . .

Dunbar finished his whisky, and quietly replaced the glass upon the table, looking from Sowerby to Stringer with unmistakable significance. Stringer emptied his glass of rum, and Sowerby disposed of his stout.

"I got thith letter lath night," continued the breeches-maker, bending forward confidentially over the table. (The document looked at least twelve months old.) "I got thith letter latht night with thethe three fiverth in it; and not havin' no friendth in London—I'm an American thitithen, by birth,—Levinthky, my name ith—Abraham Levinthky—I'm a Noo Englander. Well, not havin' no friendth in London, and theein' you three gentlemen thittin' here, I took the liberty" . . .

Dunbar stood up, glared at Levinsky, and stalked out of the billard-room, followed by his equally indignant satellites. Having gained the outer door:

"Of all the blasted impudence!" he said, turning to Sowerby and Stringer; but there was a glint of merriment in the fierce eyes. "Can you beat that? Did you tumble to his game?"

Sowerby stared at Stringer, and Stringer stared at Sowerby.

"Except," began the latter in a voice hushed with amazement, "that he's got the coolest cheek of any mortal being I ever met." . . .

Dunbar's grim face relaxed, and he laughed boyishly, his square shoulders shaking.

"He was leading up to the confidence trick!" he said, between laughs. "Damn it all, man, it was the old confidence trick! The idea of a confidence-merchant spreading out his wares before three C. I. D. men!"

He was choking with laughter again; and now, Sowerby and Stringer having looked at one another for a moment, the surprised pair joined him in his merriment. They turned up their collars and went out into the rain, still laughing.

"That man," said Sowerby, as they walked across to the stopping place of the electric trams, "is capable of calling on the Commissioner and asking him to 'find the lady'!"

XXI

THE STUDIO IN SOHO

Certainly, such impudence as that of Mr. Levinsky is rare even in east-end London, and it may be worth while to return to the corner of the billiard-room and to study more closely this remarkable man.

He was sitting where the detectives had left him, and although their departure might have been supposed to have depressed him, actually it had had a contrary effect; he was chuckling with amusement, and, between his chuckles, addressing himself to the contents of the pewter with every mark of appreciation. Three gleaming golden teeth on the lower row, and one glittering canine, made a dazzling show every time that he smiled; he was a very greasy and a very mirthful Hebrew.

Finishing his tankard of ale, he shuffled out into the street, the line of his bent shoulders running parallel with that of his hat-brim. His hat appeared to be several sizes too large for his head, and his skull was only prevented from disappearing into the capacious crown by the intervention of his ears, which, acting as brackets, supported the whole weight of the rain-sodden structure. He mounted a tram proceeding in the same direction as that which had borne off the Scotland Yard men. Quitting this at Bow Road, he shuffled into the railway station, and from Bow Road proceeded to Liverpool Street. Emerging from the station at Liverpool Street, he entered a motor-'bus bound westward.

His neighbors, inside, readily afforded him ample elbow room; and, smiling agreeably at every one, including the conductor (who resented his good-humor) and a pretty girl in the corner seat (who found it embarrassing) he proceeded to Charing Cross. Descending from the 'bus, he passed out into Leicester Square and plunged into the network of streets which complicates the map of Soho. It will be of interest to follow him.

In a narrow turning off Greek Street, and within hail of the popular Bohemian restaurants, he paused before a doorway sandwiched between a Continental newsagent's and a tiny French café; and, having fumbled in his greasy raiment he presently produced a key, opening the door, carefully closed it behind him, and mounted the dark stair.

On the top floor he entered a studio, boasting a skylight upon which the rain was drumming steadily and drearily. Lighting a gas burner in one corner of the place which bore no evidence of being used for its legitimate purpose—he entered a little adjoining dressing-room. Hot and cold water were laid on there, and a large zinc bath stood upon the floor. With the aid of an enamel bucket, Mr. Abraham Levinsky filled the bath.

Leaving him to his ablutions, let us glance around the dressing-room. Although there was no easel in the studio, and no indication of artistic activity, the dressing-room was well stocked with costumes. Two huge dress-baskets were piled in one corner, and their contents hung upon hooks around the three available walls. A dressing table, with a triplicate mirror and a suitably shaded light, presented a spectacle reminiscent less of a model's dressing-room than of an actor's.

At the expiration of some twenty-five minutes, the door of this dressing-room opened; and although Abraham Levinsky had gone in, Abraham Levinsky did not come out!

Carefully flicking a particle of ash from a fold of his elegant, silk-lined cloak, a most distinguished looking gentleman stepped out onto the bleak and dirty studio. He wore, in addition to a graceful cloak, which was lined with silk of cardinal red, a soft black hat, rather wide brimmed and dented in a highly artistic manner, and irreproachable evening clothes; his linen was immaculate; and no valet in London could have surpassed the perfect knotting of his tie. His pearl studs were elegant and valuable; and a single eyeglass was swung about his neck by a thin, gold chain. The white gloves, which fitted perfectly, were new; and if the glossy boots were rather long in the toe-cap from an English point of view, the gold-headed malacca cane which the newcomer carried was quite *de rigueur*.

The strong clean-shaven face calls for no description here; it was the face of M. Gaston Max.

M. Max, having locked the study door, and carefully tried it to make certain of its security, descended the stairs. He peeped out cautiously into the street ere setting foot upon the pavement; but no one was in sight at the moment, and he emerged quickly, closing the door behind him, and taking shelter under the newsagent's awning. The rain continued its steady downpour, but M. Max stood there softly humming a little French melody until a taxi-cab crawled into view around the Greek Street corner.

He whistled shrilly through his teeth—the whistle of a gamin; and the cabman, glancing up and perceiving him, pulled around into the turning, and drew up by the awning.

M. Max entered the cab.

"To Frascati's," he directed.

The cabman backed out into Greek Street and drove off. This was the hour when the theaters were beginning to eject their throngs, and outside one of them, where a popular comedy had celebrated its three-hundred-and-fiftieth performance, the press of cabs and private cars was so great that M. Max found himself delayed within sight of the theater foyer.

Those patrons of the comedy who had omitted to order vehicles or who did not possess private conveyances, found themselves in a quandary to-night, and amongst those thus unfortunately situated, M. Max, watching the scene with interest, detected a lady whom he knew—none other than the delightful American whose conversation had enlivened his recent journey from Paris—Miss Denise Ryland. She was accompanied by a charming companion, who, although she was wrapped up in a warm theater cloak, seemed to be shivering disconsolately as she and her friend watched the interminable stream of vehicles filing up before the theater, and cutting them off from any chance of obtaining a cab for themselves.

M. Max acted promptly.

"Drive into that side turning!" he directed the cabman, leaning out of the window. The cabman followed his directions, and M. Max, heedless of the inclement weather, descended from the cab, dodged actively between the head lamps of a big Mercedes and the tail-light of a taxi, and stood bowing before the two ladies, his hat pressed to his bosom with one gloved hand, the other, ungloved, resting upon the gold knob of the malacca.

"Why!" cried Miss Ryland, "if it isn't . . . M. Gaston! My dear . . . M. Gaston! Come under the awning, or"—her head was wagging furiously—"you will be . . . simply drowned."

M. Max smilingly complied.

"This is M. Gaston," said Denise Ryland, turning to her companion, "the French gentleman . . . whom I met . . . in the train from . . . Paris. This is Miss Helen Cumberly, and I know you two will get on . . . famously."

M. Max acknowledged the presentation with a few simple words which served to place the oddly met trio upon a mutually easy footing. He was, *par excellence*, the polished cosmopolitan man of the world.

"Fortunately I saw your dilemma," he explained. "I have a cab on the corner yonder, and it is entirely at your service."

"Now that . . . is real good of you," declared Denise Ryland. "I think you're . . . a brick." . . .

"But, my dear Miss Ryland!" cried Helen, "we cannot possibly deprive M. Gaston of his cab on a night like this!"

"I had hoped," said the Frenchman, bowing gallantly, "that this most happy reunion might not be allowed to pass uncelebrated. Tell me if I intrude upon other plans, because I am speaking selfishly; but I was on my way to a lonely supper, and apart from the great pleasure which your company would afford me, you would be such very good Samaritans if you would join me."

Helen Cumberly, although she was succumbing rapidly to the singular fascination of M. Max, exhibited a certain hesitancy. She was no stranger to Bohemian customs, and if the distinguished Frenchman had been an old friend of her companion's, she should have accepted without demur; but she knew that the acquaintance had commenced in a Continental railway train, and her natural prudence instinctively took up a brief for the prosecution. But Denise Ryland had other views.

"My dear girl," she said, "you are not going to be so . . . crack-brained . . . as to stand here . . . arguing and contracting . . . rheumatism, lumbago . . . and other absurd complaints . . . when you know *perfectly* well that we had already arranged to go . . . to supper!" She turned to the smiling Max. "This girl needs . . . *dragging* out of . . . her morbid self . . . M. Gaston! We'll accept . . . your cab, on the distinct . . . understanding that you are to accept *our* invitation . . . to supper."

M. Max bowed agreeably.

"By all means let *my* cab take us to *your* supper," he said, laughing.

XXII

M. MAX MOUNTS CAGLIOSTRO'S STAIRCASE

At a few minutes before midnight, Helen Cumberly and Denise Ryland, escorted by the attentive Frenchman, arrived at Palace Mansions. Any distrust which Helen had experienced at first was replaced now by the esteem which every one of discrimination

(criminals excluded) formed of M. Max. She perceived in him a very exquisite gentleman, and although the acquaintance was but one hour old, counted him a friend. Denise Ryland was already quite at home in the Cumberly household, and she insisted that Dr. Cumberly would be deeply mortified should M. Gaston take his departure without making his acquaintance. Thus it came about that M. Gaston Max was presented (as "M. Gaston") to Dr. Cumberly.

Cumberly, who had learned to accept men and women upon his daughter's estimate, welcomed the resplendent Parisian hospitably; the warm, shaded lights made convivial play in the amber deeps of the decanters, and the cigars had a fire-side fragrance which M. Max found wholly irresistible.

The ladies being momentarily out of earshot, M. Gaston glancing rapidly about him, said: "May I beg a favor, Dr. Cumberly?"

"Certainly, M. Gaston," replied the physician—he was officiating at the syphon. "Say when."

"When!" said Max. "I should like to see you in Harley Street to-morrow morning."

Cumberly glanced up oddly. "Nothing wrong, I hope?"

"Oh, not professionally," smiled Max; "or perhaps I should say only semi-professionally. Can you spare me ten minutes?"

"My book is rather full in the morning, I believe," said Cumberly, frowning thoughtfully, "and without consulting it—which, since it is in Harley Street, is impossible—I scarcely know when I shall be at liberty. Could we not lunch together?"

Max blew a ring of smoke from his lips and watched it slowly dispersing.

"For certain reasons," he replied, and his odd American accent became momentarily more perceptible, "I should prefer that my visit had the appearance of being a professional one."

Cumberly was unable to conceal his surprise, but assuming that his visitor had good reason for the request, he replied after a moment's reflection:

"I should propose, then, that you come to Harley Street at, shall we say, 9.30? My earliest professional appointment is at 10. Will that inconvenience you?"

"Not at all," Max assured him; "it will suit me admirably."

With that the matter dropped for the time, since Helen and her new friend now reentered; and although Helen's manner was markedly depressed, Miss Ryland energetically turned the conversation upon the subject of the play which they had witnessed that evening.

M. Max, when he took his departure, found that the rain had ceased, and accordingly he walked up Whitehall, interesting himself in those details of midnight London life so absorbing to the visitor, though usually overlooked by the resident.

Punctually at half-past nine, a claret-colored figure appeared in sedate Harley Street. M. Gaston Max pressed the bell above which appeared:

DR. BRUCE CUMBERLY.

He was admitted by Garnham, who attended there daily during the hours when Dr. Cumberly was visible to patients, and presently found himself in the consulting room of the physician.

"Good morning, M. Gaston!" said Cumberly, rising and shaking his visitor by the hand. "Pray sit down, and let us get to business. I can give you a clear half-hour."

Max, by way of reply, selected a card from one of the several divisions of his card-case, and placed it on the table. Cumberly glanced at it and started slightly, turning and surveying his visitor with a new interest.

"You are M. Gaston Max!" he said, fixing his gray eyes upon the face of the man before him. "I understood my daughter to say" . . .

Max waved his hands, deprecatingly.

"It is in the first place to apologize," he explained, "that I am here. I was presented to your daughter in the name of Gaston—which is at least part of my own name—and because other interests were involved I found myself in the painful position of being presented to you under the same false colors" . . .

"Oh, dear, dear!" began Cumberly. "But—"

"Ah! I protest, it is true," continued Max with an inimitable movement of the shoulder; "and I regret it; but in my profession" . . .

"Which you adorn, monsieur," injected Cumberly.

"Many thanks—but in my profession these little annoyances sometimes occur. At the earliest suitable occasion, I shall reveal myself to Miss Cumberly and Miss Ryland, but at present,"—he spread his palms eloquently, and raised his eyebrows—"*morbleu!*

it is impossible."

"Certainly; I quite understand that. Your visit to London is a professional one? I am more than delighted to have met you, M. Max; your work on criminal anthroposcopy has an honored place on my shelves."

Again M. Max delivered himself of the deprecatory wave.

"You cover me with confusion," he protested; "for I fear in that book I have intruded upon sciences of which I know nothing, and of which you know much."

"On the contrary, you have contributed to those sciences, M. Max," declared the physician; "and now, do I understand that the object of your call this morning?" . . .

"In the first place it was to excuse myself—but in the second place, I come to ask your help."

He seated himself in a deep armchair—bending forward, and fixing his dark, penetrating eyes upon the physician. Cumberly, turning his own chair slightly, evinced the greatest interest in M. Max's disclosures.

"If you have been in Paris lately," continued the detective, "you will possibly have availed yourself of the opportunity—since another may not occur—of visiting the house of the famous magician, Cagliostro, on the corner of Rue St. Claude, and Boulevard Beaumarchais" . . .

"I have not been in Paris for over two years," said Cumberly, "nor was I aware that a house of that celebrated charlatan remained extant."

"Ah! Dr. Cumberly, your judgment of Cagliostro is a harsh one. We have no time for such discussion now, but I should like to debate with you this question: was Cagliostro a charlatan? However, the point is this: Owing to alterations taking place in the Boulevard Beaumarchais, some of the end houses in Rue St. Claude are being pulled down, among them Number 1, formerly occupied by the Comte de Cagliostro. At the time that the work commenced, I availed myself of a little leisure to visit that house, once so famous. I was very much interested, and found it fascinating to walk up the Grande Staircase where so many historical personages once walked to consult the seer. But great as was my interest in the apartments of Cagliostro, I was even more interested in one of the apartments in a neighboring house, into which—quite accidentally, you understand—I found myself looking."

XXIII

RAID IN THE RUE ST. CLAUDE

"I perceived," said M. Gaston Max, "that owing to the progress of the work of demolition, and owing to the carelessness of the people in charge—*nom d'un nom!* they were careless, those!—I was able, from a certain point, to look into a small room fitted up in a way very curious. There was a sort of bunk somewhat similar to that in a steamer berth, and the walls were covered with paper of a Chinese pattern—most bizarre. No one was in the room when I first perceived it, but I had not been looking in for many moments before a Chinaman entered and closed the shutters. He was hasty, this one.

"*Eh bien!* I had seen enough. I perceived that my visit to the house of Cagliostro had been dictated by a good little angel. It happened that for many months I had been in quest of the headquarters of a certain group which I knew, beyond any tiny doubt, to have its claws deep in Parisian society. I refer to an opium syndicate" . . .

Dr. Cumberly started and seemed about to speak; but he restrained himself, bending forward and awaiting the detective's next words with even keener interest than hitherto.

"I had been trying—all vainly—to trace the source from which the opium was obtained, and the place where it was used. I have devoted much attention to the subject, and have spent some twelve months in the opium provinces of China, you understand. I know how insidious a thing it is, this opium, and how dreadful a curse it may become when it gets a hold upon a community. I was formerly engaged upon a most sensational case in San Francisco; and the horrors of the discoveries which we made there— the American police and myself—have remained with me ever since. *Pardieu!* I cannot forget them! Therefore when I learnt that an organized attempt was being made to establish elaborate opium dens upon a most up-to-date plan, in Paris, I exerted myself to the utmost to break up this scheme in its infancy" . . .

Dr. Cumberly was hanging upon every word.

"Apart from the physical and moral ruin attendant upon the vice," continued Max, "the methods of this particular organization have brought financial ruin to many." He shook his finger at Dr. Cumberly as if to emphasize his certainty upon this point. "I will not go into particulars now, but there is a system of wholesale robbery—*sapristi!* of most ingenious brigandage—being practised by this group. Therefore I congratulated myself upon the inspiration which had led me to mount Cagliostro's staircase. The way in which these people had conducted their sinister trade from so public a spot as this was really wonderful, but I had already learned to respect the ingenuity of the group, or of the man at the head of it. I wasted no time; not I! We raided the house that evening" . . .

"And what did you find?" asked Dr. Cumberly, eagerly.

"We found this establishment elaborately fitted, and the whole of the fittings were American. *Eh bien!* This confirmed me in my belief that the establishment was a branch of the wealthy concern I have mentioned in San Francisco. There was also a branch in New York, apparently. We found six or eight people in the place in various stages of coma; and I cannot tell you their names because— among them were some well-known in the best society" . . .

"Good Heavens, M. Max, you surprise and shock me!"

"What I tell you is but the truth. We apprehended two low fellows who acted as servants sometimes in the place. We had records of both of them at the Bureau. And there was also a woman belonging to the same class. None of these seemed to me very important, but we were fortunate enough to capture, in addition, a Chinaman—Sen—and a certain Madame Jean—the latter the principal of the establishment!"

"What! a woman?"

"*Morbleu!* a woman—exactly! You are surprised? Yes; and I was surprised, but full inquiry convinced me that Madame Jean was the chief of staff. We had conducted the raid at night, of course, and because of the big names, we hushed it up. We can do these things in Paris so much more easily than is possible here in London." He illustrated, delivering a kick upon the person of an imaginary malefactor. "*Cochon! Va!*" he shrugged. "It is finished!

"The place was arranged with Oriental magnificence. The reception-room—if I can so term that apartment—was like the scene of Rimsky Korsakov's *Shéhérezade;* I could see that very heavy charges were made at this establishment. I will not bore you with further particulars, but I will tell you of my disappointment."

"Your disappointment?"

"Yes, I was disappointed. True, I had brought about the closing of that house, but of the huge sums of money fraudulently obtained from victims, I could find no trace in the accounts of Madame Jean. She defied me with silence, simply declining to give any account of herself beyond admitting that she conduted an hotel at which opium might be smoked if desired. *Blagueur!* Sen, the Chinaman, who professed to speak nothing but Chinese—ah! *cochon!*—was equally a difficult case, *Nom d'un nom!* I was in despair, for apart from frauds connected with the concern, I had more than small suspicions that at least one death—that of a wealthy banker—could be laid at the doors of the establishment in Rue St. Claude." . . .

Dr. Cumberly bent yet lower, watching the speaker's face.

"A murder!" he whispered.

"I do not say so," replied Max, "but it certainly might have been. The case then must, indeed, have ended miserably, as far as I was concerned, if I had not chanced upon a letter which the otherwise prudent Madame Jean had forgotten to destroy. *Triomphe!* It was a letter of instruction, and definitely it proved that she was no more than a kind of glorified *conciérge*, and that the chief of the opium group was in London."

"Undoubtedly in London. There was no address on the letter, and no date, and it was curiously signed: Mr. King."

"Mr. King!"

Dr. Cumberly rose slowly from his chair, and took a step toward M. Max.

"You are interested?" said the detective, and shrugged his shoulders, whilst his mobile mouth shaped itself in a grim smile. *"Pardieu!* I knew you would be! Acting upon another clue which the letter—priceless letter—contained, I visited the Crédit Lyonnais. I discovered that an account had been opened there by Mr. Henry Leroux of London on behalf of his wife, Mira Leroux, to the amount of a thousand pounds."

"A thousand pounds—really!" cried Dr. Cumberly, drawing his heavy brows together—"as much as that?"

"Certainly. It was for a thousand pounds," repeated Max, "and the whole of that amount had been drawn out."

"The whole thousand?"

"The whole thousand; *nom d'un p'tit bonhomme!* The whole thousand! Acting, as I have said, upon the information in this always priceless letter, I confronted Madame Jean and the manager of the bank with each other. *Morbleu!* 'This,' he said, 'is Mira Leroux of London!' " . . .

"What!" cried Cumberly, seemingly quite stupefied by this last revelation.

Max spread wide his palms, and the flexible lips expressed sympathy with the doctor's stupefaction.

"It is as I tell you," he continued. "This Madame Jean had been posing as Mrs. Leroux, and in some way, which I was unable to understand, her signature had been accepted by the Crédit Lyonnais. I examined the specimen signature which had been forwarded to them by the London County and Suburban Bank, and I perceived, at once, that it was not a case of common forgery. The signatures were identical" . . .

"Therefore," said Cumberly, and he was thinking of Henry Leroux, whom Fate delighted in buffeting—"therefore, the Crédit Lyonnais is not responsible?"

"Most decidedly not responsible," agreed Max. "So you see I now have two reasons for coming to London: one, to visit the London County and Suburban Bank, and the other to find . . . Mr. King. The first part of my mission I have performed successfully; but the second" . . . again he shrugged, and the lines of his mouth were humorous.

Dr. Cumberly began to walk up and down the carpet.

"Poor Leroux!" he muttered—"poor Leroux."

"Ah! poor Leroux, indeed," said Max. "He is so typical a victim of this most infernal group!"

"What!" Dr. Cumberly turned in his promenade and stared at the detective—"he's not the only one?"

"My dear sir," said Max, gently, "the victims of Mr. King are truly as the sands of Arabia."

"Good heavens!" muttered Dr. Cumberly; "good heavens!"

"I came immediately to London," continued Max, "and presented myself at New Scotland Yard. There I discovered that my inquiry was complicated by a ghastly crime which had been committed in the flat of Mr.

Leroux; but I learned, also, that Mr. King was concerned in this crime—his name had been found upon a scrap of paper clenched in the murdered woman's hand!"

"I was present when it was found," said Dr. Cumberly.

"I know you were," replied Max. "In short, I discovered that the Palace Mansions murder case was my case, and that my case was the Palace Mansions case. *Eh bien!* the mystery of the Paris draft did not detain me long. A call upon the manager of the London County and Suburban Bank at Charing Cross revealed to me the whole plot. The real Mrs. Leroux had never visited that bank; it was Madame Jean, posing as Mrs. Leroux, who went there and wrote the specimen signature, accompanied by a certain Soames, a butler" . . .

"I know him!" said Dr. Cumberly, grimly, "the blackguard!"

"Truly a blackguard, truly a big, dirty blackguard! But it is such *canaille* as this that Mr. King discovers and uses for his own ends. Paris society, I know for a fact, has many such a cankerworm in its heart. Oh! it is a big case, a very big case. Poor Mr. Leroux being confined to his bed—ah! I pity him— I took the opportunity to visit his flat in Palace Mansions with Inspector Dunbar, and I obtained further evidence showing how the conspiracy had been conducted; yes. For instance, Dunbar's notebook showed me that Mr. Leroux was accustomed to receive letters from Mrs. Leroux whilst she was supposed to be in Paris. I actually discovered some of those letters, and they bore no dates. This, if they came from a woman, was not remarkable, but, upon one of them I found something that *was* remarkable. It was still in its envelope, you must understand, this letter, its envelope bearing the Paris postmark. But impressed upon the paper I discovered a second post-mark, which, by means of a simple process, and the use of a magnifying glass, I made out to be *Bow, East!*"

"What!"

"Do you understand? This letter, and others doubtless, had been enclosed in an envelope and despatched to Paris from Bow, East? In short, Mrs. Leroux wrote those letters before she left London; Soames never posted them, but handed them over to some representative of Mr. King; this other, in turn, posted them to Madame Jean in Paris! *Morbleu!* these are clever rogues! This which I

was fortunate enough to discover had been on top, you understand, this *billet*, and the outer envelope being very heavily stamped, that below retained the impress of the postmark."

"Poor Leroux!" said Cumberly again, with suppressed emotion. "That unsuspecting, kindly soul has been drawn into the meshes of this conspiracy. How they have been wound around him, until." . . .

"He knows the truth about his wife?" asked Max, suddenly glancing up at the physician, "that she is not in Paris?"

"I, myself, broke the painful news to him," replied Cumberly—"after a consultation with Miss Ryland and my daughter. I considered it my duty to tell him, but I cannot disguise from myself that it hastened, if it did not directly occasion, his breakdown."

"Yes, yes," said Max; "we have been very fortunate however in diverting the attention of the press from the absence of Mrs. Leroux throughout this time. *Nom d'un nom!* Had they got to know about the scrap of paper found in the dead woman's hand, I fear that this would have been impossible."

"I do not doubt that it would have been impossible, knowing the London press," replied Dr. Cumberly, "but I, too, am glad that it has been achieved; for in the light of your Paris discoveries, I begin at last to understand."

"You were not Mrs. Leroux's medical adviser?"

"I was not," replied Cumberly, glancing sharply at Max. "Good heavens, to think that I had never realized the truth!"

"It is not so wonderful at all. Of course, as I have seen from the evidence which you gave to the police, you knew that Mrs. Vernon was addicted to the use of opium?"

"It was perfectly evident," replied Cumberly; "painfully evident. I will not go into particulars, but her entire constitution was undermined by the habit. I may add, however, that I did not associate the vice with her violent end, except" . . .

"Ah!" interrupted Max, shaking his finger at the physician, "you are coming to the point upon which you disagreed with the divisional surgeon! Now, it is an important point. You are of opinion that the injection in Mrs. Vernon's shoulder—which could not have been self-administered" . . .

"She was not addicted to the use of the needle," interrupted Cumberly; "she was an opium *smoker*."

"Quite so, quite so," said Max: "it makes the point all the more clear. You are of opinion that this injection was made at least eight hours before the woman's death?"

"At least eight hours—yes."

"Eh bien!" said Max; "and have you had extensive experience of such injections?"

Dr. Cumberly stared at him in some surprise.

"In a general way," he said, "a fair number of such cases have come under my notice; but it chances that one of my patients, a regular patient—is addicted to the vice."

"Injections?"

"Only as a makeshift. He has periodical bouts of opium smoking—what I may term deliberate debauches."

"Ah!" Max was keenly interested. "This patient is a member of good society?"

"He's a member of Parliament," replied Cumberly, a faint, humorous glint creeping into his gray eyes; "but, of course, that is not an answer to your question! Yes, he is of an old family, and is engaged to the daughter of a peer."

"Dr. Cumberly," said Max, "in a case like the present—apart from the fact that the happiness—*pardieu!* the life—of one of your own friends is involved . . . should you count it a breach of professional etiquette to divulge the name of that patient?"

It was a disturbing question; a momentous question for a fashionable physician to be called upon to answer thus suddenly. Dr. Cumberly, who had resumed his promenade of the carpet, stopped with his back to M. Max, and stared out of the window into Harley Street.

M. Max, a man of refined susceptibilities, came to his aid, diplomatically.

"It is perhaps overmuch to ask you," he said. "I can settle the problem in a more simple manner. Inspector Dunbar will ask you for this gentleman's name, and you, as witness in the case, cannot refuse to give it."

"I can refuse until I stand in the witness-box!" replied Cumberly, turning, a wry smile upon his face.

"With the result," interposed Max, "that the ends of justice might be defeated, and the wrong man hanged!"

"True," said Cumberly; "I am splitting hairs. It is distinctly a breach of professional etiquette, nevertheless, and I cannot disguise the fact from myself. However, since

the knowledge will never go any further, and since tremendous issues are at stake, I will give you the name of my opium patient. It is Sir Brian Malpas!"

"I am much indebted to you, Dr. Cumberly," said Max; "a thousand thanks;" but in his eyes there was a far-away look. "Malpas—Malpas! Where in this case have I met with the name of Malpas?" . . .

"Inspector Dunbar may possibly have mentioned it to you in reference to the evidence of Mr. John Exel, M. P. Mr. Exel, you may remember" . . .

"I have it!" cried Max; *"Nom d'un nom!* I have it! It was from Sir Brian Malpas that he had parted at the corner of Victoria Street on the night of the murder, is it not so?"

"Your memory is very good, M. Max!"

"Then Mr. Exel is a personal friend of Sir Brian Malpas?"

"Excellent! Kismet aids me still! I come to you hoping that you may be acquainted with the constitution of Mrs. Leroux, but no! behold me disappointed in this. Then—*morbleu!* among your patients I find a possible client of the opium syndicate!"

"What! Malpas? Good God! I had not thought of that! Of course, he must retire somewhere from the ken of society to indulge in these opium orgies" . . .

"Quite so. I have hopes. Since it would never do for Sir Brian Malpas to know who I am and what I seek, a roundabout introduction is provided by kindly Providence— Ah! that good little angel of mine!—in the person of Mr. John Exel, M. P."

"I will introduce you to Mr. Exel with pleasure."

"Eh bien! Let it be arranged as soon as possible," said M. Max. "To Mr. John Exel I will be, as to Miss Ryland (*morbleu!* I hate me!) and Miss Cumberly (*pardieu!* I loathe myself!), M. Gaston! It is ten o'clock, and already I hear your first patient ringing at the front-door bell. Good morning, Dr. Cumberly."

Dr. Cumberly grasped his hand cordially.

"Good morning, M. Max!"

The famous detective was indeed retiring, when:

"M. Max!"

He turned—and looked into the troubled gray eyes of Dr. Cumberly.

"You would ask me where is she—Mrs. Leroux?" he said. "My friend—I may call you my friend, may I not?—I cannot say if she is living or is dead. Some little I know of the Chinese, quite a little; *nom de dieu!* . . . I hope she is dead!'' . . .

XXIV

OPIUM

Denise Ryland was lunching that day with Dr. Cumberly and his daughter at Palace Mansions; and as was usually the case when this trio met, the conversation turned upon the mystery.

"I have just seen Leroux," said the physician, as he took his seat, "and I have told him that he must go for a drive to-morrow. I have released him from his room, and given him the run of the place again, but until he can get right away, complete recovery is impossible. A little cheerful company might be useful, though. You might look in and see him for a while, Helen?"

Helen met her father's eyes, gravely, and replied, with perfect composure, "I will do so with pleasure. Miss Ryland will come with me."

"Suppose," said Denise Ryland, assuming her most truculent air, "you leave off . . . talking in that . . . frigid manner . . . my dear. Considering that Mira . . . Leroux and I were . . . old friends, and that you . . . are old friends of hers, too, and considering that I spend . . . my life amongst . . . people who very sensibly call . . . one another . . . by their Christian names, forget that my name is Ryland, and call me . . . Denise!"

"I should love to!" cried Helen Cumberly; "in fact, I wanted to do so the very first time I saw you; perhaps because Mira Leroux always referred to you as Denise" . . .

"May I also avail myself of the privilege?" inquired Dr. Cumberly with gravity, "and may I hope that you will return the compliment?"

"I cannot . . . do it!" declared Denise Ryland, firmly. "A doctor . . . should never be known by any other name than . . . Doctor. If I heard any one refer to my own . . . physician as Jack or . . . Bill, or Dick . . . I should lose *all* faith in him at once!"

As the lunch proceeded, Dr. Cumberly gradually grew more silent, seeming to be employed with his own thoughts; and although his daughter and Denise Ryland were discussing the very matter that engaged his own attention, he took no part in the conversation for some time. Then:

"I agree with you!" he said, suddenly, interrupting Helen; "the greatest blow of all to Leroux was the knowledge that his wife had been deceiving him."

"He invited . . . deceit!" proclaimed Denise Ryland, "by his . . . criminal neglect."

"Oh! how can you say so!" cried Helen, turning her gray eyes upon the speaker reproachfully; "he deserves—"

"He certainly deserves to know the real truth," concluded Dr. Cumberly; "but would it relieve his mind or otherwise?"

Denise Ryland and Helen looked at him in silent surprise.

"The truth?" began the latter—"Do you mean that you know—where she is" . . .

"If I knew that," replied Dr. Cumberly, "I should know everything; the mystery of the Palace Mansions murder would be a mystery no longer. But I know one thing: Mrs. Leroux's absence has nothing to do with any love affair."

"What!" exclaimed Denise Ryland. "There isn't another man . . . in the case? You can't tell me" . . .

"But I *do* tell you!" said Dr. Cumberly; "I *assure* you."

"And you have not told—Mr. Leroux?" said Helen incredulously. "You have *not* told him—although you know that the thought— of *that* is?" . . .

"Is practically killing him? No, I have not told him yet. For—would my news act as a palliative or as an irritant?"

"That depends," pronounced Denise Ryland, "on the nature of . . . your news."

"I suppose I have no right to conceal it from him. Therefore, we will tell him to-day. But although, beyond doubt, his mind will be relieved upon one point, the real facts are almost, if not quite, as bad."

"I learnt, this morning," he continued, lighting a cigarette, "certain facts which, had I been half as clever as I supposed myself, I should have deduced from the data already in my possession. I was aware, of course, that the unhappy victim—Mrs. Vernon—was addicted to the use of opium, and if a tangible link were necessary, it existed in the form of the written fragment which I myself took from the dead woman's hand." . . .

"A link!" said Denise Ryland.

"A link between Mrs. Vernon and Mrs.

Leroux," explained the physician. "You see, it had never occurred to me that they knew one another." . . .

"And did they?" questioned his daughter, eagerly.

"It is almost certain that they were acquainted, at any rate; and in view of certain symptoms, which, without giving them much consideration, I nevertheless had detected in Mrs. Leroux, I am disposed to think that the bond of sympathy which existed between them was" . . .

He seemed to hesitate, looking at his daughter, whose gray eyes were fixed upon him intently, and then at Denise Ryland, who, with her chin resting upon her hands, and her elbows propped upon the table, was literally glaring at him.

"Opium!" he said.

A look of horror began slowly to steal over Helen Cumberly's face; Denise Ryland's head commenced to sway from side to side. But neither woman spoke.

"By the courtesy of Inspector Dunbar," continued Dr. Cumberly, "I have been enabled to keep in touch with the developments of the case, as you know; and he had noted as a significant fact that the late Mrs. Vernon's periodical visits to Scotland corresponded, curiously, with those of Mrs. Leroux to Paris. I don't mean in regard to date; although in one or two instances (notably Mrs. Vernon's last journey to Scotland, and that of Mrs. Leroux to Paris), there was similarity even in this particular. A certain Mr. Debnam—the late Horace Vernon's solicitor—placed an absurd construction upon this" . . .

"Do you mean," interrupted Helen in a strained voice, "that he—insinuated that Mrs. Vernon" . . .

"He had an idea that she visited Leroux—yes," replied her father hastily. "It was one of those absurd and irritating theories, which, instinctively, we know to be wrong, but which, if asked for evidence, we cannot hope to *prove* to be wrong."

"It is outrageous!" cried Helen, her eyes flashing indignantly; "Mr. Debnam should be ashamed of himself!"

Dr. Cumberly smiled rather sadly.

"In this world," he said, "we have to count with the Debnams. One's own private knowledge of a man's character is not worth a brass farthing as legal evidence. But I am happy to say that Dunbar completely pooh-poohed the idea."

"I like Inspector Dunbar!" declared Helen; "he is so strong—a splendid man!"

Denise Ryland stared at her cynically, but made no remark.

"The inspector and myself," continued Dr. Cumberly, "attached altogether a different significance to the circumstances. I am pleased to tell you that Debnam's unpleasant theories are already proved fallacious; the case goes deeper, far deeper, than a mere intrigue of that kind. In short, I am now assured—I cannot, unfortunately, name the source of my new information—but I am assured, that Mrs. Leroux, as well as Mrs. Vernon, was addicted to the opium vice." . . .

"Oh, my God! how horrible!" whispered Helen.

"A certain notorious character," resumed Dr. Cumberly . . .

"Soames!" snapped Denise Ryland. "Since I heard . . . that man's name I knew him for . . . a villain . . . of the worst possible . . . description . . . imaginable."

"Soames," replied Dr. Cumberly, smiling slightly, "was one of the group, beyond doubt—for I may as well explain that we are dealing with an elaborate organization; but the chief member, to whom I have referred, is a greater one than Soames. He is a certain shadowy being, known as Mr. King."

"The name on the paper!" said Helen, quickly. "But of course the police have been looking for Mr. King all along?"

"In a general way—yes; but as we have thousands of Kings in London alone, the task is a stupendous one. The information which I received this morning narrows down the search immensely; for it points to Mr. King being the chief, or president, of a sort of opium syndicate, and, furthermore, it points to his being a Chinaman."

"A Chinaman!" cried Denise and Helen together.

"It is not absolutely certain, but it is more than probable. The point is that Mrs. Leroux has not eloped with some unknown lover; she is in one of the opium establishments of Mr. King."

"Do you mean that she is detained there?" asked Helen.

"It appears to me, now, to be certain that she is. My hypothesis is that she was an habitué of this place, as also was Mrs. Vernon. These unhappy women, by means of elaborate plans, made on their behalf by the

syndicate, indulged in periodical opium orgies. It was a game well worth the candle,
as the saying goes, from the syndicate's
standpoint; for Mrs. Leroux, alone, has paid
no less than a thousand pounds to the opium
group!"

"A thousand pounds!" cried Denise Ryland. "You don't mean to tell me that that . . .
silly fool . . . of a man, Harry Leroux . . . has
allowed himself to be swindled of . . . all that
money?"

"There is not the slightest doubt about it,"
Dr. Cumberly assured her; "he opened a credit
to that amount in Paris, and the entire sum
has been absorbed by Mr. King!"

"It's almost incredible!" said Helen.

"I quite agree with you," replied her father.
"Of course, most people know that there are
opium dens in London, as in almost every
other big city, but the existence of these palatial establishments, conducted by Mr. King,
although undoubtedly a fact, is a fact difficult
to accept. It doesn't seem possible that such
a place can be conducted secretly; whereas I
am assured that all the efforts of Scotland
Yard thus far have failed to locate the site of
the London branch."

"But surely," cried Denise Ryland, nostrils dilated indignantly, "some of the . . .
customers of this . . . disgusting place . . .
can be followed?" . . .

"The difficulty is to identify them," explained Cumberly. "Opium smoking is essentially a secret vice; a man does not visit
an opium den openly as he would visit his
club; and the elaborate precautions adopted
by the women are illustrated in the case of
Mrs. Vernon, and in the case of Mrs. Leroux.
It is a pathetic fact almost daily brought home
to me, that women who acquire a drug habit
become more rapidly and more entirely enslaved by it than does a man. It becomes the
center of the woman's existence; it becomes
her god: all other claims, social and domestic, are disregarded. Upon this knowledge,
Mr. King has established his undoubtedly
extensive enterprise." . . .

Dr. Cumberly stood up.

"I will go down and see Leroux," he announced quietly. "His sorrow hitherto has
been secondary to his indignation. Possibly
ignorance in this case is preferable to the
truth, but nevertheless I am determined to
tell him what I know. Give me ten minutes
or so, and then join me. Are you agreeable?"

"Quite," said Helen.

Dr. Cumberly departed upon his self-
imposed mission.

XXV

FATE'S SHUTTLECOCK

Some ten minutes later, Helen Cumberly and
Denise Ryland were in turn admitted to Henry
Leroux's flat. They found him seated on a
couch in his dining-room, wearing the inevitable dressing-gown. Dr. Cumberly, his
hands clasped behind him, stood looking out
of the window.

Leroux's pallor now was most remarkable; his complexion had assumed an ivory
whiteness which lent his face a sort of
statuesque beauty. He was cleanly shaven
(somewhat of a novelty), and his hair was
brushed back from his brow. But the dark
blue eyes were very tragic.

He rose at sight of his new visitors, and
a faint color momentarily tinged his cheeks.
Helen Cumberly grasped his outstretched
hand, then looked away quickly to where her
father was standing.

"I almost thought," said Leroux, "that you
had deserted me."

"No," said Helen, seeming to speak with
an effort—"we—my father, thought—that
you needed quiet."

Denise Ryland nodded grimly.

"But now," she said, in her most truculent manner. "we are going to . . . drag you
out of . . . your morbid . . . self . . . for a
change . . . which you need . . . if ever a
man . . . needed it."

"I have just prescribed a drive," said Dr.
Cumberly, turning to them, "for to-morrow
morning; with lunch at Richmond and a walk
across the park, rejoining the car at the Bushey
Gate, and so home to tea."

Henry Leroux looked eagerly at Helen in
silent appeal. He seemed to fear that she
would refuse.

"Do you mean that you have included us
in the prescription, father?" she asked.

"Certainly; you are an essential part of it."

"It will be fine," said the girl quietly; "I
shall enjoy it."

"Ah!" said Leroux, with a faint note of
contentment in his voice; and he reseated
himself.

There was an interval of somewhat awkward silence, to be broken by Denise Ryland.

"Dr. Cumberly has told you the news?" she asked, dropping for the moment her syncopated and pugnacious manner.

Leroux closed his eyes and leant back upon the couch.

"Yes," he replied. "And to think that I am a useless wreck—a poor parody of a man—whilst—Mira is . . . Oh, God! help me!—God help *her!*"

He was visibly contending with his emotions; and Helen Cumberly found herself forced to turn her head aside.

"I have been blind," continued Leroux, in a forced, monotonous voice. "That Mira has not—deceived me, in the worst sense of the word, is in no way due to my care of her. I recognize that, and I accept my punishment; for I deserved it. But what now overwhelms me is the knowledge, the frightful knowledge, that in a sense I have misjudged her, that I have remained here inert, making no effort, thinking her absence voluntary, whilst—God help her!—she has been" . . .

"Once again, Leroux," interrupted Dr. Cumberly, "I must ask you not to take too black a view. I blame myself more than I blame you, for having failed to perceive what as an intimate friend I had every opportunity to perceive; that your wife was acquiring the opium habit. You have told me that you count her as dead"—he stood beside Leroux, resting both hands upon the bowed shoulders—"I have not encouraged you to change that view. One who has cultivated—the—vice, to a point where protracted absences become necessary—you understand me?—is, so far as my experience goes" . . .

"Incurable! I quite understand," jerked Leroux. "A thousand times better dead, indeed."

"The facts as I see them," resumed the physician, "as I see them, are these: by some fatality, at present inexplicable, a victim of the opium syndicate met her death in this flat. Realizing that the inquiries brought to bear would inevitably lead to the cross-examination of Mrs. Leroux, the opium syndicate has detained her; was forced to detain her."

"Where is the place," began Leroux, in a voice rising higher with every syllable—"where is the infamous den to which—to which" . . .

Dr. Cumberly pressed his hands firmly upon the speaker's shoulders.

"It is only a question of time, Leroux," he said, "and you will have the satisfaction of knowing that—though at a great cost to yourself—this dreadful evil has been stamped out, that this yellow peril has been torn from the heart of society. Now, I must leave you for the present; but rest assured that everything possible is being done to close the nets about Mr. King."

"Ah!" whispered Leroux, "*Mr. King!*"

"The circle is narrowing," continued the physician. "I may not divulge confidences; but a very clever man—the greatest practical criminologist in Europe—is devoting the whole of his time, night and day, to this object."

Helen Cumberly and Denise Ryland exhibited a keen interest in the words, but Leroux, with closed eyes, merely nodded in a dull way. Shortly, Dr. Cumberly took his departure, and, Helen looking at her companion interrogatively:—

"I think," said Denise Ryland, addressing Leroux, "that you should not over-tax your strength at present." She walked across to where he sat, and examined some proofslips lying upon the little table beside the couch. " 'Martin Zeda,' " she said, with a certain high disdain. "Leave 'Martin Zeda' alone for once, and read a really cheerful book!"

Leroux forced a smile to his lips.

"The correction of these proofs," he said diffidently, "exacts no great mental strain, but is sufficient to—distract my mind. Work, after all, is nature's own sedative."

"I rather agree with Mr. Leroux, Denise," said Helen;—"and really you must allow him to know best."

"Thank you," said Leroux, meeting her eyes momentarily. "I feared that I was about to be sent to bed like a naughty boy!"

"I hope it's fine to-morrow," said Helen rapidly. "A drive to Richmond will be quite delightful."

"I think, myself," agreed Leroux, "that it will hasten my recovery to breathe the fresh air once again."

Knowing how eagerly he longed for health and strength, and to what purpose, the girl found something very pathetic in the words.

"I wish you were well enough to come out this afternoon," she said; "I am going to a private view at Olaf van Noord's studio. It is sure to be an extraordinary afternoon. He is the god of the Soho futurists, you know. And his pictures are the weirdest nightmares imaginable. One always meets such singular people there, too, and I am honored in receiving an invitation to represent the *Planet!*"

"I consider," said Denise Ryland, head wagging furiously again, "that the man is . . . mad. He had an exhibition . . . in Paris . . . and everybody . . . laughed at him . . . simply *laughed* at him."

"But financially, he is very successful," added Helen.

"Financially!" exclaimed Denise Ryland, *"Financially!* To criticize a man's work . . . financially, is about as . . . sensible as . . . to judge the Venus . . . de Milo . . . by weight!—or to sell the works . . . of Leonardo . . . da Vinci by the . . . yard! Olaf van Noord is nothing but . . . a fool . . . of the worst possible . . . description . . . imaginable."

"He is at least an entertaining fool!" protested Helen, laughingly.

"A mountebank!" cried Denise Ryland; "a clown . . . a pantaloon . . . a whole family of . . . idiots . . . rolled into one!"

"It seems unkind to run away and leave you here—in your loneliness," said Helen to Leroux; "but really I must be off to the wilds of Soho." . . .

"To-morrow," said Leroux, standing up and fixing his eyes upon her lingeringly, "will be a red-letter day. I have no right to complain, whilst such good friends remain to me—such true friends." . . .

XXVI

"OUR LADY OF THE POPPIES"

A number of visitors were sprinkled about Olaf van Noord's large and dirty studio, these being made up for the most part of those weird and nondescript enthusiasts who seek to erect an apocryphal Montmartre in the plains of Soho. One or two ordinary mortals, representing the Press, leavened the throng, but the entire gathering—"advanced" and unenlightened alike—seemed to be drawn to a common focus: a large canvas placed advantageously in the southeast corner of the studio, where it enjoyed all the benefit of a pure and equably suffused light.

Seated apart from his worshipers upon a little sketching stool, and handling a remarkably long, amber cigarette-holder with much grace, was Olaf van Noord. He had hair of so light a yellow as sometimes to appear white, worn very long, brushed back from his brow and cut squarely all around behind, lending him a medieval appearance. He wore a slight mustache carefully pointed; and his scanty vandyke beard could not entirely conceal the weakness of his chin. His complexion had the color and general appearance of drawing-paper, and in his large blue eyes was an eerie hint of sightlessness. He was attired in a light tweed suit cut in an American pattern, and out from his low collar flowed a black French knot.

Olaf van Noord rose to meet Helen Cumberly and Denise Ryland, advancing across the floor with the measured gait of a tragic actor. He greeted them aloofly, and a little negro boy proffered tiny cups of China tea. Denise Ryland distended her nostrils as her gaze swept the picture-covered walls; but she seemed to approve of the tea.

The artist next extended to them an ivory box containing little yellow-wrapped cigarettes. Helen Cumberly smilingly refused, but Denise Ryland took one of the cigarettes, sniffed at it superciliously—and then replaced it in the box.

"It has a most . . . egregiously horrible . . . odor," she commented.

"They are a special brand," explained Olaf van Noord, distractedly, "which I have imported for me from Smyrna. They contain a small percentage of opium."

"Opium!" exclaimed Denise Ryland, glaring at the speaker and then at Helen Cumberly, as though the latter were responsible in some way for the vices of the painter.

"Yes," he said, reclosing the box, and pacing somberly to the door to greet a new arrival.

"Did you ever in all your life," said Denise Ryland, glancing about her, "see such an exhibition . . . of nightmares?"

Certainly, the criticism was not without justification; the dauby-looking oil-paintings, incomprehensible water-colors, and riotous charcoal sketches which formed the mural decoration of the studio were distinctly "advanced." But, since the center of interest seemed to be the large canvas on the easel, the two moved to the edges of the group of spectators and began to examine this masterpiece. A very puzzled newspaperman joined them, bending and whispering to Helen Cumberly:

"Are you going to notice the thing seriously? Personally, I am writing it up as a practical joke! We are giving him half a column—Lord knows what for!—but I can't see how to handle it except as funny stuff."

"But, for heaven's sake . . . what does he . . . *call* it?" muttered Denise Ryland, holding a pair of gold rimmed pince-nez before her eyes, and shifting them to and fro in an endeavor to focus the canvas.

" 'Our Lady of the Poppies,' " replied the journalist. "Do you think it's intended to mean anything in particular?"

The question was no light one; it embodied a problem not readily solved. The scene depicted, and depicted with a skill, with a technical mastery of the bizarre that had in it something horrible—was a long narrow room—or, properly, cavern. The walls apparently were hewn from black rock, and at regular intervals, placed some three feet from these gleaming walls, uprose slender golden pillars supporting a kind of fretwork arch which entirely masked the ceiling. The point of sight adopted by the painter was peculiar. One apparently looked down into this apartment from some spot elevated fourteen feet or more above the floor level. The floor, which was black and polished, was strewn with tiger skins; and little, inlaid tables and garishly colored cushions were spread about in confusion, whilst cushioned divans occupied the visible corners of the place. The lighting was very "advanced": a lamp, having a kaleidoscopic shade, swung from the center of the roof low into the room and furnished all the illumination.

Three doors were visible; one, directly in line at the further end of the place, apparently of carved ebony inlaid with ivory; another, on the right, of lemon wood or something allied to it, and inlaid with a design in some emerald hued material; with a third, corresponding door, on the left, just barely visible to the spectator.

Two figures appeared. One was that of a Chinaman in a green robe scarcely distinguishable from the cushions surrounding him, who crouched upon the divan to the left of the central door, smoking a long bamboo pipe. His face was the leering face of a yellow satyr. But, dominating the composition, and so conceived in form, in color, and in lighting, as to claim the attention centrally, so that the other extravagant details became but a setting for it, was another figure.

Upon a slender ivory pedestal crouched a golden dragon, and before the pedestal was placed a huge Chinese vase of the indeter-

minate pink seen in the heart of a rose, and so skilfully colored as to suggest an internal luminousness. The vase was loaded with a mass of exotic poppies, a riotous splash of color; whilst beside this vase, and slightly in front of the pedestal, stood the figure presumably intended to represent the Lady of the Poppies who gave title to the picture.

The figure was that of an Eastern girl, slight and supple, and possessing a devilish and forbidding grace. Her short hair formed a black smudge upon the canvas, and cast a dense shadow upon her face. The composition was infinitely daring; for out of this shadow shone the great black eyes, their diablerie most cunningly insinuated; whilst with a brilliant exclusion of detail—by means of two strokes of the brush steeped in brightest vermilion, and one seemingly haphazard splash of dead white—an evil and abandoned smile was made to greet the spectator.

To the waist, the figure was a study in satin nudity, whence, from a jeweled girdle, light draperies swept downward, covering the feet and swinging, a shimmering curve out into the foreground of the canvas, the curve being cut off in its apogee by the gold frame.

Above her head, this girl of demoniacal beauty held a bunch of poppies seemingly torn from the vase: this, with her left hand; with her right she pointed, tauntingly, at her beholder.

In comparison with the effected futurism of the other pictures in the studio, "Our Lady of the Poppies," beyond question was a great painting. From a point where the entire composition might be taken in by the eye, the uncanny scene glowed with highly colored detail; but, exclude the scheme of the composition, and focus the eye upon any one item—the golden dragon—the seated Chinaman—the ebony door—the silk-shaded lamp; it had no detail whatever: one beheld a meaningless mass of colors. Individually, no one section of the canvas had life, had meaning; but, as a whole, it glowed, it lived—it was genius. Above all, it was uncanny.

This, Denise Ryland fully realized, but critics had grown so used to treating the work of Olaf van Noord as a joke, that "Our Lady of the Poppies" in all probability would never be judged seriously.

"What does it mean, Mr. van Noord?" asked Helen Cumberly, leaving the group of worshipers standing hushed in rapture before the canvas and approaching the painter. "Is there some occult significance in the title?"

"It is a priestess," replied the artist, in his dreamy fashion. . . .

"A priestess?"

"A priestess of the temple." . . .

Helen Cumberly glanced again at the astonishing picture.

"Do you mean," she began, "that there is a living original?"

Olaf van Noord bowed absently, and left her side to greet one who at that moment entered the studio. Something magnetic in the personality of the newcomer drew all eyes from the canvas to the figure on the threshold. The artist was removing garish tiger skin furs from the shoulders of the girl—for the new arrival was a girl, a Eurasian girl.

She wore a tiger skin motor-coat, and a little, close-fitting, turban-like cap of the same. The coat removed, she stood revealed in a clinging gown of silk; and her feet were shod in little amber colored slippers with green buckles. The bodice of her dress opened in a surprising V, displaying the satin texture of her neck and shoulders, and enhancing the barbaric character of her appearance. Her jet black hair was confined by no band or comb, but protruded Bishareen-like around the shapely head. Without doubt, this was the Lady of the Poppies—the original of the picture.

"Dear friends," said Olaf van Noord, taking the girl's hand, and walking into the studio, "permit me to present my model!"

Following, came a slightly built man who carried himself with a stoop; an olive faced man, who squinted frightfully, and who dressed immaculately.

"What a most . . . extraordinary-looking creature!" whispered Denise Ryland to Helen. "She has undoubted attractions of . . . a hellish sort . . . if I may use . . . the term."

"She is the strangest looking girl I have ever seen in my life," replied Helen, who found herself unable to turn her eyes away from Olaf van Noord's model. "Surely she is not a professional model!"

The chatty reporter (his name was Crockett) confided to Helen Cumberly:

"She is not exactly a professional model, I think, Miss Cumberly, but she is one of the van Noord set, and is often to be seen in the more exclusive restaurants, and sometimes in the Café Royal."

"She is possibly a member of the theatrical profession?"

"I think not. She is the only really strange figure (if we exclude Olaf) in this group of poseurs. She is half Burmese, I believe, and a native of Moulmein."

"Most extraordinary creature!" muttered Denise Ryland, focussing upon the Eurasian her gold rimmed glasses—"most extraordinary." She glanced around at the company in general. "I really begin to feel . . . more and more as though I were . . . in a private lunatic . . . asylum. That picture . . . beyond doubt is the work . . . of a madman . . . a perfect . . . madman!"

"I, also, begin to be conscious of an uncomfortable sensation," said Helen, glancing about her almost apprehensively. "Am I dreaming, or did some one else enter the studio, immediately behind that girl?"

"A squinting man . . . yes!"

"But a third person?"

"No, my dear . . . look for yourself. As you say . . . you are . . . dreaming. It's not to be wondered . . . at!"

Helen laughed, but very uneasily. Evidently it had been an illusion, but an unpleasant illusion; for she should have been prepared to swear that not two, but three people had entered! Moreover, although she was unable to detect the presence of any third stranger in the studio, the persuasion that this third person actually was present remained with her, unaccountably, and uncannily.

The lady of the tiger skins was surrounded by an admiring group of unusuals, and Helen, who had turned again to the big canvas, suddenly became aware that the little cross-eyed man was bowing and beaming radiantly before her.

"May I be allowed," said Olaf van Noord who stood beside him, "to present my friend Mr. Gianapolis, my dear Miss Cumberly?" . . .

Helen Cumberly found herself compelled to acknowledge the introduction, although she formed an immediate, instinctive distaste for Mr. Gianapolis. But he made such obvious attempts to please, and was so really entertaining a talker, that she unbent towards him a little. His admiration, too, was unconcealed; and no pretty woman, however great her common sense, is entirely admiration-proof.

"Do you not think 'Our Lady of the Poppies' remarkable?" said Gianapolis, pleasantly.

"I think," replied Denise Ryland,—to whom, also, the Greek had been presented by Olaf van Noord, "that it indicates . . . a disordered . . . imagination on the part of . . . its creator."

"It is a technical masterpiece," replied the Greek, smiling, "but hardly a work of imagination; for you have seen the original—of the principal figure, and"—he turned to Helen Cumberly—"one need not go very far East for such an interior as that depicted."

"What!" Helen knitted her brows, prettily—"you do not suggest that such an apartment actually exists either East or West?"

Gianapolis beamed radiantly.

"You would, perhaps, like to see such an apartment?" he suggested.

"I should, certainly," replied Helen Cumberly. "Not even in a stage setting have I seen anything like it."

"You have never been to the East?"

"Never, unfortunately. I have desired to go for years, and hope to go some day."

"In Smyrna you may see such rooms; possibly in Port Said—certainly in Cairo. In Constantinople—yes! But perhaps in Paris; and—who knows?—Sir Richard Burton explored Mecca, but who has explored London?"

Helen Cumberly watched him curiously.

"You excite my curiosity," she said. "Don't you think"—turning to Denise Ryland—"he is most tantalizing?"

Denise Ryland distended her nostrils scornfully.

"He is telling . . . fairy tales," she declared. "He thinks . . . we are . . . silly!"

"On the contrary," declared Gianapolis; "I flatter myself that I am too good a judge of character to make that mistake."

Helen Cumberly absorbed his entire attention; in everything he sought to claim her interest; and when, ere taking their departure, the girl and her friend walked around the studio to view the other pictures, Gianapolis was the attendant cavalier, and so well as one might judge, in his case, his glance rarely strayed from the piquant beauty of Helen.

When they departed, it was Gianapolis, and not Olaf van Noord, who escorted them to the door and downstairs to the street. The red lips of the Eurasian smiled upon her circle of adulators, but her eyes—her unfathomable eyes—followed every movement of the Greek.

XXVII

GROVE OF A MILLION APES

Four men sauntered up the grand staircase and entered the huge smoking-room of the Radical Club as Big Ben was chiming the hour of eleven o'clock. Any curious observer who had cared to consult the visitor's book in the hall, wherein the two lines last written were not yet dry, would have found the following entries:

VISITOR	RESIDENCE	INTROD'ING MEMBER
Dr. Bruce Cumberly	London	John Exel
M. Gaston	Paris	Brian Malpas

The smoking-room was fairly full, but a corner near the big open grate had just been vacated, and here, about a round table, the four disposed themselves. Our French acquaintance being in evening dress had perforce confined himself in his sartorial eccentricities to a flowing silk knot in place of the more conventional, neat bow. He was already upon delightfully friendly terms with the frigid Exel and the aristocratic Sir Brian Malpas. Few natures were proof against the geniality of the brilliant Frenchman.

Conversation drifted, derelict, from one topic to another, now seized by this current of thought, now by that; and M. Gaston Max made no perceptible attempt to steer it in any given direction. But presently:

"I was reading a very entertaining article," said Exel, turning his monocle upon the physician, "in the *Planet* to-day, from the pen of Miss Cumberly; Ah! dealing with Olaf van Noord."

Sir Brian Malpas suddenly became keenly interested.

"You mean in reference to his new picture, 'Our Lady of the Poppies'?" he said.

"Yes," replied Exel, "but I was unaware that you knew van Noord?"

"I do not know him," said Sir Brian, "I should very much like to meet him. But directly the picture is on view to the public I shall certainly subscribe my half-crown."

"My own idea," drawled Exel, "was that Miss Cumberly's article probably was more interesting than the picture or the painter. Her description of the canvas was certainly most vivid; and I, myself, for a moment, experienced an inclination to see the thing. I feel sure, however, that I should be disappointed."

"I think you are wrong," interposed Cumberly. "Helen is enthusiastic about the picture, and even Miss Ryland, whom you have met and who is a somewhat severe critic, admits that it is out of the ordinary."

Max, who covertly had been watching the face of Sir Brian Malpas, said at this point:

"I would not miss it for anything, after reading Miss Cumberly's account of it. When are you thinking of going to see it, Sir Brian? I might arrange to join you."

"Directly the exhibition is opened," replied the baronet, lapsing again into his dreamy manner. "Ring me up when you are going, and I will join you."

"But you might be otherwise engaged?"

"I never permit business," said Sir Brian, "to interfere with pleasure."

The words sounded absurd, but, singularly, the statement was true. Sir Brian had won his political position by sheer brilliancy. He was utterly unreliable and totally indifferent to that code of social obligations which ordinarily binds his class. He held his place by force of intellect, and it was said of him that had he possessed the faintest conception of his duties toward his fellow men, nothing could have prevented him from becoming Prime Minister. He was a puzzle to all who knew him. Following a most brilliant speech in the House, which would win admiration and applause from end to end of the Empire, he would, perhaps on the following day, exhibit something very like stupidity in debate. He would rise to address the House and take his seat again without having uttered a word. He was eccentric, said his admirers, but there were others who looked deeper for an explanation, yet failed to find one, and were thrown back upon theories.

M. Max, by strategy, masterful because it was simple, so arranged matters that at about twelve o'clock he found himself strolling with Sir Brian Malpas toward the latter's chambers in Piccadilly.

A man who wore a raincoat with the collar turned up and buttoned tightly about his throat, and whose peculiar bowler hat seemed to be so tightly pressed upon his head that it might have been glued there, detached himself from the shadows of the neighboring cabrank as M. Gaston Max and Sir Brian Malpas quitted the Club, and followed them at a discreet distance.

It was a clear, fine night, and both gentlemen formed conspicuous figures, Sir Brian because of his unusual height and upright military bearing, and the Frenchman by reason of his picturesque cloak and hat. Up Northumberland Avenue, across Trafalgar Square and so on up to Piccadilly Circus went the two, deep in conversation; with the tireless man in the raincoat always dogging their footsteps. So the procession proceeded on, along Piccadilly. Then Sir Brian and M. Max turned into the door of a block of chambers, and a constable, who chanced to be passing at the moment, touched his helmet to the baronet.

As the two were entering the lift, the follower came up level with the doorway and abreast of the constable; the top portion of a very red face showed between the collar of the raincoat and the brim of the hat, together with a pair of inquiring blue eyes.

"Reeves!" said the follower, addressing the constable.

The latter turned and stared for a moment at the speaker; then saluted hurriedly.

"Don't do that!" snapped the proprietor of the bowler; "you should know better! Who was that gentleman?"

"Sir Brian Malpas, sir."

"Sir Brian Malpas?"

"Yes, sir."

"And the other?"

"I don't know, sir. I have never seen him before."

"H'm!" grunted Detective-Sergeant Sowerby, walking across the road toward the Park with his hands thrust deep in his pockets; "I have! What the deuce is Max up to? I wonder if Dunbar knows about this move?"

He propped himself up against the railings, scarcely knowing what he expected to gain by remaining there, but finding the place as well suited to reflection as any other. He shared with Dunbar a dread that the famous Frenchman would bring the case to a successful conclusion unaided by Scotland Yard, thus casting professional discredit upon Dunbar and himself.

His presence at that spot was largely due to accident. He had chanced to be passing the Club when Sir Brian and M. Max had come out, and, fearful that the presence of the tall stranger portended some new move on the Frenchman's part, Sowerby had followed, hoping to glean something by persistency when clues were unobtainable by other means. He had had no time to make inquiries of the porter of the Club respecting the identity of M. Max's companion, and thus, as has appeared, he did not obtain the desired information until his arrival in Piccadilly.

Turning over these matters in his mind, Sowerby stood watching the block of buildings across the road. He saw a light spring into being in a room overlooking Piccadilly, a room boasting a handsome balcony. This took place some two minutes after the departure of the lift bearing Sir Brian and his guest upward; so that Sowerby permitted himself to conclude that the room with the balcony belonged to Sir Brian Malpas.

He watched the lighted window aimlessly and speculated upon the nature of the conversation then taking place up there above him. Had he possessed the attributes of a sparrow, he thought, he might have flown up to that balcony and have "got level" with this infernally clever Frenchman who was almost certainly going to pull off the case under the very nose of Scotland Yard.

In short, his reflections were becoming somewhat bitter; and persuaded that he had nothing to gain by remaining there any longer he was about to walk off, when his really remarkable persistency received a trivial reward.

One of the windows communicating with the balcony was suddenly thrown open, so that Sowerby had a distant view of the corner of a picture, of the extreme top of a bookcase, and of a patch of white ceiling in the room above; furthermore he had a clear sight of the man who opened the window, and who now turned and reentered the room. The man was Sir Brian Malpas.

Heedless of the roaring traffic stream, upon the brink of which he stood, heedless of all who passed him by, Sowerby gazed aloft, seeking to project himself, as it were, into that lighted room. Not being an accomplished clairvoyant, he remained in all his component parts upon the pavement of Piccadilly; but ours is the privilege to succeed where Sowerby failed, and the comedy being enacted in the room above should prove well deserving of study.

To the tactful diplomacy of M. Gaston Max, the task of securing from Sir Brian an invitation to step up into his chambers in order to smoke a final cigar was no heavy one. He seated himself in a deep armchair, at the baronet's invitation, and accepted a very fine cigar, contentedly, sniffing at the old cognac with the appreciation of a connoisseur, ere holding it under the syphon.

He glanced around the room, noting the character of the ornaments, and looked up at the big book-shelf which was near to him; these rapid inquiries dictated the following remark: "You have lived in China, Sir Brian?"

Sir Brian surveyed him with mild surprise.

"Yes," he replied; "I was for some time at the Embassy in Pekin."

His guest nodded, blowing a ring of smoke from his lips and tracing its hazy outline with the lighted end of his cigar.

"I, too, have been in China," he said slowly.

"What, really! I had no idea."

"Yes—I have been in China . . . I" . . .

M. Gaston grew suddenly deathly pale and his fingers began to twitch alarmingly. He stared before him with wide-opened eyes and began to cough and to choke as if suffocating—dying.

Sir Brian Malpas leapt to his feet with an exclamation of concern. His visitor weakly waved him away, gasping: "It is nothing . . . it will . . . pass off. Oh! *mon dieu!*" . . .

Sir Brian ran and opened one of the windows to admit more air to the apartment. He turned and looked back anxiously at the man in the armchair. M. Gaston, twitching in a pitiful manner and still frightfully pale, was clutching the chair-arms and glaring straight in front of him. Sir Brian started slightly and advanced to his visitor's side.

The burning cigar lay upon the carpet beside the chair, and Sir Brian took it up and tossed it into the grate. As he did so he looked searchingly into the eyes of M. Gaston. The pupils were extraordinarily dilated. . . .

"Do you feel better?" asked Sir Brian.

"Much better," muttered M. Gaston, his face twitching nervously—"much better."

"Are you subject to these attacks?"

"Since—I was in China—yes, unfortunately."

Sir Brian tugged at his fair mustache and seemed about to speak, then turned aside, and, walking to the table, poured out a peg of brandy and offered it to his guest.

"Thanks," said M. Gaston; "many thanks indeed, but already I recover. There is only one thing that would hasten my recovery, and that, I fear, is not available."

"What is that?"

He looked again at M. Gaston's eyes with their very dilated pupils.

"Opium!" whispered M. Gaston.

"What! you . . . you" . . .

"I acquired the custom in China," replied

the Frenchman, his voice gradually growing stronger; "and for many years, now, I have regarded opium as essential to my well-being. Unfortunately business has detained me in London, and I have been forced to fast for an unusually long time. My outraged constitution is protesting—that is all."

He shrugged his shoulders and glanced up at his host with an odd smile.

"You have my sympathy," said Sir Brian. . . .

"In Paris," continued the visitor, "I am a member of a select and cozy little club; near the Boulevard Beaumarchais . . . ."

"I have heard of it," interjected Malpas—"on the Rue St. Claude?"

"That indeed is its situation," replied the other with surprise. "You know someone who is a member?"

Sir Brian Malpas hesitated for ten seconds or more; then, crossing the room and reclosing the window, he turned, facing his visitor across the large room.

"I was a member, myself, during the time that I lived in Paris," he said, in a hurried manner which did not entirely serve to cover his confusion.

"My dear Sir Brian! We have at least one taste in common!"

Sir Brian Malpas passed his hand across his brow with a weary gesture well-known to fellow Members of Parliament, for it often presaged the abrupt termination of a promising speech.

"I curse the day that I was appointed to Pekin," he said; "for it was in Pekin that I acquired the opium habit. I thought to make it my servant; it has made me" . . .

"What! you would give it up?"

Sir Brian surveyed the speaker with surprise again.

"Do you doubt it?"

"My dear Sir Brian!" cried the Frenchman, now completely restored, "my real life is lived in the land of the poppies; my other life is but a shadow! *Morbleur* to be an outcast from that garden of bliss is to me torture excruciating. For the past three months I have regularly met in my trances." . . .

Sir Brian shuddered coldly.

"In my explorations of that wonderland," continued the Frenchman, "a most fascinating Eastern girl. Ah! I cannot describe her; for when, at a time like this, I seek to conjure up her image,—*nom d'um nom!* do you know, I can think of nothing but a serpent!"

"A serpent!"

"A serpent, exactly. Yet, when I actually meet her in the land of the poppies, she is a dusky Cleopatra in whose arms I forget the world—even the world of the poppy. We float down the stream together, always in an Indian bark canoe, and this stream runs through orange groves. Numberless apes—millions of apes, inhabit these groves, and as we two float along, they hurl orange blossoms—orange blossoms, you understand—until the canoe is filled with them. I assure you, monsieur, that I perform these delightful journeys regularly, and to be deprived of the key which opens the gate of this wonderland, is to me like being exiled from a loved one. *Pardieu!* that grove of apes! *Morbleu!* my witch of the dusky eyes! Yet, as I have told you, owing to some trick of my brain, whilst I can experience an intense longing for that companion of my dreams, my waking attempts to visualize her provide nothing but the image" . . .

"Of a serpent," concluded Sir Brian, smiling pathetically. "You are indeed an enthusiast, M. Gaston, and to me a new type. I had supposed that every slave of the drug cursed his servitude and loathed and despised himself." . . .

"Ah, monsieur! to *me* those words sound almost like a sacrilege!"

"But," continued Sir Brian, "your remarks interest me strangely; for two reasons. First, they confirm your assertion that you are, or were, an habitué of the Rue St. Claude, and secondly, they revive in my mind an old fancy—a superstition."

"What is that, Sir Brian?" inquired M. Max, whose opium vision was a faithful imitation of one related to him by an actual frequenter of the establishment near the Boulevard Beaumarchais.

"Only once before, M. Gaston, have I compared notes with a fellow opium-smoker, and he, also, was a patron of Madame Jean; he, also, met in his dreams that Eastern Circe, in the grove of apes, just as I" . . .

"*Morbleu!* Yes?"

"As *I* meet her!"

"But this is astounding!" cried Max, who actually thought it so. "Your fancy—your superstition—was this: that only habitués of Rue St. Claude met, in poppyland, this vision? And in your fancy you are now confirmed?"

"It is singular, at least."

"It is more than that, Sir Brian! Can it be that some intelligence presides over that establishment and exercises—shall I call it a hypnotic influence upon the inmates?"

M. Max put the question with sincere interest.

"One does not *always* meet her," murmured Sir Brian. "But—yes, it is possible. for I have since renewed those experiences in London."

"What! in London?"

"Are you remaining for some time longer in London?"

"Alas! for several weeks yet."

"Then I will introduce you to a gentleman who can secure you admission to an establishment in London—where you may even hope sometimes to find the orange grove—to meet your dream-bride!"

"What!" cried M. Gaston, rising to his feet, his eyes bright with gratitude, "you will do that?"

"With pleasure," said Sir Brian Malpas, wearily; "nor am I jealous! But—no! do not thank me, for I do not share your views upon the subject, monsieur. You are a devout worshiper; I, an unhappy slave!"

XXVIII

THE OPIUM AGENT

Into the Palm Court of the Hotel Astoria, Mr. Gianapolis came, radiant and bowing. M. Gaston rose to greet his visitor. M. Gaston was arrayed in a light gray suit and wore a violet tie of very chaste design; his complexion had assumed a quality of sallowness, and the pupils of his eyes had acquired (as on the occasion of his visit to the chambers of Sir Brian Malpas) a *chatoyant* quality; they alternately dilated and contracted in a most remarkable manner—in a manner which attracted the immediate attention of Mr. Gianapolis.

"My dear sir," he said, speaking in French, "you suffer. I perceive how grievously you suffer; and you have been denied that panacea which beneficent nature designed for the service of mankind. A certain gentleman known to both of us (we brethren of the poppy are all nameless) has advised me of your requirements—and here I am."

"You are welcome," declared M. Gaston.

He rose and grasped eagerly the hand of the Greek, at the same time looking about the Palm Court suspiciously. "You can relieve my sufferings?"

Mr. Gianapolis seated himself beside the Frenchman.

"I perceive," he said, "that you are of those who abjure the heresies of De Quincey. How little he knew, that De Quincey, of the true ritual of the poppy! He regarded it as the German regards his lager, whereas we know—you and I—that it is an Eleusinian mystery; that true communicants must retreat to the temple of the goddess if they would partake of Paradise with her."

"It is perhaps a question of temperament," said M. Gaston, speaking in a singularly tremulous voice. "De Quincey apparently possessed the type of constitution which is cerebrally stimulated by opium. To such a being the golden gates are closed; and the Easterners, whom he despised for what he termed their beastly lethargies, have taught me the real secret of the poppy. I do not employ opium as an aid to my social activities; I regard it as nepenthe from them and as a key to a brighter realm. It has been my custom, M. Gianapolis, for many years, periodically to visit that fairyland. In Paris I regularly arranged my affairs in such a manner that I found myself occasionally at liberty to spend two or three days, as the case might be, in the company of my bright friends who haunted the Boulevard Beaumarchais."

"Ah! Our acquaintance has mentioned something of this to me, Monsieur. You knew Madame Jean?"

"The dear Madame Jean! Name of a name! She was the hierophant of my Paris Temple" . . .

"And Sen?"

"Our excellent Sen! Splendid man! It was from the hands of the worthy Sen, the incomparable Sen, that I received the key to the gate! Ah! how I have suffered since the accursed business has exiled me from the" . . .

"I feel for you," declared Gianapolis, warmly; "I, too, have worshiped at the shrine; and although I cannot promise that the London establishment to which I shall introduce you is comparable with that over which Madame Jean formerly presided" . . .

"Formerly?" exclaimed M. Gaston, with lifted eyebrows. "You do not tell me" . . .

"My friend," said Gianapolis, "in Europe we are less enlightened upon certain matters than in Smyrna, in Constantinople—in Cairo. The impertinent police have closed the establishment in the Rue St. Claude!"

"Ah!" exclaimed M. Gaston, striking his brow, "misery! I shall return to Paris, then, only to die?"

"I would suggest, monsieur," said Gianapolis, tapping him confidentially upon the breast, "that you periodically visit London in future. The journey is a short one, and already, I am happy to say, the London establishment (conducted by Mr. Ho-Pin of Canton—a most accomplished gentleman, and a graduate of London)—enjoys the patronage of several distinguished citizens of Paris, of Brussels, of Vienna, and elsewhere."

"You offer me life!" declared M. Gaston, gratefully. "The commoner establishments, for the convenience of sailors and others of that class, at Dieppe, Calais,"—he shrugged his shoulders, comprehensively—"are impossible as resorts. In catering for the true devotees—for those who, unlike De Quincey, plunge and do not dabble—for those who seek to explore the ultimate regions of poppyland, for those who have learnt the mystery from the real masters in Asia and not in Europe—the enterprise conducted by Madame Jean supplied a want long and bitterly experienced. I rejoice to know that London has not been neglected." . . .

"My dear friend!" cried Gianapolis enthusiasticallly, "no important city has been neglected! A high priest of the cult has arisen, and from a parent lodge in Pekin he has extended his offices to kindred lodges in most of the capitals of Europe and Asia; he has not neglected the Near East, and America owes him a national debt of gratitude."

"Ah! the great man!" murmured M. Gaston, with closed eyes. "As an old habitué of the Rue St. Claude, I divine that you refer to Mr. King?"

"Beyond doubt," whispered Gianapolis, imparting a quality of awe to his voice. "From you, my friend, I will have no secrets; but"—he glanced about him crookedly, and lowered his voice to an impressive whisper—"the police, as you are aware" . . .

"Curse their interference!" said M. Gaston.

"Curse it indeed; but the police persist in believing, or in pretending to believe, that any establishment patronized by lovers of the magic resin must necessarily be a resort of criminals."

"Pah!"

"Whilst this absurd state of affairs prevails, it is advisable, it is more than advisable, it is imperative, that all of us should be secret. The . . . raid—unpleasant word!—upon the establishment in Paris—was so unexpected that there was no time to advise patrons; but the admirable tact of the French authorities ensured the suppression of all names. Since—always as a protective measure—no business relationship exists between any two of Mr. King's establishments (each one being entirely self-governed) some difficulty is being experienced, I believe, in obtaining the names of those who patronized Madame Jean. But I am doubly glad to have met you, M. Gaston, for not only can I put you in touch with the London establishment, but I can impress upon you the necessity of preserving absolute silence" . . .

M. Gaston extended his palms eloquently.

"To me," he declared, "the name of Mr. King is a sacred symbol."

"It is to all of us!" responded the Greek, devoutly.

M. Gaston in turn became confidential, bending toward Gianapolis so that, as the shadow of the Greek fell upon his face, his pupils contracted catlike.

"How often have I prayed," he whispered, "for a sight of that remarkable man!"

A look of horror, real or simulated, appeared upon the countenance of Gianapolis.

"To see—Mr. King!" he breathed. "My dear friend, I declare to you by all that I hold sacred that I—though one of the earliest patrons of the first establishment, that in Pekin—have never seen Mr. King!"

"He is so cautious and so clever as that?"

"Even as cautious and even as clever—yes! Though every branch of the enterprise in the world were destroyed, no man would ever see Mr. King; he would remain but a *name!*"

"You will arrange for me to visit the house of—Ho-Pin, did you say?—immediately?"

"To-day, if you wish," said Gianapolis, brightly.

"My funds," continued M. Gaston, shrugging his shoulders, "are not limitless at the moment; and until I receive a remittance from Paris" . . .

The brow of Mr. Gianapolis darkened slightly.

"Our clientele here," he replied, "is a very wealthy one, and the fees are slightly higher than in Paris. An entrance fee of fifty guineas is charged, and an annual subscription of the same amount" . . .

"But," exclaimed M. Gaston, "I shall not be in London for so long as a year! In a week or a fortnight from now, I shall be on my way to America!"

"You will receive an introduction to the New York representative, and your membership will be available for any of the United

States establishments."

"But I am going to South America."

"At Buenos Aires is one of the largest branches."

"But I am not going to Buenos Aires! I am going with a prospecting party to Yucatan."

"You must be well aware, monsieur, that to go to Yucatan is to exile yourself from all that life holds for you."

"I can take a supply" . . .

"You will die, monsieur! Already you suffer abominably" . . .

"I do not suffer because of any lack of the specific," said M. Gaston wearily; "for if I were entirely unable to obtain possession of it, I should most certainly die. But I suffer because, living as I do at present in a public hotel, I am unable to embark upon a protracted voyage into those realms which hold so much for me" . . .

"I offer you the means" . . .

"But to charge me one hundred guineas, since I cannot possibly avail myself of the full privileges, is to rob me—is to trade upon my condition!" M. Gaston was feebly indignant.

"Let it be twenty-five guineas, monsieur," said the Greek, reflectively, "entitling you to two visits."

"Good! good!" cried M. Gaston. "Shall I write you a check?"

"You mistake me," said Gianapolis. "I am in no way connected with the management of the establishment. You will settle this business matter with Mr. Ho-Pin" . . .

"Yes, yes!"

"To whom I will introduce you this evening. Checks, as you must be aware, are unacceptable. I will meet you at Piccadilly Circus, outside the entrance to the London Pavilion, at nine o'clock this evening, and you will bring with you the twenty-five guineas in cash. You will arrange to absent yourself during the following day?"

"Of course, of course! At nine o'clock at Piccadilly Circus?"

"Exactly."

M. Gaston, this business satisfactorily completed, made his way to his own room by a somewhat devious route, not wishing to encounter anyone of his numerous acquaintances whilst in an apparent state of ill-health so calculated to excite compassion. He avoided the lift and ascended the many stairs to his small apartment.

Here he rectified the sallowness of his complexion, which was due, not to outraged nature, but to the arts of make-up. His dilated pupils (a phenomenon traceable to drops of belladonna) he was compelled to suffer for the present; but since their condition tended temporarily to impair his sight, he determined to remain in his room until the time for the appointment with Gianapolis.

"So!" he muttered—"we have branches in Europe, Asia, Africa and America! *Eh, bien!* to find all those would occupy five hundred detectives for a whole year. I have a better plan: crush the spider and the winds of heaven will disperse his web!"

XXIX

M. MAX OF LONDON
AND M. MAX OF PARIS

He seated himself in a cane armchair and, whilst the facts were fresh in his memory, made elaborate notes upon the recent conversation with the Greek. He had achieved almost more than he could have hoped for; but, knowing something of the elaborate organization of the opium group, he recognized that he owed some part of his information to the sense of security which this admirably conducted machine inspired in its mechanics. The introduction from Sir Brian Malpas had worked wonders, without doubt; and his own intimate knowledge of the establishment adjoining the Boulevard Beaumarchais, far from arousing the suspicions of Gianapolis, had evidently strengthened the latter's conviction that he had to deal with a confirmed opium slave.

The French detective congratulated himself upon the completeness of his Paris operation. It was evident that the French police had succeeded in suppressing all communication between the detained members of the Rue St. Claude den and the head office—which he shrewdly suspected to be situated in London. So confident were the group in the self-contained properties of each of their branches that the raid of any one establishment meant for them nothing more than a temporary financial loss. Failing the clue supplied by the draft on Paris, the case, so far as he was concerned, indeed, must have terminated with the raiding of the opium house. He reflected that he owed that precious discovery primarily to the promptness with which he had conducted the raid—to the finding of the letter (the *one* incriminating letter) from Mr. King.

Evidently the group remained in ignorance of the fact that the little arrangement at the Crédit Lyonnais had been discovered. He surveyed—and his eyes twinkled humorously—a small photograph which was contained in his writing-case.

It represented a very typical Parisian gentleman, with a carefully trimmed square beard and well brushed mustache, wearing pince-nez and a white silk knot at his neck. The photograph was cut from a French magazine, and beneath it appeared the legend:

"M. Gaston Max, Service de Sûrète."

There was marked genius in the conspicuous dressing of M. Gaston Max, who, as M. Gaston, was now patronizing the Hotel Astoria. For whilst there was nothing furtive, nothing secret, about this gentleman, the closest scrutiny (and because he invited it, he was never subjected to it) must have failed to detect any resemblance between M. Gaston of the Hotel Astoria and M. Gaston Max of the Service de Sûrète.

And which was the original M. Gaston Max? Was the M. Max of the magazine photograph a disguised M. Max? or was that the veritable M. Max, and was the patron of the Astoria a disguised M. Max? It is quite possible that M. Gaston Max, himself, could not have answered that question, so true an artist was he; and it is quite certain that had the occasion arisen he would have refused to do so.

He partook of a light dinner in his own room, and having changed into evening dress, went out to meet Mr. Gianapolis. The latter was on the spot punctually at nine o'clock, and taking the Frenchman familiarly by the arm, he hailed a taxi-cab, giving the man the directions, "To Victoria-Suburban." Then, turning to his companion, he whispered: "Evening dress? And you must return in daylight."

M. Max felt himself to be flushing like a girl. It was an error of artistry that he had committed; a heinous crime! "So silly of me!" he muttered.

"No matter," replied the Greek, genially.

The cab started. M. Max, though silently reproaching himself, made mental notes of the destination. He had not renewed his sallow complexion, for reasons of his own, and his dilated pupils were beginning to contract again, facts which were not very evident, however, in the poor light. He was very twitchy, nevertheless, and the face of the man beside him was that of a sympathetic vulture, if such a creature can be imagined. He inquired casually if the new patron had brought his money with him, but for the most part his conversation turned upon China, with which country he seemed to be well acquainted. Arrived at Victoria, Mr. Gianapolis discharged the cab, and again taking the Frenchman by the arm, walked with him some twenty paces away from the station. A car suddenly pulled up almost beside them.

Ere M. Max had time to note those details in which he was most interested, Gianapolis had opened the door of the limousine, and the Frenchman found himself within, beside Gianapolis, and behind drawn blinds, speeding he knew not in what direction!

"I suppose I should apologize, my dear M. Gaston," said the Greek; and, although unable to see him, for there was little light in the car, M. Max seemed to *feel* him smiling—"but this little device has proved so useful hitherto. In the event of any of those troubles—wretched police interferences—arising, and of officious people obtaining possession of a patron's name, he is spared the necessity of perjuring himself in any way" . . .

"Perhaps I do not entirely understand you, monsieur?" said M. Max.

"It is so simple. The police are determined to raid one of our establishments: they adopt the course of tracking an habitué. This is not impossible. They question him; they ask, 'Do you know a Mr. King?' He replies that he knows no such person, has never seen, has never spoken with him! I assure you that official inquiries have gone thus far already, in New York, for example; but to what end? They say, 'Where is the establishment of a Mr. King to which you have gone on such and such an occasion?' He replies with perfect truth, 'I do not know.' Believe me this little device is quite in your own interest, M. Gaston."

"But when again I feel myself compelled to resort to the solace of the pipe, how then?"

"So simple! You will step to the telephone and ask for this number: East 18642. You will then ask for Mr. King, and an appointment will be made; I will meet you as I met you this evening—and all will be well."

M. Max began to perceive that he had to deal with a scheme even more elaborate than hitherto he had conjectured. These were very clever people, and through the whole complicated network, as through the petal of a poppy one may trace the veins, he traced the guiding will—the power of a tortuous Eastern mind. The system was truly Chinese in its elaborate, uncanny mystifications.

In some covered place that was very dark, the car stopped, and Gianapolis, leaping out with agility, assisted M. Max to descend.

This was a covered courtyard, only lighted by the head-lamps of the limousine.

"Take my hand," directed the Greek.

M. Max complied, and was conducted through a low doorway and on to descending steps.

Dimly, he heard the gear of the car reversed, and knew that the limousine was backing out from the courtyard. The door behind him was closed, and he heard no more. A dim light shone out below.

He descended, walking more confidently now that the way was visible. A moment later he stood upon the threshold of an apartment which calls for no further description at this place; he stood in the doorway of the incredible, unforgettable cave of the golden dragon; he looked into the beetle eyes of Ho-Pin!

Ho-Pin bowed before him, smiling his mirthless smile. In his left hand he held an amber cigarette tube in which a cigarette smoldered gently, sending up a gray pencil of smoke into the breathless, perfumed air.

"Mr. Ho-Pin," said Gianapolis, indicating the Chinaman, "who will attend to your requirements. This is our new friend from Paris, introduced by Sir B.M——, M. Gaston."

"You are vewry welcome," said the Chinaman in his monotonous, metallic voice. "I understand that a fee of twenty-five guineas"—he bowed again, still smiling.

The visitor took out his pocket-book and laid five notes, one sovereign, and two half-crowns upon a little ebony table beside him. Ho-Pin bowed again and waved his hand toward the lemon-colored door on the left.

"Good night, M. Gaston!" said Gianapolis, in radiant benediction.

"*Au revoir, monsieur!*"

M. Max followed Ho-Pin to Block A and was conducted to a room at the extreme right of the matting-lined corridor. He glanced about it curiously.

"If you will pwrepare for your flight into the subliminal," said Ho-Pin, bowing in the doorway, "I shall pwresently wreturn with your wings."

In the cave of the golden dragon, Gianapolis sat smoking upon one of the divans. The silence of the place was extraordinary; unnatural, in the very heart of busy commercial London. Ho-Pin reappeared and standing in the open doorway of Block A sharply clapped his hands three times.

Said, the Egyptian, came out of the door at the further end of the place, bearing a brass tray upon which were a little brass lamp of Oriental manufacture wherein burned a blue spirituous flame, a Japanese, lacquered box not much larger than a snuff-box, and a long and most curiously carved pipe of wood inlaid with metal and having a metal bowl. Bearing this, he crossed the room, passed Ho-Pin, and entered the corridor beyond.

"You have, of course, put him in the observation room?" said Gianapolis.

Ho-Pin regarded the speaker unemotionally.

"Assuwredly," he replied; "for since he visits us for the first time, Mr. King will wish to see him" . . .

A faint shadow momentarily crossed the swarthy face of the Greek at mention of that name *Mr. King.* The servants of Mr. King, from the highest to the lowest, served him for gain . . . and from fear.

XXX

MAHARA

Utter silence had claimed again the cave of the golden dragon. Gianapolis sat alone in the place. smoking a cigarette, and gazing crookedly at the image on the ivory pedestal. Then, glancing at his wrist-watch, he stood up, and, stepping to the entrance door, was about to open it . . .

"Ah, so! You go—already?"—

Gianapolis started back as though he had put his foot upon a viper, and turned.

The Eurasian, wearing her yellow, Chinese dress, and with a red poppy in her hair, stood watching him through half-shut eyes, slowly waving her little fan before her face. Gianapolis attempted the radiant smile, but its brilliancy was somewhat forced tonight.

"Yes, I must be off," he said hurriedly; "I have to see someone—a future client, I think!"

"A future client—yes!"—the long black eyes were closed almost entirely now. "Who is it—this future client, that you have to see?"

"My dear Mahâra! How odd of you to ask that" . . .

"It is odd of me?—so! . . . It is odd of me that I thinking to wonder why you alway running away from me now?"

"Run away from you! My dear little Mahâra!"—He approached the dusky beauty with a certain timidity as one might seek to caress a tiger-cat—"Surely you know" . . .

She struck down his hand with a sharp blow of her closed fan, darting at him a look from the brilliant eyes which was a living flame.

Resting one hand upon her hip, she stood with her right foot thrust forward from beneath the yellow robe and pivoting upon the heel of its little slipper. Her head tilted, she watched him through lowered lashes.

"It was not so with you in Moulmein," she said, her silvery voice lowered caressingly. "Do you remember with me a night beside the Irawaddi?—where was that I wonder? Was it in Prome?—Perhaps, yes? . . . you threatened me to leap in, if . . . and I think to believe you!—I believing you!"

"Mahâra!" cried Gianapolis, and sought to seize her in his arms.

Again she struck down his hand with the little fan, watching him continuously and with no change of expression. But the smoldering fire in those eyes told of a greater flame which consumed her slender body and was potent enough to consume many a victim upon its altar. Gianapolis' yellow skin assumed a faintly mottled appearance.

"Whatever is the matter?" he inquired plaintively.

"So you must be off—yes? I hear you say it; I asking you who to meet?"

"Why do you speak in English?" said Gianapolis with a faint irritation. "Let us talk . . ."

She struck him lightly on the face with her fan; but he clenched his teeth and suppressed an ugly exclamation.

"Who was it?" she asked, musically, "that say to me, 'to hear you speaking English—like rippling water'?"

"You are mad!" muttered Gianapolis, beginning to drill the points of his mustache as was his manner in moments of agitation. His crooked eyes were fixed upon the face of the girl. "You go too far."

"Be watching, my friend, that you also go not too far."

The tones were silvery as ever, but the menace unmistakable. Gianapolis forced a harsh laugh and brushed up his mustache furiously.

"What are you driving at?" he demanded, with some return of self-confidence. "Am I to be treated to another exhibition of your insane jealousies?" . . .

"Ah!" The girl's eyes opened widely; she darted another venomous glance at him. "I am sure now, I am sure!"

"My dear Mahâra, you talk nonsense!"

"Ah!"

She glided sinuously toward him, still with one hand resting upon her hip, stood almost touching his shoulder and raised her beautiful wicked face to his, peering at him through half-closed eyes, and resting the hand which grasped the fan lightly upon his arm.

"You think I do not see? You think I do not watch?"—softer and softer grew the silvery voice—"at Olaf van Noord's studio you think I do not hear? Perhaps you not thinking to care if I see and hear—for it seem you not seeing nor hearing me. I watch and I see. Is it her so soft brown hair? That color of hair is so more prettier than ugly black! Is it her English eyes? Eyes that born in the dark forest of Burma so hideous and so like the eyes of the apes! Is it her white skin and her red cheeks? A brown skin—though someone, there was, that say it is satin of heaven—is so tiresome; when no more it is a new toy it does not interest" . . .

"Really," muttered Gianapolis, uneasily, "I think you must be mad! I don't know what you are talking about."

"Liar!"

One lithe step forward the Eurasian sprang, and, at the word, brought down the fan with all her strength across Gianapolis' eyes.

He staggered away from her, uttering a hoarse cry and instinctively raising his arms to guard himself from further attack; but the girl stood poised again, her hand upon her hip; and swinging her right toe to and fro. Gianapolis, applying his handkerchief to his eyes, squinted at her furiously.

"Liar!" she repeated, and her voice had something of a soothing whisper. "I say to you, be so careful that you go not too far—with me! I do what I do, not because I am a poor fool" . . .

"It's funny," declared Gianapolis, an emotional catch in his voice—"it's damn funny for you—for you—to adopt these airs with me! Why, you went to Olaf van" . . .

"Stop!" cried the girl furiously, and sprang at him panther-like, so that he fell back again in confusion, stumbled and collapsed upon a divan, with upraised, warding arms. "You Greek rat! you skinny Greek rat! Be careful what you think to say to me—to *me!* to *me!* Olaf van Noord—the poor, white-faced corpse-man! He is only one of Said's mummies! Be careful what you think to say to me . . . Oh! be careful—be very careful! It is dangerous of any friend of—*Mr. King*" . . .

Gianapolis glanced at her furtively.

"It is dangerous of anyone in a house of—*Mr. King* to think to make attachments,"—she hissed the words beneath her breath—"outside of ourselves. *Mr. King* would not be glad to hear of it . . . I do not like to tell it to *Mr. King*" . . .

Gianapolis rose to his feet, unsteadily, and stretched out his arms in supplication.

"Mahâra!" he said, "don't treat me like this! dear little Mahâra! what have I done to you? Tell me!—only tell me!"

"Shall I tell it in English?" asked the Eurasian softly. Her eyes now were nearly closed; "or does it worry you that I speak so ugly" . . .

"Mahâra!" . . .

"I only say, be so very careful."

He made a final, bold attempt to throw his arms about her, but she slipped from his grasp and ran lightly across the room.

"Go! hurry off!" she said, bending forward and pointing at him with her fan, her eyes widely opened and blazing—"but remember—there is danger! There is Said, who creeps silently, like the jackal" . . .

She opened the ebony door and darted into the corridor beyond, closing the door behind her.

Gianapolis looked about him in a dazed manner, and yet again applied his handkerchief to his stinging eyes. Whoever could have seen him now must have failed to recognize the radiant Gianapolis so well-known in Bohemian society, the Gianapolis about whom floated a halo of mystery, but who at all times was such a good fellow and so debonair. He took up his hat and gloves, turned, and resolutely strode to the door. Once he glanced back over his shoulder, but shrugged with a sort of self-contempt, and ascended to the top of the steps.

With a key which he selected from a large bunch in his pocket, he opened the door, and stepped out into the garage, carefully closing the door behind him. An electric pocket-lamp served him with sufficient light to find his way out into the lane, and very shortly he was proceeding along Limehouse Causeway. At the moment, indignation was the major emotion ruling his mind; he resented the form which his anger assumed, for it was a passion of rebellion, and rebellion is only possible in servants. It is the part of a slave resenting the lash. He was an unscrupulous, unmoral man, not lacking in courage of a sort; and upon the conquest of Mahâra, the visible mouthpiece of Mr. King, he had entered in much the same spirit as that actuating a Kanaka who dives for pearls in a shark-infested lagoon. He had sought a slave, and lo! the slave was become the master! Otherwise whence this spirit of rebellion . . . this fear?

He occupied himself with such profitless reflections up to the time that he came to the electric trams; but, from thence onward, his mind became otherwise engaged. On his way to Piccadilly Circus that same evening, he had chanced to find himself upon a crowded pavement walking immediately behind Denise Ryland and Helen Cumberly. His esthetic, Greek soul had been fired at first sight of the beauty of the latter; and now, his heart had leaped ecstatically. His first impulse, of course, had been to join the two ladies; but Gianapolis had trained himself to suspect all impulses.

Therefore he had drawn near—near enough to overhear their conversation without proclaiming himself. What he learned by this eavesdropping he counted of peculiar value.

Helen Cumberly was arranging to dine with her friend at the latter's hotel that evening. "But I want to be home early," he had heard the girl say, "so if I leave you at about ten o'clock I can walk to Palace Mansions. No! you need not come with me; I enjoy a lonely walk through the streets of London in the evening" . . .

Gianapolis registered a mental vow that Helen's walk should not be a lonely one. He did not flatter himself upon the possession of a pleasing exterior, but, from experience, he knew that with women he had a winning way.

Now, his mind aglow with roseate possibilities, he stepped from the tram in the neighborhood of Shoreditch, and chartered a taxicab. From this he descended at the corner of Arundel Street and strolled along westward in the direction of the hotel patronized by Miss Ryland. At a corner from which he could command a view of the entrance, he paused and consulted his watch.

It was nearly twenty minutes past ten. Mentally, he cursed Mahâra, who perhaps had caused him to let slip this golden opportunity. But his was not a character easily discouraged; he lighted a cigarette and prepared himself to wait, in the hope that the girl had not yet left her friend.

Gianapolis was a man capable of the uttermost sacrifices upon either of two shrines; that of Mammon, or that of Eros. His was a temperament (truly characteristic of his race) which can build up a structure painfully, year by year, suffering unutterable privations in the cause of its growth, only to shatter it at a blow for a woman's smile. He was a true member of that brotherhood, represented throughout the bazaars of the East, of those singular shopkeepers who live by commercial rapine, who, demanding a hundred piastres for an embroidered shawl from a plain woman, will exchange it with a pretty one for a perfumed handkerchief. Externally of London, he was internally of the Levant.

His vigil lasted but a quarter of an hour. At twenty-five minutes to eleven, Helen Cumberly came running down the steps of the hotel and hurried toward the Strand. Like a shadow, Gianapolis, throwing away a half-smoked cigarette, glided around the corner, paused and so timed his return that he literally ran into the girl as she entered the main thoroughfare.

He started back.

"Why!" he cried, "Miss Cumberly!"

Helen checked a frown, and hastily substituted a smile.

"How odd that I should meet you here, Mr. Gianapolis," she smiled.

"Most extraordinary! I was on my way to visit a friend in Victoria Street upon a rather urgent matter. May I venture to hope that your path lies in a similar direction?"

Helen Cumberly, deceived by his suave manner (for how was she to know that the Greek had learnt her address from Crockett, the reporter?), found herself at a loss for an excuse. Her remarkably pretty mouth was drawn down to one corner, inducing a dimple of perplexity in her left cheek. She had that breadth between the eyes which, whilst of an attribute of perfect beauty, indicates an active mind, and is often found in Scotch women; now, by the slight raising of her eyebrows, this space was accentuated. But Helen's rapid thinking availed her not at all.

"Had you proposed to walk?" inquired Gianapolis, bending deferentially and taking his place beside her with a confidence which showed that her opportunity for repelling his attentions was past.

"Yes," she said, hesitatingly; "but—I fear I am detaining you." . . .

Of two evils she was choosing the lesser; the idea of being confined in a cab with this ever-smiling Greek was unthinkable.

"Oh, my dear Miss Cumberly!" cried Gianapolis, beaming radiantly, "it is a greater pleasure than I can express to you, and then for two friends who are proceeding in the same direction to walk apart would be quite absurd, would it not?"

The term "friend" was not pleasing to Helen's ears; Mr. Gianapolis went far too fast. But she recognized her helplessness, and accepted this cavalier with as good a grace as possible.

He immediately began to talk of Olaf van Noord and his pictures, whilst Helen hurried along as though her life depended upon her speed. Sometimes, on the pretense of piloting her at crossings, Gianapolis would take her arm; and this contact she found most disagreeable; but on the whole his conduct was respectful to the point of servility.

A pretty woman who is not wholly obsessed by her personal charms, learns more of the ways of mankind than it is vouchsafed to her plainer sister ever to know; and in the crooked eyes of Gianapolis, Helen Cumberly read a world of unuttered things, and drew her own conclusions. These several conclusions dictated a single course; avoidance of Gianapolis in future.

Fortunately, Helen Cumberly's self-chosen path in life had taught her how to handle the nascent and undesirable lover. She chatted upon the subject of art, and fenced adroitly whenever the Greek sought to introduce the slightest personal element into the conversation. Nevertheless, she was relieved when at last she found herself in the familiar Square with her foot upon the steps of Palace Mansions.

"Good night, Mr. Gianapolis!" she said, and frankly offered her hand.

The Greek raised it to his lips with exaggerated courtesy, and retained it, looking into her eyes in his crooked fashion.

"We both move in the world of art and letters; may I hope that this meeting will not be our last?"

"I am always wandering about between

Fleet Street and Soho," laughed Helen. "It is quite certain we shall run into each other again before long. Good night, and thank you so much!"

She darted into the hallway, and ran lightly up the stairs. Opening the flat door with her key, she entered and closed it behind her, sighing with relief to be free of the over-attentive Greek. Some impulse prompted her to enter her own room, and, without turning up the light, to peer down into the Square.

Gianapolis was descending the steps. On the pavement he stood and looked up at the windows, lingeringly; then he turned and walked away.

Helen Cumberly stifled an exclamation.

As the Greek gained the corner of the Square and was lost from view, a lithe figure—kin of the shadows which had masked it—became detached from the other shadows beneath the trees of the central garden and stood, a vague silhouette seemingly looking up at her window as Gianapolis had looked.

Helen leaned her hands upon the ledge and peered intently down. The figure was a vague blur in the darkness, but it was moving away along by the rails . . . following Gianapolis. No clear glimpse she had of it, for bat-like, it avoided the light, this sinister shape—and was gone.

XXXI

MUSK AND ROSES

It is time to rejoin M. Gaston Max in the catacombs of Ho-Pin. Having prepared himself for drugged repose in the small but luxurious apartment to which he had been conducted by the Chinaman, he awaited with interest the next development. This took the form of the arrival of an Egyptian attendant, white-robed, red-slippered, and wearing the inevitable tarboosh. Upon the brass tray which he carried were arranged the necessities of the opium smoker. Placing the tray upon a little table beside the bed, he extracted from the lacquered box a piece of gummy substance upon the end of a long needle. This he twisted around, skilfully, in the lamp flame until it acquired a blue spirituous flame of its own. He dropped it into the bowl of the carven pipe and silently placed the pipe in M. Max's hand.

Max, with simulated eagerness, rested the mouthpiece between his lips and *exhaled* rapturously.

Said stood watching him, without the slightest expression of interest being perceptible upon his immobile face. For some time the Frenchman made pretense of inhaling, gently, the potent vapor, lying propped upon one elbow; then, allowing his head gradually to droop, he closed his eyes and lay back upon the silken pillow.

Once more he exhaled feebly ere permitting the pipe to drop from his listless grasp. The mouthpiece yet rested between his lips, but the lower lip was beginning to drop. Finally, the pipe slipped through his fingers on to the rich carpet, and he lay inert, head thrown back, and revealing his lower teeth. The nauseating fumes of opium loaded the atmosphere.

Said silently picked up the pipe, placed it upon the tray and retired, closing the door in the same noiseless manner that characterized all his movements.

For a time, M. Max lay inert, glancing about the place through the veil of his lashes. He perceived no evidence of surveillance, therefore he ventured fully to open his eyes; but he did not move his head.

With the skill in summarizing detail at a glance which contributed largely to make him the great criminal investigator that he was, he noted those particulars which at an earlier time had occasioned the astonishment of Soames.

M. Max was too deeply versed in his art to attempt any further investigations, yet; he contented himself with learning as much as was possible without moving in any way; and whilst he lay there awaiting whatever might come, the door opened noiselessly—to admit Ho-Pin.

He was about to be submitted to a supreme test, for which, however, he was not unprepared. He lay with closed eyes, breathing nasally.

Ho-Pin, his face a smiling, mirthless mask, bent over the bed. Adeptly, he seized the right eyelid of M. Max, and rolled it back over his forefinger, disclosing the eyeball. M. Max, anticipating this test of the genuineness of his coma, had rolled up his eyes at the moment of Ho-Pin's approach, so that now only the white of the sclerotic showed. His trained nerves did not betray him. He lay like a dead man, never flinching.

Ho-Pin, releasing the eyelid, muttered

something gutturally, and stole away from the bed as silently as he had approached it. Very methodically he commenced to search through M. Max's effects, commencing with the discarded garments. He examined the maker's marks upon these, and scrutinized the buttons closely. He turned out all the pockets, counted the contents of the purse, and of the notecase, examined the name inside M. Max's hat, and explored the lining in a manner which aroused the detective's professional admiration. Watch and pocket-knife, Ho-Pin inspected with interest. The little hand-bag which M. Max had brought with him, containing a few toilet necessaries, was overhauled religiously. So much the detective observed through his lowered lashes.

Then Ho-Pin again approached the bed and M. Max became again a dead man.

The silken pyjamas which the detective wore were subjected to gentle examination by the sensitive fingers of the Chinaman, and those same fingers crept beetle-like beneath the pillow.

Silently, Ho-Pin stole from the room and silently closed the door.

M. Max permitted himself a long breath of relief. It was an ordeal through which few men could have passed triumphant.

The *silence* of the place next attracted the inquirer's attention. He had noted this silence at the moment that he entered the cave of the golden dragon, but here it was even more marked; so that he divined, even before he had examined the walls, that the apartment was rendered sound-proof in the manner of a public telephone cabinet. It was a significant circumstance to which he allotted its full value.

But the question uppermost in his mind at the moment was this: Was the time come yet to commence his explorations?

Patience was included in his complement, and, knowing that he had the night before him, he preferred to wait. In this he did well. Considerable time elapsed, possibly half-an-hour . . . and again the door opened.

M. Max was conscious of a momentary nervous tremor; for now a *woman* stood regarding him. She wore a Chinese costume; a huge red poppy was in her hair. Her beauty was magnificently evil; she had the grace of a gazelle and the eyes of a sorceress. He had deceived Ho-Pin, but could he deceive this Eurasian with the witch-eyes wherein burnt ancient wisdom?

He felt rather than saw her approach; for now he ventured to peep no more. She touched him lightly upon the mouth with her fingers and laughed a little low, rippling laugh, the sound of which seemed to trickle along his sensory nerves, icily. She bent over him—lower—lower—and lower yet; until, above the nauseating odor of the place he could smell the musk perfume of her hair. Yet lower she bent; with every nerve in his body he could feel her nearing presence. . . .

She kissed him on the lips.

Again she laughed, in that wicked, eerie glee.

M. Max was conscious of the most singular, the maddest impulses; it was one of the supreme moments of his life. He knew that all depended upon his absolute immobility; yet something in his brain was prompting him—prompting him—to gather the witch to his breast; to return that poisonous, that vampirish kiss, and then to crush out life from the small lithe body.

Sternly he fought down these strange promptings, which he knew to emanate hypnotically from the brain of the creature bending over him.

"Oh, my beautiful dead-baby," she said, softly, and her voice was low, and weirdly sweet. "Oh, my new baby, how I love you, my dead one!" Again she laughed, a musical peal. "I will creep to you in the poppyland where you go . . . and you shall twine your fingers in my hair and pull my red mouth down to you, kissing me . . . kissing me, until you stifle and you die of my love . . . Oh! my beautiful mummy-baby . . . my baby." . . .

The witch-crooning died away into a murmur; and the Frenchman became conscious of the withdrawal of that presence from the room. No sound came to tell of the reclosing of the door; but the obsession was removed, the spell raised.

Again he inhaled deeply the tainted air, and again he opened his eyes.

He had no warranty to suppose that he should remain unmolested during the remainder of the night. The strange words of the Eurasian he did not construe literally; yet could he be certain that he was secure? . . . Nay! he could be certain that he was *not!*

The shaded lamp was swung in such a position that most of the light was directed upon him where he lay, whilst the walls of the room were bathed in a purple shadow. Behind him and above him, directly over the head of the bunk, a faint sound—a sound inaudible except in such a dead silence as that prevailing—told of some shutter being raised or opened. He had trained himself to watch beneath lowered lids without betraying that he was doing so by the slightest nervous twitching. Now, as he watched the purple shaded lamp above him, he observed that it was swaying and moving very gently, whereas hitherto it had floated motionless in the still air.

No other sound came to guide him, and to have glanced upward would have been to betray all.

For the second time that night he became aware of one who watched him, became conscious of observation without the guaranty of his physical senses. And beneath this new surveillance, there grew up such a revulsion of his inner being as he had rarely experienced. The perfume of *roses* became perceptible; and for some occult reason, its fragrance *disgusted.*

It was as though a faint draught from the opened shutter poured into the apartment an impalpable cloud of evil; the very soul of the Eurasian, had it taken vapory form and enveloped him, could not have created a greater turmoil of his senses than this!

Some sinister and definitely malignant intelligence was focussed upon him; or was this a chimera of his imagination? Could it be that now he was become *en rapport* with the thought-forms created in that chamber by its successive occupants?

Scores, perhaps hundreds of brains had there partaken of the unholy sacrament of opium; thousands, millions of evil carnivals had trailed in impish procession about that bed. He knew enough of the creative power of thought to be aware that a sensitive mind coming into contact with such an atmosphere could not fail to respond in some degree to the suggestions, to the elemental hypnosis, of the place.

Was he, owing to his self-induced receptivity of mind, redreaming the evil dreams of those who had occupied that bed before him?

It might be so, but, whatever the explanation, he found himself unable to shake off that uncanny sensation of being watched, studied, by a powerful and inimical intelligence.

Mr. King! . . . Mr. King was watching him! The director of that group, whose structure was founded upon the wreckage of human souls, was watching him! Because of a certain sympathy which existed between his present emotions and those which had threatened to obsess him whilst the Eurasian was in the room, he half believed that it was she who peered down at him, now . . . or she, and another.

The lamp swung gently to and fro, turning slowly to the right and then revolving again to the left, giving life in its gyrations to the intermingled figures on the walls. The atmosphere of the room was nauseating; it was beginning to overpower him. . . .

Creative power of thought . . . what startling possibilities it opened up. Almost it seemed, if Sir Brian Malpas were to be credited, that the collective mind-force of a group of opium smokers had created the "glamor" of a woman—an Oriental woman—who visited them regularly in their trances. Or had that vision a prototype in the flesh—whom he had seen? . . .

Creative power of thought . . . *Mr. King!* He was pursuing Mr. King; whilst Mr. King might be nothing more than a thought-form— a creation of cumulative thought—an elemental spirit which became visible to his subjects, his victims, which had power over them; which could slay them as the "shell" slew Frankenstein, his creator; which could materialize: . . . Mr. King might be the Spirit of Opium. . . .

The faint clicking sound was repeated.

Beads of perspiration stood upon M. Max's forehead; his imagination had been running away with him. God! this was a house of fear! He controlled himself, but only by dint of a tremendous effort of will.

Stealthily watching the lamp, he saw that the arc described by its gyrations was diminishing with each successive swing, and, as he watched, its movements grew slighter and slighter, until finally it became quite stationary again, floating, purple and motionless, upon the stagnant air.

Very slowly, he ventured to change his position, for his long ordeal was beginning to induce cramp. The faint creaking of the metal bunk seemed, in the dead stillness and to his highly-tensed senses, like the rattling of castanets.

For ten minutes he lay in his new postion; then moved slightly again and waited for fully three-quarters of an hour. Nothing happened, and he now determined to proceed with his inquiries.

Sitting upon the edge of the bunk, he looked about him, first directing his attention to that portion of the wall immediately above. So cunningly was the trap contrived that he could find no trace of its existence. Carefully balancing himself upon the rails on either side of the bunk, he stood up and peered closely about that part of the wall from which the sound had seemd to come. He even ran his fingers lightly over the paper, up as high as he could reach; but not the slightest crevice was perceptible. He began to doubt the evidence of his own senses.

Unless his accursed imagination had been playing him tricks, a trap of some kind had been opened above his head and someone had looked in at him; yet—and his fingers were trained to such work—he was prepared to swear that the surface of the Chinese paper covering the wall was perfectly continuous. He drummed upon it lightly with his finger-tips, here and there over the surface above the bed. And in this fashion he became enlightened.

A portion, roughly a foot in height and two feet long, yielded a slightly different note to his drumming; whereby he knew that that part of the paper was not *attached* to the wall. He perceived the truth. The trap, when closed, fitted flush with the back of the wall-paper, and this paper (although when pasted upon the walls it showed no evidence of the fact) must be *transparent*.

From some dark place beyond, it was possible to peer in *through* the rectangular patch of paper as through a window, at the occupant of the bunk below, upon whom the shaded lamp directly poured its rays!

He examined more closely a lower part of the wall, which did not fall within the shadow of the purple lamp-shade; for he was thinking of the draught which had followed the opening of the trap. By this examination he learnt two things: The explanation of the draught, and that of a peculiar property possessed by the mural decorations. These (as Soames had observed before him) assumed a new form if one stared at them closely; other figures, figures human and animal, seemed to take shape and to peer out from *behind* the more obvious designs which were perceptible at a glance. The longer and the closer one studied these singular walls, the more evident the *under* design became, until it usurped the field of vision entirely. It was a bewildering delusion; but M. Max had solved the mystery.

There were *two* designs; the first, an intricate Chinese pattern, was painted or printed

upon material like the finest gauze. This was attached over a second and vividly colored pattern upon thick parchment-like paper— as he learnt by the application of the point of his pocket-knife.

The observation trap was covered with this paper, and fitted so nicely in the opening that his fingers had failed to detect, through the superimposed gauze, the slightest irregularity there. But, the trap opened, a perfectly clear view of the room could be obtained through the gauze, which, by reason of its texture, also admitted a current of air.

This matter settled, M. Max proceeded carefully to examine the entire room foot by foot. Opening the door in one corner, he entered the bathroom, in which, as in the outer apartment, an electric light was burning. No window was discoverable, and not even an opening for ventilation purposes. The latter fact he might have deduced from the stagnation of the atmosphere.

Half an hour or more he spent in this fashion, without having discovered anything beyond the secret of the observation trap. Again he took out his pocket-knife, which was a large one with a handsome mother-o'-pearl handle. Although Mr. Ho-Pin had examined this carefully, he had solved only half of its secrets. M. Max extracted a little pair of tweezers from the slot in which they were lodged—as Ho-Pin had not neglected to do; but Ho-Pin, having looked at the tweezers, had returned them to their place: M. Max did not do so. He opened the entire knife as though it had been a box, and revealed within it a tiny set of appliances designed principally for the desecration of locks!

Selecting one of these, he took up his watch from the table upon which it lay, and approached the door. It possessed a lever handle of the Continental pattern, and M. Max silently prayed that this might not be a snare and a delusion, but that the lock below might be of the same manufacture.

In order to settle the point, he held the face of his watch close to the keyhole, wound its knob in the wrong direction, and lo! it became an electric lamp!

One glance he cast into the tiny cavity, then dropped back upon the bunk, twisting his mobile mouth in that half smile at once humorous and despairful.

"*Nom d'un p'tit bonhomme!*—a Yale!" he muttered. "To open that without noise is impossible! Damn!"

M. Max threw himself back upon the pillow, and for an hour afterward lay deep in silent reflection.

He had cigarettes in his case and should have liked to smoke, but feared to take the risk of scenting the air with a perfume so unorthodox.

He had gained something by his exploit, but not all that he had hoped for; clearly his part now was to await what the morning should bring.

XXXII

BLUE BLINDS

Morning brought the silent opening of the door, and the entrance of Said, the Egyptian, bearing a tiny Chinese tea service upon a lacquered tray.

But M. Max lay in a seemingly deathly stupor, and from this the impassive Oriental had great difficulty in arousing him. Said, having shaken some symptoms of life into the limp form of M. Max, filled the little cup with fragrant China tea, and, supporting the dazed man, held the beverage to his lips. With his eyes but slightly opened, and with all his weight resting upon the arm of the Egyptian, he gulped the hot tea, and noted that it was of exquisite quality.

Theine is an antidote to opium, and M. Max accordingly became somewhat restored, and lay staring at the Oriental, and blinking his eyes foolishly.

Said, leaving the tea service upon the little table, glided from the room. Something else the Egyptian had left upon the tray in addition to the dainty vessels of porcelain; it was a steel ring containing a dozen or more keys. Most of these keys lay fanwise and bunched together, but one lay isolated and pointing in an opposite direction. It was a Yale key—the key of the door!

Silently as a shadow, M. Max glided into the bathroom, and silently, swiftly, returned, carrying a cake of soap. Three clear, sharp impressions, he secured of the Yale, the soap leaving no trace of the operation upon the metal. He dropped the precious soap tablet into his open bag.

In a state of semi-torpor, M. Max sprawled upon the bed for ten minutes or more, during which time, as he noted, the door re-

mained ajar. Then there entered a figure which seemed wildly out of place in the establishment of Ho-Pin. It was that of a butler, most accurately dressed and most deferential in all his highly-trained movements. His dark hair was neatly brushed, and his face, which had a pinched appearance, was composed in that "if-it-is-entirely-agreeable-to-you-Sir" expression, typical of his class.

The unhealthy, yellow skin of the new arrival, which harmonized so ill with the clear whites of his little furtive eyes, interested M. Max extraordinarily. M. Max was blinking like a week-old kitten, and one could have sworn that he was but hazily conscious of his surroundings; whereas in reality he was memorizing the cranial peculiarities of the new arrival, the shape of his nose, the disposition of his ears; the exact hue of his eyes; the presence of a discolored tooth in his lower jaw, which a fish-like, nervous trick of opening and closing the mouth periodically revealed.

"Good morning, sir!" said the valet, gently rubbing his palms together and bending over the bed.

M. Max inhaled deeply, stared in glassy fashion, but in no way indicated that he had heard the words.

The valet shook him gently by the shoulder.

"Good morning, sir. Shall I prepare your bath?"

"She is a serpent!" muttered M. Max, tossing one arm weakly above his head . . . "all yellow. . . . But roses are growing in the mud . . . of the river!"

"If you will take your bath, sir," insisted the man in black, "I shall be ready to shave you when you return."

"Bath . . . shave me!"

M. Max began to rub his eyes and to stare uncomprehendingly at the speaker.

"Yes, sir; good morning, sir,"—there was another bow and more rubbing of palms.

"Ah!—of course! *Morbleu!* This is Paris. . . ."

"No, sir, excuse me, sir, London. Bath hot or cold, sir?"

"Cold," replied M. Max, struggling upright with apparent difficulty; "yes,—cold."

"Very good, sir. Have you brought your own razor, sir?"

"Yes, yes," muttered Max—"in the bag—in that bag."

"I will fill the bath, sir."

The bath being duly filled, M. Max, throwing about his shoulders a magnificent silk kimono which he found upon the armchair, steered a zigzag course to the bathroom. His tooth-brush had been put in place by the attentive valet; there was an abundance of clean towels, soaps, bath salts, with other necessities and luxuries of the toilet. M. Max, following his bath, saw fit to evidence a return to mental clarity; and whilst he was being shaved he sought to enter into conversation with the valet. But the latter was singularly reticent, and again M. Max changed his tactics. He perceived here a golden opportunity which he must not allow to slip through his fingers.

"Would you like to earn a hundred pounds?" he demanded abruptly, gazing into the beady eyes of the man bending over him.

Soames almost dropped the razor. His state of alarm was truly pitiable; he glanced to the right, he glanced to the left, he glanced over his shoulder, up at the ceiling and down at the floor.

"Excuse me, sir," he said, nervously; "I don't think I quite understand you, sir?"

"It is quite simple," replied M. Max. "I asked you if you had some use for a hundred pounds. Because if you have, I will meet you at any place you like to mention and bring with me cash to that amount!"

"Hush, sir!—for God's sake, hush, sir!" whispered Soames.

A dew of perspiration was glistening upon his forehead, and it was fortunate that he had finished shaving M. Max, for his hand was trembling furiously. He made a pretense of hurrying with towels, bay rum, and powder spray, but the beady eyes were ever glancing to right and left and all about.

M. Max, who throughout this time had been reflecting, made a second move.

"Another fifty, or possibly another hundred, could be earned as easily," he said, with assumed carelessness. "I may add that this will not be offered again, and . . . that you will shortly be out of employment, with worse to follow."

Soames began to exhibit signs of collapse.

"Oh, my God!" he muttered, "what shall I do? I can't promise—I can't promise; but I might—I *might* look in at the 'Three Nuns' on Friday evening about nine o'clock." . . .

He hastily scooped up M. Max's belongings, thrust them into the handbag and closed it. M. Max was now fully dressed and ready to depart. He placed a sovereign in the valet's ready palm.

"That's an appointment," he said softly.

Said entered and stood bowing in the doorway.

"Good morning, sir, good morning," muttered Soames, and covertly he wiped the perspiration from his brow with the corner of a towel—"good morning, and thank you very much."

M. Max, buttoning his light overcoat in order to conceal the fact that he wore evening dress, entered the corridor, and followed the Egyptian into the cave of the golden dragon. Ho-Pin, sleek and smiling, received him there. Ho-Pin was smoking the inevitable cigarette in the long tube, and, opening the door, he silently led the way up the steps into the covered courtyard, Said following with the handbag. The limousine stood there, dimly visible in the darkness. Said placed the handbag upon the seat inside, and Ho-Pin assisted M. Max to enter, closing the door upon him, but leaning through the open window to shake his hand. The Chinaman's hand was icily cold and limp.

"*Au wrevoir*, my dear fwriend," he said in his metallic voice. "I hope to have the pleasure of gwreeting you again vewry shortly."

With that he pulled up the window from the outside, and the occupant of the limousine found himself in impenetrable darkness; for dark blue blinds covered all the windows. He lay back, endeavoring to determine what should be his next move. The car started with a perfect action, and without the slightest jolt or jar. By reason of the light which suddenly shone in through the chinks of the blinds, he knew that he was outside the covered courtyard; then he became aware that a sharp turning had been taken to the left, followed almost immediately, by one to the right.

He directed his attention to the blinds.

"Ah! *nom d'un nom!* they are clever—these!"

The blinds worked in little vertical grooves and had each a tiny lock. The blinds covering the glass doors on either side were attached to the adjustable windows; so that when Ho-Pin had raised the window, he had also closed the blind! And these windows operated automatically, and defied all M. Max's efforts to open them!

He was effectively boxed in and unable

to form the slightest impression of his surroundings. He threw himself back upon the soft cushions with a muttered curse of vexation; but the mobile mouth was twisted into that wryly humorous smile. Always, M. Max was a philosopher.

At the end of a drive of some twenty-five minutes or less, the car stopped—the door was opened, and the radiant Gianapolis extended both hands to the occupant.

"My dear M. Gaston!" he cried, "how glad I am to see you looking so well! Hand me your bag, I beg of you!"

M. Max placed the bag in the extended hand of Gianapolis, and leapt out upon the pavement.

"This way, my dear friend!" cried the Greek, grasping him warmly by the arm.

The Frenchman found himself being led along toward the head of the car; and, at the same moment, Said reversed the gear and backed away. M. Max was foiled in his hopes of learning the number of the limousine.

He glanced about him wonderingly.

"You are in Temple Gardens, M. Gaston," explained the Greek, "and here, unless I am greatly mistaken, comes a disengaged taxicab. You will drive to your hotel?"

"Yes, to my hotel," replied M. Max. "And whenever you wish to avail yourself of your privilege, and pay a second visit to the establishment presided over by Mr. Ho-Pin, you remember the number?"

"I remember the number," replied M. Max.

The cab hailed by Gianapolis drew up beside the two, and M. Max entered it.

"Good morning, M. Gaston."

"Good morning, Mr. Gianapolis."

XXXIII

LOGIC VS. INTUITION

And now, Henry Leroux, Denise Ryland and Helen Cumberly were speeding along the Richmond Road beneath a sky which smiled upon Leroux's convalescence; for this was a perfect autumn morning which ordinarily had gladdened him, but which saddened him today.

The sun shone and the sky was blue; a pleasant breeze played upon his cheeks; whilst Mira, his wife, was . . .

He knew that he had come perilously near to the borderland beyond which are gibbering, mowing things: that he had stood upon the frontier of insanity; and realizing the futility of such reflections, he struggled to banish them from his mind, for his mind was not yet healed—and he must be whole, be sane, if he would take part in the work, which, now, strangers were doing, whilst he—whilst he was a useless hulk.

Denise Ryland had been very voluble at the commencement of the drive, but, as it progressed, had grown gradually silent, and now sat with her brows working up and down and with a little network of wrinkles alternately appearing and disappearing above the bridge of her nose. A self-reliant woman, it was irksome to her to know herself outside the circle of activity revolving around the mysterious Mr. King. She had had one interview with Inspector Dunbar, merely in order that she might give personal testimony to the fact that Mira Leroux had not visited her that year in Paris. Of the shrewd Scotsman she had formed the poorest opinion; and indeed she never had been known to express admiration for, or even the slightest confidence in, any man breathing. The amiable M. Gaston possessed virtues which appealed to her, but whilst she admitted that his conversation was entertaining and his general behavior good, she always spoke with the utmost contempt of his sartorial splendor.

Now, with the days and the weeks slipping by, and with the spectacle before her of poor Leroux, a mere shadow of his former self, with the case, so far as she could perceive, at a standstill, and with the police (she firmly believed) doing "absolutely . . . nothing . . . whatever"—Denise Ryland recognized that what was lacking in the investigation was that intuition and wit which only a clever woman could bring to bear upon it, and of which she, in particular, possessed an unlimited reserve.

The car sped on toward the purer atmosphere of the riverside, and even the clouds of dust, which periodically enveloped them, with the passing of each motor-'bus, and which at the commencement of the drive had inspired her to several notable and syncopated outbursts, now left her unmoved.

She thought that at last she perceived the secret working of that Providence which ever dances attendance at the elbow of accomplished womankind. Following the lead set by "H. C." in the *Planet* ("H. C." was Helen Cumberly's *nom de plume*) and by Crocket in the *Daily Monitor*, the London Press had taken Olaf van Noord to its bosom; and his exhibition in the Little Gallery was an established financial success, whilst "Our Lady of the Poppies" (which had, of course, been rejected by the Royal Academy) promised to be the picture of the year.

Mentally, Denise Ryland was again surveying that remarkable composition; mentally she was surveying Olaf van Noord's model, also. Into the scheme slowly forming in her brain, the yellow-wrapped cigarette containing "a small percentage of opium" fitted likewise. Finally, but not last in importance, the Greek gentleman, Mr. Gianapolis, formed a unit of the whole.

Denise Ryland had always despised those detective creations which abound in French literature; perceiving in their marvelous deductions a tortured logic incompatible with the classic models. She prided herself upon her logic, possibly because it was a quality which she lacked, and probably because she confused it with intuition, of which, to do her justice, she possessed an unusual share. Now, this intuition was at work, at work well and truly; and the result which this mental contortionist ascribed to pure reason was nearer to the truth than a real logician could well have hoped to attain by confining himself to legitimate data. In short, she had determined to her own satisfaction that Mr. Gianapolis was the clue to the mystery; that Mr. Gianapolis was not (as she had once supposed) enacting the part of an amiable liar when he declared that there were, in London, such apartments as that represented by Olaf van Noord; that Mr. Gianapolis was acquainted with the present whereabouts of Mrs. Leroux; that Mr. Gianapolis knew who murdered Iris Vernon; and that Scotland Yard was a benevolent institution for the support of those of enfeebled intellect.

These results achieved, she broke her long silence at the moment that the car was turning into Richmond High Street.

"My dear!" she exclaimed, clutching Helen's arm, "I see it all!"

"Oh!" cried the girl, "how you startled me! I thought you were ill or that you had seen something frightful." . . .

"I *have* . . . seen something . . . frightful," declared Denise Ryland. She glared across at the haggard Leroux. "Harry . . . Leroux," she continued, "it is very fortunate . . . that I came to London . . . very fortunate."

"I am sincerely glad that you did," answered the novelist, with one of his kindly, weary smiles.

"My dear," said Denise Ryland, turning again to Helen Cumberly, "you say you met that . . . cross-eyed . . . being . . . Gianapolis, again?"

"Good Heavens!" cried Helen; "I thought I should never get rid of him; a most loathsome man!"

"My dear . . . child"—Denise squeezed her tightly by the arm, and peered into her face, intently—"cul-tivate . . . *deliberately* cultivate that man's acquaintance!"

Helen stared at her friend as though she suspected the latter's sanity.

"I am afraid I do not understand at all," she said, breathlessly.

"I am positive that I do not," declared Leroux, who was as much surprised as Helen. "In the first place I am not acquainted with this cross-eyed being."

"You are . . . out of this!" cried Denise Ryland with a sweeping movement of the left hand; "entirely . . . out of it! This is no *man's* . . . business." . . .

"But my dear Denise!" exclaimed Helen. . . .

"I beseech you; I entreat you; . . . I *order* . . . you to cul-tivate . . . that . . . execrable . . . being."

"Perhaps," said Helen, with eyes widely opened, "you will condescend to give me some slight reason why I should do anything so extraordinary and undesirable?"

"Undesirable!" cried Denise. "On the contrary; . . . it is *most* . . . desirable! It is essential. The wretched . . . cross-eyed . . . creature has presumed to fall in love . . . with you." . . .

"Oh!" cried Helen, flushing, and glancing rapidly at Leroux, who now was thoroughly interested, "please do not talk nonsense!"

"It is no . . . nonsense. It is the finger . . . of Providence. Do you know where you can find . . . him?"

"Not exactly; but I have a shrewd suspicion," again she glanced in an embarrassed way at Leroux, "that he will know where to find *me*."

"Who is this presumptuous person?" inquired the novelist, leaning forward, his dark blue eyes aglow with interest.

"Never mind," replied Denise Ryland, "you will know . . . soon enough. In the meantime . . . as I am simply . . . starving, suppose we see about . . . lunch?"

Moved by some unaccountable impulse, Helen extended her hand to Leroux, who took it quietly in his own and held it, looking down at the slim fingers as though he derived strength and healing from their touch.

"Poor boy," she said softly.

XXXIV

M. MAX REPORTS PROGRESS

Detective-Sergeant Sowerby was seated in Dunbar's room at New Scotland Yard. Some days had elapsed since that critical moment when, all unaware of the fact, they had stood within three yards of the much-wanted Soames, in the fauteuils of the east-end music-hall. Every clue thus far investigated had proved a cul-de-sac. Dunbar, who had literally been working night and day, now began to show evidence of his giant toils. The tawny eyes were as keen as ever, and the whole man as forceful as of old, but in the intervals of conversation, his lids would droop wearily; he would only arouse himself by a perceptible effort.

Sowerby, whose bowler hat lay upon Dunbar's table, was clad in the familiar raincoat, and his ruddy cheerfulness had abated not one whit.

"Have you ever read 'The Adventures of Martin Zeda'?" he asked suddenly, breaking a silence of some minutes' duration.

Dunbar looked up with a start, as . . .

"Never!" he replied; "I'm not wasting my time with magazine trash."

"It's not trash," said Sowerby, assuming that unnatural air of reflection which sat upon him so ill. "I've looked up the volumes of the *Ludgate Magazine* in our local library, and I've read all the series with much interest."

Dunbar leaned forward, watching him frowningly.

"I should have thought," he replied, "that you had enough to do without wasting your time in that way!"

"*Is* it a waste of time?" inquired Sowerby, raising his eyebrows in a manner which lent him a marked resemblance to a famous comedian. "I tell you that the man who can work out plots like those might be a second Jack-the-Ripper and not a soul the wiser!" . . .

"Ah!"

"I've never met a more innocent *looking* man, I'll allow; but if you'll read the

Adventures of Martin Zeda,' you'll know that" . . .

"Tosh!" snapped Dunbar, irritably; "your ideas of psychology would make a Manx cat laugh! I suppose, on the same analogy, you think the leader-writers of the dailies could run the Government better than the Cabinet does it?"

"I think it very likely" . . .

"Tosh! Is there anybody in London knows more about the inside workings of crime than the Commissioner? You will admit there isn't; very good. Accordingly to your ideas, the Commissioner must be the biggest blackguard in the Metropolis! I have said it twice before, and I'll be saying it again, Sowerby: *tosh!*"

"Well," said Sowerby with an offended air, "has anybody ever seen Mr. King?"

"What are you driving at?"

"I am driving at this: somebody known in certain circles as Mr. King is at the bottom of this mystery. It is highly probable that Mr. King himself murdered Mrs. Vernon. On the evidence of your own notes, nobody left Palace Mansions between the time of the crime and the arrival of witnesses. Therefore, *one* of your witnesses must be a liar; and the liar is Mr. King!"

Inspector Dunbar glared at his subordinate. But the latter continued undaunted:—

"You won't believe it's Leroux; therefore it must be either Mr. Exel, Dr. Cumberly, or Miss Cumberly." . . .

Inspector Dunbar stood up very suddenly, thrusting his chair from him with much violence.

"Do you recollect the matter of Soames leaving Palace Mansions?" he snapped.

Sowerby's air of serio-comic defiance began to leave him. He scratched his head reflectively.

"Soames got away like that because no one was expecting him to do it. In the same way, neither Leroux, Exel, nor Dr. Cumberly knew that there was any one else *in* the flat at the very time when the murderer was making his escape. The cases are identical. They were not looking for a fugitive. He had gone before the search commenced. A clever man could have slipped out in a hundred different ways unobserved. Sowerby, you are . . ."

What Sowerby was, did not come to light at the moment; for, the door quietly opened and in walked M. Gaston Max arrayed in his inimitable traveling coat, and holding his hat of velour in his gloved hand. He bowed politely.

"Good morning, gentlemen," he said.

"Good morning," said Dunbar and Sowerby together.

Sowerby hastened to place a chair for the distinguished visitor. M. Max, thanking him with a bow, took his seat, and from an inside pocket extracted a notebook.

"There are some little points," he said with a deprecating wave of the hand, "which I should like to confirm." He opened the book, sought the wanted page, and continued: "Do either of you know a person answering to the following description: Height, about four feet eight-and-a-half inches, medium build and carries himself with a nervous stoop. Has a habit of rubbing his palms together when addressing anyone. Has plump hands with rather tapering fingers, and a growth of reddish down upon the backs thereof, indicating that he has red or reddish hair. His chin recedes slightly and is pointed, with a slight cleft parallel with the mouth and situated equidistant from the base of the chin and the lower lip. A nervous mannerism of the latter periodically reveals the lower teeth, one of which, that immediately below the left canine, is much discolored. He is clean-shaven, but may at some time have worn whiskers. His eyes are small and ferret-like, set very closely together and of a ruddy brown color. His nose is wide at the bridge, but narrows to an unusual point at the end. In profile it is irregular, or may have been broken at some time. He has scanty eyebrows set very high, and a low forehead with two faint, vertical wrinkles starting from the inner points of the eyebrows. His natural complexion is probably sallow, and his hair (as hitherto mentioned) either red or of sandy color. His ears are set far back, and the lobes are thin and pointed. His hair is perfectly straight and sparse, and there is a depression of the cheeks where one would expect to find a prominence: that is—at the cheekbone. The cranial development is unusual. The skull slopes back from the crown at a remarkable angle, there being no protuberance at the back, but instead a straight slope to the spine, sometimes seen in the Teutonic races, and in this case much exaggerated. Viewed from the front the skull is narrow, the temples depressed, and the crown bulging over the ears, and receding to a ridge on top. In profile the forehead is almost apelike in size and contour . . . ."

"Soames!" exclaimed Inspector Dunbar, Leaping to his feet, and bringing both his palms with a simultaneous bang upon the table before him—"Soames, by God!"

M. Max, shrugging and smiling slightly, returned his notebook to his pocket, and, taking out a cigar-case, placed it, open, upon the table, inviting both his confrères, with a gesture, to avail themselves of its contents.

"I thought so," he said simply. "I am glad."

Sowerby selected a cigar in a dazed manner, but Dunbar, ignoring the presence of the cigar-case, leant forward across the table, his eyes blazing, and his small, even, lower teeth revealed in a sort of grim smile.

"M. Max," he said tensely—"you are a clever man! Where have you got him?"

"I have not got him," replied the Frenchman, selecting and lighting one of his own cigars. "He is much too useful to be locked up" . . .

"But" . . .

"But yes, my dear Inspector—he is safe; oh! he is quite safe. And on Tuesday night he is going to introduce us to Mr. King!"

"Mr. King!" roared Dunbar; and in three strides of the long legs he was around the table and standing before the Frenchman.

In passing he swept Sowerby's hat on to the floor, and Sowerby, picking it up, began mechanically to brush it with his left sleeve, smoking furiously the while.

"Soames," continued M. Max, quietly—"he is now known as Lucas, by the way—is a man of very remarkable character; a fact indicated by his quite unusual skull. He has no more will than this cigar"—he held the cigar up between his fingers, illustratively—"but of stupid pig obstinacy, that canaille—saligaud!—has enough for all the cattle in Europe! He is like a man who knows that he stands upon a sinking ship, yet, who whilst promising to take the plunge every moment, hesitates and will continue to hesitate until someone pushes him in. Pardieu! I push! Because of his pig obstinacy I am compelled to take risks most unnecessary. He will not consent, that Soames, to open the door for us . . ."

"What door?" snapped Dunbar.

"The door of the establishment of Mr. King," explained Max, blandly.

"But where is it?"

"It is somewhere between Limehouse Causeway—is it not called so?—and the riverside. But although I have been there, myself, I can tell you no more . . . ."

"What! you have been there yourself?"

"But yes—most decidedly. I was there some nights ago. But they are ingenious, ah! they are so ingenious!—so Chinese! I should not have known even the little I do know if it were not for the inquiries which I made last week. I knew that the letters to Mr. Leroux which were supposed to come from Paris were handed by Soames to some one who posted them to Paris from Bow, East. You remember how I found the impression of the postmark?"

Dunbar nodded, his eyes glistening; for that discovery of the Frenchman's had filled him with a sort of envious admiration.

"Well, then," continued Max, "I knew that the inquiry would lead me to your east-end, and I suspected that I was dealing with Chinamen; therefore, suitably attired, of course, I wandered about in those interesting slums on more than one occasion; and I concluded that the only district in which a Chinaman could live without exciting curiosity was that which lies off the West India Dock Road." . . .

Dunbar nodded significantly at Sowerby, as who should say: "What did I tell you about this man?"

"On one of these visits," continued the Frenchman, and a smile struggled for expression upon his mobile lips, "I met you two gentlemen with a Mr.—I think he is called Stringer—" . . .

"You met us!" exclaimed Sowerby.

"My sense of humor quite overcoming me," replied M. Max, "I even tried to swindle you. I think I did the trick very badly!"

Dunbar and Sowerby were staring at one another amazedly.

"It was in the corner of a public house billiard-room," added the Frenchman, with twinkling eyes; "I adopted the ill-used name of Levinsky on that occasion." . . .

Dunbar began to punch his left palm and to stride up and down the floor; whilst Sowerby, his blue eyes opened quite roundly, watched M. Max as a schoolboy watches an illusionist.

"Therefore," continued M. Max, "I shall ask you to have a party ready on Tuesday night in Limehouse Causeway—suitably concealed, of course; and as I am almost sure that the haunt of Mr. King is actually upon the riverside (I heard one little river sound as I was coming away) a launch party might cooperate with you in affecting the raid."

"The raid!" said Dunbar, turning from a point by the window, and looking back at the Frenchman. "Do you seriously tell me that we are going to raid Mr. King's on Tuesday night?"

"Most certainly," was the confident reply. "I had hoped to form one of the raiding party; but *nom d'un nom!*"—he shrugged, in his graceful fashion—"I must be one of the rescued!"

"Of the rescued!"

"You see I visited that establishment as a smoker of opium" . . .

"You took that risk?"

"It was no greater risk than is run by quite a number of people socially well known in London, my dear Inspector Dunbar! I was introduced by an habitué and a member of the best society; and since nobody knows that Gaston Max is in London—that Gaston Max has any business in hand likely to bring him to London—*pardieu*, what danger did I incur? But, excepting the lobby—the cave of the dragon (a stranger apartment even than that in the Rue St. Claude) and the Chinese cubiculum where I spent the night—*mon dieu!* what a night!—I saw nothing of the establishment" . . .

"But you must know where it is!" cried Dunbar.

"I was driven there in a closed limousine, and driven away in the same vehicle" . . .

"You got the number?"

"It was impossible. These are clever people! But it must be a simple matter, Inspector, to trace a fine car like that which regularly appears in those east-end streets?"

"Every constable in the division must be acquainted with it," replied Dunbar, confidently. "I'll know all about that car inside the next hour!"

"If on Tuesday night you could arrange to have it followed," continued M. Max, "it would simplify matters. What I have done is this: I have bought the man, Soames—up to a point. But so deadly is his fear of the mysterious Mr. King that although he has agreed to assist me in my plans, he will not consent to divulge an atom of information until the raid is successfully performed."

"Then for heaven's sake what *is* he going to do?"

"Visitors to the establishment (it is managed by a certain Mr. Ho-Pin; make a note of him, that Ho-Pin) having received the necessary dose of opium are locked in for the night. On Tuesday, Soames, who acts as valet to poor fools using the place, has agreed—

for a price—to unlock the door of the room in which *I* shall be" . . .

"What!" cried Dunbar, "you are going to risk yourself alone in that place *again?*"

"I have paid a very heavy fee," replied the Frenchman with his odd smile, "and it entitles me to a second visit; I shall pay that second visit on Tuesday night, and my danger will be no greater than on the first occasion."

"But Soames may betray you!"

"Fear nothing; I have measured my Soames, not only anthropologically, but otherwise. I fear only his folly, not his knavery. He will not betray me. *Morbleu!* he is too much a frightened man. I do not know what has taken place; but I could see that, assured of escaping the police for complicity in the murder, he would turn King's evidence immediately" . . .

"And you gave him that assurance?"

"At first I did not reveal myself. I weighed up my man very carefully; I measured that Soames-pig. I had several stories in readiness, but his character indicated which I should use. Therefore, suddenly I arrested him!"

"Arrested him?"

"*Pardieu!* I arrested him very quietly in a corner of the bar of 'Three Nuns' public house. My course was justified. He saw that the reign of his mysterious Mr. King was nearing its close, and that I was his only hope" . . .

"But still he refused" . . .

"His refusal to reveal anything whatever under those circumstances impressed me more than all. It showed me that in Mr. King I had to deal with a really wonderful and powerful man; a man who ruled by means of *fear;* a man of gigantic force. I had taken the pattern of the key fitting the Yale lock of the door of my room, and I secured a duplicate immediately. Soames has not access to the keys, you understand. I must rely upon my diplomacy to secure the same room again—all turns upon that; and at an hour after midnight, or later if advisable, Soames has agreed to let me out. Beyond this, I could induce him to do nothing—nothing whatever. *Cochon!* Therefore, having got out of the locked room, I must rely upon my own wits—and the Browning pistol which I have presented to Soames together with the duplicate key" . . .

"Why not go armed?" asked Dunbar.

"One's clothes are searched, my dear Inspector, by an expert! I have given the key,

the pistol, and the implements of the housebreaker (a very neat set which fits easily into the breast-pocket) to Soames, to conceal in his private room at the establishment until Tuesday night. All turns upon my securing the same apartment. If I am unable to do so, the arrangements for the raid will have to be postponed. Opium smokers are faddists essentially, however, and I think I can manage to pretend that I have formed a strange penchant for this particular cubiculum" . . .

"By whom were you introduced to the place?" asked Dunbar, leaning back against the table and facing the Frenchman.

"That I cannot in honor divulge," was the reply; "but the representative of Mr. King who actually admitted me to the establishment is one Gianapolis; address unknown, but telephone number 18642 East. Make a note of him, that Gianapolis."

"I'll arrest him in the morning," said Sowerby, writing furiously in his notebook.

"*Nom d'un p'tit bonhomme!* M. Sowerby, you will do nothing of that foolish description, my dear friend," said Max; and Dunbar glared at the unfortunate sergeant. "Nothing whatever must be done to arouse suspicion between now and the moment of the raid. You must be circumspect—ah, *morbleu!* so circumspect. By all means trace this Mr. Gianapolis; yes. But do not let him *suspect* that he is being traced" . . .

XXXV

TRACKER TRACKED

Helen Cumberly and Denise Ryland peered from the window of the former's room into the dusk of the Square, until their eyes ached with the strain of an exercise so unnatural.

"I tell you," said Denise with emphasis, "that . . . sooner or later . . . he will come prowling . . . around. The mere fact that he did not appear . . . last night . . . counts for nothing. His own crooked . . . plans no doubt detain him . . . very often . . . at night."

Helen sighed wearily. Denise Ryland's scheme was extremely distasteful to her, but whenever she thought of the pathetic eyes of Leroux she found new determination. Several times she had essayed to analyze the motives which actuated her; always she feared to pursue such inquiries beyond a certain point. Now that she was beginning to share her friend's views upon the matter, all social plans sank into insignificance, and she lived only in the hope of again meeting Gianapolis, of tracing out the opium group, and of finding Mrs. Leroux. In what state did she hope and expect to find her? This was a double question which kept her wakeful through the dreary watches of the night. . . .

"Look!"

Denise Ryland grasped her by the arm, pointing out into the darkened Square. A furtive figure crossed from the northeast corner into the shade of some trees and might be vaguely detected coming nearer and nearer.

"There he is!" whispered Denise Ryland, excitedly; "I told you he couldn't . . . keep away. I know that kind of brute. There is nobody at home, so listen: I will watch . . . from the drawing-room, and you . . . light up here and move about . . . as if preparing to go out."

Helen, aware that she was flushed with excitement, fell in with the proposal readily; and having switched on the lights in her room and put on her hat so that her moving shadow was thrown upon the casement curtain, she turned out the light again and ran to rejoin her friend. She found the latter peering eagerly from the window of the drawing-room.

"He thinks you are coming out!" gasped Denise. "He has slipped . . . around the corner. He will pretend to be . . . passing . . . this way . . . the cross-eyed . . . hypocrite. Do you feel capable . . . of the task?"

"Quite," Helen declared, her cheeks flushed and her eyes sparkling. "You will follow us as arranged; for heaven's sake, don't lose us!"

"If the doctor knew of this," breathed Denise, "he would never . . . forgive me. But no woman . . . no true woman . . . could refuse to undertake . . . so palpable . . . a duty" . . .

Helen Cumberly, wearing a warm, golfing jersey over her dress, with a woolen cap to match, ran lightly down the stairs and out into the Square, carrying a letter. She walked along to the pillar-box, and having examined the address upon the envelope with great care, by the light of an adjacent lamp, posted the letter, turned—and there, radiant and bowing, stood Mr. Gianapolis.

"Kismet is really most kind to me!" he cried. "My friend, who lives, as I think I mentioned once before, in Peer's Chambers, evidently radiates good luck. I last had the good fortune to meet you when on my way

to see him, and I now meet you again within five minutes of leaving him! My dear Miss Cumberly, I trust you are quite well?"

"Quite," said Helen, holding out her hand. "I am awfully glad to see you again, Mr. Gianapolis!"

He was distinctly encouraged by her tone. He bent forward confidentially.

"The night is young," he said; and his smile was radiant. "May I hope that your expedition does not terminate at this post-box?"

Helen glanced at him doubtfully, and then down at her jersey. Gianapolis was unfeignedly delighted with her naïveté.

"Surely you don't want to be seen with me in this extraordinary costume!" she challenged . .

"My dear Miss Cumberly, it is simply enchanting! A girl with such a figure as yours never looks better than when she dresses sportily!"

The latent vulgarity of the man was escaping from the bondage in which ordinarily he confined it. A real passion had him in its grip, and the real Gianapolis was speaking. Helen hesitated for one fateful moment; it was going to be even worse than she had anticipated. She glanced up at Palace Mansions.

Across a curtained window moved a shadow, that of a man wearing a long gown and having his hands clasped behind him, whose head showed as an indistinct blur because the hair was wildly disordered. This shadow passed from side to side of the window and was lost from view. It was the shadow of Henry Leroux.

"I am afraid I have a lot of work to do," said Helen, with a little catch in her voice.

"My dear Miss Cumberly," cried Gianapolis, eagerly, placing his hand upon her arm, "it is precisely of your work that I wish to speak to you! Your work is familiar to me— I never miss a line of it; and knowing how you delight in the outré and how inimitably you can describe scenes of Bohemian life, I had hoped, since it was my privilege to meet you, that you would accept my services as cicerone to some of the lesser-known resorts of Bohemian London. Your article, 'Dinner in Soho,' was a delightful piece of observation, and the third—I think it was the third— of the same series: 'Curiosities of the Café Royal,' was equally good. But your powers of observation would be given greater play in any one of the three establishments to which I should be honored to escort you."

Helen Cumberly, though perfectly self-reliant, as only the modern girl journalist can be, was fully aware that, not being of the flat-haired, bespectacled type, she was called upon to exercise rather more care in her selection of companions for copy-hunting expeditions than was necessary in the case of certain fellow-members of the Scribes' Club. No power on earth could have induced her to accept such an invitation from such a man, under ordinary circumstances; even now, with so definite and important an object in view, she hesitated. The scheme might lead to nothing; Denise Ryland (horrible thought!) might lose the track; the track might lead to no place of importance, so far as her real inquiry was concerned.

In this hour of emergency, new and wiser ideas were flooding her brain. For instance, they might have admitted Inspector Dunbar to the plot. With Inspector Dunbar dogging her steps, she should have felt perfectly safe; but Denise—she had every respect for Denise's reasoning powers, and force of character—yet Denise nevertheless might fail her.

She glanced into the crooked eyes of Gianapolis, then up again at Palace Mansions.

The shadow of Henry Leroux recrossed the cream-curtained window.

"So early in the evening," pursued the Greek, rapidly, "the more interesting types will hardly have arrived; nevertheless, at the Memphis Café" . . .

"Memphis Café!" muttered Helen, glancing at him rapidly; "what an odd name."

"Ah! My dear Miss Cumberly!" cried Gianapolis, with triumph—"I knew that you had never heard of the true haunts of Bohemia! The Memphis Café—it is actually a club—was founded by Olaf van Noord two years ago, and at present has a membership including some of the most famous artistic folk of London; not only painters, but authors, composers, actors, actresses. I may add that the peerage, male and female, is represented."

"It is actually a gaming-house, I suppose?" said Helen, shrewdly.

"A gaming-house? Not at all! If what you wish to see is play for high stakes, it is not to the Memphis Café you must go. I can show you Society losing its money in thousands, if the spectacle would amuse you. I only await your orders" . . .

"You certainly interest me," said Helen;

and indeed this half-glimpse into phases of London life hidden from the world—even from the greater part of the ever-peering journalistic world—was not lacking in fascination.

The planning of a scheme in its entirety constitutes a mental effort which not infrequently blinds us to the shortcomings of certain essential details. Denise's plan, a good one in many respects, had the fault of being over-elaborate. Now, when it was too late to advise her friend of any amendment, Helen perceived that there was no occasion for her to suffer the society of Gianapolis.

To bid him good evening, and then to follow him, herself, was a plan much superior to that of keeping him company whilst Denise followed both!

Moreover, he would then be much more likely to go home, or to some address which it would be useful to know. What a *very* womanish scheme theirs had been, after all; Helen told herself that the most stupid man imaginable could have placed his finger upon its weak spot immediately.

But her mind was made up. If it were possible, she would warn Denise of the change of plan; if it were not, then she must rely upon her friend to see through the ruse which she was about to practise upon the Greek.

"Good night, Mr. Gianapolis!" she said abruptly, and held out her hand to the smiling man. His smile faded. "I should love to join you, but really you must know that it's impossible. I will arrange to make up a party, with pleasure, if you will let me know where I can 'phone you?"

"But," he began . . .

"Many thanks, it's really impossible; there are limits even to the escapades allowed under the cloak of 'Copy'! Where can I communicate with you?"

"Oh! how disappointed I am! But I must permit you to know your own wishes better than I can hope to know them, Miss Cumberly. Therefore"—Helen was persistently holding out her hand—"good night! Might I venture to telephone to *you* in the morning? We could then come to some arrangement, no doubt" . . .

"You might not find me at home" . . .

"But at nine o'clock!"

"It allows me no time to make up my party!"

"But such a party must not exceed three: yourself and two others" . . .

"Nevertheless, it has to be arranged."

"I shall ring up to-morrow evening, and if you are not at home, your maid will tell me when you are expected to return."

Helen quite clearly perceived that no address and no telephone number were forthcoming.

"You are committing yourself to endless and unnecessary trouble, Mr. Gianapolis, but if you really wish to do as you suggest, let it be so. Good night!"

She barely touched his extended hand, turned, and ran fleetly back toward the door of Palace Mansions. Ere reaching the entrance, however, she dropped a handkerchief, stooped to recover it, and glanced back rapidly.

Gianapolis was just turning the corner.

Helen perceived the unmistakable form of Denise Ryland lurking in the Palace Mansions doorway, and, waving frantically to her friend, who was nonplussed at this change of tactics, she hurried back again to the corner and peeped cautiously after the retreating Greek.

There was a cab rank some fifty paces beyond, with three taxis stationed there. If Gianapolis chartered a cab, and she were compelled to follow in another, would Denise come upon the scene in time to take up the prearranged rôle of sleuth-hound?

Gianapolis hesitated only for a few seconds; then, shrugging his shoulders, he stepped out into the road and into the first cab on the rank. The man cranked his engine, leapt into his seat and drove off. Helen Cumberly, ignoring the curious stares of the two remaining taxi-men, ran out from the shelter of the corner and jumped into the next cab, crying breathlessly:

"Follow that cab! Don't let the man in it suspect, but follow, and don't lose sight of it!"

They were off!

Helen glanced ahead quickly, and was just in time to see Gianapolis' cab disappear; then, leaning out of the window, she indulged in an extravagant pantomime for the benefit of Denise Ryland, who was hurrying after her.

"Take the next cab and follow *me!*" she cried, whilst her friend raised her hand to her ear the better to detect the words. "I cannot wait for you or the track will be lost" . . .

Helen's cab swung around the corner—and she was not by any means certain that Denise Ryland had understood her; but to have delayed would have been fatal, and she

must rely upon her friend's powers of penetration to form a third in this singular procession.

Whilst these thoughts were passing in the pursuer's mind, Gianapolis, lighting a cigarette, had thrown himself back in a corner of the cab and was mentally reviewing the events of the evening—that is, those events which were associated with Helen Cumberly. He was disappointed but hopeful: at any rate he had suffered no definite repulse. Without doubt, his reflections had been less roseate had he known that he was followed, not only by two, but by *three* trackers.

He had suspected for some time now, and the suspicion had made him uneasy, that his movements were being watched. Police surveillance he did not fear; his arrangements were too complete, he believed, to occasion him any ground for anxiety even though half the Criminal Investigation Department were engaged in dogging his every movement. He understood police methods very thoroughly, and all his experience told him that this elusive shadow which latterly had joined him unbidden, and of whose presence he was specially conscious whenever his steps led toward Palace Mansions, was no police officer.

He had two theories respecting the shadow—or, more properly, one theory which was divisible into two parts; and neither part was conducive to peace of mind. Many years, crowded with many happenings, some of which he would fain forget, had passed since the day when he had entered the service of Mr. King, in Pekin. The enterprises of Mr. King were always of a secret nature, and he well remembered the fate of a certain Burmese gentleman of Rangoon who had attempted to throw the light of publicity into the dark places of these affairs.

From a confidant of the doomed man, Gianapolis had learned, fully a month before a mysterious end had come to the Burman, how the latter (by profession a money-lender) had complained of being shadowed night and day by someone or something, of whom or of which he could never succeed in obtaining so much as a glimpse.

Gianapolis shuddered. These were morbid reflections, for, since he had no thought of betraying Mr. King, he had no occasion to apprehend a fate similar to that of the unfortunate money-lender of Rangoon. It was a very profitable service, that of Mr. King, yet there were times when the fear of his employer struck a chill to his heart; there were times when almost he wished to be done with it all . . .

By Whitechapel Station he discharged the cab, and, standing on the pavement, lighted a new cigarette from the glowing stump of the old one. A fair amount of traffic passed along the Whitechapel Road, for the night was yet young; therefore Gianapolis attached no importance to the fact that almost at the moment when his own cab turned and was driven away, a second cab swung around the corner of Mount Street and disappeared.

But, could he have seen the big limousine drawn up to the pavement some fifty yards west of London Hospital, his reflections must have been terrible, indeed.

Fate willed that he should know nothing of this matter, and, his thoughts automatically reverting again to Helen Cumberly, he enjoyed that imaginary companionship throughout the remainder of his walk, which led him along Cambridge Road, and from thence, by a devious route, to the northern end of Globe Road.

It may be enlightening to leave Gianapolis for a moment and to return to Mount Street.

Helen Cumberly's cabman, seeing the cab ahead pull up outside the railway station, turned around the nearest corner on the right (as has already appeared), and there stopped. Helen, who also had observed the maneuver of the taxi ahead, hastily descended, and giving the man half-a-sovereign, said rapidly:

"I must follow on foot now, I am afraid! but as I don't know this district at all, could you bring the cab along without attracting attention, and manage to keep me in sight?"

"I'll try, miss," replied the man, with alacrity; "but it won't be an easy job."

"Do your best," cried Helen, and ran off rapidly around the corner, and into Whitechapel Road.

She was just in time to see Gianapolis throw away the stump of his first cigarette and stroll off, smoking a second. She rejoiced that she was inconspicuously dressed, but, simple as was her attire, it did not fail to attract coarse comment from some whom she jostled on her way. She ignored all this, however, and, at a discreet distance followed the Greek, never losing sight of him for more than a moment.

When, leaving Cambridge Road—a considerable thoroughfare—he plunged into a turning, crooked and uninviting, which ran roughly at right angles with the former, she hesitated, but only for an instant. Not another pedestrian was visible in the street,

which was very narrow and ill-lighted, but she plainly saw Gianapolis passing under a street-lamp some thirty yards along. Glancing back in quest of the cabman, but failing to perceive him, she resumed the pursuit.

She was nearly come to the end of the street (Gianapolis already had disappeared into an even narrower turning on the left) when a bright light suddenly swept from behind and cast her shadow far out in front of her upon the muddy road. She heard the faint thudding of a motor, but did not look back, for she was confident that this was the taxi-man following. She crept to the corner and peered around it; Gianapolis had disappeared.

The light grew brighter—brighter yet; and, with the engine running very silently, the car came up almost beside her. She considered this unwise on the man's part, yet welcomed his presence, for in this place not a soul was visible, and for the first time she began to feel afraid . . .

A shawl, or some kind of silken wrap, was suddenly thrown over her head!

She shrieked frenziedly, but the arm of her captor was now clasped tightly about her mouth and head. She felt herself to be suffocating. The silken thing which enveloped her was redolent of the perfume of roses; it was stifling her. She fought furiously, but her arms were now seized in an irresistible grasp, and she felt herself lifted—and placed upon a cushioned seat.

Instantly there was a forward movement of the vehicle which she had mistaken for a taxi-cab, . . . and she knew that she was speeding through those unknown east-end streets—God! to what destination?

She could not cry out, for she was fighting for air—she seemed to be encircled by a swirling cloud of purplish mist. On—and on—and on, she was borne; she knew that she must have been drugged in some way, for consciousness was slipping—slipping . . .

Helpless as a child in that embrace which never faltered, she was lifted again and carried down many steps. Insensibility was very near now, but with all the will that was hers she struggled to fend it off. She felt herself laid down upon soft cushions . . .

A guttural voice was speaking, from a vast distance away:

"What is this that you bwring us, Mahâra?"

Answered a sweet, silvery voice:

"Does it matter to you what I bringing? It is one I hate—hate—*hate!* There will be *two* cases of 'ginger' to go away some day instead of *one*—that is all! *Said, yälla!"*

"Your pwrimitive passions will wruin us" . . .

The silvery voice grew even more silvery: "Do you quarrel with me, Ho-Pin, my friend?"

"This is England, not Burma! Giana-polis" . . .

"Ah! Whisper—*whisper* it to *him,* and" . . .

Oblivion closed in upon Helen Cumberly; she seemed to be sinking into the heart of a giant rose.

XXXVI

IN DUNBAR'S ROOM

Dr. Cumberly, his face unusually pale, stood over by the window of Inspector Dunbar's room, his hands locked behind him. In the chair nearest to the window sat Henry Leroux, so muffled up in a fur-collared motor-coat that little of his face was visible; but his eyes were tragic as he leant forward resting his elbows upon his knees and twirling his cap between his thin fingers. He was watching Inspector Dunbar intently; only glancing from the gaunt face of the detective occasionally to look at Denise Ryland, who sat close to the table. At such times his gaze was pathetically reproachful, but always rather sorrowful than angry.

As for Miss Ryland, her habitual self-confidence seemed somewhat to have deserted her, and it was almost with respectful interest that she followed Dunbar's examination of a cabman who, standing cap in hand, completed the party so strangely come together at that late hour.

"This is what you have said," declared Dunbar, taking up an official form, and, with a movement of his hand warning the taxi-man to pay attention: " 'I, Frederick Dean, motor-cab driver, was standing on the rank in Little Abbey Street to-night at about a quarter to nine. My cab was the second on the rank. A young lady who wore, I remember, a woolen cap and jersey, with a blue serge skirt, ran out from the corner of the Square and directed me to follow the cab in front of me, which had just been chartered by a dark man wearing a black overcoat and silk hat. She ordered me to keep him in sight; and as I drove off I heard her calling from the window of my cab to another lady who

seemed to be following her. I was unable to see this other lady, but my fare addressed her as "Denise." I followed the first cab to Whitechapel Station; and as I saw it stop there, I swung into Mount Street. The lady gave me half-a-sovereign, and told me that she proposed to follow the man on foot. She asked me if I could manage to keep her in sight, without letting my cab be seen by the man she was following. I said I would try, and I crept along at some distance behind her, going as slowly as possible until she went into a turning branching off to the right of Cambridge Road; I don't know the name of this street. She was some distance ahead of me, for I had had trouble in crossing Whitechapel Road.

" 'A big limousine had passed me a moment before, but as an electric tram was just going by on my off-side, between me and the limousine, I don't know where the limousine went. When I was clear of the tram I could not see it, and it may have gone down Cambridge Road and then down the same turning as the lady. I pulled up at the end of this turning, and could not see a sign of any one. It was quite deserted right to the end, and although I drove down, bore around to the right and finally came out near the top of Globe Road, I did not pass anyone. I waited about the district for over a quarter-of-an-hour and then drove straight to the police station, and they sent me on here to Scotland Yard to report what had occurred.'

"Have you anything to add to that?" said Dunbar, fixing his tawny eyes upon the cab-man.

"Nothing at all," replied the man—a very spruce and intelligent specimen of his class and one who, although he had moved with the times, yet retained a slightly horsey appearance, which indicated that he had not always been a mechanical Jehu.

"It is quite satisfactory as far as it goes," muttered Dunbar. "I'll get you to sign it now and we need not detain you any longer."

"There is not the slightest doubt," said Dr. Cumberly, stepping forward and speaking in an unusually harsh voice, "that Helen endeavored to track this man Gianapolis, and was abducted by him or his associates. The limousine was the car of which we have heard so much" . . .

"If my cabman had not been such a . . . fool," broke in Denise Ryland, clasping her hands, "we should have had a different . . . tale to tell."

"I have no wish to reproach anybody,"

said Dunbar, sternly; "but I feel called upon to remark, madam, that you ought to have known better than to interfere in a case like this; a case in which we are dealing with a desperate and clever gang."

For once in her life Denise Ryland found herself unable to retort suitably. The mildly reproachful gaze of Leroux she could not meet; and although Dr. Cumberly had spoken no word of complaint against her, from his pale face she persistently turned away her eyes.

The cabman having departed, the door almost immediately reopened, and Sergeant Sowerby came in.

"Ah! there you are, Sowerby!" cried Dunbar, standing up and leaning eagerly across the table. "You have the particulars respecting the limousine?"

Sergeant Sowerby, removing his hat and carefully placing it upon the only vacant chair in the room, extracted a bulging notebook from a pocket concealed beneath his raincoat, cleared his throat, and reported as follows:

"There is only one car known to members of that division which answers to the description of the one wanted. This is a high-power, French car which seems to have been registered first in Paris, where it was made, then in Cairo, and lastly in London. It is the property of the gentleman whose telephone number is 18642 East—Mr. I. Gianapolis; and the reason of its frequent presence in the neighborhood of the West India Dock Road, is this: it is kept in a garage in Wharf-End Lane, off Limehouse Causeway. I have interviewed two constables at present on that beat, and they tell me that there is nothing mysterious about the car except that the chauffeur is a foreigner who speaks no English. He is often to be seen cleaning the car in the garage, and both the men are in the habit of exchanging good evening with him when passing the end of the lane. They rarely go that far, however, as it leads nowhere."

"But if you have the telephone number of this man, Gianapolis," cried Dr. Cumberly, "you must also have his address" . . .

"We obtained both from the Eastern Exchange," interrupted Inspector Dunbar. "The instrument, number 18642 East, is installed in an office in Globe Road. The office, which is situated in a converted private dwelling, bears a brass plate simply inscribed, 'I. Gianapolis, London and Smyrna.' "

"What is the man's reputed business?" jerked Cumberly.

"We have not quite got to the bottom of that, yet," replied Sowerby; "but he is an agent of some kind, and evidently in a large way of business, as he runs a very fine car, and seems to live principally in different hotels. I am told that he is an importer of Turkish cigarettes and" . . .

"He is an importer and exporter of *hashish!*" snapped Dunbar irritably. "If I could clap my eyes upon him I should know him at once! I tell you, Sowerby, he is the man who was convicted last year of exporting *hashish* to Egypt in faked packing-cases which contained pottery ware, ostensibly, but had false bottoms filled with cakes of *hashish*" . . .

"But," began Dr. Cumberly . . .

"But because he came before a silly bench," snapped Dunbar, his eyes flashing angrily, "he got off with a fine—a heavy one, certainly, but he could well afford to pay it. It is that kind of judicial folly which ties the hands of Scotland Yard!"

"What makes you so confident that this is the man?" asked the physician.

"He was convicted under the name of G. Ionagis," replied the detective; "which I believe to be either his real name or his real name transposed. Do you follow me? I. Gianapolis is Ionagis Gianapolis, and G. Ionagis is Gianapolis Ionagis. I was not associated with the *hashish* case; he stored the stuff in a china warehouse within the city precincts, and at that time he did not come within my sphere. But I looked into it privately, and I could see that the prosecution was merely skimming the surface; we are only beginning to get down to the depths *now*."

Dr. Cumberly raised his hand to his head in a distracted manner.

"Surely," he said, and he was evidently exercising a great restraint upon himself— "surely we're wasting time. The office in Globe Road should be raided without delay. No stone should be left unturned to effect the immediate arrest of this man Gianapolis or Ionagis. Why, God almighty! while we are talking here, my daughter" . . .

"*Morbleu!* who talks of arresting Gianapolis?" inquired the voice of a man who silently had entered the room.

All turned their heads; and there in the doorway stood M. Gaston Max.

"Thank God you've come!" said Dunbar with sincerity. He dropped back into his chair, a strong man exhausted. "This case is getting beyond me!"

Denise Ryland was staring at the Frenchman as if fascinated. He, for his part, having glanced around the room, seemed called upon to give her some explanation of his presence.

"Madame," he said, bowing in his courtly way, "only because of very great interests did I dare to conceal my true identity. My name is Gaston, that is true, but only so far as it goes. My real name is Gaston Max, and you who live in Paris will perhaps have heard it."

"Gaston Max!" cried Denise Ryland, springing upright as though galvanized; "you are M. Gaston Max! But you are not the least bit in the world like" . . .

"Myself?" said the Frenchman, smiling. "Madame, it is only a man fortunate enough to possess no enemies who can dare to be like himself."

He bowed to her in an oddly conclusive manner, and turned again to Inspector Dunbar.

"I am summoned in haste," he said; "tell me quickly of this new development."

Sowerby snatched his hat from the vacant chair, and politely placed the chair for M. Max to sit upon. The Frenchman, always courteous, gently forced Sergeant Sowerby himself to occupy the chair, silencing his muttered protests with upraised hand. The matter settled, he lowered his hand, and, resting it fraternally upon the sergeant's shoulder, listened to Inspector Dunbar's account of what had occurred that night. No one interrupted the Inspector until he was come to the end of his narrative.

"*Mille tonnerres!*" then exclaimed M. Max; and, holding a finger of his glove between his teeth, he tugged so sharply that a long rent appeared in the suede.

His eyes were on fire; the whole man quivered with electric force.

In silence that group watched the celebrated Frenchman; instinctively they looked to him for aid. It is at such times that personality proclaims itself. Here was the last court of appeal, to which came Dr. Cumberly and Inspector Dunbar alike; whose pronouncement they awaited, not questioning that it would be final.

"To-morrow night," began Max, speaking in a very low voice, "we raid the headquarters of Ho-Pin. This disappearance of your daughter, Dr. Cumberly, is frightful; it could not have been foreseen or it should have been prevented. But the least mistake now, and"—he looked at Dr. Cumberly as if apologizing for his barbed words—"she

may never return!"

"My God!" groaned the physician, and momentarily dropped his face into his hands.

But almost immediately he recovered himself and with his mouth drawn into a grim straight line, looked again at M. Max, who continued:

"I do not think that this abduction was planned by the group; I think it was an accident and that they were forced, in self-protection, to detain your daughter, who unwisely—*morbleu!* how unwisely!—forced herself into their secrets. To arrest Gianapolis (even if that were possible) would be to close their doors to us permanently; and as we do not even know the situation of those doors, that would be to ruin everything. Whether Miss Cumberly is confined in the establishment of Ho-Pin or somewhere else, I cannot say; whether she is a captive of Gianapolis or of Mr. King, I do not know. But I know that the usual conduct of the establishment is not being interrupted at present; for only half-an-hour ago I telephoned to Mr. Gianapolis!"

"At Globe Road?" snapped Dunbar, with a flash of the tawny eyes.

"At Globe Road—yes (oh! they would not detain her there!). Mr. Gianapolis was present to speak to me. He met me very agreeably in the matter of occupying my old room in the delightful Chinese hotel of Mr. Ho-Pin. Therefore"—he swept his left hand around forensically, as if to include the whole of the company—"to-morrow night at eleven o'clock I shall be meeting Mr. Gianapolis at Piccadilly Circus, and later we shall join the limousine and be driven to the establishment of Ho-Pin." He turned to Inspector Dunbar. "Your arrangements for watching all the approaches to the suspected area are no doubt complete?"

"Not a stray cat," said Dunbar with emphasis, "can approach Limehouse Causeway or Pennyfields, or any of the environs of the place, to-morrow night after ten o'clock, without the fact being reported to me! You will know at the moment that you step from the limousine that a cyclist scout, carefully concealed, is close at your heels with a whole troupe to follow; and if, as you suspect, the den adjoins the river bank, a police cutter will be lying at the nearest available point."

"*Eh bien!*" said M. Max; then, turning to Denise Ryland and Dr. Cumberly, and shrugging his shoulders: "you see, frightful as your suspense must be, to make any foolish arrests to-night, to move in this matter at all to-night—would be a case of more haste and less speed" . . .

"But," groaned Cumberly, "is Helen to lie in that foul, unspeakable den until the small hours of to-morrow morning? Good God! they may" . . .

"There is one little point," interrupted M. Max with upraised hand, "which makes it impossible that we should move to-night— quite apart from the advisability of such a movement. We do not know exactly where this place is situated. What can we do?" He shrugged his shoulders, and, with raised eyebrows, stared at Dr. Cumberly.

"It is fairly evident," replied the other slowly, and with a repetition of the weary upraising of his hand to his head, "it is fairly evident that the garage used by the man Gianapolis must be very near to—most probably adjoining—the entrance to this place of which you speak."

"Quite true," agreed the Frenchman. "But these are clever, these people of Mr. King. They are Chinese, remember, and the Chinese—ah, I know it!—are the most mysterious and most cunning people in the world. The entrance to the cave of black and gold will not be as wide as a cathedral door. A thousand men might search this garage, which, as Detective Sowerby" (he clapped the latter on the shoulder) "informed me this afternoon, is situated in Wharf-End Lane— all day and all night, and become none the wiser. To-morrow evening"—he lowered his voice—"I myself, shall be not outside, but inside that secret place; I shall be the *concierge* for one night—*Eh bien*, that *concierge* will admit the policeman!"

A groan issued from Dr. Cumberly's lips; and M. Max, with ready sympathy, crossed the room and placed his hands upon the physician's shoulders, looking steadfastly into his eyes.

"I understand, Dr. Cumberly," he said, and his voice was caressing as a woman's. *"Pardieu!* I understand. To wait is agony; but you, who are a physician, know that to wait sometimes is necessary. Have courage, my friend, have courage!"

XXXVII

THE WHISTLE

Luke Soames, buttoning up his black coat,

stood in the darkness, listening.

His constitutional distaste for leaping blindfolded had been over-ridden by circumstance. He felt himself to be a puppet of Fate, and he drifted with the tide because he lacked the strength to swim against it. That will-o'-the-wisp sense of security which had cheered him when first he had realized how much he owed to the protective wings of Mr. King had been rudely extinguished upon the very day of its birth; he had learnt that Mr. King was a sinister protector; and almost hourly he lived again through the events of that night when, all unwittingly, he had become a witness of strange happenings in the catacombs.

Soames had counted himself a lost man that night; the only point which he had considered debatable was whether he should be strangled or poisoned. That his employers were determined upon his death, he was assured; yet he had lived through the night, had learnt from his watch that the morning was arrived . . . and had seen the flecks at the roots of his dyed hair, blanched by the terrors of that vigil—of that watching, from moment to moment, for the second coming of Ho-Pin. . . .

Yes, the morning had dawned, and with it a faint courage. He had shaved and prepared himself for his singular duties, and Said had brought him his breakfast as usual. The day had passed uneventfully, and once, meeting Ho-Pin, he had found himself greeted with the same mirthless smile but with no menace. Perhaps they had believed his story, or had disbelieved it but realized that he was too closely bound to them to be dangerous.

Then his mind had reverted to the conversation overheard in the music-hall. Should he seek to curry favor with his employers by acquainting them with the fact that, contrary to Gianapolis' assertion, an important clue had fallen into the hands of the police? Did they know this already? So profound was his belief in the omniscience of the invisible Mr. King that he could not believe that Power ignorant of anything appertaining to himself.

Yet it was possible that those in the catacombs were unaware how Scotland Yard, night and day, quested for Mr. King. The papers made no mention of it; but then the papers made no mention of another fact— the absence of Mrs. Leroux. Now that he was no longer panic-ridden, he could mentally reconstruct that scene of horror, could hear

again, imaginatively, the shrieks of the maltreated woman. Perhaps this same active
imagination of his was playing him tricks,
but, her voice . . . Always he preferred to
dismiss these ideas.

He feared Ho-Pin in the same way that
an average man fears a tarantula, and he was
only too happy to avoid the ever smiling
Chinaman; so that the days passed on, and,
finding himself unmolested and the affairs
of the catacombs proceeding apparently as
usual, he kept his information to himself,
uncertain if he shared it with his employers
or otherwise, but hesitating to put the matter
to the test—always fearful to approach Ho-
Pin, the beetlesque.

But this could not continue indefinitely;
at least he must speak to Ho-Pin in order to
obtain leave of absence. For, since that unforgettable night, he had lived the life of a
cave-man indeed, and now began to pine for
the wider vault of heaven. Meeting the impassive Chinaman in the corridor one morning, on his way to valet one of the living
dead, Soames ventured to stop him.

"Excuse me, sir," he said, confusedly, "but
would there be any objection to my going
out on Friday evening for an hour?"

"Not at all, Soames," replied Ho-Pin, with
his mirthless smile: "you may go at six, wreturn at ten."

Ho-Pin passed on.

Soames heaved a gentle sigh of relief. The
painful incident was forgotten, then. He hurried into the room, the door of which Said
was holding open, quite eager for his unsavory work.

In crossing its threshold, he crossed out
of his new peace into a mental turmoil greater
in its complexities than any he yet had known;
he met M. Gaston Max, and his vague doubts
respecting the omniscience of Mr. King were
suddenly reinforced.

Soames' perturbation was so great on that
occasion that he feared it must unfailingly
be noticed. He realized that now he was definitely in communication with the enemies
of Mr. King! Ah; but Mr. King did not know
how formidable was the armament of those
enemies! He (Soames) had over-rated Mr.
King; and because that invisible being could
inspire Fear in an inconceivable degree, he
had thought him all-powerful. Now, he realized that Mr. King was unaware of the existence of at least one clue held by the police;
was unaware that his name was associated
with the Palace Mansions murder.

The catacombs of Ho-Pin were a sinking
ship, and Soames was first of the rats to leave.

He kept his appointment at the "Three
Nuns" as has appeared; he accepted the
blood-money that was offered him, and he
returned to the garage adjoining Kan-Suh
Concessions, that night, hugging in his bosom
a leather case containing implements by
means whereof his new accomplice designed
to admit the police to the cave of the golden
dragon.

Also, in the pocket of his overcoat, he had
a neat Browning pistol; and when the door
at the back of the garage was opened for him
by Said, he found that the touch of this little
weapon sent a thrill of assurance through
him, and he began to conceive a sentiment
for the unknown investigator to whom he
was bound, akin to that which formerly he
had cherished for Mr. King!

Now the time was come.

The people of the catacombs acquired a
supersensitive power of hearing, and Soames
was able at this time to detect, as he sat or
lay in his own room, the movements of persons in the corridor outside and even in the
cave of the golden dragon. That mysterious
trap in the wall gave him many qualms, and
to-night he had glanced at it a thousand times.
He held the pistol in his hand, and buttoned
up within his coat was the leather case. Only
remained the opening of his door in order
to learn if the lights were extinguished in the
corridor.

He did not anticipate any serious difficulty, provided he could overcome his constitutional nervousness. In his waistcoat
pocket was a brand new Yale key which, his
latest employer had assured him, fitted the
lock of the end door of Block A. The door
between the cave of the dragon and Block A
was never locked, so far as Soames was aware,
nor was that opening from the corridor in
which his own room was situated. Therefore, only a few moments—fearful moments,
certainly—need intervene, ere he should have
a companion; and within a few minutes of
that time, the police—his friends!—would be
there to protect him! He recognized that the
law, after all, was omnipotent, and of all
masters was the master to be served.

There was no light in the corridor. Leaving his door ajar, he tiptoed cautiously along
toward the cave. Assuring himself once again
that the pistol lay in his pocket, he fumbled
for the lever which opened the door, found
it, depressed it, and stepped quietly forward
in his slippered feet.

The unmistakable odor of the place assailed his nostrils. All was in darkness, and absolute silence prevailed. He had a rough idea of the positions of the various little tables, and he stepped cautiously in order to skirt them; but evidently he had made a miscalculation. Something caught his foot, and with a muffled thud he sprawled upon the floor, barely missing one of the tables which he had been at such pains to avoid.

Trembling like a man with an ague, he lay there, breathing in short, staccato breaths, and clutching the pistol in his pocket. Certainly he had made no great noise, but . . . Nothing stirred.

Soames summoned up courage to rise and to approach again the door of Block A. Without further mishap he reached it, opened it, and entered the blackness of the corridor. He could make no mistake in regard to the door, for it was the end one. He stole quietly along, his fingers touching the matting, until he came in contact with the corner angle; then, feeling along from the wall until he touched the strip of bamboo which marked the end of the door, he probed about gently with the key; for he knew to within an inch or so where the keyhole was situated.

Ah! he had it! His hand trembling slightly, he sought to insert the key in the lock. It defied his efforts. He felt it gently with the fingers of his left hand, thinking that he might have been endeavoring to insert the key with the irregular edge downward, and not uppermost; but no—such was not the case.

Again he tried, and with no better result. His nerves were threatening to overcome him, now; he had not counted upon any such hitch as this: but fear sharpened his wits. He recollected the fall which he had sustained, and how he had been precipitated upon the polished floor, outside.

Could he have mistaken his direction? Was it not possible that owing to his momentary panic, he had arisen, facing not the door at the foot of the steps, as he had supposed, but that by which a moment earlier he had entered the cave of the golden dragon?

Desperation was with him now; he was gone too far to draw back. Trailing his fingers along the matting covering of the wall, he retraced his steps, came to the open door, and reentered the apartment of the dragon. He complimented himself, fearfully, upon his own address, for he was inspired with an idea whereby he might determine his position. Picking his way among the little tables and the silken ottomans, he groped about with his hands in the impenetrable darkness for the pedestal supporting the dragon. At last his fingers touched the ivory. He slid them downward, feeling for the great vase of poppies which always stood before the golden image. . . .

The vase was on the *left* and not on the *right* of the pedestal. His theory was correct; he had been groping in the mysterious precincts of that Block B which he had never entered, which he had never seen any one else enter, and from whence he had never known any one to emerge! It was the fall that had confused him; now, he took his bearings anew, bent down to feel for any tables that might lie in his path, and crept across the apartment toward the door which he sought.

Ah! this time there could be no mistake! He depressed the lever handle, and, as the door swung open before him, crept furtively into the corridor.

Repeating the process whereby he had determined the position of the end door, he fumbled once again for the keyhole. He found it with even less difficulty than he had experienced in the wrong corridor, inserted the key in the lock, and with intense satisfaction felt it slip into place.

He inhaled a long breath of the lifeless air, turned the key, and threw the door open. One step forward he took . . .

A whistle (God! he knew it!) a low, minor whistle, wavered through the stillness. He was enveloped, mantled, choked, by the perfume of *roses!*

The door, which, although it had opened easily, had seemed to be a remarkably heavy one, swung to behind him; he heard the click of the lock. Like a trapped animal, he turned, leaped back, and found his quivering hands in contact with books—books—books . . .

A lamp lighted up in the center of the room.

Soames turned and stood pressed closely against the book-shelves, against the bookshelves which magically had grown up in front of the door by which he had entered. He was in the place of books and roses—in the haunt of *Mr. King!*

A great clarity of mind came to him, as it comes to a drowning man; he knew that those endless passages, through which once he had been led in darkness, did not exist, that he had been deceived, had been guided along the same corridor again and again; he knew that this room of roses did not lie at the heart of a labyrinth, but almost adjoined the cave of the golden dragon.

He knew that he was a poor, blind fool;

that his plotting had been known to those whom he had thought to betray; that the new key which had opened a way into this place of dread was not the key which his accomplice had given him. He knew that that upon which he had tripped at the outset of his journey had been set in his path by cunning design, in order that the fall might confuse his sense of direction. He knew that the great vase of poppies had been moved, that night. . . .

God! his brain became a seething furnace. There, before him, upstood the sandalwood screen, with one corner of the table projecting beyond it. Nothing of life was visible in the perfumed place, where deathly silence prevailed. . . .

No lion has greater courage than a cornered rat. Soames plucked the pistol from his pocket and fired at the screen—*once!*—*twice!*

He heard the muffled report, saw the flash of the little weapon, saw the two holes in the carven woodwork, and gained a greater, hysterical courage—the courage of a coward's desperation.

Immediately before him was a little ebony table, bearing a silver bowl, laden to the brim with sulphur-colored roses. He overturned the table with his foot, laughing wildly. In three strides he leapt across the room, grasped the sandalwood screen, and hurled it to the floor. . . .

In the instant of its fall, he became as Lot's wife. The pistol dropped from his nerveless grasp, thudding gently on the carpet, and, with his fingers crooked paralytically, he stood swaying . . . and looking into the face of *Mr. King!*

Soames' body already was as rigid as it would be in death; his mind was numbed—useless. But his outraged soul forced utterance from the lips of the man.

A scream, a scream to have made the angels shudder, to have inspired pity in the devils of Hell, burst from him. Two yellow hands leaped at his throat. . . .

XXXVIII

THE SECRET TRAPS

M. Gaston Max, from his silken bed in the catacombs of Ho-Pin, watched the hand of his watch which lay upon the little table be-side him. Already it was past two o'clock, and no sign had come from Soames; a hundred times his imagination had almost tricked him into believing that the door was opening; but always the idea had been illusory and due to the purple shadow of the lamp-shade which overcast that side of the room and the door.

He had experienced no difficulty in arranging with Gianapolis to occupy the same room as formerly; and, close student of human nature though he was, he had been unable to detect in the Greek's manner, when they had met that night, the slightest restraint, the slightest evidence of uneasiness. His reception by Ho-Pin had varied scarce one iota from that accorded him on his first visit to the cave of the golden dragon. The immobile Egyptian had brought him the opium, and had departed silently as before. On this occasion, the trap above the bed had not been opened. But hour after hour had passed, uneventfully, silently, in that still, suffocating room. . . .

A key in the lock!—yes, a key was being inserted in the lock! He must take no unnecessary risks; it might be another than Soames. He waited—the faint sound of fumbling ceased. Still, he waited, listening intently.

Half-past-two. If it had been Soames, why had he withdrawn? M. Max arose noiselessly and looked about him. He was undecided what to do, when . . .

Two shots, followed by a most appalling shriek—the more frightful because it was muffled; the shriek of a man *in extremis*, of one who stands upon the brink of Eternity, brought him up rigid, tense, with fists clenched, with eyes glaring; wrought within this fearless investigator an emotion akin to terror.

Just that one gruesome cry there was and silence again.

What did it mean?

M. Max began hastily to dress. He discovered, in endeavoring to fasten his collar, that his skin was wet with cold perspiration.

"Pardieu!" he said, twisting his mouth into that wry smile, "I know, now, the meaning of fright!"

He was ever glancing toward the door, not hopefully as hitherto, but apprehensively, fearfully.

That shriek in the night might portend merely the delirium of some other occupant of the catacombs; but the shots . . .

"It was *Soames!*" he whispered aloud; "I have risked too much; I am fast in the rat-trap!"

He looked about him for a possible weapon. The time for inactivity was past. It would be horrible to die in that reeking place, whilst outside, it might be, immediately above his head, Dunbar and the others waited and watched.

The construction of the metal bunk attracted his attention. As in the case of steamer bunks one of the rails—that nearer to the door—was detachable in order to facilitate the making of the bed. Rapidly, nervously, he unscrewed it; but the hinges were riveted to the main structure, and after a brief examination he shrugged his shoulders despairingly. Then, he recollected that in the adjoining bathroom there was a metal towel rail, nickeled, and with a heavy knock at either end, attached by two brackets to the wall.

He ran into the inner room and eagerly examined these fastenings. They were attached by small steel screws. In an instant he was at work with the blade of his pocket-knife. Six screws in all there were to be dealt with, three at either end. The fifth snapped the blade and he uttered an exclamation of dismay. But the shortened implement proved to be an even better screw-driver than the original blade, and half a minute later he found himself in possession of a club such as would have delighted the soul of Hercules.

He managed to unscrew one of the knobs, and thus to slide off from the bar the bracket attachments; then, replacing the knob, he weighed the bar in his hand, appreciatively. His mind now was wholly composed, and his course determined. He crossed the little room and rapped loudly upon the door.

The rapping sounded muffled and dim in that sound-proof place. Nothing happened, and thrice he repeated the rapping with like negative results. But he had learnt something: the door was a very heavy one.

He made a note of the circumstance, although it did not interfere with the plan which he had in mind. Wheeling the armchair up beside the bed, he mounted upon its two arms and, *once—twice—thrice*—crashed the knob of the iron bar against that part of the wall which concealed the trap.

Here the result was immediate. At every blow of the bar the trap behind yielded. A fourth blow sent the knob crashing through the gauze material, and far out into some dark place beyond. There was a sound as of a number of books falling.

He had burst the trap.

Up on the back of the chair he mounted, resting his bar against the wall, and began in feverish haste to tear away the gauze concealing the rectangular opening.

An almost overpowering perfume of roses was wafted into his face. In front of him was blackness.

Having torn away all the gauze, he learned that the opening was some two feet long by one foot high. Resting the bar across the ledge he extended his head and shoulders forward through this opening into the rose-scented place beyond, and without any great effort drew himself up with his hands, so that, provided he could find some support upon the other side, it would be a simple matter to draw himself through entirely.

He felt about with his fingers, right and left, and in doing so disturbed another row of books, which fell upon the floor beneath him. He had apparently come out in the middle of a large book-shelf. To the left of him projected the paper-covered door of the trap, at right angles; above and below were book-laden shelves, and on the right there had been other books, until his questing fingers had disturbed them.

M. Max, despite his weight, was an agile man. Clutching the shelf beneath, he worked his way along to the right, gradually creeping further and further into the darkened room, until at last he could draw his feet through the opening and crouch sideways upon the shelf.

He lowered his left foot, sought for and found another shelf beneath, and descended as by a ladder to the thickly carpeted floor. Grasping the end of the bar, he pulled that weapon down; then he twisted the button which converted his timepiece into an electric lantern, and, holding the bar in one tensely quivering hand, looked rapidly about him.

This was a library; a small library, with bowls of roses set upon tables, shelves, in gaps between the books, and one lying overturned upon the floor. Although it was almost drowned by their overpowering perfume, he detected a faint smell of powder. In one corner stood a large writing-table with papers strewn carelessly upon it. Its appointments were markedly Chinese in character, from the singular, gold inkwell to the jade paperweight; markedly Chinese—and—*feminine*. A very handsome screen lay upon the floor in front of this table, and the rich carpet he noted to be disordered as if a struggle had taken place upon it. But, most singular circumstance of all, and most disturbing . . . there was no door to this room!

For a moment he failed to appreciate the entire significance of this. A secret room difficult to enter he could comprehend, but a secret room difficult to *quit* passed his comprehension completely. Moreover, he was no better off for his exploit.

Three minutes sufficed him in which to examine the shelves covering the four walls of the room from floor to ceiling. None of the books were dummies, and slowly the fact began to dawn upon his mind that what at first he had assumed to be a rather simple device, was, in truth, almost incomprehensible.

For how, in the name of Sanity, did the occupant of this room—and obviously it was occupied at times—enter and leave it?

"Ah!" he muttered, shining the light upon a row of yellow-bound volumes from which he had commenced his tour of inspection and to which that tour had now led him back, "it is uncanny—this!"

He glanced back at the rectangular patch of light which marked the trap whereby he had entered this supernormal room. It was situated close to one corner of the library, and, acting upon an idea which came to him (any idea was better than none) he proceeded to throw down the books occupying the corresponding position at the other end of the shelf.

A second trap was revealed, identical with that through which he had entered!

It was fastened with a neat brass bolt; and, standing upon one of the little Persian tables—from which he removed a silver bowl of roses—he opened this trap and looked into the lighted room beyond. He saw an apartment almost identical with that which he himself recently had quitted; but in one particular it differed. It was occupied . . . *and by a woman!*

Arrayed in a gossamer nightrobe she lay in the bed, beneath the trap, her sunken face matching the silken whiteness. Her thin arms drooped listlessly over the rails of the bunk, and upon her left hand M. Max perceived a wedding ring. Her hair, flaxen in the electric light, was spread about in wildest disorder upon the pillow, and a breath of fetid air assailed his nostrils as he pressed his face close to the gauze masking the opening in

order to peer closely at this victim of the catacombs.

He watched the silken covering of her bosom, intently, but failed to detect the slightest movement.

"*Morbleu!*" he muttered, "is she dead?"

He rent the gauze with a sweep of his left hand, and standing upon the bottom shelf of the case, craned forward into the room, looking all about him. A purple shaded lamp burnt above the bed as in the adjoining apartment which he himself had occupied. There were dainty feminine trifles littered in the big armchair, and a motor-coat hung upon the hook of the bathroom door. A small cabin-trunk in one corner of the room bore the initials: "M. L."

Max dropped back into the incredible library with a stifled gasp.

"*Pardieu!*" he said. "It is Mrs. Leroux that I have found!"

A moment he stood looking from trap to trap; then turned and surveyed again the impassable walls, the rows of works, few of which were European, some of them bound in vellum, some in pigskin, and one row of huge volumes, ten in number, on the bottom shelf, in crocodile hide.

"It is weird, this!" he muttered, "nightmare!"—turning the light from row to row. "How is this lamp lighted that swings here?"

He began to search for the switch, and, even before he found it, had made up his mind that, once discovered, it would not only enable him more fully to illuminate the library, but would constitute a valuable clue.

At last he found it, situated at the back of one of the shelves, and set above a row of four small books, so that it could readily be reached by inserting the hand.

He flooded the place with light; and perceived at a glance that a length of white flex crossing the ceiling enabled anyone seated at the table to ignite the lamp from there also. Then, replacing his torch in his pocket, and assuring himself that the iron bar lay within easy reach, he began deliberately to remove all of the books from the shelves covering that side of the room upon which the switch was situated. His theory was a sound one; he argued that the natural and proper place for such a switch in such a room would be immediately inside the door, so that one entering could ignite the lamp without having to grope in the darkness. He was encouraged, furthermore, by the fact that at a point some four feet to the left of this switch there was a gap in the bookcases, running from floor to ceiling; a gap no more than four inches across.

Having removed every book from its position, save three, which occupied a shelf on a level with his shoulder and adjoining the gap, he desisted wearily, for many of the volumes were weighty, and the heat of the room was almost insufferable. He dropped with a sigh upon a silk ottoman close beside him. . . .

A short, staccato, muffled report split the heavy silence... and a little round hole appeared in the woodwork of the book-shelf before which, an instant earlier, M. Max had been standing—in the woodwork of that shelf, which had been upon a level with his head.

In one giant leap he hurled himself across the room— . . . as a second bullet pierced the yellow silk of the ottoman.

Close under the trap he crouched, staring up, fearful-eyed. . . .

A yellow hand and arm—a hand and arm of great nervous strength and of the hue of old ivory, directed a pistol through the opening above him. As he leaped, the hand was depressed with a lightning movement, but, lunging suddenly upward, Max seized the barrel of the pistol, and with a powerful wrench, twisted it from the grasp of the yellow hand. It was his own Browning!

At the time—in that moment of intense nervous excitement—he ascribed his sensations to his swift bout with Death—with Death who almost had conquered; but later, even now, as he wrenched the weapon into his grasp, he wondered if physical fear could wholly account for the sickening revulsion which held him back from that rectangular opening in the bookcase. He thought that he recognized in this a kindred horror—as distinct from terror—to that which had come to him with the odor of roses through this very trap, upon the night of his first visit to the catacombs of Ho-Pin.

It was not as the fear which one has of a dangerous wild beast, but as the loathing which is inspired by a thing diseased, leprous, contagious. . . .

A mighty effort of will was called for, but he managed to achieve it. He drew himself upright, breathing very rapidly, and looked through into the room—the room which he had occupied, and from which a moment ago the murderous yellow hand had protruded.

That room was empty . . . empty as he had left it!

"Mille tonneres! he has escaped me!" he cried aloud, and the words did not seem of his own choosing.

Who had escaped? Someone—man or woman; rather some *thing*, which, yellow handed, had sought to murder him!

Max ran across to the second trap and looked down at the woman whom he knew, beyond doubt, to be Mrs. Leroux. She lay in her death-like trance, unmoved.

Strung up to uttermost tension, he looked down at her and listened—listened, intently.

Above the fumes of the apartment in which the woman lay, a stifling odor of roses was clearly perceptible. The whole place was tropically hot. Not a sound, save the creaking of the shelf beneath him, broke the heavy stillness.

XXXIX

THE LABYRINTH

Feverishly, Max clutched at the last three books upon the shelf adjoining the gap. Of these, the center volume, a work bound in yellow calf and bearing no title, proved to be irremovable; right and left it could be inclined, but not moved outward. It masked the lever handle of the door!

But that door was locked.

Max, with upraised arms, swept the perspiration from his brows and eyes; he leant dizzily up against the door which defied him; his mind was working with febrile rapidity. He placed the pistol in his pocket, and, recrossing the room, mounted up again upon the shelves, and crept through into the apartment beyond, from which the yellow hand had protruded. He dropped, panting, upon the bed, then, eagerly leaping to the door, grasped the handle.

"Pardieu!" he muttered, "it is unlocked!"

Though the light was still burning in this room, the corridor outside was in darkness. He pressed the button of the ingenious lamp which was also a watch, and made for the door communicating with the cave of the dragon. It was readily to be detected by reason of its visible handle; the other doors being externally indistinguishable from the rest of the matting-covered wall.

The cave of the dragon proved to be empty, and in darkness. He ran across its polished floor and opened at random the door immediately facing him. A corridor similar to the one which he had just quitted was revealed. Another door was visible at one end, and to this he ran, pulled it open, stepped through the opening, and found himself back in the cave of the dragon!

"Morbleu!" he muttered, "it is bewildering—this!"

Yet another door, this time one of ebony, he opened; and yet another matting-lined corridor presented itself to his gaze. He swept it with the ray of the little lamp, detected a door, opened it, and entered a similar suite to those with which he already was familiar. It was empty, but, unlike the one which he himself had tenanted, this suite possessed two doors, the second opening out of the bathroom. To this he ran; it was unlocked; he opened it, stepped ahead . . . and was back again in the cave of the dragon.

"Mon dieu!" he cried, "this is Chinese—quite Chinese!"

He stood looking about him, flashing the ray of light upon doors which were opened and upon openings in the walls where properly there should have been no doors.

"I am too late!" he muttered; "they had information of this and they have 'unloaded.' That they intend to fly the country is proven by their leaving Mrs. Leroux behind. *Ah, nom d'un nom*, the good God grant that they have left also." . . .

Coincident with his thoughts of her, the voice of Helen Cumberly reached his ears! He stood there quivering in every nerve, as: *"Help! Help!"* followed by a choking, inarticulate cry, came, muffled, from somewhere—he could not determine where.

But the voice was the voice of Helen Cumberly. He raised his left fist and beat his brow as if to urge his brain to super-activity. Then, leaping, he was off.

Door after door he threw open, crying, "Miss Cumberly! Miss Cumberly! Where are you? Have courage! Help is here!"

But the silence remained unbroken—and always his wild search brought him back to the accursed cave of the golden dragon. He began to grow dizzy; he felt that his brain was bursting. For somewhere—somewhere but a few yards removed from him—a woman was in extreme peril!

Clutching dizzily at the pedestal of the dragon, he cried at the top of his voice:—

"Miss Cumberly! For the good God's sake answer me! Where are you?"

"Here, M. Max!" he was answered; "the door on your right . . . and then to your right again—quick! *quick!* Saints! she has killed me!"

It was Gianapolis who spoke!

Max hurled himself through the doorway indicated, falling up against the matting wall by reason of the impetus of his leap. He turned, leaped on, and one of the panels was slightly ajar; it was a masked door. Within was darkness out of which came the sounds of a great turmoil, as of wild beasts in conflict.

Max kicked the door fully open and flashed the ray of the torch into the room. It poured its cold light upon a group which, like some masterpiece of classic statuary, was to remain etched indelibly upon his mind.

Helen Cumberly lay, her head and shoulders pressed back upon the silken pillows of the bed, with both hands clutching the wrist of the Eurasian and striving to wrench the latter's fingers from her throat, in the white skin of which they were bloodily embedded. With his left arm about the face and head of the devilish half-caste, and grasping with his right hand her slender right wrist—putting forth all his strength to hold it back—was Gianapolis!

His face was of a grayish pallor and clammy with sweat; his crooked eyes had the glare of madness. The lithe body of the Eurasian writhing in his grasp seemed to possess the strength of two strong men; for palpably the Greek was weakening. His left sleeve was torn to shreds—to bloody shreds beneath the teeth of the wild thing with which he fought; and lower, lower, always nearer to the throat of the victim, the slender, yellow arm forced itself, forced the tiny hand clutching a poniard no larger than a hatpin but sharp as an adder's tooth.

"Hold her!" whispered Gianapolis in a voice barely audible, as Max burst into the room. "She came back for this and . . . I followed her. She has the strength of . . . a tigress!"

Max hurled himself into the mêlée, grasping the wrist of the Eurasian below where it was clutched by Gianapolis. Nodding to the Greek to release his hold, he twisted it smartly upward.

The dagger fell upon the floor, and with an animal shriek of rage, the Eurasian tottered back. Max caught her about the waist and tossed her unceremoniously into a corner of the room.

Helen Cumberly slipped from the bed, and lay very white and still upon the garish carpet, with four tiny red streams trickling from the nail punctures in her throat. Max stooped and raised her shoulders; he glanced at the Greek, who, quivering in all his limbs, and on the verge of collapse, only kept himself upright by dint of clutching at the side of the doorway. Max realized that Gianapolis was past aiding him; his own resources were nearly exhausted, but, stooping, he managed to lift the girl and to carry her out into the corridor.

"Follow me!" he gasped, glancing back at Gianapolis; "*Morbleu*, make an effort! The keys—the keys!"

Laying Helen Cumberly upon one of the raised divans, with her head resting upon a silken cushion, Max, teeth tightly clenched and dreadfully conscious that his strength was failing him, waited for Gianapolis. Out from the corridor the Greek came staggering, and Max now perceived that he was bleeding profusely from a wound in the breast.

"She came back," whispered Gianapolis, clutching at the Frenchman for support . . . "the hellcat! . . . I did not know . . . that . . . Miss . . . Cumberly was here. As God is my witness I did not know! But I followed . . . *her*—Mahâra . . . thank God I did! She has finished me, I think, but"—he lowered the crooked eyes to the form of Helen Cumberly—"never mind . . . Saints!"

He reeled and sank upon his knees. He clutched at the edge of his coat and raised it to his lips, wherefrom blood was gushing forth. Max stooped eagerly, for as the Greek had collapsed upon the floor, he had heard the rattle of keys.

"She had . . . the keys," whispered Gianapolis. "They have . . . tabs . . . upon them . . . Mrs. Leroux . . . number 3 B. The door to the stair"—very, very slowly, he inclined his head toward the ebony door near which Max was standing—"is marked X. The door . . . at the top—into garage . . . B."

"Tell me," said Max, his arm about the dying man's shoulders—"try to tell me: who killed Mrs. Vernon and why?"

"*Mr. King!*" came in a rattling voice. "Because of the . . . carelessness of someone . . . Mrs. Vernon wandered into the room . . . of Mrs. Leroux. She seems to have had a fit of remorse . . . or something like it. She begged Mrs. Leroux to pull up . . . before . . . too late. Ho-Pin arrived just as she

was crying to . . . Mrs. Leroux . . . and asking if she could ever forgive her . . . for bringing her here. . . . It was Mrs. Vernon who . . . introduced Mrs. . . . Leroux. Ho-Pin heard her . . . say that she . . . would tell . . . Leroux the truth . . . as the only means" . . .

"Yes, yes, *morbleu!* I understand! And then?"

"Ho-Pin knows . . . women . . . like a book. He thought Mrs. Vernon would . . . shirk the scandal. We used to send our women . . . to Nurse Proctor's, then . . . to steady up a bit . . . We let Mrs. Vernon go . . . as usual. The scene with . . . Mrs. Leroux had shaken . . . her and she fainted . . . in the car . . . Victoria Street. . . . I was with her. Nurse Proctor had . . . God! I am dying! . . . a time with her; . . . she got so hysterical that they had to . . . detain her . . . and three days later . . . her husband died; Proctor, the . . . fool . . . somehow left a paper containing the news in Mrs. Vernon's room. . . . They had had to administer an injection that afternoon . . . and they thought she was . . . sleeping." . . .

"*Morbleu!* Yes, yes!—a supreme effort, my friend!"

"Directly Ho-Pin heard of Vernon's death, he knew that his hold . . . on Mrs. Vernon . . . was lost. . . . He . . . and Mahâra . . . and . . . *Mr. King* . . . drove straight to . . . Gillingham . . . Street . . . to . . . arrange. . . . Ah! . . . she rushed like a mad woman into the street, a moment before . . . they arrived. A cab was passing, and" . . .

"I know this! I know this! What happened at Palace Mansions?"

The Greek's voice grew fainter.

"Mr. King followed . . . her . . . upstairs. Too late; . . . but whilst Leroux was in . . . Cumberly's flat . . . leaving door open . . . Mr. King went . . . in . . . Mahâra . . . was watching . . . gave signal . . . whistle . . . of someone's approach. It was thought . . . Mr. King . . . had secured *all* the message . . . Mrs. Vernon . . . was . . . writing. . . . Mr. King opened the door of . . . the lift-shaft . . . lift not working . . . climbed down that way . . . and out by door on . . . ground floor . . . when Mr. . . . the Member of Parliament . . . went upstairs." . . .

"Ah! *pardieu!* one last word! *Who is Mr. King?*"

Gianapolis lurched forward, his eyes glazing, half raised his arm—pointing back into the cave of the dragon—and dropped, face downward, on the floor, with a crimson pool forming slowly about his head.

An unfamiliar sound had begun to disturb the silence of the catacombs. Max glanced at the white face of Helen Cumberly, then directed the ray of the little lamp toward the further end of the apartment. A steady stream of dirty water was pouring into the cave of the dragon through the open door ahead of him.

Into the disc of light, leaped, fantastic, the witch figure of the Eurasian. She turned and faced him, threw up both her arms, and laughed shrilly, insanely. Then she turned and ran like a hare, her yellow silk dress gleaming in the moving ray. Inhaling sibilantly, Max leaped after her. In three strides he found his foot splashing in water. An instant he hesitated. Through the corridor ahead of him sped the yellow figure, and right to the end. The seemingly solid wall opened before her; it was another masked door.

Max crossed the threshold hard upon her heels. Three descending steps were ahead of him, and then a long brick tunnel in which swirled fully three feet of water, which, slowly rising, was gradually flooding the cave of the dragon.

On went the Eurasian, up to her waist in the flood, with Max gaining upon her, now, at every stride. There was a damp freshness in the air of the passage, and a sort of mist seemed to float above the water. This mist had a familiar smell. . . .

They were approaching the river, and there was a fog to-night!

Even as he realized the fact, the quarry vanished, and the ray of light from Max's lamp impinged upon the opening in an iron sluice gate. The Eurasian had passed it, but Max realized that he must lower his head if he would follow. He ducked rapidly, almost touching the muddy water with his face. A bank of yellow fog instantly enveloped him, and he pulled up short, for, instinctively, he knew that another step might precipitate him into the Thames.

He strove to peer about him, but the feeble ray of the lamp was incapable of penetrating the fog. He groped with his fingers, right and left, and presently found slimy wooden steps. He drew himself closely to these, and directed the light upon them. They led upward. He mounted cautiously, and was clear of the oily water, now, and upon a sort of gangway above which lowered a green

and rotting wooden roof.

Obviously, the tide was rising; and, after seeking vainly to peer through the fog ahead, he turned and descended the steps again, finding himself now nearly up to his armpits in water. He just managed to get in under the sluice gate without actually submerging his head, and to regain the brick tunnel.

He paused for a moment, hoping to be able to lower the gate, but the apparatus was out of his reach, and he had nothing to stand upon to aid him in manipulating it.

Three or four inches of water now flooded the cave of the golden dragon. Max pulled the keys from his pocket, and unlocked the door at the foot of the steps. He turned, resting the electric lamp upon one of the little ebony tables, and lifting Helen Cumberly, carried her half-way up the steps, depositing her there with her back to the wall. He staggered down again; his remarkable physical resources were at an end; it must be another's work to rescue Mrs. Leroux. He stooped over Gianapolis, and turned his head. The crooked eyes glared up at him deathly.

"May the good God forgive you," he whispered. "You tried to make your peace with Him."

The sound of muffled blows began to be audible from the head of the steps. Max staggered out of the cave of the golden dragon. A slight freshness and dampness was visible in its atmosphere, and the gentle gurgling of water broke its heavy stillness. There was a new quality come into it, and, strangely, an old quality gone out from it. As he lifted the lamp from the table—now standing in slowly moving water—the place seemed no longer to be the cave of the golden dragon he had known. . . .

He mounted the steps again, with difficulty, resting his shaking hands upon the walls. Shattering blows were being delivered upon the door, above.

"Dunbar!" he cried feebly, stepping aside to avoid Helen Cumberly, where she lay. "Dunbar!" . . .

XL

DAWN AT THE NORE

The river police seemed to be floating, suspended in the fog, which now was so dense that the water beneath was invisible. Inspector Rogers, who was in charge, fastened up his coat collar about his neck and turned to Stringer, the Scotland Yard man, who sat beside him in the stern of the cutter gloomily silent.

"Time's wearing on," said Rogers, and his voice was muffled by the fog as though he were speaking from inside a box. "There must be some hitch."

"Work it out for yourself," said the C. I. D. man gruffly. "We know that the office in Globe Road belongs to Gianapolis, and according to the Eastern Exchange he was constantly ringing up East 39951; that's the warehouse of Kan-Suh Concessions. He garages his car next door to the said warehouse, and to-night our scouts follow Gianapolis and Max from Piccadilly Circus to Waterloo Station, where they discharge the taxi and pick up Gianapolis' limousine. Still followed, they drive—where? Straight to the garage at the back of that wharf yonder! Neither Gianapolis, Max, nor the chauffeur come out of the garage. I said, and I still say, that we should have broken in at once, but Dunbar was always pigheaded, and he thinks Max is a tin god." . . .

"Well, there's no sign from Max," said Rogers; "and as we aren't ten yards above the wharf, we cannot fail to hear the signal. For my part I never noticed anything suspicious, and never had anything reported, about this ginger firm, and where the swell dope-shop I've heard about can be situated, beats me. It can't very well be *under* the place, or it would be below the level of the blessed river!"

"This waiting makes me sick!" growled Stringer. "If I understand aright—and I'm not sure that I do—there are two women tucked away there somewhere in that place"— he jerked his thumb aimlessly into the fog; "and here we are hanging about with enough men in yards, in doorways, behind walls, and freezing on the river, to raid the Houses of Parliament!"

"It's a pity we didn't get the word from the hospitals before Max was actually inside," said Rogers. "For three wealthy ladies to be driven to three public hospitals in a sort of semi-conscious condition, with symptoms of opium, on the same evening isn't natural. It points to the fact that the boss of the den has *unloaded!* He's been thoughtful where his lady clients were concerned, but probably the men have simply been kicked out and left to shift for themselves. If we only knew one of them it might be confirmed."

"It's not worth worrying about, now," growled Stringer. "Let's have a look at the time."

He fumbled inside his overcoat and tugged out his watch.

"Here's a light," said Rogers, and shone the ray of an electric torch upon the watch-face.

"A quarter-to-three," grumbled Stringer. "There may be murder going on, and here we are." . . .

A sudden clamor arose upon the shore, near by; a sound as of sledge-hammers at work. But above this pierced shrilly the call of a police whistle.

"What's that?" snapped Rogers, leaping up. "Stand by there!"

The sound of the whistle grew near and nearer; then came a voice—that of Sergeant Sowerby—hailing them through the fog.

"Dunbar's in! But the gang have escaped! They've got to a motor launch twenty yards down, on the end of the creek"* . . .

But already the police boat was away.

"Let her go!" shouted Rogers—"close inshore! Keep a sharp lookout for a cutter, boys!"

Stringer, aroused now to excitement, went blundering forward through the fog, joining the men in the bows. Four pairs of eyes were peering through the mist, the damnable, yellow mist that veiled all things.

"Curse the fog!" said Stringer; "it's just our damn luck!"

"Cutter 'hoy!" bawled a man at his side suddenly, one of the river police more used to the mists of the Thames. "Cutter on the port bow, sir!"

"Keep her in sight," shouted Rogers from the stern; "don't lose her for your lives!"

Stringer, at imminent peril of precipitating himself into the water, was craning out over the bows and staring until his eyes smarted.

"Don't you see her?" said one of the men on the lookout. "She carries no lights, of course, but you can just make out the streak of her wake."

Harder, harder stared Stringer, and now a faint, lighter smudge in the blackness, ahead and below, proclaimed itself the wake of some rapidly traveling craft.

"I can hear her motor!" said another voice.

Stringer began, now, also to listen.

Muffled sirens were hooting dismally all about Limehouse Reach, and he knew that this random dash through the night was fraught with extreme danger, since this was a narrow and congested part of the great highway. But, listen as he might, he could not detect the sounds referred to.

The brazen roar of a big steamer's siren rose up before them. Rogers turned the head of the cutter sharply to starboard but did not slacken speed. The continuous roar grew deeper, grew louder.

"Sharp lookout there!" cried the inspector from the stern.

Suddenly over their bows uprose a black mass.

"My God!" cried Stringer, and fell back with upraised arms as if hoping to fend off that giant menace.

He lurched, as the cutter was again diverted sharply from its course, and must have fallen under the very bows of the oncoming liner, had not one of the lookouts caught him by the collar and jerked him sharply back into the boat.

A blaze of light burst out over them, and there were conflicting voices raised one in opposition to another. Above them all, even above the beating of the twin screws and the churning of the inky water, arose that of an officer from the bridge of the steamer.

"Where the flaming hell are *you* going?" inquired this stentorian voice; "haven't you got any blasted eyes and ears" . . .

High on the wash of the liner rode the police boat; down she plunged again, and began to roll perilously; up again—swimming it seemed upon frothing milk.

The clangor of bells, of voices, and of churning screws died, remote, astern.

"Damn close shave!" cried Rogers. "It must be clear ahead; they've just run into it."

One of the men on the lookout in the bows, who had never departed from his duty for an instant throughout this frightful commotion, now reported:

"Cutter crossing our bow, sir! Getting back to her course."

"Keep her in view," roared Rogers.

"Port, sir!"

"How's that?"

"Starboard, easy!"

"Keep her in view!"

"As she is, sir!"

Again they settled down to the pursuit, and it began to dawn upon Stringer's mind that the boat ahead must be engined identically with that of the police; for whilst they certainly gained nothing upon her, neither did they lose.

"Try a hail," cried Rogers from the stern. "We may be chasing the wrong boat!"

"Cutter 'hoy!" bellowed the man beside Stringer, using his hands in lieu of a megaphone—"heave to!"

"Give 'em 'in the King's name!' " directed Rogers again.

"Cutter 'hoy," roared the man through his trumpeted hands,—"heave to—in the King's name!"

Stringer glared through the fog, clutching at the shoulder of the shouter almost convulsively.

"Take no notice, sir," reported the man.

"Then it's the gang!" cried Rogers from the stern; "and we haven't made a mistake. Where the blazes are we?"

"Well on the way to Blackwall Reach, sir," answered someone. "Fog lifting ahead."

"It's the rain that's doing it," said the man beside Stringer.

Even as he spoke, a drop of rain fell upon the back of Stringer's hand. This was the prelude; then, with ever-increasing force, down came the rain in torrents, smearing out the fog from the atmosphere, as a painter, with a sponge, might wipe a color from his canvas. Long tails of yellow vapor, twining—twining—but always coiling downward, floated like snakes about them; and the oily waters of the Thames became pock-marked in the growing light.

Stringer now quite clearly discerned the quarry—a very rakish-looking motor cutter, painted black, and speeding seaward ahead of them. He quivered with excitement.

"Do you know the boat?" cried Rogers, addressing his crew in general.

"No, sir," reported his second-in-command; she's a stranger to me. They must have kept her hidden somewhere." He turned and looked back into the group of faces, all directed toward the strange craft. "Do any of you know her?" he demanded.

A general shaking of heads proclaimed the negative.

"But she can shift," said one of the men. "They must have been going slow through the fog; she's creeping up to ten or twelve knots now, I should reckon."

"Your reckoning's a trifle out!" snapped Rogers, irritably, from the stern; "but she's certainly showing us her heels. Can't we put somebody ashore and have her cut off lower down?"

"While we're doing that," cried Stringer, excitedly, "she would land somewhere and we should lose the gang!"

"That's right," reluctantly agreed Rogers. "Can you see any of her people?"

Through the sheets of rain all peered eagerly.

"She seems to be pretty well loaded," reported the man beside Stringer, "but I can't make her out very well."

"Are we doing our damnedest?" inquired Rogers.

"We are, sir," reported the engineer; "she hasn't got another oat in her!"

Rogers muttered something beneath his breath, and sat there glaring ahead at the boat ever gaining upon her pursuer.

"So long as we keep her in sight," said Stringer, "our purpose is served. She can't land anybody."

"At her present rate," replied the man upon whose shoulders he was leaning, "she'll be out of sight by the time we get to Tilbury or she'll have hit a barge and gone to the bottom!"

"I'll eat my hat if I lose her!" declared Rogers angrily. "How the blazes they slipped away from the wharf beats me!"

"They didn't slip away from the wharf," cried Stringer over his shoulder. "You heard what Sowerby said; they lay in the creek below the wharf, and there was some passageway underneath."

"But damn it all, man!" cried Rogers, "it's high tide; they must be a gang of bally mermaids. Why, we were almost level with the wharf when we left, and if they came from *below* that, as you say, they must have been below water!"

"There they are, anyway," growled Stringer.

Mile after mile that singular chase continued through the night. With every revolution of the screw, the banks to right and left seemed to recede, as the Thames grew wider and wider. A faint saltiness was perceptible in the air; and Stringer, moistening his dry lips, noted the saline taste.

The shipping grew more scattered. Whereas, at first, when the fog had begun to lift, they had passed wondering faces peering at them from lighters and small steamers, tow boats and larger anchored craft, now they raced, pigmy and remote, upon open waters, and through the raindrift gray hulls showed, distant, and the banks were a faint blur. It seemed absurd that, with all those vessels about, they nevertheless could take no steps to seek assistance in cutting off the boat which they were pursuing, but must drive on through the rain, ever losing, ever dropping behind that black speck ahead.

A faint swell began to be perceptible. Stringer, who throughout the whole pursuit thus far had retained his hold upon the man in the bows, discovered that his fingers were cramped. He had much difficulty in releasing that convulsive grip.

"Thank you!" said the man, smiling, when at last the detective released his grip. "I'll admit I'd scarcely noticed it myself, but now I come to think of it, you've been fastened onto me like a vise for over two hours!"

"Two hours!" cried Stringer; and, crouching down to steady himself, for the cutter was beginning to roll heavily, he pulled out his watch, and in the gray light inspected the dial.

It was true! They had been racing seaward for some hours!

"Good God!" he muttered.

He stood up again, unsteadily, feet wide apart, and peered ahead through the grayness.

The banks he could not see. Far away on the port bow a long gray shape lay—a moored vessel. To starboard were faint blurs, indistinguishable, insignificant; ahead, a black dot with a faint comet-like tail—the pursued cutter—and ahead of that, again, a streak across the blackness, with another dot slightly to the left of the quarry . . .

He turned and looked along the police boat, noting that whereas, upon the former occasion of his looking, forms and faces had been but dimly visible, now he could distinguish them all quite clearly. The dawn was breaking.

"Where are we?" he inquired hoarsely.

"We're about one mile northeast of Sheerness and two miles southwest of the Nore Light!" announced Rogers—and he laughed, but not in a particularly mirthful manner.

Stringer temporarily found himself without words.

"Cutter heading for the open sea, sir," announced a man in the bows, unnecessarily.

"Quite so," snapped Rogers. "So are you!"

"We have got them beaten," said Stringer, a faint note of triumph in his voice. "We've given them no chance to land."

"If this breeze freshens much," replied Rogers, with sardonic humor, "they'll be giving *us* a fine chance to sink!"

Indeed, although Stringer's excitement had prevented him from heeding the circumstance, an ever-freshening breeze was blowing in his face, and he noted now that, quite mechanically, he had removed his bowler hat at some time earlier in the pursuit and had placed it in the bottom of the boat. His hair was blown in the wind, which sang merrily in his ears, and the cutter, as her course was slightly altered by Rogers, ceased to roll and began to pitch in a manner very disconcerting to the landsman.

"It'll be rather fresh outside, sir," said one of the men, doubtfully. "We're miles and miles below our proper patrol" . . .

"Once we're clear of the bank it'll be more than fresh," replied Rogers; "but if they're bound for France, or Sweden, or Denmark, that's *our* destination, too!" . . .

On—and on—and on they drove. The Nore Light lay astern; they were drenched with spray. Now green water began to spout over the nose of the laboring craft.

"I've only enough juice to run us back to Tilbury, sir, if we put about now!" came the shouted report.

"It's easy to *talk!*" roared Rogers. "If one of these big 'uns gets us broadside on, our number's up!" . . .

"Cutter putting over for Sheppey coast, sir!" bellowed the man in the bows.

Stringer raised himself, weakly, and sought to peer through the driving spray and rainmist.

"By God! *They've turned—turtle!*" . . .

"Stand by with belts!" bellowed Rogers.

Rapidly life belts were unlashed; and, ahead, to port, to starboard, brine-stung eyes glared out from the reeling craft. Gray in the nascent dawn stretched the tossing sea about them; and lonely they rode upon its billows.

"*Port! port! hard a-port!*" screamed the lookout.

But Rogers, grimly watching the oncoming billows, knew that to essay the maneuver at that moment meant swamping the cutter. Straight ahead they drove. A wave, higher than any they yet had had to ride, came boiling down upon them . . . and twisting, writhing, upcasting imploring arms to the elements—the implacable elements—a girl, a dark girl, entwined, imprisoned in silken garments, swept upon its crest!

Out shot a cork belt into the boiling sea . . . and fell beyond her reach. She was swept past the cutter. A second belt was hurled from the stern . . .

The Eurasian, uttering a wailing cry like that of a seabird, strove to grasp it . . .

Close beside her, out of the wave, uprose a yellow hand, grasping—seeking—clutching. It fastened itself into the meshes of her floating hair . . .

"Here goes!" roared Rogers.

They plunged down into an oily trough; they turned; a second wave grew up above them, threateningly, built its terrible wall higher and higher over their side. Round they swung, and round, and round . . .

Down swept the eager wave . . . down—down—down . . . It lapped over the stern of the cutter; the tiny craft staggered, and paused, tremulous—dragged back by that iron grip of old Neptune—then leaped on—away—headed back into the Thames estuary, triumphant.

"God's mercy!" whispered Stringer—"that was touch-and-go!"

No living thing moved upon the waters.

XLI

WESTMINSTER—MIDNIGHT

Detective-Sergeant Sowerby reported himself in Inspector Dunbar's room at New Scotland Yard.

"I have completed my inquiries in Wharfend Lane" he said; and pulling out his bulging pocket-book, he consulted it gravely.

Inspector Dunbar looked up.

"Anything important?" he asked.

"We cannot trace the makers of the sanitary fittings, and so forth, but they are all of American pattern. There's nothing in the nature of a trademark to be found from end to end of the place; even the iron sluice-gate at the bottom of the brick tunnel has had the makers' name chipped off, apparently with a cold chisel. So you see they were prepared for all emergencies!"

"Evidently," said Dunbar, resting his chin on the palms of his hands and his elbows upon the table.

"The office and warehouse staff of the ginger importing concern are innocent enough, as you know already. Kan-suh Concessions was conducted merely as a blind, of course, but it enabled the Chinaman, Ho-Pin, to appear in Wharf-end Lane at all times of the day and night without exciting suspicion. He was supposed to be the manager, of course. The presence of the wharf is sufficient to explain how they managed to build the place without exciting suspicion. They probably had all the material landed there labeled as preserved ginger, and they would take it down below at night, long after the office and warehouse Staff of Concessions had gone home.

The workmen probably came and went by way of the river, also, commencing work after nightfall and going away before business commenced in the morning."

"It beats me," said Dunbar, reflectively, "how masons, plumbers, decorators, and all the other artisans necessary for a job of that description, could have been kept quiet."

"Foreigners!" said Sowerby triumphantly. "I'll undertake to say there wasn't an Englishman on the job. The whole of the gang was probably imported from abroad somewhere, boarded and lodged during the day-time in the neighborhood of Limehouse, and watched by Mr. Ho-Pin or somebody else until the job was finished; then shipped back home again. It's easily done if money is no object."

"That's right enough," agreed Dunbar; "I have no doubt you've hit upon the truth. But now that the place has been dismantled, what does it look like? I haven't had time to come down myself, but I intend to do so before it's closed up."

"Well," said Sowerby, turning over a page of his notebook, "it looks like a series of vaults, and the Rev. Mr. Firmingham, a local vicar whom I got to inspect it this morning, assures me, positively, that it's a crypt."

"A crypt!" exclaimed Dunbar, fixing his eyes upon his subordinate.

"A crypt—exactly. A firm dealing in grease occupied the warehouse before Kan-Suh Concessions rented it, and they never seem to have suspected that the place possessed any cellars. The actual owner of the property, Sir James Crozel, an ex-Lord Mayor, who is also ground landlord of the big works on the other side of the lane, had no more idea than the man in the moon that there were any cellars beneath the place. You see the vaults are below the present level of the Thames at high tide; that's why nobody ever suspected their existence. Also, an examination of the bare walls—now stripped— shows that they were pretty well filled up to the top with ancient débris, to within a few years ago, at any rate."

"You mean that our Chinese friends excavated them?"

"No doubt about it. They were every bit of twenty feet below the present street level, and, being right on the bank of the Thames, nobody would have thought of looking for them unless he knew they were there."

"What do you mean exactly, Sowerby?" said Dunbar, taking out his fountain-pen and tapping his teeth with it.

"I mean," said Sowerby, "that someone connected with the gang must have located the site of these vaults from some very old map or book."

"I think you said that the Reverend Somebody-or-Other avers that they were a crypt?"

"He does; and when he pointed out to me the way the pillars were placed, as if to support the nave of a church, I felt disposed to agree with him. The place where the golden dragon used to stand (it isn't really gold, by the way!) would be under the central aisle, as it were; then there's a kind of side aisle on the right and left and a large space at top and bottom. The pillars are stone and of very early Norman pattern, and the last three or four steps leading down to the place appear to belong to the original structure. I tell you it's the crypt of some old forgotten Norman church or monastery chapel."

"Most extraordinary!" muttered Dunbar. "But I suppose it is possible enough. Probably the church was burnt or destroyed in some other way; deposits of river mud would gradually cover up the remaining ruins; then in later times, when the banks of the Thames were properly attended to, the site of the place would be entirely forgotten, of course. Most extraordinary!"

"That's the reverend gentleman's view, at any rate," said Sowerby, "and he's written three books on the subject of early Norman churches! He even goes so far as to say that he has heard—as a sort of legend—of the existence of a very large Carmelite monastery, accommodating over two hundred brothers, which stood somewhere adjoining the Thames within the area now covered by Limehouse Causeway and Pennyfields. There is a little turning not far from the wharf, known locally—it does not appear upon any map—as Prickler's Lane; and my friend, the vicar, tells me that he has held the theory for a long time"—Sowerby referred to his notebook with great solemnity—"that this is a corruption of Pré-aux-Clerce Lane."

"H'm!" said Dunbar; "very ingenious, at any rate. Anything else?"

"Nothing much," said Sowerby, scanning his notes, "that you don't know already. There was some very good stuff in the place—Oriental ware and so on, a library of books which I'm told is unique, a tremendous stock of opium and *hashish*. It's a perfect maze of doors and observation-traps. There's a small kitchen at the end, near the head of the tunnel—which, by the way, could be used as a means of entrance and exit at low tide. All the electric power came through the meter of Kan-Suh Concessions."

"I see," said Dunbar, reflectively, glancing at his watch; "in a word, we know everything except" . . .

"What's that?" said Sowerby, looking up.

"The identity of Mr. King!" replied the inspector, reaching for his hat which lay upon the table.

Sowerby replaced his book in his pocket.

"I wonder if any of the bodies will ever come ashore?" he said.

"God knows!" rapped Dunbar; "we can't even guess how many were aboard. You might as well come along, Sowerby, I've just heard from Dr. Cumberly. Mrs. Leroux" . . .

"Dead?"

"Dying," replied the inspector; "expected to go at any moment. But the doctor tells me that she may—it's just possible—recover consciousness before the end; and there's a bare chance" . . .

"I see," said Sowerby eagerly; "of course she must know!"

The two hastened to Palace Mansions. Despite the lateness of the hour, Whitehall was thronged with vehicles, and all the glitter and noise of midnight London surrounded them.

"It only seems like yesterday evening," said Dunbar, as they mounted the stair of Palace Mansions, "that I came here to take charge of the case. Damme! it's been the most exciting I've ever handled, and it's certainly the most disappointing."

"It is indeed," said Sowerby, gloomily, pressing the bell-button at the side of Henry Leroux's door.

The door was opened by Garnham; and these two, fresh from the noise and bustle of London's streets, stepped into the hushed atmosphere of the flat where already a Visitant, unseen but potent, was arrived, and now was beckoning, shadowlike, to Mira Leroux.

"Will you please sit down and wait," said Garnham, placing chairs for the two Scotland Yard men in the dining-room.

"Who's inside?" whispered Dunbar, with that note of awe in his voice which such a scene always produces; and he nodded in the direction of the lobby.

"Mr. Leroux, sir," replied the man, "the nurse, Miss Cumberly, Dr. Cumberly and Miss Ryland" . . .

"No one else?" asked the detective sharply.

"And Mr. Gaston Max," added the man.

"You'll find whisky and cigars upon the table there, sir."

He left the room. Dunbar glanced across at Sowerby, his tufted brows raised, and a wry smile upon his face.

"In at the death, Sowerby!" he said grimly, and lifted the stopper from the cut-glass decanter.

In the room where Mira Leroux lay, so near to the Borderland that her always ethereal appearance was now positively appalling, a hushed group stood about the bed.

"I think she is awake, doctor," whispered the nurse softly, peering into the emaciated face of the patient.

Mira Leroux opened her eyes and smiled at Dr. Cumberly, who was bending over her. The poor faded eyes turned from the face of the physician to that of Denise Ryland, then to M. Max, wonderingly; next to Helen, whereupon an indescribable expression crept into them; and finally to Henry Leroux, who, with bowed head, sat in the chair beside her. She feebly extended her thin hand and laid it upon his hair. He looked up, taking the hand in his own. The eyes of the dying woman filled with tears as she turned them from the face of Leroux to Helen Cumberly—who was weeping silently.

"Look after . . . him," whispered Mira Leroux.

Her hand dropped and she closed her eyes again. Cumberly bent forward suddenly, glancing back at M. Max who stood in a remote corner of the room watching this scene.

Big Ben commenced to chime the hour of midnight. That frightful coincidence so startled Leroux that he looked up and almost rose from his chair in his agitation. Indeed it startled Cumberly, also, but did not divert him from his purpose.

"It is now or never!" he whispered.

He took the seemingly lifeless hand in his own, and bending over Mira Leroux, spoke softly in her ear:

"Mrs. Leroux," he said, "there is something which we all would ask you to tell us; we ask it for a reason—believe me."

Throughout the latter part of this scene the big clock had been chiming the hour, and now was beating out the twelve strokes of midnight; had struck six of them and was about to strike the seventh.

Seven! boomed the clock.

Mira Leroux opened her eyes and looked up into the face of the physician.

Eight! . . .

"Who," whispered Dr. Cumberly, "is he?"

Nine!

In the silence following the clock-stroke, Mira Leroux spoke almost inaudibly.

"You mean . . . *Mr. King?*"

Ten!

"Yes, yes! Did you ever *see* him?" . . .

Every head in the room was craned forward; every spectator tensed up to the highest ultimate point.

"Yes," said Mira Leroux quite clearly; "I saw him, Dr. Cumberly . . . He is" . . .

Eleven!

Mira Leroux moved her head and smiled at Helen Cumberly; then seemed to sink deeper into the downy billows of the bed. Dr. Cumberly stood up very slowly, and turned, looking from face to face.

"It is finished," he said—"we shall never know!"

But Henry Leroux and Helen Cumberly, their glances meeting across the bed of the dead Mira, knew that for them it was not finished, but that Mr. King, the invisible, invisibly had linked them.

Twelve! . . .

Dope

" Are you ready for us, Sin? " asked Sir Lucien

Part First

KAZMAH THE DREAM-READER

Chapter I

A MESSAGE FOR IRVIN

Monte Irvin, alderman of the city and prospective Lord Mayor of London, paced restlessly from end to end of the well-appointed library of his house in Prince's Gate. Between his teeth he gripped the stump of a burnt-out cigar. A tiny spaniel lay beside the fire, his beady black eyes following the nervous movements of the master of the house.

At the age of forty-five Monte Irvin was not ill-looking, and, indeed, was sometimes spoken of as handsome. His figure was full without being corpulent; his well-groomed black hair and moustache and fresh if rather coarse complexion, together with the dignity of his upright carriage, lent him something of a military air. This he assiduously cultivated as befitting an ex-Territorial officer, although as he had seen no active service he modestly refrained from using any title of rank.

Some quality in his brilliant smile, an Oriental expressiveness of the dark eyes beneath their drooping lids, hinted a Semitic strain; but it was otherwise not marked in his appearance, which was free from vulgarity, whilst essentially that of a successful man of affairs.

In fact, Monte Irvin had made a success of every affair in life with the lamentable exception of his marriage. Of late his forehead had grown lined, and those business friends who had known him for a man of abstemious habits had observed in the City chophouse at which he lunched almost daily that whereas formerly he had been a noted trencherman, he now ate little but drank much.

Suddenly the spaniel leapt up with that feverish, spider-like activity of the toy species and began to bark.

Monte Irvin paused in his restless patrol and listened.

"Lie down!" he said. "Be quiet."

The spaniel ran to the door, sniffing eagerly. A muffled sound of voices became audible, and Irvin, following a moment of hesitation, crossed and opened the door. The dog ran out, yapping in his irritating staccato

fashion, and an expression of hope faded from Irvin's face as he saw a tall fair girl standing in the hallway talking to Hinkes, the butler. She wore a soiled Burberry, high-legged tan boots, and a peaked cap of distinctly military appearance. Irvin would have retired again, but the girl glanced up and saw him where he stood by the library door. He summoned up a smile and advanced.

"Good evening, Miss Halley," he said, striving to speak genially—for of all of his wife's friends he liked Margaret Halley the best. "Were you expecting to find Rita at home?"

The girl's expression was vaguely troubled. She had the clear complexion and bright eyes of perfect health, but to-night her eyes seemed over-bright, whilst her face was slightly pale.

"Yes," she replied; "that is, I hoped she might be at home."

"I am afraid I cannot tell you when she is likely to return. But please come in, and I will make inquiries."

"Oh, no, I would rather you did not trouble and I won't stay, thank you nevertheless. I expect she will ring me up when she comes in."

"Is there any message I can give her?"

"Well"—she hesitated for an instant—"you might tell her, if you would, that I only returned home at eight o'clock, so that I could not come around any earlier." She glanced rapidly at Irvin, biting her lip. "I wish I could have seen her," she added in a low voice.

"She wishes to see you particularly?"

"Yes. She left a note this afternoon." Again she glanced at him in a troubled way. "Well, I suppose it cannot be helped," she added and smilingly extended her hand. "Good night, Mr. Irvin. Don't bother to come to the door."

But Irvin passed Hinkes and walked out under the porch with Margaret Halley. Humid yellow mist floated past the street lamps, and seemed to have gathered in a moving reef around the little runabout car which was standing outside the house, its motor chattering tremulously.

"Phew! a beastly night!" he said. "Foggy and wet."

"It's a brute isn't it," said the girl laughingly, and turned on the steps so that the light shining out of the hallway gleamed on her white teeth and upraised eyes. She was pulling on big, ugly, furred gloves, and Monte Irvin mentally contrasted her fresh, athletic type of beauty with the delicate, exotic charm of his wife.

She opened the door of the little car, got in and drove off, waving one hugely gloved hand to Irvin as he stood in the porch looking after her. When the red tail-light had vanished in the mist he returned to the house and re-entered the library. If only all his wife's friends were like Margaret Halley, he mused, he might have been spared the insupportable misgivings which were goading him to madness. His mind filled with poisonous suspicions, he resumed his pacing of the library, awaiting and dreading that which should confirm his blackest theories. He was unaware of the fact that throughout the interview he had held the stump of cigar between his teeth. He held it there yet, pacing, pacing up and down the long room.

Then came the expected summons. The telephone bell rang. Monte Irvin clenched his hands and inhaled deeply. His color changed in a manner that would have aroused a physician's interest. Regaining his self-possession by a visible effort, he crossed to a small side-table upon which the instrument rested. Rolling the cigar stump into the left corner of his mouth, he took up the receiver.

"Hallo!" he said.

"Someone named Brisley, sir, wishes——"

"Put him through to me here."

"Very good, sir."

A short interval, then:

"Yes?" said Monte Irvin.

"My name is Brisley. I have a message for Mr. Monte Irvin."

"Monte Irvin speaking. Anything to report, Brisley?"

Irvin's deep, rich voice was not entirely under control.

"Yes, sir. The lady drove by taxicab from Prince's Gate to Albemarle Street."

"Ah!"

"Went up to chambers of Sir Lucien Pyne and was admitted."

"Well?"

"Twenty minutes later came out. Lady was with Sir Lucien. Both walked around to Old Bond Street. The Honorable Quentin Gray—"

"Ah!" breathed Irvin.

"—Overtook them there. He got out of a cab. He joined them. All three up to apartments of a professional crystal-gazer styling himself Kazmah 'the dream-reader.' "

A puzzled expression began to steal over the face of Monte Irvin. At sound of the telephone bell he had paled somewhat. Now he began to recover his habitual florid coloring.

"Go on," he directed, for the speaker had paused.

"Seven to ten minutes later," resumed the nasal voice, "Mr. Gray came down. He hailed a passing cab, but man refused to stop. Mr. Gray seemed to be very irritable."

The fact that the invisible speaker was reading from a notebook he betrayed by his monotonous intonation and abbreviated sentences, which resembled those of a constable giving evidence in a police court.

"He walked off rapidly in direction of Piccadilly. Colleague followed. Near the Ritz he obtained a cab. He returned in same to Old Bond Street. He ran upstairs and was gone from four-and-a-half to five minutes. He then came down again. He was very pale and agitated. He discharged cab and walked away. Colleague followed. He saw Mr. Gray enter Prince's Restaurant. In the hall Mr. Gray met a gent unknown by sight to colleague. Following some conversation both gents went in to dinner. They are there now. Speaking from Dover Street Tube."

"Yes, yes. But the lady?"

"A native, possibly Egyptian, apparently servant of Kazmah, came out a few minutes after Mr. Gray had gone for cab, and went away. Sir Lucien Pyne and lady are still in Kazmah's rooms."

"What!" cried Irvin, pulling out his watch and glancing at the disk. "But it's after eight o'clock!"

"Yes, sir. The place is all shut up, and other offices in block closed at six. Door of Kazmah's is locked. I knocked and got no reply."

"Damn it! You're talking nonsense! There must be another exit."

"No, sir. Colleague has just relieved me. Left two gents over their wine at Prince's."

Monte Irvin's color began to fade slowly.

"Then it's Pyne!" he whispered. The hand which held the receiver shook. "Brisley—meet me at the Piccadilly end of Bond Street. I am coming now."

He put down the telephone, crossed to the wall and pressed a button. The cigar stump held firmly between his teeth, he stood on the rug before the hearth, facing the door.

Presently it opened and Hinkes came in.

"The car is ready, Hinkes?"

"Yes, sir, as you ordered. Shall Pattison come round to the door?"

"At once."

"Very good, sir."

He withdrew, closing the door quietly, and Monte Irvin stood staring across the library at the full-length portrait in oils of his wife in the pierrot dress which she had worn in the third act of *The Maid of the Masque*.

The clock in the hall struck half-past eight.

Chapter II

THE APARTMENTS OF KAZMAH

It was rather less than two hours earlier on the same evening that Quentin Gray came out of the confectioner's shop in Old Bond Street carrying a neat parcel. Yellow dusk was closing down upon this bazaar of the New Babylon, and many of the dealers in precious gems, vendors of rich stuffs, and makers of modes had already deserted their shops. Smartly dressed show-girls, saleswomen, girl clerks and others crowded the pavements, which at high noon had been thronged with ladies of fashion. Here a tailor's staff, there a hatter's lingered awhile as iron shutters and gratings were secured, and bidding one another good night, separated and made off towards Tube and 'bus. The working day was ended. Society was dressing for dinner.

Gray was about to enter the cab which awaited him, and his fresh-colored, boyish face wore an expression of eager expectancy, which must have betrayed the fact to an experienced beholder that he was hurrying to keep an agreeable appointment. Then, his hand resting on the handle of the cab-door, this expression suddenly changed to one of alert suspicion.

A tall, dark man, accompanied by a woman muffled in grey furs and wearing a silk scarf over her hair, had passed on foot along the opposite side of the street. Gray had seen them through the cab windows.

His smooth brow wrinkled and his mouth tightened to a thin straight line beneath the fair "regulation" moustache. He fumbled under his overcoat for loose silver, drew out a handful and paid off the taximan.

Sometimes walking in the gutter in order to avoid the throngs upon the pavement, regardless of the fact that his glossy dress-boots were becoming spattered with mud, Gray hurried off in pursuit of the pair. Twenty yards ahead he overtook them, as they were on the point of passing a picture dealer's window, from which yellow light streamed forth into the humid dusk. They were walking slowly, and Gray stopped in front of them.

"Hallo, you two!" he cried. "Where are you off to? I was on my way to call for you, Rita."

Flushed and boyish he stood before them, and his annoyance was increased by their failure to conceal the fact that his appearance was embarrassing if not unwelcome. Mrs. Monte Irvin was a petite, pretty woman, although some of the more wonderful bronzed tints of her hair suggested the employment of henna, and her naturally lovely complexion was delicately and artistically enhanced by art. Nevertheless, the flower-like face peeping out from the folds of a gauzy scarf, like a rose from a mist, whilst her soft little chin nestled into the fur, might have explained even in the case of an older man the infatuation which Quentin Gray was at no pains to hide.

She glanced up at her companion, Sir Lucien Pyne, a swarthy, cynical type of aristocrat, imperturbably. Then: "I had left a note for you, Quentin," she said hurriedly. She seemed to be in a dangerously high-strung condition.

"But I have booked a table and a box," cried Gray, with a hint of juvenile petulance.

"My dear Gray," said Sir Lucien coolly, "we are men of the world—and we do not look for consistency in womenfolk. Mrs. Irvin has decided to consult a palmist or a hypnotist or some such occult authority before dining with you this evening. Doubtless she seeks to learn if the play to which you propose to take her is an amusing one."

His smile of sardonic amusement Gray found to be almost insupportable, and although Sir Lucien refrained from looking at Mrs. Irvin whilst he spoke, it was evident enough that his words held some covert significance, for:

"You know perfectly well that I have a particular reason for seeing him," she said.

"A woman's particular reason is a man's feeble excuse," murmured Sir Lucien rudely. "At least, according to a learned Arabian philosopher."

"I was going to meet you at Prince's," said

Mrs. Irvin hurriedly, and again glancing at Gray. There was a pathetic hesitancy in her manner, the hesitancy of a weak woman who adheres to a purpose only by supreme effort.

"Might I ask," said Gray, "the name of the person you are going to consult?"

Again she hesitated and glanced rapidly at Sir Lucien, but he was staring coolly in another direction.

"Kazmah," she replied in a low voice.

"Kazmah!" cried Gray. "The man who sells perfume and pretends to read dreams? What an extraordinary notion. Wouldn't tomorrow do? He will surely have shut up shop?"

"I have been at pains to ascertain," replied Sir Lucien, "at Mrs. Irvin's express desire, that the man of mystery is still in session and will receive her."

Beneath the mask of nonchalance which he wore it might have been possible to detect excitement repressed with difficulty; and had Gray been more composed and not obsessed with the idea that Sir Lucien had deliberately intruded upon his plans for the evening, he could not have failed to perceive that Mrs. Monte Irvin was feverishly preoccupied with matters having no relation to dinner and the theatre. But his private suspicions grew only the more acute.

"Then if the dinner is not off," he said, "may I come along and wait for you?"

"At Kazmah's?" asked Mrs. Irvin. "Certainly." She turned to Sir Lucien. "Shall you wait? It isn't much use as I'm dining with Quentin."

"If I do not intrude," replied the baronet, "I will accompany you as far as the cave of the oracle, and then bid you good night."

The trio proceeded along Old Bond Street. Quentin Gray regarded the story of Kazmah as a very poor lie devised on the spur of the moment. If he had been less infatuated, his natural sense of dignity must have dictated an offer to release Mrs. Irvin from her engagement. But jealousy stimulates the worst instincts and destroys the best. He was determined to attach himself as closely as the Old Man of the Sea attached himself to Es-Sindibad, in order that the lie might be unmasked. Mrs. Irvin's palpable embarrassment and nervousness he ascribed to her perception of his design.

A group of shop girls and others waiting for 'buses rendered it impossible for the three to keep abreast, and Gray, falling to the rear, stepped upon the foot of a little man who was walking close behind them.

"Sorry, sir," said the man, suppressing an exclamation of pain—for the fault had been Gray's.

Gray muttered an ungenerous acknowledgment, all anxiety to regain the side of Mrs. Irvin; for she seemed to be speaking rapidly and excitedly to Sir Lucien.

He recovered his place as the two turned in at a lighted doorway. Upon the wall was a bronze plate bearing the inscription:

KAZMAH

Second Floor

Gray fully expected Mrs. Irvin to suggest that he should return later. But without a word she began to ascend the stairs. Gray followed, Sir Lucien standing aside to give him precedence.

On the second floor was a door painted in Oriental fashion. It possessed neither bell nor knocker, but as one stepped upon the threshold this door opened noiselessly as if dumbly inviting the visitor to enter the square apartment discovered. This apartment was richly furnished in the Arab manner, and lighted by a fine brass lamp swung upon chains from the painted ceiling. The intricate perforations of the lamp were inset with colored glass, and the result was a subdued and warm illumination. Odd-looking Oriental vessels, long-necked lidded jars, jugs with tenuous spouts and squat bowls possessing engraved and figured covers emerged from the shadows of niches. A low divan with gaily colored mattresses extended from the door around one corner of the room where it terminated beside a kind of *mushrabîyeh* cabinet or cupboard. Beyond this cabinet was a long, low counter laden with statuettes of Nile gods, amulets, mummy-beads and little stoppered flasks of blue enamel ware. There were two glass cases filled with other strange-looking antiquities. A faint perfume was perceptible.

Sir Lucien entering last of the party, the door closed behind him, and from the cabinet on the right of the divan a young Egyptian stepped out. He wore the customary white robe, red sash and red slippers, and a *tarbûsh*, the little scarlet cap commonly called a fez, was set upon his head. He walked to a door on the left of the counter, and slid it noiselessly open. Bowing gravely:

"The Sheikh el Kazmah awaits," he said, speaking with the soft intonation of a native of Upper Egypt.

It now became evident, even to the infatuated Gray, that Mrs. Irvin was laboring under the influence of tremendous excitement. She turned to him quickly, and he thought that her face looked almost haggard, whilst her eyes seemed to have changed color— become lighter, although he could not be certain that this latter effect was not due to the peculiar illumination of the room. But when she spoke her voice was unsteady.

"Will you see if you can find a cab," she said. "It is so difficult at night, and my shoes will get frightfully muddy crossing Piccadilly. I shall not be more than a few minutes." She walked through the doorway, the Egyptian standing aside as she passed. He followed her, but came out again almost immediately, reclosed the door, and retired into the cabinet, which was evidently his private cubicle.

Silence claimed the apartment. Sir Lucien threw himself nonchalantly upon the divan, and took out his cigarette-case.

"Will you have a cigarette, Gray?" he asked.

"No thanks," replied the other, in tones of smothered hostility. He was ill at ease, and paced the apartment nervously. Pyne lighted a cigarette, and tossed the extinguished match into a brass bowl.

"I think," said Gray jerkily, "I shall go for a cab. Are you remaining?"

"I am dining at the club," answered Pyne, "but I can wait until you return." "As you wish," jerked Gray. "I don't expect to be long."

He walked rapidly to the outer door, which opened at his approach and closed noiselessly behind him as he made his exit.

Chapter III

KAZMAH

Mrs. Monte Irvin entered the inner room. The air was heavy with the perfume of frankincense which smouldered in a brass vessel set upon a tray. This was the audience chamber of Kazmah. In marked contrast to the overcrowded appointments, divans and cupboards of the first room, it was sparsely furnished. The floor was thickly carpeted, but save for an ornate inlaid table upon which stood the tray and incense-burner, and a long, low-cushioned seat placed immediately beneath a hanging lamp burning dimly in a globular green shade, it was devoid of decoration. The walls were draped with green curtains, so that except for the presence of the painted door, the four sides of the apartment appeared to be uniform.

Having conducted Mrs. Irvin to the seat, the Egyptian bowed and retired again through the doorway by which they had entered. The visitor found herself alone.

She moved nervously, staring across at the blank wall before her. With her little satin shoe she tapped the carpet, biting her under lip and seeming to be listening. Nothing stirred. Not even an echo of busy Bond Street penetrated to the place. Mrs Irvin unfastened her cloak and allowed it to fall back upon the settee. Her bare shoulders looked waxen and unnatural in the weird light which shone down upon them. She was breathing rapidly.

The minutes passed by in unbroken silence. So still was the room that Mrs. Irvin could hear the faint crackling sound made by the burning charcoal in the brass vessel near her. Wisps of blue-grey smoke arose through the perforated lid and she began to watch them fascinatedly, so lithe they seemed, like wraiths of serpents creeping up the green draperies.

So she was seated, her foot still restlessly tapping, but her gaze arrested by the hypnotic movements of the smoke, when at last a sound from the outer world penetrated the room. A church clock struck the hour of seven, its clangor intruding upon the silence only as a muffled boom. Almost coincident with the last stroke came the sweeter note of a silver gong from somewhere close at hand.

Mrs. Irvin started, and her eyes turned instantly in the direction of the greenly draped wall before her. Her pupils had grown suddenly dilated, and she clenched her hands tightly.

The light above her head went out.

Now that the moment was come to which she had looked forward with mingled hope and terror, long-pent-up emotion threatened to overcome her, and she trembled wildly.

Out of the darkness dawned a vague light and in it a shape seemed to take form. As the light increased the effect was as though part of the wall had become transparent so as to reveal the interior of an inner room where a figure was seated in a massive ebony chair. The figure was that of an Oriental, richly robed and wearing a white turban. His long slim hands, of the color of old ivory, rested upon the arms of the chair, and on the first finger of the right hand gleamed a big talismanic ring. The face of the seated man was lowered, but from under heavy brows his abnormally large eyes regarded her fixedly.

So dim the light remained that it was impossible to discern the details with anything like clearness, but that the clean-shaven face of the man with those wonderful eyes was strikingly and intellectually handsome there could be no doubt.

This was Kazmah, "the dream reader," and although Mrs. Irvin had seen him before, his statuesque repose and the weirdness of his unfaltering gaze thrilled her uncannily.

Kazmah slightly raised his hand in greeting: the big ring glittered in the subdued light.

"Tell me your dream," came a curious mocking voice; "and I will read its portent."

Such was the set formula with which Kazmah opened all interviews. He spoke with a slight and not unmusical accent. He lowered his hand again. The gaze of those brilliant eyes remained fixed upon the woman's face. Moistening her lips, Mrs. Irvin spoke.

"Dreams! What I have to say does not belong to dreams, but to reality!" She laughed unmirthfully. "You know well enough why I am here."

She paused.

"Why are you here?"

"You know! You know!" Suddenly into her voice had come the unmistakable note of hysteria. "Your theatrical tricks do not impress me. I know what you are! A spy—an eavesdropper who watches—watches, and listens! But you may go too far! I am nearly desperate—do you understand?—nearly desperate. Speak! Move! Answer me!"

But Kazmah preserved his uncanny repose.

"You are distracted," he said. "I am sorry for you. But why do you come to *me* with your stories of desperation? You have insisted upon seeing me. I am here."

"And you play with me—taunt me!"

"The remedy is in your hands."

"For the last time, I tell you I will never do it! Never, never, never!"

"Then why do you complain? If you cannot afford to pay for your amusements, and you refuse to compromise in a simple manner, why do you approach *me?*"

"Oh, my God!" She moaned and swayed dizzily—"have pity on me! Who are you, what are you, that you can bring ruin on a woman because—" She uttered a choking sound, but continued hoarsely, "Raise your head. Let me see your face. As heaven is my witness, I am ruined—ruined!"

"To-morrow——"

"I cannot wait for to-morrow——"

That quivering, hoarse cry betrayed a condition of desperate febrile excitement. Mrs. Irvin was capable of proceeding to the wildest extremities. Clearly the mysterious Egyptian recognized this to be the case, for slowly raising his hand:

"I will communicate with you," he said, and the words were spoken almost hurriedly. "Depart in peace—" a formula wherewith he terminated every séance. He lowered his hand.

The silver gong sounded again—and the dim light began to fade.

Thereupon the unhappy woman acted; the long suppressed outburst came at last. Stepping rapidly to the green transparent veil behind which Kazmah was seated, she wrenched it asunder and leapt toward the figure in the black chair.

"You shall not trick me!" she panted. "Hear me out or I go straight to the police—now—now!"

She grasped the hands of Kazmah as they rested motionless, on the chair-arms.

Complete darkness came.

Out of it rose a husky, terrified cry—a second, louder cry; and then a long, wailing scream . . . horror-laden as that of one who has touched some slumbering reptile. . . .

Chapter IV

THE CLOSED DOOR

Rather less than five minutes later a taxicab drew up in Old Bond Street, and from it Quentin Gray leapt out impetuously and ran in at the doorway leading to Kazmah's stairs. So hurried was his progress that he collided violently with a little man who, carrying himself with a pronounced stoop, was slinking furtively out.

The little man reeled at the impact and almost fell, but:

"Hang it all!" cried Gray irritably. "Why the devil don't you look where you're going!"

He glared angrily into the face of the other. It was a peculiar and remembered face, notable because of a long, sharp, hooked nose and very little, foxy, brown eyes; a sly face to which a small, fair moustache only added insignificance. It was crowned by a wide-brimmed bowler hat which the man wore pressed down upon his ears like a Jew peddlar.

"Why!" cried Gray, "This is the second time to-night you have jostled me!"

He thought he had recognized the man for the same who had been following himself, Mrs. Irvin and Sir Lucien Pyne along Old Bond Street.

A smile, intended to be propitiatory, appeared upon the pale face.

"No, sir, excuse me, sir——"

"Don't deny it!" said Gray angrily. "If I had the time I should give you in charge as a suspicious loiterer."

Calling to the cabman to wait, he ran up the stairs to the second floor landing. Before the painted door bearing the name of Kazmah he halted, and as the door did not open, stamped impatiently, but with no better result.

At that, since there was neither bell nor knocker, he raised his fist and banged loudly.

No one responded to the summons.

"Hi, there!" he shouted. "Open the door! Pyne! Rita!"

Again he banged—and yet again. Then he paused, listening, his ear pressed to the panel.

He could detect no sound of movement within. Fists clenched, he stood staring at the closed door, and his fresh color slowly deserted him and left him pale.

"Damn him!" he muttered savagely. "Damn him! he has fooled me!"

Passionate and self-willed, he was shaken by a storm of murderous anger. That Pyne had planned this trick, with Rita Irvin's consent, he did not doubt, and his passive dislike of the man became active hatred. Of the woman he dared not think. He had for long looked upon Sir Lucien in the light of a rival, and the irregularity of his own infatuation for another's wife in no degree lessened his resentment.

Again he pressed his ear to the door, and listened intently. Perhaps they were hiding within. Perhaps this charlatan, Kazmah, was an accomplice in the pay of Sir Lucien. Perhaps this was a secret place of rendezvous.

To the manifest absurdity of such a conjecture he was blind in his anger. But that he was helpless, befooled, he recognized; and with a final muttered imprecation he turned and slowly descended the stair. A lingering hope was dispelled when, looking right and left along Bond Street, he failed to perceive the missing pair.

The cabman glanced at him interrogatively. "I shall not require you," said Gray, and gave the man half-a-crown.

Busy with his poisonous conjectures, he remained all unaware of the presence of a furtive, stooping figure which lurked behind the railings of the arcade at this point linking Old Bond Street to Albemarle Street. Nor had the stooping stranger any wish to attract Gray's attention. Most of the shops in the narrow lane were already closed, although the florist's at the corner remained open, but of the shadow which lay along the greater part of the arcade this alert watcher took every advantage. From the recess formed by a shop door he peered out at Gray, where the light of a street lamp fell upon him, studying his face, his movements, with unrelaxing vigilance.

Gray, following some moments of indecision, strode off towards Piccadilly. The little man came out cautiously from his hiding-place and looked after him. Out of a dark porch, ten paces along Bond Street, appeared a burly figure to fall into step a few yards behind Gray. The little man licked his lips appreciatively and returned to the doorway below the premises of Kazmah.

Reaching Piccadilly, Gray stood for a time on the corner, indifferent to the jostling of passers-by. Finally he crossed, walked along to the Prince's Restaurant, and entered the lobby. He glanced at his wrist-watch. It registered the hour of seven-twenty-five.

He cancelled his order for a table and was standing staring moodily towards the entrance when the doors swung open and a man entered who stepped straight up to him, hand extended, and:

"Glad to see you, Gray," he said. "What's the trouble?"

Quentin Gray stared as if incredulous at the speaker, and it was with an unmistakable note of welcome in his voice that he replied:

"Seton! Seton Pasha!"

The frown disappeared from Gray's forehead, and he gripped the other's hand in hearty greeting. But:

"Stick to plain Seton!" said the new-comer, glancing rapidly about him. "Ottoman titles are not fashionable."

The speaker was a man of arresting personality. Above medium height, well but leanly built, the face of Seton "Pasha" was burned to a deeper shade than England's wintry sun is capable of producing. He wore a close-trimmed beard and moustache, and the bronze on his cheeks enhanced the brightness of his grey eyes and rendered very noticable a slight frosting of the dark hair above his temples. He had the indescribable air of a "sure" man, a sound man to have beside one in a tight place; and looking into the rather grim face, Quentin Gray felt suddenly ashamed of himself. From Seton Pasha he knew that he could keep nothing back, he knew that presently he should find himself telling this quiet, brown-skinned man the whole story of his humiliation—and he knew that Seton would not spare his feelings.

"My dear fellow," he said, "you must pardon me if I sometimes fail to respect your wishes in this matter. When I left the East the name of Seton Pasha was on everybody's tongue. But are you alone?"

"I am. I only arrived in London to-night and in England this morning."

"Were you thinking of dining here?"

"No; I saw you through the doorway as I was passing. But this will do as well as another place. I gather that you are disengaged. Perhaps you will dine with me?"

"Splendid!" cried Gray. "Wait a moment. Perhaps my table hasn't gone!"

He ran off in his boyish, impetuous fashion, and Seton watched him, smiling quietly.

The table proved to be available, and ere long the two were discussing an excellent dinner. Gray lost much of his irritability and began to talk coherently upon topics of general interest. Presently, following an interval during which he had been covertly watching his companion:

"Do you know, Seton," he said, "you are the one man in London whose company I could have tolerated to-night."

"My arrival was peculiarly opportune."

"Your arrivals are always peculiarly opportune." Gray stared at Seton with an expression of puzzled admiration. "I don't think I shall ever understand your turning up immediately before the Senussi raid in

Egypt. Do you remember? I was with the armored cars."

"I remember perfectly."

"Then you vanished in the same mysterious fashion, and the C.O. was a sphinx on the subject. I next saw you strolling out of the gate of Baghdad. How the devil you'd got to Baghdad, considering that you didn't come with us and that you weren't with the cavalry, heaven only knows!"

"No," said Seton judicially, gazing through his uplifted wine-glass; "when one comes to consider the matter without prejudice it is certainly odd. But do I know the lady to whose non-appearance I owe the pleasure of your company to night?"

Quentin Gray stared at him blankly.

"Really, Seton, you amaze me. Did I say that I had an appointment with a lady?"

"My dear Gray, when I see a man standing biting his nails and glaring out into Piccadilly from a restaurant entrance I ask myself a question. When I learn that he has just cancelled an order for a table for two I answer it."

Gray laughed. "You always make me feel so infernally young, Seton."

"Good!"

"Yes, it's good to feel young, but bad to feel a young fool; and that's what I feel—and what I am. Listen!"

Leaning across the table so that the light of the shaded lamp fell fully upon his flushed, eager face, Gray, not without embarrassment, told his companion of the "dirty trick"—so he phrased it—which Sir Lucien Pyne had played upon him. In conclusion:

"What would you do, Seton?" he asked.

Seton sat regarding him in silence with a cool, calculating stare which some men had termed insolent, absently tapping his teeth with the gold rim of a monocle which he carried but apparently never used for any other purpose; and it was at about this time that a long, low car passed near the door of the restaurant, crossing the traffic stream of Piccadilly to draw up at the corner of Old Bond Street.

From the car Monte Irvin alighted and, telling the man to wait, set out on foot. Ten paces along Bond Street he encountered a small, stooping figure which became detached from the shadows of a shop door. The light of a street lamp shone down upon the sharp, hooked nose and into the cunning little brown eyes of Brisley, of Spinker's Detective Agency. Monte Irvin started.

"Ah, Brisley!" he said, "I was looking for you. Are they still there?"

"Probably, sir." Brisley licked his lips. "My colleague, Gunn, reports no one came out whilst I was away 'phoning."

"But the whole thing seems preposterous. Are there no other offices in the block where they might be?"

"I personally saw Mr. Gray, Sir Lucien Pyne and the lady go into Kazmah's. At that time—roughly, ten to seven—all the other offices had been closed, approximately, one hour."

"There is absolutely no possibility that they might have come out unseen by you?"

"None, sir. I should not have troubled a client if in doubt. Here's Gunn."

Old Bond Street now was darkened and deserted; the yellow mist had turned to fine rain, and Gunn, his hands thrust in his pockets, was sheltering under the porch of the arcade. Gunn possessed a purple complexion which attained to full vigor of coloring in the nasal region. His moustache of dirty grey was stained brown in the centre as if by frequent potations of stout, and his bulky figure was artificially enlarged by the presence of two overcoats, the outer of which was a waterproof and the inner a blue garment appreciably longer both in sleeve and skirt than the former. The effect produced was one of great novelty. Gunn touched the brim of his soft felt hat, which he wore turned down all round apparently in imitation of a flower-pot.

"All snug, sir," he said, hoarsely and confidentially, bending forward and breathing the words into Irvin's ear. "Snug as a bee in a hive. You're as good as a bachelor again."

Monte Irvin mentally recoiled.

"Lead the way to the door of this place," he said tersely.

"Yes, sir, this way, sir. Be careful of the step there. You may remark that the outer door is not yet closed. I am informed upon reliable authority as the last to go locks the door. Hence we perceive that the last has not yet gone. It is likewise opened by the first to come of a mornin'. Here we are, sir; door on the right."

The landing was in darkness, but as Gunn spoke he directed the ray of a pocket lamp upon a bronze plate bearing the name "Kazmah." He rested one hand upon his hip.

"All snug," he repeated; "as snug as a eel in mud. The *decree nisi* is yours, sir. As an alderman of the City of London and a Justice

of the Peace you are entitled to call a police officer——"

"Hold your tongue!" rapped Irvin. "You've been drinking: and I place no reliance whatever in your evidence. I do not believe that my wife or any one else but ourselves is upon these premises."

The watery eyes of the insulted man protruded unnaturally. "Drinkin'!" he whispered, "drink—"

But indignation now deprived Gunn of speech and:

"Excuse me, sir," interrupted the nasal voice of Brisley, "but I can absolutely answer for Gunn. Reputation of the Agency at stake. Worked with us for three years. Parties undoubtedly on the premises as reported."

"Drink—" whispered Gunn.

"I shall be glad," said Monte Irvin, and his voice shook emotionally, "if you will lend me your pocket lamp. I am naturally upset. Will you kindly both go downstairs. I will call if I want you."

The two men obeyed, Gunn muttering hoarsely to Brisley; and Monte Irvin was left standing on the landing, the lamp in his hand. He waited until he knew from the sound of their footsteps that the pair had regained the street, then, resting his arm against the closed door, and pressing his forehead to the damp sleeve of his coat, he stood awhile, the lamp, which he held limply, shining down upon the floor.

His lips moved, and almost inaudibly he murmured his wife's name.

Chapter V

THE DOOR IS OPENED

Quentin Gray and Seton strolled out of Prince's and both paused whilst Seton lighted a long black cheroot.

"It seems a pity to waste that box," said Gray. "Suppose we look in at the Gaiety for an hour?"

His humor was vastly improved, and he watched the passing throngs with an expression more suited to his boyish good looks than that of anger and mortification which had rested upon him an hour earlier.

Seton Pasha tossed a match into the road.

"My official business is finished for the day," he replied. "I place myself unreservedly in your hands."

"Well, then," began Gray—and paused.

A long, low car, the chauffeur temporarily detained by the stoppage of a motor 'bus ahead, had slowed up within three yards of the spot where they were standing. Gray seized Seton's arm in a fierce grip.

"Seton," he said, his voice betraying intense excitement, "look! There is Monte Irvin!"

"In the car?"

"Yes, yes! But—he has two *police* with him! Seton! what can it mean?"

The car moved away, swinging to the right across the traffic stream and clearly heading for Old Bond Street. Quentin Gray's mercurial color deserted him, and he turned to Seton a face grown suddenly pale.

"Good God," he whispered, "something has happened to Rita!"

Neglectful of his personal safety, he plunged out into the traffic, dodging this way and that, and making after Monte Irvin's car. Of the fact that his friend was close beside him he remained unaware until, on the corner of Old Bond Street, a firm grip settled upon his shoulder. Gray turned angrily. But the grip was immovable, and he found himself staring into the unemotional face of Seton Pasha.

"Seton, for God's sake, don't detain me! I must learn what's wrong."

"Pull up, Gray."

Quentin Gray clenched his teeth.

"Listen to me, Seton. This is no time for interference. I—"

"You are about to become involved in some very unsavory business; and I repeat—pull up. In a moment we shall learn all there is to be learned. But are you determined openly to thrust yourself into the family affairs of Mr. Monte Irvin?"

"If anything has happened to Rita I'll kill that damned cur Pyne!"

"You are determined to intrude upon this man in your present frame of mind at a time of evident trouble?"

But Gray was deaf to the promptings of prudence and good taste alike.

"I'm going to see the thing through," he said hoarsely.

"Quite so. Rely upon me. But endeavor to behave more like a man of the world and less like a dangerous lunatic, or we shall quarrel atrociously."

Quentin Gray audibly gnashed his teeth, but the cool stare of the other's eyes was quelling, and now as their glances met and clashed, a sympathetic smile softened the lines of Seton's grim mouth, and:

"I quite understand, old chap," he said, linking his arm in Gray's. "But can't you see how important it is, for everybody's sake, that we should tackle the thing coolly?"

"Seton"—Gray's voice broke—"I'm sorry. I know I'm mad; but I was with her only an hour ago, and now—"

"And now 'her' husband appears on the scene accompanied by a police inspector and a sergeant. What are your relations with Mr. Monte Irvin?"

They were walking rapidly again along Bond Street.

"What do you mean, Seton?" asked Gray.

"I mean does he approve of your friendship with his wife, or is it a clandestine affair?"

"Clandestine?—certainly not. I was on my way to call at the house when I met her with Pyne this evening."

"That is what I wanted to know. Very well; since you intend to follow the thing up, it simplifies matters somewhat. Here is the car."

"At Kazmah's door! What in heaven's name does it mean?"

"It means that we shall get a very poor reception if we intrude. Question the chauffeur."

But Gray had already approached the man, who touched his cap in recognition.

"What's the trouble, Pattison?" he demanded breathlessly. "I saw police in the car a moment ago."

"Yes, sir. I don't rightly know, sir, what's happened. But Mr. Irvin drove from home to the corner of old Bond Street a quarter of an hour ago and told me to wait, then came back again and drove round to Vine Street to fetch the police. They're inside now."

Even as he spoke, with excitement ill concealed, a police-sergeant came out of the doorway, and:

"Move on, there," he said to Seton and Gray. "You mustn't hang about this door."

"Excuse me, Sergeant," cried Gray, "but if the matter concerns Mrs. Monte Irvin I can probably supply information."

The Sergeant stared at him hard, saw that both he and his friend wore evening dress, and grew proportionately respectful.

"What is your name, sir?" he asked. "I'll mention it to the officer in charge."

"Quentin Gray. Inform Mr. Monte Irvin that I wish to speak to him."

"Very good, sir." He turned to the chauffeur. "Hand me out the bag I gave you at Vine Street."

Pattison leaned over the door at the front of the car, and brought out a big leather grip. With this in hand the police-sergeant returned into the doorway.

"We're in for it now," said Seton grimly, "whatever it is."

Gray returned no answer, moving restlessly up and down before the door in a fever of excitement and dread. Presently the Sergeant reappeared.

"Step this way, please," he said.

Followed by Seton and Gray he led the way up to the landing before Kazmah's apartments. It was vaguely lighted by two police-lanterns. Four men were standing there, and four pairs of eyes were focussed upon the stair-head.

Monte Irvin, his features a distressing ashen color, spoke.

"That you, Gray?" Quentin Gray would not have recognized the voice. "Thanks for offering your help. God knows I need all I can get. You were with Rita to-night. What happened? Where is she?"

"Heaven knows where she is!" cried Gray. "I left her here with Pyne shortly after seven o'clock."

He paused, fixing his gaze upon the face of Brisley, whose shifty eyes avoided him and who was licking his lips in the manner of a dog who has seen the whip.

"Why," said Gray, "I believe you are the fellow who has been following me all night for some reason."

He stepped toward the foxy little man but: "Never mind, Gray," interrupted Irvin. "*I* was to blame. But he was following my wife, not you. Tell me quickly: Why did she come here?"

Gray raised his hand to his brow with a gesture of bewilderment.

"To consult this man, Kazmah. I actually saw her enter the inner room, I went to get a cab, and when I returned the door was locked."

"You knocked?"

"Of course. I made no end of a row. But I could get no reply and went away."

Monte Irvin turned, a pathetic figure, to the Inspector who stood beside him.

"We may as well proceed, Inspector Whiteleaf," he said. "Mr. Gray's evidence throws no light on the matter at all."

"Very well, sir," was the reply; "we have the warrant, and have given the usual notice to whoever may be hiding inside. Burton!"

The Sergeant stepped forward, placed the leather bag on the floor, and stooping, opened it, revealing a number of burglarious-looking instruments.

"Shall I try to cut through the panel?" he asked.

"No, no!" cried Monte Irvin. "Waste no time. You have a crowbar there. Force the door from its hinges. Hurry, man!"

"It doesn't work on hinges!" Gray interrupted excitedly. "It slides to the right by means of some arrangement concealed under the mat."

"Pass that lantern," directed Burton, glancing over his shoulder to Gunn.

Setting it beside him, the Sergeant knelt and examined the threshold of the door.

"A metal plate," he said. "The weight moves a lever, I suppose, which opens the door if it isn't locked. The lock will be on the left of the door as it opens to the right. Let's see what we can do."

He stood up, crowbar in hand, and inserted the chisel blade of the implement between the edge of the door and the doorcase.

"Hold steady!" said the Inspector, standing at his elbow.

The dull metallic sound of hammer blows on steel echoed queerly around the well of the staircase. Brisley and Gunn, standing very close together on the bottom step of the stair to the third floor, watched the police furtively. Irvin and Gray found a common fascination in the door itself, and Seton, cheroot in mouth, looked from group to group with quiet interest.

"Right!" cried the Sergeant.

The blows ceased.

Firmly grasping the bar, Burton brought all his weight to bear upon it. There was a dull, cracking sound and a sort of rasping. The door moved slightly.

"There's where it locks!" said the Inspector, directing the light of a lantern upon the crevice created. "Three inches lower. But it may be bolted as well."

"We'll soon get at the bolts," replied Burton, the lust of destruction now strong upon him.

Wrenching the crowbar from its place he attacked the lower panel of the door, and amid a loud splintering and crashing created a hole big enough to allow of the passage of a hand and arm.

The Inspector reached in, groped about,

and then uttered an exclamation of triumph.

"I've unfastened the bolt," he said. "If there isn't another at the top you ought to be able to force the door now, Burton."

The jimmy was thrust back into position, and:

"Stand clear!" cried Burton.

Again he threw his weight upon the bar— and again.

"Drive it further in!" said Monte Irvin; and snatching up the heavy hammer, he rained blows upon the steel butt. "Now try."

Burton exerted himself to the utmost.

"Take hold up here, someone!" he panted. "Two of us can pull."

Gray leapt forward, and the pair of them bent to the task.

There came a dull report of parting mechanism, more sound of splintering wood . . . and the door rolled open!

A moment of tense silence, then:

"Is anyone inside there?" cried the Inspector loudly.

Not a sound came from the dark interior.

"The lantern!" whispered Monte Irvin.

He stumbled into the room, from which a heavy smell of perfume swept out upon the landing. Quentin Gray, snatching the lantern from the floor, where it had been replaced, was the next to enter.

"Look for the switch, and turn the lights on!" called the Inspector, following.

Even as he spoke, Gray had found the switch, and the apartment of Kazmah became flooded with subdued light.

A glance showed it to be unoccupied.

Gray ran across to the *mushrabîyeh* cabinet and jerked the curtains aside. There was no one in the cabinet. It contained a chair and a table. Upon the latter was a telephone and some papers and books.

"This way!" he cried, his voice high pitched and unnatural.

He burst through the doorway into the inner room which he had seen Mrs. Irvin enter. The air was laden with the smell of frankincense.

"A lantern!" he called. "I left one on the divan."

But Monte Irvin had caught it up and was already at his elbow. His hand was shaking so that the light danced wildly now upon the carpet, now upon the green walls. This room also was deserted. A black gap in the curtain showed where the material had been roughly torn. Suddenly:

"My God, look!" muttered the Inspector, who, with the others, now stood in the curious draped apartment.

A thin stream of blood was trickling out from beneath the torn hangings!

Monte Irvin staggered and fell back against the Inspector, clutching at him for support. But Sergeant Burton, who carried the second lantern, crossed the room and wrenched the green draperies bodily from their fastenings.

They had masked a wooden partition or stout screen, having an aperture in the centre which could be closed by means of another of the sliding doors. A space some five feet deep was thus walled off from this second room. It contained a massive ebony chair. Behind the chair, and dividing the second room into yet a third section, extended another wooden partition in one end of which was an ordinary office door; and immediately at the back of the chair appeared a little opening or window, some three feet up from the floor.

The sound of a groan, followed by that of a dull thud, came from the outer room.

"Hullo!" cried Inspector Whiteleaf. "Mr. Irvin has fainted. Lend a hand."

"I am here," replied the quiet voice of Seton Pasha.

"My God!" whispered Gray. "Seton! Seton!"

"Touch nothing," cried the Inspector from outside, "until I come!"

And now the narrow apartment became filled with all the awe-stricken company, only excepting Monte Irvin, and Brisley, who was attending to the swooning man.

Flat upon the floor, between the door and the ebony chair, arms extended and eyes staring upward at the ceiling, lay Sir Lucien Pyne, his white shirt front redly dyed. In the hush which had fallen, the footsteps of Inspector Whiteleaf sounded loudly as he opened the final door, and swept the interior of an inner room with the rays of the lantern.

The room was barely furnished as an office. There was another half-glazed door opening on to a narrow corridor. This door was locked.

"*Pyne!*" whispered Gray, pale now to the lips. "Do you understand, Seton? It's Pyne! Look! He has been stabbed!"

Sergeant Burton knelt down and gingerly laid his hand upon the stained linen over the breast of Sir Lucien.

"Dead?" asked the Inspector, speaking from the inner doorway.

"Yes."

"You say, sir," turning to Quentin Gray, "that this is Sir Lucien Pyne?"

"Yes."

Inspector Whiteleaf rather clumsily removed his cap. The odor of Seton's cheroot announced itself above the Oriental perfume with which the place was laden.

"Burton!"

"Yes?"

"See if this telephone in the office is in order. It appears to be an extension from the outer room."

While the others stood grouped about that still figure on the floor, Sergeant Burton entered the little office.

"Hello!" he cried. "Yes?" A momentary interval, then: "It's all right, sir. What number?"

"Gentlemen," said the Inspector, firmly and authoritatively, "I am about to telephone to Vine Street for instructions. No one will leave the premises."

Amid an intense hush:

"Regent 201," called Sergeant Burton.

Chapter VI

RED KERRY

Chief Inspector Kerry, of the Criminal Investigation Department, stood before the empty grate of his cheerless office in New Scotland Yard, one hand thrust into the pocket of his blue reefer jacket and the other twirling a malacca cane, which was heavily silver-mounted and which must have excited the envy of every sergeant-major beholding it. Chief Inspector Kerry wore a very narrow-brimmed bowler hat, having two ventilation holes conspicuously placed immediately above the band. He wore this hat tilted forward and to the right.

"Red Kerry" wholly merited his sobriquet, for the man was as red as fire. His hair, which he wore cropped close as a pugilist's, was brilliantly red, and so was his short, wiry, aggressive moustache. His complexion was red, and from beneath his straight red eyebrows he surveyed the world with a pair of unblinking, intolerant steel-blue eyes. He never smoked in public, as his taste inclined towards Irish twist and a short clay pipe; but he was addicted to the use of chewing-gum, and as he chewed—and he chewed incessantly—he revealed a perfect row of large,

white, and positively savage-looking teeth. High cheek bones and prominent maxillary muscles enhanced the truculence indicated by his chin.

But, next to this truculence, which was the first and most alarming trait to intrude itself upon the observer's attention, the outstanding characteristics of Chief Inspector Kerry was his compact neatness. Of no more than medium height but with shoulders like an acrobat, he had slim, straight legs and the feet of a dancing master. His attire, from the square-pointed collar down to the neat black brogues, was spotless. His reefer jacket fitted him faultlessly, but his trousers were cut so unfashionably narrow that the protuberant thigh muscles and the line of a highly developed calf could quite easily be discerned. The hand twirling the cane was small but also muscular, freckled and covered with light down. Red Kerry was built on the lines of a whippet, but carried the equipment of an Irish terrier.

The telephone bell rang. Inspector Kerry moved his square shoulders in a manner oddly suggestive of a wrestler, laid the malacca cane on the mantleshelf, and crossed to the table. Taking up the telephone:

"Yes?" he said, and his voice was high-pitched and imperious.

He listened for a moment.

"Very good, sir."

He replaced the receiver, took up a wet oilskin overall from the back of a chair and the cane from the mantleshelf. Then, rolling chewing-gum from one corner of his mouth into the other, he snapped off the electric light and walked from the room.

Along the corridor he went with a lithe, silent step, moving from the hips and swinging his shoulders. Before a door marked "Private" he paused. From his waistcoat pocket he took a little silver convex mirror and surveyed himself critically therein. He adjusted his neat tie, replaced the mirror, knocked at the door and entered the room of the Assistant Commissioner.

This important official was a man constructed on huge principles, a man of military bearing, having tired eyes and a bewildered manner. He conveyed the impression that the collection of documents, books, telephones, and other paraphernalia bestrewing his table had reduced him to a state of stupor. He looked up wearily and met the fierce gaze of the chief inspector with a glance almost apologetic.

"Ah, Chief Inspector Kerry?" he said, with vague surprise. "Yes. I told you to come. Really, I ought to have been at home hours ago. It's most unfortunate. I have to do the work of three men. This *is* your department, is it not, Chief Inspector?"

He handed Kerry a slip of paper, at which the Chief Inspector stared fiercely.

"Murder!" rapped Kerry. "Sir Lucien Pyne. Yes, sir, I am still on duty."

His speech, in moments of interest, must have suggested to one overhearing him from an adjoining room, for instance, the operation of a telegraphic instrument. He gave to every syllable the value of a rap and certain words he terminated with an audible snap of the teeth.

"Ah," murmured the Assistant Commissioner. "Yes. Divisional Inspector—Somebody (I cannot read the name) has detained all the parties. But you had better report at Vine Street. It appears to be a big case."

He sighed wearily.

"Very good, sir. With your permission I will glance at Sir Lucien's pedigree."

"Certainly—certainly," said the Assistant Commissioner, waving one large hand in the direction of a bookshelf.

Kerry crossed the room, laid his oilskin and cane upon a chair, and from the shelf where it reposed took a squat volume. The Assistant Commissioner, hand pressed to brow, began to study a document which lay before him.

"Here we are," said Kerry, *sotto voce.* "Pyne, Sir Lucien St. Aubyn, fourth baronet, son of General Sir Christian Pyne, K.C.B. H'm! Born Malta. . . . Oriel College; first in classics. . . . H'm. Blue. . . . India, Burma. . . . Contested Wigan. . . . . attached British Legation. . . . H'm! . . ."

He returned the book to its place, took up his overall and cane, and:

"Very good, sir," he said. "I will proceed to Vine Street."

"Certainly—certainly," murmured the Assistant Commissioner, glancing up absently. "Good night."

"Good night, sir."

"Oh, Chief Inspector!"

Kerry turned, his hand on the door-knob. "Sir?"

"I—er—what was I going to say? Oh, yes! The social importance of the murdered man raises the case from the—er—you follow me? Public interest will become acute, no doubt. I have therefore selected you for your well known discretion. I met Sir Lucien once. Very sad. Good night."

"Good night, sir."

Kerry passed out into the corridor, closing the door quietly. The Assistant Commissioner was a man for whom he entertained the highest respect. Despite the bewildered air and wandering manner, he knew this big, tired-looking soldier for an administrator of infinite capacity and inexhaustive energy.

Proceeding to a room further along the corridor, Chief Inspector Kerry opened the door and looked in.

"Detective-sergeant Coombes." he snapped and rolled chewing-gum from side to side of his mouth.

Detective-sergeant Coombes, a plump, short man having lank black hair and a smile of sly contentment perpetually adorning his round face, rose hurriedly from the chair upon which he had been seated. Another man who was in the room rose also, as if galvanized by the glare of the fierce blue eyes.

"I'm going to Vine Street," said Kerry succinctly; "you're coming with me," turned, and went on his way.

Two taxicabs were standing in the yard, and into the first of these Inspector Kerry stepped, followed by Coombes, the latter breathing heavily and carrying his hat in his hand, since he had not yet found time to put it on.

"Vine Street," shouted Kerry. "Brisk."

He leaned back in the cab, chewing industriously.

Coombes, having somewhat recovered his breath, essayed speech.

"Is it something big?" he asked.

"Sure," snapped Kerry. "Do they send *me* to stop dog-fights?"

Knowing the man and recognizing the mood, Coombes became silent, and this silence he did not break all the way to Vine Street. At the station:

"Wait," said Chief Inspector Kerry, and went swinging in, carrying his overall and having the malacca cane tucked under his arm.

A few minutes later he came out again and reentered the cab.

"Piccadilly corner of Old Bond Street," he directed the man.

"Is it burglary?" asked Detective-sergeant Coombes with interest.

"No," said Kerry. "It's murder; and there seems to be stacks of evidence. Sharpen your pencil."

"Oh!" murmured Coombes.

They were almost immediately at their destination, and Chief Inspector Kerry, dismissing the cabman, set off along Bond Street with his lithe, swinging gait, looking all about him intently. Rain had ceased, but the air was damp and chilly, and few pedestrians were to be seen.

A car was standing before Kazmah's premises, the chauffeur walking up and down on the pavement and flapping his hands across his chest in order to restore circulation. The Chief Inspector stopped.

"Hi, my man!" he said.

The chauffeur stood still.

"Whose car?"

"Mr. Monte Irvin's."

Kerry turned on his heel and stepped to the office door. It was ajar, and Kerry, taking an electric torch from his overall pocket, flashed the light upon the name-plate. He stood for a moment, chewing and looking up the darkened stairs. Then, torch in hand, he ascended.

Kazmah's door was closed, and the Chief Inspector rapped loudly. It was opened at once by Sergeant Burton, and Kerry entered, followed by Coombes.

The room at first sight seemed to be extremely crowded. Monte Irvin, very pale and haggard, sat upon the divan beside Quentin Gray. Seton was standing near the cabinet, smoking. These three had evidently been conversing at the time of the detective's arrival with an alert-looking, clean-shaven man whose bag, umbrella, and silk hat stood upon one of the little inlaid tables. Just inside the second door were Brisley and Gunn, both palpably ill at ease, and glancing at Inspector Whiteleaf, who had been interrogating them.

Kerry chewed silently for a moment, bestowing a fierce stare upon each face in turn, then:

"Who's in charge?" he snapped.

"I am," replied Whiteleaf.

"Why is the lower door open?"

"I thought——"

"Don't think. Shut the door. Post your Sergeant inside. No one is to go out. Grab anybody who comes in. Where's the body?"

"This way," said Inspector Whiteleaf hurriedly; then, over his shoulder: "Go down to the door, Burton."

He led Kerry towards the inner room, Coombes at his heels. Brisley and Gunn stood aside to give them passage; Gray and Monte Irvin prepared to follow. At the doorway

Kerry turned.

"You will all be good enough to stay where you are," he said. He directed the aggressive stare in Seton's direction. "And if the gentleman smoking a cheroot is not satisfied that he has quite destroyed any clue perceptible by the sense of smell I should be glad to send out for some fireworks."

He tossed his oilskin and his cane on the divan and went into the room of séance, savagely biting at a piece of apparently indestructible chewing-gum.

The torn green curtain had been laid aside and the electric lights turned on in the inside rooms. Pallid, Sir Lucien Pyne lay by the ebony chair glaring horribly upward.

Always with the keen eyes glancing this way and that, Inspector Kerry crossed the little audience room and entered the enclosure contained between the two screens. By the side of the dead man he stood, looking down silently. Then he dropped upon one knee and peered closely into the white face. He looked up.

"He has not been moved?"

"No."

Kerry bent yet lower, staring closely at a discolored abrasion on Sir Lucien's forehead. His glance wandered from thence to the carved ebony chair. Still kneeling, he drew from his waistcoat pocket a powerful lens contained in a washleather bag. He began to examine the back and sides of the chair. Once he laid his finger lightly on a protruding point of the carving, and then scrutinised his finger through the glass. He examined the dead man's hands, his nails, his garments. Then he crawled about, peering closely at the carpet.

He stood up suddenly. "The doctor," he snapped.

Inspector Whiteleaf retired, but returned immediately with the clean-shaven man to whom Monte Irvin had been talking when Kerry arrived.

"Good evening, doctor," said Kerry. "Do I know your name? Start your notes, Coombes."

"My name is Dr. Wilbur Weston, and I live in Albemarle Street."

"Who called you?"

"Inspector Whiteleaf telephoned to me about half an hour ago."

"You examined the dead man?"

"I did."

"You avoided moving him?

"It was unnecessary to move him. He was

dead, and the wound was in the left shoulder. I pulled his coat open and unbuttoned his shirt. That was all."

"How long dead?"

"I should say he had been dead not more than an hour when I saw him."

"What had caused death?"

"The stab of some long, narrow-bladed weapon; such as a stiletto."

"Why a stiletto?" Kerry's fierce eyes challenged him. "Did you ever see a wound made by a stiletto?"

"Several—in Italy, and one at Saffron Hill. They are characterised by very little external bleeding."

"Right, doctor. It had reached his heart?"

"Yes. The blow was delivered from behind."

"How do you know?"

"The direction of the wound is forward. I have seen an almost identical wound in the case of an Italian woman stabbed by a jealous rival."

"He would fall on his back."

"Oh, no. He would fall on his face, almost certainly."

"But he lies on his back."

"In my opinion he had been moved."

"Right. I know he had. Good night, doctor. See him out, Inspector."

Dr. Weston seemed rather startled by this abrupt dismissal, but the steel-blue eyes of Inspector Kerry were already bent again upon the dead man, and, murmuring "good night," the doctor took his departure, followed by Whiteleaf.

"Shut this door," snapped Kerry after the Inspector. "I will call when I want you. You stay, Coombes. Got it all down?"

Sergeant Coombes scratched his head with the end of a pencil, and:

"Yes," he said, with hesitancy. "That is, except the word after 'narrow-bladed weapon such as a——' I've got what looks like 'steel-hatto.' "

Kerry glared.

"Try taking the cotton-wool out of your ears," he suggested. "The word was stiletto, s-t-i-l-e-t-t-o—stiletto."

"Oh," said Coombes, "thanks."

Silence fell between the two men from Scotland Yard. Kerry stood awhile, chewing and staring at the ghastly face of Sir Lucien. Then:

"Go through all pockets," he directed.

Sergeant Coombes placed his notebook and pencil upon the seat of the chair and set to work. Kerry entered the inside room or office. It contained a writing-table (upon which was a telephone and a pile of old newspapers), a cabinet, and two chairs. Upon one of the chairs lay a crush-hat, a cane, and an overcoat. He glanced at some of the newspapers, then opened the drawers of the writing-table. They were empty. The cabinet proved to be locked, and a door which he saw must open upon a narrow passage running beside the suite of rooms was locked also. There was nothing in the pockets of the overcoat, but inside the hat he found pasted the initials L. P. He rolled chewing-gum, stared reflectively at the little window immediately above the table, through which a glimpse might be obtained of the ebony chair, and went out again.

"Nothing," reported Coombes.

"What do you mean—nothing?"

"His pockets are empty!"

"All of them?"

"Every one."

"Good," said Kerry. "Make a note of it. He wears a real pearl stud and a good signet ring; also a gold wrist watch, face broken and hands stopped at seven-fifteen. That was the time he died. He was stabbed from behind as he stood where I'm standing now, fell forward, struck his head on the leg of the chair, and lay face downwards."

"I've got that," muttered Coombes. "What stopped the watch?"

"Broken as he fell. There are tiny fragments of glass stuck in the carpet, showing the exact position in which his body originally lay; and for God's sake stop smiling."

Kerry threw open the door.

"Who first found the body?" he demanded of the silent company.

"I did," cried Quentin Gray, coming forward. "I and Seton Pasha."

"Seton Pasha!" Kerry's teeth snapped together, so that he seemed to bite off the words. "I don't see a Turk present."

Seton smiled quietly.

"My friend uses a title which was conferred upon me some years ago by the ex-Khedive," he said. "My name is Greville Seton."

Inspector Kerry glanced back across his shoulder.

"Notes," he said. "Unlock your ears, Coombes." He looked at Gray. "What is your name?"

"Quentin Gray."

"Who are you, and in what way are you concerned in this case?"

"I am the son of Lord Wrexborough, and I——"

He paused, glancing helplessly at Seton. He had recognized that the first mention of Rita Irvin's name in the police evidence must be made by himself.

"Speak up, sir," snapped Kerry. "Sergeant Coombes is deaf."

Gray's face flushed, and his eyes gleamed angrily.

"I should be glad, Inspector," he said, "if you would remember that the dead man was a personal acquaintance and that other friends are concerned in this ghastly affair."

"Coombes will remember it," replied Kerry frigidly. "He's taking notes."

"Look here——" began Gray.

Seton laid his hand upon the angry man's shoulder.

"Pull up, Gray," he said quietly. "Pull up, old chap." He turned his cool regard upon Chief Inspector Kerry, twirling the cord of his monocle about one finger. "I may remark, Inspector Kerry—for I understand this to be your name—that your conduct of the inquiry is not always characterised by the best possible taste."

Kerry rolled chewing-gum, meeting Seton's gaze with a stare intolerant and aggressive. He imparted that odd writhing movement to his shoulders.

"For my conduct I am responsible to the Commissioner," he replied. "And if he's not satisfied the Commissioner can have my written resignation at any hour in the twenty-four that he's short of a pipe-lighter. If it would not inconvenience you to keep quiet for two minutes I will continue my examination of this witness."

Chapter VII

FURTHER EVIDENCE

The examination of Quentin Gray was three times interrupted by telephone messages from Vine Street; and to the unsatisfactory character of these the growing irascibility of Chief Inspector Kerry bore testimony. Then the divisional surgeon arrived, and Burton incurred the wrath of the Chief Inspector by

deserting his post to show the doctor upstairs.

"If inspired idiocy can help the law," shouted Kerry, "the man who did this job is as good as dead!" He turned his fierce gaze in Gray's direction. "Thank you, sir. I need trouble you no further."

"Do you wish me to remain?"

"No. Inspector Whiteleaf, see these two gentlemen past the Sergeant on duty."

"But damn it all!" cried Gray, his pent-up emotions at last demanding an outlet, "I won't submit to your infernal dragooning! Do you realize that while you're standing here, doing nothing—absolutely nothing—an unhappy woman is——"

"I realize," snapped Kerry, showing his teeth in canine fashion, "that if you're not outside in ten seconds there's going to be a cloud of dust on the stairs!"

White with passion, Gray was on the point of uttering other angry and provocative words when Seton took his arm in a firm grip. "Gray!" he said sharply. "You leave with me now or I leave alone."

The two walked from the room, followed by Whiteleaf. As they disappeared:

"Read out all the *times* mentioned in the last witness's evidence," directed Kerry, undisturbed by the rencontre.

Sergeant Coombes smiled rather uneasily, consulting his notebook.

" 'At about half-past six I drove to Bond Street.' " he began.

"I said the *times*," rapped Kerry. "I know to what they refer. Just give me the times as mentioned."

"Oh," murmured Coombes, "yes. 'About half-past six.' " He ran his finger down the page. " 'A quarter to seven.' 'Seven o'clock.' 'Twenty-five minutes past seven.' 'Eight o'clock.' "

"Stop!" said Kerry. "That's enough." He fixed a baleful glance upon Gunn, who from a point of the room discreetly distant from the terrible red man was watching with watery eyes. "Who's the smart in all the overcoats?" he demanded.

"My name is James Gunn," replied this greatly insulted man in a husky voice.

"Who are you? What are you? What are you doing here?"

"I'm employed by Spinker's Agency, and——"

"Oh!" shouted Kerry, moving his shoulders. He approached the speaker and glared menancingly into his purple face. "Ho, ho! So you're one of the queer birds out of that roost, are you? Spinker's Agency! Ah, yes!" He fixed his gaze now upon the pale features of Brisley. "I've seen you before, haven't I?"

"Yes, Chief Inspector," said Brisley, lick-ing his lips. "Hayward's Heath. We have been retained by——"

"*You* have been retained!" shouted Kerry. "*You* have!"

He twisted round upon his heel, facing Monte Irvin. Angry words trembled on his tongue. But at sight of the broken man who sat there alone, haggard, a subtle change of expression crept into his fierce eyes; and when he spoke again the high-pitched voice was almost gentle. "You had employed these men, sir, to watch——"

He paused, glancing towards Whiteleaf, who had just entered again, and then in the direction of the inner room where the divisional surgeon was at work.

"To watch my wife, Inspector. Thank you; but all the world will know to-morrow. I might as well get used to it."

Monte Irvin's pallor grew positively alarming. He swayed suddenly and extended his hands in a significant groping fashion. Kerry sprang forward and supported him.

"All right, Inspector—all right." muttered Irvin. "Thank you. It has been a great shock. At first I feared——"

"You thought your wife had been attacked, I understand? Well—it's not so bad as that, sir. I am going to walk downstairs to the car with you."

"But there is so much you will want to know——"

"It can keep until to-morrow. I've enough work in this peep-show here to have me busy all night. Come along. Lean on my arm."

Monte Irvin rose unsteadily. He knew that there was cardiac trouble in his family, but he had never realized before the meaning of his heritage. He felt physically ill.

"Inspector"—his voice was a mere whisper—"have you any theory to explain——"

"Mrs. Irvin's disappearance? Don't worry, sir. Without exactly having a theory I think I may say that in my opinion she will turn up presently."

"God bless you," murmured Irvin, as Kerry assisted him out on to the landing.

Inspector Whiteleaf held back the sliding door, the mechanism of which had been bro-ken so that the door now automatically remained half closed.

"Funny, isn't it," said Gunn, as the two disappeared and Inspector Whiteleaf re-entered, "that a man should be so upset about the disappearance of a woman he was going to divorce?"

"Damn funny!" said Whiteleaf, whose temper was badly frayed by contact with Kerry. "I should have a good laugh if I were you."

He crossed the room, going in to where the surgeon was examining the victim of this mysterious crime. Gunn stared after him dismally.

"A person doesn't get much sympathy from the police, Brisley." he declared. "That one's almost as bad as *him*," jerking his thumb in the direction of the landing.

Brisley smiled in a somewhat sickly manner.

"Red Kerry is a holy terror," he agreed, *sotto voce*, glancing aside to where Coombes was checking his notes. "Look out! Here he comes."

"Now," cried Kerry, swinging into the room, "what's the game? Plotting to defeat the ends of justice?"

He stood with hands thrust in reefer pockets, feet wide apart, glancing fiercely from Brisley to Gunn, and from Gunn back again to Brisley. Neither of the representatives of Spinker's Agency ventured any remark, and:

"How long have you been watching Mrs. Monte Irvin?" demanded Kerry.

"Nearly a fortnight," replied Brisley.

"Got your evidence in writing?"

"Yes."

"Up to to-night?"

"Yes."

"Dictate to Sergeant Coombes."

He turned on his heel and crossed to the divan upon which his oilskin overall was lying. Rapidly he removed his reefer and his waistcoat, folded them, and placed them neatly beside his overall. He retained his bowler at its jaunty angle.

A cud of presumably flavorless chewing-gum he deposited in a brass bowl, and from a little packet which he had taken out of his jacket pocket he drew a fresh piece, redolent of mint. This he put into his mouth, and returned the packet to its resting-place. A slim, trim figure, he stood looking round him reflectively.

"Now," he muttered, "what about it?"

Chapter VIII

KERRY CONSULTS THE ORACLE

The clock of Brixton Town Hall was striking the hour of 1 a.m. as Chief Inspector Kerry inserted his key in the lock of the door of his house in Spenser Road.

A light was burning in the hallway, and from the little dining-room on the left the reflection of a cheerful fire danced upon the white paint of the half-open door. Kerry deposited his hat, cane, and overall upon the rack, and moving very quietly entered the room and turned on the light. A modestly furnished and scrupulously neat apartment was revealed. On the sheepskin rug before the fire a Manx cat was dozing beside a pair of carpet slippers. On the table some kind of cold repast was laid, the viands concealed under china covers. At a large bottle of Guiness's Extra Stout Kerry looked with particular appreciation.

He heaved a long sigh of contentment, and opened the bottle of stout. Having poured out a glass of the black and foaming liquid and satisfied an evidently urgent thirst, he explored beneath the covers, and presently was seated before a spread of ham and tongue, tomatoes, and bread and butter.

A door opened somewhere upstairs, and:

"Is that yoursel', Dan?" inquired a deep but musical female voice.

"Sure it is," replied Kerry; and no one who had heard the high official tones of the imperious Chief Inspector would have supposed that they could be so softened and modulated. "You should have been asleep hours ago, Mary."

"Have ye to go out again?"

"I have, bad luck; but don't trouble to come down. I've all I want and more."

"If 'tis a new case I'll come down."

"It's the devil's own case; but you'll get your death of cold."

Sounds of movement in the room above followed, and presently footsteps on the stairs. Mrs. Kerry, enveloped in a woollen dressing-gown, which obviously belonged to the Inspector, came into the room. Upon her Kerry directed a look from which all fierceness had been effaced, and which expressed only an undying admiration. And, indeed, Mary Kerry was in many respects a remarkable character. Half an inch taller than Kerry, she fully merited the compliment designed by that trite apothegm, "a fine woman." Large-boned but shapely, as she came in with her long dark hair neatly plaited, it seemed to her husband—who had remained her lover—that he saw before him the rosy-cheeked lass whom ten years before he had met and claimed on the chilly shores of Loch Broom. By all her neighbors Mrs. Kerry was looked upon as a proud, reserved person, who had held herself much aloof since her husband had become Chief Inspector; and the reputation enjoyed by Red Kerry was that of an aggressive and uncompanionable man. Now here was a lover's meeting, not lacking the shy, downward glance of dark eyes as steel-blue eyes flashed frank admiration.

Kerry, who quarrelled with everybody except the Assistant Commissioner, had only found one cause of quarrel with Mary. He was a devout Roman Catholic, and for five years he had clung with the bull-dog tenacity which was his to the belief that he could convert his wife to the faith of Rome. She remained true to the Scottish Free Church, in whose precepts she had been reared, and at the end of the five years Kerry gave it up and admired her all the more for her Caledonian strength of mind. Many and heated were the debates he had held with worthy Father O'Callaghan respecting the validity of a marriage not solemnized by a priest, but of late years he had grown reconciled to the parting of the ways on Sunday morning; and as the early mass was over before the Scottish service he was regularly to be seen outside a certain Presbyterian chapel waiting for his heretical spouse.

He pulled her down on to his knee and kissed her.

"It's twelve hours since I saw you," he said.

She rested her arm on the back of the saddle-back chair, and her dark head close beside Kerry's fiery red one.

"I kenned ye had a new case on," she said, "when it grew so late. How long can ye stay?"

"An hour. No more. There's a lot to do before the papers come out in the morning. By breakfast time all England, including the murderer, will know I'm in charge of the case. I wish I could muzzle the Press."

"'Tis a murder, then? The Lord gi'e us grace. Ye'll be wishin' to tell me?"

"Yes. I'm stumped!"

"Ye've time for a rest an' a smoke. Put

ye're slippers on."

"I've no time for that, Mary."

She stood up and took the slippers from the hearth.

"Put ye're slippers on," she repeated firmly.

Kerry stooped without another word and began to unlace his brogues. Meanwhile from a side-table his wife brought a silver tobacco-box and a stumpy Irish clay. The slippers substituted for his shoes, Kerry lovingly filled the cracked and blackened bowl with strong Irish twist, which he first teased carefully in his palm. The bowl rested almost under his nostrils when he put the pipe in his mouth, and how he contrived to light it without burning his moustache was not readily apparent. He succeeded, however, and soon was puffing clouds of pungent smoke into the air with the utmost contentment.

"Now," said his wife, seating herself upon the arm of the chair, "tell me, Dan."

Thereupon began a procedure identical to that which had characterized the outset of every successful case of the Chief Inspector. He rapidly outlined the complexities of the affair in Old Bond Street, and Mary Kerry surveyed the problem with a curious and almost fey detachment of mind, which enabled her to see light where all was darkness to the man on the spot.

With the clarity of a trained observer Kerry described the apartments of Kazmah, the exact place where the murdered man had been found, and the construction of the rooms. He gave the essential points from the evidence of the several witnesses, quoting the exact times at which various episodes had taken place. Mary Kerry, looking straightly before her with unseeing eyes, listened in silence until he ceased speaking; then:

"There are really but twa rooms," she said, in a faraway voice, "but the second o' these is parteetioned into three parts?"

"That's it."

"A door frae the landing opens upon the fairst room, a door frae a passage opens upon the second. Where does yon passage lead?"

"From the main stair along beside Kazmah's rooms to a small back stair. This back stair goes from top to bottom of the building, from the end of the same hallway as the main stair."

"There is nae ither way out but by the front door?"

"No."

"Then if the evidence o' the Spinker man is above suspeecion, Mrs. Irvin and this Kazmah were still on the premises when ye arrived?"

"Exactly. I gathered that much at Vine Street before I went on to Bond Street. The whole block was surrounded five minutes after my arrival, and it still is."

"What ither offices are in this passage?"

"None. It's a blank wall on the left, and one door on the right—the one opening into the Kazmah office. There are other premises on the same floor, but they are across the landing."

"What premises?"

"A solicitor and a commission agent."

"The floor below?"

"It's all occupied by a modiste, Rénan."

"The top floor?"

"Cubanis Cigarette Company, a Servants' Agency, and an electrician."

"Nae more?"

"No more."

"Where does yon back stair open on the topmaist floor?"

"In a corridor similar to that alongside Kazmah's. It has two windows on the right overlooking a narrow roof and the top of the arcade, and on the left is the Cubanis Cigarette Company. The other offices are across the landing."

Mary Kerry stared into space awhile.

"Kazmah and Mrs. Irvin could ha' come down to the fairst floor, or gane up to the thaird floor unseen by the Spinker man," she said dreamily.

"But they couldn't have reached the street, my dear!" cried Kerry.

"No—they couldn'a ha' gained the street."

She became silent again, her husband watching her expectantly. Then:

"If puir Sir Lucien Pyne was killed at a quarter after seven—the time his watch was broken—the native sairvent did no' kill him. Frae the Spinker's evidence the black man went awa' before then," she said. "Mrs. Irvin?"

Kerry shook his head.

"From all accounts a slip of a woman," he replied. "It was a strong hand that struck the blow."

"Kazmah?"

"Probably."

"Mr. Quentin Gray came back wi' a cab and went upstairs, frae the Spinker's evidence, at aboot a quarter after seven, and came doon five meenites later sair pale an' fretful."

Kerry surrounded himself and the speaker with wreaths of stifling smoke.

"We have only the bare word of Mr. Gray that he didn't go in again, Mary; but I believe him. He's a hot-headed fool, but square."

"Then 'twas yon Kazmah," announced Mrs. Kerry. "Who is Kazmah?"

Her husband laughed shortly.

"That's the point at which I got stumped," he replied. "We've heard of him at the Yard, of course, and we know that under the cloak of a dealer in Eastern perfumes he carried on a fortune-telling business. He managed to avoid prosection, though. It took me over an hour to-night to explore the thought-reading mechanism; it's a sort of Maskelyne's Mysteries worked from the inside room. But who Kazmah is or what's his nationality I know no more than the man in the moon."

"Pairfume?" queried the far-away voice.

"Yes, Mary. The first room is a sort of miniature scent bazaar. There are funny little imitation antique flasks of Kazmah preparations, creams, perfumes and incense, also small square wooden boxes of a kind of Turkish delight, and a stock of Egyptian mummy beads, statuettes, and the like, which may be genuine for all I know."

"Nae books or letters?"

"Not a thing, except his own advertisements, a telephone directory, and so on."

"The inside office bureau?"

"Empty as Mother Hubbard's cupboard!"

"The place was ransacked by the same folk that emptied the dead man's pockets so as tae leave nae clue," pronounced the sibyl-like voice. "Mr. Gray said he had choc'lates wi' him. Where did he leave them?"

"Mary, you're a wonder!" exclaimed the admiring Kerry. "The box was lying on the divan in the first room where he said he had left it on going out for a cab."

"Does nane o' the evidence show if Mrs. Irvin had been to Kazmah's before?"

"Yes. She went there fairly regularly to buy perfume."

"No' for the fortune-tellin'?"

"No. According to Mr. Gray, to buy perfume."

"Had Mr. Gray been there wi' her before?"

"No. Sir Lucien Pyne seems to have been her pretty constant companion."

"Do you suspect she was his lady-love?"

"I believe Mr. Gray suspects something of the kind."

"And Mr. Gray?"

"He is not such an old friend as Sir Lucien was. But I fancy nevertheless it was Mr. Gray that her husband doubted."

"Do ye suspect the puir soul had cause, Dan?"

"No," replied Kerry promptly; "I don't. The boy is mad about her, but I fancy she just liked his company. He's the heir of Lord Wrexborough, and Mrs. Irvin used to be a stage beauty. It's a usual state of affairs, and more often than not means nothing."

"I dinna ken sich folks," declared Mary Kerry. "They a'most desairve all they get. They are bound tae come tae nae guid end. Where did ye say Sir Lucien lived?"

"Albemarle Street; just round the corner."

"Ye told me he only kepit twa sairvents: a cook-hoosekeper, who lived awa', an' a man—a foreigner?"

"A kind of half-baked Dago, named Juan Mareno. A citizen of the United States according to his own account."

"Ye dinna like Juan Mareno?"

"He's a hateful swine!" flashed Kerry, with sudden venom. "I'm watching Mareno very closely. Coombes is at work upon Sir Lucien's papers. His life was a bit of a mystery. He seems to have had no relations living, and I can't find that he even employed a solicitor."

"Ye'll be sairchin' for yon Egyptian?"

"The servant? Yes. We'll have him by the morning, and then we shall know who Kazmah is. Meanwhile, in which of the offices is Kazmah hiding?"

Mary Kerry was silent for so long that her husband repeated the question:

"In which of the offices is Kazmah hiding?"

"In nane," she said dreamily. "Ye surrounded the buildings too late, I ken."

"Eh!" cried Kerry, turning his head excitedly. "But the man Brisley was at the door all night!"

"It doesna' matter. They have escapit."

Kerry scratched his close-cropped head in angry perplexity.

"You're always right, Mary," he said. "But hang me if—— Never mind! When we get the servant we'll soon get Kazmah."

"Aye," murmured his wife. "If ye hae na' got Kazmah the now."

"But—Mary! This isn't helping me! It's mystifying me deeper than ever!"

"It's no' clear eno', Dan. But for sure behind this mystery o' the death o' Sir Lucien there's a darker mystery still; sair dark. 'Tis the biggest case ye ever had. Dinna look for Kazmah. Look tae find why the woman went tae him; and try tae find the meanin' o' the sma' window behind the big chair. . . . yes"— she seemed to be staring at some distant visible object—"watch the man Mareno—"

"But—Mrs. Irvin——"

"Is in God's guid keepin'—"

"You don't think she's dead!"

"She is wairse than dead. Her sins have found her out." The fey light suddenly left her eyes, and they became filled with tears. She turned impulsively to her husband. "Oh, Dan! Ye must find her! Ye must find her! Puir weak hairt—dinna ye ken how she is suffering!"

"My dear," he said, putting his arms around her, "what is it? What is it?"

She brushed the tears from her eyes and tried to smile. " 'Tis something like the second sight, Dan," she answered simply. "And it's escapit me again. I a'most had the clue to it a'. Oh, there's some horrible wickedness in it, an' cruelty an' shame."

The clock on the mantelshelf began to peal. Kerry was watching his wife's rosy face with a mixture of loving admiration and wonder. She looked so very bonny and placid and capable that he was puzzled anew at the strange gift which she seemingly inherited from her mother, who had been equally shrewd, equally comely and similarly endowed.

"God bless us all!" he said, kissed her heartily, and stood up. "Back to bed you go, my dear. I must be off. There's Mr. Irvin to see in the morning, too."

A few minutes later he was swinging through the deserted streets, his mind wholly occupied with lover-like reflections to the exclusion of those professional matters which properly should have been engaging his attention. As he passed the end of a narrow court near the railway station, the gleam of his silver mounted malacca attracted the attention of a couple of loafers who were leaning one on either side of an iron pillar in the shadow of the unsavory alley. Not another pedestrian was in sight, and only the remote night-sounds of London broke the silence.

Twenty paces beyond, the footpads silently closed in upon their prey. The taller of the pair reached him first, only to receive a back-handed blow full in his face which sent him reeling a couple of yards.

Round leapt the assaulted man to face his second assailant.

"If you two smarts really want handling," he rapped ferociously, "say the word, and I'll bash you flat."

As he turned, the light of a neighboring lamp shone down upon the savage face, and a smothered yell came from the shorter ruffian:

"Blimey, Bill! It's *Red Kerry!*"

Whereupon, as men pursued by devils, the pair made off like the wind!

Kerry glared after the retreating figures for a moment, and a grin of fierce satisfaction revealed his gleaming teeth. He turned again and swung on his way toward the main road. The incident had done him good. It had banished domestic matters from his mind; and he was become again the highly trained champion of justice, standing, an unseen buckler, between society and the criminal.

Chapter IX

A PACKET OF CIGARETTES

Following their dismissal by Chief Inspector Kerry, Seton and Gray walked around to the latter's chambers in Piccadilly. They proceeded in silence, Gray too angry for speech, and Seton busy with reflections. As the man admitted them:

"Has anyone 'phoned, Willis?" asked Gray.

"No one, sir."

They entered a large room which combined the characteristics of a library with those of a military gymnasium. Gray went to a side table and mixed drinks. Placing a glass before Seton, he emptied his own at a draught.

"If you'll excuse me for a moment," he said, "I should like to ring up and see if by any possible chance there's news of Rita."

He walked out to the telephone, and Seton heard him making a call. Then:

"Hullo! Is that you, Hinkes?" he asked. . . . "Yes; speaking. Is Mrs. Irvin at home?"

A few moments of silence followed, and:

"Thanks! Good-bye," said Gray.

He rejoined his friend.

"Nothing," he reported, and made a gesture of angry resignation. "Evidently Hinkes is still unaware of what has happened. Irvin hasn't returned yet. Seton, this business is driving me mad."

He refilled his glass, and having looked in his cigarette-case, began to ransack a small cupboard.

"Damn it all!" he exclaimed. "I haven't got a cigarette in the place!"

"I don't smoke them myself," said Seton, "but I can offer you a cheroot."

"Thanks. They are a trifle too strong. Hullo! here are some."

From the back of a shelf he produced a small, plain brown packet, and took out of it a cigarette at which he stared oddly. Seton, smoking one of the inevitable cheroots, watched him, tapping his teeth with the rim of his eyeglass.

"Poor old Pyne!" muttered Gray, and, looking up, met the inquiring glance. "Pyne left these here only the other day," he explained awkwardly. "I don't know where he got them, but they are something very special. I suppose I might as well——"

He lighted one, and, uttering a weary sigh, threw himself into a deep leather-covered arm-chair. Almost immediately he was up again. The telephone bell had rung. His eyes alight with hope, he ran out, leaving the door open so that his conversation was again audible to the visitor.

"Yes, yes, speaking. What?" His tone changed. "Oh, it's you, Margaret. What? . . . Certainly, delighted. No, there's nobody here but old Seton Pasha. What? You've heard the fellows talk about him who were out East. . . . Yes, that's the chap. . . . Come right along."

"You don't propose to lionise me, I hope, Gray?" said Seton, as Gray returned to his seat.

The other laughed.

"I forgot you could hear me," he admitted. "It's my cousin, Margaret Halley. You'll like her. She's a tip-top girl, but eccentric. Goes in for pilling."

"Pilling?" inquired Seton gravely.

"Doctoring. She's an M.R.C.S., and only about twenty-four or so. Fearfully clever kid; makes me feel an infant."

"Flat heels, spectacles, and a judicial manner?"

"Flat heels, yes. But not the other. She's awfully pretty, and used to look simply terrific in khaki. She was an M.O. in Serbia, you know, and afterwards at some nurses' hospital in Kent. She's started in practice for herself now round in Dover Street. I wonder what she wants."

Silence fell between them; for, although prompted by different reasons, both were undesirous of discussing the tragedy; and this silence prevailed until the ringing of the doorbell announced the arrival of the girl. Willis opening the door, she entered composedly, and Gray introduced Seton.

"I am so glad to have met you at last, Mr. Seton," she said laughingly. "From Quentin's many accounts I had formed the opinion that you were a kind of *Arabian Nights* myth."

"I am glad to disappoint you," replied Seton, finding something very refreshing in the company of this pretty girl, who wore a creased Burberry, and stray locks of whose abundant bright hair floated about her face in the most careless fashion imaginable.

She turned to her cousin, frowning in a rather puzzled way.

"Whatever have you been burning here?" she asked. "There is such a curious smell in the room."

Gray laughed more heartily than he had laughed that night, glancing in Seton's direction.

"So much for your taste in cigars!" he cried.

"Oh!" said Margaret, "I'm sure it's not Mr. Seton's cigar. It isn't a smell of tobacco."

"I don't believe they're *made* of tobacco!" cried Gray, laughing louder yet, although his merriment was forced.

Seton smiled good-naturedly at the joke, but he had perceived at the moment of Margaret's entrance the fact that her gaiety also was assumed. Serious business had dictated her visit, and he wondered the more to note how deeply this odor, real or fancied, seemed to intrigue her.

She sat down in the chair which Gray placed by the fireside, and her cousin unceremoniously slid the brown packet of cigarettes across the little table in her direction.

"Try one of these, Margaret," he said. "They are great, and will quite drown the unpleasant odor of which you complain."

Whereupon the observant Seton saw a quick change take place in the girl's expression. She had the same clear coloring as her cousin, and now this freshness deserted her cheeks, and her pretty face became quite pale. She was staring at the brown packet. "Where did you get them?" she asked quietly.

A smile faded from Gray's lips. Those five words had translated him in spirit to that green-draped room in which Sir Lucien Pyne was lying dead. He glanced at Seton in the appealing way which sometimes made him appear so boyish.

"Er—from Pyne," he replied. "I must tell you, Margaret——"

"Sir Lucien Pyne?" she interrupted.

"Yes."

"Not from Rita Irvin?"

Quentin Gray started upright in his chair. "No! But why do you mention her?"

Margaret bit her lip in sudden perplexity. "Oh, I don't know." She glanced apologetically toward Seton. He rose immediately.

"My dear Miss Halley," he said, "I perceive, indeed I had perceived all along, that you have something of a private nature to communicate to your cousin."

But Gray stood up, and:

"Seton! . . . Margaret!" he said, looking from one to the other. "I mean to say, Margaret, if you've anything to tell me about Rita . . . Have you? Have you?"

He fixed his gaze eagerly upon her.

"I have—yes."

Seton prepared to take his leave, but Gray impetuously thrust him back, immediately turning again to his cousin.

"Perhaps you haven't heard, Margaret," he began.

"I have heard what has happened to-night—to Sir Lucien."

Both men stared at her silently for a moment.

"Seton has been with me all the time," said Gray. "If he will consent to stay, with your permission, Margaret, I should like him to do so."

"Why, certainly," agreed the girl. "In fact, I shall be glad of his advice."

Seton inclined his head, and without another word resumed his seat. Gray was too excited to sit down again. He stood on the tiger-skin rug before the fender, watching his cousin and smoking furiously.

"Firstly, then," continued Maragaret, "please throw that cigarette in the fire, Quentin."

Gray removed the cigarette from between his lips, and stared at it dazedly. He looked at the girl, and the clear grey eyes were watching him with an inscrutable expression.

"Right-o!" he said awkwardly, and tossed the cigarette in the fire. "You used to smoke like a furnace, Margaret. Is this some new 'cult'?"

"I still smoke a great deal more than is good for me," she confessed; "but I don't

smoke opium."

The effect of these words upon the two men who listened was curious. Gray turned an angry glance upon the brown packet lying on the table, and "Faugh!" he exclaimed, and drawing a handkerchief from his sleeve began disgustedly to wipe his lips. Seton stared hard at the speaker, tossed his cheroot into the fire, and taking up the packet withdrew a cigarette and sniffed at it critically. Margaret watched him.

He tore the wrapping off, and tasted a strand of the tobacco.

"Good heavens!" he whispered. "Gray, these things are doped!"

Chapter X

SIR LUCIEN'S STUDY WINDOW

Old Bond Street presented a gloomy and deserted prospect to Chief Inspector Kerry as he turned out of Piccadilly and swung along toward the premises of Kazmah. He glanced at the names on some of the shop windows as he passed, and wondered if the furriers, jewelers and other merchants dealing in costly wares properly appreciated the services of the Metropolitan Police Force. He thought of the peacefully slumbering tradesmen in their suburban homes, the safety of their stocks wholly dependent upon the vigilance of that Unsleeping Eye—for to an unsleeping eye he mentally compared the service of which he was a member.

A constable stood on duty before the door of the block. Red Kerry was known by sight and reputation to every member of the force, and the constable saluted as the celebrated Chief Inspector appeared.

"Anything to report, constable?"

"Yes, sir."

"What?"

"The ambulance has been for the body, and another gentleman has been."

Kerry stared at the man.

"Another gentleman? Who the devil's the other gentleman?"

"I don't know, sir. He came with Inspector Whiteleaf, and was inside for nearly an hour."

"Inspector Whiteleaf is off duty. What time was this?"

"Twelve-thirty, sir."

Kerry chewed reflectively ere nodding to

the man and passing on.

"Another gentleman!" he muttered, entering the hallway. "Why didn't Inspector Warley report this? Who the devil——" Deep in thought he walked upstairs, finding his way by the light of the pocket torch which he carried. A second constable was on duty at Kazmah's door. He saluted.

"Anything to report?" rapped Kerry.

"Yes, sir. The body has been removed, and the gentleman with Inspector——"

"Damn that for a tale! Describe this gentleman."

"Rather tall, pale, dark, clean-shaven. Wore a fur-collared overcoat, collar turned up. He was accompanied by Inspector Whiteleaf."

"H'm. Anything else?"

"Yes. About an hour ago I heard a noise on the next floor——"

"Eh!" snapped Kerry, and shone the light suddenly into the man's face so that he blinked furiously. "Eh? What kind of noise?"

"Very slight. Like something moving."

"Like *something!* Like *what* thing? A cat or an elephant?"

"More like, say, a box or a piece of furniture."

"And you did—what?"

"I went up to the top landing and listened."

"What did you hear?"

"Nothing at all."

Chief Inspector Kerry chewed audibly.

"All quiet?" he snapped.

"Absolutely. But I'm certain I heard something all the same."

"How long had Inspector Whiteleaf and this dark horse in the fur coat been gone at the time you heard the noise?"

"About half an hour, sir."

"Do you think the noise came from the landing or from one of the offices above?"

"An office I should say. It was very dim."

Chief Inspector Kerry pushed upon the broken door, and walked into the rooms of Kazmah. Flashing the ray of his torch on the wall, he found the switch and snapped up the lights. He removed his overall and tossed it on a divan with his cane. Then, tilting his bowler further forward, he thrust his hands into his reefer pockets, and stood staring toward the door, beyond which lay the room of the murder, in darkness.

"Who is he?" he muttered. "What's it mean?"

Taking up the torch, he walked through and turned on the lights in the inner rooms. For a long time he stood staring at the little square window low down behind the ebony chair, striving to imagine uses for it as his wife had urged him to do. The globular green lamp in the second apartment was worked by three switches situated in the inside room, and he had discovered that in this way the visitor who came to consult Kazmah was treated to the illusion of a gradually falling darkness. Then, the door in the first partition being opened, whoever sat in the ebony chair would become visible by the gradual uncovering of a light situated above the chair. On this light being covered again the figure would apparently fade away.

It was ingenious, and, so far, quite clear. But two things badly puzzled the inquirer; the little window down behind the chair, and the fact that all the arrangements for raising and lowering the lights were situated not in the narrow chamber in which Kazmah's chair stood, and in which Sir Lucien had been found, but in the room behind it—the room with which the little window communicated.

The table upon which the telephone rested was set immediately under this mysterious window, the window was provided with a green blind; and the switchboard controlling the complicated lighting scheme was also within reach of anyone seated at the table.

Kerry rolled mint gum from side to side of his mouth, and absently tried the handle of the door opening out from this interior room—evidently the office of the establishment—into the corridor. He knew it to be locked. Turning, he walked through the suite and out on to the landing, passing the constable and going upstairs to the top floor, torch in hand.

From the main landing he walked along the narrow corridor until he stood at the head of the back stairs. The door nearest to him bore the name: "Cubanis Cigarette Company." He tried the handle. The door was locked, as he had anticipated. Kneeling down, he peered into the keyhole, holding the electric torch close beside his face and chewing industriously.

Ere long he stood up, descended again, but by the back stair, and stood staring reflectively at the door communicating with Kazmah's inner room. Then, walking along the corridor to where the man stood on the landing, he went in again to the mysterious apartments, but only to get his cane and his overall and to turn out the lights.

Five minutes later he was ringing the late Sir Lucien's door-bell.

A constable admitted him, and he walked straight through into the study where Coombes, looking very tired but smiling undauntedly, sat at a littered table studying piles of documents.

"Anything to report?" rapped Kerry.

"The man, Mareno, has gone to bed, and the expert from the Home Office has been——"

Inspector Kerry brought his cane down with a crash upon the table, whereat Coombes started nervously.

"So that's it!" he shouted furiously, "an 'expert from the Home Office'! So that's the dark horse in the fur coat. Coombes! I'm fed up to the back teeth with this gun from the Home Office! If I'm not to have entire charge of the case I'll throw it up. I'll stand for no blasted overseer checking my work! Wait till I see the Assistant Commissioner! What the devil has the job to do with the Home Office!"

"Can't say," murmured Coombes. "But he's evidently a big bug from the way Whiteleaf treated him. He instructed me to stay in the kitchen and keep an eye on Mareno while he prowled about in here."

"Instructed you!" cried Kerry, his teeth gleaming and his steel-blue eyes creating upon Coombes' mind an impression that they were emitting sparks. *"Instructed* you! I'll ask you a question, Detective-sergeant Coombes: Who is in charge of this case?"

"Well, I thought you were."

"You *thought* I was?"

"Well, you are."

"I am? Very well—you were saying—?"

"I was saying that I went into the kitchen——"

"Before that! Something about 'instructed.' "

Poor Coombes smiled pathetically.

"Look here," he said, bravely meeting the ferocious glare of his superior, "as man to man, what could I do?"

"You could stop smiling!" snapped Kerry. "Hell!" He paced several times up and down the room. "Go ahead, Coombes."

"Well, there's nothing much to report. I stayed in the kitchen, and the man from the Home Office was in here alone for about half an hour."

"Alone?"

"Inspector Whiteleaf stayed in the dining-room."

"Had he been 'instructed' too?"

"I expect so. I think he just came along as a sort of guide."

"Ah!" muttered Kerry savagely, "a sort of guide! Any idea what the bogey man did in here?"

"He opened the window. I heard him."

"That's funny. It's exactly what I'm going to do! This smart from Whitehall hasn't got a corner in notions yet, Coombes."

The room was a large and lofty one, and had been used by a former tenant as a studio. The toplights had been roofed over by Sir Lucien, however, but the raised platform, approached by two steps, which had probably been used as a model's throne, was a permanent fixture of the apartment. It was backed now by bookcases, except where a blue plush curtain was draped before a French window.

Kerry drew the curtain back, and threw open the folding leaves of the window. He found himself looking out upon the leads of Albemarle Street. No stars and no moon showed through the grey clouds draping the wintry sky, but a dim and ghostly half-light nevertheless rendered the ugly expanse visible from where he stood.

On one side loomed a huge tank, to the brink of which a rickety wooden ladder invited the explorer to ascend. Beyond it were a series of iron gangways and ladders forming part of the fire emergency arrangements of the neighboring institution. Straight ahead a section of building jutted up and revealed two small windows, which seemed to regard him like watching eyes.

He walked out on to the roof, looking all about him. Beyond the tank opened a frowning gully—the Arcade connecting Albemarle Street with Old Bond Street; on the other hand, the scheme of fire gangways was continued. He began to cross the leads, going in the direction of Bond Street. Coombes watched him from the study. When he came to the more northerly of the two windows which had attracted his attention, he knelt down and flashed the ray of his torch through the glass.

A kind of small warehouse was revealed, containing stacks of packages. Immediately inside the window was a rough wooden table, and on this table lay a number of smaller packages, apparently containing cigarettes.

Kerry turned his attention to the fastening of the window. A glance showed him that it was unlocked. Resting the torch on the leads, he grasped the sash and gently raised the window, noting that it opened almost noise-lessly. Then, taking up the torch again, he stooped and stepped in on to the table below.

It moved slightly beneath his weight. One of the legs was shorter than its fellows. But he reached the floor as quietly as possible, and instantly snapped off the light of the torch.

A heavy step sounded from outside—someone was mounting the stairs—and a disk of light suddenly appeared upon the ground-glass panel of the door.

Kerry stood quite still, chewing steadily.

"Who's there?" came the voice of the constable posted on Kazmah's landing.

The inspector made no reply.

"Is there anyone here?" cried the man.

The disk of light disappeared, and the alert constable could be heard moving along the corridor to inspect the other offices. But the ray had shone upon the frosted glass long enough to enable Kerry to read the words painted there in square black letters. They had appeared reversed, of course, and had read thus:

CUBANIS CIGARETTE CO.

Chapter XI

THE DRUG SYNDICATE

At six-thirty that morning Margaret Halley was aroused by her maid—the latter but half awake—and sitting up in bed and switching on the lamp, she looked at the card which the servant had brought to her, and read the following:

CHIEF INSPECTOR KERRY,
C.I.D.

New Scotland Yard, S.W.1.

"Oh, dear," she said sleepily, "what an appallingly early visitor. Is the bath ready yet, Janet?"

"I'm afraid not," replied the maid, a plain, elderly woman of the old-fashioned useful servant type. "Shall I take a kettle into the bathroom?"

"Yes—that will have to do. Tell Inspector Kerry that I shall not be long."

Five minutes later Margaret entered her little consulting-room, where Kerry, having adjusted his tie, was standing before the mirror in the overmantel, staring at a large photograph of the charming lady doctor in military uniform. Kerry's fierce eyes sparkled appreciatively as his glance rested on the tall figure arrayed in a woollen dressing-gown, the masculine style of which by no means disguised the beauty of Margaret's athletic figure. She had hastily arranged her bright hair with deliberate neglect of all affectation. She belonged to that ultra-modern school which scorns to sue masculine admiration, but which cannot dispense with it nevertheless. She aspired to be assessed upon an intellectual basis, an ambition which her unfortunate good looks rendered difficult of achievement.

"Good morning, Inspector," she said composedly. "I was expecting you."

"Really, miss?" Kerry stared curiously. "Then you know what I've come about?"

"I think so. Won't you sit down? I am afraid the room is rather cold. Is it about—Sir Lucien Pyne?"

"Well," replied Kerry, "it concerns him certainly. I've been in communication by telephone with Hinkes, Mr. Monte Irvin's butler, and from him I learned that you were professionally attending Mrs. Irvin."

"I was not her regular medical adviser, but——"

Margaret hesitated, glancing rapidly at the Inspector, and then down at the writing-table before which she was seated. She began to tap the blotting-pad with an ivory paper-knife. Kerry was watching her intently.

"Upon your evidence, Miss Halley," he said rapidly, "may depend the life of the missing woman."

"Oh!" cried Margaret, "whatever can have happened to her? I rang up as late as two o'clock this morning; after that I abandoned hope."

"There's something underlying the case that I don't understand, miss. I look to you to put me wise."

She turned to him impulsively.

"I will tell you all I know, Inspector," she said. "I will be perfectly frank with you."

"Good!" rapped Kerry. "Now—you have known Mrs. Monte Irvin for some time?"

"For about two years."

"You didn't know her when she was on the stage?"

"No. I met her at a Red Cross concert at which she sang."

"Do you think she loved her husband?"

"I know she did."

"Was there any—prior attachment?"

"Not that I know of."

"Mr. Quentin Gray?"

Margaret smiled, rather mirthlessly.

"He is my cousin, Inspector, and it was I who introduced him to Rita Irvin. I sincerely wish I had never done so. He lost his head completely."

"There was nothing in Mrs. Irvin's attitude towards him to justify her husband's jealousy?"

"She was always frightfully indiscreet, Inspector, but nothing more. You see, she is greatly admired, and is used to the company of silly, adoring men. Her husband doesn't really understand the ways of these Bohemian folks. I knew it would lead to trouble, sooner or later."

"Ah!"

Chief Inspector Kerry thrust his hands into the pockets of his jacket.

"Now—Sir Lucien?"

Margaret tapped more rapidly with the paper-knife.

"Sir Lucien belonged to a set of which Rita had been a member during her stage career. I think—he admired her; in fact, I believe he had offered her marriage. But she did not care for him in the least—in that way."

"Then in what way did she care for him?" rapped Kerry.

"Well—now we are coming to the point." Momentarily she hesitated; then: "They were both addicted——"

"Yes?"

"——To drugs."

"Eh?" Kerry's eyes grew hard and fierce in a moment. "What drugs?"

"All sorts of drugs. Shortly after I became acquainted with Rita Irvin I learned that she was a victim of the drug habit, and I tried to cure her. I regret to say that I failed. At that time she had acquired a taste for opium."

Kerry said not a word, and Margaret raised her head and looked at him pathetically.

"I can see that you have no pity for the victims of this ghastly vice, Inspector Kerry," she said.

"I haven't!" he snapped fiercely. "I admit I haven't, miss. It's bad enough in the heathens, but for an Englishwoman to dope herself is downright unchristian and beastly."

"Yet I have come across so many of these

cases, during the war and since, that I have begun to understand how easy, how dreadfully easy it is, for a woman especially, to fall into the fatal habit. Bereavement, or that most frightful of all mental agonies, suspense, will too often lead the poor victim into the path that promises forgetfulness. Rita Irvin's case is less excusable. I think she must have begun drug-taking because of the mental and nervous exhaustion resulting from late hours and over-much gaiety. The demands of her profession proved too great for her impaired nervous energy, and she sought some stimulant which would enable her to appear bright on the stage when actually she should have been recuperating, in sleep, that loss of vital force which can be recuperated in no other way."

"But *opium!*" snapped Kerry.

"I am afraid her other drug habits had impaired her will, and shaken her self-control. She was tempted to try opium by its promise of a new and novel excitement."

"Her husband, I take it, was ignorant of all this?"

"I believe he was. Quentin—Mr. Gray—had no idea of it either."

"Then it was Sir Lucien Pyne who was in her confidence in the matter?"

Margaret nodded slowly, still tapping the blotting-pad.

"He used to accompany her to places where drugs could be obtained, and on several occasions—I cannot say how many—I believe he went with her to some den in Chinatown. It may have been due to Mr. Irvin's discovery that his wife could not satisfactorily account for some of these absences from home which led him to suspect her fidelity."

"Ah!" said Kerry hardly, "I shouldn't wonder. And now"—he thrust out a pointing finger—"where did she get these drugs?"

Margaret met the fierce stare composedly.

"I have said that I shall be quite frank," she replied. "In my opinion she obtained them from Kazmah."

"Kazmah!" shouted Kerry. "Excuse me, miss, but I see I've been wearing blinkers without knowing it! Kazmah's was a dope-shop?"

"That has been my belief for a long time, Inspector. I may add that I have never been able to obtain a shred of evidence to prove it. I am so keenly interested in seeing the people who pander to this horrible vice unmasked and dealt with as they merit, that I have tried many times to find out if my suspicion was correct."

Inspector Kerry was writhing his shoulders excitedly. "Did you ever visit Kazmah?" he asked.

"Yes. I asked Rita Irvin to take me, but she refused, and I could see that the request embarrassed her. So I went alone."

"Describe exactly what took place."

Margaret Halley stared reflectively at the blotting-pad for a moment, and then described a typical séance at Kazmah's. In conclusion:

"As I came away," she said, "I bought a bottle of every kind of perfume on sale, some of the incense, and also a box of sweetmeat; but they all proved to be perfectly harmless. I analyzed them."

Kerry's eyes glistened with admiration.

"We could do with you at the Yard, miss," he said. "Excuse me for saying so."

Margaret smiled rather wanly.

"Now—this man Kazmah," resumed the Chief Inspector. "Did you ever see him again?"

"Never. I have been trying for months and months to find out who he is."

Kerry's face became very grim.

"About ten trained men are trying to find that out at the present moment!" he rapped. "Do you think he wore a make-up?"

"He may have done so," Margaret admitted. "But his features were obviously undisguised, and his eyes one would recognize anywhere. They were larger than any human eyes I have ever seen."

"He couldn't have been the Egyptian who looked after the shop, for instance?"

"Impossible! He did not remotely resemble him. Besides, the man to whom you refer remained outside to receive other visitors. Oh, that's out of the question, Inspector."

"The light was very dim?"

"Very dim indeed, and Kazmah never once raised his head. Indeed, except for a dignified gesture of greeting and one of dismissal, he never moved. His immobility was rather uncanny."

Kerry began to pace up and down the narrow room, and:

"He bore no resemblance to the late Sir Lucien Pyne, for instance?" he rapped.

Margaret laughed outright and her laughter was so inoffensive and so musical that the Chief Inspector laughed also.

"That's more hopeless than ever!" she said. "Poor Sir Lucien had strong, harsh features

and rather small eyes. He wore a moustache, too. But Sir Lucien, I feel sure, was one of Kazmah's clients."

"Ah!" said Kerry. "And what leads you to suppose, Miss Halley, that this Kazmah dealt in drugs?"

"Well, you see, Rita Irvin was always going there to buy perfumes, and she frequently sent her maid as well."

"But"—Kerry stared—"you say that the perfume was harmless."

"That which was sold to casual visitors was harmless, Inspector. But I strongly suspect that regular clients were supplied with something quite different. You see, I know no fewer than thirty unfortunate women in the West End of London alone who are simply helpless slaves to various drugs, and I think it more than a coincidence that upon their dressing-tables I have almost invariably found one or more of Kazmah's peculiar antique flasks."

Chief Inspector Kerry's jaw muscles protruded conspicuously.

"You speak of patients?" he asked.

Margaret nodded her head.

"When a woman becomes addicted to the drug habit," she explained, "she sometimes shuns her regular medical adviser. I have many patients who came to me originally simply because they dared not face their family doctor. In fact, since I gave up Army work, my little practice has threatened to develop into that of a drug-habit specialist."

"Have you taxed any of these people with obtaining drugs from Kazmah?"

"Not directly. It would have been undiplomatic. But I have tried to surprise them into telling me. Unfortunately, these poor people are as cunning as any other kind of maniac; for, of course, it becomes a form of mania. They recognize that confession might lead to a stoppage of supplies—the eventuality they most dread."

"Did you examine the contents of any of these flasks found on dressing-tables?"

"I rarely had an opportunity; but when I did they proved to contain perfume when they contained anything."

"H'm," mused Kerry, and although in deference to Margaret, he had denied himself chewing-gum, his jaws worked automatically. "I gather that Mrs. Monte Irvin had expressed a wish to see you last night?"

"Yes. Apparently she was threatened with a shortage of cocaine——"

"Cocaine was her drug?"

"One of them. She had tried them all, poor, silly girl! You must understand that for an habitual drugtaker suddenly to be deprived of drugs would lead to complete collapse, perhaps death. And during the last few days I had noticed a peculiar nervous symptom in Rita Irvin which had interested me. Finally, the day before yesterday, she confessed that her usual source of supply had been closed to her. Her words were very vague, but I gathered that some form of coercion was being employed."

"With what object?"

"I have no idea. But she used the words, 'They will drive me mad,' and seemed to be in a dangerously nervous condition. She said that she was going to make a final attempt to obtain a supply of the poison which had become indispensable to her. 'I cannot do without it!' she said. 'But if they refuse, will *you* give me some?' "

"What did you say?"

"I begged of her, as I had done on many previous occasions, to place herself in my hands. But she evaded a direct answer, as is the way of one addicted to this vice. 'If I cannot get some by to-morrow,' she said, 'I shall go mad, or dead. Can I rely on you?'

"I told her that I would prescribe cocaine for her on the distinct understanding that from the first dose she was to place herself under my care for a cure."

"She agreed?"

"She agreed. Yesterday afternoon, while I was away at an important case, she came here. Poor Rita!" Margaret's soft voice trembled. "Look—she left this note."

From a letter-rack she took a square sheet of paper and handed it to the Chief Inspector. He bent his fierce eyes upon the writing—large, irregular and shaky.

" 'Dear Margaret,' " he read aloud. " 'Why aren't you at home? I am wild with pain, and feel I am going mad. Come to me *directly* you return, and bring enough to keep me alive. I——' Hullo! there's no finish!"

He glanced up from the page. Margaret Halley's eyes were dim.

"She despaired of my coming and went to Kazmah," she said. "Can you doubt that that was what she went for?"

"No!" snapped Kerry savagely; "I can't. But do you mean to tell me, Miss Halley, that Mrs. Irvin couldn't get cocaine anywhere else? I know for a fact that it's smuggled in regularly, and there's more than one receiver."

Margaret looked at him strangely.

"I know it, too, Inspector," she said quietly. "Owing to the lack of enterprise on the part of our British drug-houses, even reputable chemists are sometimes dependent upon illicit stock from Japan and America. But you know that the price of these smuggled drugs has latterly become so high as to be prohibitive in many cases?"

"I don't. What are you driving at, miss?"

"At this: Somebody had made a corner in contraband drugs. The most wicked syndicate that ever was formed has got control of the lives of, it may be, thousands of drug-slaves!"

Kerry's teeth closed with a sharp snap.

"At last," he said, "I see where the smart from the Home Office comes in."

"The Secretary of State has appointed a special independent commissioner to inquire into this hellish traffic," replied Margaret quietly. "I am glad to say that I have helped in getting this done by the representations which I have made to my uncle, Lord Wrexborough. But I give you my word, Inspector Kerry, that I have withheld nothing from you any more than from him."

"Him!" snapped Kerry, eyes fiercely ablaze.

"From the Home Office representative—before whom I have already given evidence."

Chief Inspector Kerry took up his hat, cane and overall from the chair upon which he had placed them, and, his face a savage red mask, bowed with a fine courtesy. He burned to learn particulars; he disdained to obtain them from a woman.

"Good morning, Miss Halley," he said. "I am greatly indebted to you."

He walked stiffly from the room and out of the flat without waiting for a servant to open the door.

Part Second

MRS. SIN

Chapter XII

THE MAID OF THE MASQUE

The past life of Mrs. Monte Irvin, in which at this time three distinct groups of investigators became interested—namely, those of Whitehall, Scotland Yard, and Fleet Street—was of a character to have horrified the prudish, but to have excited the compassion of the wise.

Daughter of a struggling suburban solicitor, Rita Esden, at the age of seventeen, from a delicate and rather commonplace child began to develop into a singularly pretty girl of an elusive and fascinating type of beauty, almost ethereal in her dainty coloring, and possessed of large and remarkably fine eyes, together with a wealth of copper-red hair, a crown which seemed too heavy for her slender neck to support. Her father viewed her increasing charms and ever-growing list of admirers with the gloomy apprehension of a disappointed man who had come to look upon each gift of the gods as a new sorrow cunningly disguised. Her mother, on the contrary, fanned the girl's natural vanity and ambition with a success which rarely attended the enterprises of this foolish old woman, and Rita proving to be endowed with a moderately good voice, a stage career was determined upon without reference to the contrary wishes of Mr. Esden.

Following the usual brief "training" which is counted sufficient for an aspirant to musical comedy honors, Rita, by the prefixing of two letters to her name, set out to conquer the play-going world as Rita Dresden.

Two years of hard work and disappointment served to dispel the girl's illusions. She learned to appreciate at its true value that masculine admiration which, in an unusual degree, she had the power to excite. Those of her admirers who were in a position to assist her professionally were only prepared to use their influence upon terms which she was unprepared to accept. Those whose intentions were strictly creditable, by some malignancy of fate, possessed no influence whatever. She came to regard herself as a peculiarly unlucky girl, being ignorant of the fact that Fortune, an impish hierophant, imposes identical tests upon every candidate who aspires to the throne of a limelight princess.

Matters stood thus when a new suitor appeared in the person of Sir Lucien Pyne. When his card was brought up to Rita, her heart leaped because of a mingled emotion of triumph and fear which the sight of the baronet's name had occasioned. He was a director of the syndicate in whose production she was playing—a man referred to with awe by every girl in the company as having it in his power to make or mar a professional reputation. Not that he took any active part in the affairs of the concern; on the contrary, he was an aristocrat who held himself aloof from all matters smacking of commerce, but at the same time one who invested his money shrewdly. Sir Lucien's protegée of to-day was London's idol of to-morrow, and even before Rita had spoken to him she had found and won a spiritual battle between her true self and that vain, admiration-loving Rita Dresden who favored capitulation.

She knew that Sir Lucien's card represented a sign-post at the cross-roads where many a girl, pretty but not exceptionally talented, had hesitated with beating heart. It was no longer a question of remaining a member of the chorus (and understudy for a small part) or of accepting promotion to "lead" in a new production; it was that of accepting whatever Sir Lucien chose to offer—or of retiring from the profession so far as this powerful syndicate was concerned.

Such was the reputation enjoyed at this time by Sir Lucien Pyne among those who had every opportunity of forming an accurate opinion.

Nevertheless, Rita was determined not to succumb without a struggle. She did not count herself untalented nor a girl to be lightly valued, and Sir Lucien might prove to be less black than rumor had painted him. As presently appeared, both in her judgment of herself and in that of Sir Lucien, she was at least partially correct. He was very courteous, very respectful, and highly attentive.

Her less favored companions smiled significantly when the familiar Rolls-Royce appeared at the stage door night after night, never doubting that Rita Dresden was chosen to "star" in the forthcoming production, but, with rare exceptions, frankly envying her this good fortune.

Rita made no attempt to disillusion them, recognizing that it must fail. She was resigned to being misjudged. If she could achieve success at that price, success would have been purchased cheaply.

That Sir Lucien was deeply infatuated she was not slow to discover, and with an address perfected by experience and a determination to avoid the easy path inherited from a father whose scrupulous honesty had ruined his professional prospects, she set to work to win esteem as well as admiration.

Sir Lucien was first surprised, then piqued, and finally interested by such unusual tactics. The second phase was the dangerous one for Rita, and during a certain luncheon at Romanos her fate hung in the balance. Sir Lucien realized that he was in peril of losing his head over this tantalizingly pretty girl who gracefully kept him at a distance, fencing with an adroitness which was baffling, and Sir Lucien Pyne had set out with no intention of doing anything so preposterous as falling in love. Keenly intuitive, Rita scented danger and made a bold move. Carelessly rolling a bread-crumb along the cloth:

"I am giving up the stage when the run finishes," she said.

"Indeed," replied Sir Lucien imperturbably. "Why?"

"I am tired of stage life. I have been invited to go and live with my uncle in New York and have decided to accept. You see"—she bestowed upon him a swift glance of her brilliant eyes—"men in the theatrical world are not all like you. Real friends, I mean. It isn't very nice, sometimes."

Sir Lucien deliberately lighted a cigarette. If Rita was bluffing, he mused, she had the pluck to make good her bluff. And if she did so? He dropped the extinguished match upon a plate. Did he care? He glanced at the girl, who was smiling at an acquaintance on the other side of the room. Fortune's wheel spins upon a needle point. By an artistic performance occupying less than two minutes, but suggesting that Rita possessed qualities which one day might spell success, she had decided her fate. Her heart was beating like a hammer in her breast, but she preserved an attitude of easy indifference. Without for a moment believing in the American uncle, Sir Lucien did believe, correctly, that Rita Dresden was about to elude him. He realized, too, that he was infinitely more interested than he had ever been hitherto, and more interested than he had intended to become.

This seemingly trivial conversation was a turning point, and twelve months later Rita Dresden was playing the title rôle in *The Maid of the Masque*. Sir Lucien had discovered himself to be really in love with her, and he might quite possibly have offered her marriage even if a dangerous rival had not appeared to goad him to that desperate leap—for so he regarded it.

Monte Irvin, although considerably Rita's senior, had much to commend him in the eyes of the girl—and in the eyes of her mother, who still retained a curious influence over her daughter. He was much more wealthy than Pyne, and although the latter was a baronet, Irvin was certain to be knighted ere long, so that Rita would secure the appendage of "Lady" in either case. Also, his reputation promised a more reliable husband than Sir Lucien could be expected to make. Moreover, Rita liked him, whereas she had never sincerely liked and trusted Sir Lucien. And there was a final reason—of which Mrs. Esden knew nothing.

On the first night that Rita had been entrusted with a part of any consequence—and this was shortly after the conversation at Romanos—she had discovered herself to be in a state of hopeless panic. All her scheming and fencing would have availed her nothing if she were to break down at the critical moment. It was an eventuality which Sir Lucien had foreseen, and he seized the opportunity at once of securing a new hold upon the girl and of rendering her more pliable than he had hitherto found her to be. At this time the idea of marriage had not presented itself to Sir Lucien.

Some hours before the performance he detected her condition of abject fright . . . and from his waistcoat pocket he took a little gold snuff-box.

At first the girl declined to follow advice which instinctively she distrusted, and Sir Lucien was too clever to urge it upon her. But he glanced casually at his wrist-watch—and poor Rita shuddered. The gold box was hidden again in the baronet's pocket.

To analyze the process which thereupon took place in Rita's mind would be a barren task, since its result was a foregone conclusion. Daring ambition rather than any merely abstract virtue was the keynote of her character. She had rebuffed the advances of Sir Lucien as she had rebuffed others, primarily because her aim in life was set higher than mere success in light comedy. This she counted but a means to a more desirable end— a wealthy marriage. To the achievement of such an alliance the presence of an accepted lover would be an obstacle; and true love Rita Dresden had never known. Yet, short of this final sacrifice which some women so lightly made, there were few scruples which she was not prepared to discard in furtherance of her designs. Her morality, then, was diplomatic, for the vice of ambition may sometimes make for virtue.

Rita's vivacious beauty and perfect self-possession on the fateful night earned her a permanent place in stageland: Rita Dresden became a "star." She had won a long and hard-fought battle; but in avoiding one master she had abandoned herself to another.

The triumph of her début left her strangely exhausted. She dreaded the coming of the second night almost as keenly as she had dreaded the ordeal of the first. She struggled, poor victim, and only increased her terrors. Not until the clock showed her that in twenty minutes she must make her first entrance did she succumb. But Sir Lucien's gold snuff-box lay upon her dressing-table— and she was trembling. When at last she heard the sustained note of the oboe in the orchestra giving the pitch to the answering violins, she raised the jewelled lid of the box.

So she entered upon the path which leads down to destruction, and since to conjure with the drug which pharmacists know as methylbenzoyl ecgonine is to raise the demon Insomnia, ere long she found herself exploring strange by-paths in quest of sleep.

By the time that she was entrusted with the leading part in *The Maid of the Masque*, she herself did not recognize how tenacious was the hold which this fatal habit had secured upon her. In the company of Sir Lucien Pyne she met other devotees, and for a time came to regard her unnatural mode of existence as something inseparable from the Bohemian life. To the horrible side of it she was blind.

It was her meeting with Monte Irvin during the run of this successful play which first awakened a dawning comprehension; not because she ascribed his admiration to her artificial vivacity, but because she realized the strength of the link subsisting between herself and Sir Lucien. She liked and respected Irvin, and as a result began to view her conduct from a new standpoint. His life was so entirely open and free from reproach, while part of her own was dark and secret. She conceived a desire to be done with that dark and secret life.

This was a shadow-land over which Sir Lucien Pyne presided, and which must be kept hidden from Monte Irvin; and it was not until she thus contemplated cutting herself adrift from it all that she perceived the Gordian knot which bound her to the drug coterie. How far, yet how smoothly, by all but imperceptible stages she had glided down the stream since that night when the gold box had lain upon her dressing-table! Kazmah's drug store in Bond Street had few secrets for her; or so she believed. She knew that the establishment of the strange, immobile Egyptian was a source from which drugs could always be obtained; she knew that the dream-reading business served some double purpose; but she did not know the identity of Kazmah.

Two of the most insidious drugs familiar to modern pharmacy were wooing her to slavery, and there was no strong hand to hold her back. Even the presence of her mother might have offered some slight deterrent at this stage of Rita's descent, but the girl had quitted her suburban home as soon as her salary had rendered her sufficiently independent to do so, and had established herself in a small but elegant flat situated in the heart of theatreland.

But if she had walked blindly into the clutches of cocaine and veronal, her subsequent experiments with *chandu* were prompted by indefensible curiosity, and a false vanity which urged her to do everything that was "done" by the ultra-smart and vicious set of which she had become a member.

Her first introduction to opium-smoking was made under the auspices of an American comedian then appearing in London, an old devotee of the poppy; and it took place shortly after Sir Lucien Pyne had proposed marriage to Rita. This proposal she had not rejected outright; she had pleaded time for consideration. Monte Irvin was away, and Rita secretly hoped that on his return he would declare himself. Meanwhile she indulged in every new craze which became fashionable among her associates. A *chandu* party took place at the American's flat in Duke Street; and Rita, who had been invited, and who had consented to go with Sir Lucien Pyne, met there for the first time the woman variously known as "Lola" and "Mrs. Sin."

Chapter XIII

A CHANDU PARTY

From the restaurant at which she had had supper with Sir Lucien, Rita proceeded to Duke Street. Alighting from Pyne's car at the door, they went up to the flat of the organizer of the opium party—Mr. Cyrus Kilfane. One other guest was already present—a slender, fair woman, who was introduced by the American as Mollie Gretna, but whose weakly pretty face Rita recognized as that of a notorious society divorcée, foremost in the van of every new craze, a past-mistress of the smartest vices.

Kilfane had sallow, expressionless features and drooping, light-colored eyes. His straw-hued hair, brushed back from a sloping brow, hung lankly down upon his coat-collar. Long familiarity with China's ruling vice and contact with those who practiced it had brought about that mysterious physical alteration—apparently reflecting a mental change—so often to be seen in one who has consorted with Chinamen. Even the light eyes seemed to have grown slightly oblique; the voice, the unimpassioned greeting, were those of a son of Cathay. He carried himself with a stoop and had a queer, shuffling gait.

"Ah, my dear daughter," he murmured in a solemnly facetious manner, "how glad I am to welcome you to our poppy circle."

He slowly turned his half-closed eyes in Pyne's direction, and slowly turned them back again.

"Do you seek forgetfulness of old joys?" he asked. "This is my own case and Pyne's. Or do you, as Mollie does, seek new joys—youth's eternal quest?"

Rita laughed with a careless abandon which belonged to that part of her character veiled from the outer world.

"I think I agree with Miss Gretna," she said lightly. "There is not so much happiness in life that I want to forget the little I have had."

"Happiness," murmured Kilfane. "There is no real happiness. Happiness is smoke. Let us smoke."

"I am curious, but half afraid," declared Rita. "I have heard that opium sometimes has no other effect than to make one frightfully ill."

"Oh, my dear!" cried Miss Gretna, with a foolish giggling laugh. "you will love it! Such fascinating dreams! Such delightful adventures!"

"Other drugs," drawled Sir Lucien, "merely stimulate one's normal mental activities. *Chandu* is a key to another life. Cocaine, for instance, enhances our capacity for work. It is only a heretic like De Quincey who prostitutes the magic gum to such base purposes. *Chandu* is misunderstood in Europe; in Asia it is the companion of the æsthete's leisure."

"But surely," said Rita, "one pipe of opium will not produce all these wonders."

"Some people never experience them at all," interrupted Miss Gretna. "The great idea is to get into a comfortable position, and just resign yourself—let yourself go. Oh, it's heavenly!"

Cyrus Kilfane turned his dull eyes in Rita's direction.

"A question of temperament and adaptability," he murmured. "De Quincey, Pyne"—slowly turning towards the baronet—"is didactic, of course; but his *Confessions* may be true, nevertheless. He forgets, you see, that he possessed an unusual constitution, and the temperament of a Norwegian herring. He forgets, too, that he was a laudanum drinker, not an opium smoker. Now you, my daughter"—the lustreless eyes again sought Rita's flushed face—"are vivid—intensely vital. If you can succeed in resigning yourself to the hypnosis induced your experiences will be delightful. Trust your Uncle Cy."

Leaving Rita chatting with Miss Gretna, Kilfane took Pyne aside, offering him a cigarette from an ornate, jewelled case.

"Hello," said the baronet, "can you still get these?"

"With the utmost difficulty." murmured Kilfane, returning the case to his pocket. "Lola charges me five guineas a hundred for them, and only supplies them as a favor. I shall be glad to get back home, Pyne. The right stuff is the wrong price in London."

Sir Lucien laughed sardonically, lighting Kilfane's cigarette and then his own.

"I find it so myself," he said. "Everything except opium is to be had at Kazmah's, and nothing except opium interests me."

"He supplies me with cocaine," murmured the comedian. "His figure works out, as nearly as I can estimate it, at 10s. 7½d. a grain. I saw him about it yesterday afternoon, pointing out to the brown guy that as the wholesale price is roughly 2¼d., I regarded his margin of profit as somewhat broad."

"Indeed!"

"The first time I had ever seen him, Pyne. I brought an introduction from Dr. Silver, of New York, and Kazmah supplied me without question—at a price."

"You always saw Rashîd?"

"Yes. If there were other visitors I waited. But yesterday I made a personal appointment with Kazmah. He pretended to think I had come to have a dream interpreted. He is clever, Pyne. He never moved a muscle throughout the interview. But finally he assured me that all the receivers in England had amalgamated, and that the price he charged represented a very narrow margin of profit. Of course he is a liar. He is making a fortune. Do you know him, personally?"

"No," replied Sir Lucien. "Outside his Bond Street home of mystery he is unknown. A clever man, as you say. You obtain your opium from Lola?"

"Yes. Kazmah sent her to me. She keeps me on ridiculously low rations, and if I had not brought my own outfit I don't think she would have sold me one. Of course, her game is beating up clients for the Limehouse dive."

"You have visited 'The House of a Hundred Raptures'?"

"Many times, at week-ends. Opium, like wine, is better enjoyed in company."

"Does she post you the opium?"

"Oh, no; my man goes to Limehouse for it. Ah! here she is."

A woman came in, carrying a brown leather attaché case. She had left her hat and coat in the hall, and wore a smart blue serge skirt and a white blouse. She was not tall, but she possessed a remarkably beautiful figure which the cut of her garments was not intended to disguise; and her height was appreciably increased by a pair of suéde shoes having the most wonderful heels which Rita ever remembered to have seen worn on or off the stage. They seemed to make her small feet appear smaller, and lent to her slender ankles an exaggerated frontal curve.

Her hair was of that true, glossy black which suggests the blue sheen of raven's plumage, and her thickly fringed eyes were dark and southern as her hair. She had full, voluptuous lips, and a bold self-assurance. In the swift, calculating glance which she cast about the room there was something greedy and evil; and when it rested upon Rita Dresden's dainty beauty to the evil greed was added cruelty.

"Another little sister, dear Lola," murmured Kilfane. "Of course, you know who it is? This, my daughter," turning the sleepy glance towards Rita, "is our officiating priestess, Mrs. Sin."

The woman so strangely named revealed her gleaming teeth in a swift, unpleasant smile; then her nostrils dilated and she glanced about her suspiciously.

"Someone smokes the *chandu* cigarettes," she said, speaking in a low tone which, nevertheless, failed to disguise her harsh voice, and with a very marked accent.

"I am the offender, dear Lola," said Kilfane, dreamily waving his cigarette towards her. "I have managed to make the last hundred spin out. You have brought me a new supply?"

"Oh no, indeed," replied Mrs. Sin, tossing her head in a manner oddly reminiscent of a once famous Spanish dancer. "Next Tuesday you get some more. Ah! it is no good! You talk and talk and it cannot alter anything. Until they come I cannot give them to you."

"But it appears to me," murmured Kilfane, "that the supply is always growing less."

"Of course. The best goes all to Edinburgh now. I have only three sticks of Yezd left of all my stock."

"But the cigarettes——"

"Are from Buenos Ayres? Yes. But Buenos Ayres must get the opium before we get the cigarettes, eh? Five cases come to London on Tuesday, Cy. Be of good courage, my dear."

She patted the sallow cheek of the American with her jewelled fingers, and turned aside, glancing about her.

"Yes," murmured Kilfane. "We are all present, Lola. I have had the room prepared. Come, my chidren, let us enter the poppy portico."

He opened a door and stood aside, waving one thin yellow hand between the first two fingers of which smouldered the drugged cigarette. Led by Mrs. Sin, the company filed into an apartment evidently intended for a drawing-room, but which had been hastily transformed into an opium divan.

Tables, chairs, and other items of furniture had been stacked against one of the walls and the floor spread with rugs, skins, and numerous silk cushions. A gas fire was alight, but before it had been placed an ornate Japanese screen whereon birds of dazzling plumage hovered amid the leaves of gilded palm trees. In the centre of the room stood a small card-table, and upon it were a large brass tray and an ivory pedestal exquisitely carved in the form of a nude figure having one arm upraised. The figure supported a lamp, the light of which was subdued by a barrel-shaped shade of Chinese workmanship.

Mollie Gretna giggled hysterically.

"Make yourself comfortable, dear," she cried to Rita, dropping down upon a heap of cushions stacked in a recess beside the fireplace. "I am going to take off my shoes. The last time, Cyrus, when I woke up my feet were quite numb."

"You should come down to my place," said Mrs. Sin, setting the leather case on the little card-table beside the lamp. "You have there your own little room and silken sheets to lie in, and it is quiet—so quiet."

"Oh!" cried Mollie Gretna, "I *must* come! But I daren't go alone. Will you come with me, dear?" turning to Rita.

"I don't know," was the reply. "I may not like opium."

"But if you do—and I know you will?"

"Why," said Rita, glancing rapidly at Pyne, "I suppose it would be a novel experience."

"Let me arrange it for you," came the harsh voice of Mrs. Sin. "Lucy will drive you both down—won't you, my dear?" The shadowed eyes glanced aside at Sir Lucien Pyne.

"Certainly," he replied. "I am always at the ladies' service."

Rita Dresden settled herself luxuriously into a nest of silk and fur in another corner of the room, regarding the baronet coquettishly through her half-lowered lashes.

"I won't go unless it is my party, Lucy," she said. "You must let me pay."

"A detail," murmured Pyne, crossing and standing beside her.

Interest now became centred upon the preparations being made by Mrs. Sin. From the attaché case she took out a lacquered box,

silken-lined like a jewel-casket. It contained four singular-looking pipes, the parts of which she began to fit together. The first and largest of these had a thick bamboo stem, an amber mouthpiece, and a tiny, disproportionate bowl of brass. The second was much smaller and was of some dark, highly-polished wood, mounted with silver conceived in an ornate Chinese design representing a long-tailed lizard. The mouthpiece was of jade. The third and fourth pipes were yet smaller, a perfectly matched pair in figured ivory of exquisite workmanship, delicately gold-mounted.

"These for the ladies," said Mrs. Sin, holding up the pair. "You"—glancing at Kilfane—"have got your own pipe, I know."

She laid them upon the tray, and now took out of the case a little copper lamp, a smaller lacquered box and a silver spatula, her jewelled fingers handling the queer implements with a familiarity bred of habit.

"What a strange woman!" whispered Rita to Pyne. "Is she an Oriental?"

"Cuban-Jewess," he replied in a low voice.

Mrs. Sin carefully lighted the lamp, which burned with a short, bluish flame, and, opening the lacquered box, she dipped the spatula into the thick gummy substance which it contained and twisted the little instrument round and round between her fingers, presently withdrawing it with a globule of *chandu*, about the size of a bean, adhering to the end. She glanced aside at Kilfane.

"Chinese way, eh?" she said.

She began to twirl the prepared opium above the flame of the lamp. From it a slight, sickly smelling vapor arose. No one spoke, but all watched her closely; and Rita was conscious of a growing, pleasurable excitement. When by evaporation the *chandu* had become reduced to the size of a small pea, and a vague spirituous blue flame began to dance round the end of the spatula, Mrs. Sin pressed it adroitly into the tiny bowl of one of the ivory pipes, having first held the bowl inverted for a moment over the lamp. She turned to Rita.

"The guest of the evening," she said. "Do not be afraid. Inhale—oh, so gentle—and blow the smoke from the nostrils. You know how to smoke?"

"The same as a cigarette?" asked Rita excitedly, as Mrs. Sin bent over her.

"The same, but very, very gentle."

Rita took the pipe and raised the mouthpiece to her lips.

Chapter XIV

IN THE SHADE OF
THE LONELY PALM

Persian opium of good quality contains from ten to fifteen per cent. of morphine, and *chandu* made from opium of Yezd would contain perhaps twenty-five per cent. of this potent drug; but because in the act of smoking distillation occurs, nothing like this quantity of morphine reaches the smoker. To the distilling process, also, may be due the different symptoms resulting from smoking *chandu* and injecting morphia—or drinking tincture of opium, as De Quincey did.

Rita found the flavor of the preparation to be not entirely unpleasant. Having overcome an initial aversion, caused by its marked medicinal tang, she grew reconciled to it and finished her first smoke without experiencing any other effect than a sensation of placid contentment. Deftly, Mrs. Sin renewed the pipe. Silence had fallen upon the party.

The second "pill" was no more than half consumed when a growing feeling of nausea seized upon the novice, becoming so marked that she dropped the ivory pipe weakly and uttered a faint moan.

Instantly, silently, Mrs. Sin was beside her.

"Lean forward—so," she whispered, softly, as if fearful of intruding her voice upon these sacred rites. "In a moment you will be better. Then, if you feel faint, lie back. It is the sleep. Do not fight against it."

The influence of the stronger will prevailed. Self-control and judgment are qualities among the first to succumb to opium. Rita ceased to think longingly of the clean, fresh air, of escape from these sickly fumes which seemed now to fill the room with a moving vapor. She bent forward, her chin resting upon her breast, and gradually the deathly sickness passed. Mentally, she underwent a change, too. From an active state of resistance the ego traversed a descending curve ending in absolute passivity. The floor had seemingly begun to revolve and was moving insidiously, so that the pattern of the carpet formed a series of concentric rings. She found this imaginary phenomenon to be soothing rather than otherwise, and resigned herself almost eagerly to the delusion.

Mrs. Sin allowed her to fall back upon the cushions—so gently and so slowly that the operation appeared to occupy several minutes and to resemble that of sinking into innumerable layers of swansdown. The sinuous figure bending over her grew taller with the passage of each minute, until the dark eyes of Mrs. Sin were looking down at Rita from a dizzy elevation. As often occurs in the case of a neurotic subject, delusion as to time and space had followed the depression of the sensory cells.

But surely, she mused, this could not be Mrs. Sin who towered so loftily above her. Of course, how absurd to imagine that a woman could remain thus motionless for so many hours. And Rita thought, now, that she had been lying for several hours beneath the shadow of that tall, graceful, and protective shape.

Why—it was a slender palm-tree, which stretched its fanlike foliage over her! Far, far above her head the long, dusty green fronds projected from the mast-like trunk. The sun, a ball of fiery brass, burned directly in the zenith, so that the shadow of the foliage lay like a carpet about her feet. That which she had mistaken for the ever-receding eyes of Mrs. Sin, wondering with a delightful vagueness why they seemed constantly to change color, proved to be a pair of brilliantly plumaged parrakeets perched upon a lofty branch of the palm.

This was an equatorial noon, and even if she had not found herself to be under the influence of a delicious abstraction Rita would not have moved; for, excepting the friendly palm, not another vestige of vegetation was visible right away to the horizon; nothing but an ocean of sand whereon no living thing moved. She and the parrakeets were alone in the heart of the Great Sahara.

But stay! Many, many miles away, a speck on the dusty carpet of the desert, something moved! Hours must elapse before that tiny figure, provided it were approaching, could reach the solitary palm. Delightedly, Rita contemplated the infinity of time. Even if the figure moved ever so slowly, she should be waiting there beneath the palm to witness its arrival. Already, she had been there for a period which she was far too indolent to strive to compute—a week, perhaps. She turned her attention to the parrakeets. One of them was moving, and she noted with delight that it had perceived her far below and was endeavoring to draw the attention of its less observant companion to her presence. For many hours she lay watching it and wondering why, since the one bird was so singularly intelligent, its companion was equally dull. When she lowered her eyes and looked out again across the sands, the figure had approached so close as to be recognizable.

It was that of Mrs. Sin. Rita appreciated the fitness of her presence, and experienced no surprise, only a mild curiosity. This curiosity was not concerned with Mrs. Sin herself, but with the nature of the burden which she bore upon her head.

She was dressed in a manner which Rita dreamily thought would have been inadequate in England, or even in Cuba, but which was appropriate in the Great Sahara. How exquisitely she carried herself, mused the dreamer; no doubt this fine carriage was due in part to her wearing golden shoes with heels like stilts, and in part to her having been trained to bear heavy burdens upon her head. Rita remembered that Sir Lucien had once described to her the elegant deportment of the Arab women, ascribing it to their custom of carrying water-jars in that way.

The appearance of the speck on the horizon had marked the height of her trance. Her recognition of Mrs. Sin had signalized the decline of the *chandu* influence. Now, the intrusion of a definite, uncontorted memory was evidence of returning cerebral activity.

Rita had no recollection of the sunset; indeed, she had failed to perceive any change in the form and position of the shadow cast by the foliage. It had spread, an ebony patch, equally about the bole of the tree, so that the sun must have been immediately overhead. But, of course, she had lain watching the parrakeets for several hours, and now night had fallen. The desert mounds were touched with silver, the sky was a nest of diamonds, and the moon cast a shadow of the palm like a bar of ebony right across the prospect to the rim of the sky dome.

Mrs. Sin stood before her, one half of her lithe body concealed by this strange black shadow and the other half gleaming in the moonlight so that she resembled a beautiful ivory statue which some iconoclast had cut in two.

Placing her burden upon the ground, Mrs. Sin knelt down before Rita and reverently kissed her hand, whispering: "I am your slave, my poppy queen."

She spoke in a strange language, no doubt some African tongue, but one which Rita understood perfectly. Then she laid one hand upon the object which she had carried on her head, and which now proved to be a large lacquered casket covered with Chinese figures and bound by three hoops of gold. It had a very curious shape.

"Do you command that the chest be opened?" she asked.

"Yes," answered Rita languidly.

Mrs. Sin threw up the lid, and from the interior of the casket, which, because of the glare of the moonlight, seemed every moment to assume a new form, drew out a bronze lamp.

"The sacred lamp," she whispered, and placed it on the sand. "Do you command that it be lighted?"

Rita inclined her head.

The lamp became lighted; in what manner she did not observe, nor was she curious to learn. Next from the large casket Mrs. Sin took another smaller casket and a very long, tapering silver bodkin. The first casket had perceptibly increased in size. It was certainly much larger than Rita had supposed; for now out from its shadowy interior Mrs. Sin began to take pipes—long pipes and short pipes, pipes of gold and pipes of silver, pipes of ivory and pipes of jade. Some were carved to represent the heads of demons, some had the bodies of serpents wreathed about them; others were encrusted with precious gems, and filled the night with the venomous sheen of emeralds, the blood-rays of rubies and golden glow of topaz, while the spear-points of diamonds flashed a challenge to the stars.

"Do you command that the pipes be lighted?" asked the harsh voice.

Rita desired to answer, "No"; but heard herself saying, "Yes."

Thereupon, from a thousand bowls, linking that lonely palm to the remote horizon, a thousand elfin fires arose—blue-tongued and spirituous. Grey pencillings of smoke stole straightly upward to the sky, so that look where she would Rita could discern nothing but these countless thin, faintly wavering, vertical lines of vapor.

The dimensions of the lacquered casket had increased so vastly as to conceal the kneeling figure of Mrs. Sin; and staring at it wonderingly, Rita suddenly perceived that it was not an ordinary casket. She knew at last why its shape had struck her as being unusual.

It was a Chinese coffin.

The smell of the burning opium was stifling her. Those remorseless threads of smoke were closing in, twining themselves about her throat. It was becoming cold, too, and the moonlight was growing dim. The position of the moon had changed, of course, as the night had stolen on towards morning, and now it hung dimly before her. The smoke obscured it.

But was this smoke obscuring the moon? Rita moved her hands for the first time since she had found herself under the palm tree, weakly fending off those vaporous tentacles which were seeking to entwine themselves about her throat. Of course, it was not smoke obscuring the moon, she decided; it was a lamp, upheld by an ivory figure—a lamp with a Chinese shade.

A subdued roaring sound became audible; and this was occasioned by the gas fire, burning behind the Japanese screen on which gaily plumaged birds sported in the branches of golden palms. Rita raised her hands to her eyes. Mist obscured her sight. Swiftly, now, reality was asserting itself and banishing the phantasmagoria conjured up by *chandu.*

In her dim, cushioned corner Mollie Gretna lay back against the wall, her face pale and her weak mouth foolishly agape. Cyrus Kilfane was indistinguishable from the pile of rugs amid which he sprawled by the table, and of Sir Lucien Pyne nothing was to be seen but the outstretched legs and feet which projected grotesquely from a recess. Seated, Oriental fashion, upon an improvised divan near the grand piano and propped up by a number of garish cushions, Rita beheld Mrs. Sin. The long bamboo pipe had fallen from her listless fingers. Her face wore an expression of mystic rapture like that characterizing the features of some Chinese Buddhas.

Fear, unaccountable but uncontrollable, suddenly seized upon Rita. She felt weak and dizzy, but she struggled partly upright.

"Lucy!" she whispered.

Her voice was not under control, and once more she strove to call to Pyne.

"Lucy!" came the hoarse whisper again.

The fire continued its muted roaring, but no other sound answered to the appeal. A horror of the companionship in which she found herself thereupon took possession of the girl. She must escape from these sleepers, whose spirits had been expelled by the potent necromancer, opium, from these empty tenements whose occupants had fled. The idea of the cool night air in the open streets was delicious.

She staggered to her feet, swaying drunkenly, but determined to reach the door. She shuddered, because of a feeling of internal chill which assailed her, but step by step crept across the room, opened the door, and tottered out into the hallway. There was no sound in the flat. Presumably Kilfane's man had retired, or perhaps he, too, was a devotee.

Rita's fur coat hung upon the rack, and although her fingers appeared to have lost all their strength and her arm to have become weak as that of an infant, she succeeded in detaching the coat from the hook. Not pausing to put it on, she opened the door and stumbled out on to the darkened landing. Whereas her first impulse had been to awaken someone, preferably Sir Lucien, now her sole desire was to escape undetected.

She began to feel less dizzy, and having paused for a moment on the landing, she succeeded in getting her coat on. Then she closed the door as quietly as possible, and clutching the handrail began to grope her way downstairs. There was only one flight, she remembered, and a short passage leading to the street door. She reached the passage without mishap, and saw a faint light ahead.

The fastenings gave her some trouble, but finally her efforts were successful, and she found herself standing in deserted Duke Street. There was no moon, but the sky was cloudless. She had no idea of the time, but because of the stillness of the surrounding streets she knew that it must be very late. She set out for her flat, walking slowly and wondering what explanation she should offer if a constable observed her.

Oxford Street showed deserted as far as the eye could reach, and her light footsteps seemed to awaken a hundred echoes. Having proceeded for some distance without meeting anyone, she observed—and experienced a childish alarm—the head-lights of an approaching car. Instantly the idea of hiding presented itself to her, but so rapidly did the big automobile speed along the empty thoroughfare that Rita was just passing a street lamp as the car raced by, and she must therefore have been clearly visible to the occupants.

Never for a moment glancing aside, Rita pressed on as quickly as she could. Then her vague alarm became actual terror. She heard the brakes being applied to the car, and heard the gritty sound of the tires upon the roadway as the vehicle's headlong progress was suddenly checked. She had been seen—perhaps recognized; and whoever was in the car proposed to return to speak to her.

If her strength had allowed she would have run, but now it threatened to desert her altogether and she tottered weakly. A pattering of footsteps came from behind. Someone was running back to overtake her. Recognizing escape to be impossible, Rita turned just as the runner came up with her.

"Rita!" he cried, rather breathlessly. "Miss Dresden!"

She stood very still, looking at the speaker. It was Monte Irvin.

Chapter XV

METAMORPHOSIS

As Irvin seized her hands and looked at her eagerly, half-fearfully, Rita achieved sufficient composure to speak.

"Oh, Mr. Irvin," she said, and found that her voice was not entirely normal, "what must you think——"

He continued to hold her hands, and:

"I think you are very indiscreet to be out alone at three o'clock in the morning," he answered gently. "I was recalled to London by urgent business, and returned by road—fortunately, since I have met you."

"How can I explain——"

"I don't ask you to explain—Miss Dresden. I have no right and no desire to ask. But I wish I had the right to advise you."

"How good you are," she began; "and I——"

Her voice failed her completely, and her sensitive lips began to tremble. Monte Irvin drew her arm under his own and led her back to meet the car, which the chauffeur had turned and which was now approaching.

"I will drive you home," he said, "and if I may call in the morning I should like to do so."

Rita nodded. She could not trust herself to speak again. And having placed her in the car, Monte Irvin sat beside her, reclaiming her hand and grasping it reassuringly and sympathetically throughout the short drive. They parted at her door.

"Good night," said Irvin, speaking very deliberately because of an almost uncontrollable desire which possessed him to take Rita in his arms, to hold her fast, to protect her from her own pathetic self and from those influences, dimly perceived about her, but which intuitively he knew to be evil.

"If I call at eleven will that be too early?"

"No," she whispered. "Please come early. There is a matinée to-morrow."

"You mean to-day," he corrected. "Poor little girl, how tired you will be. Good night."

"Good night," she said, almost inaudibly.

She entered, and, having closed the door, stood leaning against it for several minutes. Weakness and nausea threatened to overcome her anew, and she felt that if she essayed another step she must collapse upon the floor. Her maid was in bed, and had not been awakened by Rita's entrance. After a time she managed to grope her way to her bedroom, where, turning up the light, she sank down helplessly upon the bed.

Her mental state was peculiar, and her thoughts revolved about the journey from Oxford Street homeward. A thousand times she mentally repeated the journey, speaking the same words over and over again, and hearing Monte Irvin's replies.

In those few minutes during which they had been together her sentiments in regard to him had undergone a change. She had always respected Irvin, but this respect had been curiously compounded of the personal and the mercenary; his well-ordered establishment at Prince's Gate had loomed behind the figure of the man forming a pleasing background to the portrait. Without being showy he was a splendid "match" for any woman. His wife would have access to good society, and would enjoy every luxury that wealth could procure. This was the picture lovingly painted and constantly retouched by Rita's mother.

Now it had vanished. The background was gone, and only the man remained; the strong, reserved man whose deep voice had spoken so gently, whose devotion was so true and unselfish that he only sought to shield and protect her from follies the nature of which he did not even seek to learn. She was stripped of her vanity, and felt loathsome and unworthy of such a love.

"Oh," she moaned, rocking to and fro. "I hate myself—I hate myself!"

Now that the victory so long desired seemed at last about to be won, she hesitated to grasp the prize. One solacing reflection she had. She would put the errors of the past behind her. Many times of late she had found herself longing to be done with the feverish life of the stage. Envied by those who had been her companions in the old chorus days, and any one of whom would have counted ambition crowned could she have played *The Maid of the Masque*, Rita thought otherwise. The ducal mansions and rose-bowered Riviera hotels through which she moved nightly had no charm for her; she sighed for reality, and had wearied long ago of the canvas palaces and the artificial Southern moonlight. In fact, stage life had never truly appealed to her—save as a means to an end.

Again and yet again her weary brain reviewed the episodes of the night since she had left Cyrus Kilfane's flat, so that nearly an hour had elapsed before she felt capable of the operation of undressing. Finally, however, she undressed, shuddering although the room was warmed by an electric radiator. The weakness and sickness had left her, but she was quite wide awake, although her brain demanded rest from that incessant review of the events of the evening.

She put on a warm wrap and seated herself at the dressing-table, studying her face critically. She saw that she was somewhat pale and that she had an indefinable air of dishevelment. Also she detected shadows beneath her eyes, the pupils of which were curiously contracted. Automatically, as a result of habit, she unlocked her jewel-case and took out a tiny phial containing minute cachets. She shook several out on to the palm of her hand, and then paused, staring at her reflection in the mirror.

For fully half a minute she hesitated, then:

"I shall never close my eyes all night if I don't!" she whispered, as if in reply to a spoken protest: "and I should be a wreck in the morning."

Thus, in the very apogee of her resolve to reform, did she drive one more rivet into the manacles which held her captive to Kazmah and Company.

Upon a little spirit-stove stood a covered vessel containing milk, which was placed there nightly by Rita's maid. She lighted the burner and warmed the milk. Then, swallowing three of the cachets from the phial, she drank the milk. Each cachet contained three decigrams of malourea, the insidious drug notorious under its trade name of Veronal.

She slept deeply, and was not awakened until ten o'clock. Her breakfast consisted of a cup of strong coffee; but when Monte Irvin arrived at eleven Rita exhibited no sign of nerve exhaustion. She looked bright and charming, and Irvin's heart leapt hotly in his breast at sight of her.

Following some desultory and unnatural conversation:

"May I speak quite frankly to you?" he said, drawing his chair nearer to the settee upon which Rita was seated.

She glanced at him swiftly. "Of course," she replied. "Is it—about my late hours?"

He shook his head, smiling rather sadly.

"That is only one phase of your rather feverish life, little girl," he said. "I don't mean that I want to lecture you or reproach you. I only want to ask you if you are satisfied?"

"Satisfied?" echoed Rita, twirling a tassel that hung from a cushion beside her.

"Yes. You have achieved success in your profession." He strove in vain to banish bitterness from his voice. "You are a 'star,' and your photograph is to be seen frequently in the smartest illustrated papers. You are clever and beautiful and have hosts of admirers. But—are you satisfied?"

She stared absently at the silk tassel, twirling it about her white fingers more and more rapidly. Then:

"No," she answered softly.

Monte Irvin hesitated for a moment ere bending forward and grasping her hands.

"I am glad you are not satisfied," he whispered. "I always knew you had a soul for something higher—better."

She avoided his ardent gaze, but he moved to the settee beside her and looked into the bewitching face.

"Would it be a great sacrifice to give it all up?" he whispered in a yet lower tone.

Rita shook her head, persistently staring at the tassel.

"For me?"

She gave him a swift, half-frightened glance, pressing her hands against his breast and leaning back.

"Oh, you don't know me—you don't know me!" she said, the good that was in her touched to life by the man's sincerity. "I don't—deserve it."

"Rita!" he murmured. "I won't hear you say that!"

"You know nothing about my friends—about my life——"

"I know that I want you for my wife, so that I can protect you from those 'friends.'" He took her in his arms, and she surrendered her lips to him.

"My sweet little girl," he whispered. "I

cannot believe it—yet."

But the die was cast, and when Rita went to the theatre to dress for the afternoon performance she was pledged to sever her connection with the stage on the termination of her contract. She had luncheon with Monte Irvin, and had listened almost dazedly to his plans for the future. His wealth was even greater than her mother had estimated it to be, and Rita's most cherished dreams were dwarfed by the prospects which Monte Irvin opened up before her. It almost seemed as though he knew and shared her dearest ambitions. She was to winter beneath real Southern palms and to possess a cruising yacht, not one of boards and canvas like that which figured in *The Maid of the Masque.*

Real Southern palms, she mused guiltily, not those conjured up by opium. That he was solicitous for her health the nature of his schemes revealed. They were to visit Switzerland, and proceed thence to a villa which he owned in Italy. Christmas they would spend in Cairo, explore the Nile to Assouan in a private *dahabîyeh*, and return home via the Riviera in time to greet the English spring. Rita's delicate, swiftly changing color, her almost ethereal figure, her intense nervous energy he ascribed to a delicate constitution.

She wondered if she would ever dare to tell him the truth; if she ought to tell him.

Pyne came to her dressing-room just before the performance began. He had telephoned at an early hour in the morning, and had learned from her maid that Rita had come home safely and was asleep. Rita had expected him; but the influence of Monte Irvin, from whom she had parted at the stage-door, had prevailed until she actually heard Sir Lucien's voice in the corridor. She had resolutely refrained from looking at the little jewelled casket, engraved "From Lucy to Rita," which lay in her make-up box upon the table. But the imminence of an ordeal which she dreaded intensely weakened her resolution. She swiftly dipped a little nail-file into the white powder which the box contained; and when Pyne came in she turned to him composedly.

"I am so sorry if I gave you a scare last night, Lucy," she said. "But I woke up feeling sick, and I had to go out into the fresh air."

"I was certainly alarmed," drawled Pyne, whose swarthy face looked more than usually worn in the hard light created by the competition between the dressing-room lamps and the grey wintry daylight which crept through the windows. "Do you feel quite fit again?"

"Quite, thanks." Rita glanced at a ring which she had not possessed three hours before. "Oh, Lucy—I don't know how to tell you——"

She turned in her chair, looking up wistfully at Pyne, who was standing behind her. His jaw hardened, and his glance sought the white hand upon which the costly gems glittered. He coughed nervously.

"Perhaps"—his drawling manner of speech temporarily deserted him; he spoke jerkily—"perhaps—I can guess."

She watched him in a pathetic way, and there was a threat of tears in her beautiful eyes; for whatever his earlier intentions may have been, Sir Lucien had proved a staunch friend and, according to his own peculiar code, an honorable lover.

"Is it—Irvin?" he asked jerkily.

Rita nodded, and a tear glistened upon her darkened lashes.

Sir Lucien cleared his throat again, then coolly extended his hand, once more master of his emotions.

"Congratulations, Rita," he said. "The better man wins. I hope you will be very happy."

He turned and walked quietly out of the dressing-room.

Chapter XVI

LIMEHOUSE

It was on the following Tuesday evening that Mrs. Sin came to the theatre, accompanied by Mollie Gretna. Rita instructed that she should be shown up to the dressing-room. The personality of this singular woman interested her keenly. Mrs. Sin was well known in certain Bohemian quarters, but was always spoken of as one speaks of a pet vice. Not to know Mrs. Sin was to be outside the magic circle which embraced the exclusively smart people who practiced the latest absurdities.

The so-called artistic temperament is compounded of great strength and great weakness; its virtues are whiter than those of ordinary people and its vices blacker. For such a personality Mrs. Sin embodied the idea of secret pleasure. Her bold good looks repelled Rita, but the knowledge in her dark eyes was alluring.

"I arrange for you for Saturday night," she said. "Cy Kilfane is coming with Mollie, and you bring Lucy, eh?"

"Oh," replied Rita hesitatingly, "I am sorry you have gone to so much trouble."

"No trouble, my dear," Mrs. Sin asssured her. "Just a little matter of business, and you can pay the bill when it suits you."

"I am frightfully excited!" cried Mollie Gretna. "It is so nice of you to have asked me to join your party. Of course Cy goes practically every week, but I have always wanted another girl to go with. Oh, I shall be in a perfectly delicious panic when I find myself all among funny Chinamen and things! I think there is something so magnificently wicked-looking about a pigtail—and the very name of Limehouse thrills me to the soul!"

That fixity of purpose which had enabled Rita to avoid the cunning snares set for her feet and to snatch triumph from the very cauldron of shame without burning her fingers availed her not at all in dealing with Mrs. Sin. The image of Monte receded before this appeal to the secret pleasure-loving woman, of insatiable curiosity, primitive and unmoral, who dwells, according to a modern cynic philosopher, within every daughter of Eve touched by the fire of genius.

She accepted the arrangement for Saturday, and before her visitors had left the dressing-room her mind was busy with plausible deceits to cover the sojourn in Chinatown. Something of Mollie Gretna's foolish enthusiasm had communicated itself to Rita.

Later in the evening Sir Lucien called, and on hearing of the scheme grew silent. Rita, glancing at his reflection in the mirror, detected a black and angry look upon his face. She turned to him.

"Why, Lucy," she said, "don't you want me to go?"

He smiled in his sardonic fashion.

"Your wishes are mine, Rita," he replied.

She was watching him closely.

"But you don't seem keen," she persisted. "Are you angry with me?"

"Angry?"

"We are still friends, aren't we?"

"Of course. Do you doubt my friendship?"

Rita's maid came in to assist her in changing for the third act, and Pyne went out of the room. But, in spite of his assurances, Rita could not forget that fierce, almost savage expression which had appeared upon his face

when she had told him of Mrs. Sin's visit.

Later she taxed him on the point, but he suffered her inquiry with imperturbable sangfroid, and she found herself no wiser respecting the cause of his annoyance. Painful twinges of conscience came during the ensuing days, when she found herself in her fiancé's company, but she never once seriously contemplated dropping the acquaintance of Mrs. Sin.

She thought, vaguely, as she had many times thought before, of cutting adrift from the entire clique, but there was no return of that sincere emotional desire to reform which she had experienced on the day that Monte Irvin had taken her hand, in blind trust, and had asked her to be his wife. Had she analyzed, or been capable of analyzing, her intentions with regard to the future, she would have learned that daily they inclined more and more towards compromise. The drug habit was sapping will and weakening moral, insidiously, imperceptibly. She was caught in a current of that "sacred river" seen in an opium-trance by Coleridge, and which ran—

> "Through caverns measureless to man
> Down to a sunless sea."

Pyne's big car was at the stage-door on the fateful Saturday night, for Rita had brought her dressing-case to the theatre, and having called for Kilfane and Mollie Gretna they were to proceed direct to Limehouse.

Rita, as she entered the car, noticed that Juan Mareno, Sir Lucien's man, and not the chauffeur with whom she was acquainted, sat at the wheel. As they drove off:

"Why is Mareno driving to-night, Lucy?" she asked.

Sir Lucien glanced aside at her.

"He is in my confidence," he replied. "Fraser is not."

"Oh, I see. You don't want Fraser to know about the Limehouse journey?"

"Naturally I don't. He would talk to all the men at the garage, and from South Audleystreet the tit-bit of scandal would percolate through every stratum of society."

Rita was silent for a few moments, then:

"Were you thinking about Monte?" she asked diffidently.

Pyne laughed.

"He would scarcely approve, would he?"

"No," replied Rita. "Was that why you were angry when I told you I was going?"

"This 'anger,' to which you constantly

revert, had no existence outside your own imagination, Rita. But"—he hesitated—"you will have to consider your position, dear, now that you are the future Mrs. Monte."

Rita felt her cheeks flush, and she did not reply immediately.

"I don't understand you, Lucy," she declared at last. "How odd you are."

"Am I? Well, never mind. We will talk about my eccentricity later. Here is Cyrus."

Kilfane was standing in the entrance to the stage door of the theatre at which he was playing. As the car drew up he lifted two leather grips on to the step, and Mareno, descending, took charge of them.

"Come along, Mollie," said Kilfane, looking back.

Miss Gretna, very excited, ran out and got into the car beside Rita. Pyne lowered two of the collapsible seats for Kilfane and himself, and the party set out for Limehouse.

"Oh!" cried the fair-haired Mollie, grasping Rita's hand, "my heart began palpitating with excitement the moment I woke up this morning! How calm you are, dear."

"I am only calm outside," laughed Rita.

The *joie de vivre* and apparently unimpaired vitality of this woman, for whom (if half that which rumor whispered were true) vice had no secrets, astonished Rita. Her physical resources were unusual, no doubt, because the demand made upon them by her mental activities was slight.

As the car sped along the Strand, where theatre-goers might still be seen making for tube, omnibus, and tramcar, and entered Fleet Street, where the car and taxi-cab traffic was less, a mutual silence fell upon the party. Two at least of the travellers were watching the lighted windows of the great newspaper offices with a vague sense of foreboding, and thinking how, bound upon a secret purpose, they were passing along the avenue of publicity. It is well that man lacks prescience. Neither Rita nor Sir Lucien could divine that a day was shortly to come when the hidden presses which throbbed about them that night should be busy with the story of the murder of one and disappearance of the other.

Around St. Paul's Churchyard whirled the car, its engine running strongly and almost noiselessly. The great bell of St. Paul's boomed out the half-hour.

"Oh!" cried Mollie Gretna, "how that made me jump! What a beautifully gloomy sound!"

Kilfane murmured some inaudible reply, but neither Pyne nor Rita spoke.

Cornhill and Leadenhall Street, along which presently their route lay, offered a prospect of lamp-lighted emptiness, but at Aldgate they found themselves amid East End throngs which afforded a marked contrast to those crowding theatreland; and from thence through Whitechapel and the seemingly endless Commercial Road it was a different world into which they had penetrated.

Rita hitherto had never seen the East End on a Saturday night, and the spectacle afforded by these busy marts, lighted by naphtha flames, in whose smoky glare Jews and Jewesses, Poles, Swedes, Easterns, dagoes, and halfcastes moved feverishly, was a fascinating one. She thought how utterly alien they were, these men and women of a world unknown to that society upon whose borders she dwelled; she wondered how they lived, where they lived, why they lived. The wet pavements were crowded with nondescript humanity, the night was filled with the unmusical voices of Hebrew hucksters, and the air laden with the smoky odor of their lamps. Tramcars and motor-'buses were packed unwholesomely with these children of shadowland drawn together from the seven seas by the magnet of London.

She glanced at Pyne, but he was seemingly lost in abstraction, and Kilfane appeared to be asleep. Mollie Gretna was staring eagerly out on the opposite side of the car at a group of three dago sailors, whom Mareno had nearly run down, but she turned at that moment and caught Rita's glance.

"Don't you simply love it!" she cried. "Some of those men were really handsome, dear. If they would only wash I am sure I could adore them!"

"Even such charms as yours can be bought at too high a price," drawled Sir Lucien. "They would gladly do murder for you, but never wash."

Crossing Limehouse Canal, the car swung to the right into West India Dock Road. The uproar of the commercial thoroughfare was left far behind. Dark, narrow streets and sinister-looking alleys lay right and left of them, and into one of the narrowest and least inviting of all Mareno turned the car.

In the dimly-lighted doorway of a corner house the figure of a Chinaman showed as a motionless silhouette.

"Oh!" sighed Mollie Gretna rapturously, "a Chinaman! I begin to feel deliciously sinful!"

The car came to a standstill.

"We get out here and walk," said Sir Lucien. "It would not be wise to drive further. Mareno will deliver our baggage by hand presently."

"But we shall all be murdered," cried Mollie, "murdered in cold blood! I am dreadfully frightened!"

"Something of the kind is quite likely," drawled Sir Lucien, "if you draw attention to our presence in the neighborhood so deliberately. Walk ahead, Kilfane, with Mollie. Rita and I will follow at a discreet distance. Leave the door ajar."

Temporarily subdued by Pyne's icy manner, Miss Gretna became silent, and went on ahead with Cyrus Kilfane, who had preserved an almost unbroken silence throughout the journey. Rita and Sir Lucien followed slowly.

"What a creepy neighborhood," whispered Rita. "Look! Someone is standing in that doorway over there, watching us."

"Take no notice," he replied. "A cat could not pass along this street unobserved by the Chinese, but they will not interfere with us provided we do not interfere with them."

Kilfane had turned to the right into a narrow court, at the entrance to which stood an iron pillar. As he and his companion passed under the lamp in a rusty bracket which projected from the wall, they vanished into a place of shadows. There was a ceaseless chorus of distant machinery, and above it rose the grinding and rattling solo of a steam winch. Once a siren hooted apparently quite near them, and looking upward at a tangled, indeterminable mass which overhung the street at this point, Rita suddenly recognized it for a ship's bow-sprit.

"Why," she said, "we are right on the bank of the river!"

"Not quite," answered Pyne. "We are skirting a dock basin. We are nearly at our destination."

Passing in turn under the lamp, they entered the narrow court, and from a doorway immediately on the left a faint light shone out upon the wet pavement. Pyne pushed the door fully open and held it for Rita to enter. As she did so:

"Hello! hello!" croaked a harsh voice. "Number one p'lice chop, lo! Sin Sin Wa!"

The uncanny cracked voice proceeded to give an excellent imitation of a police whistle, and concluded with that of the clicking of castanets.

"Shut the door, Lucy," came the murmurous tones of Kilfane from the gloom of the stuffy little room, in the centre of which stood a stove wherefrom had proceeded the dim light shining out upon the pavement. "Light up, Sin Sin."

"Sin Sin Wa! Sin Sin Wa!" shrieked the voice, and again came the rattling of imaginary castanets. "Smartest leg in Buenos Ayres—Buenos Ayres—p'lice chop—p'lice chop, lo!"

"Oh," whispered Mollie Gretna, in the darkness, "I believe I am going to scream!"

Pyne closed the door, and a dimly discernible figure on the opposite side of the room stooped and opened a little cupboard in which was a lighted ship's lantern. The lantern being lifted out and set upon a rough table near the stove, it became possible to view the apartment and its occupants.

It was a small, low-ceiled place, having two doors, one opening upon the street and the other upon a narrow, uncarpeted passage. The window was boarded up. The ceiling had once been whitewashed and a few limp, dark fragments of paper still adhering to the walls proved that some forgotten decorator had exercised his art upon them in the past. A piece of well-worn matting lay upon the floor, and there were two chairs, a table, and a number of empty tea-chests in the room.

Upon one of the tea-chests placed beside the cupboard which had contained the lantern a Chinaman was seated. His skin was of so light a yellow color as to approximate to dirty white, and his face was pock-marked from neck to crown. He wore long, snakelike moustaches, which hung down below his chin. They grew from the extreme outer edges of his upper lip, the centre of which, usually the most hirsute, was hairless as the lip of an infant. He possessed the longest and thickest pigtail which could possibly grow upon a human scalp, and his left eye was permanently closed, so that a smile which adorned his extraordinary countenance seemed to lack the sympathy of his surviving eye, which, oblique, beady, held no mirth in its glittering depths.

The garments of the one-eyed Chinaman, who sat complacently smiling at the visitors, consisted of a loose blouse, blue trousers tucked into grey socks, and a pair of those native, thick-soled slippers which suggest to a Western critic the acme of discomfort. A raven, black as a bird of ebony, perched upon the Chinaman's shoulder, head a-tilt, surveying the newcomers with a beady, glittering left eye which strangely resembled the beady, glittering right eye of the Chinaman. For, singular, uncanny circumstance, this was a one-eyed raven which sat upon the shoulder of his one-eyed master!

Mollie Gretna uttered a stifled cry. "Oh!" she whispered. "I knew I was going to scream!"

The eye of Sin Sin Wa turned momentarily in her direction, but otherwise he did not stir a muscle.

"Are you ready for us, Sin?" asked Sir Lucien.

"All leady. Lola hab gotchee topside loom leady," replied the Chinaman in a soft, crooning voice.

"Go ahead, Kilfane," directed Sir Lucien.

He glanced at Rita, who was standing very near him, surveying the evil little room and its owner with ill-concealed disgust.

"This is merely the foyer, Rita," he said, smiling slightly. "The state apartments are upstairs and in the adjoining house."

"Oh," she murmured—and no more.

Kilfane and Mollie Gretna were passing through the inner doorway, and Mollie turned.

"Isn't it loathsomely delightful?" she cried.

"Smartest leg in Buenos Ayres!" shrieked the raven. "Sin Sin, Sin Sin!"

Uttering a frightened exclamation, Mollie disappeared along the passage. Sir Lucien indicated to Rita that she was to follow; and he, passing through last of the party, closed the door behind him.

Sin Sin Wa never moved, and the raven, settling down upon the Chinaman's shoulder, closed his serviceable eye.

Chapter XVII

THE BLACK SMOKE

Up an uncarpeted stair Cyrus Kilfane led the party, and into a kind of lumber-room lighted by a tin oil lamp and filled to overflowing with heterogeneous and unsavory rubbish. Here were garments, male and female, no less than five dilapidated bowler hats, more tea-chests, broken lamps, tattered fragments of cocoanut-matting, steel bed-laths and straw mattresses, ruins of chairs—the whole diffusing an indescribably unpleasant odor.

Opening a cupboard door, Kilfane revealed a number of pendent, ragged garments, and two more bowler hats. Holding the garments aside, he banged upon the back of the cupboard—three blows, a pause, and then two blows.

Following a brief interval, during which even Mollie Gretna was held silent by the strangeness of the proceedings,

"Who is it?" inquired a muffled voice.

"Cy and the crowd," answered Kilfane.

Thereupon ensued a grating noise, and hats and garments swung suddenly backward, revealing a doorway in which Mrs. Sin stood framed. She wore a Japanese kimona of embroidered green silk and a pair of green and gold brocaded slippers which possessed higher heels than Rita remembered to have seen even Mrs. Sin mounted upon before. Her ankles were bare, and it was impossible to determine in what manner she was clad beneath the kimona. Undoubtedly she had a certain dark beauty, of a bold, abandoned type.

"Come right in," she directed. "Mind your head, Lucy."

The quartette filed through into a carpeted corridor, and Mrs. Sin reclosed the false back of the cupboard, which, viewed from the other side, proved to be a door fitted into a recess in the corridor of the adjoining house. This recess ceased to exist when a second and heavier door was closed upon the first.

"You know," murmured Kilfane, "old Sin Sin has his uses, Lola. Those doors are perfectly made."

"Pooh!" scoffed the woman, with a flash of her dark eyes; "he is half a ship's carpenter and half an ape!"

She moved along the passage, her arm linked in that of Sir Lucien. The others followed, and:

"Is she truly *married* to that dreadful Chinaman?" whispered Mollie Gretna.

"Yes, I believe so," murmured Kilfane. "She is known as Mrs. Sin Sin Wa."

"Oh!" Mollie's eyes opened widely. "I almost envy her! I have read that Chinamen tie their wives to beams in the roof and lash them with leather thongs until they swoon. I could die for a man who lashed me with leather thongs. Englishmen are so ridiculously gentle to women."

Opening a door on the left of the corridor, Mrs. Sin displayed a room screened off into three sections. One shaded lamp high up near the ceiling served to light all the cubicles, which were heated by small charcoal stoves. These cubicles were identical in shape and appointment, each being draped with quaint Chinese tapestry and containing rugs, a silken divan, an armchair, and a low, Eastern table.

"Choose for yourself," said Mrs. Sin, turning to Rita and Mollie Gretna. "Nobody else come to-night. You two in this room, eh? Next door each other for company."

She withdrew, leaving the two girls together. Mollie clasped her hands ecstatically.

"Oh, my dear!" she said. "What do you think of it all?"

"Well," confessed Rita, looking about her, "personally I feel rather nervous."

"My dear!" cried Mollie. "I am simply quivering with delicious terror!"

Rita became silent again, looking about her, and listening. The harsh voice of the Cuban-Jewess could be heard from a neighboring room, but otherwise a perfect stillness reigned in the house of Sin Sin Wa. She remembered that Mrs. Sin had said, "It is quiet—so quiet."

"The idea of undressing and reclining on these divans in real Oriental fashion," declared Mollie, giggling, "makes me feel that I am an odalisque already. I have dreamed that I was an odalisque, dear—after smoking, you know. It was heavenly. At least, I don't know that 'heavenly' is quite the right word."

And now that evil spirit of abandonment came to Rita—communicated to her, possibly, by her companion. Dread, together with a certain sense of moral reluctance, departed; and she began to enjoy the adventure at last. It was as though something in the faintly perfumed atmosphere of the place had entered into her blood, driving out reserve and stifling conscience.

When Sir Lucien reappeared she ran to him excitedly, her charming face flushed and her eyes sparkling.

"Oh, Lucy," she cried, "how long will our things be? I'm keen to smoke!"

His jaw hardened, and when he spoke it was with a drawl more marked than usual.

"Mareno will be here almost immediately," he answered.

The tone constituted a rebuff, and Rita's coquetry deserted her, leaving her mortified and piqued. She stared at Pyne, biting her lip.

"You don't like me to-night," she declared. "If I look ugly, it's your fault; you told me to wear this horrid old costume!"

He laughed in a forced, unnatural way.

"You are quite well aware that you could never look otherwise than maddeningly beautiful," he said harshly. "Do you want me to recall the fact to you again that you are shortly to be Monte Irvin's wife—or should you prefer me to remind you that you have declined to be mine?"

Turning slowly, he walked away, but:

"Oh, Lucy!" whispered Rita.

He paused, looking back.

"I know now why you didn't want me to come," she said. "I—I'm sorry."

The hard look left Sir Lucien's face immediately and was replaced by a curious, indefinable expression, an expression which rarely appeared there.

"You only know half the reason," he replied softly.

At that moment Mrs. Sin came in, followed by Mareno carrying two dressing-cases. Mollie Gretna had run off to Kilfane, and could be heard talking loudly in another room; but, called by Mrs. Sin, she now returned, wide-eyed with excitement.

Mrs. Sin cast a lightning glance at Sir Lucien, and then addressed Rita.

"Which of these three rooms you choose?" she asked, revealing her teeth in one of those rapid smiles which were mirthless as the eternal smile of Sin Sin Wa.

"Oh," said Rita hurriedly, "I don't know. Which do you want, Mollie?"

"I love this end one!" cried Mollie. "It has cushions which simply reek of Oriental voluptuousness and cruelty. It reminds me of a delicious book I have been reading called *Musk, Hashish, and Blood.*"

"Hashish!" said Mrs. Sin, and laughed harshly. "One night you shall eat the hashish, and then——"

She snapped her fingers, glancing from Rita to Pyne.

"Oh, really? Is that a promise?" asked Mollie eagerly.

"No, no," answered Mrs. Sin. "It is a threat!"

Something in the tone of her voice as she uttered the last four words in mock dramatic fashion caused Mollie and Rita to stare at one another questioningly. That suddenly altered tone had awakened an elusive memory, but neither of them could succeed in identifying it.

Mareno, a lean, swarthy fellow, his foreign cast of countenance accentuated by close-cut side-whiskers, deposited Miss Gretna's case in the cubicle which she had selected and, Rita pointing to that adjoining it, he disposed the second case beside the divan and departed silently. As the sound of a closing door reached them:

"You notice how quiet it is?" asked Mrs. Sin.

"Yes," replied Rita. "It is extraordinarily quiet."

"This an empty house—'To let,'" explained Mrs. Sin. "We watch it stay so. Sin the landlord, see? Windows all boarded up and everything padded. No sound outside, no sound inside. Sin call it the 'House of a Hundred Raptures,' after the one he have in Buenos Ayres."

The voice of Cyrus Kilfane came, querulous, from a neighboring room.

"Lola, my dear, I am almost ready."

"Ho!" Mrs. Sin uttered a deep-toned laugh. "He is a glutton for *chandu!* I am coming, Cy."

She turned and went out. Sir Lucien paused for a moment, permitting her to pass, and:

"Good night, Rita," he said in a low voice. "Happy dreams!"

He moved away.

"Lucy!" called Rita softly.

"Yes?"

"Is it—is it really safe here?"

Pyne glanced over his shoulder towards the retreating figure of Mrs. Sin, then:

"I shall be awake," he replied. "I would rather you had not come, but since you are here you must go through with it." He glanced again along the narrow passage created by the presence of the partitions, and spoke in a voice lower yet. "You have never really trusted me, Rita. You were wise. But you can trust me now. Good night, dear."

He walked out of the room and along the carpeted corridor to a little apartment at the back of the house, furnished comfortably but in execrably bad taste. A cheerful fire was burning in the grate, the flue of which had been ingeniously diverted by Sin Sin Wa so that the smoke issued from a chimney of the adjoining premises. On the mantelshelf, which was garishly draped, were a number of photographs of Mrs. Sin in Spanish dancing costume.

Pyne seated himself in an armchair and lighted a cigarette. Except for the ticking of a clock the room was silent as a padded cell. Upon a little Moorish table beside a deep, low settee lay a complete opium-smoking outfit.

Lolling back in the chair and crossing his legs, Sir Lucien became lost in abstraction, and he was thus seated when, some ten minutes later, Mrs. Sin came in.

"Ah!" she said, her harsh voice softened to a whisper. "I wondered. So you wait to smoke with me?"

Pyne slowly turned his head, staring at her as she stood in the doorway, one hand resting on her hip and her shapely figure boldly outlined by the kimona.

"No," he replied. "I don't want to smoke. Are they all provided for?"

Mrs. Sin shook her head.

"Not Cy," she said. "Two pipes are nothing to him. He will need two more—perhaps three. But you are not going to smoke?"

"Not to-night, Lola."

She frowned, and was about to speak, when:

"Lola, my dear," came a distant, querulous murmur. "Give me another pipe."

Mrs. Sin tossed her head, turned, and went out again. Sir Lucien lighted another cigarette. When finally the woman came back, Cyrus Kilfane had presumably attained the opium-smoker's paradise, for Lola closed the door and seated herself upon the arm of Sir Lucien's chair. She bent down, resting her dusky cheek against his.

"You smoke with me?" she whispered coaxingly.

"No, Lola, not to-night," he said, patting her jewel-laden hand and looking aside into the dark eyes which were watching him intently.

Mrs. Sin became silent for a few moments.

"Something has changed in you," she said at last. "You are different—lately."

"Indeed!" drawled Sir Lucien. "Possibly you are right. Others have said the same thing."

"You have lots of money now. Your investments have been good. You want to become respectable, eh?"

Pyne smiled sardonically.

"Respectability is a question of appearance," he replied. "The change to which you refer would seem to go deeper."

"Very likely," murmured Mrs. Sin. "I know why you don't smoke. You have promised your pretty little friend that you will stay awake and see that nobody tries to cut her sweet white throat."

Sir Lucien listened imperturbably.

"She is certainly nervous," he admitted coolly. "I may add that I am sorry I brought her here."

"Oh," said Mrs. Sin, her voice rising half a note. "Then why do you bring her to the House?"

"She made the arrangement herself, and I took the easier path. I am considering your interests as much as my own, Lola. She is about to marry Monte Irvin, and if his suspicions were aroused he is quite capable of digging down to the 'Hundred Raptures.' "

"You brought her to Kazmah's."

"She was not at that time engaged to Irvin."

"Ah, I see. And now everybody says you are changed. Yes, she is a charming friend."

Pyne looked up into the half-veiled dark eyes.

"She never has been and never can be any more to me, Lola," he said.

At those words, designed to placate, the fire which smouldered in Lola's breast burst into sudden flame. She leapt to her feet, confronting Sir Lucien.

"I know! I know!" she cried harshly. "Do you think I am blind? If she had been like any of the others, do you suppose it would have mattered to *me*? But you *respect* her— you *respect* her!"

Eyes blazing and hands clenched, she stood before him, a woman mad with jealousy, not of a successful rival but of a respected one. She quivered with passion, and Pyne, perceiving his mistake too late, only preserved his wonted composure by dint of a great effort. He grasped Lola and drew her down on to the arm of the chair by sheer force, for she resisted savagely. His ready wit had been at work, and:

"What a little spitfire you are," he said, firmly grasping her arms which felt rigid to the touch. "Surely you can understand? Rita amused me, at first; then, when I found she was going to marry Monte Irvin I didn't bother about her any more. In fact, because I like and admire Irvin, I tried to keep her away from the dope. We don't want trouble with a man of that type, who has all sorts of influence; besides, Monte Irvin is a good fellow."

Gradually, as he spoke, the rigid arms relaxed and the lithe body ceased to quiver. Finally, Lola sank back against his shoulder, sighing.

"I don't believe you," she whispered. "You are telling me lies. But you have always told me lies; one more does not matter, I suppose. How strong you are. You have hurt my wrists.

You will smoke with me now?"

For a moment Pyne hesitated; then:

"Very well," he said. "Go and lie down. I will roast the *chandu*."

Chapter XVIII

THE DREAM OF SIN SIN WA

For an habitual opium-smoker to abstain when the fumes of *chandu* actually reach his nostrils is a feat of will-power difficult adequately to appraise. An ordinary tobacco smoker cannot remain for long among those who are enjoying the fragrant weed without catching the infection and beginning to smoke also. Twice to redouble the lure of my lady Nicotine would be but loosely to estimate the seduction of the Spirit of the Poppy; yet Sir Lucien Pyne smoked one pipe with Mrs. Sin, and perceiving her to be already in a state of dreamy abstraction, loaded a second, but in his own case with a fragment of cigarette stump which smouldered in a tray upon the table. His was that rare type of character whose possessor remains master of his vices.

Following the fourth pipe—Pyne, after the second, had ceased to trouble to repeat his feat of legerdemain—"the sleep" claimed Mrs. Sin. Her languorous eyes closed, and her face assumed that rapt expression of Buddha-like beatitude which Rita had observed at Kilfane's flat. According to some scientific works on the subject, sleep is not invariably induced in the case of Europeans by the use of *chandu*. Loosely, this is true. But this type of European never becomes an habitué; the habitué always sleeps. That dream-world to which opium alone holds the key becomes the real world—for the delights of which the smoker gladly resigns all mundane interests. The exiled Chinaman returns again to the sampan of his boyhood, floating joyously on the waters of some willow-lined canal; the Malay hears once more the mystic whispering in the mangrove swamps, or scents the fragrance of nutmeg and cinnamon in the far-off golden Chersonese. Mrs. Sin doubtless lived anew the triumphs of earlier days in Buenos Ayres, when she had been La Belle Lola, the greatly beloved, and before she had met and married Sin Sin Wa. *Chandu* gives much, but claims all, and he who would open the poppy-gates must close the door of ambition and bid farewell to manhood.

Sir Lucien stood looking at the woman, and although one pipe had affected him but slightly, his imagination momentarily ran riot and a pageant of his life swept before him, so that his jaw grew hard and grim and he clenched his hands convulsively. An unbroken stillness prevailed in the opium-house of Sin Sin Wa.

Recovering from his fit of abstraction, Pyne, casting a final keen glance at the sleeper, walked out of the room. He looked along the carpeted corridor in the direction of the cubicles, paused, and then opened the heavy door masking the recess behind the cupboard. Next opening the false back of the cupboard, he passed through to the lumber-room beyond, and partly closed the second door.

He descended the stair and went along the passage; but ere he reached the door of the room on the ground floor:

"Hello! hello Sin Sin! Sin Win Wa!" croaked the raven. "Number one p'lice chop, lo!" The note of a police whistle followed, rendered with uncanny fidelity.

Pyne entered the room. It presented the same aspect as when he had left it. The ship's lantern stood upon the table, and Sin Sin Wa sat upon the tea-chest, the great black bird perched on his shoulder. The fire in the stove had burned lower, and its downcast glow revealed less mercilessly the dirty condition of the floor. Otherwise no one, nothing, seemed to have been disturbed. Pyne leaned against the doorpost, taking out and lighting a cigarette. The eye of Sin Sin Wa glanced sideways at him.

"Well, Sin Sin," said Sir Lucien, dropping a match and extinguishing it under his foot, "you see I am not smoking *chandu* to-night."

"No smokee," murmured the Chinaman. "Velly good stuff."

"Yes, the stuff is all right, Sin."

"Number one ploper," crooned Sin Sin Wa, and relapsed into smiling silence.

"Number one p'lice," croaked the raven sleepily. "Smartest——" He even attempted the castanets imitation, but was overcome by drowsiness.

For a while Sir Lucien stood watching the singular pair and smiling in his ironical fashion. The motive which had prompted him to leave the neighboring house and to seek the companionship of Sin Sin Wa was so obscure and belonged so peculiarly to the superdelicacies of chivalry, that already he was laughing at himself. But, nevertheless, in this house

and not in its secret annex of a Hundred Raptures he designed to spend the night. Presently:

"Hon'lable p'lice patlol come 'long plenty soon," murmured Sin Sin Wa.

"Indeed?" said Sir Lucien, glancing at his wrist-watch. "The door is open above."

Sin Sin Wa raised one yellow forefinger, without moving either hand from the knee upon which it rested, and shook it slightly to and fro.

"Allee lightee," he murmured. "No bhobbery. Allee peaceful fellers."

"Will they want to come in?"

"Wantchee dlink," replied Sin Sin Wa.

"Oh, I see. If I go out into the passage it will be all right?"

"Allee lightee."

Even as he softly crooned the words came a heavy squelch of rubbers upon the wet pavement outside, followed by a rapping on the door. Sin Sin Wa glanced aside at Sir Lucien, and the latter immediately withdrew, partly closing the door. The Chinaman shuffled across and admitted two constables. The raven, remaining perched upon his shoulder, shrieked, "Smartest leg in Buenos Ayres," and, fully awakened, rattled invisible castanets.

The police strode into the stuffy little room without ceremony, a pair of burly fellows, fresh-complexioned, and genial as men are wont to be who have reached a welcome resting-place on a damp and cheerless night. They stood by the stove, warming their hands; and one of them stooped, took up the little poker, and stirred the embers to a brighter glow.

"Been havin' a pipe, Sin?" he asked, winking at his companion. "I can smell something like opium!"

"No smokee opium," murmured Sin Sin Wa complacently. "Smokee Woodbine."

"Ho, ho!" laughed the other constable. "I *don't* think."

"You likee tly one piecee pipee one time?" inquired the Chinaman. "Gotchee fliend makee smokee."

The man who had poked the fire slapped his companion on the back.

"Now's your chance, Jim!" he cried. "You always said you'd like to have a cut at it."

"H'm!" muttered the other. "A 'double' o' that fifteen over-proof Jamaica of yours, Sin, would hit me in a tender spot to-night."

"Lum?" murmured Sin Sin blandly. "No hab got."

He resumed his seat on the tea-chest, and the raven muttered sleepily, "Sin Sin—Sin——"

"H'm!" repeated the constable.

He raised the skirt of his heavy top-coat, and from his trouser-pocket drew out a leather purse. The eye of Sin Sin Wa remained fixed upon a distant corner of the room. From the purse the constable took a shilling, ringing it loudly upon the table.

"Double rum, miss, please!" he said, facetiously. "There's no treatin' allowed nowadays, so my pal's payin' for his own!"

"I stood *yours* last night, Jim, anyway!" cried the other, grinning. "Go on, stump up!"

Jim rang a second shilling on the table.

"*Two* double rums!" he called.

Sin Sin Wa reached a long arm into the little cupboard beside him and withdrew a bottle and a glass. Leaning forward he placed bottle and glass on the table, and adroitly swept the coins into his yellow palm.

"Number one p'lice chop," croaked the raven.

"You're right, old bird!" said Jim, pouring out a stiff peg of the spirit and disposing of it at a draught. "We should freeze to death on this blasted riverside beat if it wasn't for Sin Sin."

He measured out a second portion for his companion, and the latter drank the raw spirit off as though it had been ale, replaced the glass on the table, and having adjusted his belt and lantern in that characteristic way which belongs exclusively to members of the Metropolitan Police Force, turned and departed.

"Good night, Sin," he said, opening the door.

"So-long," mumured the Chinaman.

"Good night, old bird," cried Jim following his colleague.

"So-long."

The door closed, and Sin Sin Wa, shuffling across, rebolted it. As Sir Lucien came out from his hiding-place Sin Sin Wa returned to his seat on the tea-chest, first putting the glass, unwashed, and the rum bottle back in the cupboard.

To the ordinary observer the Chinaman presents an inscrutable mystery. His seemingly unemotional character and his racial inability to express his thoughts intelligibly in any European tongue stamp him as a creature apart, and one whom many are prone erroneously to classify very low in the human scale and not far above the ape. Sir Lucien usually spoke to Sin Sin Wa in English, and the other replied in that weird jargon known as "pidgin." But the Sin Sin Wa who murmured gibberish and the Sin Sin Wa who could converse upon many and curious subjects in his own language were two different beings—as Sir Lucien was aware. Now, as the one-eyed Chinaman resumed his seat and the one-eyed raven sank into slumber, Pyne suddenly spoke in Chinese, a tongue which he understood as it is understood by few Englishmen; that strange, sibilant speech which is alien from all Western conceptions of oral intercourse as the Chinese institutions and ideals are alien from those of the rest of the civilized world.

"So you make a profit on your rum, Sin Sin Wa," he said ironically, "at the same time that you keep in the good graces of the police?"

Sin Sin Wa's expression underwent a subtle change at the sound of his native language. He moved his hands and became slightly animated.

"A great people of the West, most honorable sir," he replied in the pure mandarin dialect, "claim credit for having said that 'business is business.' Yet he who thus expressed himself was a Chinaman."

"You surprise me."

"The wise man must often find occasion for surprise, most honorable sir."

Sir Lucien lighted a cigarette.

"I sometimes wonder, Sin Sin Wa," he said slowly, "what your aim in life can be. Your father was neither a ship's carpenter nor a shopkeeper. This I know. Your age I do not know and cannot guess; but you are no longer young. You covet wealth. For what purpose, Sin Sin Wa?"

Standing behind the Chinaman, Sir Lucien's dark face, since he made no effort to hide his feelings, revealed the fact that he attached to this seemingly abstract discussion a greater importance than his tone of voice might have led one to suppose. Sin Sin Wa remained silent for some time, then:

"Most honorable sir," he replied, "when I have smoked the opium, before my eyes—for in dreams I have two—a certain picture arises. It is that of a farm in the province of Ho-Nan. Beyond the farm stretch paddy-fields as far as one can see. Men and women and boys and girls move about the farm, happy in their labors; and far, far away dwell the mountain gods, who send the great Yellow River sweeping down through the valleys where the poppy is in bloom. It is to possess that farm, most honorable sir, and those paddy-fields that I covet wealth."

"And in spite of the opium which you consume, you have never lost sight of this ideal?"

"Never."

"But—your wife?"

Sin Sin Wa performed a curious shrugging movement, peculiarly racial.

"A man may not always have the same wife," he replied cryptically. "The honorable wife who now attends to my requirements, laboring unselfishly in my miserable house and scorning the love of other men as she has always done—and as an honorable and upright woman is expected to do—may one day be gathered to her ancestors. A man never knows. Or she may leave me. I am not a good husband. It may be that some little maiden of Ho-Nan, mild-eyed like the musk-deer and modest and tender, will consent to minister to my old age. Who knows?"

Sir Lucien blew a thick cloud of tobacco smoke into the room, and:

"She will never love you, Sin Sin Wa," he said, almost sadly. "She will come to your house only to cheat you."

Sin Sin Wa repeated the eloquent shrug.

"We have a saying in Ho-Nan, most honorable sir," he answered, "and it is this: 'He who has tasted the poppy-cup has nothing to ask of love.' She will cook for me, this little one, and stroke my brow when I am weary, and light my pipe. My eye will rest upon her with pleasure. It is all I ask."

There came a soft rapping on the outer door—three raps, a pause, and then two raps. The raven opened his beady eye.

"Sin Sin Wa," he croaked, "number one p'lice chop, lo!"

Sin Sin Wa glanced aside at Sir Lucien.

"The traffic. A consignment of opium," he said. "Sam Tûk calls."

Sir Lucien consulted his watch, and:

"I should like to go with you, Sin Sin Wa," he said. "Would it be safe to leave the house—with the upper door unlocked?"

Sin Sin Wa glanced at him again.

"All are sleeping, most honorable sir?"

"All."

"I will lock the room above and the outer door. It is safe."

He raised a yellow hand, and the raven stepped sedately from his shoulder on to his wrist.

"Come, Tling-a-Ling," crooned Sin Sin Wa,

"you go to bed, my little black friend, and one day you, too, shall see the paddy-fields of Ho-Nan."

Opening the useful cupboard, he stooped, and in hopped the raven. Sin Sin Wa closed the cupboard, and stepped out into the passage.

"I will bring you a coat and a cap and scarf," he said. "Your magnificient apparel would be out of place among the low pigs who wait in my other disgusting cellar to rob me. Forgive my improper absence for one moment, most honorable sir."

Chapter XIX

THE TRAFFIC

Sir Lucien came out into the alley wearing a greasy cloth cap pulled down over his eyes and an old overall, the collar turned up about a red woollen muffler which enveloped the lower part of his face. The odor of the outfit was disgusting, but this man's double life had brought him so frequently in contact with all forms of uncleanness, including that of the Far East, compared with which the dirt of the West is hygienic, that he suffered it without complaint.

A Chinese "boy" of indeterminable age, wearing a slop-shop suit and a cap, was waiting outside the door, and when Sin Sin Wa appeared, carefully locking up, he muttered something rapidly in his own sibilant language.

Sin Sin Wa made no reply. To his indoor attire he had added a pea-jacket and a bowler hat; and the oddly assorted trio set off westward, following the bank of the Thames in the direction of Limehouse Basin. The narrow, ill-lighted streets were quite deserted, but from the river and the riverside arose that ceaseless jangle of industry which belongs to the great port of London. On the Surrey shore whistles shrieked, and endless moving chains set up their monstrous clangor into the night. Human voices sometimes rose above the din of machinery.

In silence the three pursued their way, crossing inlets and circling around basins dimly divined, turning to the right into a lane flanked by high, eyeless walls, and again to the left, finally to emerge nearly opposite a dilapidated gateway giving access to a small wharf. On the rickety gates bills were posted announcing, "This Wharf to Let." The annexed building appeared to be a mere shell. To the right again they turned, and once more to the left, halting before a two-story brick house which had apparently been converted into a barber's shop. In one of the grimy windows were some loose packets of cigarettes, a soapmaker's advertisement, and a card:

SAM TÛK
BARBER

Opening the door with a key which he carried, the boy admitted Sir Lucien and Sin Sin Wa to the dimly-lighted interior of a room the pretensions of which to be regarded as a shaving saloon were supported by the presence of two chairs, a filthy towel, and a broken mug. Sin Sin Wa shuffled across to another door, and, followed by Sir Lucien, descended a stone stair to a little cellar apparently intended for storing coal. A tin lamp stood upon the bottom step.

Removing the lamp from the step, Sin Sin Wa set it on the cellar floor, which was black with coal dust, then closed and bolted the door. A heap of nondescript litter lay piled in a corner of the cellar. This Sin Sin Wa disturbed sufficiently to reveal a movable slab in the roughly paved floor. It was so ingeniously concealed by coal dust that one who had sought it unaided must have experienced great difficulty in detecting it. Furthermore, it could only be raised in the following manner:

A piece of strong iron wire, which lay among the other litter, was inserted in a narrow slot, apparently a crack in the stone. About an inch of the end of the wire being bent outward to form a right angle, when the seemingly useless piece of scrap-iron had been thrust through the slab and turned, it formed a handle by means of which the trap could be raised.

Again Sin Sin Wa took up the lamp, placing it at the brink of the opening revealed. A pair of wooden steps rested below, and Sir Lucien, who evidently was no stranger to the establishment, descended awkwardly, since there was barely room for a big man to pass. He found himself in the mouth of a low passage, unpaved and shored up with rough timbers in the manner of a mine-working. Sin Sin Wa followed with the lamp, drawing the slab down into its place behind him.

Stooping forward and bending his knees, Sir Lucien made his way along the passage, the Chinaman following. It was of considerable length, and terminated before a strong door bearing a massive lock. Sin Sin Wa reached over the stooping figure of Sir Lucien and unfastened the lock. The two emerged in a kind of dug-out. Part of it had evidently been in existence before the ingenious Sin Sin Wa had exercised his skill upon it, and was of solid brickwork and stone-paved; palpably a storage vault. But it had been altered to suit the Chinaman's purpose, and one end—that in which the passage came out—was timbered. It contained a long counter and many shelves; also a large oil-stove and a number of pots, pans, and queer-looking jars. On the counter stood a ship's lantern. The shelves were laden with packages and bottles. Behind the counter sat a venerable and perfectly bald Chinaman. The only trace of hair upon his countenence grew on the shrunken upper lip—mere wisps of white down. His skin was shrivelled like that of a preserved fig, and he wore big horn-rimmed spectacles. He never once exhibited the slightest evidence of life, and his head and face, and the horn-rimmed spectacles, might quite easily have passed for those of an unwrapped mummy. This was Sam Tûk.

Bending over a box upon which rested a canvas-bound package was a burly seaman engaged in unknotting the twine with which the canvas was kept in place. As Sin Sin Wa and Sir Lucien came in he looked up, revealing a red-bearded, ugly face, very puffy under the eyes.

"Wotcher, Sin Sin!" he said gruffly. "Who's your long pal?"

"Fliend," murmured Sin Sin Wa complacently. "You gotchee *pukka* stuff thisee time, George?"

"I allus brings the *pukka* stuff!" roared the seaman, ceasing to fumble with the knots and glaring at Sin Sin Wa. "Wotcher mean—*pukka* stuff?"

"Gotchee no use for blan," murmured Sin Sin Wa. "Gotchee no use for tin-tack. Gotchee no use for glue."

"Bran!" roared the man, his glance and pose very menacing. "Tin-tacks and glue! Who the flamin' 'ell ever tried to sell *you* glue?"

"Me only wantchee lemindee you," said Sin Sin Wa. "No pidgin."

"George" glared for a moment, breathing heavily; then he stooped and resumed his task, Sin Sin Wa and Sir Lucien watching him in silence. A sound of lapping water was faintly audible.

Opening the canvas wrappings, the man began to take out and place upon the counter a number of reddish balls of "leaf" opium, varying in weight from about eight ounces to a pound or more.

"H'm!" murmured Sin Sin Wa. "Smyrna stuff."

From a pocket of his pea-jacket he drew a long bodkin, and taking up one of the largest balls he thrust the bodkin in and then withdrew it, the steel stained a coffee color. Sin Sin Wa smelled and tasted the substance adhering to the bodkin, weighed the ball reflectively in his yellow palm, and then set it aside. He took up a second, whereupon:

" 'Alf a mo', guvnor!" cried the seaman furiously. "D'you think I'm going to wait 'ere while you prods about in all the blasted lot? It's damn near high tide—I shan't get out. 'Alf time! Savvy? Shove it on the scales!"

Sin Sin Wa shook his head.

"Too muchee slick. Too muchee bhobbery," he murmured. "Sin Sin Wa gotchee sabby what him catchee buy or no pidgin."

"What's the game?" inquired George menacingly. "Don't you know a cake o' Smyrna when you smells it?"

"No sabby lead chop till ploddem withee dipper," explained the Chinaman, imperturbably.

"Lead!" shouted the man. "There ain't no bloody lead in 'em!"

"H'm," murmured Sin Sin Wa smilingly. "So fashion, eh? All velly ploper."

He calmly inserted the bodkin in the second cake; seemed to meet with some obstruction, and laid the ball down upon the counter. From beneath his jacket he took out a clasp-knife attached to a steel chain. Undeterred by a savage roar from the purveyor, he cut the sticky mass in half, and digging his long nails into one of the halves, brought out two lead shots. He directed a glance of his beady eye upon the man.

"Bloody liar," he murmured sweetly. "Lobber."

"Who's a robber?" shouted George, his face flushing darkly, and apparently not resenting the earlier innuendo; "who's a robber?"

"One sarcee Smyrna feller packee stuff so fashion," murmured Sin Sin Wa. "Thief-feller lobbee poor sailorman."

George jerked his peaked cap from his head, revealing a tangle of unkempt red hair. He scratched his skull with savage vigor.

"Blimey!" he said pathetically. " 'Ere's a go! I been done brown, guv'nor."

"Lough luck," murmured Sin Sin Wa, and resumed his examination of the cakes of opium.

The man watched him now in silence, only broken by exclamations of "Blimey" and "Flaming hell" when more shot was discovered. The test concluded:

"Gotchee some more?" asked Sin Sin Wa.

From the canvas wrapping George took out and tossed on the counter a square packet wrapped in grease-paper.

"H'm," murmured Sin Sin Wa, "Patna. Where you catchee?"

"Off of a lascar," growled the man.

The cake of Indian opium was submitted to the same careful scrutiny as that which the balls of Turkish had already undergone, but the Patna opium proved to be unadulterated. Reaching over the counter Sin Sin Wa produced a pair of scales, and, watched keenly by George, weighed the leaf and then the cake.

"Ten-six Smyrna; one 'leben Patna," muttered Sin Sin Wa. "You catchee eighty jimmies."

"Eh?" roared George. "Eighty quid! Eighty quid! Flamin' blind o' Riley! D'you think I'm up the pole? Eighty quid? You're barmy!"

"Eighty-ten," murmured Sin Sin Wa. "Eighty jimmies opium; ten bob lead."

"I give more'n that for it!" cried the seaman. "An' I damn near hit a police boat comin' in, too!"

Sir Lucien spoke a few words rapidly in Chinese. Sin Sin Wa performed his curious Oriental shrug, and taking a fat leather wallet from his hip-pocket, counted out the sum of eighty-five pounds upon the counter.

"You catchee eighty-five," he murmured. "Too muchee plice."

The man grabbed the money and pocketed it without a word of acknowledgment. He turned and strode along the room, his heavy, iron-clamped boots ringing on the paved floor.

"Fetch a glim, Sin Sin," he cried. "I'll never get out if I don't jump to it."

Sin Sin Wa took the lantern from the counter and followed. Opening a door at the further end of the place, he set the lantern at the head of three descending wooden steps discovered. With the opening of the door the sound of lapping water had grown perceptibly louder. George clattered down the steps, which led to a second but much stouter door. Sin Sin Wa followed, nearly closing the first door, so that only a faint streak of light crept down to them.

The second door was opened, and the clangor of the Surrey shore suddenly proclaimed itself. Cold, damp air touched them, and the faint light of the lantern above cast their shadows over unctuous gliding water, which lapped the step upon which they stood. Slimy shapes uprose dim and ghostly from its darkly moving surface.

A boat was swinging from a ring beside the door, and into it George tumbled. He unhitched the lashings, and strongly thrust the boat out upon the water. Coming to the first of the dim shapes, he grasped it and thereby propelled the skiff to another beyond. These indistinct shapes were the piles supporting the structure of a wharf.

"Good night, guv'nor!" he cried hoarsely.

"So-long," muttered Sin Sin Wa.

He waited until the boat was swallowed in the deeper shadows, then reclosed the water-gate and ascended to the room where Sir Lucien awaited. Such was the receiving office of Sin Sin Wa. While the wharf remained untenanted it was not likely to be discovered by the authorities, for even at low tide the river-door was invisible from passing craft. Prospective lesses who had taken the trouble to inquire about the rental had learned that it was so high as to be prohibitive.

Sin Sin Wa paid fair prices and paid cash. This was no more than a commercial necessity; for those who have opium, cocaine, veronal, or heroin to sell can always find a ready market in London and elsewhere. But one sufficiently curious and clever enough to have solved the riddle of the vacant wharf would have discovered that the mysterious owner who showed himself so loath to accept reasonable offers for the property could well afford to be thus independent. Those who control "the traffic" control El Dorado—a city of gold which, unlike the fabled Manoa, actually exists and yields its riches to the unscrupulous adventurer.

Smiling his mirthless, eternal smile, Sin Sin Wa placed the newly purchased stock upon a shelf immediately behind Sam Tûk; and Sam Tûk exhibited the first evidence of animation which had escaped him throughout the progress of the "deal." He slowly nodded his hairless head.

Chapter XX

KAZMAH'S METHODS

Rita Dresden married Monte Irvin in the spring and bade farewell to the stage. The goal long held in view was attained at last. But another farewell which at one time she had contemplated eagerly no longer appeared desirable or even possible. To cocamania had been added a tolerance for opium, and at the last *chandu* party given by Cyrus Kilfane she had learned that she could smoke nearly as much opium as the American habitué.

The altered attitude of Sir Lucien surprised and annoyed her. He, who had first introduced her to the spirit of the coca leaf and to the goddess of the poppy, seemed suddenly to have determined to convince her of the folly of these communions. He only succeeded in losing her confidence. She twice visited the "House of a Hundred Raptures" with Mollie Gretna, and once with Mollie and Kilfane, unknown to Sir Lucien.

Urgent affairs of some kind necessitated his leaving England a few weeks before the date fixed for Rita's wedding, and as Kilfane had already returned to America, Rita recognized with a certain dismay that she would be left to her own resources—handicapped by the presence of a watchful husband.

This subtle change in her view of Monte Irvin she was incapable of appreciating, for Rita was no psychologist. But the effect of the drug habit was pointedly illustrated by the fact that in a period of little more than six months, from regarding Monte Irvin as a rock of refuge—a chance of salvation—she had come to regard him in the light of an obstacle to her indulgence. Not that her respect had diminished. She really loved at last, and so well that the idea of discovery by this man whose wholesomeness was the trait of character which most potently attracted her, was too appalling to be contemplated. The chance of discovery would be enhanced, she recognized, by the absence of her friends and accomplices.

Of course she was acquainted with many other devotees. In fact, she met so many of them that she had grown reconciled to her habits, believing them to be common to all "smart" people—a part of the Bohemian life. The truth of the matter was that she had become a prominent member of a coterie closely knit and associated by a bond of mutual vice—a kind of masonry whereof Kazmah of Bond Street was Grand Master and Mrs. Sin Grand Mistress.

The relations existing between Kazmah and his clients were of a most peculiar nature, too, and must have piqued the curiosity of anyone but a drug-slave. Having seen him once, in his oracular cave, Rita had been accepted as one of the initiated. Thereafter she had had no occasion to interview the strange, immobile Egyptian, nor had she experienced any desire to do so. The method of obtaining drugs was a simple one. She had merely to present herself at the establishment in Bond Street and to purchase either a flask of perfume or a box of sweetmeats. There were several varieties of perfume, and each corresponded to a particular drug. The sweetmeats corresponded to morphine. Rashîd, the attendant, knew all Kazmah's clients, and with the box or flask he gave them a quantity of the required drug. This scheme was precautionary. For if a visitor should chance to be challenged on leaving the place, there was the legitimate purchase to show in evidence of the purpose of the visit.

No conversation was necessary: merely the selection of a scent and the exchange of a sum of money. Rashîd retired to wrap up the purchase, and with it a second and smaller package was slipped into the customer's hand. That the prices charged were excessive—nay, ridiculous—did not concern Rita, for, in common with the rest of her kind, she was careless of expenditure.

Chandu, alone, Kazmah did not sell. He sold morphine, tincture of opium, and other preparations; but those who sought the solace of the pipe were compelled to deal with Mrs. Sin. She would arrange *chandu* parties, or would prepare the "Hundred Raptures" in Limehouse for visitors; but, except in the form of opiated cigarettes, she could rarely be induced to part with any of the precious gum. Thus she cleverly kept a firm hold upon the devotees of the poppy.

Drug-takers form a kind of brotherhood, and outside the charmed circle they are secretive as members of the Mafia, the Camorra, or the Catouse-Menegant. In this secrecy, which, indeed, is a recognized symptom of drug mania, lay Kazmah's security. Rita experienced no desire to peer behind the veil which, literally and metaphorically, he had placed between himself and the world. At first she had been vaguely curious, and had questioned Sir Lucien and others, but nobody seemed to know the real identity of Kazmah, and nobody seemed to care provided that he continued to supply drugs. They all led secret, veiled lives, these slaves of the laboratory, and that Kazmah should do likewise did not surprise them: he had excellent reasons.

During this early stage of faint curiosity she had suggested to Sir Lucien that for Kazmah to conduct a dream-reading business seemed to be to add to the likelihood of police interference.

The baronet had smiled sardonically.

"It is an additional safeguard," he had assured her. "It corresponds to the method of a notorious Paris assassin who was very generally regarded by the police as a cunning pickpocket. Kazmah's business of 'dream-reading' does not actually come within the Act. He is clever enough for that. Remember, he does not profess to tell fortunes. It also enables him to balk idle curiosity."

At the time of her marriage Rita was hopelessly in the toils, and had been really panic-stricken at the prospect—once so golden—of a protracted sojourn abroad. The war, which rendered travel impossible, she regarded rather in the light of a heaven-sent boon. Irvin, though personally favoring a quiet ceremony, recognized that Rita cherished a desire to quit theatreland in a chariot of fire, and accordingly the wedding was on a scale of magnificence which outshone that of any other celebrated during the season. Even the lugubrious Mr. Esden, who gave his daughter away, was seen to smile twice. Mrs. Esden moved in a rarified atmosphere of gratified ambition and parental pride, which no doubt closely resembled that which the angels breathe.

It was during the early days of her married life, and while Sir Lucien was still abroad, that Rita began to experience difficulty in obtaining the drugs which she required. She had lost touch to a certain extent with her former associates; but she had retained her maid, Nina, and the girl regularly went to Kazmah's and returned with the little flasks of perfume. When an accredited representative was sent upon such a mission, Kazmah dispatched the drugs disguised in a scent flask; but on each successive occasion that

Nina went to him the prices increased, and finally became so exorbitant that even Rita grew astonished and dismayed.

She mentioned the matter to another habitué, a lady of title addicted to the use of the hypodermic syringe, and learned that she (Rita) was being charged nearly twice as much as her friend.

"I should bring the man to his senses, dear," said her ladyship. "I know a doctor who will be only too glad to supply you. When I say a doctor, he is no longer recognized by the B.M.A., but he's none the less clever and kind for all that."

To the clever and kind medical man Rita repaired on the following day, bearing a written introduction from her friend. The discredited physician supplied her for a short time, charging only moderate fees. Then, suddenly, this second source of supply was closed. The man declared that he was being watched by the police, and that he dared not continue to supply her with cocaine and veronal. His shifty eyes gave the lie to his words, but he was firm in his resolution, whatever may have led him to it, and Rita was driven back to Kazmah. His charges had become more extortionate than ever, but her need was imperative. Nevertheless, she endeavored to find another drug dealer, and after a time was again successful.

At a certain supper club she was introduced to a suave little man, quite palpably an uninterned alien, who smilingly offered to provide her with any drug to be found in the British Pharmacopeia, at most moderate charges. With this little German-Jew villain she made a pact, reflecting that, provided that his wares were of good quality, she had triumphed over Kazmah.

The craving for *chandu* seized her sometimes and refused to be exorcised by morphia, laudanum, or any other form of opium; but she had not dared to spend a night at the "House of a Hundred Raptures" since her marriage. Her new German friend volunteered to supply the necessary gum, outfit, and to provide an apartment where she might safely indulge in smoking. She declined—at first. But finally, on Mollie Gretna's return from France, where she had been acting as a nurse, Rita and Mollie accepted the suave alien's invitation to spend an evening in his private opium divan.

Many thousands of careers were wrecked by the war, and to the war and the consequent absence of her husband Rita undoubtedly owed her relapse into opium-smoking. That she would have continued secretly to employ cocaine, veronal, and possibly morphine was probable enough; but the constant society of Monte Irvin must have made it extremely difficult for her to indulge the craving for *chandu*. She began to regret the gaiety of her old life. Loneliness and monotony plunged her into a state of suicidal depression, and she grasped eagerly at every promise of excitement.

It was at about this time that she met Margaret Halley, and between the two, so contrary in disposition, a close friendship arose. The girl doctor ere long discovered Rita's secret, of course, and the discovery was hastened by an event which occured shortly after they had become acquainted.

The suave alien gentlemen disappeared.

That was the entire story in five words—or all of the story that Rita ever learned. His apartments were labelled "To Let," and the night clubs knew him no more. Rita for a time was deprived of drugs, and the nervous collapse which resulted revealed to Margaret Halley's trained perceptions the truth respecting her friend.

Kazmah's terms proved to be more outrageous than ever, but Rita found herself again compelled to resort to the Egyptian. She went personally to the rooms in Old Bond Street and arranged with Rashîd to see Kazmah on the following day, Friday, for Kazmah only received visitors by appointment. As it chanced, Sir Lucien Pyne returned to England on Thursday night and called upon Rita at Prince's Gate. She welcomed him as a friend in need, unfolding the pitiful story, to the truth of which her nervous condition bore eloquent testimony.

Sir Lucien began to pace up and down the charming little room in which Rita had received him. She watched him, haggard-eyed. Presently:

"Leave Kazmah to me," he said. "If you visit him he will merely shield himself behind the mystical business, or assure you that he is making no profit on his sales. Kilfane had similar trouble with him."

"Then *you* will see him?" asked Rita.

"I will make a point of interviewing him in the morning. Meanwhile, if you will send Nina around to Albemarle Street in about an hour I will see what can be done."

"Oh, Lucy," whispered Rita, "what a pal you are."

Sir Lucien smiled in his cold fashion.

"I try to be," he said enigmatically; "but I don't always succeed." He turned to her. "Have you ever thought of giving up this doping?" he asked. "Have you ever realized that with increasing tolerance the quantities must increase as well, and that a day is sure to come when——"

Rita repressed a nervous shudder.

"You are trying to frighten me," she replied. "You have tried before; I don't know why. But it's no good, Lucy. You know I cannot give it up."

"You can try."

"I don't want to try!" she cried irritably. "It will be time enough when Monte is back again, and we can really 'live.' This wretched existence, with everything restricted and rationed, and all one's friends in Flanders or Mesopotamia or somewhere, drives me mad! I tell you I should die, Lucy, if I tried to do without it now."

The hollow pretence of reform contemplated in a hazy future did not deceive Sir Lucien. He suppressed a sigh, and changed the topic of conversation.

Chapter XXI

THE CIGARETTES FROM BUENOS AYRES

Sir Lucien's intervention proved successful. Kazmah's charges became more modest, and Rita no longer found it necessary to deprive herself of hats and dresses in order to obtain drugs. But, nevertheless, these were not the halcyon days of old. She was now surrounded by spies. It was necessary to resort to all kinds of subterfuge in order to cover her expenditures at the establishment in Old Bond Street. Her husband never questioned her outlay, but on the other hand it was expedient to be armed against the possibly of his doing so, and Rita's debts were accumulating formidably.

Then there was Margaret Halley to consider. Rita had never hitherto given her confidence to anyone who was not addicted to the same practices as herself, and she frequently experienced embarrassment beneath the grave scrutiny of Margaret's watchful eyes. In another this attitude of gentle disapproval would have been irritating, but Rita loved and admired Margaret, and suffered accordingly.

As for Sir Lucien, she had ceased to understand him. An impalpable barrier seemed to have arisen between them. The inner man had become inaccessible. Her mind was not subtle enough to grasp the real explanation of this change in her old lover. Being based upon wrong premises, her inferences were necessarily wide of the truth, and she believed that Sir Lucien was jealous of Margaret's cousin, Quentin Gray.

Gray met Rita at Margaret Halley's flat shortly after he had returned home from service in the East, and he immediately conceived a violent infatuation for this pretty friend of his cousin's. In this respect his conduct was in no way peculiar. Few men were proof against the seductive Mrs. Monte Irvin, not because she designedly encouraged admiration, but because she was one of those fortunately rare characters who inspire it without conscious effort. Her appeal to men was sweetly feminine and quite lacking in that self-assertive and masculine "take me or leave me" attitude which characterizes some of the beauties of to-day. There was nothing abstract about her delicate loveliness, yet her charm was not wholly physical. Many women disliked her.

At dance, theatre, and concert Quentin Gray played the doting cavalier; and Rita, who was used to at least one such adoring attendant, accepted his homage without demur. Monte Irvin returned to civil life, but Rita showed no disposition to dispense with her new admirer. Both Gray and Sir Lucien had become frequent visitors at Prince's Gate, and Irvin, who understood his wife's character up to a point, made them his friends.

Shortly after Monte Irvin's return Sir Lucien taxed Rita again with her increasing subjection to drugs. She was in a particularly gay humor, as the supplies from Kazmah had been regular, and she laughingly fenced with him when he reminded her of her declared intention to reform when her husband should return.

"You are really as bad as Margaret," she declared. "There is nothing the matter with me. You talk of 'curing' me as though I were ill. Physician, heal thyself!"

The sardonic smile momentarily showed upon Pyne's face, and:

"I know when and where to pull up, Rita," he said. "A woman never knows this. If I were deprived of opium to-morrow I could get along without it."

"I have given up opium," replied Rita. "It's too much trouble, and the last time

Mollie and I went——"

She paused, glancing quickly at Sir Lucien.

"Go on," he said grimly. "I know you have been to Sin Sin Wa's. What happened the last time?"

"Well," continued Rita hurriedly, "Monte seemed to be vaguely suspicious. Besides, Mrs. Sin charged me most preposterously. I really cannot afford it, Lucy."

"I am glad you cannot. But what I was about to say was this: suppose *you* were to be deprived, not of *chandu*, but of cocaine and veronal, do you know what would happen to you?"

"Oh!" whispered Rita, "why *will* you persist in trying to frighten me! I am not going to be deprived of them."

"I persist, dear, because I want you to try, gradually, to depend less upon drugs, so that if the worst should happen you would have a chance."

Rita stood up and faced him, biting her lip.

"Lucy," she said, "do you mean that Kazmah——"

"I mean that anything might happen, Rita. After all, we do possess a police service in London, and one day there might be an accident. Kazmah has certain influence, but it may be withdrawn. Rita, won't you try?"

She was watching him closely, and now the pupils of her beautiful eyes became dilated.

"You know something," she said slowly, "which you are keeping from me."

He laughed and turned aside.

"I know that I am compelled to leave England again, Rita, for a time; and I should be a happier man if I knew that you were not so utterly dependent upon Kazmah."

"Oh, Lucy, are you going away again?"

"I must. But I shall not be absent long, I hope."

Rita sank down upon the settee from which she had risen, and was silent for some time; then:

"I *will* try, Lucy," she promised. "I will go to Margaret Halley, as she is always asking me to do."

"Good girl," said Pyne quietly. "It is just a question of making the effort, Rita. You will succeed, with Margaret's help."

A short time later Sir Lucien left England, but throughout the last week that he remained in London Rita spent a great part of every day in his company. She had latterly begun to experience an odd kind of remorse

for her treatment of the inscrutably reserved baronet. His earlier intentions she had not forgotten, but she had long ago forgiven them; and now she often felt sorry for this man whom she had deliberately used as a stepping-stone to fortune.

Gray was quite unable to conceal his jealousy. He seemed to think that he had a proprietary right to Mrs. Monte Irvin's society, and during the week preceding Sir Lucien's departure Gray came perilously near to making himself ridiculous on more than one occasion.

One night, on leaving a theatre, Rita suggested to Pyne that they should proceed to a supper club for an hour. "It will be like old times," she said.

"But your husband is expecting you," protested Sir Lucien.

"Let's ring him up and ask him to join us. He won't, but he cannot very well object then."

As a result they presently found themselves descending a broad carpeted stairway. From the rooms below arose the strains of an American melody. Dancing was in progress, or, rather, one of those orgiastic ceremonies which passed for dancing during this pagan period. Just by the foot of the stairs they paused and surveyed the scene.

"Why," said Rita, "there is Quentin—glaring insanely, silly boy."

"Do you see whom he is with?" asked Sir Lucien.

"Mollie Gretna."

"But I mean the woman sitting down."

Rita stood on tiptoe, trying to obtain a view, and suddenly:

"Oh!" she exclaimed; "Mrs. Sin!"

The dance at that moment concluding, they crossed the floor and joined the party. Mrs. Sin greeted them with one of her rapid, mirthless smiles. She was wearing a gown noticeable, but not for quantity, even in that semi-draped assembly. Mollie Gretna giggled rapturously. But Gray's swiftly changing color betrayed a mood which he tried in vain to conceal by his manner. Having exchanged a few words with the new arrivals, he evidently realized that he could not trust himself to remain longer, and:

"Now I must be off," he said awkwardly. "I have an appointment—important business. Good night, everybody."

He turned away and hurried from the room. Rita flushed slightly and exchanged a glance with Sir Lucien. Mrs. Sin, who had been watching the three intently, did not fail to perceive this glance. Mollie Gretna characteristically said a silly thing.

"Oh!" she cried. "I wonder whatever is the matter with him! He looks as though he had gone mad!"

"It is perhaps his heart," said Mrs. Sin harshly, and she raised her bold dark eyes to Sir Lucien's face.

"Oh, please don't talk about hearts," cried Rita, wilfully misunderstanding. "Monte has a weak heart, and it frightens me."

"So?" murmured Mrs. Sin. "Poor fellow."

"*I* think a weak heart is most romantic," declared Mollie Gretna.

But Gray's behavior had cast a shadow upon the party which even Mollie's empty light-hearted chatter was powerless to dispel, and when, shortly after midnight, Sir Lucien drove Rita home to Prince's Gate, they were very silent throughout the journey. Just before the car reached the house:

"Where does Mrs. Sin live?" asked Rita, although it was not of Mrs. Sin that she had been thinking.

"In Limehouse, I believe," replied Sir Lucien; "at The House. But I fancy she has rooms somewhere in town also."

He stayed only a few minutes at Prince's Gate, and as the car returned along Piccadilly Sir Lucien, glancing upward towards the windows of a tall block of chambers facing the Green Park, observed a light in one of them. Acting upon a sudden impulse, he raised the speaking-tube.

"Pull up, Fraser," he directed.

The chauffeur stopped the car and Sir Lucien alighted, glancing at the clock inside as he did so, and smiling at his own quixotic behavior. He entered an imposing doorway and rang one of the bells. There was an interval of two minutes or so, when the door opened and a man looked out.

"Is that you, Willis?" asked Pyne.

"Oh, I beg pardon, Sir Lucien. I didn't know you in the dark."

"Has Mr. Gray retired yet?"

"Not yet. Will you please follow me, Sir Lucien. The stairway lights are off."

A few moments later Sir Lucien was shown into the apartment of Gray's which oddly combined the atmosphere of a gymnasium with that of a study. Gray, wearing a dressing-gown and having a pipe in his mouth, was standing up to receive his visitor, his face rather pale and the expression of his lips at variance with that in his eyes. But:

"Hello, Pyne," he said quietly. "Anything wrong—or have you just looked in for a smoke?"

Sir Lucien smiled a trifle sadly.

"I wanted a chat, Gray," he replied. "I'm leaving town to-morrow, or I should not have intruded at such an unearthly hour."

"No intrusion," muttered Gray; "try the armchair—no, the big one. It's more comfortable." He raised his voice: "Willis, bring some fluid!"

Sir Lucien sat down, and from the pocket of his dinner jacket took out a plain brown packet of cigarettes and selected one.

"Here," said Gray, "have a cigar!"

"No, thanks," replied Pyne. "I rarely smoke anything but these."

"Never seen that kind of packet before," declared Gray. "What brand are they?"

"No particular brand. They are imported from Buenos Ayres, I believe."

Willis having brought in a tray of refreshments and departed again, Sir Lucien came at once to the point.

"I really called, Gray," he said, "to clear up any misunderstanding there may be in regard to Rita Irvin."

Quentin Gray looked up suddenly when he heard Rita's name, and:

"What misunderstanding?" he asked.

"Regarding the nature of my friendship with her," answered Sir Lucien coolly. "Now, I am going to speak quite bluntly, Gray, because I like Rita and I respect her. I also like and respect Monte Irvin; and I don't want you, or anybody else, to think that Rita and I are, or ever have been, anything more than pals. I have known her long enough to have learned that she sails straight, and has always sailed straight. Now—listen, Gray, please. You embarrassed me to-night, old chap, and you embarrassed Rita. It was unnecessary." He paused, and then added slowly: "She is as sacred to me, Gray, as she is to you—and we are both friends of Monte Irvin."

For a moment Quentin Gray's fiery temper flickered up, as his heightened color showed, but the coolness of the older and cleverer man prevailed. Gray laughed, stood up, and held out his hand.

"You're right, Pyne!" he said. "But she's damn pretty!" He uttered a loud sigh. "If only she were not married!"

Sir Lucien gripped the outstretched hand, but his answering smile had much pathos in it.

"If only she were not, Gray," he echoed.

He took his departure shortly afterwards, absently leaving a brown packet of cigarettes upon the table. It was an accident. Yet there were few, when the truth respecting Sir Lucien Pyne became known, who did not believe it to have been a deliberate act, designed to lure Quentin Gray into the path of the poppy.

Chapter XXII

THE STRANGLE-HOLD

Less than a month later Rita was in a state of desperation again. Kazmah's prices had soared above anything that he had hitherto extorted. Her bank account, as usual, was greatly overdrawn, and creditors of all kinds were beginning to press for payment. Then, crowning catastrophe, Monte Irvin, for the first time during their married life, began to take an interest in Rita's reckless expenditure. By a combination of adverse circumstances, she, the wife of one of the wealthiest aldermen of the City of London, awakened to the fact that literally she had no money.

She pawned as much of her jewellery as she could safely dispose of, and temporarily silenced the more threatening tradespeople; but Kazmah declined to give credit, and cheques had never been acceptable at the establishment in Old Bond Street.

Rita feverishly renewed her old quest, seeking in all directions for some less extortionate purveyor. But none was to be found. The selfishness and secretiveness of the drug slave made it difficult for her to learn on what terms others obtained Kazmah's precious goods; but although his prices undoubtedly varied, she was convinced that no one of all his clients was so cruelly victimized as she.

Mollie Gretna endeavored to obtain an extra supply to help Rita, but Kazmah evidently saw through the device, and the endeavor proved a failure.

She demanded to see Kazmah, but Rashîd, the Egyptian, blandly assured her that "the Sheikh-el-Kazmah" was away. She cast discretion to the winds and wrote to him, protesting that it was utterly impossible for her to raise so much ready money as he demanded, and begging him to grant her a small supply or to accept the letter as a promissory note to be redeemed in three months. No

answer was received, but when Rita again called at Old Bond Street, Rashîd proposed one of the few compromises which the frenzied woman found herself unwilling to accept.

"The Sheikh-el-Kazmah say, my lady, your friend Mr. Gray never come to him. If you bring him it will be all right."

Rita found herself stricken dumb by this cool proposal. The degradation which awaits the drug slave had never been more succinctly expounded to her. She was to employ Gray's foolish devotion for the commercial advantage of Kazmah. Of course Gray might any day become one of the three wealthiest peers in the realm. She divined the meaning of Kazmah's hitherto incomprehensible harshness (or believed that she did); she saw what was expected of her. "My God!" she whispered. "I have not come to that yet."

Rashîd she knew to be incorruptible or powerless, and she turned away, trembling, and left the place, whose faint perfume of frankincense had latterly become hateful to her.

She was at this time bordering upon a state of collapse. Insomnia, which latterly had defied dangerously increased doses of veronal, was telling upon nerve and brain. Now, her head aching so that she often wondered how long she could retain sanity, she found herself deprived not only of cocaine, but also of malourea. Margaret Halley was her last hope, and to Margaret she hastened on the day before the tragedy which was destined to bring to light the sinister operations of the Kazmah group.

Although, perhaps mercifully, she was unaware of the fact, representatives of Spinker's Agency had been following her during the whole of the preceding fortnight. That Rita was in desperate trouble of some kind her husband had not failed to perceive, and her reticence had quite naturally led him to a certain conclusion. He had sought to win her confidence by every conceivable means and had failed. At last had come doubt—and the hateful interview with Spinker.

As Rita turned in at the doorway below Margaret's flat, then, Brisley was lighting a cigarette in the shelter of a porch nearly opposite, and Gunn was not far away.

Margaret immediately perceived that her friend's condition was alarming. But she realized that whatever the cause to which it might be due, it gave her the opportunity for which she had been waiting. She wrote

a prescription containing one grain of cocaine, but declined firmly to issue others unless Rita authorized her, in writing, to
undertake a cure of the drug habit.

Rita's disjointed statements pointed to a
conspiracy of some kind on the part of those
who had been supplying her with drugs, but
Margaret knew from experience that to exhibit curiosity in regard to the matter would
be merely to provoke evasions.

A hopeless day and a pain-racked, sleepless night found Kazmah's unhappy victim
in the mood for any measure, however desperate, which should promise even temporary relief. Monte Irvin went out very early,
and at about eleven o'clock Rita rang up
Kazmah's, but only to be informed by Rashîd,
who replied, that Kazmah was still away.
"This evening he tell me that he see your
friend if he come, my lady——" As if the
Fates sought to test her endurance to the
utmost, Quentin Gray called shortly afterwards and invited her to dine with him and
go to a theatre that evening.

For five age-long seconds Rita hesitated.
If no plan offered itself by nightfall she knew
that her last scruple would be conquered.
"After all," whispered a voice within her
brain, "Quentin is a man. Even if I took him
to Kazmah's and he was in some way induced to try opium, or even cocaine, he would
probably never become addicted to drug-
taking. But I should have done my part——"

"Very well, Quentin," she heard herself
saying aloud. "Will you call for me?"

But when he had gone Rita sat for more
than half an hour, quite still, her hands
clenched and her face a tragic mask. (Gunn,
of Spinker's Agency, reported telephonically
to Monte Irvin in the City that the Hon.
Quentin Gray had called and had remained
about twenty-five minutes; that he had proceeded to the Prince's Restaurant, and from
there to Mudie's, where he had booked a box
at the Gaiety Theatre.)

Towards the fall of dusk the more dreadful symptoms which attend upon a sudden
cessation of the use of cocaine by a victim of
cocainophagia began to assert themselves
again. Rita searched wildly in the lining of
her jewel-case to discover if even a milligram
of the drug had by chance fallen there from
the little gold box. But the quest was in vain.

As a final resort she determined to go to
Margaret Halley again.

She hurried to Dover Street, and her last
hope was shattered. Margaret was out, and

Janet had no idea when she was likely to
return. Rita had much ado to prevent herself
from bursting into tears. She scribbled a few
lines, without quite knowing what she was
writing, sealed the paper in an envelope, and
left it on Margaret's table.

Of returning to Prince's Gate and dressing
for the evening, she had only a hazy impression. The hammer-beats in her head were
depriving her of reasoning power, and she
felt cold, numbed, although a big fire blazed
in her room. Then as she sat before her mirror, drearily wondering if her face really
looked as drawn and haggard as the image
in the glass, or if definite delusions were beginning, Nina came in and spoke to her. Some
moments elapsed before Rita could grasp the
meaning of the girl's words.

"Sir Lucien Pyne has rung up, Madam,
and wishes to speak to you."

Sir Lucien! Sir Lucien had come back? Rita
experienced a swift return of feverish energy. Half dressed as she was, and without
pausing to take a wrap, she ran out to the
telephone.

Never had a man's voice sounded so sweet
as that of Sir Lucien when he spoke across
the wires. He was at Albemarle Street, and
Rita, wasting no time in explanations, begged
him to await her there. In another ten minutes she had completed her toilette and had
sent Nina to 'phone a cab. (One of the minor
details of his wife's behavior which latterly
had aroused Irvin's distrust was her frequent
employment of public vehicles in preference
to either of the cars.)

Quentin Gray she had quite forgotten,
until, as she was about to leave:

"Is there any message for Mr. Gray,
Madam?" inquired Nina naïvely.

"Oh!" cried Rita. "Of course! Quick! Give
me some paper and a pencil."

She wrote a hasty note, merely asking Gray
to proceed to the restaurant, where she
promised to join him, left it in charge of the
maid, and hurried off to Albemarle Street.

Mareno, the silent, yellow-faced servant
who had driven the car on the night of Rita's
first visit to Limehouse, admitted her. He
showed her immediately into the lofty study,
where Sir Lucien awaited.

"Oh, Lucy—Lucy!" she cried, almost before the door had closed behind Mareno. "I
am desperate—desperate!"

Sir Lucien placed a chair for her. His face
looked very drawn and grim. But Rita was
in too highly strung a condition to observe

this fact, or indeed to observe anything.

"Tell me," he said gently.

And in a torrent of disconnected, barely coherent language, the tortured woman told him of Kazmah's attempt to force her to lure Quentin Gray into the drug coterie. Sir Lucien stood behind her chair, and the icy reserve which habitually rendered his face an impenetrable mask deserted him as the story of Rita's treatment at the hands of the Egyptian of Bond Street was unfolded in all its sordid hideousness. Rita's soft, musical voice, for which of old she had been famous, shook and wavered; her pose, her twitching gestures, all told of a nervous agony bordering on prostration or worse. Finally:

"He dare not refuse *you!*" she cried. "Ring him up and insist upon him seeing me tonight!"

"*I* will see him, Rita."

She turned to him, wild-eyed.

"You shall not! You shall not!" she said. "I am going to speak to that man face to face, and if he is human he must listen to me. Oh! I have realized the hold he has upon me, Lucy! I know what it means, this disappearance of all the others who used to sell what Kazmah sells. If I am to suffer, *he* shall not escape! I swear it. Either he listens to me to-night or I go straight to the police!"

"Be calm, little girl," whispered Sir Lucien, and he laid his hand upon her shoulder.

But she leapt up, her pupils suddenly dilating and her delicate nostrils twitching in a manner which unmistakably pointed to the impossibility of thwarting her if sanity were to be retained.

"Ring him up, Lucy," she repeated in a low voice. "He is there. Now that I have someone behind me I see my way at last!"

"There may, nevertheless, be a better way," said Sir Lucien; but he added quickly: "Very well, dear, I will do as you wish. I have a little cocaine, which I will give you."

He went out to the telephone, carefully closing the study door.

That he had counted upon the influence of the drug to reduce Rita to a more reasonable frame of mind was undoubtedly the fact, for presently as they proceeded on foot towards Old Bond Street he reverted to something like his old ironical manner. But Rita's determination was curiously fixed. Unmoved by every kind of appeal, she proceeded to the appointment which Sir Lucien had made—ignorant of that which Fate held in store for her—and Sir Lucien, also humanly blind, walked on to meet his death.

Part Third

THE MAN FROM WHITEHALL

Chapter XXIII

CHIEF INSPECTOR KERRY RESIGNS

"Come in," said the Assistant Commissioner. The door opened and Chief Inspector Kerry entered. His face was as fresh-looking, his attire as spruce and his eyes were as bright, as though he had slept well, enjoyed his bath and partaken of an excellent breakfast. Whereas he had not been to bed during the preceding twenty-four hours, had breakfasted upon biscuits and coffee, and had spent the night and early morning in ceaseless toil. Nevertheless he had found time to visit a hairdressing saloon, for he prided himself upon the nicety of his personal appearance.

He laid his hat, cane and overall upon a chair, and from a pocket of his reefer jacket took out a big notebook.

"Good morning, sir," he said.

"Good morning, Chief Inspector," replied the Assistant Commissioner. "Pray be seated. No doubt"—he suppressed a weary sigh—"you have a long report to make. I observe that some of the papers have the news of Sir Lucien Pyne's death."

Chief Inspector Kerry smiled savagely.

"Twenty pressmen are sitting downstairs," he said, "waiting for particulars. One of them got into my room." He opened his notebook. "He didn't stay long."

The Assistant Commissioner gazed wearily at his blotting-pad, striking imaginary chords upon the table-edge with his large widely extended fingers. He cleared his throat.

"Er—Chief Inspector," he said, "I fully recognize the difficulties which—you follow me? But the Press is the Press. Neither you nor I could hope to battle against such an institution even if we desired to do so. Where active resistance is useless, a little tact—you quite understand?"

"Quite, sir. Rely upon me," replied Kerry. "But I didn't mean to open my mouth until I had reported to you. Now, sir, here is a précis of evidence, nearly complete, written out clearly by Sergeant Coombes. You would probably prefer to read it?"

"Yes, yes, I will read it. But has Sergeant Coombes been on duty all night?"

"He has, sir, and so have I. Sergeant Coombes went home an hour ago."

"Ah," murmured the Assistant Commissioner.

He took the notebook from Kerry, and resting his head upon his hand began to read. Kerry sat very upright in his chair, chewing slowly and watching the profile of the reader with his unwavering steel-blue eyes. The reading was twice punctuated by telephone messages, but the Assistant Commissioner apparently possessed the Napoleonic faculty of doing two things at once; for his gaze travelled uninterruptedly along the lines of the report throughout the time that he issued telephonic instructions.

When he had arrived at the final page of Coombes' neat, schoolboy writing, he did not look up for a minute or more, continuing to rest his head in the palm of his hand. Then:

"So far you have not succeeded in establishing the identity of the missing man, Kazmah?" he said.

"Not so far, sir," replied Kerry, enunciating the words with characteristic swift precision, each syllable distinct as the rap of a typewriter. "Inspector Whiteleaf, of Vine Street, has questioned all constables in the Piccadilly area, and we have seen members of the staffs of many shops and offices in the neighborhood, but no one is familiar with the appearance of the missing man."

"Ah—now, the Egyptian servant?"

Inspector Kerry moved his shoulders restlessly.

"Rashîd is his name. Many of the people in the neighborhood knew him by sight, and at five o'clock this morning one of my assistants had the good luck to find out, from an Arab coffee-house keeper named Abdulla, where Rashîd lived. He paid a visit to the place—it's off the West India Dock Road—half an hour later. But Rashîd had gone. I regret to report that all traces of him have been lost."

"Ah—considering this circumstance side by side with the facts that no scrap of evidence has come to light in the Kazmah premises and that the late Sir Lucien's private books and papers cannot be found, what do you deduce, Chief Inspector?"

"My report indicates what I deduce, sir!

An accomplice of Kazmah's must have been in Sir Lucien's household! Kazmah and Mrs. Irvin can only have left the premises by going up to the roof and across the leads to Sir Lucien's flat in Albemarle Street. I shall charge the man Juan Mareno."

"What has he to say?" murmured the Assistant Commissioner, absently turning over the pages of the notebook. "Ah, yes. 'Claims to be a citizen of the United States but has produced no papers. Engaged by Sir Lucien Pyne in San Francisco. Professes to have no evidence to offer. Admitted Mrs. Monte Irvin to Sir Lucien's flat on night of murder. Sir Lucien and Mrs. Irvin went out together shortly afterwards, and Sir Lucien ordered him (Mareno) to go for the car to garage in South Audley Street and drive to club, where Sir Lucien proposed to dine. Mareno claims to have followed instructions. After waiting near club for an hour, learned from hall porter that Sir Lucien had not been there that evening. Drove car back to garage and returned to Albemarle Street shortly after eight o'clock.' H'm. Is this confirmed in any way?"

Kerry's teeth snapped together viciously. "Up to a point it is, sir. The club porter remembers Mareno inquiring about Sir Lucien, and the people at the garage testify that he took out the car and returned it as stated."

"No one has come forward who actually saw him waiting outside the club?"

"No one. But unfortunately it was a dark, misty night, and cars waiting for club members stand in a narrow side turning. Mareno is a surly brute, and he might have waited an hour without speaking to a soul. Unless another chauffeur happened to notice and recognize the car nobody would be any wiser."

The Assistant Commissioner sighed, glancing up for the first time.

"You don't think he waited outside the club at all?" he said.

"I don't, sir!" rapped Kerry.

The Assistant Commissioner rested his head upon his hand again.

"It doesn't seem to be germane to your case, Chief Inspector, in any event. There is no question of an alibi. Sir Lucien's wristwatch was broken at seven-fifteen—evidently at the time of his death; and this man Mareno does not claim to have left the flat until after that hour."

"I know it, sir," said Kerry. "He took out the car at half-past seven. What I want to know is where he went to!"

The Assistant Commissioner glanced rapidly into the speaker's fierce eyes.

"From what you have gathered respecting the appearance of Kazmah, does it seem possible that Mareno may be Kazmah?"

"It does not, sir. Kazmah has been described to me, at first hand and at second hand. All descriptions tally in one respect: Kazmah has remarkably large eyes. In Miss Halley's evidence you will note that she refers to them as 'larger than any human eyes I have ever seen.' Now, Mareno has eyes like a pig!"

"Then I take it you are charging him as accessory?"

"Exactly, sir. Somebody got Kazmah and Mrs. Irvin away, and it can only have been Mareno. Sir Lucien had no other resident servant; he was a man who lived almost entirely at restaurants and clubs. Again, somebody cleaned up his papers, and it was somebody who knew where to look for them."

"Quite so—quite so," murmured the Assistant Commissioner. "Of course, we shall learn to-day something of his affairs from his banker. He must have banked *somewhere*. But surely, Chief Inspector, there is a safe or private bureau in his flat?"

"There is, sir," said Kerry grimly; "a safe. I had it opened at six o'clock this morning. It had been hastily cleaned out; not a doubt of it. I expect Sir Lucien carried the keys on his person. You will remember, sir, that his pockets had been emptied?"

"H'm," mused the Assistant Commissioner. "This Cubanis Cigarette Company, Chief Inspector?"

"Dummy goods!" rapped Kerry. "A blind. Just a back entrance to Kazmah's office. Premises were leased on behalf of an agent. This agent—a reputable man of business—paid the rent quarterly. I've seen him."

"And who was his client?" asked the Assistant Commissioner, displaying a faint trace of interest.

"A certain Mr. Isaacs!"

"Who can be traced?"

"Who can't be traced!"

"His checks?"

Chief Inspector Kerry smiled, so that his large white teeth gleamed savagely.

"Mr. Isaacs represented himself as a dealer in Covent Garden who was leasing the office for a lady friend, and who desired, for domestic reasons, to cover his tracks. As ready money in large amounts changes hands in the market, Mr. Isaacs paid ready money to the agent. Beyond doubt the real source of the ready money was Kazmah's."

"But his address?"

"A hotel in Covent Garden."

"Where he lives?"

"Where he is known to the booking-clerk, a girl who allowed him to have letters addressed there. A man of smoke, sir, acting on behalf of someone in the background."

"Ah! and these Bond Street premises have been occupied by Kazmah for the past eight years?"

"So I am told. I have yet to see representatives of the landlord. I may add that Sir Lucien Pyne had lived in Albemarle Street for about the same time."

Wearily raising his head:

"The point is certainly significant," said the Assistant Commissioner. "Now we come to the drug traffic, Chief Inspector. You have found no trace of drugs on the premises?"

"Not a grain, sir!"

"In the office of the cigarette firm?"

"No."

"By the way, was there no staff attached to the latter concern?"

Kerry chewed viciously.

"No business of any kind seems to have been done there," he replied. "An office-boy employed by the solicitor on the same floor as Kazmah has seen a man, and also a woman, go up to the third floor on several occasions, and he seems to think they went to the Cubanis office. But he's not sure, and he can give no useful description of the parties, anyway. Nobody in the building has ever seen the door open before this morning."

The Assistant Commissioner sighed yet more wearily.

"Apart from the suspicions of Miss Margaret Halley, you have no sound basis for supposing that Kazmah dealt in prohibited drugs?" he inquired.

"The evidence of Miss Halley, the letter left for her by Mrs. Irvin, and the fact that Mrs. Irvin said, in the presence of Mr. Quentin Gray, that she had 'a particular reason' for seeing Kazmah, point to it unmistakably, sir. Then, I have seen Mrs. Irvin's maid. (Mr. Monte Irvin is still too unwell to be interrogated.) The girl was very frightened, but she admitted outright that she had been in the habit of going regularly to Kazmah for certain perfumes. She wouldn't admit that she knew the flasks contained cocaine

or veronal, but she did admit that her mistress had been addicted to the drug habit for several years. It began when she was on the stage."

"Ah, yes," murmured the Assistant Commissioner; "she was Rita Dresden, was she not—*The Maid of the Masque?* A very pretty and talented actress. A pity—a great pity. So the girl, characteristically, is trying to save herself?"

"She is," said Kerry grimly. "But it cuts no ice. There is another point. After this report was made out, a message reached me from Miss Halley, as a result of which I visited Mr. Quentin Gray early this morning."

"Dear, dear," sighed the Assistant Commissioner, "your intense zeal and activity are admirable, Chief Inspector, but appalling. And what did you learn?"

From an inside pocket Chief Inspector Kerry took out a plain brown paper packet containing several cigarettes and laid the packet on the table.

"I got these, sir," he said grimly. "They were left at Mr. Gray's house some weeks ago by the late Sir Lucien. They are doped."

The Assistant Commissioner, his head resting upon his hand, gazed abstractedly at the packet. "If only you could trace the source of supply," he murmured.

"That brings me to my last point, sir. From Mrs. Irvin's maid I learned that her mistress was acquainted with a certain Mrs. Sin."

"Mrs. Sin? Incredible name."

"She's a woman reputed to be married to a Chinaman. Inspector Whiteleaf, of Vine Street, knows her by sight as one of the nightclub birds—a sort of mysterious fungus, sir, flowering in the dark and fattening on gilded fools. Unless I'm greatly mistaken, Mrs. Sin is the link between the doped cigarettes and the missing Kazmah."

"Does anyone know where she lives?"

"Lots of 'em know!" snapped Kerry. "But it's making them speak."

"To whom do you more particularly refer, Chief Inspector?"

"To the moneyed asses and the brainless women belonging to a certain West End set, sir," said Kerry savagely. "They go in for every monstrosity from Buenos Ayres, Port Said and Pekin. They get up dances that would make a wooden horse blush. They eat *hashish* and they smoke opium. They inject morphine, and they would have their hair dyed blue if they heard it was 'being done.' "

"Ah," sighed the Assistant Commissioner, "a very delicate and complex case, Chief Inspector. The agony of mind which Mr. Irvin must be suffering is too horrible for one to contemplate. An admirable man, too; honorable and generous. I can conceive no theory to account for the disappearance of Mrs. Irvin other than that she was a party to the murder."

"No sir," said Kerry guardedly. "But we have the dope clue to work on. That the Chinese receive stuff in the East End and that it's sold in the West End every constable in the force is well aware. Leman Street is getting busy, and every shady case in the Piccadilly area will be beaten up within the next twenty-four hours, too. It's purely departmental, sir, from now onwards, and merely a question of time. Therefore I don't doubt the issue."

Kerry paused, cleared his throat, and produced a foolscap envelope which he laid upon the table before the Assistant Commissioner.

"With very deep regret, sir," he said, "after a long and agreeable association with the Criminal Investigation Department, I have to tender you this."

The Assistant Commissioner took up the envelope and stared at it vaguely.

"Ah, yes, Chief Inspector," he murmured. "Perhaps I fail entirely to follow you; I am somewhat overworked, as you know. What does this envelope contain?"

"My resignation, sir," replied Kerry.

Chapter XXIV

TO INTRODUCE 719

Some moments of silence followed. Sounds of traffic from the Embankment penetrated dimly to the room of the Assistant Commissioner; ringing of tram bells and that vague sustained noise which is created by the whirring of countless wheels along hard pavements. Finally:

"You have selected a curious moment to retire, Chief Inspector," said the Assistant Commissioner. "Your prospects were never better. No doubt you have considered the question of your pension?"

"I know what I'm giving up, sir," replied Kerry.

The Assistant Commissioner slowly revolved in his chair and gazed sadly at the speaker. Chief Inspector Kerry met his glance with that fearless, unflinching stare which lent him so formidable an appearance.

"You might care to favor me with some explanation which I can lay before the Chief Commissioner?"

Kerry snapped his white teeth together viciously.

"May I take it, sir, that you accept my resignation?"

"Certainly not. I will place it before the responsible authority. I can do no more."

"Without disrespect, sir, I want to speak to you as man to man. As a private citizen I could do it. As your subordinate I can't."

The Assistant Commissioner sighed, stroking his neatly brushed hair with one large hand.

"Equally without disrespect, Chief Inspector," he murmured, "it is news for me to learn that you have ever refrained from speaking your mind either in my presence or in the presence of any man."

Kerry smiled, unable wholly to conceal a sense of gratified vanity.

"Well, sir," he said, "you have my resignation before you, and I'm prepared to abide by the consequences. What I want to say is this: I'm a man that has worked hard all his life to earn the respect and the trust of his employers. I am supposed to be Chief Inspector of this department, and as Chief Inspector I'll kow-tow to nothing on two legs once I've been put in charge of a case. I work right in the sunshine. There's no grafting about me. I draw my salary every week, and any man that says I earn sixpence in the dark is at liberty to walk right in here and deposit his funeral expenses. If I'm supposed to be under a cloud—there's my reply. But I demand a public inquiry."

At ever increasing speed, succinctly, viciously he rapped out the words. His red face grew more red, and his steel-blue eyes more fierce. The Assistant Commissioner exhibited bewilderment. As the high tones ceased:

"Really, Chief Inspector," he said, "you pain and surprise me. I do not profess to be ignorant of the cause of your—annoyance. But perhaps if I acquaint you with the facts of my own position in the matter you will be open to reconsider your decision."

Kerry cleared his throat loudly.

"I won't work in the dark, sir," he declared truculently. "I'd rather be a pavement artist and my own master than Chief Inspector with an unknown spy following me about."

"Quite so—quite so." The Assistant Commissioner was wonderfully patient. "Very well, Chief Inspector. It cannot enhance my personal dignity to admit the fact, but I'm nearly as much in the dark as yourself."

"What's that, sir?" Kerry sat bolt upright, staring at the speaker.

"At a late hour last night the Secretary of State communicated in person with the Chief Commissioner—at the latter's town residence. He instructed him to offer every facility to a newly appointed agent of the Home Office who was empowered to conduct an official inquiry into the drug traffic. As a result Vine Street was advised that the Home Office investigator would proceed at once to Kazmah's premises, and from thence wherever available clues might lead him. For some reason which has not yet been explained to me, this investigator chooses to preserve a strict anonymity."

Traces of irritation became perceptible in the weary voice. Kerry staring, in silence, the Assistant Commissioner continued:

"I have been advised that this nameless agent is in a position to establish his bona fides at any time, as he bears a number of these cards. You see, Chief Inspector, I am frank with you."

From a table drawer the Assistant Commissioner took a visiting-card, which he handed to Kerry. The latter stared at it as one stares at a rare specimen. It was the card of Lord Wrexborough, His Majesty's Principal Secretary of State for the Home Department, and in the cramped caligraphy of his lordship it bore a brief note, initialled, thus:

To introduce 719

Lord Wrexborough (ⓦ)

Great Cumberland Place, W. 1

Some moments of silence followed; then:

"Seven-one-nine," said Kerry in a high, strained voice. "Why seven-one-nine? And why all this hocus-pocus? Am I to understand, sir, that not only myself but all the Criminal Investigation Department is under a cloud?"

The Assistant Commissioner stroked his hair.

"You are to understand, Chief Inspector, that for the first time throughout my period of office I find myself out of touch with the Chief Commissioner. It is not departmental for me to say so, but I believe the Chief Commissioner finds himself similarly out of touch with the Secretary of State. Apparently very powerful influences are at work, and the line of conduct taken up by the Home Office suggests to my mind that collusion between the receivers and distributors of drugs and the police is suspected by someone. That being so, possibly out of a sense of fairness to all officially concerned, the committee which I understand has been appointed to inquire into the traffic has decided to treat us all alike, from myself down to the rawest constable. It's highly irritating and preposterous, of course, but I cannot disguise from you or from myself that we are on trial, Chief Inspector!"

Kerry stood up and slowly moved his square shoulders in the manner of an athlete about to attempt a feat of weight-lifting. From the Assistant Commissioner's table he took the envelope which contained his resignation, and tore it into several portions. These he deposited in a waste-paper basket.

"That's that!" he said. "I am very deeply indebted to you, sir. I know now what to tell the Press."

The Assistant Commissioner glanced up.

"Not a word about 719," he said; "of course, you understand this?"

"If we don't exist as far as 719 is concerned, sir," said Kerry in his most snappy tones, "719 means nothing to me!"

"Quite so—quite so. Of course, I may be wrong in the motives which I ascribe to this Whitehall agent, but misunderstanding is certain to arise out of a system of such deliberate mystification, which can only be compared to that employed by the Russian police under the Tsars."

Half an hour later Chief Inspector Kerry came out of New Scotland Yard, and, walking down on to the Embankment, boarded a Norwood tramcar. The weather remained damp and gloomy, but upon the red face of Chief Inspector Kerry, as he mounted to the upper deck of the car, rested an expression which might have been described as one of cheery truculence. Where other passengers, coat collars upturned, gazed gloomily from the windows at the yellow murk overhanging the river, Kerry looked briskly about him, smiling pleasurably.

He was homeward bound, and when he presently alighted and went swinging along Spenser Road towards his house, he was still smiling. He regarded the case as having developed into a competition between himself and the man appointed by Whitehall. And it was just such a position, disconcerting to one of less aggressive temperament, which stimulated Chief Inspector Kerry and put him in high good humor.

Mrs. Kerry, arrayed in a serviceable raincoat, and wearing a plain felt hat, was standing by the dining-room door as Kerry entered. She had a basket on her arm. "I was waiting for ye, Dan," she said simply.

He kissed her affectionately, put his arm about her waist, and the two entered the cosy little room. By no ordinary human means was it possible that Mary Kerry should have known that her husband would come home at that time, but he was so used to her prescience in this respect that he offered no comment. She "kenned" his approach always, and at times when his life had been in danger—and these were not of infrequent occurrence—Mary Kerry, if sleeping, had awakened, trembling, though the scene of peril were a hundred miles away, and if awake had blanched and known a deadly sudden fear.

"Ye'll be goin' to bed?" she asked.

"For three hours, Mary. Don't fail to rouse me if I oversleep."

"Is it clear to ye yet?"

"Nearly clear. The dark thing you saw behind it all, Mary, was dope! Kazmah's is a secret drug-syndicate. They've appointed a Home Office agent, and he's working independently of us, but . . ."

His teeth came together with a snap.

"Oh, Dan," said his wife, "it's a race? Drugs? A Home Office agent? Dan, they think the Force is in it?"

"They do!" rapped Kerry. "I'm for Leman Street in three hours. If there's double-dealing behind it, then the mugs are in the East End, and it's folly, not knavery, I'm looking for. It's a race, Mary, and the credit of the Service is at stake! No, my dear, I'll have a snack when I wake. You're going shopping?"

"I am, Dan. I'd ha' started, but I wanted to see ye when ye came hame. If ye've only three hours go straight up the now. I'll ha'

something hot a' ready when ye waken."

Ten minutes later Kerry was in bed, his short clay pipe between his teeth, and *The Meditations of Marcus Aurelius* in his hand. Such was his customary sleeping-draught, and it had never been known to fail. Half a pipe of Irish twist and three pages of the sad imperial author invariably plunged Chief Inspector Kerry into healthy slumber.

Chapter XXV

NIGHT-LIFE OF SOHO

It was close upon midnight when Detective-sergeant Coombes appeared in a certain narrow West End thoroughfare, which was lined with taxicabs and private cars. He wore a dark overcoat and a tweed cap, and although his chin was buried in the genial folds of a woollen comforter, and his cap was pulled over his eyes, his sly smile could easily be detected even in the dim light afforded by the car lamps. He seemed to have business of a mysterious nature among the cabmen; for with each of them in turn he conducted a brief conversation, passing unobtrusively from cab to cab, and making certain entries in a notebook. Finally he disapeared. No one actually saw him go, and no one had actually seen him arrive. At one moment, however, he was there; in the next he was gone.

Five minutes later Chief Inspector Kerry entered the street. His dark overcoat and white silk muffler concealed a spruce dress suit, a fact betrayed by black, braided trousers, unusually tight-fitting, and boots which almost glittered. He carried the silver-headed malacca cane, and had retained his narrow-brimmed bowler at its customary jaunty angle.

Passing the lines of waiting vehicles, he walked into the entrance of a popular night-club which faced the narrow street. On a lounge immediately inside the doorway a heated young man was sitting fanning his dancing partner and gazing into her weakly pretty face in vacuous adoration.

Kerry paused for a moment, staring at the pair. The man returned his stare, looking him up and down in a manner meant to be contemptuous. Kerry's fierce, intolerant gaze became transferred to the face and then the figure of the woman. He tilted his hat further forward and turned aside. The woman's glance followed him, to the marked disgust of her companion.

"Oh," she whispered, "what a delightfully savage man! He looks positively uncivilized. I have no doubt he drags women about by their hair. I *do* hope he's a member!"

Mollie Gretna spoke loudly enough for Kerry to hear her, but unmoved by her admiration he stepped up to the reception office. He was in high good humor. He had spent the afternoon agreeably, interviewing certain officials charged with policing the East End of London, and had succeeded, to quote his own language, in "getting a gale up." Despite the coldness of the weather, he had left two inspectors and a speechlessly indignant superintendent bathed in perspiration.

"Are you a member, sir?" inquired the girl behind the desk.

Kerry smiled genially. A newsboy thrust open the swing-door, yelling: "Bond Street murder! A fresh *development*. Late speshul!"

"Oh!" cried Mollie Gretna to her companion, "get me a paper. Be quick! I am so excited!"

Kerry took up a pen, and in large bold hand-writing inscribed the following across two pages of the visitors' book:

"Chief Inspector Kerry.
Criminal Investigation
Department."

He laid a card on the open book, and, thrusting his cane under his arm, walked to the head of the stairs.

"Cloak-room on the right, sir," said an attendant.

Kerry paused, glancing over his shoulder and chewing audibly. Then he settled his hat more firmly upon his red head and descended the stairs. The attendant went to inspect the visitors' book, but Mollie Gretna was at the desk before him, and:

"Oh, Bill!" she cried to her annoyed cavalier, "it's Inspector Kerry—who is in charge of poor Lucy's murder! Oh, Bill! this is lovely! Something is going to happen! Do come down!"

Followed by the obedient but reluctant "Bill," Mollie ran downstairs, and almost into the arms of a tall dark girl, who, carrying a purple opera cloak, was coming up.

"You're not going yet, Dickey?" asked Mollie, throwing her arms around the other's waist.

"Ssh!" whispered "Dickey." "Inspector

Kerry is here! You don't want to be called as a witness at nasty inquests and things, do you?"

"Good heavens, my dear, no! But why should I be?"

"Why should any of us? But don't you see they are looking for the people who used to go to Kazmah's? It's in the paper to-night. We shall all be served with *subpoenas*. I'm off!"

Escaping from Mollie's embrace, the tall girl ran up the stairs, kissing her hand to Bill as she passed. Mollie hesitated, looking all about the crowded room for Chief Inspector Kerry. Presently she saw him, standing nearly opposite the stairway, his intolerant blue eyes turning right and left, so that the fierce glance seemed to miss nothing and no one in the room. Hands thrust in his overcoat pockets and his cane held under his arms, he inspected the place and its occupants as a very aggressive country cousin might inspect the monkey-house at the Zoo. To Mollie's intense disappointment he persistently avoided looking in her direction.

Although a popular dance was on the point of commencing, several visitors had suddenly determined to leave. Kerry pretended to be ignorant of the sensation which his appearance had created, passing slowly along the room and submitting group after group to deliberate scrutiny; but as news flies through an Eastern bazaar the name of the celebrated detective, whose association with London's latest crime was mentioned by every evening paper in the kingdom, sped now on magic wings; so that there was a muted *charivari* out of which, in every key from bass to soprano, arose ever and anon the words "Chief Inspector Kerry."

"It's perfectly ridiculous but characteristically English," drawled one young man, standing beside Mollie Gretna, "to send out a bally red-headed policeman in preposterous glad-rags to look for a clever criminal. Kerry is well known to all the crooks, and nobody could mistake him. Damn silly— damn silly!"

As "damn silly" Kerry's open scrutiny of the members and visitors must have appeared to others, but it was a deliberate policy very popular with the Chief Inspector, and termed by him "beating." Possessed of an undisguisable personality, Kerry had found a way of employing his natural physical peculiarities to his professional advantage. Where other investigators worked in the dark, secretly, Red Kerry sought the limelight—at the right time. That every hour lost in getting on the track of the mysterious Kazmah was a point gained by the equally mysterious man from Whitehall he felt assured, and although the elaborate but hidden mechanism of New Scotland Yard was at work seeking out the patrons of the Bond Street drug-shop, Kerry was indisposed to await the result.

He had been in the night club only about ten minutes, but during those ten minutes fully a dozen people had more or less hurriedly departed. Because of the arrangements already made by Sergeant Coombes, the addresses of many of these departing visitors would be in Kerry's possession ere the night was much older. And why should they have fled, incontinent, if not for the reason that they feared to become involved in the Kazmah affair? All the cabmen had been warned; and those fugitives who had private cars would be followed.

It was a curious scene which Kerry surveyed, a scene to have interested philosopher and politician alike. For here were representatives of every stratum of society, although some of those standing for the lower strata were suitably disguised. The peerage was well represented, so was Judah; there were women entitled to wear coronets dancing with men entitled to wear the broad arrow, and men whose forefathers had signed Magna Charta dancing with chorus girls from the revues and musical comedies.

Waiting until the dance was fully in progress, Inspector Kerry walked slowly around the room in the direction of the stair. Parties seated at tables were treated each to an intolerant stare, alcoves were inspected and more than one waiter meeting the gaze of the steely eyes, felt a prickling of conscience and recalled past peccadilloes.

Bill had claimed Mollie Gretna for the dance, but:

"No, Bill," she had replied, watching Kerry as if enthralled; "I don't want to dance. I am watching Chief Inspector Kerry."

"That's evident," complained the young man. "Perhaps you would like to spend the rest of the night in Bow Street?"

"Oh," whispered Mollie, "I should love it! I have never been arrested, but if ever I am I hope it will be by Chief Inspector Kerry. I am positive he would haul me away in handcuffs!"

When Kerry came to the foot of the stairs, Mollie quite deliberately got in his way, mur-mured an apology, and gave him a sidelong gaze through lowered lashes, which was more eloquent than any thesis. He smiled with fierce geniality, looked her up and down, and proceeded to mount the stairs, with never a backward glance.

His genius for criminal investigation possessed definite limitations. He could not perhaps have been expected in tactics so completely opposed to those which he had anticipated to recognize the presence of a valuable witness. Student of human nature though undoubtedly he was, he had not solved the mystery of that outstanding exception which seems to be involved in every rule.

Thus, a fellow with a low forehead and a weakly receding chin, Kerry classified as a dullard, a witling, unaware that if the brow were but low enough and the chin virtually absent altogether he might stand in the presence of a second Daniel. Physiognomy is a subtle science, and the exceptions to its rules are often of a sensational character. In the same way Kerry looked for evasion, and, where possible, flight, on the part of one possessing a guilty conscience. Mollie Gretna was a phenomenal exception to a rule otherwise sound. And even one familiar with criminal psychology might be forgiven for failing to detect guilt in a woman anxious to make the acquaintance of a prominent member of the Criminal Investigation Department.

Pausing for a moment in the entrance of the club, and chewing reflectively, Kerry swung open the door and walked out into the street. He had one more cover to "beat," and he set off briskly, plunging into the mazes of Soho, crossing Wardour Street into Old Compton Street, and proceeding thence in the direction of Shaftesbury Avenue. Turning to the right on entering the narrow thoroughfare for which he was bound, he stopped and whistled softly. He stood in the entrance to a court; and from further up the court came an answering whistle.

Kerry came out of the court again, and proceeded some twenty paces along the street to a restaurant. The windows showed no light, but the door remained open, and Kerry entered without hesitation, crossed a darkened room and found himself in a passage where a man was seated in a little apartment like that of a stage-door keeper. He stood up, on hearing Kerry's tread, peering out at the newcomer.

"The restaurant is closed, sir."

"Tell me a better one," rapped Kerry. "I want to go upstairs."

"Your card, sir."

Kerry revealed his teeth in a savage smile and tossed his card on to the desk before the concierge. He passed on, mounting the stairs at the end of the passage. Dimly a bell rang; and on the first landing Kerry met a heavily built foreign gentleman, who bowed.

"My dear Chief Inspector," he said gutturally, "what is this, please? I trust nothing is wrong, eh?"

"Nothing," replied Kerry. "I just want to look round."

"A few friends," explained the suave alien, rubbing his hands together and still bowing, "remain playing dominoes with me."

"Very good," rapped Kerry. "Well, if you think we have given them time to hide the 'wheel' we'll go in. Oh, don't explain. I'm not worrying about stickle-backs to-night. I'm out for salmon."

He opened a door on the left of the landing and entered a large room which offered evidence of having been hastily evacuated by a considerable company. A red and white figured cloth of a type much used in Continental cafés had been spread upon a long table, and three foreigners, two men and an elderly woman, were bending over a row of dominoes set upon one corner of the table. Apparently the men were playing and the woman was watching. But there was a dense cloud of cigar smoke in the room, and mingled with its pungency were sweeter scents. A number of empty champagne bottles stood upon a sideboard and an elegant silk theatre-bag lay on a chair.

"H'm," said Kerry, glaring fiercely from the bottles to the players, who covertly were watching him. "How you two smarts can tell a domino from a door-knocker after cracking a dozen magnums gets me guessing."

He took up the scented bag and gravely handed it to the old woman.

"You have mislaid your bag, madam," he said. "But, fortunately, I noticed it as I came in."

He turned the glance of his fierce eyes upon the man who had met him on the landing, and who had followed him into the room.

"Third floor, von Hindenburg," he rapped, "Don't argue. Lead the way."

For one dangerous moment the man's brow lowered and his heavy face grew blackly menacing. He exchanged a swift look with his friends seated at the disguised roulette table. Kerry's jaw muscles protruded enormously.

"Give me another answer like that," he said in a tone of cold ferocity, "and I'll kick you from here to Paradise."

"No offense—no offense," muttered the man, quailing before the savagery of the formidable Chief Inspector. "You come this way, please. Some ladies call upon me this evening, and I do not want to frighten them."

"No," said Kerry, "you wouldn't, naturally." He stood aside as a door at the further end of the room was opened. "After you, my friend; I said 'lead the way.' "

They mounted to the third floor of the restaurant. The room which they had just quitted was used as an auxiliary dining and supper-room before midnight, as Kerry knew. After midnight the centre table was unmasked, and from thence onward to dawn, sometimes, was surrounded by roulette players. The third floor he had never visited, but he had a shrewd idea that it was not entirely reserved for the private use of the proprietor.

A babel of voices died away as the two men walked into a room rather smaller than that below and furnished with little tables, café fashion. At one end was a grand piano and a platform before which a velvet curtain was draped. Some twenty people, men and women, were in the place, standing looking towards the entrance. Most of the men and all the women but one were in evening dress; but, despite this common armor of respectability, they did not all belong to respectable society.

Two of the women Kerry recognized as bearers of titles, and one was familiar to him as a screen-beauty. The others were unclassifiable, but all were fashionably dressed with the exception of a masculine-looking lady who had apparently come straight off a golf course, and who later was proved to be a well-known advocate of woman's rights. The men all belonged to familiar types. Some of them were Jews.

Kerry, his feet widely apart and his hands thrust in his overcoat pockets, stood staring at face after face and chewing slowly. The proprietor glanced apologetically at his patrons and shrugged. Silence fell upon the company. Then:

"I am a police officer," said Kerry sharply. "You will file out past me, and I want a card from each of you. Those who have no cards will write name and address here."

He drew a long envelope and a pencil from a pocket of his dinner jacket. Laying the envelope and pencil on one of the little tables:

"Quick march!" he snapped. "You, sir——" shooting out his forefinger in the direction of a tall, fair young man, "step out!"

Glancing helplessly about him, the young man obeyed, and approaching Kerry:

"I say, officer," he whispered nervously, "can't you manage to keep my name out of it? I mean to say, my people will kick up the deuce. Anything up to a tenner . . . ."

The whisper faded away. Kerry's expression had grown positively ferocious.

"Put your card on the table," he said tersely, "and get out while my hands stay in my pockets!"

Hurriedly the noble youth (he was the elder son of an earl) complied, and departed. Then, one by one, the rest of the company filed past the Chief Inspector. He challenged no one until a Jew smilingly laid a card on the table bearing the legend: "Mr. John Jones, Lincoln's Inn Fields."

"Hi!" rapped Kerry, grasping the man's arm. "One moment, Mr. 'Jones'! The card I want is in the other case. D'you take me for a mug? That 'Jones' trick was tried on Noah by the blue-faced baboon!"

His perception of character was wonderful. At some of the cards he did not even glance; and upon the women he wasted no time at all. He took it for granted that they would all give false names, but since each of them would be followed it did not matter. When at last the room emptied, he turned to the scowling proprietor, and:

"That's that!" he said. "I've had no instructions about your establishment, my friend, and as I've seen nothing improper going on I'm making no charge, at the moment. I don't want to know what sort of show takes place on your platform, and I don't want to know anything about you that I don't know already. You're a Swiss subject and a dark horse."

He gathered up the cards from the table, glancing at them carelessly. He did not expect to gain much from his possession of these names and addresses. It was among the women that he counted upon finding patrons of Kazmah and Company. But as he was about to drop the cards into his overcoat pocket, one of them, which bore a written note, attracted his attention.

At this card he stared like a man amazed; his face grew more and more red, and:

"Hell!" he said—"Hell! which of 'em was it?"

The card contained the following:—

To introduce 719

Lord Wrexborough ⓦ

Great Cumberland Place, W. 1

Chapter XXVI

THE MOODS OF MOLLIE

Early the following morning Margaret Halley called upon Mollie Gretna.

Mollie's personality did not attract Margaret. The two had nothing in common, but Margaret was well aware of the nature of the tie which had bound Rita Irvin to this empty and decadent representative of English aristocracy. Mollie Gretna was entitled to append the words "The Honorable" to her name, but not only did she refrain from doing so but she even preferred to be known as "Gretna"—the style of one of the family estates.

This pseudonym she had adopted shortly after her divorce, when she had attempted to take up a stage career. But although the experience had proved disastrous, she had retained the *nom de guerre,* and during the past four years had several times appeared at war charity garden-parties as a classical dancer—to the great delight of the guests and greater disgust of her family. Her maternal uncle, head of her house, said to be the most blasé member of the British peerage, and known as "the noble tortoise," was generally considered to have pronounced the final verdict upon his golden-haired niece when he declared "she is almost amusing."

Mollie received her visitor with extravagant expressions of welcome.

"My dear Miss Halley," she cried, "how perfectly sweet of you to come to see me! Of course, I can guess what you have called about. Look! I have every paper published this morning in London! Every one! Oh! poor, darling little Rita! What *can* have become of her!"

Tears glistened upon her carefully made-up lashes and so deep did her grief seem to be that one would never have suspected that she had spent the greater part of the night playing bridge at a "mixed" club in Dover Street, and from thence had proceeded to a military "breakfast-dance."

"It is indeed a ghastly tragedy," said Margaret. "It seems incredible that she cannot be traced."

"Absolutely incredible!" declared Mollie, opening a large box of cigarettes. "Will you have one, dear?"

"No thanks. By the way, they are not from Buenos Ayres, I suppose?"

Mollie, cigarette in hand, stared, round-eyed, and:

"Oh, my dear Miss Halley!" she cried, "what an idea! Such a funny thing to suggest."

Margaret smiled coolly.

"Poor Sir Lucien used to smoke cigarettes of that kind," she explained, "and I thought perhaps you smoked them, too."

Mollie shook her head and lighted the cigarette.

"He gave me one once, and it made me feel quite sick," she declared.

Margaret glanced at the speaker, and knew immediately that Mollie had determined to deny all knowledge of the drug coterie. Because there is no problem of psychology harder than that offered by a perverted mind, Margaret was misled in ascribing this secrecy to a desire to avoid becoming involved in a scandal. Therefore:

"Do you quite realize, Miss Gretna," she said quietly, "that every hour wasted now in tracing Rita may mean, must mean, an hour of agony for her?"

"Oh, don't! please don't!" cried Mollie, clasping her hands. "I cannot bear to think of it."

"God knows in whose hands she is. Then there is poor Mr. Irvin. He is utterly prostrated. One shudders to contemplate his torture as the hours and the days go by and no news comes of Rita."

"Oh, my dear! you are making me cry!" exclaimed Mollie. "If only I could do something to help. . . ."

Margaret was studying her closely, and now for the first time she detected sincere

emotion in Mollie's voice—and unforced tears in her eyes. Hope was reborn.

"Perhaps you can," she continued, speaking gently. "You knew all Rita's friends and all Sir Lucien's. You must have met the woman called Mrs. Sin?"

"Mrs. Sin," whispered Mollie, staring in a frightened way so that the pupils of her eyes slowly enlarged. "What about Mrs. Sin?"

"Well, you see, they seem to think that through Mrs. Sin they will be able to trace Kazmah; and wherever Kazmah is one would expect to find poor Rita."

Mollie lowered her head for a moment, then glanced quickly at the speaker, and quickly away again.

"Please let me explain just what I mean," continued Margaret. "It seems to be impossible to find anybody in London who will admit having known Mrs. Sin or Kazmah. They are all afraid of being involved in the case, of course. Now, if you can help, don't hesitate for that reason. A special commission has been appointed by Lord Wrexborough to deal with the case, and their agent is working quite independently of the police. Anything which you care to tell him will be treated as strictly confidential; but think what it may mean to Rita."

Mollie clasped her hands about her right knee and rocked to and fro in her chair.

"No one knows who Kazmah is," she said.

"But a number of people seem to know Mrs. Sin. I am sure you must have met her?"

"If I say that I know her, shall I be called as a witness?"

"Certainly not. I can assure you of that."

Mollie continued to rock to and fro.

"But if I were to tell the police I should have to go to court, I suppose?"

"I suppose so," replied Margaret. "I am afraid I am dreadfully ignorant of such matters. It might depend upon whether you spoke to a high official or to a subordinate one; an ordinary policeman for instance. But the Home Office agent has nothing whatever to do with Scotland Yard."

Mollie stood up in order to reach an ash-tray, and:

"I really don't think I have anything to say, Miss Halley," she declared. "I have certainly met Mrs. Sin, but I know nothing whatever about her, except I believe she is a Jewess."

Margaret sighed, looking up wistfully into Mollie's face. "Are you quite sure?" she pleaded. "Oh, Miss Gretna, if you know anything—anything—don't hide it how. It may mean so much."

"Oh, I quite understand that," cried Mollie. "My heart simply aches and aches when I think of poor, sweet little Rita. But—really I don't think I can be of the least tiny bit of use."

Their glances met; and Margaret read hostility in the shallow eyes. Mollie, who had been wavering, now for some reason had become confirmed in her original determination to remain silent. Margaret stood up.

"It is no good, then," she said. "We must hope that Rita will be traced by the police. Good-bye, Miss Gretna. I am so sorry you cannot help."

"And so am I!" declared Mollie. "It is perfectly sweet of you to take such an interest, and I feel a positive *worm*. But what can I do?"

As Margaret was stepping into her little runabout car, which awaited her at the door, a theory presented itself to account for Mollie's sudden hostility. It had developed, apparently, as a result of Margaret's reference to the Home Office inquiry. Of course! Mollie would naturally be antagonistic to a commission appointed to suppress the drug traffic.

Convinced that this was the correct explanation, Margaret drove away, reflecting bitterly that she had been guilty of a strategical error which it was now too late to rectify.

In common with others, Kerry among them, who had come in contact with that perverted intelligence, she misjudged Mollie's motives. In the first place, the latter had no wish to avoid publicity, and in the second place—although she sometimes wondered vaguely what she should do when her stock of drugs became exhausted—Mollie was prompted by no particular animosity toward the Home Office inquiry. She had merely perceived a suitable opportunity to make the acquaintance of the fierce red Chief Inspector, and at the same time to secure notoriety for herself.

Ere Margaret's car had progressed a hundred yards from the door, Mollie was at the telephone.

"City 400, please," she said.

An interval elapsed, then:

"Is that the Commissioner's office, New Scotland Yard?" she asked.

A voice replied that it was.

"Could you put me through to Chief Inspector Kerry?"

"What name?" inquired the voice.

Mollie hesitated for three seconds, and then gave her family name.

"Very well, madam," said the voice respectfully. "Please hold on, and I will enquire if the Chief Inspector is here."

Mollie's heart was beating rapidly with pleasurable excitement, and she was as confused as a maiden at her first rendezvous. Then:

"Hello," said the voice.

"Yes?"

"I am sorry, madam. But Chief Inspector Kerry is off duty."

"Oh dear!" sighed Mollie, "what a pity. Can you tell me where I could find him?"

"I am afraid not, madam. It is against the rules to give private addresses of members of any department."

"Oh, very well." She sighed again. "Thank you."

She replaced the receiver and stood biting her finger thoughtfully. She was making a mental inventory of her many admirers and wondering which of them could help her. Suddenly she came to a decision on the point. Taking up the receiver:

"Victoria 8440, please," she said.

Still biting one finger she waited, until:

"Foreign Office," announced a voice.

"Please put me through to Mr. Archie Boden-Shaw," she said.

Ere long that official's secretary was inquiring her name, and a moment later:

"Is that you, Archie?" said Mollie. "Yes! Mollie speaking. No, please listen, Archie! You can get to know everything at the Foreign Office, and I want you to find out for me the private address of Chief Inspector Kerry, who is in charge of the Bond Street murder case. Don't be silly! I've asked Scotland Yard, but they won't tell me. *You* can find out. . . . It doesn't matter why I want to know. . . . Just ring me up and tell me. I *must* know in half an hour. Yes, I shall be seeing you to-night. Good-bye. . . ."

Less than half an hour later, the obedient Archie rang up, and Mollie, all excitement, wrote the following address in a dainty scented notebook which she carried in her handbag.

CHIEF INSPECTOR KERRY,
67 Spenser Road, Brixton.

Chapter XXVII

CROWN EVIDENCE

The appearance of the violet-enamelled motor brougham upholstered in cream, and driven by a chauffeur in a violet and cream livery, created some slight sensation in Spenser Road, S.E. Mollie Gretna's conspicuous car was familiar enough to residents in the West End of London, but to lower middle-class suburbia it came as something of a shock. More than one window curtain moved suspiciously, suggesting a hidden but watchful presence, when the glittering vehicle stopped before the gate of number 67; and the lady at number 68 seized an evidently rare opportunity to come out and polish her letter-box.

She was rewarded by an unobstructed view of the smartest woman in London (thus spake society paragraphers) and of the most expensive set of furs in Europe, also of a perfectly gowned slim figure. Of Mollie's disdainful face, with its slightly uptilted nose, she had no more than a glimpse.

A neat maid, evidently Scotch, admitted the dazzling visitor to number 67; and Spenser Road waited and wondered. It was something to do with the Bond Street murder! Small girls appeared from doorways suddenly opened and darted off to advise less-watchful neighbors.

Kerry, who had been at work until close upon dawn in the mysterious underworld of Soho, was sleeping, but Mrs. Kerry received Mollie in a formal little drawing-room, which, unlike the cosy, homely dining-room, possessed that frigid atmosphere which belongs to uninhabited apartments. In a rather handsome cabinet were a number of trophies associated with the detective's successful cases. The cabinet itself was a present from a Regent Street firm for whom Kerry had recovered valuable property.

Mary Kerry, dressed in a plain blouse and skirt, exhibited no trace of nervousness in the presence of her aristocratic and fashionable caller. Indeed, Mollie afterwards declared that "she was quite a ladylike person. But rather tin tabernacley, my dear."

"Did ye wish to see Chief Inspector Kerry parteecularly?" asked Mary, watching her visitor with calm, observant eyes.

"Oh, most particularly!" cried Mollie, in a flutter of excitement. "Of course I don't know *what* you must think of me for calling

at such a preposterous hour, but there are some things that simply can't wait."

"Aye," murmured Mrs. Kerry. " 'Twill be yon Bond Street affair?"

"Oh, yes, it is, Mrs. Kerry. Doesn't the very name of Bond Street turn your blood cold? I am simply shivering with fear!"

"As the wife of a Chief Inspector I am maybe more used to tragedies than yoursel', madam. But it surely is a sair grim business. My husband is resting the now. He was hard at work a' the night. Nae doubt ye'll be wishin' to see him privately?"

"Oh, if you please. I am sorry to disturb him. I can imagine that he must be literally exhausted after spending a whole night among dreadful people."

Mary Kerry stood up.

"If ye'll excuse me for a moment I'll awaken him," she said. "Our household is sma'."

"Oh, of course!" I quite understand, Mrs. Kerry! So sorry. But so good of you."

"Might I offer ye a glass o' sherry an' a biscuit?"

"I simply couldn't *dream* of troubling you! Please don't suggest such a thing. I feel covered with guilt already. Many thanks nevertheless."

Mary Kerry withdrew, leaving Mollie alone. As soon as the door closed Mollie stood up and began to inspect the trophies in the cabinet. She was far too restless and excited to remain sitting down. She looked at the presentation clock on the mantelpiece and puzzled over the signatures engraved upon a large silver dish which commemorated the joy displayed by the Criminal Investigation Department upon the occasion of Kerry's promotion to the post of Chief Inspector.

The door opened and Kerry came in. He had arisen and completed his toilet in several seconds less than five minutes. But his spotlessly neat attire would have survived inspection by the most lynx-eyed martinet in the Brigade of Guards. As he smiled at his visitor with fierce geniality, Mollie blushed like a young girl.

Chief Inspector Kerry was a much bigger man than she had believed him to be. The impression left upon her memory by his brief appearance at the night club had been that of a small, dapper figure. Now, as he stood in the little drawing-room, she saw that he was not much if anything below the average height of Englishmen, and that he possessed wonderfully broad shoulders. In fact, Kerry was deceptive. His compact neatness and the smallness of his feet and hands, together with those swift, lithe movements which commonly belong to men of light physique, curiously combined to deceive the beholder, but masked eleven stones of bone and muscle.

"Very good of you to offer information, miss," he said. "I'm willing to admit that I can do with it."

He opened a bureau and took out a writing-block and a fountain pen. Then he turned and stared hard at Mollie. She quickly lowered her eyes.

"Excuse me," said Kerry; "but didn't I see you somewhere last night?"

"Yes," she said. "I was sitting just inside the door at——"

"Right! I remember," interrupted Kerry. He continued to stare. "Before you say any more, miss, I have to remind you that I am a police officer, and that you may be called upon to swear to the truth of any information you may give me."

"Oh, of course! I know."

"You know? Very well, then; we can get on. Who gave you my address?"

At the question, so abruptly asked, Mollie felt herself blushing again. It was delightful to know that she could still blush. "Oh—I . . . that is, I asked Scotland Yard——"

She bestowed a swift, half-veiled glance at her interrogator, but he offered her no help, and:

"They wouldn't tell me," she continued. "So—I had to find out. You see, I heard you were trying to get information which I thought perhaps I could give."

"So you went to the trouble to find my private address rather than to the nearest police station," said Kerry. "Might I ask you from whom you heard that I wanted this information?"

"Well—it's in the papers, isn't it?"

"It is certainly. But it occurred to me that someone might have told you as well."

"Actually, someone did: Miss Margaret Halley."

"Good!" rapped Kerry. "Now we're coming to it. She told you to come to me?"

"Oh no!" cried Mollie—"she didn't. She told me to tell *her* so that she could tell someone connected with the Home Office."

"Eh?" said Kerry; "eh?" He bent forward, staring fiercely. "Please tell me exactly what Miss Halley wanted to know."

The intensity of his gaze Mollie found very perturbing, but:

"She wanted me to tell her where Mrs.

Sin lived," she replied.

Kerry experienced a quickening of the pulse. In the failure of the C.I.D. to trace the abode of the notorious Mrs. Sin he had suspected double-dealing. He counted it unbelievable that a figure so conspicuous in certain circles could evade official quest even for forty-eight hours. K Division's explanation, too, that there were no less than eighty Chinamen resident in and about Limehouse whose names either began or ended with Sin, he looked upon as a paltry evasion. That very morning he had awakened from a species of nightmare wherein "719" had affected the arrest of Kazmah and Mrs. Sin and rescued Mrs. Irvin from the clutches of the former. Now—here was hope. "719" would seem to be as hopelessly in the dark as everybody else.

"You refused?" he rapped.

"Of course I did, Inspector," said Mollie, with a timid, tender glance. "I thought you were the proper person to tell."

"Then you know?" asked Kerry, unable to conceal his eagerness.

"Yes," sighed Mollie. "Unfortunately—I know. Oh, Inspector, how can I explain it to you?"

"Don't trouble, miss. Just give me the address and I'll ask no questions!"

His keenness was thrilling, infectious. As a result of the night's "beating" he had a list of some twenty names whose owners might have been patrons of Kazmah and some of whom might know Mrs. Sin. But he had learned from bitter experience how difficult it was to induce such people to give useful evidence. There was practically no means of forcing them to speak if they chose, from selfish motives, to be silent. They could be forced to appear in court, but anything elicited in public was worse than useless. Furthermore, Kerry could not afford to wait. Mollie replied excitedly:

"Oh, Inspector, I know you will think me simply an appalling person when I tell you; but I have been to Mrs. Sin's house—The House of a Hundred Raptures she calls it——"

"Yes, yes! But—the address?"

"However can I tell you the address, Inspector? I could drive you there, but I haven't the very haziest idea of the name of the horrible street! One drives along dreadful roads where there are stalls and Jews for quite an interminable time, and then over a sort of canal, and then round to the right all among ships and horrid Chinamen. Then, there is a doorway in a little court, and Mrs. Sin's husband sits inside a smelly room with a positively ferocious raven who shrieks about legs and policemen! Oh! can I ever forget it!"

"One moment, miss, one moment," said Kerry, keeping an iron control upon himself. "What is the name of Mrs. Sin's husband?"

"Oh, let me think! I can always remember it by recalling the croak of the raven." She raised one hand to her brow, posing reflectively, and began to murmur:

"Sin Sin Ah . . . Sin Sin Jar . . . Sin Sin— oh! I have it! Sin Sin *Wa!*"

"Good!" rapped Kerry, and made a note on the block. "Sin Sin *Wa;* and he has a pet raven, you say, who talks?"

"Who positively talks like some horrid old woman!" cried Mollie. "He has only one eye."

"The raven?"

"The raven, yes—and also the Chinaman."

"What!"

"Oh! it's a nightmare to behold them together!" declared Mollie, clasping her hands and bending forward.

She was gaining courage, and now looked almost boldly into the fierce eyes of the Chief Inspector.

"Describe the house," he said succinctly. "Take your time and use your own words."

Thereupon Mollie launched into a description of Sin Sin Wa's opium-house. Kerry, his eyes fixed upon her face, listened silently. Then:

"These little rooms are really next door?" he asked.

"I suppose so, Inspector. We always went through the back of a cupboard!"

"Can you give me names of others who used this place?"

"Well"—Mollie hesitated—"poor Rita, of course, and Sir Lucien. Then, Cyrus Kilfane used to go."

"Kilfane? The American actor?"

"Yes."

"H'm. He's back in America; Sir Lucien is dead; and Mrs. Irvin is missing. Nobody else?"

Mollie shook her head.

"Who first took you there?"

"Cyrus Kilfane."

"Not Sir Lucien?"

"Oh, no! But both of them had been before."

"What was Kazmah's connection with Mrs. Sin and her husband?"

"I have no idea, Inspector. Kazmah used to supply cocaine and veronal and trional and heroin, but those who wanted to smoke opium he sent to Mrs. Sin."

"What! he gave them her address?"

"No, no! He gave her *their* address."

"I see. She called?"

"Yes. Oh, Inspector"—Mollie bent farther forward—"I can see in your eyes that you think I am fabulously wicked! Shall I be arrested?"

Kerry coughed drily and stood up.

"Probably not, miss. But you may be required to give evidence."

"Oh, actually?" cried Mollie, also standing up and approaching nearer.

"Yes. Shall you object?"

Mollie looked into his eyes.

"Not if I can be of the slightest assistance to *you,* Inspector."

A theory to explain why this social butterfly had sought him out as a recipient of her compromising confidences presented itself to Kerry's mind. He was a modest man, having neither time nor inclination for gallantries, and this was the first occasion throughout his professional career upon which he had obtained valuable evidence on the strength of his personal attractions. He doubted the accuracy of his deduction. But, Mollie at that moment lowering her lashes and then rapidly raising them again, Kerry was compelled to accept his own astonishing theory.

"And she is the daughter of a peer!" he reflected. "No wonder it has been hard to get evidence." He glanced rapidly in the direction of the door. There were several details which were by no means clear, but he decided to act upon the information already given and to get rid of his visitor without delay. Where some of the most dangerous criminals in Europe and America had failed, Mollie Gretna had succeeded in making Red Kerry nervous.

"I am much indebted to you, miss," he said, and opened the door.

"Oh, it has been delightful to confess to you, Inspector!" declared Mollie. "I will give you my card, and I shall expect you to come to me for any further information you may want. If I have to be brought to court, *you* will tell me, won't you?"

"Rely upon me, miss," replied Kerry shortly.

He escorted Mollie to her brougham, observed by no less than six discreetly hidden neighbors. And as the brougham was driven off she waved her hand to him! Kerry felt a hot flush spreading over his red countenance, for the veiled onlookers had not escaped his attention. As he re-entered the house:

"Yon's a bad woman," said his wife, emerging from the dining-room.

"I believe you may be right, Mary," replied Kerry confusedly.

"I kenned it when fairst I set een upon her painted face. I kenned it the now when she lookit sideways at ye. If yon's a grand lady, she's a woman o' puir repute. The Lord gi'e us grace."

Chapter XXVIII

THE GILDED JOSS

London was fog-bound. The threat of the past week had been no empty one. Towards the hour of each wintry sunset had come the yellow racks, hastening dusk and driving folks more speedily homeward to their firesides. The dull reports of fog-signals had become a part of the metropolitan bombination, but hitherto the choking mist had not secured a strangle-hold.

Now, however, it had triumphed, casting its thick net over the city as if eager to stifle the pulsing life of the new Babylon. In the neighborhood of the Docks its density was extraordinary, and the purlieus of Limehouse became mere mysterious gullies of smoke impossible to navigate unless one were very familiar with their intricacies and dangers.

Chief Inspector Kerry, wearing a cardigan under his oilskins, tapped the pavement with the point of his malacca like a blind man. No glimmer of light could he perceive. He could not even see his companion.

"Hell!" he snapped irritably, as his foot touched a brick wall, "where the devil are you, constable?"

"Here beside you, sir," answered P.C. Bryce, of K Division, his guide.

"Which side?"

"Here, sir."

The constable grasped Kerry's arm.

"But we've walked slap into a damn brick wall!"

"Keep the wall on your left, sir, and it's all clear ahead."

"Clear be damned!" said Kerry. "Are we nearly there?"

"About a dozen paces and we shall see the lamp—if it's been lighted."

"And if not we shall stroll into the river, I suppose?"

"No danger of that. Even if the lamp's out, we shall strike the iron pillar."

"I don't doubt it," said Kerry grimly.

They proceeded at a slow pace. Dull reports and a vague clangor were audible. These sounds were so deadened by the clammy mist that they might have proceeded from some gnome's workshop deep in the bowels of the earth. The blows of a pile-driver at work on the Surrey shore suggested to Kerry's mind the phantom crew of Hendrick Hudson at their game of ninepins in the Katskill Mountains. Suddenly:

"Is that you, Bryce?" he asked.

"I'm here, sir," replied the voice of the constable from beside him.

"H'm, then there's someone else about." He raised his voice. "Hi, there! have you lost your way?"

Kerry stood still, listening. But no one answered to his call.

"I'll swear there was someone just behind us, Bryce!"

"There was, sir. I saw someone, too. A Chinese resident, probably. Here we are!"

• A sound of banging became audible, and on advancing another two paces, Kerry found himself beside Bryce before a low closed door.

"Hello! hello!" croaked a dim voice. "Number one p'lice chop, lo! Sin Sin Wa!"

The flat note of a police whistle followed.

"Sin Sin is at home," declared Bryce. "That's the raven."

"Does he take the thing about with him, then?"

"I don't think so. But he puts it in a cupboard when he goes out, and it never talks unless it can see a light."

Bolts were unfastened and the door was opened. Out through the moving curtain of fog shone the red glow from a stove. A grotesque silhouette appeared outlined upon the dim redness.

"You wantchee me?" crooned Sin Sin Wa.

"I do!" rapped Kerry. "I've called to look for opium."

He stepped past the Chinaman into the dimly lighted room. As he did so, the cause of an apparent deformity which had characterized the outline of Sin Sin Wa became apparent. From his left shoulder the raven partly arose, moving his big wings, and:

"Smartest leg!" it shrieked in Kerry's ear

and rattled imaginary castenets.

The Chief Inspector started, involuntarily. "Damn the thing!" he muttered. "Come in, Bryce, and shut the door. What's this?"

On a tea-chest set beside the glowing stove, the little door of which was open, stood a highly polished squat wooden image, gilded and colored red and green. It was that of a leering Chinaman, possibly designed to represent Buddha, and its jade eyes seemed to blink knowingly in the dancing rays from the stove.

"Sin Sin Wa's joss," murmured the proprietor, as Bryce closed the outer door. "Me shinee him up; makee joss glad. Number one piecee joss."

Kerry turned and stared into the pockmarked smiling face. Seen in that dim light it was not unlike the carved face of the image, save that the latter possessed two open eyes and the Chinaman but one. The details of the room were indiscernible, lost in yellowish shadow, but the eye of the raven and the eye of Sin Sin Wa glittered like strange jewels.

"H'm" said Kerry. "Sorry to interrupt your devotions. Light us."

"Allee velly ploper," crooned Sin Sin Wa.

He took up the joss tenderly and bore it across the room. Opening a little cupboard set low down near the floor he discovered a lighted lantern. This he took out and set upon the dirty table. Then he placed the image on a shelf in the cupboard and turned smilingly to his visitors.

"Number one p'lice!" shrieked the raven.

"Here!" snapped Kerry. "Put that damn thing to bed!"

"Velly good," murmured Sin Sin Wa complacently.

He raised his hand to his shoulder and the raven stepped sedately from shoulder to wrist. Sin Sin Wa stooped.

"Come, Tling-a-Ling," he said softly. "You catchee sleepee."

The raven stepped down from his wrist and walked into the cupboard.

"So fashion, lo!" said Sin Sin Wa, closing the door.

He seated himself upon a tea-chest beside the useful cupboard, resting his hands upon his knees and smiling.

Kerry, chewing steadily, had watched the proceedings in silence, but now:

"Constable Bryce," he said crisply, "you recognize this man as Sin Sin Wa, the occupier of the house?"

"Yes, sir," replied Bryce.

He was not wholly at ease, and persistently avoided the Chinaman's oblique, beady eye.

"In the ordinary course of your duty you frequently pass along this street?"

"It's the limit of the Limehouse beat, sir. Poplar patrols on the other side."

"So that at this point, or hereabout, you would sometimes meet the constable on the next beat?"

"Well, sir," Bryce hesitated, clearing his throat, "this street isn't properly in his district."

"I didn't say it was!" snapped Kerry, glaring fiercely at the embarrassed constable. "I said you would sometimes meet him here."

"Yes, sometimes."

"Sometimes. Right. Did you ever come in here?"

The constable ventured a swift glance at the savage red face, and:

"Yes, sir, now and then," he confessed. "Just for a warm on a cold night, maybe."

"Allee velly welcome," murmured Sin Sin Wa.

Kerry never for a moment removed his fixed gaze from the face of Bryce.

"Now, my lad," he said, "I'm going to ask you another question. I'm not saying a word about the warm on a cold night. We're all human. But—did you ever see or hear or smell anything suspicious in this house?"

"Never," affirmed the constable earnestly.

"Did anything ever take place that suggested to your mind that Sin Sin Wa might be concealing something—upstairs, for instance?"

"Never a thing, sir. There's never been a complaint about him."

"Allee velly ploper," crooned Sin Sin Wa.

Kerry stared intently for some moments at Bryce; then, turning suddenly to Sin Sin Wa:

"I want to see your wife," he said. "Fetch her!"

Sin Sin Wa gently patted his knees.

"She velly bad woman," he declared. "She no hab topside pidgin."

"Don't talk!" shouted Kerry. "Fetch her!"

Sin Sin Wa turned his hands palms upward.

"Me no hab gotchee wifee," he murmured.

Kerry took one pace forward.

"Fetch her," he said; "or——" He drew a pair of handcuffs from the pocket of his oilskin.

"Velly bad luck," murmured Sin Sin Wa. "Catchee tlouble for wifee no got."

He extended his wrists, meeting the angry glare of the Chief Inspector with a smile of resignation. Kerry bit savagely at his chewing-gum, glancing aside at Bryce.

"Did you ever see his wife?" he snapped.

"No, sir. I didn't know he had one."

"No habgotchee," murmured Sin Sin Wa. "She velly bad woman."

"For the last time," said Kerry, stooping and thrusting his face forward so that his nose was only some six inches from that of Sin Sin Wa, "where's Mrs. Sin?"

"Catchee lun off," replied the Chinaman blandly. "Velly bad woman. Tlief woman. Catchee stealee alla my dollars!"

"Eh!"

Kerry stood upright, moving his shoulders and rattling the handcuffs.

"Comee here when Sin Sin Wa hab gone for catchee shavee, liftee alla my dollars, and— *pff! chee*-lo!"

He raised his hand and blew imaginary fluff into space. Kerry stared down at him with an expresion in which animal ferocity and helplessness were oddly blended. Then:

"Bryce," he said, "stay here. I'm going to search the house."

"Very good, sir."

Kerry turned again to the Chinaman.

"Is there anyone upstairs?" he demanded.

"Nobody hab. Sin Sin Wa alla samee lonesome. Catchee shinum him joss."

Kerry dropped the handcuffs back into the pocket of his overall and took out an electric torch. With never another glance at Sin Sin Wa he went out into the passage and began to mount the stairs, presently finding himself in a room filled with all sorts of unsavory rubbish and containing a large cupboard. He uttered an exclamation of triumph.

Crossing the littered floor, and picking his way amid broken cane chairs, teachests, discarded garments and bedlaths, he threw open the cupboard door. Before him hung a row of ragged clothes and a number of bowler hats. Directing the ray of the torch upon the unsavory collection, he snatched coats and hats from the hooks upon which they depended and hurled them impatiently upon the floor.

When the cupboard was empty he stepped into it and began to bang upon the back. The savagery of his expression grew more marked than usual, and as he chewed his maxillary muscles protruded extraordinarily.

"If ever I sounded a brick wall," he muttered, "I'm doing it now."

Tap where he would—and he tapped with his knuckles and with the bone ferrule of his cane—there was nothing in the resulting sound to suggest that that part of the wall behind the cupboard was less solid than any other part.

He examined the room rapidly, then passed into another one adjoining it, which was evidently used as a bedroom. The latter faced towards the court and did not come in contact with the wall of the neighboring house. In both rooms the windows were fastened, and judging from the state of the fasteners were never opened. In that containing the cupboard outside shutters were also closed. Despite this sealing-up of the apartments, traces of fog hung in the air. Kerry descended the stairs.

Snapping off the light of his torch, he stood, feet wide apart, staring at Sin Sin Wa. The latter, smiling imperturbably, yellow hands resting upon knees, sat quite still on the teachest. Constable Bryce was seated on a corner of the table, looking curiously awkward in his tweed overcoat and bowler hat, which garments quite failed to disguise the policeman. He stood up as Kerry entered. Then:

"There used to be a door between this house and the next," said Kerry succinctly. "My information is exact and given by someone who has often used that door."

"Bloody liar," murmured Sin Sin Wa.

"What!" shouted Kerry. "What did you say, you yellow-faced mongrel!"

He clenched his fists and strode towards the Chinaman.

"Sarcee feller catchee pullee leg," explained the unmoved Sin Sin Wa. "Velly bad man tellee lie for makee bhoberry—getchee poor Chinaman in tlouble."

In the fog-bound silence Kerry could very distinctly be heard chewing. He turned suddenly to Bryce.

"Go back and fetch two men," he directed. "I should never find my way."

"Very good, sir."

Bryce stepped to the door, unable to hide the relief which he experienced, and opened it. The fog was so dense that it looked like a yellow curtain hung in the opening.

"Phew!" said Bryce. "I may be some little time, sir."

"Quite likely. But don't stop to pick daisies."

The constable went out, closing the door.

Kerry laid his cane on the table, then stooped and tossed a cud of chewing-gum into the stove. From his waistcoat pocket he drew out a fresh piece and placed it between his teeth. Drawing a tea-chest closer to the stove, he seated himself and stared intently into the glowing heart of the fire.

Sin Sin Wa extended his arm and opened the little cupboard.

"Number one p'lice," croaked the raven drowsily.

"You catchee sleepee, Tling-a-Ling," said Sin Sin Wa.

He took out the green-eyed joss, set it tenderly upon a corner of the table, and closed the cupboard door. With a piece of chamois leather, which he sometimes dipped into a little square tin, he began to polish the hideous figure.

Chapter XXIX

DOUBTS AND FEARS

Monte Irvin raised his head and stared dully at Margaret Halley. It was very quiet in the library of the big old-fashioned house at Prince's Gate. A faint crackling sound which proceeded from the fire was clearly audible. Margaret's grey eyes were anxiously watching the man whose pose as he sat in the deep, saddle-back chair so curiously suggested collapse.

"Drugs," he whispered. "Drugs."

Few of his City associates would have recognized the voice; all would have been shocked to see the change which had taken place in the man.

"You really understand why I have told you, Mr. Irvin, don't you?" said Margaret almost pleadingly. "Dr. Burton thought you should not be told, but then Dr. Burton did not know you were going to ask me point blank. And I thought it better that you should know the truth, bad as it is, rather than——"

"Rather than suspect—worse things," whispered Irvin. "Of course, you were right, Miss Halley. I am very, very grateful to you for telling me. I realize what courage it must have called for. Believe me, I shall always remember——"

He broke off, staring across the room at his wife's portrait. Then:

"If only I had known," he added.

Irvin exhibited greater composure than Margaret had ventured to anticipate. She was confirmed in her opinion that he should be told the truth.

"I would have told you long ago," she said, "if I had thought that any good could result from my doing so. Frankly, I had hoped to cure Rita of the habit, and I believe I might have succeeded in time."

"There has been no mention of drugs in connection with the case," said Monte Irvin, speaking monotonously. "In the Press, I mean."

"Hitherto there has not," she replied. "But there is a hint of it in one of this evening's papers, and I determined to give you the exact facts so far as they are known to me before some garbled account came to your ears."

"Thank you," he said, "thank you. I had felt for a long time that I was getting out of touch with Rita, that she had other confidants. Have you any idea who they are, Miss Halley?"

He raised his eyes, looking at her pathetically. Margaret hesitated; then:

"Well," she replied, "I am afraid Nina knew."

"Her maid?"

"I think she must have known."

He sighed.

"The police have interrogated her," he said. "Probably she is being watched."

"Oh, I don't think she knows anything about the drug syndicate," declared Margaret. "She merely acted as confidential messenger. Poor Sir Lucien Pyne, I am sure, was addicted to drugs."

"Do you think"—Irvin spoke in a very low voice—"do you think he led her into the habit?"

Margaret bit her lip, staring down at the red carpet.

"I would hate to slander a man who can never defend himself," she replied finally. "But—I have sometimes thought he did."

Silence fell. Both were contemplating a theory which neither dared to express in words.

"You see," continued Margaret, "it is evident that this man Kazmah was patronized by people so highly placed that it is hopeless to look for information from them. Again, such people have influence. I don't suggest that they are using it to protect Kazmah, but I have no doubt they are doing so to protect themselves."

Monte Irvin raised his eyes to her face. A weary, sad look had come into them.

"You mean that it may be to somebody's interest to hush up the matter as much as possible?"

Margaret nodded her head.

"The prevalence of the drug habit in society—especially in London society—is a secret which has remained hidden so long from the general public," she replied, "that one cannot help looking for bribery and corruption. The stage is made the scapegoat whenever the voice of scandal breathes the word 'dope,' but we rarely hear the names of the worst offenders even whispered. I have thought for a long time that the authorities must know the names of the receivers and distributors of cocaine, veronal, opium, and the other drugs, huge quantities of which find their way regularly to the West End of London. Pharmacists sometimes experience the greatest difficulty in obtaining the drugs which they legitimately require, and the prices have increased extraordinarily. Cocaine, for instance, has gone up from five and sixpence an ounce to eighty-seven shillings, and heroin from three and sixpence to over forty shillings, while opium that was once about twenty shillings a pound is now eight times the price."

Monte Irvin listened attentively.

"In the course of my Guildhall duties," he said slowly, "I have been brought in contact frequently with police officers of all ranks. If influential people are really at work protecting these villains who deal illicitly in drugs, I don't think, and I am not prepared to believe, that they have corrupted the police."

"Neither do I believe so, Mr. Irvin!" said Margaret eagerly.

"But," Irvin pursued, exhibiting greater animation, "you inform me that a Home Office commissioner has been appointed. What does that mean, if not that Lord Wrexborough distrusts the police?"

"Well, you see, the police seemed to be unable, or unwilling, to do anything in the matter. Of course, this may have been due to the fact that the traffic was so skillfully handled that it defied their inquiries."

"Take, as an instance, Chief Inspector Kerry," continued Irvin. "He has exhibited the utmost delicacy and consideration in his dealings with me, but I'll swear that a whiter man never breathed."

"Oh, really, Mr. Irvin, I don't think for a moment that men of that class are suspected of being concerned. Indeed, I don't believe any active collusion is suspected at all."

"Lord Wrexborough thinks that Scotland Yard hasn't got an officer clever enough for the dope people?"

"Quite possibly."

"I take it that he has put up a secret service man?"

"I believe—that is, I know he has."

Monte Irvin was watching Margaret's face, and despite the dull misery which deadened his usually quick perceptions, he detected a heightened color and a faint change of expression. He did not question her further upon the point, but:

"God knows I welcome all the help that offers," he said. "Lord Wrexborough is your uncle, Miss Halley; but do you think this secret commission business quite fair to Scotland Yard?"

Margaret stared for some moments at the carpet, then raised her grey eyes and looked earnestly at the speaker. She had learned in the brief time that had elapsed since this black sorrow had come upon him to understand what it was in the character of Monte Irvin which had attracted Rita. It afforded an illustration of that obscure law governing the magnetism which subsists between diverse natures. For not all the agony of mind which he suffered could hide or mar the cleanness and honesty of purpose which were Monte Irvin's outstanding qualities.

"No," Margaret replied; "honestly, I don't. And I feel rather guilty about it, too, because I have been urging uncle to take such a step for quite a long time. You see"—she glanced at Irvin wistfully—"I am brought in contact with so many victims of the drug habit. I believe the police are hampered; and these people who deal in drugs manage in some way to evade the law. The Home Office agent will report to a committee appointed by Lord Wrexborough, and then, you see, if it is found necessary to do so, there will be special legislation."

Monte Irvin sighed wearily, and his glance strayed in the direction of the telephone on the side-table. He seemed to be constantly listening for something which he expected but dreaded to hear. Whenever the toy spaniel which lay curled up on the rug before the fire moved or looked towards the door, Irvin started and his expression changed.

"This suspense," he said jerkily, "this suspense is so hard to bear."

"Oh, Mr. Irvin, your courage is wonderful," replied Margaret earnestly. "But he"— she hastily corrected herself—"everybody is convinced that Rita is safe. Under some strange misapprehension regarding this awful tragedy she has run away into hiding. Probably she has been induced to do so by those interested in preventing her from giving evidence."

Monte Irvin's eyes lighted up strangely. "Is that the opinion of the Home Office agent?" he asked.

"Yes."

"Inspector Kerry shares it," declared Irvin. "Please God they are right."

"It is the only possible explanation," said Margaret. "Any hour now we may expect news of her."

"You don't think," pursued Monte Irvin, "that anybody—anybody—suspects Rita of being concerned in the death of Sir Lucien?"

He fixed a gaze of pathetic inquiry upon her face.

"Of course not!" she cried. "How ridiculous it would be."

"Yes," he murmured, "it would be ridiculous."

Margaret stood up.

"I am quite relieved now that I have done what I conceived to be my duty, Mr. Irvin," she said. "And, bad as the truth may be, it is better than doubt, after all. You must look after yourself, you know. When Rita comes back we shall have a big task before us to wean her from her old habits." She met his glance frankly. "But we shall succeed."

"How you cheer me," whispered Monte Irvin emotionally. "You are the truest friend that Rita ever had, Miss Halley. You will keep in touch with me, will you not?"

"Of course. Next to yourself there is no one so sincerely interested as I am. I love Rita as I should have loved a sister if I had had one. Please don't stand up. Dr. Burton has told you to avoid all exertion for a week or more, I know."

Monte Irvin grasped her outstretched hand.

"Any news which reaches me," he said, "I will communicate immediately. Thank you. In times of trouble we learn to know our real friends."

Chapter XXX

THE FIGHT IN THE DARK

Towards eleven o'clock at night the fog began slightly to lift. As Kerry crossed the bridge

over Limehouse Canal he could vaguely discern the dirty water below, and street lamps showed dimly, surrounded each by a halo of yellow mist. Fog signals were booming on the railway, and from the great docks in the neighborhood mechanical clashings and hammerings were audible.

Turning to the right, Kerry walked on for some distance, and then suddenly stepped into the entrance to a narrow cul-de-sac and stood quite still.

A conviction had been growing upon him during the past twelve hours that someone was persistently and cleverly dogging his footsteps. He had first detected the presence of this mysterious follower outside the house of Sin Sin Wa, but the density of the fog had made it impossible for him to obtain a glimpse of the man's face. He was convinced, too, that he had been followed back to Leman Street, and from there to New Scotland Yard. Now, again he became aware of this persistent presence, and hoped at last to confront the spy.

Slow footsteps, the footsteps of someone proceeding with the utmost caution, came along the pavement. Kerry stood close to the wall of the court, one hand in a pocket of his overall, waiting and chewing.

Nearer came the footsteps—and nearer. A shadowy figure appeared only a yard or so away from the watchful Chief Inspector. Thereupon he acted.

With one surprising spring he hurled himself upon the unprepared man, grasped him by his coat collar, and shone the light of an electric torch fully into his face.

"Hell!" he snapped. "The smart from Spinker's!"

The ray of the torch lighted up the mean, pinched face of Brisley, blanched now by fright, gleamed upon the sharp, hooked nose and into the cunning little brown eyes. Brisley licked his lips. In Kerry's muscular grip he bore quite a remarkable resemblance to a rat in the jaws of a terrier.

"Ho, ho!" continued the Chief Inspector, showing his teeth savagely. "So we let Scotland Yard make the pie, and then we steal all the plums, do we?"

He shook the frightened man until Brisley's broad brimmed bowler was shaken off, revealing the receding brow and scanty neutral-colored hair.

"We let Scotland Yard work night and day, and then we present our rat-faced selves to Mr. Monte Irvin and say we have 'found the lady' do we?'' Another vigorous shake followed. ''We track Chief Inspectors of the Criminal Investigation Department, do we? We do, eh? We are dirty, skulking mongrels, aren't we? We require to be kicked from Limehouse to Paradise, don't we?'' He suddenly released Brisley. ''So we shall be!'' he shouted furiously.

Hot upon the promise came the deed.

Brisley sent up a howl of pain as Kerry's right brogue came into violent contact with his person. The assault almost lifted him off his feet, and hatless as he was he set off, running as a man runs whose life depends upon his speed. The sound of his pattering footsteps was echoed from wall to wall of the cul-de-sac until finally it was swallowed up in the fog.

Kerry stood listening for some moments, then, directing a furious kick upon the bowler which lay at his feet, he snapped off the light of the torch and pursued his way. The lesser mystery was solved, but the greater was before him.

He had made a careful study of the geography of the neighborhood, and although the fog was still dense enough to be confusing, he found his way without much difficulty to the street for which he was bound. Some fifteen paces along the narrow thoroughfare he came upon someone standing by a closed door set in a high brick wall. The street contained no dwelling houses, and except for the solitary figure by the door was deserted and silent. Kerry took out his torch and shone a white ring upon the smiling countenance of Detective-sergeant Coombes.

''If that smile gets any worse,'' he said irritably, ''they'll have to move your ears back. Anything to report?''

''Sin Sin Wa went to bed an hour ago.''

''Any visitors?''

''No.''

''Has he been out?''

''No.''

''Got the ladder?''

''Yes.''

''All quiet in the neighborhood?''

''All quiet.''

''Good.''

The street in which this conversation took place was one running roughly parallel to that in which the house of Sin Sin Wa was situated. A detailed search of the Chinaman's premises had failed to bring to light any scrap of evidence to show that opium had ever been smoked there. Of the door

described by Mollie Gretna, and said to communicate with the adjoining establishment, not a trace could be found. But the fact that such a door had existed did not rest solely upon Mollie's testimony. From one of the ''beat-ups'' interviewed that day, Kerry had succeeded in extracting confirmatory evidence.

Inquiries conducted in the neighborhood of Poplar had brought to light the fact that four of the houses in this particular street, including that occupied by Sin Sin Wa and that adjoining it, belonged to a certain Mr. Jacobs, said to reside abroad. Mr. Jacob's rents were collected by an estate agent, and sent to an address in San Francisco. For some reason not evident to this man of business, Mr. Jacobs demanded a rental for the house next to Sin Sin Wa's, which was out of all proportion to the value of the property. Hence it had remained vacant for a number of years. The windows were broken and boarded up, as was the door.

Kerry realized that the circumstance of the landlord of ''The House of a Hundred Raptures'' being named Jacobs, and the lessee of the Cubanis Cigarette Company's premises in Old Bond Street being named Isaacs, might be no more than a coincidence. Nevertheless it was odd. He had determined to explore the place without unduly advertising his intentions.

Two modes of entrance presented themselves. There was a trap on the roof, but in order to reach it access would have to be obtained to one of the other houses in the row, which also possessed a roof-trap; or there were four windows overlooking a little back yard, two upstairs and two down.

By means of a short ladder which Coombes had brought for the purpose Kerry climbed on to the wall and dropped into the yard.

''The jemmy!'' he said softly.

Coombes, also mounting, dropped the required implement. Kerry caught it deftly, and in a very few minutes had wrenched away the rough planking nailed over one of the lower windows, without making very much noise.

''Shall I come down?'' inquired Coombes in muffled tones from the top of the wall.

''No,'' rapped Kerry. ''Hide the ladder again. If I want help I'll whistle. Catch!''

He tossed the jemmy up to Coombes, and Coombes succeeded in catching it. Then Kerry raised the glassless sash of the window and stepped into a little room, which he surveyed by the light of his electric torch. It was filthy and littered with rubbish, but showed no sign of having been occupied for a long time. The ceiling was nearly black, and so were the walls. He went out into a narrow passage similar to that in the house of Sin Sin Wa and leading to a stair.

Walking quietly, he began to ascend. Mollie Gretna's description of the opium-house had been most detailed and lurid, and he was prepared for some extravagant scene.

He found three bare, dirty rooms, having all the windows boarded up.

"Hell!" he said succinctly.

Resting his torch upon a dust-coated ledge of the room, which presumably was situated in the front of the house, he deposited a cud of chewing-gum in the empty grate and lovingly selected a fresh piece from the packet which he always carried. Once more chewing he returned to the narrow passage, which he knew must be that in which the secret doorway had opened.

It was uncarpeted and dirty, and the walls were covered with faded filthy paper, the original color and design of which were quite lost. There was not the slightest evidence that a door had ever existed in any part of the wall. Following a detailed examination, Kerry returned his magnifying glass to the washleather bag and the bag to his waistcoat pocket.

"H'm," he said, thinking aloud, "Sin Sin Wa may have only one eye, but it's a good eye."

He raised his glance to the blackened ceiling of the passage, and saw that the trap giving access to the roof was situated immediately above him. He directed the ray of the torch upon it. In the next moment he had snapped off the light and was creeping silently towards the door of the front room.

The trap had moved slightly!

Gaining the doorway, Kerry stood just inside the room and waited. He became conscious of a kind of joyous excitement, which claimed him at such moments; an eagerness and a lust of action. But he stood perfectly still, listening and waiting.

There came a faint creaking sound, and a new damp chilliness was added to the stale atmosphere of the passage. Someone had quietly raised the trap.

Cutting through the blackness like a scimitar shone a ray of light from above, widening as it descended and ending in a white patch on the floor. It was moved to and fro.

Then it disappeared. Another vague creaking sound followed—that caused by a man's weight being imposed upon a wooden framework.

Finally came a thud on the bare boards of the floor.

Complete silence ensued. Kerry waited, muscles tense and brain alert. He even suspended the chewing operation. A dull, padding sound reached his ears.

From the quality of the thud which had told of the intruder's drop from the trap to the floor, Kerry had deduced that he wore rubber-soled shoes. Now, the sound which he could hear was that of the stranger's furtive footsteps. He was approaching the doorway in which Kerry was standing.

Just behind the open door Kerry waited. And unheralded by any further sound to tell of his approach, the intruder suddenly shone a ray of light right into the room. He was on the threshold; only the door concealed him from Kerry, and concealed Kerry from the new-comer.

The disc of light cast into the dirty room grew smaller. The man with the torch was entering. A hand which grasped a magazine pistol appeared beyond the edge of the door, and Kerry's period of inactivity came to an end. Leaning back he adroitly kicked the weapon from the hand of the man who held it!

There was a smothered cry of pain, and the pistol fell clattering on the floor. The light went out, too. As it vanished Kerry leapt from his hiding-place. Snapping on the light of his own pocket lamp, he ran out into the passage.

Crack! came the report of a pistol.

Kerry dropped flat on the floor. He had not counted on the intruder being armed with *two* pistols! His pocket lamp, still alight, fell beside him, and he lay in a curiously rigid attitude on his side, one knee drawn up and his arm thrown across his face.

Carefully avoiding the path of light cast by the fallen torch, the unseen stranger approached silently. Pistol in hand, he bent; nearer and nearer, striving to see the face of the prostrate man. Kerry lay deathly still. The other dropped on one knee and bent closely over him. . . .

Swiftly as a lash Kerry's arm was whipped around the man's neck, and helpless he pitched over on to his head! Uttering a small groan, he lay heavy and still across Kerry's body.

"Flames!" muttered the Chief Inspector, extricating himself; "I didn't mean to break his neck."

He took up the electric torch, and shone it upon the face of the man on the floor. It was a dirty, unshaven face, unevenly tanned, as though the man had worn a beard until quite recently and had come from a hot climate. He was attired in a manner which suggested that he might be a ship's fireman save that he wore canvas shoes having rubber soles.

Kerry stood watching him for some moments. Then he groped behind him with one foot until he found the pistol, the second pistol which the man had dropped as he pitched on his skull. Kerry picked it up, and resting the electric torch upon the crown of his neat bowler hat—which lay upon the floor—he stooped, pistol in hand, and searched the pockets of the prostrate man, who had begun to breathe stertorously. In the breast pocket he found a leather wallet of good quality; and at this he stared, a curious expression coming into his fierce eyes. He opened it, and found Treasury notes, some official-looking papers, and a number of cards. Upon one of these cards he directed the light, and this is what he read:

To introduce 719

Lord Wrexborough Ⓦ

Great Cumberland Place, W. 1

"God's truth!" gasped Kerry. "It's the man from Whitehall!"

The stertorous breathing ceased, and a very dirty hand was thrust up to him.

"I'm glad you spoke, Chief Inspector Kerry," drawled a vaguely familiar voice. "I was just about to kick you in the back of the neck!"

Kerry dropped the wallet and grasped the proffered hand. "719" stood up, smiling grimly. Footsteps were clattering on the stairs. Coombes had heard the shot.

"Sir," said Kerry, "if ever you need a testimonial to your efficiency at this game, my address is Sixty-seven Spenser Road, Brix-

ton. We've met before."

"We have, Chief Inspector," was the reply. "We met at Kazmah's, and later at a certain gambling den in Soho."

The pseudo fireman dragged a big cigar-case from his hip-pocket.

"I'm known as Seton Pasha. Can I offer you a cheroot?"

Chapter XXXI

THE STORY OF 719

In a top back room of the end house in the street which also boasted the residence of Sin Sin Wa, Seton Pasha and Chief Inspector Kerry sat one on either side of a dirty deal table. Seton smoked and Kerry chewed. A smoky oil lamp burned upon the table, and two notebooks lay beside it.

"It is certainly odd," Seton was saying, "that you failed to break my neck. But I have made it a practice since taking up my residence here to wear a cap heavily padded. I apprehend sandbags and pieces of loaded tubing."

"The tube is not made," declared Kerry, "which can do the job. You're harder to kill than a Chinese Jew."

"Your own escape is almost equally remarkable," added Seton. "I rarely miss at such short range. But you had nearly broken my wrist with that kick."

"I'm sorry," said Kerry. "You should always bang a door wide open suddenly before you enter into a suspected room. Anybody standing behind usually stops it with his head."

"I am indebted for the hint, Chief Inspector. We all have something to learn."

"Well, sir, we've laid our cards on the table, and you'll admit we've both got a lot to learn before we see daylight. I'll be obliged if you'll put me wise to your game. I take it you began work on the very night of the murder?"

"I did. By a pure accident—the finding of an opiated cigarette in Mr. Gray's rooms—I perceived that the business which had led to my recall from the East was involved in the Bond Street mystery. Frankly, Chief Inspector, I doubted at that time if it were possible for you and me to work together. I decided to work alone. A beard which I had worn in the East, for purposes of disguise, I shaved off; and because the skin was whiter where the hair had grown than elsewhere, I found it necessary after shaving to powder my face heavily. This accounts for the description given to you of a man with a pale face. Even now the coloring is irregular, as you may notice.

"Deciding to work anonymously, I went post haste to Lord Wrexborough and made certain arrangements whereby I became known to the responsible authorities as '719.' The explanation of these figures is a simple one. My name is Greville Seton. G is the seventh letter in the alphabet, and S the nineteenth; hence—'seven–nineteen.'

"The increase of the drug traffic and the failure of the police to cope with it had led to the institution of a Home Office inquiry, you see. It was suspected that the traffic was in the hands of Orientals, and in looking about for a confidential agent to make certain inquiries, my name cropped up. I was at that time employed by the Foreign Office, but Lord Wrexborough borrowed me." Seton smiled at his own expression. "Every facility was offered to me, as you know. And that my investigations led me to the same conclusion as your own, my presence as lessee of this room, in the person of John Smiles, seaman, sufficiently demonstrates."

"H'm," said Kerry, "and I take it your investigations have also led you to the conclusion that our hands are clean?"

Seton Pasha fixed his cool regard upon the speaker.

"Personally, I never doubted this, Chief Inspector," he declared. "I believed, and I still believe, that the people who traffic in drugs are clever enough to keep in the good books of the local police. It is a case of clever *camouflage*, rather than corruption."

"Ah," snapped Kerry. "I was waiting to hear you mention it. So long as we know. I'm not a man that stands for being pointed at. I've got a boy at a good public school, but if ever he said he was ashamed of his father, the day he said it would be a day he'd never forget!"

Seton Pasha smiled grimly and changed the topic.

"Let us see," he said, "if we are any nearer to the heart of the mystery of Kazmah. You were at the Regent Street bank today, I understand, at which the late Sir Lucien Pyne had an account?"

"I was," replied Kerry. "Next to his theatrical enterprise his chief source of income

seems to have been a certain Jose Santos Company, of Buenos Ayres. We've traced Kazmah's account, too. But no one at the bank has ever seen him. The missing Rashîd always paid in. Checks were signed 'Mohammed el-Kazmah,' in which name the account had been opened. From the amount standing to his credit there it's evident that the proceeds of the dope business went elsewhere."

"Where do you think they went?" asked Seton quietly, watching Kerry.

"Well," rapped Kerry, "I think the same as you. I've got two eyes and I can see out of both of them."

"And you think?"

"I think they went to the Jose Santos Company, of Buenos Ayres!"

"Right!" cried Seton. "I feel sure of it. We may never know how it was all arranged or who was concerned, but I am convinced that Mr. Isaacs, lessee of the Cubanis Cigarette Company offices, Mr. Jacobs (my landlord!), Mohammed el-Kazmah—whoever he may be—the untraceable Mrs. Sin Sin Wa, and another, were all shareholders of the Jose Santos Company."

"I'm with you. By 'another' you mean?"

"Sir Lucien! It's horrible, but I'm afraid it's true."

They became silent for a while. Kerry chewed and Seton smoked. Then:

"The significance of the fact that Sir Lucien's study window was no more than forty paces across the leads from a well-oiled window of the Cubanis Company will not have escaped you," said Seton. "I performed the journey just ahead of you, I believe. Then Sir Lucien had lived in Buenos Ayres; that was before he came into the title, and at a time, I am told, when he was not overburdened with wealth. His man, Mareno, is indisputably some kind of a South American, and he can give no satisfactory account of his movements on the night of the murder.

"That we have to deal with a powerful drug syndicate there can be no doubt. The late Sir Lucien may not have been a director, but I feel sure he was financially interested. Kazmah's was the distributing office, and the importer——"

"Was Sin Sin Wa!" cried Kerry, his eyes gleaming savagely. "He's as clever and cunning as all the rest of Chinatown put together. Somewhere not a hundred miles from this spot where we are now there's a store of stuff big enough to dope all Europe!"

"And there's something else," said Seton quietly, knocking a cone of grey ash from his cheroot on to the dirty floor. "Kazmah is hiding there in all probability, if he hasn't got clear away—and Mrs. Monte Irvin is being held a prisoner!"

"If they haven't——"

"For Irvin's sake I hope not, Chief Inspector. There are two very curious points in the case—apart from the mystery which surrounds the man Kazmah: the fact that Mareno, palpably an accomplice, stayed to face the music, and the fact that Sin Sin Wa likewise has made no effort to escape. Do you see what it means? They are covering the big man—Kazmah. Once he and Mrs. Irvin are out of the way, we can prove nothing against Mareno and Sin Sin Wa! And the most we could do for Mrs. Sin would be to convict her of selling opium."

"To do even that we should have to take a witness to court," said Kerry gloomily; "and all the satisfaction we'd get would be to see her charged ten pounds!"

Silence fell between them again. It was that kind of sympathetic silence which is only possible where harmony exists; and, indeed, of all the things strange and bazarre which characterized the inquiry, this sudden amity between Kerry and Seton Pasha was not the least remarkable. It represented the fruit of a mutual respect.

There was something about the lean, unshaven face of Seton Pasha, and something, too, in his bright grey eyes which, allowing for difference of coloring, might have reminded a close observer of Kerry's fierce countenance. The tokens of iron determination and utter indifference to danger were perceptible in both. And although Seton was dark and turning slightly grey, while Kerry was as red as a man well could be, that they possessed several common traits of character was a fact which the dissimilarity of their complexions wholly failed to conceal. But while Seton Pasha hid the grimness of his nature beneath a sort of humorous reserve, the dangerous side of Kerry was displayed in his open truculence.

Seated there in that Limehouse attic, a smoky lamp burning on the table between them, and one gripping the stump of a cheroot between his teeth, while the other chewed steadily, they presented a combination which none but a fool would have lightly challenged.

"Sin Sin Wa is cunning," said Seton suddenly. "He is a very clever man. Watch him as closely as you like, he will never lead you to the 'store.' In the character of John Smiles I had some conversation with him this morning, and I formed the same opinion as yourself. He is waiting for something; and he is certain of his ground. I have a premonition, Chief Inspector, that whoever else may fall into the net, Sin Sin Wa will slip out. We have one big chance."

"What's that?" rapped Kerry.

"The dope syndicate can only have got contol of 'the traffic' in one way—by paying big prices and buying out competitors. If they cease to carry on for even a week they lose their control. The people who bring the stuff over from Japan, South America, India, Holland, and so forth will sell somewhere else if they can't sell to Kazmah and Company. Therefore we want to watch the ships from likely ports, or, better still, get among the men who do the smuggling. There must be resorts along the riverside used by people of that class. We might pick up information there."

Kerry smiled savagely.

"I've got half a dozen good men doing every dive from Wapping to Gravesend," he answered. "But if you think it worth looking into personally, say the word."

"Well, my dear sir,"—Seton Pasha tossed the end of his cheroot into the empty grate—"what else can we do?"

Kerry banged his fist on the table.

"You're right!" he snapped. "We're stuck! But anything's better than nothing. We'll start here and now; and the first joint we'll make for is Dougal's."

"Dougal's?" echoed Seton Pasha.

"That's it—Dougal's. A danger spot on the Isle of Dogs used by the lowest type of sea-faring men, and not barred to Arabs, Chinks, and other gaily colored fowl. If there's any chat going on about dope, we'll hear it in Dougal's."

Seton Pasha stood up, smiling grimly.

"Dougal's it shall be," he said.

Chapter XXXII

ON THE ISLE OF DOGS

As the police boat left Limehouse Pier, a clammy south-easterly breeze blowing upstream lifted the fog in clearly defined layers, an effect very singular to behold. At one moment a great arc-lamp burning above the Lavender Pond of the Surrey Commercial Dock shot out a yellowish light across the Thames. Then, as suddenly as it had come, the light vanished again as a stratum of mist floated before it.

The creaking of the oars sounded muffled and ghostly, and none of the men in the boat seemed to be inclined to converse. Heading across stream they made for the unseen promontory of the Isle of Dogs. Navigation was suspended, and they reached mid-stream without seeing a ship's light. Then came the damp wind again to lift the fog, and ahead of them they discerned one of the General Steam Navigation Company's boats awaiting an opportunity to make her dock at the head of Deptford Creek. The clamor of an iron-works on the Millwall shore burst loudly upon their ears, and away astern the lights of the Surrey Dock shone out once more. Hugging the bank they pursued a southerly course, and from Limehouse Reach crept down to Greenwich Reach.

Fog closed in upon them, a curtain obscuring both light and sound. When the breeze came again it had gathered force, and it drove the mist before it in wreathing banks, and brought to their ears a dull lowing and to their nostrils a farmyard odor from the cattle pens. Ghostly flames, leaping and falling, leaping and falling, showed where a gasworks lay on the Greenwich bank ahead.

Eastward swept the river now, and fresher blew the breeze. As they rounded the blunt point of the "Isle" the fog banks went swirling past them astern, and the lights on either shore showed clearly ahead. A ship's siren began to roar somewhere behind them. The steamer which they had passed was about to pursue her course.

Closer in-shore drew the boat, passing a series of wharves, and beyond these a tract of waste, desolate bank very gloomy in the half light and apparently boasting no habitation of man. The activities of the Green-wich bank seemed remote, and the desolation of the Isle of Dogs very near, touching them intimately with its peculiar gloom.

A light sprang into view some little distance inland, notable because it shone lonely in an expanse of utter blackness. Kerry broke the long silence.

"Dougal's," he said. "Put us ashore here."

The police boat was pulled in under a rickety wooden structure, beneath which the Thames water whispered eerily; and Kerry and Seton disembarked, mounting a short flight of slimy wooden steps and crossing a roughly planked place on to a shingly slope. Climbing this, they were on damp waste ground, pathless and uninviting.

"Dougal's is being watched," said Kerry. "I think I told you?"

"Yes," replied Seton. "But I have formed the opinion that the dope gang is too clever for the ordinary type of man. Sin Sin Wa is an instance of what I mean. Neither you nor I doubt that he is a receiver of drugs—perhaps *the* receiver; but where is our case? The only real link connecting him with the West-End habitué is his wife. And she has conveniently deserted him! We cannot possibly prove that she hasn't while he chooses to maintain that she has."

"H'm," grunted Kerry, abruptly changing the subject. "I hope I'm not recognized here."

"Have you visited the place before?"

"Some years ago. Unless there are any old hands on view to-night, I don't think I shall be spotted."

He wore a heavy and threadbare overcoat, which was several sizes too large for him, a muffler, and a tweed cap—the outfit supplied by Seton Pasha; and he had a very vivid and unpleasant recollection of his appearance as viewed in his little pocket-mirror before leaving Seton's room. As they proceeded across the muddy wilderness towards the light which marked the site of Dougal's, they presented a picture of a sufficiently villainous pair.

The ground was irregular, and the path wound sinuously about mounds of rubbish; so that often the guiding light was lost, and they stumbled blindly among nondescript litter, which apparently represented the accumulation of centuries. But finally they turned a corner formed by a stack of rusty scrap iron, and found a long, low building before them. From a ground-floor window light streamed out upon the fragments of rubbish strewing the ground, from amid which sickly weeds uprose as if in defiance of nature's laws. Seton paused, and:

"What is Dougal's exactly?" he asked; "a public house?"

"No," rapped Kerry. "It's a coffee-shop used by the dockers. You'll see when we get inside. The place never closes so far as I know, and if we made 'em close there would be a dock strike."

He crossed and pushed open the swing door. As Seton entered at his heels, a babel of coarse voices struck upon his ears and he found himself in a superheated atmosphere suggestive of shag, stale spirits, and imperfectly washed humanity.

Dougal's proved to be a kind of hut of wood and corrugated iron, not unlike an army canteen. There were two counters, one at either end, and two large American stoves. Oil lamps hung from the beams, and the furniture was made up of trestle tables, rough wooden chairs, and empty barrels. Coarse, thick curtains covered all the windows but one. The counter further from the entrance was laden with articles of food, such as pies, tins of bully-beef, and "saveloys," while the other was devoted to liquid refreshment in the form of ginger-beer and cider (or so the casks were conspicuously labelled), tea, coffee, and cocoa.

The place was uncomfortably crowded, the patrons congregating more especially around the two stoves. There were men who looked like dock laborers, seamen, and riverside loafers; lascars, Chinese, Arabs, and dagoes; and at the "solid" counter there presided a red-armed, brawny woman, fierce of mien and ready of tongue, while a huge Irishman, possessing a broken nose and deficient teeth, ruled the "liquid" department with a rod of iron and a flow of language which shocked even Kerry. This formidable ruffian, a retired warrior of the ring, was Dougal, said to be the strongest man from Tower Hill to the River Lea.

As they entered, several of the patrons glanced at them curiously, but no one seemed to be particularly interested. Kerry wore his cap pulled well down over his fierce eyes, and had the collar of his topcoat turned up.

He looked about him, as if expecting to recognize someone; and as they made their way to Dougal's counter, a big fellow dressed in the manner of a dock laborer stepped up to the Chief Inspector and clapped him on the shoulder.

"Have one with me, Mike," he said, winking. "The coffee's good."

Kerry bent towards him swiftly, and:

"Anybody here, Jervis?" he whispered.

"George Martin is at the bar. I've had the tip that he 'traffics.' You'll remember he figured in my last report, sir."

Kerry nodded, and the trio elbowed their way to the counter. The pseudo dock hand was a detective attached to Leman Street,

and one who knew the night birds of East End London as few men outside their own circles knew them.

"Three coffees, Pat," he cried, leaning across the shoulder of a heavy, red-headed fellow who lolled against the counter. "And two lumps of sugar in each."

"To hell wid yer sugar!" roared Dougal, grasping three cups deftly in one hairy hand and filling them from a steaming urn. "There's no more sugar tonight."

"Not any *brown* sugar?" asked the customer.

"Yez can have one tayspoon of brown, and no more to–night," cried Dougal.

He stooped rapidly below the counter, then pushed the three cups of coffee towards the detective. The latter tossed a shilling down, at which Dougal glared ferociously.

" 'Twas wid sugar ye said!" he roared.

A second shilling followed. Dougal swept both coins into a drawer and turned to another customer, who was also clamoring for coffee. Securing their cups with difficulty, for the red-headed man surlily refused to budge, they retired to a comparatively quiet spot, and Seton tasted the hot beverage.

"H'm," he said. "Rum! Good rum, too!"

"It's a nice position for me," snapped Kerry. "I *don't* think! I would remind you that there's a police station actually on this blessed island. If there was a dive like Dougal's anywhere West it would be raided as a matter of course. But to shut Dougal's would be to raise hell. There are two laws in England, sir; one for Piccadilly and the other for the Isle of Dogs!"

He sipped his coffee with appreciation. Jervis looked about him cautiously, and:

"That's George—the red-headed hooligan against the counter," he said. "He's been liquoring up pretty freely, and I shouldn't be surprised to find that he's got a job on to-night. He has a skiff beached below here, and I think he's waiting for the tide."

"Good!" rapped Kerry. "Where can we find a boat?"

"Well," Jervis smiled. "There are several lying there if you didn't come in an R.P. boat."

"We did. But I'll dismiss it. We want a small boat."

"Very good, sir. We shall have to pinch one!"

"That doesn't matter," declared Kerry, glancing at Seton with a sudden twinkle discernible in his steely eyes. "What do you say, sir?"

"I agree with you entirely," replied Seton quietly. "We must find a boat, and lie off somewhere to watch for George. He should be worth following."

"We'll be moving, then," said the Leman Street detective. "It will be high tide in an hour."

They finished their coffee as quickly as possible; the stuff was not far below boiling-point. Then Jervis returned the cups to the counter.

"Good night, Pat!" he cried, and rejoined Seton and Kerry.

As they came out into the desolation of the scrap heaps, the last traces of fog had disappeared and a steady breeze came up the river, fresh and salty from the Nore. Jervis led them in a north-easterly direction, threading a way through pyramids of rubbish, until with the wind in their teeth they came out upon the river bank at a point where the shore shelved steeply downwards. A number of boats lay on the shingle.

"We're pretty well opposite Greenwich Marshes," said Jervis. "You can just see one of the big gasometers. The end boat is George's."

"Have you searched it?" rapped Kerry, placing a fresh piece of chewing-gum between his teeth.

"I have, sir. Oh, he's too wise for that!"

"I propose," said Seton briskly, "that we borrow one of the other boats and pull down stream to where that short pier juts out. We can hide behind it and watch for our man. I take it he'll be bound up-stream, and the tide will help us to follow him quietly."

"Right," said Kerry. "We'll take the small dinghy. It's big enough."

He turned to Jervis.

"Nip across to the wooden stairs," he directed, "and tell Inspector White to stand by, but to keep out of sight. If we've started before you return, go back and join him."

"Very good, sir."

Jervis turned and disappeared into the mazes of rubbish, as Seton and Kerry grasped the boat and ran it down into the rising tide. Kerry boarding, Seton thrust it out into the river and climbed in over the stern.

"Phew! The current drags like a tow-boat!" said Kerry.

They were being drawn rapidly up-stream. But as Kerry seized the oars and began to pull steadily, this progress was checked. He could make little actual headway, however.

"The tide races round this bend like fury," he said. "Bear on the oars, sir."

Seton thereupon came to Kerry's assistance, and gradually the dinghy crept upon its course, until, below the little pier, they found a sheltered spot, where it was possible to run in and lie hidden. As they won this haven:

"Quiet!" said Seton. "Don't move the oars. Look! We were only just in time!"

Immediately above them, where the boats were beached, a man was coming down the slope, carrying a hurricane lantern. As Kerry and Seton watched, the man raised the lantern and swung it to and fro.

"Watch!" whispered Seton. "He's signalling to the Greenwich bank!"

Kerry's teeth snapped savagely together, and he chewed but made no reply, until:

"There it is!" he said rapidly. "On the marshes!"

A speck of light in the darkness it showed, a distant moving lantern on the curtain of the night. Although few would have credited Kerry with the virtue, he was a man of cultured imagination, and it seemed to him, as it seemed to Seton Pasha, that the dim light symbolized the life of the missing woman, of the woman who hovered between the gay world from which tragically she had vanished and some Chinese hell upon whose brink she hovered. Neither of the watchers was thinking of the crime and the criminal, of Sir Lucien Pyne or Kazmah, but of Mrs. Monte Irvin, mysterious victim of a mysterious tragedy. "Oh, Dan! ye must find her! ye must find her! Puir weak hairt—dinna ye ken how she is suffering!" Clairvoyantly, to Kerry's ears was borne an echo of his wife's words.

"The traffic!" he whispered. "If we lose George Martin to-night we deserve to lose the case!"

"I agree, Chief Inspector," said Seton quietly.

The grating sound made by a boat thrust out from a shingle beach came to their ears above the whispering of the tide. A ghostly figure in the dim light, George Martin clambered into his craft and took to the oars.

"If he's for the Greenwich bank," said Seton grimly, "he has a stiff task."

But for the Greenwich bank the boat was headed; and pulling mightily against the current, the man struck out into mid-stream.

They watched him for some time, silently, noting how he fought against the tide, sturdily heading for the point at which the signal had shown. Then:

"What do you suggest?" asked Seton. He may follow the Surrey bank up-stream."

"I suggest," said Kerry, "that we drift. Once in Limehouse Reach we'll hear him. There are no pleasure parties punting about that stretch."

"Let us pull out, then. I propose that we wait for him at some convenient point between the West India Dock and Limehouse Basin."

"Good," rapped Kerry, thrusting the boat out into the fierce current. "You may have spent a long time in the East, sir, but you're fairly wise on the geography of the lower Thames."

Gripped in the strongly running tide they were borne smoothly up-stream, using the oars merely for the purpose of steering. The gloomy mystery of the London river claimed them and imposed silence upon them, until familiar landmarks told of the northern bend of the Thames, and the light above the Lavender Pond shove out upon the unctuously moving water.

Each pulling a scull they headed in for the left bank.

"There's a wharf ahead," said Seton, looking back over his shoulder. "If we put in beside it we can wait there unobserved."

"Good enough," said Kerry.

They bent to the oars, stealing stroke by stroke out of the grip of the tide, and presently came to a tiny pool above the wharf structure, where it was possible to lie undisturbed by the eager current.

Those limitations which are common to all humanity and that guile which is peculiar to the Chinese veiled the fact from their ken that the deserted wharf, in whose shelter they lay, was at once the roof and the gateway of Sin Sin Wa's receiving office!

As the boat drew in to the bank, a Chinese boy who was standing on the wharf retired into the shadows. From a spot visible downstream but invisible to the men in the boat, he signalled constantly with a hurricane lantern.

Three men from New Scotland Yard were watching the house of Sin Sin Wa, and Sin Sin Wa had given no sign of animation since, some hours earlier, he had extinguished his bedroom light. Yet George, drifting noiselessly up-stream, received a signal to the effect "police" while Seton Pasha and Chief Inspector Kerry lay below the biggest dope cache in London. Seton sometimes swore under his breath. Kerry chewed incessantly. But George never came.

At that eerie hour of the night when all things living, from the lowest to the highest, nor excepting Mother Earth herself, grow chilled, when all Nature's perishable handiwork feels the touch of death—a wild, sudden cry rang out, a wailing, sorrowful cry, that seemed to come from nowhere, from everywhere, from the bank, from the stream; that rose and fell and died sobbing into the hushed whisper of the tide.

Seton's hand fastened like a vise on to Kerry's shoulder, and:

"Merciful God!" he whispered; "what was it? *Who* was it?"

"If it wasn't a spirit it was a woman," replied Kerry hoarsely; "and a woman very near to her end."

"Kerry!"—Seton Pasha had dropped all formality—"Kerry—if it calls for all the men that Scotland Yard can muster, we must search every building, down to the smallest rathole in the floor, on this bank—and do it by dawn!"

"We'll do it," rapped Kerry.

Chapter XXXIII

CHINESE MAGIC

Detective-Sergeant Coombes and three assistants watched the house of Sin Sin Wa, and any one of the three would have been prepared to swear "on the Book" that Sin Sin Wa was sleeping. But he who watches a Chinaman watches an illusionist. He must approach his task in the spirit of a psychical inquirer who seeks to trap a bogus medium. The great Robert Houdin, one of the master wizards of modern times, quitted Petrograd by two gates at the same hour according to credible witnesses; but his performance sinks into insignificance beside that of a Chinese predecessor who flourished under one of the Ming emperors. The palace of this potentate was approached by gates, each having twelve locks, and each being watched by twelve guards. Nevertheless a distinguished member of the wizard family not only gained access to the imperial presence but also departed again unseen by any of the guards, and leaving all the gates locked behind him! If Detective-sergeant Coombes had known this story he might not have experienced such complete confidence.

That door of Sin Sin Wa's establishment which gave upon a little backyard was oiled both lock and hinge so that it opened noiselessly. Like a shadow, like a ghost, Sin Sin Wa crept forth, closing the door behind him. He carried a sort of canvas kit-bag, so that one observing him might have concluded that he was "moving."

Resting his bag against the end wall, he climbed up by means of holes in the neglected brickwork until he could peer over the top. A faint smell of tobacco smoke greeted him: a detective was standing in the lane below. Soundlessly, Sin Sin Wa descended again. Raising his bag he lifted it lovingly until it rested upright upon the top of the wall and against the side of the house. The night was dark and still. Only a confused beating sound on the Surrey bank rose above the murmur of sleeping London.

From the rubbish amid which he stood, Sin Sin Wa selected a piece of rusty barrel-hoop. Cautiously he mounted upon a wooden structure built against the end wall and raised himself upright, surveying the prospect. Then he hurled the fragment of iron far along the lane, so that it bounded upon a strip of corrugated roofing in a yard twice removed from his own, and fell clattering among a neighbor's rubbish.

A short exclamation came from the detective in the lane. He could be heard walking swiftly away in the direction of the disturbance. And ere he had gone six paces, Sin Sin Wa was bending like an inverted U over the wall and was lowering his precious bag to the ground. Like a cat he sprang across and dropped noiselessly beside it.

"Hello! Who's there?" cried the detective, standing by the wall of the house which Sin Sin Wa had selected as a target.

Sin Sin Wa, bag in hand, trotted, soft of foot, across the lane and into the shadow of the dock-building. By the time that the C.I.D. man had decided to climb up and investigate the mysterious noise, Sin Sin Wa was on the other side of the canal and rapping gently upon the door of Sam Tûk's hairdressing establishment.

The door was opened so quickly as to suggest that someone had been posted there for the purpose. Sin Sin Wa entered and the door was closed again.

"Light, Ah Fung," he said in Chinese. "What news?"

The boy who had admitted him took a lamp from under a sort of rough counter and turned to Sin Sin Wa.

"George came with the boat, master, but I signalled to him that the red policeman and the agent who has hired the end room were watching."

"They are gone?"

"They gather men at the head depôt and are searching house from house. She who sleeps below awoke and cried out. They heard her cry."

"George waits?"

"He waits, master. He will wait long if the gain is great."

"Good."

Sin Sin Wa shuffled across to the cellar stairs, followed by Ah Fung with the lamp. He descended, and, brushing away the carefully spread coal dust, inserted the piece of bent wire into the crevice and raised the secret trap. Bearing his bag upon his shoulder he went down into the tunnel.

"Reclose the door, Ah Fung," he said softly; "and be watchful."

As the boy replaced the stone trap, Sin Sin Wa struck a match. Then, having the lighted match held in one hand and carrying the bag in the other, he crept along the low passage to the door of the cache. Dropping the smouldering match-end, he opened the door and entered that secret warehouse for which so many people were seeking.

Seated in a cane chair by the oil-stove was the shrivelled figure of Sam Tûk, his bald head lolling sideways so that his big horn-rimmed spectacles resembled a figure 8. On the counter was set a ship's lantern. As Sin Sin Wa came in Sam Tûk slowly raised his head.

No greetings were exchanged, but Sin Sin Wa untied the neck of his kit-bag and drew out a large wicker cage. Thereupon: "Hello! hello!" remarked the occupant drowsily. "Number one p'lice chop lo! Sin Sin Wa— Sin Sin . . ."

"Come, my Tling-a-Ling," crooned Sin Sin Wa.

He opened the front of the cage and out stepped the raven on to his wrist. Sin Sin Wa raised his arm and Tling-a-Ling settled himself contentedly upon his master's shoulder.

Placing the empty cage on the counter, Sin Sin Wa plunged his hand down into the bag and drew out the gleaming wooden joss. This he set beside the cage. With never a glance at the mummy figure of Sam Tûk, he walked around the counter, raven on shoulder, and grasping the end of the laden shelves, he pulled the last section smoothly to the left, showing that it was attached to a sliding door. The establishments of Sin Sin Wa were as full of surprises as a Sicilian trinket-box.

The double purpose of the timbering which had been added to this old storage vault was now revealed. It not only served to enlarge the store-room, but also shut off from view a second portion of the cellar, smaller than the first, and containing appointments which indicated that it was sometimes inhabited.

There was an oil-stove in the room, which, like that adjoining it, was evidently unprovided with any proper means of ventilation. A paper-shaded lamp hung from the low roof. The floor was covered with matting, and there were arm-chairs, a divan and other items of furniture, which had been removed from Mrs. Sin's sanctum in the dismantled House of a Hundred Raptures. In a recess a bed was placed, and as Sin Sin Wa came in Mrs. Sin was standing by the bed looking down at a woman who lay there.

Mrs. Sin wore her kimona of embroidered green silk and made a striking picture in that sordid setting. Her black hair she had dyed a fashionable shade of red. She glanced rapidly across her shoulder at Sin Sin Wa—a glance of contempt with which was mingled faint distrust.

"So," she said, in Chinese, "you have come at last."

Sin Sin Wa smiled. "They watched the old fox," he replied. "But their eyes were as the eyes of the mole."

Still aside, contemptuously, the woman regarded him, and:

"Suppose they are keener than you think?" she said. "Are you sure you have not led them—here?"

"The snail may not pursue the hawk," murmured Sin Sin Wa; "nor the eye of the bat follow his flight."

"Smartest leg," remarked the raven.

"Yes, yes, my little friend," crooned Sin Sin Wa, "very soon now you shall see the paddy-fields of Ho-Nan and watch the great Yellow River sweeping eastward to the sea."

"Pah!" said Mrs. Sin. "Much—very much—you care about the paddy-fields of Ho-Nan, and little, oh, very little, about the dollars and the traffic! You have my papers?"

"All are complete. With those dollars for which I care not, a man might buy the world—if he had but enough of the dollars. You are well known in Poplar as 'Mrs. Jacobs,' and your identity is easily established—as 'Mrs. Jacobs.' You join the *Mahratta* at the Albert Dock. I have bought you a post as stewardess."

Mrs. Sin tossed her head. "And Juan?"

"What can they prove against your Juan if *you* are missing?"

Mrs. Sin nodded towards the bed.

With slow and shuffling steps Sin Sin Wa approached. He continued to smile, but his glittering eye held even less of mirth than usual. Tucking his hands into his sleeves, he stood and looked down—at Rita Irvin.

Her face had acquired a waxen quality, but some of her delicate coloring still lingered, lending her a ghastly and mask-like aspect. Her nostrils and lips were blanched, however, and possessed a curiously pinched appearance. It was impossible to detect the fact that she breathed, and her long lashes lay motionless upon her cheeks.

Sin Sin Wa studied her silently for some time, then:

"Yes," he murmured, "she is beautiful. But women are like adder's eggs. He is a fool who warms them in his bosom." He turned his slow regard upon Mrs. Sin. "You have stained your hair to look even as hers. It was discreet, my wife. But one is beautiful and many-shadowed like a copper vase, and the other is like a winter sunset on the poppy-fields. You remind me of the angry red policeman, and I tremble."

"Tremble as much as you like," said Mrs. Sin scornfully, "but *do* something, think; don't leave everything to me. She screamed to-night—and someone heard her. They are searching the river bank from door to door."

"Lo!" murmured Sin Sin Wa, "even this I had learned, nor failed to heed the beating of a distant drum. And why did she scream?"

"I was—keeping her asleep; and the prick of the needle woke her."

"Tchée, tchée," crooned Sin Sin Wa, his voice sinking lower and lower and his eye nearly closing. "But still she lives—and is beautiful."

"Beautiful!" mocked Mrs. Sin. "A doll-woman, bloodless and nerveless!"

"So—so. Yet she, so bloodless and nerveless, unmasked the secret of Kazmah, and she, so bloodless and nerveless, struck down——"

Mrs. Sin ground her teeth together audibly.

"Yes, yes!" she said in sibilant Chinese. "She is a robber, a thief, a murderess." She bent over the unconscious woman, her jewel-laden fingers crooked and menacing. "With my bare hands I would strangle her, but——"

"There must be no marks of violence when she is found in the river. Tchée, chée—it is a pity."

"Number one p'lice chop, lo!" croaked the raven, following this remark with the police-whistle imitation.

Mrs. Sin turned and stared fiercely at the one-eyed bird.

"Why do you bring that evil, croaking thing here?" she demanded. "Have we not enough risks?"

Sin Sin Wa smiled patiently.

"Too many," he murmured. "For failure is nothing but the taking of seven risks when

six were enough. Come—let us settle our affairs. The 'Jacobs' account is closed, but it is only a question of hours or days before the police learn that the wharf as well as the house belongs to someone of that name. We have drawn our last dollar from the traffic, my wife. Our stock we are resigned to lose. So let us settle our affairs."

"Smartest—smartest," croaked Tling-a-Ling, and rattled ghostly castanets.

Chapter XXXIV

ABOVE AND BELOW

Thank the guid God I see ye alive, Dan," said Mary Kerry.

Having her husband's dressing-gown over her night attire, and her usually neat hair in great disorder, she stood just within the doorway of the little dining-room at Spenser Road, her face haggard and the fey light in her eyes. Kerry, seated in the armchair dressed as he had come in from the street, a parody of his neat self with mud on his shoes and streaks of green slime on his overall, raised his face from his hands and stared at her wearily.

"I awakened wi' a cry at some hour afore the dawn," she whispered, stretching out her hands and looking like a wild-eyed prophetess of old. "My hairt beat sair fast and then grew caud. I droppit on my knees and prayed as I ha' ne'er prayed afore. Dan, Dan, I thought ye were gane from me."

"I nearly was," said Kerry, a faint spark of his old truculency lighting up the weary eyes. "The man from Whitehall only missed me by a miracle."

" 'Twas the miracle o' prayer, Dan," declared his wife in a low, awe-stricken voice. "For as I prayed, a great comfort came to me an' a great peace. The second sight was wi' me, Dan, and I saw, no' yersel'—whereby I seemed to ken that ye were safe—but a puir dying soul stretched on a bed o' sorrow. At the fuit o' the bed was standing a fearsome figure o' a man—yellow and wicked, wi' his hands tuckit in his sleeves. I thought 'twas a veesion that was opening up tae me and that a' was about to be made clear, when as though a curtain had been droppit before my een, it went awa' an' I kenned it nae more; but plain—plain, I heerd the howling o' a dog."

Kerry started and clutched the arms of the chair.

"A dog!" he said. "A dog!"

"The howling o' a sma' dog," declared his wife; "and I thought 'twas a portent, an' the great fear came o'er me again. But as I prayed 'twas unfolden to me that the portent was no' for yersel' but for her—the puir weak hairt ye ha' tae save."

She ceased speaking and the strange fey light left her eyes. She dropped upon her knees beside Kerry, bending her head and throwing her arms about him. He glanced down at her tenderly and laid his hands upon her shoulders; but he was preoccupied, and the next moment, his jaws moving mechanically, he was staring straight before him.

"A dog," he muttered, "a dog!"

Mary Kerry did not move; until, a light of understanding coming into Kerry's fierce eyes, he slowly raised her and stood upright himself.

"I have it!" he said. "Mary, the case is won! Twenty men have spent the night and early morning beating the river bank so that the very rats have been driven from their holes. Twenty men have failed where a dog would have succeeded. Mary, I must be off."

"Ye're no goin' out again, Dan. Ye're weary tae death."

"I must, my dear, and it's *you* who send me."

"But, Dan, where are ye goin'?"

Kerry grabbed his hat and cane from the sideboard upon which they lay, and:

"I'm going for the dog!" he rapped.

Weary as he was and travel-stained, for once neglectful of that neatness upon which he prided himself, he set out, hope reborn in his heart. His assertion that the very rats had been driven from their holes was scarce an exaggeration. A search-party of twenty men, hastily mustered and conducted by Kerry and Seton Pasha, had explored every house, every shop, every wharf, and, as Kerry believed, every cellar adjoining the bank, between Limehouse Basin and the dock gates. Where access had been denied them or where no one had resided they had never hesitated to force an entrance. But no trace had they found of those whom they sought.

For the first time within Kerry's memory, or, indeed, within the memory of any member of the Criminal Investigation Department, Detective-sergeant Coombes had ceased to smile when the appalling truth was revealed to him that Sin Sin Wa had vanished—that Sin Sin Wa had mysteriously joined that invisible company which included Kazmah, Mrs. Sin and Mrs. Monte Irvin. Not a word of reprimand did the Chief Inspector utter, but his eyes seemed to emit sparks. Hands plunged deeply in his pockets he had turned away, and not even Seton Pasha had dared speak to him for fully five minutes.

Kerry began to regard the one-eyed Chinaman with a superstitious fear which he strove in vain to stifle. That any man could have succeeded in converting a *chandu-khân* such as that described by Mollie Gretna into a filthy deserted dwelling such as that visited by Kerry, within the space of some thirty-six hours, was wellnigh incredible. But the Chief Inspector had deduced (correctly) that the exotic appointments depicted by Mollie were all of a detachable nature—merely masking the filthiness beneath; so that at the shortest notice the House of a Hundred Raptures could be dismantled. The communicating door was a larger proposition, but that it was one within the compass of Sin Sin Wa its effectual disapearance sufficiently demonstrated.

Doubtless (Kerry mused savagely) the appointments of the opium-house had been smuggled into that magically hidden cache which now concealed the conjurer Sin Sin Wa as well as the other members of the Kazmah company. How any man of flesh and blood could have escaped from a six-roomed house surrounded by detectives surpassed Kerry's powers of imagination. How any apartment large enough to contain a mouse, much less half a dozen human beings, could exist anywhere within the area covered by the search-party he failed to understand, nor was he prepared to admit it humanly possible.

Kerry chartered a taxicab by Brixton Town Hall and directed the man to drive to Princes Gate. To the curious glances of certain of his neighbors who had never before seen the Chief Inspector otherwise than a model of cleanliness and spruceness he was indifferent. But the manner in which the taxi-driver looked him up and down penetrated through the veil of abstraction which hitherto had rendered Kerry impervious to all external impressions, and:

"Give me another look like that, my lad," he snapped furiously, "and I'll bash your head through your blasted wind-screen."

A ready retort trembled upon the cabman's tongue, but a glance into the savage blue eyes reduced him to fearful silence. Kerry entered the cab and banged the door; and the man drove off positively trembling with indignation.

Deep in reflection the Chief Inspector was driven westward through the early morning traffic. Fine rain was falling, and the streets presented that curiously drab appearance which only London streets can present in all its dreary perfection. Workers bound City-ward fought for places inside trams and buses. A hundred human comedies and tragedies were to be witnessed upon the highways; but to all of them Kerry was blind as he was deaf to the din of workaday Babylon. In spirit he was roaming the bank of Old Father Thames where the river sweeps eastward below Limehouse Causeway—wonder-stricken before the magic of the one-eyed wizard who could at will efface himself as an artist rubs out a drawing, who could *camouflage* a drug warehouse so successfully that human skill, however closely addressed to the task, failed utterly to detect its whereabouts. Above the discord of the busy streets he heard again and again that cry in the night which had come from a hapless prisoner whom they were powerless to succor. He beat his cane upon the floor of the cab and swore savagely and loudly. The intimidated cabman, believing these demonstrations designed to urge him to a greater speed, performed feats of driving calculated to jeopardize his license. But still the savage passenger stamped and cursed, so that the cabby began to believe that a madman was seated behind him.

At the corner of Kennington Oval Kerry was effectually aroused to the realities. A little runabout car passed his cab, coming from a southerly direction. Proceeding at a rapid speed it was lost in the traffic ahead. Unconsciously Kerry had glanced at the oc-cupants and had recognized Margaret Halley and Seton Pasha. The old spirit of rivalry between himself and the man from Whitehall leapt up hotly within Kerry's breast. "Now where the hell has *he* been!" he muttered.

As a matter of fact, Seton Pasha, acting upon a suggestion of Margaret's had been to Brixton Prison to interview Juan Mareno who lay there under arrest. Contents bills an-nouncing this arrest as the latest public de-velopment in the Bond Street murder case were to be seen upon every news-stand; yet the problem of that which had brought Seton to the south of London was one with which

Kerry grappled in vain. He had parted from the Home Office agent in the early hours of the morning, and their parting had been one of mutual despair which neither had sought to disguise.

It was a coincidence which a student of human nature might have regarded as sig-nificant, that whereas Kerry had taken his troubles home to his wife, Seton Pasha had sought inspiration from Margaret Halley; and whereas the guidance of Mary Kerry had led the Chief Inspector to hurry in quest of Rita Irvin's spaniel, the result of Seton's interview with Margaret had been an equally hurried journey to the big jail.

Unhappily Seton had failed to elicit the slightest information from the saturnine Mareno. Unmoved alike by promises or threats, he had coolly adhered to his original evidence.

So, while the authorities worked fever-ishly and all England reading of the arrest of Mareno inquired indignantly, "But who is Kazmah, and where is Mrs. Monte Irvin?" Sin Sin Wa placidly pursued his arrange-ments for immediate departure to the paddy-fields of Ho-Nan, and sometimes in the weird crooning voice with which he addressed the raven he would sing a monotonous chant dealing with the valley of the Yellow River where the opium-poppy grows. Hidden in the cunning vault, the search had passed above him; and watchful on a quay on the Surrey shore whereto his dinghy was fas-tened, George Martin awaited the signal which should tell him that Kazmah and Company were ready to leave. Any time af-ter dark he expected to see the waving lan-tern and to collect his last payment from the traffic.

At the very hour that Kerry was hastening to Princes Gate, Sin Sin Wa sat before the stove in the drug cache, the green-eyed joss upon his knee. With a fragment of chamois leather he lovingly polished the leering idol, crooning softly to himself and smiling his mirthless smile. Perched upon his shoulder the raven studied this operation with ap-parent interest, his solitary eye glittering bead-like. Upon the opposite side of the stove sat the ancient Sam Tûk, and at intervals of five minutes or more he would slowly nod his hairless head.

The sliding door which concealed the in-ner room was partly open, and from the opening there shone forth a dim red light, cast by the paper-shaded lamp which illuminated the place. The coarse voice of the Cuban-Jewess rose and fell in a ceaseless half-muttered soliloquy, indescribably unpleasant but to which Sin Sin Wa was evidently indifferent.

Propped up amid cushions on the divan which once had formed part of the furniture of the House of a Hundred Raptures, Mrs. Sin was smoking opium. The long bamboo pipe had fallen from her listless fingers, and her dark eyes were partly glazed. Buddha-like immobility was claiming her, but it had not yet effaced that expression of murderous malice with which the smoker contemplated the unconscious woman who lay upon the bed at the other end of the room.

As the moments passed the eyes of Mrs. Sin grew more and more glazed. Her harsh voice became softened, and presently: "Ah!" she whispered; "so you wait to smoke with me?"

Immobile she sat propped up amid the cushions, and only her full lips moved.

"Two pipes are nothing to Cy," she murmured. "He smokes five. But you are not going to smoke?"

Again she paused, then:

"Ah, my Lucy. You smoke with *me?*" she whispered coaxingly.

Chandu had opened the poppy gates. Mrs. Sin was conversing with her dead lover.

"Something has changed you," she sighed. "You are different—lately. You have lots of money now. Your investments have been good. You want to become—respectable, eh?"

Slightly—ever so slightly—the red lips curled upwards. No sound of life came from the woman lying white and still in the bed. But through the partly open door crept snatches of Sin Sin Wa's crooning melody.

"Yet once," she murmured, "yet once I seemed beautiful to you, Lucy. For La Belle Lola you forgot that English pride." She laughed softly. "You forgot Sin Sin Wa. If there had been no Lola you would never have escaped from Buenos Ayres with your life, my Lucy. You forgot that English pride, and did not ask me where I got them from—the ten thousand dollars to buy your 'honor' back."

She became silent, as if listening to the dead man's reply. Finally:

"No—I do not reproach you, my dear," she whispered. "You have paid me back a thousand fold, and Sin Sin Wa, the old fox, grows rich and fat. To-day we hold the traffic in our hands, Lucy. The old fox cares only

for his money. Before it is too late let us go—you and I. Do you remember Havana, and the two months of heaven we spent there? Oh, let us go back to Havana, Lucy. Kazmah has made us rich. Let Kazmah die. . . . You smoke with me?"

Again she became silent, then:

"Very likely," she murmured; "very likely I know why you don't smoke. You have promised your pretty little friend that you will stay awake and see that nobody tries to cut her sweet white throat."

She paused momentarily, then muttered something rapidly in Spanish, followed by a short, guttural phrase in Chinese.

"Why do you bring her to the house?" she whispered hoarsely. "And you brought her to Kazmah's. Ah! I see. Now everybody says you are changed. Yes . . . she is a charming friend."

The Buddha-like face became suddenly contorted, and as suddenly grew placid again.

"I know! I know!" Mrs. Sin muttered harshly. "Do you think I am blind! If she had been like any of the others, do you suppose it would have mattered to *me?* But you *respect* her—you *respect.* . . ." Her voice died away to an almost inaudible whisper: "I don't believe you. You are telling me lies. But you have always told me lies; one more does not matter, I suppose. . . . How strong you are. You have hurt my wrists. You will smoke with me now?"

She ceased speaking abruptly, and abruptly resumed again:

"And I do as you wish—I do as you wish. How can I keep her from it except by making the price so high that she cannot afford to buy it? I tell you I do it. I bargain for the pink and white boy, Quentin, because I want her to be indebted to him—because I want her to be so sorry for him that she lets him take her away from *you!* Why should you *respect* her——"

Silence fell upon the drugged speaker. Sin Sin Wa could be heard crooning softly about the Yellow River and the mountain gods who sent it sweeping down through the valleys where the opium-poppy grows.

"Go, Juan," hissed Mrs. Sin. "I say—*go!*"

Her voice changed eerily to a deep, mocking bass; and Rita Irvin lying, a pallid wraith of her once lovely self, upon the untidy bed, stirred slightly—her lashes quivering. Her eyes opened and stared straight upward at the low, dirty ceiling, horror growing in their shadowy depths.

Chapter XXXV

BEYOND THE VEIL

Rita Irvin's awakening was no awakening in the usually accepted sense of the word; it did not even represent a lifting of the veil which cut her off from the world, but no more than a momentary perception of the existence of such a veil and of the existence of something behind it. Upon the veil, in grey smoke, the name "Kazmah" was written in moving characters. Beyond the veil, dimly divined, was life.

As of old the victims of the Inquisition, waking or dreaming, beheld ever before them the instrument of their torture, so before this woman's racked and half-numbed mind panoramically passed, an endless pageant, the incidents of the night which had cut her off from living men and women. She tottered on the border-line which divides sanity from madness. She was learning what Sir Lucien had meant when, once, long long ago, in some remote time when she was young and happy and had belonged to a living world, he had said "a day is sure to come——" It had come, that "day." It had dawned when she had torn the veil before Kazmah—and that veil had enveloped her ever since. All that had preceded the fatal act was blotted out, blurred and indistinct; all that had succeeded it lived eternally, passing, an endless pageant, before her tortured mind.

The horror of the moment when she had touched the hands of the man seated in the big ebony chair was of such kind that no subsequent terrors had supplanted it. For those long, slim hands of the color of old ivory were cold, rigid, lifeless—the hands of a corpse! Thus the pageant began, and it continued as hereafter, memory and delusion taking the stage in turn.

*   *   *   *   *

Complete darkness came.

Rita uttered a wild cry of horror and loathing, shrinking back from the thing which sat in the ebony chair. She felt that consciousness was slipping from her; felt herself falling, and shrieked to know herself helpless and alone with Kazmah. She groped for support, but found none; and, moaning, she sank down, and was unconscious of her fall.

A voice awakened her. Someone knelt beside her in the darkness, supporting her; someone who spoke wildly, despairingly, but with a strange, emotional reverence curbing the passion in his voice.

"Rita—my Rita! What have they done to you? Speak to me. . . . Oh, God! spare her to me. . . . Let her hate me for ever, but spare her—spare her. Rita, speak to me! I tried, heaven hear me, to save you, little girl. I only want you to be happy——"

She felt herself being lifted gently, tenderly. And as though the man's passionate entreaty had called her back from the dead, she reentered into life and strove to realize what had happened.

Sir Lucien was supporting her, and she found it hard to credit the fact that it was he, the hard, nonchalant man of the world she knew, who had spoken. She clutched his arm with both hands.

"Oh, Lucy!" she whispered. "I am so frightened—and so ill."

"Thank God," he said huskily, "she is alive. Lean against me and try to stand up. We must get away from here."

Rita managed to stand upright, clinging wildly to Sir Lucien. A square, vaguely luminous opening became visible to her. Against it, silhouetted, she could discern part of the outline of Kazmah's chair. She drew back, uttering a low, sobbing cry. Sir Lucien supported her, and:

"Don't be afraid, dear," he said reassuringly. "Nothing shall hurt you."

He pushed open a door, and through it shone the same vague light which she had seen in the opening behind the chair. Sir Lucien spoke rapidly in a language which sounded like Spanish. He was answered by a perfect torrent of words in the same tongue.

Fiercely he cried something back at the hidden speaker.

A shriek of rage, of frenzy, came out of the darkness. Rita felt that consciousness was about to leave her again. She swayed forward dizzily, and a figure which seemed to belong to delirium—a lithe shadow out of which gleamed a pair of wild eyes—leapt upon her. A knife glittered. . . .

In order to have repelled the attack, Sir Lucien would have had to release Rita, who was clinging to him, weak and terror-stricken. Instead he threw himself before her. . . . She saw the knife enter his shoulder. . . .

Through absolute darkness she sank down into a land of chaotic nightmare horrors. Great bells clanged maddeningly. Impish hands plucked at her garments, dragged her hair. She was hurried this way and that, bruised, torn, and tossed helpless upon a sea of liquid brass. Through vast avenues lined with yellow, immobile Chinese faces she was borne upon a bier. Oblique eyes looked into hers. Knives which glittered greenly in the light of lamps globular and suspended in immeasurable space, were hurled at her in showers. . . .

Sir Lucien stood before her, supporting her; and all the knives buried themselves in his body. She tried to cry out, but no sound could she utter. Darkness fell again. . . .

A Chinaman was bending over her. His hands were tucked in his loose sleeves. He smiled, and his smile was hideous but friendly. He was strangely like Sin Sin Wa, save that he did not lack an eye.

Rita found herself lying in an untidy bed in a room laden with opium fumes and dimly lighted. On a table beside her were the remains of a meal. She strove to recall having partaken of food, but was unsuccessful. . . .

There came a blank—then a sharp, stabbing pain in her right arm. She thought it was the knife, and shrieked wildly again and again. . . .

Years seemingly elapsed, years of agony spent amid oblique eyes which floated in space unattached to any visible body, amid reeking fumes and sounds of ceaseless conflict. Once she heard the cry of some bird, and thought it must be the parakeet which eternally sat on a branch of a lonely palm in the heart of the Great Sahara. . . . Then, one night, when she lay shrinking from the plucking yellow hands which reached out of the darkness:

"Tell me your dream," boomed a deep, mocking voice; "and I will read its portent!"

She opened her eyes. She lay in the untidy bed in the room which was laden with the fumes of *chandu*. She stared upward at the low, dirty ceiling.

"Why do you come to *me* with your stories of desperation?" continued the mocking voice. "You have insisted upon seeing me. I am here."

Rita managed to move her head so that she could see more of the room.

On a divan at the other end of the place, propped up by a number of garish cushions, Rita beheld Mrs. Sin. The long bamboo pipe had fallen from her listless fingers. Her face wore an expression of mystic rapture, like that characterizing the features of some Chinese Buddhas. . . .

In the other corner of the divan, contemplating her from under heavy brows, sat *Kazmah*. . . .

Chapter XXXVI

SAM TÛK MOVES

Chinatown was being watched as Chinatown had never been watched before, even during the most stringent enforcement of the Defence of the Realm Act. K Division was on its mettle, and Scotland Yard had sent to aid Chief Inspector Kerry every man that could be spared to the task. The River Police, too, were aflame with zeal; for every officer in the service whose work lay east of London Bridge had appropriated to himself the stigma implied by the creation of Lord Wrexborough's commision.

"Corners" in foodstuffs, metals, and other indispensable commodities are appreciated by every man, because every man knows such things to exist; but a corner in drugs was something which the East End police authorities found very difficult to grasp. They could not free their minds of the traditional idea that every second Chinaman in the Causeway was a small importer. They were seeking a hundred lesser stores instead of one greater one. Not all Seton's quiet explanations nor Kerry's savage language could wean the higher local officials from their ancient beliefs. They failed to conceive the idea of a wealthy syndicate conducted by an educated Chinaman, and backed, covered, and protected by a crooked gentleman and accomplished man of affairs.

Perhaps they knew and perhaps they knew not, that during the period ruled by D.O.R.A. as much as £25 was paid by habitués for one pipe of *chandu*. The power of gold is often badly estimated by an official whose horizon is marked by a pension. This is mere lack of imagination, and no more reflects discredit upon a man than lack of hair on his crown or of color in his cheeks. Nevertheless, it may prove very annoying.

Towards the close of an afternoon which symbolized the worst that London's particular climate can do in the matter of drizzling rain and gloom, Chief Inspector Kerry, carrying an irritable toy spaniel, came out of a turning which forms a V with Limehouse Canal, into a narrow street which runs parallel with the Thames. He had arrived at the conclusion that the neighborhood was sown so thickly with detectives that one could not throw a stone without hitting one. Yet Sin Sin Wa had quietly left his abode and had disappeared from official ken.

Three times within the past ten minutes the spaniel had tried to bite Kerry, nor was Kerry blind to the amusement which his burden had occasioned among the men of K Division whom he had met on his travels. Finally, as he came out into the riverside lane, the illtempered little animal essayed a fourth, and successful, attempt, burying his wicked white teeth in the Chief Inspector's wrist.

Kerry hooked his fingers into the dog's collar, swung the yapping animal above his head, and hurled it from him into the gloom and rain mist.

"Hell take the blasted thing!" he shouted. "I'm done with it!"

He tenderly sucked his wounded wrist, and picking up his cane, which he had dropped, he looked about him and swore savagely. Of Seton Pasha he had had news several times during the day, and he was aware that the Home Office agent was not idle. But to that old rivalry which had leapt up anew when he had seen Seton near Kennington Oval had succeeded a sort of despair; so that now he would have welcomed the information that Seton had triumphed where he had failed. A furious hatred of the one-eyed Chinaman around whom he was convinced the mystery centred had grown up within his mind. At that hour he would gladly have resigned his post and sacrificed his pension to know that Sin Sin Wa was under lock and key. His outlook was official, and accordingly peculiar. He regarded the murder of Sir Lucien Pyne and the flight or abduction of Mrs. Monte Irvin as mere minor incidents in a case wherein Sin Sin Wa figured as the chief culprit. Nothing had acted so powerfully to bring about this conviction in the mind of the Chief Inspector as the inexplicable disappearance of the Chinaman under circumstances which had apparently precluded such a possibility.

A whimpering cry came to Kerry's ears; and because beneath the mask of ferocity which he wore a humane man was concealed: "Flames!" he snapped; "perhaps I've broken the poor little devil's leg."

Shaking a cascade of water from the brim of his neat bowler, he set off through the murk towards the spot from whence the cries

of the spaniel seemed to proceed. A few paces brought him to the door of a dirty little shop. In a window close beside it appeared the legend:

SAM TÛK,
BARBER.

The spaniel crouched by the door whining and scratching, and as Kerry came up it raised its beady black eyes to him with a look which, while it was not unfearful, held an unmistakable appeal. Kerry stood watching the dog for a moment, and as he watched he became conscious of an exhilarated pulse.

He tried the door and found it to be open. Thereupon he entered a dirty little shop, which he remembered to have searched in person in the grey dawn of the day which now was entering upon a premature dusk. The dog ran in past him, crossed the gloomy shop, and raced down into a tiny coal cellar, which likewise had been submitted during the early hours of the morning to careful scrutiny under the directions of the Chief Inspector.

A Chinese boy, who had been the only occupant of the place on that occasion and who had given his name as Ah Fung, was surprised by the sudden entrance of man and dog in the act of spreading coal dust with his fingers upon a portion of the paved floor. He came to his feet with a leap and confronted Kerry. The spaniel began to scratch feverishly upon the spot where the coal dust had been artificially spread. Kerry's eyes gleamed like steel. He shot out his hand and grasped the Chinaman by his long hair. "Open that trap," he said, "or I'll break you in half!"

Ah Fung's oblique eyes regarded him with an expression difficult to analyze, but partly it was murderous. He made no attempt to obey the order. Meanwhile the dog, whining and scratching furiously, had exposed the greater part of a stone slab somewhat larger than those adjoining it, and having a large crack or fissure in one end.

"For the last time," said Kerry, drawing the man's head back so that his breath began to whistle through his nostrils, "open that trap."

As he spoke he released Ah Fung, and Ah Fung made one wild leap towards the stairs. Kerry's fist caught him behind the ear as he sprang, and he went down like a dead man upon a small heap of coal which filled the angle of the cellar.

Breathing rapidly and having his teeth so tightly clenched that his maxillary muscles protruded lumpishly, Kerry stood looking at the fallen man. But Ah Fung did not move.

The dog had ceased to scratch, and now stood uttering short staccato barks and looking up at the Chief Inspector. Otherwise there was no sound in the house, above or below.

Kerry stooped, and with his handkerchief scrupulously dusted the stone slab. The spaniel, resentment forgotten, danced excitedly beside him and barked continuously.

"There's some sort of hook to fit in that crack," muttered Kerry.

He began to hunt about among the débris which littered one end of the cellar, testing fragment after fragment, but failing to find any piece of scrap to suit his purpose. By sheer perseverance rather than by any process of reasoning, he finally hit upon the piece of bent wire which was the key to this door of Sin Sin Wa's drug warehouse.

One short exclamation of triumph he muttered at the moment that his glance rested upon it, and five seconds later he had the trapdoor open and was peering down into the narrow pit in which wooden steps rested. The spaniel began to bark wildly, whereupon Kerry grasped him, tucked him under his arm, and ran up to the room above, where he deposited the furiously wriggling animal. He stepped quickly back again and closed the upper door. By this act he plunged the cellar into complete darkness, and accordingly he took out from the pocket of his rain-drenched overall the electric torch which he always carried. Directing its ray downwards into the cellar, he perceived Ah Fung move and toss his hand above his head. He also detected a faint rattling sound.

"Ah!" said Kerry.

He descended, and stooping over the unconscious man extracted from the pocket of his baggy blue trousers four keys upon a ring. At these Kerry stared eagerly. Two of them belonged to yale locks; the third was a simple English barrel-key, which probably fitted a padlock; but the fourth was large and complicated.

"Looks like the key of a jail," he said aloud.

He spoke with unconscious prescience. This was the key of the door of the vault. Removing his overall, Kerry laid it with his cane upon the scrap-heap, then he climbed down the ladder and found himself in the mouth of that low timbered tunnel, like a trenchwork, which owed its existence to the cunning craftsmanship of Sin Sin Wa. Stooping uncomfortably, he made his way along the passage until the massive door confronted him. He was in no doubt as to which key to employ; his mental condition was such that he was indifferent to the dangers which probably lay before him.

The well-oiled lock operated smoothly. Kerry pushed the door open and stepped briskly into the vault.

His movements, from the moment that he had opened the trap, had been swift and as nearly noiseless as the difficulties of the task had permitted. Nevertheless, they had not been so silent as to escape the attention of the preternaturally acute Sin Sin Wa. Kerry found the place occupied only by the aged Sam Tûk. A bright fire burned in the stove, and a ship's lantern stood upon the counter. Dense chemical fumes rendered the air difficult to breathe; but the shelves, once laden with the largest illicit collection of drugs in London, were bare.

Kerry's fierce eyes moved right and left; his jaws worked automatically. Sam Tûk sat motionless, his hands concealed in his sleeves, bending decrepitly forward in his chair. Then:

"Hi! Guy Fawkes!" rapped Kerry, striding forward "Who's been letting off fire-works?"

Sam Tûk nodded senilely, but spoke not a word.

Kerry stooped and stared into the heart of the fire. A dense coat of white ash lay upon the embers. He grasped the shoulder of the aged Chinaman, and pushed him back so that he could look into the bleared eyes behind the owlish spectacles.

"Been cleaning up the 'evidence,' eh?" he shouted. "This joint stinks of opium and a score of other dopes. Where are the gang?" He shook the yielding, ancient frame. "Where's the smart with one eye?"

But Sam Tûk merely nodded; and as Kerry released his hold sank forth again, nodding incessantly.

"H'm, you're a hard case," said the Chief Inspector. "A couple of witnesses like you and the jury would retire to Bedlam!"

He stood glaring fiercely at the limp frame of the old Chinaman, and as he glared his expression changed. Lying on the dirty floor not a yard from Sam Tûk's feet was a ball of leaf opium!

"Ha!" exclaimed Kerry, and he stooped to pick it up.

As he did so, with a lightning movement of which the most astute observer could never have supposed him capable, Sam Tûk whipped a loaded rubber tube from his sleeve and struck Kerry a shrewd blow across the back of the skull.

The Chief Inspector, without word or cry, collapsed upon his knees, and then fell gently forward—forward—and toppled face downwards before his assailant. His bowler fell off and rolled across the dirty floor.

Sam Tûk sank deeply into his chair, and his toothless jaws worked convulsively. The skinny hand which clutched the piece of tubing twitched and shook, so that the primitive deadly weapon fell from its wielder's grasp.

Silently, that set of empty shelves nearest to the inner wall of the vault slid open, and Sin Sin Wa came out. He, too, carried his hands tucked in his sleeves, and his yellow, pock-marked face wore its eternal smile.

"Well done," he crooned softly in Chinese. "Well done, bald father of wisdom. The dogs draw near, but the old fox sleeps not."

Chapter XXXVII

SETON PASHA REPORTS

At about the time that the fearless Chief Inspector was entering the estabishment of Sam Tûk, Seton Pasha was reporting to Lord Wrexborough in Whitehall. His nautical disguise had served its purpose, and he had now finally abandoned it, recognizing that he had to deal with a criminal of genius to whom disguise merely afforded matter for amusement.

In his proper person, as Greville Seton, he afforded a marked contrast to that John Smiles, a seaman, who had sat in a top room in Limehouse with Chief Inspector Kerry. And although he had to report failure, the grim, bronzed face and bright grey eyes must have inspired in the heart of any thoughtful observer confidence in ultimate success. Lord Wrexborough, silverhaired, florid and dignified, sat before a vast table laden with neatly arranged dispatch-boxes, books, documents tied with red tape, and other impressive impedimenta which characterize the table of a Secretary of State. Quentin Gray, unable to conceal his condition of nervous excitement, stared from a window down into Whitehall.

"I take it, then, Seton," Lord Wrexborough was saying, "that in your opinion—although perhaps it is somewhat hastily formed—there is and has been no connivance between officials and receivers of drugs?"

"That is my opinion, sir. The traffic has gradually and ingeniously been 'ringed' by a wealthy group. Small dealers have been bought out or driven out, and to-day I believe it would be difficult, if not impossible, to obtain opium, cocaine, or veronal illicitly anywhere in London. Kazmah and Company had the available stock cornered. Of course, now that they are out of business, no doubt others will step in. It is a trade that can never be suppressed under existing laws."

"I see, I see," muttered Lord Wrexborough, adjusting his pince-nez. "You also believe that Kazmah and Company are in hiding within what you term"—he consulted a written page—"the 'Causeway area'? And you believe that the man called Sin Sin Wa is the head of the organization?"

"I believe that the late Sir Lucien Pyne was the actual head of the group," said Seton bluntly. "But Sin Sin Wa is the acting head. In view of his physical peculiarities, I don't quite see how he's going to escape us, either, sir. His wife has a fighting chance, and as for Mohammed el-Kazmah, he might sail for anywhere to-morrow, and we should never know. You see, we have no description of the man."

"His passports?" murmured Lord Wrexborough.

Seton Pasha smiled grimly.

"Not an insurmountable difficulty, sir," he replied; "but Sin Sin Wa is a marked man. He has the longest and thickest pigtail which I ever saw on a human scalp. I take it he is a Southerner of the old school; therefore, he won't cut it off. He has also only one eye, and while there are many one-eyed Chinamen, there are few one-eyed Chinamen who possess pigtails like a battleship's hawser. Furthermore, he travels with a talking raven, and I'll swear he won't leave it behind. On the other hand, he is endowed with an amount of craft which comes very near to genius."

"And—Mrs. Monte Irvin?"

Quentin Gray turned suddenly, and his boyish face was very pale.

"Seton, Seton!" he said. "For God's sake tell me the truth! Do you think——"

He stopped, choking emotionally. Seton

Pasha watched him with that cool, confident stare which could either soothe or irritate; and——

"She was alive this morning, Gray," he replied quietly; "we heard her. You may take it from me that they will offer her no violence. I shall say no more."

Lord Wrexborough cleared his throat and took up a document from the table.

"Your remark raises another point, Quentin," he said sternly, "which has to be settled to-day. Your appointment to Cairo was confirmed this morning. You sail on Tuesday."

Quentin Gray turned again abruptly and stared out of the window.

"You're practically kicking me out, sir," he said. "I don't know what I've done."

"You have done nothing," replied Lord Wrexborough, "which an honorable man may not do. But in common with many others similarly circumstanced, you seem inclined, now that your military duties are at an end, to regard life as a sort of perpetual 'leave.' I speak frankly before Seton because I know that he agrees with me. My friend the Foreign Secretary has generously offered you an appointment which opens up a career that should not—I repeat, that should not prove less successful than his own."

Gray turned, and his face had flushed deeply.

"I know that Margaret has been scaring you about Rita Irvin," he said, "but on my word, sir, there was no need to do it."

He met Seton Pasha's cool regard, and:

"Margaret's one of the best," he added. I know you agree with me?"

A faint suggestion of added color came into Seton's tanned cheeks.

"I do, Gray," he answered quietly. "I believe you are good enough to look upon me as a real friend; therefore allow me to add my advice, for what it is worth, to that of Lord Wrexborough and your cousin: take the Egyptian appointment. I know where it will lead. You can do no good by remaining in London; and when we find Mrs. Irvin your presence would be an embarrassment to the unhappy man who waits for news at Princes Gate. I am frank, but it's my way."

He held out his hand, smiling. Quentin Gray's mercurial complexion was changing again, but:

"Good old Seton!" he said, rather huskily, and gripped the outstretched hand. "For Irvin's sake, save her!"

He turned to his father.

"Thank you, sir," he added; "you are always right. I shall be ready on Tuesday. I suppose you are off again, Seton?"

"I am," was the reply. "Chief Inspector Kerry is moving heaven and earth to find the Kazmah establishment, and I don't want to come in a poor second."

Lord Wrexborough cleared his throat and turned in the padded revolving chair.

"Honestly, Seton," he said, "what do think of your chance of success?"

Seton Pasha smiled grimly.

"Many ascribe success to wit," he replied, "and failure to bad luck; but the Arab says 'Kismet.' "

Chapter XXXVIII

THE SONG OF SIN SIN WA

Mrs. Sin, aroused by her husband from the deep opium sleep, came out into the fume-laden vault. Her dyed hair was disarranged, and her dark eyes stared glassily before her; but even in this half-drugged state she bore herself with the lithe carriage of a dancer, swinging her hips lazily and pointing the toes of her high-heeled slippers.

"Awake, my wife," crooned Sin Sin Wa. "Only a fool seeks the black smoke when the jackals sit in a ring."

Mrs. Sin gave him a glance of smiling contempt—a glance which, passing him, rested finally upon the prone body of Chief Inspector Kerry lying stretched upon the floor before the stove. Her pupils contracted to mere pin-points and then dilated blackly. She recoiled a step, fighting with the stupor which her illtimed indulgence had left behind.

At this moment Kerry groaned loudly, tossed his arm out with a convulsive movement, and rolled over on to his side, drawing up his knees.

The eye of Sin Sin Wa gleamed strangely, but he did not move, and Sam Tûk, who sat huddled in his chair where his feet almost touched the fallen man, stirred never a muscle. But Mrs. Sin, who still moved in a semi-phantasmagoric world, swiftly raised the hem of her kimona, affording a glimpse of a shapely silk-clad limb. From a sheath attached to her garter she drew a thin stilletto. Curiously feline, she crouched, as if about to spring.

Sin Sin Wa extended his hand, grasping his wife's wrist.

"O, woman of indifferent intelligence," he said in his queer sibilant language, "since when has murder gone unpunished in these British dominions?"

Mrs. Sin snatched her wrist from his grasp, falling back wild-eyed.

"Yellow ape! yellow ape!" she said hoarsely. "One more does not matter—now."

"One more?" crooned Sin Sin Wa, glancing curiously at Kerry.

"They are here! We are trapped!"

"No, no," said Sin Sin Wa. "He is a brave man; he comes alone."

He paused and then suddenly resumed in pidgin English:

"You likee killa him, eh?"

Perhaps unconscious that she did so, Mrs. Sin replied also in English:

"No, I am mad. Let me think, old fool!"

She dropped the stiletto and raised her hand dazedly to her brow.

"You gotchee tired of knifee chop, eh?" murmured Sin Sin Wa.

Mrs. Sin clenched her hands, holding them rigidly against her hips; and, nostrils dilated, she stared at the smiling Chinaman.

"What do you mean?" she demanded.

Sin Sin Wa performed his curious Oriental shrug.

"You putta topside pidgin on Sir Lucy alla lightee," he murmured. "Givee him hell alla velly ploper."

The pupils of the woman's eyes contracted again, and remained so. She laughed hoarsely and tossed her head.

"Who told you that?" she asked contemptuously. "It was the doll-woman who killed him—I have said so."

"*You* tella me so—*hoi, hoi!* But old Sin Sin Wa catchee wonder. Lo!"—he extended a yellow forefinger, pointing at his wife—"Mrs. Sin make him catchee die! No bhobbery, no palaber. Sin Sin Wa gotchee you sized up allee timee."

Mrs. Sin snapped her fingers under his nose then stooped, picked up the stiletto, and swiftly restored it to its sheath. Her hands resting upon her hips, she came forward, until her dark evil face almost touched the yellow, smiling face of Sin Sin Wa.

"Listen, old fool," she said in a low, husky voice; "I have done with you, ape-man, for good! Yes! I killed Lucy, *I* killed him! He belonged to *me*—until that pink and white thing took him away. I am glad I killed him.

If I cannot have him neither can she. But I was mad all the same."

She glanced down at Kerry, and:

"Tie him up," she directed, "and send him to sleep. And understand, Sin, we've shared out for the last time. You go your way and I go mine. No stinking Yellow River for me. New York is good enough until it's safe to go to Buenos Ayres."

"Smartest leg in Buenos Ayres," croaked the raven from his wicker cage, which was set upon the counter.

Sin Sin Wa regarded him smilingly.

"Yes, yes, my little friend," he crooned in Chinese, while Tling-a-Ling rattled ghostly castanets. "In Ho-Nan they will say that you are a devil and I am a wizard. That which is unknown is always thought to be magical, my Tling-a-Ling."

Mrs. Sin, who was rapidly throwing off the effects of opium and recovering her normal self-confident personality, glanced at her husband scornfully.

"Tell me," she said, "what has happened? How did he come here?"

"Blinga lilly doggy," murmured Sin Sin Wa. "Knockee Ah Fung on him head and comee down here, lo. Ah Fung allee lightee now—topside. Chasee lilly doggy. Allee velly ploper. No bhobbery."

"Talk less and act more," said Mrs. Sin. "Tie him up, and if you *must* talk, talk Chinese. Tie him up."

She pointed to Kerry. Sin Sin Wa tucked his hands into his sleeves and shuffled towards the masked door communicating with the inner room.

"Only by intelligent speech are we distinguished from the other animals," he murmured in Chinese.

Entering the inner room, he began to extricate a long piece of thin rope from amid a tangle of other materials with which it was complicated. Mrs. Sin stood looking down at the fallen man. Neither Kerry nor Sam Tûk gave the slightest evidence of life. And as Sin Sin Wa disentangled yard upon yard of rope from the bundle on the floor by the bed where Rita Irvin lay in her long troubled sleep, he crooned a queer song. It was in the Ho-Nan dialect and intelligible to himself alone.

"*Shöa, the evil woman* (he chanted), *the woman of many strange loves. . . .*
Shöa, the ghoul. . . .
Lo, the Yellow River leaps forth from the nostrils of the mountain god. . . .

Shöa, the betrayer of men. . . .
Blood is on her brow.
Lo, the betrayer is betrayed. Death sits at
*   her elbow.*
See, the Yellow River bears a corpse upon
*   its tide . . .*
Dead men hear her secret.
Shöa, the ghoul. . . .
Shö, the evil woman. Death sits at her
*   elbow.*
Black, the vultures flock about her. . . .
Lo, the Yellow River leaps forth from the
*   nostrils of the mountain god."*

Meanwhile Kerry, laying motionless at the feet of Sam Tûk, was doing some hard and rapid thinking. He had recovered consciousness a few moments before Mrs. Sin had come into the vault from the inner room. There were those, Seton Pasha among them, who would have regarded the groan and convulsive movements of Kerry's body with keen suspicion. And because the Chief Inspector suffered from no illusions respecting the genius of Sin Sin Wa, the apparent failure of the one-eyed Chinaman to recognize these preparations for attack nonplussed the Chief Inspector. His outstanding vice as an investigator was the directness of his own methods and of his mental outlook, so that he frequently experienced great difficulty in penetrating to the motives of a tortuous brain such as that of Sin Sin Wa.

That Sin Sin Wa thought him to be still unconscious he did not believe. He was confident that his tactics had deceived the Jewess, but he entertained an almost superstitious respect for the cleverness of the Chinaman. The trick with the ball of leaf opium was painfully fresh in his memory.

Kerry, in common with many members of the Criminal Investigation Department, rarely carried firearms. He was a man with a profound belief in his bare hands—aided when necessary by his agile feet. At the moment that Sin Sin Wa had checked the woman's murderous and half insane outburst Kerry had been contemplating attack. The sudden change of language on the part of the Chinaman had arrested him in the act; and, realizing that he was listening to a confession which placed the hangman's rope about the neck of Mrs. Sin, he lay still and wondered.

Why had Sin Sin Wa forced his wife to betray herself? To clear Mareno? To clear Mrs. Irvin—or to save his own skin?

It was a frightful puzzle for Kerry. Then—

where was Kazmah? That Mrs. Irvin, probably in a drugged condition, lay somewhere in that mysterious inner room Kerry felt fairly sure. His maltreated skull was humming like a bee-hive and aching intensely, but the man was tough as men are made, and he could not only think clearly, but was capable of swift and dangerous action.

He believed that he could tackle the Chinaman with fair prospects of success; and women, however murderous, he habitually disregarded as adversaries. But the mummy-like, deceptive Sam Tûk was not negligible, and Kazmah remained an unknown quantity.

From under that protective arm, cast across his face, Kerry's fierce eyes peered out across the dirty floor. Then quickly he shut his eyes again.

Sin Sin Wa, crooning his strange song, came in carrying a coil of rope—and a Mauser pistol!

"P'licemanee gotchee sleepee," he murmured, "or maybe he catchee die!"

He tossed the rope to his wife, who stood silent, tapping the floor with one slim restless foot.

"Number one top-side tie up," he crooned. "Sin Sin Wa watchee withum gun!"

Kerry lay like a dead man; for in the Chinaman's voice were menace and warning.

Chapter XXXIX

THE EMPTY WHARF

The suspected area of Limehouse was closely invested as any fortress of old when Seton Pasha once more found himself approaching that painfully familiar neighborhood. He had spoken to several pickets, and had gathered no news of interest, except that none of them had seen Chief Inspector Kerry since some time shortly before dusk. Seton, newly from more genial climes, shivered as he contemplated the misty, rain-swept streets, deserted and but dimly lighted by an occasional lamp. The hooting of a steam siren on the river seemed to be in harmony with the prevailing gloom, and the most confirmed optimist must have suffered depression amid those surroundings.

He had no definite plan of action. Every line of inquiry hitherto followed had led to nothing but disappointment. With most of

the details concerning the elaborate organ-
iztion of the Kazmah group either gathered
or in sight, the whereabouts of the surviving
members remained a profound mystery. From
the Chinese no information could be obtained. Distrust of the police resides deep
within the Chinese heart; for the Chinaman,
and not unjustly, regards the police as ever
ready to accuse him and ever unwilling to
defend him; knows himself for a pariah capable of the worst crimes, and who may
therefore be robbed, beaten and even murdered by his white neighbors with impunity.
But when the police seek information from
Chinatown, Chinatown takes its revenge—
and is silent.

Out on the river, above and below Limehouse, patrols watched for signals from the
Asiatic quarter, and from a carefully selected
spot on the Surrey side George Martin
watched also. Not even the lure of a neighboring tavern could draw him from his post.
Hour after hour he waited patiently—Sin Sin
Wa paid fair prices, and to-night he bought
neither opium nor cocaine, but liberty.

Seton Pasha, passing from point to point,
and nowhere receiving news of Kerry, began
to experience a certain anxiety respecting the
safety of the intrepid Chief Inspector. His
mind filled with troubled conjectures, he
passed the house formerly occupied by the
one-eyed Chinaman—where he found Detective-sergeant Coombes on duty and very
much on the alert—and followed the bank
of the Thames in the direction of Limehouse
Basin. The narrow, ill-lighted street was quite
deserted. Bad weather and the presence of
many police had driven the Asiatic inhabit-
ants indoors. But from the river and the docks
arose the incessant din of industry. Whistles
shrieked and machinery clanked, and sometimes remotely came the sound of human
voices.

Musing upon the sordid mystery which
seems to underlie the whole of this dingy
quarter, Seton pursued his way, crossing inlets and circling around basins dimly divined, turning to the right into a lane flanked
by high eyeless walls, and again to the left,
finally to emerge nearly opposite a dilapidated gateway giving access to a small wharf.

All unconsciously, he was traversing the
same route as that recently pursued by the
fugitive Sin Sin Wa; but now he paused, staring at the empty wharf. The annexed building, a mere shell, had not escaped examination
by the search party, and it was with no very

definite purpose in view that Seton pushed
open the rickety gate. Doubtless Kismet, of
which the Arabs speak, dictated that he
should do so.

The tide was high, and the water whispered ghostly under the pile-supported
structure. Seton experienced a new sense of
chill which did not seem to be entirely physical as he stared out at the gloomy river prospect and listened to the uncanny whisperings
of the tide. He was about to turn back when
another sound attracted his attention. A dog
was whimpering somewhere near him.

At first he was disposed to believe that
the sound was due to some other cause, for
the deserted wharf was not a likely spot in
which to find a dog, but when to the faint
whimpering there was added a scratching
sound, Seton's last doubts vanished.

"It's a dog," he said, "a small dog."

Like Kerry, he always carried an electric
pocketlamp, and now he directed its rays
into the interior of the building.

A tiny spaniel, whining excitedly, was engaged in scratching with its paws upon the
dirty floor as though determined to dig its
way through. As the light shone upon it the
dog crouched affrightedly, and, glancing in
Seton's direction, revealed its teeth. He saw
that it was covered with mud from head to
tail, presenting a most woe-begone appearance, and the mystery of its presence there
came home to him forcibly.

It was a toy spaniel of a breed very popular among ladies of fashion, and to its collar
was still attached a tattered and muddy fragment of ribbon.

The little animal crouched in a manner
which unmistakably pointed to the fact that
it apprehended ill-treatment, but these personal fears had only a secondary place in its
mind, and with one eye on the intruder it
continued to scratch madly at the floor.

Seton acted promptly. He snapped off the
light, and, replacing the lamp in his pocket,
stepped into the building and dropped down
upon his knees beside the dog. He next lay
prone, and having rapidly cleared a space
with his sleeve of some of some of the dirt
which coated it, he applied his ear to the
floor.

In spite of that iron control which habitually he imposed upon himself, he became
aware of the fact that his heart was beating
rapidly. He had learned at Leman Street that
Kerry had brought Mrs. Irvin's dog from
Prince's Gate to aid in the search for the miss-

ing woman. He did not doubt that this was the dog which snarled and scratched excitedly beside him. Dimly he divined something of the truth. Kerry had fallen into the hands of the gang, but the dog, evidently not without difficulty, had escaped. What lay below the wharf?

Holding his breath, he crouched, listening; but not a sound could he detect.

"There's nothing here, old chap," he said to the dog.

Responsive to the friendly tone, the little animal began barking loudly with high staccato notes, which must have been audible on the Surrey shore.

Seton was profoundly mystified by the animal's behavior. He had personally searched every foot of this particular building, and was confident that it afforded no hiding-place. The behavior of the dog, however, was susceptible of only one explanation; and Seton, recognizing that the clue to the mystery lay somewhere within this ramshackle building, became seized with a conviction that he was being watched.

Standing upright, he paused for a moment, irresolute, thinking that he had detected a muffled shriek. But the riverside noises were misleading and his imagination was on fire.

That almost superstitious respect for the powers of Sin Sin Wa, which had led Chief Inspector Kerry to look upon the Chinaman as being more than humanly endowed, began to take possession of Seton Pasha. He regretted having entered the place so overtly, he regretted having shown a light. Keen eyes, vigilant, regarded him. It was perhaps a delusion, bred of the mournful night sounds, the gloom, and the uncanny resourcefulness, already proven, of the Kazmah group. But it operated powerfully.

Theories, wild, improbable, flocked to his mind. The great dope cache lay beneath his feet—and there must be some hidden entrance to it which had escaped the attention of the search-party. This in itself was not improbable, since they had devoted no more time this building than to any other in the vicinity. That wild cry in the night which struck so mournful a chill to the hearts of the watchers on the river had seemed to come out of the void of the blackness, had given but slight clue to the location of the place of captivity. Indeed, they could only surmise that it had been uttered by the missing woman. Yet in their hearts neither had

doubted it.

He determined to cause the place to be searched again, as secretly as possible; he determined to set so close a guard over it and over its approaches that none could enter or leave unobserved.

Yet Kismet, in whose omnipotence he more than half believed, had ordained otherwise; for man is merely an instrument in the hand of Fate.

Chapter XL

COIL OF THE PIGTAIL

The inner room was in darkness and the fumeladen air almost unbreathable. A dull and regular moaning sound proceeded from the corner where the bed was situated, but of the contents of the place and of its other occupant or occupants Karry had no more than a hazy idea. His imagination supplied those details which he had failed to observe. Mrs. Monte Irvin, in a dying condition, lay upon the bed, and someone or some *thing* crouched on the divan behind Kerry as he lay stretched upon the matting-covered floor. His wrists, tied behind him, gave him great pain; and since his ankles were also fastened and the end of the rope drawn taut and attached to that binding his wrists, he was rendered absolutely helpless. For one of his fiery temperament this physical impotence was maddening, and because his own handkerchief had been tied tightly around his head so as to secure between his teeth a wooden stopper of considerable size which possessed an unpleasant chemical taste and smell, even speech was denied him.

How long he had lain thus he had no means of judging accurately; but hours—long, maddening hours—seemed to have passed since, with the muzzle of Sin Sin Wa's Mauser pressed coldly to his ear, he had submitted willy-nilly to the adroit manipulations of Mrs. Sin. At first he had believed, in his confirmed masculine vanity, that it would be a simple matter to extricate himself from the fastenings made by a woman; but when, rolling him sideways, she had drawn back his heels and run the loose end of the line through the loop formed by the lashing of his wrists behind him, he had recognized a Chinese training, and had resigned himself to the inevitable. The wooden gag was a sore trial, and if it had not broken his spirit it had nearly caused him to break an artery in his impotent fury.

Into the darkened inner chamber Sin Sin Wa had dragged him, and there Kerry had lain ever since, listening to the various sounds of the place, to the coarse voice, often raised in anger, of the Cuban-Jewess, to the crooning tones of the imperturbable Chinaman. The incessant moaning of the woman on the bed sometimes became mingled with another sound more remote, which Kerry for long failed to identify; but ultimately he concluded it to be occasioned by the tide flowing under the wharf. The raven was silent, because imprisoned in his wicker cage, he had been placed in some dark spot below the counter. Very dimly from time to time a steam siren might be heard upon the river, and once the thudding of a screw-propeller told of the passage of a large vessel along Limehouse Reach.

In the eyes of Mrs. Sin Kerry had read menace, and for all their dark beauty they had reminded him of the eyes of a cornered rat. Beneath the contemptuous non-chalance which she flaunted he read terror and remorse, and a foreboding of doom—panic ill repressed, which made her dangerous as any beast at bay. The attitude of the Chinaman was more puzzling. He seemed to bear the Chief Inspector no personal animosity, and indeed, in his glittering eye, Kerry had detected a sort of mysterious light of understanding which was almost mirthful, but which bore no relation to Sin Sin Wa's perpetual smile. Kerry's respect for the one-eyed Chinaman had increased rather than diminished upon closer acquaintance. Underlying his urbanity he failed to trace any symptom of apprehension. This Sin Sin Wa, accomplice of a murderess self-confessed, evident head of a drug syndicate which had led to the establishment of a Home Office inquiry—this badly "wanted" man, whose last hiding-place, whose keep, was closely invested by the agents of the law, was the same Sin Sin Wa who had smilingly extended his wrists, inviting the manacles, when Kerry had first made his acquaintance under circumstances legally very different.

Sometimes Kerry could hear him singing his weird crooning song, and twice Mrs. Sin had shrieked blasphemous execrations at him because of it. But why should Sin Sin Wa sing? What hope had he of escape? In the case of any other criminal Kerry would have answered "None," but the ease with which this one-eyed Chinaman had departed from his abode under the very noses of four detectives had shaken the Chief Inspector's confidence in the efficiency of ordinary police methods where this Chinese conjurer was concerned. A man who could convert an elaborate opium house into a dirty ruin in so short a time, too, was capable of other miraculous feats, and it would not have surprised Kerry to learn that Sin Sin Wa, at a moment's notice, could disguise himself as a chest of tea, or pass invisible through solid walls.

For evidence that Seton Pasha or any of the men from Scotland Yard had penetrated to the secret of Sam Tûk's cellar Kerry listened in vain. What was about to happen he could not imagine, nor if his life was to be spared. In the confession so curiously extorted from Mrs. Sin by her husband he perceived a clue to this and other mysteries, but strove in vain to disentangle it from the many maddening complexities of the case.

So he mused, wearily, listening to the moaning of his fellow captive, and wondering, since no sign of life came thence, why he imagined another presence in the stuffy room or the presence of someone or of some *thing* on the divan behind him. And in upon these dreary musings broke an altercation between Mrs. Sin and her husband.

"Keep the blasted thing covered up!" she cried hoarsely.

"Tling-a-Ling wantchee catchee bleathee sometime," crooned Sin Sin Wa.

"Hallo, hallo!" croaked the raven drowsily. "Smartest—smartest—smartest leg——"

"You catchee sleepee, Tling-a-Ling," murmured the Chinaman. "Mrs. Sin no likee you palaber, lo!"

"Burn it!" cried the woman; "burn the one-eyed horror!"

But when, carrying a lighted lantern, Sin Sin Wa presently came into the inner room, he smiled as imperturbably as ever, and was unmoved so far as external evidence showed.

Sin Sin Wa set the lantern upon a Moorish coffee-table which once had stood beside the divan in Mrs. Sin's sanctum at the House of a Hundred Raptures. A significant glance—its significance an acute puzzle to the recipient—he cast upon Chief Inspector Kerry. His hands tucked in the loose sleeves of his blouse, he stood looking down at the woman who lay moaning on the bed; and:

"*Tchée, tchée,*" he crooned softly, "you hab no catchee die, my beautiful. You sniffee plenty too muchee 'white snow,' *hoi, hoi!* Velly bad woman tly makee you catchee die, but Sin Sin Wa no hab got for killee chop. Topside pidgin no good enough, lo!"

His thick, extraordinary long pigtail hanging down his back and gleaming in the rays of the lantern, he stood, head bowed, watching Rita Irvin. Because of his position on the floor, Mrs. Irvin was invisible from Kerry's point of view, but she continued to moan incessantly, and he knew that she must be unconscious of the Chinaman's scrutiny.

"Hurry, old fool!" came Mrs. Sin's harsh voice from the outer room. "In ten minutes Ah Fung will give the signal. Is she dead yet—the doll-woman?"

"She hab no catchee die," murmured Sin Sin Wa. "She still vella beautiful—*tchée!*"

It was at the moment that he spoke these words that Seton Pasha entered the empty building above and found the spaniel scratching at the paved floor. So that, as Sin Sin Wa stood looking down at the wan face of the unfortunate woman who refused to die, the dog above, excited by Seton's presence, ceased to whine and scratch and began to bark.

Faintly to the vault the sound of the high-pitched barking penetrated.

Kerry tensed his muscles and groaned impotently, feeling his heart beating like a hammer in his breast. Complete silence reigned in the outer room. Sin Sin Wa never stirred. Again the dog barked, then:

"Hallo, hallo!" shrieked the raven shrilly. "Number one p'lice chop, lo! Sin Sin Wa! Sin Sin Wa!"

There came a fierce exclamation, the sound of something being hastily overturned, of a scuffle, and:

"Sin—Sin—Wa!" croaked the raven feebly.

The words ended in a screeching cry, which was followed by a sound of wildly beating wings. Sin Sin Wa, hands tucked in sleeves, turned and walked from the inner room, closing the sliding door behind him with a movement of his shoulder.

Resting against the empty shelves, he stood and surveyed the scene in the vault.

Mrs. Sin, who had been kneeling beside the wicker cage, which was upset, was in the act of standing upright. At her feet, and not far from the motionless form of old Sam Tûk, who sat like a dummy figure in his chair before the stove, lay a palpitating mass of black feathers. Other detached feathers were sprinkled about the floor. Feebly the raven's wings beat the ground once, twice—and were still.

Sin Sin Wa uttered one sibilant word, withdrew his hands from his sleeves, and, stepping around the end of the counter, dropped upon his knees beside the raven. He touched it with long yellow fingers, then raised it and stared into the solitary eye, now glazed and sightless as its fellow. The smile had gone from the face of Sin Sin Wa.

"My Tling-a-Ling!" he moaned in his native mandarin tongue. "Speak to me, my little black friend!"

A bead of blood, like a ruby, dropped from the raven's beak. Sin Sin Wa bowed his head and knelt a while in silence; then, standing up, he reverently laid the poor bedraggled body upon a chest. He turned and looked at his wife.

Hands on hips, she confronted him, breathing rapidly, and her glance of contempt swept him up and down.

"I've often threatened to do it," she said in English. "Now I've done it. They're on the wharf. We're trapped—thanks to that black, squalling horror!"

"*Tchée, tchée!*" hissed Sin Sin Wa.

His gleaming eye fixed upon the woman unblinkingly, he began very deliberately to roll up his loose sleeves. She watched him, contempt in her glance, but her expression changed subtly, and her dark eyes grew narrowed. She looked rapidly towards Sam Tûk, but Sam Tûk never stirred.

"Old fool!" she cried at Sin Sin Wa. "What are you doing?"

But Sin Sin Wa, his sleeves rolled up above his yellow, sinewy forearms, now tossed his pigtail, serpentine, across his shoulder and touched it with his fingers, an odd, caressing movement.

"Ho!" laughed Mrs. Sin in her deep scoffing fashion; "it is for *me* you make all this bhobbery, eh? It is *me* you are going to chastise, my dear?"

She flung back her head, snapping her fingers before the silent Chinaman. He watched her, and slowly—slowly—he began to crouch, lower and lower, but always that unblinking regard remained fixed upon the face of Mrs. Sin.

The woman laughed again, more loudly. Bending her lithe body forward in mocking mimicry, she snapped her fingers, once—again—and again under Sin Sin Wa's nose. Then:

"Do you think, you blasted yellow ape, that you can frighten *me?*" she screamed, a swift flame of wrath lighting up her dark face.

In a flash she had raised the kimona and had the stiletto in her hand. But, even swifter than she, Sin Sin Wa sprang . . .

Once, twice she struck at him, and blood streamed from his left shoulder. But the pigtail, like an executioner's rope, was about the woman's throat. She uttered one smothered shriek, dropping the knife, and then was silent . . .

Her dyed hair escaped from its fastenings and descended, a ruddy torrent, about her as she writhed, silent, horrible, in the death-coil of the pigtail.

Rigidly, at arms' length, he held her, moment after moment, immovable, implacable; and when he read death in her empurpled face, a miraculous thing happened.

The "blind" eye of Sin Sin Wa opened!

A husky rattle told of the end, and he dropped the woman's body from his steely grip, disengaging the pigtail with a swift movement of his head. Opening and closing his yellow fingers to restore circulation, he stood looking down at her. He spat upon the floor at her feet.

Then, turning, he held out his arms and confronted Sam Tûk.

"Was it well done, bald father of wisdom?" he demanded hoarsely.

But old Sam Tûk, seated lumpish in his chair like some grotesque idol before whom a human sacrifice has been offered up, stirred not. The length of loaded tubing with which he had struck Kerry lay beside him where it had fallen from his nerveless hand. And the two oblique, beady eyes of Sin Sin Wa, watching, grew dim. Step by step he approached the old Chinaman, stooped, touched him, then knelt and laid his head upon the thin knees.

"Old father," he murmured, "old bald father who knew so much. To-night you know all."

For Sam Tûk was no more. At what moment he had died, whether in the excitement of striking Kerry or later, no man could have presumed to say, since, save by an occasional nod of his head, he had often simu-

lated death in life—he who was so old that he was known as "The Father of Chinatown."

Standing upright, Sin Sin Wa looked from the dead man to the dead raven. Then, tenderly raising poor Tling-a-Ling, he laid the great dishevelled bird—a weird offering—upon the knees of Sam Tûk.

"Take him with you where you travel tonight, my father," he said. "He, too, was faithful."

A cheap German clock commenced a muted clangor, for the little hammer was muffled.

Sin Sin Wa walked slowly across to the counter. Taking up the gleaming joss, he unscrewed its pedestal. Then, returning to the spot where Mrs. Sin lay, he coolly detached a leather wallet which she wore beneath her dress fastened to a girdle. Next he removed her rings, her bangles and other ornaments. He secreted all in the interior of the joss—his treasure-chest. He raised his hands and began to unplait his long pigtail, which, like his "blind" eye, was *camouflage*—a false queue attached to his own hair, which he wore but slightly longer than some Europeans and many Americans. With a small pair of scissors he clipped off his long, snake-like moustaches. . . .

Chapter XLI

THE FINDING OF KAZMAH

At a point just above the sweep of Limehouse Reach a watchful river police patrol observed a moving speck of light on the right bank of the Thames. As if in answer to the signal there came a few moments later a second moving speck at a point not far above the district once notorious in its possession of Ratcliff Highway. A third light answered from the Surrey bank, and a fourth shone out yet higher up and on the opposite side of the Thames.

The tide had just turned. As Chief Inspector Kerry had once observed, "there are no pleasure parties punting about that stretch," and, consequently, when George Martin tumbled into his skiff on the Surrey shore and began lustily to pull up stream, he was observed almost immediately by the River Police.

Pulling hard against the stream, it took

him a long time to reach his destination—stone stairs near the point from which the second light had been shown. Rain had ceased and the mist had cleared shortly after dusk, as often happens this time of year, and because the night was comparatively clear the pursuing boats had to be handled with care.

George did not disembark at the stone steps, but after waiting there for some time he began to drop down on the tide, keeping close inshore.

"He knows we've spotted him," said Sergeant Coombes, who was in one of the River Police boats. "It was at the stairs that he had to pick up his man."

Certainly, the tactics of George suggested that he had recognized surveillance, and, his purpose abandoned, now sought to efface himself without delay. Taking advantage of every shadow, he resigned his boat to the gentle current. He had actually come to the entrance of Greenwich Reach when a dock light, shining out across the river, outlined the boat yellowly.

"He's got a passenger!" said Coombes amazedly.

Inspector White, who was in charge of the cutter, rested his arm on Coombes shoulder and stared across the moving tide.

"I can see no one," he replied. "You're over anxious, Detective-sergeant—and I can understand it!"

Coombes smiled heroically.

"I may be over anxious, Inspector," he replied, "but if I lost Sin Sin Wa, the River Police had never even heard of him till the C.I.D. put'em wise."

"H'm!" muttered the Inspector. "D'you suggest we board him?"

"No," said Coombes; "let him land, but don't trouble to hide any more. Show him we're in pursuit."

No longer drifting with the outgoing tide, George Martin had now boldly taken to the oars. The River Police boat close in his wake, he headed for the blunt promontory of the Isle of Dogs. The grim pursuit went on until:

"I bet I know where he's for," said Coombes.

"So do I," declared Inspector White; "Dougal's!"

Their anticipations were realized. To the wooden stairs which served as a water-gate for the establishment on the Isle of Dogs, George Martin ran in openly; the police boat followed, and:

"You were right!" cried the Inspector; "he has somebody with him!"

A furtive figure, bearing a burden upon its shoulder, moved up the slope and disappeared. A moment later the police were leaping ashore. George deserted his boat and went running heavily after his passenger.

"After them!" cried Coombes. "That's Sin Sin Wa!"

Around the mazey, rubbish-strewn paths the pursuit went hotly. In sight of Dougal's Coombes saw the swing door open and a silhouette—that of a man who carried a bag on his shoulder—pass in. George Martin followed, but the Scotland Yard man had his hand upon his shoulder.

"Police!" he said sharply. "Who's your friend?"

George turned, red and truculent, with clenched fists.

"Mind your own bloody business!" he roared.

"Mind yours, my lad!" retorted Coombes warningly. "You're no Thames waterman. Who's your friend?"

"Wotcher mean?" shouted George. "You're up the pole or canned you are!"

"Grab him!" said Coombes, and he kicked open the door and entered the saloon, followed by Inspector White and the boat's crew.

As they appeared, the Inspector conspicuous in his uniform, backed by the group of River Police, one of whom grasped George Martin by his coat collar:

"Splits!" bellowed Dougal in a voice like a fog-horn.

Twenty cups of tea, coffee and cocoa, too hot for speedy assimilation, were spilled upon the floor.

The place as usual was crowded, more particularly in the neighborhood of the two stoves. Here were dock laborers, seamen and riverside loafers, lascars, Chinese, Arabs, negroes and dagoes. Mrs. Dougal, defiant and red, brawny arms folded and her pose as that of one contemplating a physical contest, glared from behind the "solid" counter. Dougal rested his hairy hands upon the "wet" counter and revealed his defective teeth in a vicious snarl. Many of the patrons carried light baggage, since a P and O boat, an Oriental, and the S.S. Mahratta, were sailing that night or in the early morning, and Dougal's was the favorite house of call for a doch-an-dorrich for sailormen, particularly for sailormen of color.

Upon the police group became focussed

the glances of light eyes and dark eyes, round eyes, almond-shaped eyes, and oblique eyes. Silence fell.

"We are police officers," called Coombes formally. "All papers, please."

Thereupon, without disturbance, the inspection began, and among the papers scrutinized were those of one, Chung Chow, an able-bodied Chinese seaman. But since his papers were in order, and since he possessed two eyes and wore no pigtail, he excited no more interest in the mind of Detective-sergeant Coombes than did any one of the other Chinamen in the place.

A careful search of the premises led to no better result, and George Martin accounted for his possession of a considerable sum of money found upon him by explaining that he had recently been paid off after a long voyage and had been lucky at cards.

The result of the night's traffic, then, spelled failure for British justice, the s.s. *Mahratta* sailed one stewardess short of her complement; but among the Chinese crew of another steamer Eastward bound was one, Chung Chow, formerly known as Sin Sin Wa. And sometimes in the night watches there arose before him the picture of a black bird resting upon the knees of an aged Chinaman. Beyond these figures dimly he perceived the paddy-fields of Ho-Nan and the sweeping valley of the Yellow River, where the opium poppy grows.

It was about an hour before the sailing of the ship which numbered Chung Chow among the yellow members of its crew that Seton Pasha returned once more to the deserted wharf whereon he had found Mrs. Monte Irvin's spaniel. Afterwards, in the light of ascertained facts, he condemned himself for a stupidity passing the ordinary. For while he had conducted a careful search of the wharf and adjoining premises, convinced there was a cellar of some kind below, he had omitted to look for a water-gate to this hypothetical cache.

Perhaps his self-condemnation was deserved, but in justice to the agent selected by Lord Wrexborough, it should be added that Chief Inspector Kerry had no more idea of the existence of such an entrance, and exit, than had Seton Pasha.

Leaving the dog at Leman Street then, and learning that there was no news of the missing Chief Inspector, Seton set out once more. He had been informed of the myste-

rious signals flashed from side to side of the Lower Pool, and was hourly expecting a report to the effect that Sin Sin Wa had been apprehended in the act of escaping. That Sin Sin Wa had dropped into the turgid tide from his underground hiding-place, and pushing his property—which was floatable—before him, encased in a waterproof bag, had swum out and clung to the stern of George Martin's boat as it passed close to the empty wharf, neither Seton Pasha nor any other man knew—except George Martin and Sin Sin Wa.

At a suitably dark spot the Chinaman had boarded the little craft, not without difficulty, for his wounded shoulder pained him, and had changed his sodden attire for a dry outfit which awaited him in the locker at the stern of the skiff. The cunning of the Chinese has the simplicity of true genius.

Not two paces had Seton taken on to the mystifying wharf when:

"Sam Tûk, barber! Entrance in cellar!" rapped a ghostly, muffled voice from beneath his feet. "Sam Tûk, barber! Entrance in cellar!"

Seton Pasha stood still, temporarily bereft of speech. Then, *"Kerry!"* he cried. "Kerry! Where are you?"

But apparently his voice failed to reach the invisible speaker, for:

"Sam Tûk, barber! Entrance in cellar!" repeated the voice.

Seton Pasha wasted no more time. He ran out into the narrow street. A man was on duty there.

"Call assistance!" ordered Seton briskly; "send four men to join me at the barber's shop called Sam Tûks! You know it?"

"Yes, sir; I searched it with Chief Inspector Kerry."

The note of a police whistle followed.

Ten minutes later the secret of Sam Tûk's cellar was unmasked. The place was empty, and the subterranean door locked; but it succumbed to the persistent attacks of axe and crowbar, and Seton Pasha was the first of the party to enter the vault. It was laden with chemical fumes. . . .

He found there an aged Chinaman, dead, seated by a stove in which the fire had burned very low. Sprawling across the old man's knees was the body of a raven. Lying at his feet was a woman, lithe, contorted, her face half hidden in masses of bright red hair.

"End case near the door!" rapped the voice of Kerry. "Slides to the left!"

Seton Pasha vaulted over the counter, drew

the shelves aside, and entered the inner room.

By the dim light of a lantern burning upon a moorish coffee-table he discerned an untidy bed, upon which a second woman lay, pallid.

"God!" he muttered; "this place is a morgue!"

"It certainly isn't healthy!" said an irritable voice from the floor. "But I think I might survive it if you could spare a second to untie me."

Kerry's extensive practice in chewing and the enormous development of his maxillary muscles had stood him in good stead. His keen, strong teeth had bitten through the extemporized gag, and as a result the tension of the handkerchief which had held it in place had become relaxed, enabling him to rid himself of it and to spit out the fragments of filthy-tasting wood which the biting operation had left in his mouth.

Seton turned, stooped on one knee to release the captive. . . . and found himself looking into the face of someone who sat crouched upon the divan behind the Chief Inspector. The figure was that of an Oriental, richly robed. Long, slim, ivory hands rested upon his knees, and on the first finger of the right hand gleamed a big talismanic ring. But the face, surmounted by a white turban, was wonderful, arresting in its immobile intellectual beauty; and from under the heavy brows a pair of abnormally large eyes looked out hypnotically.

"My God!" whispered Seton, then:

"If you've finished your short prayer," rapped Kerry, "set about *my* little job."

"But, Kerry—Kerry, behind you——"

"I haven't any eyes in my back hair!"

Mechanically, half fearfully, Seton touched the hands of the crouching Oriental. A low moan came from the woman in the bed, and:

"It's *Kazmah!*" gasped Seton. "Kerry . . . Kazmah is—a *wax figure!*"

"Hell!" said Chief Inspector Kerry.

Chapter XLII

A YEAR LATER

Beneath an awning spread above the balcony of one of those modern elegant flats, which today characterize Heliopolis, the City of the Sun, site of perhaps the most ancient seat of learning in the known world, a party of four

was gathered, awaiting the unique spectacle which is afforded when the sun's dying rays fade from the Libyan sands and the violet wonder of the afterglow conjures up old magical Egypt from the ashes of the desert.

"Yes," Monte Irvin was saying, "only a year ago; but, thank God, it seems more like ten! Merciful time effaces sadness but spares joy."

He turned to his wife, whose flower-like face peeped out from a nest of white fur. Covertly he squeezed her hand, and was rewarded with a swift, half coquettish glance, in which he read trust and contentment. The dreadful ordeal through which she had passed had accomplished that which no physician in Europe could have hoped for, since no physician would have dared to adopt such drastic measures. Actuated by deliberate cruelty, and with the design of bringing about her death from apparently natural causes, the Kazmah group had deprived her of cocaine for so long a period that sanity, life itself, had barely survived; but for so long a period that, surviving, she had outlived the drug craving. Kazmah had cured her!

Monte Irvin turned to the tall fair girl who sat upon the arm of a cane rest-chair beside Rita.

"But nothing can ever efface the memory of all you have done for Rita, and for me," he said; "nothing, Mrs. Seton."

"Oh," said Margaret, "my mind was away back, and that sounded—so odd."

Seton Pasha, who occupied the lounge-chair upon the broad arm of which his wife was seated, looked up, smiling into the suddenly flushed face. They were but newly returned from their honeymoon, and had just taken possession of their home, for Seton was now stationed in Cairo. He flicked a cone of ash from his cheroot.

"It seems to me that we are all more or less indebted to one another," he declared. "For instance, I might never have met you, Margaret, if I had not run into your cousin that eventful night at Princes; and Gray would not have been gazing abstractedly out of the doorway if Mrs. Irvin had joined him for dinner as arranged. One can trace every episode in life right back, and ultimately come——"

"To Kismet!" cried his wife, laughing merrily. "So before we begin dinner to-night—which is a night of reunion—I am going to propose a toast to Kismet!"

"Good!" said Seton; "we shall all drink it

gladly. Eh, Irvin?"

"Gladly, indeed," agreed Monte Irvin. "You know, Seton," he continued, "we have been wandering, Rita and I; and even since your wife handed her patient over to me cured we have covered some territory. I don't know if you or Chief Inspector Kerry has been responsible, but the press accounts of the Kazmah affair have been scanty to baldness. One stray bit of news reached us—in Colorado, I think."

"What was that, Mr. Irvin?" asked Margaret, leaning towards the speaker.

"It was about Mollie Gretna. Someone wrote and told me that she had eloped with a billiard marker—a married man with five children!"

Seton laughed heartily, and so did Margaret and Rita.

"Right!" cried Seton. "She did. When last heard of she was acting as barmaid in a Portsmouth tavern!"

But Monte Irvin did not laugh.

"Poor, foolish girl!" he said gravely. "Her life might have been so different—so useful and happy."

"I agree," replied Seton, "if she had had a husband like Kerry."

"Oh, please don't!" said Margaret. "I almost fell in love with Chief Inspector Kerry myself."

"A grand fellow!" declared her husband warmly. "The Kazmah inquiry was the triumph of his career."

Monte Irvin turned to him.

"*You* did your bit, Seton," he said quietly. "The last words Inspector Kerry spoke to me before I left England were in the nature of a splendid tribute to yourself, but I will spare your blushes."

"Kerry is as white as they're made," replied Seton; "but we should never have known for certain who killed Sir Lucien if he had not risked his life in that filthy cellar as he did."

Rita Irvin shuddered slightly and drew her furs more closely about her shoulders.

"Shall we change the conversation, dear?" whispered Margaret.

"No, please," said Rita. "You cannot imagine how curious I am to learn the true details—for, as Monte says, we have been out of touch with things, and although we were so intimately concerned, neither of us really knows the inner history of the affair to this day. Of course, we know that Kazmah was a dummy figure, posed in the big ebony

chair. He never moved, except to raise his hand, and this was done by someone seated in the inner room behind the figure. But *who* was seated there?"

Seton glanced inquiringly at his wife, and she nodded, smiling.

"Right-o!" he said. "If you will excuse me for a moment I will get my notes. Hello, here's Gray!"

A little two-seater came bowling along the road from Cairo, and drew up beneath the balcony. It was the car which had belonged to Margaret when in practice in Dover Street. Quentin Gray jumped out, waving his hand cheerily to the quartette above, and went in at the doorway. Seton walked through the flat and admitted him.

"Sorry I'm late!" cried Gray, impetuous and boyish as ever, although he looked older and had grown very bronzed. "The chief detained me."

"Go through to them," said Seton informally. "I'm getting my notes; we're going to read the thrilling story of the Kazmah mystery before dinner."

"Good enough!" cried Gray. "I'm in the dark on many points."

He had outlived his youthful infatuation, although it was probable enough that had Rita been free he would have presented himself as a suitor without delay. But the old relationship he had no desire to renew. A generous self-effacing regard had supplanted the madness of his earlier passion. Rita had changed too; she had learned to know herself and to know her husband.

So that when Seton Pasha presently rejoined his guests, he found the most complete harmony to prevail among them. He carried a bulky notebook, and, tapping his teeth with his monocle:

"Ladies and gentlemen," he began whimsically, "I will bore you with a brief account of the extraordinary facts concerning the Kazmah case."

Margaret was seated in the rest-chair which her husband had vacated, and Seton took up a position upon the ledge formed by one of the wide arms. Everyone prepared to listen, with interest undisguised.

"There were three outstanding personalities dominating what we may term the Kazmah group," continued Seton. "In order of importance they were: Sin Sin Wa, Sir Lucien Pyne and Mrs. Sin."

Rita Irvin inhaled deeply, but did not interrupt the speaker.

"I shall begin with Sir Lucien," Seton went on.

"For some years before his father's death he seems to have lived a very shady life in many parts of the world. He was a confirmed gambler, and was also somewhat unduly fond of the ladies' society. In Buenos Ayres—the exact date does not matter—he made the acquaintance of a variety artiste known as La Belle Lola, a Cuban-Jewess, good-looking and unscrupulous. I cannot say if Sir Lucien was aware from the outset of his affair with La Belle that she was a married woman. But it is certain that her husband, Sin Sin Wa, very early learned of the intrigue, and condoned it.

"How Sir Lucien came to get into the clutches of the pair I do not know. But that he did so we have ascertained beyond doubt. I think, personally, that his third vice—opium—was probably responsible. For Sin Sin Wa appears throughout in the character of a drug dealer.

"These three people really become interesting from the time that La Belle Lola quitted the stage and joined her husband in the conducting of a concern in Buenos Ayres, which was the parent, if I may use the term, of the Kazmah business later established in Bond Street. From a music-hall illusionist, who came to grief during a South American tour, they acquired the Oriental waxwork figure which subsequently mystified so many thousands of dupes. It was the work of a famous French artist in wax, and had originally been made to represent the Pharaoh, Rameses II., for a Paris exhibition. Attired in Eastern robes, and worked by a simple device which raised and lowered the right hand, it was used, firstly, in a stage performance, and secondly, in the character of 'Kazmah the Dream-reader.'

"Even at this time Sir Lucien had access to good society, or to the best society which Buenos Ayres could offer, and he was the source of the surprising revelations made to patrons by the 'dream-reader.' At first, apparently, the drug business was conducted independently of the Kazmah concern, but the facilities offered by the latter for masking the former soon became apparent to the wily Sin Sin Wa. Thereupon the affair was reorganized on the lines later adopted in Bond Street. Kazmah's became a secret dope-shop, and annexed to it was an elaborate *chandu-khân*, conducted by the Chinaman. Mrs. Sin was the go-between.

"You are all waiting to hear—or, to be exact, two are waiting to hear, Gray and Margaret already know—who spoke as Kazmah through the little window behind the chair. The deep-voiced speaker was Juan Mareno, Mrs. Sin's brother! Mrs. Sin's maiden name was Lola Mareno.

"Many of these details were provided by Mareno, who, after the death of his sister, to whom he was deeply attached, volunteered to give crown evidence. Most if them we have confirmed from other sources.

"Behold 'Kazmah the dream-reader,' then, established in Buenos Ayres. The partners in the enterprise speedily acquired considerable wealth. Sir Lucien—at this time plain Mr. Pyne—several times came home and lived in London and elsewhere like a millionaire. There is no doubt, I think, that he was seeking a suitable opportunity to establish a London branch of the business."

"My God!" said Monte Irvin. "How horrible it seems!"

"Horrible, indeed!" agreed Seton. "But there are two features of the case which, in justice to Sir Lucien, we should not overlook. He, who had been a poor man, had become a wealthy one and had tasted the sweets of wealth; also he was now hopelessly in the toils of the woman Lola.

"With the ingenious financial details of the concern, which were conducted in the style of the 'Jose Santos Company,' I need not trouble you now. We come to the second period, when the flat in Albemarle Street and the two offices in Old Bond Street became vacant and were promptly leased by Mareno, acting on Sir Lucien's behalf, and calling himself sometimes Mr. Isaacs, sometimes Mr. Jacobs, and at other times merely posing as a representative of the Jose Santos Company in some other name.

"All went well. The concern had ample capital, and was organized by clever people. Sin Sin Wa took up new quarters in Limehouse; they had actually bought half the houses in one entire street as well as a warf! And Sin Sin Wa brought with him the goodwill of an illicit drug business which already had almost assumed the dimensions of a control.

"Sir Lucien's household was a mere bluff. He rarely entertained at home, and lived himself entirely at restaurants and clubs. The private entrance to the Kazmah house of business was the back window of the Cubanis Cigarette Company's office. From thence down the back stair to Kazmah's door it was a simple matter for Mareno to pass unobserved. Sir Lucien resumed his rôle of private inquiry agent, and Mareno recited the 'revelations' from notes supplied to him.

"But the 'dream reading' part of the business was merely carried on to mask the really profitable side of the concern. We have recently learned that drugs were distributed from that one office alone to the amount of thirty thousand pounds' worth annually! This is excluding the profits of the House of a Hundred Raptures and of the private *chandu* orgies organized by Mrs. Sin.

"The Kazmah group gradually acquired control of the entire market, and we know for a fact that at one period during the war they were actually supplying smuggled cocaine, indirectly, to no fewer than twelve R.A.M.C. hospitals! The complete ramifications of the system we shall never know.

"I come now to the tragedy, or series of tragedies, which brought about the collapse of the most ingenious criminal organization which has ever flourished, probably, in any community. I will dare to be frank. Sir Lucien was the victim of a woman's jealousy. Am I to proceed?"

Seton paused, glancing at his audience; and:

"If you please," whispered Rita. "Monte knows and I know—why—she killed him. But we don't know——"

"The nasty details," said Quentin Gray. "Carry on, Seton. Are you agreeable, Irvin?"

"I am anxious to know," replied Irvin, "for I believe Sir Lucien deserved well of me, bad as he was."

Seton clapped his hands, and an Egyptian servant appeared, silently and mysteriously as is the way of his class.

"Cocktails, Mahmoud!"

The Egyptian disappeared.

"There's just time," declared Margaret, gazing out across the prospect, "before sunset."

Chapter XLIII

THE STORY OF THE CRIME

"You are all aware," Seton continued, "that Sir Lucien Pyne was an admirer of Mrs. Irvin. God knows, I hold no brief for the man, but this love of his was the one redeeming feature of a bad life. How and when it began I don't profess to know, but it became the only pure thing which he possessed. That he was instrumental in introducing you, Mrs. Irvin, to the unfortunately prevalent drug habit, you will not deny; but that he afterwards tried sincerely to redeem you from it I can positively affirm. In seeking your redemption he found his own, for I know that he was engaged at the time of his death in extricating himself from the group. You may say that he made a fortune, and was satisfied; that is *your* view, Gray. I prefer to think that he was anxious to begin a new life and to make himself more worthy of the respect of those he loved.

"There was one obstacle which proved to be too great for him—Mrs. Sin. Although Juan Mareno was the spokesman of the group, Lola Mareno was the prompter. All Sir Lucien's plans for weaning Mrs. Irvin from the habits which she had acquired were deliberately and malignantly foiled by this woman. She endeavored to inveigle Mrs. Irvin into indebtedness to you, Gray, as you know now. Failing in this, she endeavored to kill her by depriving her of that which had at the time become practically indispensable. Her venomous jealousy led her to almost suicidal measures. She risked exposure and ruin in her endeavors to dispose of one whom she looked upon as a rival.

"During Sir Lucien's several absences from London she was particularly active, and this brings me to the closing scene of the drama. On the night that you determined, in desperation, Mrs. Irvin, to see Kazmah personally, you will recall that Sir Lucien went out to telephone to him?"

Rita nodded but did not speak.

"Actually," Seton explained, "he instructed Mareno to go across the leads to Kazmah's directly you had left the flat, and to give you a certain message as 'Kazmah.' He also instructed Mareno to telephone certain orders to Rashid, the Egyptian attendant. In spite of the unforeseen meeting with Gray, all would have gone well, no doubt, if Mrs. Sin had not chanced to be on the Kazmah premises at the time that the message was received!

"I need not say that Mrs. Sin was a remarkable woman, possessing many accomplishments, among them that of mimicry. She had often amused herself by taking Mareno's place at the table behind Kazmah, and, speaking in her brother's oracular voice, had delivered the 'revelations.' Mareno was like wax in his sister's hands, and on this fateful night, when he arrived at the place—which he did a few minutes before Mrs. Irvin, Gray and Sir Lucien—Mrs. Sin premptorily ordered him to wait upstairs in the Cubanis office, and *she* took her seat in the room from which the Kazmah illusions were controlled.

"So carefully arranged was every detail of the business that Rashid, the Egyptian, was ignorant of Sir Lucien's official connection with the Kazmah concern. He had been ordered—by Mareno speaking from Sir Lucien's flat—to admit Mrs. Irvin to the room of séance and then go home. He obeyed and departed, leaving Sir Lucien in the waiting-room.

"Driven to desperation by 'Kazmah's' taunting words, we know that Mrs. Irvin penetrated to the inner room. I must slur over the details of the scene which ensued. Hearing her cry out, Sir Lucien ran to her assistance. Mrs. Sin, enraged by his manner, lost all control of her insane passion. She attempted Mrs. Irvin's life with a stiletto which habitually she carried—and Sir Lucien died like a gentleman who had lived like a blackguard. He shielded her——"

Seton paused. Margaret was biting her lip hard, and Rita was looking down so that her face could not be seen.

"The shock consequent upon the deed sobered the half crazy woman," continued the speaker. "Her usual resourcefulness returned to her. Self-preservation had to be considered before remorse. Mrs. Irvin had swooned, and"—he hesitated—"Mrs. Sin saw to it that she did not revive prematurely. Mareno was summoned from the room above. The outer door was locked.

"It affords evidence of this woman's callous coolness that she removed from the Kazmah premises, and—probably assisted by her brother, although he denies it—from the person and garments of the dead man, every scrap of evidence. They had not by any means finished the task when *you* knocked at the door, Gray. But they completed it, faultlessly, after you had gone.

"Their unconscious victim, and the figure of Kazmah, as well as every paper or other possible clue, they carried up to the Cubanis office, and from thence across the roof to Sir Lucien's study. Next, while Mareno went for the car, Mrs. Sin rifled the safe, bureaus and desks in Sir Lucien's flat, so that we had the devil's own work, as you know, to find out even the more simple facts of his everyday life.

"Not a soul ever came forward who noticed the big car being driven into Albemarle Street or who observed it outside the flat. The chances run by the pair in conveying their several strange burdens from the top floor, down the stairs and out into the street were extraordinary. Yet they succeeded unobserved. Of course, the street was imperfectly lighted, and is but little frequented after dusk.

"The journey to Limehouse was performed without discovery—aided, no doubt, by the mistiness of the night; and Mareno, returning to the West End, ingeniously inquired for Sir Lucien at his club. Learning, although he knew it already, that Sir Lucien had not been to the club that night, he returned the car to the garage and calmly went back to the flat.

"His reason for taking this dangerous step is by no means clear. According to his own account, he did it to gain time for the fugitive Mrs. Sin. You see, there was really only one witness of the crime (Mrs. Irvin) and she could not have sworn to the identity of the assassin. Rashid was warned and presumably supplied with sufficient funds to enable him to leave the country.

"Well, the woman met her deserts, no doubt at the hands of Sin Sin Wa. Kerry is sure of this. And Sin Sin Wa escaped, taking with him an enormous sum of ready money. He was the true genius of the enterprise. No one, his wife and Mareno excepted—we know of no other—suspected that the real Sin Sin Wa was clean-shaven, possessed two eyes, and no pigtail! A wonderfully clever man!"

The native servant appeared to announce that dinner was served; African dusk drew its swift curtain over the desert, and a gun spoke sharply from the Citadel. In silence the party watched the deepening velvet of the sky, witnessing the birth of a million stars, and in silence they entered the gaily lighted dining-room.

Seton Pasha moved one of the lights so as to illuminate a small oil painting which hung above the sideboard. It represented the head and shoulders of a savage-looking red man, his hair close-cropped like that of a pugilist, and his moustache trimmed in such a fashion that a row of large, fierce teeth were revealed in an expression which might have been meant for a smile. A pair of intolerant steel-blue eyes looked squarely out at the spectator.

"What a time I had," said Seton, "to get him to sit for that! But I managed to secure his wife's support, and the trick was done. *You* are down to toast Kismet, Margaret, but I am going to propose the health, long life and prosperity of Chief Inspector Kerry, of the Criminal Investigation Department."